The Tin
Tsaritsa

Rächal Monigatti

For Lynne, Lisa and Paul

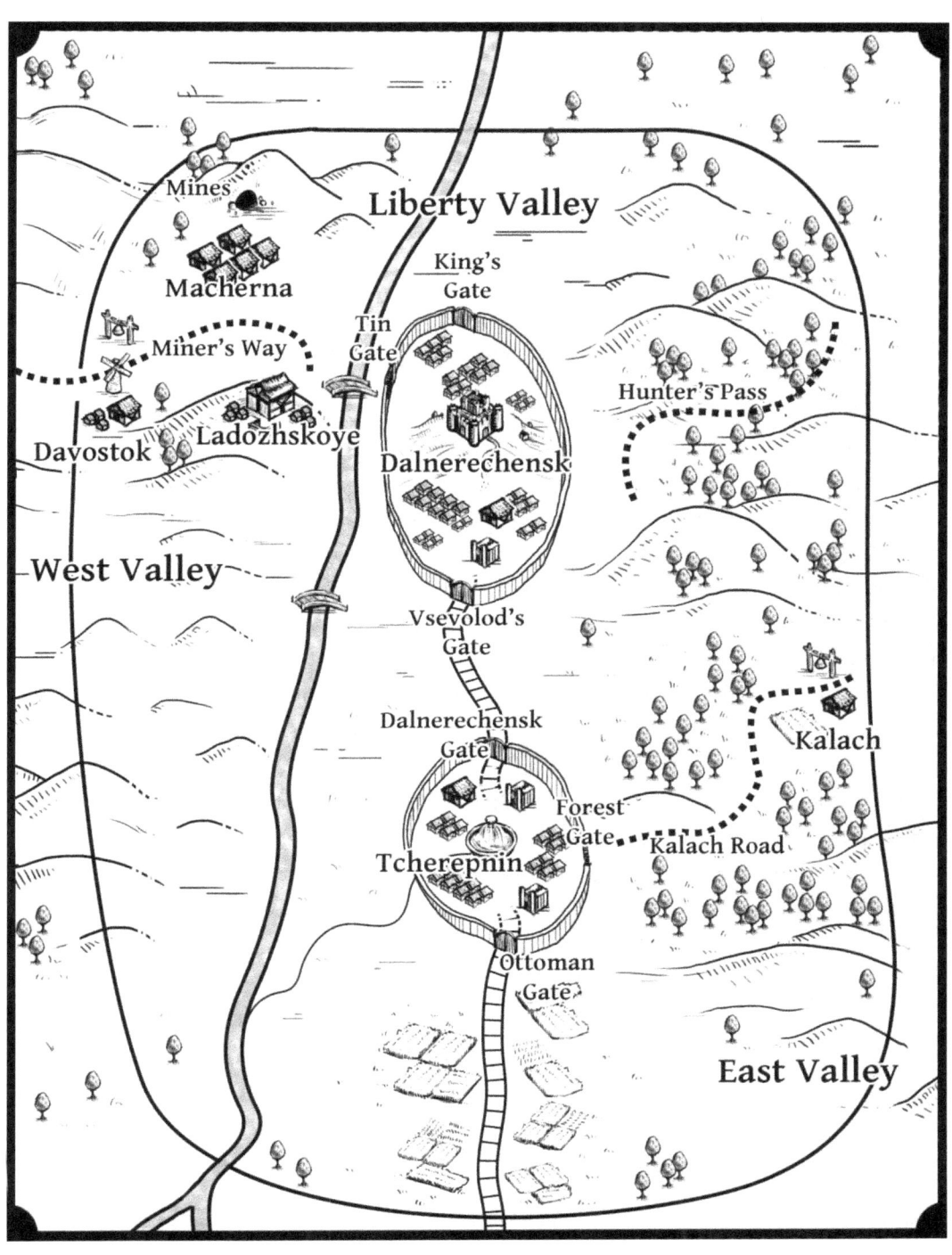

ACKNOWLEDGMENTS

I couldn't publish this book without acknowledging the help and support I have had in the many steps to its fruition. It was a three year long road with many obstacles, but thanks to the help of the following people I finally got there:

Many thanks to Marina Sisson and Polina Johnstone for their help with Russian translations, they saved many an embarrassing blunder from making it to print. Thank you to Emilie, Maureen, Paul, Lynne, Michelle and Lyall for reading my drafts and giving me feedback, it was much appreciated (and needed!)

A big thank you to Adam Schmidt for the map of the Principality of Dalnerechensk, and Sarah Foster for my cover artwork, who both patiently put up with my many changes.

Thank you to Tori and Wendy, your advice was instrumental in navigating the self-publishing world.

And finally, thank you for the love and support from my friends, family and colleagues who made all this possible. Thank you all sincerely.

PROLOGUE

April 1896

Luke Asanton squinted into the swirling dirt, watching the drill bit churn through the red dust of Texas. The grinding whine of the machine was giving him a headache and he pressed the beeswax harder into his ears, scratching the back of his neck as he did so.
'Come on...' he begged that swirling mess, willing it deeper into the rocks beneath them.

The blazing sun beat down on them relentlessly, blistering Luke's already raw skin. He scratched at it irritably, wincing at the fresh stab of pain. He was running out of time and money quickly, the last drill bits had put him in debt he would never clear unless he found something soon.

His stomach fell at that screaming, tearing sound of tortured metal. He swore, digging the wads of wax out of his ears, eyeing his friend Carlton as he cut the drill, easing it out of the hole carefully.
'It's no good' Carlton said, shouting over the bees wax and ringing in his ears, his voice strange in the sudden quiet. 'It's broken another bit Luke, it's solid rock in there.'

Luke shut his eyes, rubbing them tiredly with the heels of his hands. He was ruined. He had sold everything he owned and borrowed a lot more, and dragged three faithful workers from their homes to dig holes in the dirt in Texas. *The Lone Star State was supposed to be the land of black gold* he moaned silently, eyeing the red dust around him. He had been seduced by the miner's tales of prospectors who disturbed a rock and black geysers shot out of the ground. He hadn't realised the rocks they had to disturb were buried miles deep in the earth.

He rubbed his face, turning away from the three men that stood despondently round the drill shaft, their shoulders slumped. He thought of the money he had borrowed, more than he had ever had in his entire life, more than he had ever seen. He had charmed his way out of several banks with enough money to see him settle happily if only it was his and not borrowed. He was hovering on the edge of despair and trying desperately to cling to a hope that was fluttering further out of his reach.

His hands dropped to his sides in defeat and his eyes drifted away from the shimmering red top of the hill where they stood round the silent drill. In the distance, through a flickering, rolling heat that made the rest of the world look like a mirage, a little canvas village sat forlornly in the wilderness. It too seemed to sag unhappily; five lumpy teepees grouped around a drooping communal cooking tent, still without a chimney though it had been in use for over a month.

He dropped his eyes quickly to block out the sight of his wife Emily struggling with a basin of water she had pulled up from the well. Her white face had flashed in their direction, shooting a glance at the hill where the world was finally quiet before the dirty smudge of her thin, brown hair bowed and ducked into the cooking tent.

He suddenly regretted coming here; Emily was strained by the dirt, the constant effort to keep four men, to entertain their daughter, and all without company of her own. She had to contend with ever more ghastly animals that Laura found and let loose in their tent, squealing with laughter at the chaos it caused. Em had never complained, not even when he had sold everything they ever owned for his dream of black gold, just packed their trunks and followed him into the wilderness.

But the strain had been showing lately, Em would sit and stare at nothing for hours, or frantically scrub the place from top to bottom, from dawn till midnight. He couldn't make her suffering for nothing, for him to give up on the hole – he had been so sure about this one! Em would go mad if they went back to Boston now.

Out of the corner of his eye Luke saw a smudge of red and turned to see Laura flickering in the heat wave, bent over and waving something to a small, blurry creature he couldn't make out. *It's about the size of a large cat* he thought. *I hope it's not a skunk, or a porcupine.* The corners of his mouth twitched in spite of himself, wondering if she was laughing and giggling as it snapped and tugged at the waved torment, dragging her back and forward across the yard.

His heart swelled so painfully in his chest he caught his breath. Laura was his joy, his only treasure, the one goddamn thing he was proud of achieving in his life. She made him feel like a god when she placed her small hand in his and smiled up at him. He still remembered the colour of her cheeks and the shape of her eyelashes when he had held her in his arms for the first time. He had sworn he would give her the world if she asked for it.

'- sink another hole' Carlton finished saying, breaking into his thoughts.

'Put the last bit on it and try again' he said softly.

'What?' Carlton gasped. 'It's the last one! There's nothing there!'

Luke didn't answer, his jaw setting stubbornly. Carlton swore and threw up his hands but knew better than to argue with Luke when he was like this. He changed the drill bit, muttering under his breath, eyeing the large, discarded pile of blunt and broken bits. Luke winced as the loud whine of the drill cut back through the silence and stuffed the beeswax back into his ears, his chest hurting with the tension. *God please* he begged silently. *If not for me, then for her. She deserves better than this.*

All four dusty, tired men stared at the swirling dirt round the bit, willing it deeper, willing it to strike black gold. Carlton's thick arms shuddered above the drill and he fought to control it, fought to win against the earth. The metal began to whine protestingly and Luke grabbed the drill, forcing his weight down onto it to steady it, trying to keep it from shuddering itself apart, to keep it from blunting, ricocheting off the hard sides in the narrow shaft.

'Come on you bastard! Give her just one chance!' he screamed with frustration.

There was a tortured shriek, a metallic scream as the bit unwound itself in the deep shaft and then a low shifting growl in the bowels of the earth. The shaft filled with a rushing, rumbling sound.

The explosion knocked all four onto their backs. Luke lay stunned, watching the expanding black cloud above him. At first he thought the drill had caught fire, until the thick, viscose droplets began splashing into the red Texas dust. *It's beautiful* he whispered in awe, lying right under the black fountain, watching how it turned faintly yellow, like gold, as the hot sun shined through the liquid. *It really is black gold.*

And then he began to laugh, a quiet chuckle that grew until delirious tears were running down his face. Carlton and the men dragged him to his feet, hollering and laughing in ecstasy, hugging and slapping each other on the back, dancing round the base of the black geyser like pagans.

'I gotta tell Em!' he suddenly cried, breaking from the dance and setting off down the hill towards the sagging canvas tents. 'Em!' he yelled. 'Emily! Bring out my princess and look! Emily!'

He burst into their humble home and swept his wife into a vigorous dance, covering her thin white dress with thick oil, his words falling over themselves as he tried to tell her what he'd found, that he was sorry for all the hardship he had put her through, and all the luxuries she would now have.

'Daddy there's water on the hill!' Laura cried, running in to the one room home and he smothered her up in his arms, kissing her smooth, flushed cheeks.

'That's not water, that's oil!' he laughed, promising her a whole zoo of animals just for her. 'You will never want for anything my princess, you will have jewels and gold and – and fancy gowns and everything that rich ladies have, and you'll go horse-back riding and to fancy parties and you'll have the pick of all your husbands just you wait!'

'Oh yes!' Emily broke in, her thin, strained face shining with hysteria. 'Oh yes my girl will be made a lady. And we'll have no more of this wildness, this running around chasing your dreams into the dust of another godforsaken place, Luke. She's got to learn to be a proper lady, proper and respectable. And she won't learn it here, oh no, not in this backwards dust hole. She's going back to the city, there's a school there -'

'No!' Laura cried out. 'Don't send me away daddy!'

'Of course not princess, we've got to celebrate!' Luke grinned, Emily's words falling on ears deaf in his delirium. 'I'm going to buy both my princesses new dresses; these are all dirty!'

'You're all dirty daddy!' Laura squealed with laughter. 'You're filthy!'

'Filthy rich!' he yelled, and whooped again when equally dirty and delirious men burst in, singing and dancing; drunk on happiness, weariness, and only a little on beer.

1

September, 1903

Lady Ramkinson leaned across; the egg-thin pot held firmly, her little finger extended elegantly.

'More tea Your Majesty?' she offered, congratulating herself that neither her hand nor her voice shook.

Beneath her trained exterior Lady Ramkinson was twitching with excitement and nervousness. Her quick eyes darted round the tea setting, taking note if the milk was too warm, if the sugar cubes were still firm, if the brew was still hot. That silly girl Matilda was fidgeting in the corner of the elegant, cozy parlour and trying desperately not to look like she was eves-dropping. Lady Ramkinson inwardly sighed. By dinnertime the entire school would know Tsar Constantinovich Vakhtangov of Dalnerechensk had visited the school and taken tea with the Headmistress.

'Yes of course' he smiled, his hand not so steady as he offered the cup to be refilled.

She waited with a warm smile while he sweetened his drink and reclined, rumbling a sigh as he eased his sore back against the high leather chair, his faint blue eyes wandering around the elegant furnishings of the room; the tasteful cashmere rug, the imposing marble fireplace stocked with wood and the elegant mahogany finishings of the furniture. The room spoke of a refined woman with taste and an eye for subtle details.

Tsar Constantinovich brought the teacup slowly to his lips, aware that Lady Ramkinson had filled the cup near the top again and hoped he wouldn't spill the hot liquid on himself. *Even the tea tasted subtle and refined* he thought. He held his breath against the pain and leaned forward, selecting a shortbread biscuit from the cake stand on the small table between them and sighed again as he eased back, nibbling contentedly.

Lady Ramkinson waited, her quick, lecherous mind whirling through possible reasons why this appointment had been made. The Tsar was too old to be enrolling a daughter in the school, but perhaps a granddaughter, or great granddaughter. *Royalty* she gleamed. *Oh my reputation if I have Royalty in my school. The applications for a place will triple overnight. My school will become the most desirable school for ladies in the New World. Perhaps the most desirable anywhere on the globe.*

She had been suspicious when she had received the letter nearly three months ago informing her of the Tsar's visit. Before the gilt edged letter had arrived she had never heard of the Principality of Dalnerechensk, and she had been unable to locate it on any of her maps. It wasn't until the Family Crest stamped into the wax had been verified as an old, almost forgotten crest from Eastern Europe that she had sent a telegram back warmly inviting him to her school. Even if the Family Crest was almost forgotten it was still Royalty.

Royalty. She nearly purred it.

She brought herself sharply back from her dream of grandeur. *The little trollop's probably a disgrace to her family*, she thought meanly, not letting her smile twist into one of malice. *Better to save face in the eyes of Europe by sending her to the New World to do the best that could be done with her;*

marrying her off to a wealthy colonial where they would no longer have to bother with her.

At the thought of marriage Lady Ramkinson's mind quickly spun down other avenues of grandeur. *Marriage, that's what it is,* she thought. *My students are well known for their class, hostess skills and dutifulness.* The letter had not mentioned the possibility of enrolling a student in her school. It had been brusque and polite but not forthcoming with its details. She suddenly dismissed Matilda. *He's after a wife or an intelligent whore* she thought to herself. *Even at his age.*

'I must say I was surprised to receive a letter from the Principality of Dalnerechensk' she smiled sweetly, carefully digging for information when they were alone.

'Your school has been highly recommended, Lady Ramkinson' he answered.

'I have an excellent reputation for the education of ladies' she said helpfully.

'Quite.'

The Tsar finished his tea and set the cup on the saucer, the china rattling as he unsteadily placed it on the table. He brushed the crumbs from the front of his smart black uniform, the sun glinting through the parlour windows catching in the gold buttons and the fine red trim on his shoulders. His tired eyes drifted to the keyhole, knowing that eyes and ears were on the other side, straining for gossip. He heaved a gentle sigh of acceptance, and slight regret, and began to speak.

'I have come on behalf of my son, Crown Prince *Velikij Knjaz* Aleksei of Dalnerechensk, who believes that it is time to produce an heir to the throne. We are but a small, traditional community, and it is a custom that the choice of bride must be approved of by the father of the groom. For this wisdom His Royal Highness has expressed complete faith in me and has appointed me to seek a Lady suitable to become his wife.'

Lady Ramkinson's thoughts crashed to a halt, hardly knowing whether to laugh or scoff at the absurdity of his words. *Naturally parents wanted to approve of their offspring's choice of suitable spouse, but this was the New World and a new century, it was rare even for the politically minded unions of European Royalty to marry without ever seeing their future partner.* That the Prince was disinterested in a wife was nothing new, Lady Ramkinson was not so green to know some men despised all things feminine. But those in the public eye had to mind public opinion and at least maintain the outward appearance of married civility.

She said nothing, rearranging her expression into something compassionate while her quick thoughts churned away inside her. *Why was he looking for a bride in the New World when the houses of Europe were swollen with daughters just waiting to be wedded and bedded? Was the Prince Regent horribly disfigured, or crippled in some way, that made even those who would marry swine for pearls turn down his proposals?* Her mean mind turned to the Principality itself. *No one would marry a swine if he were king of naught but mud.*

Whatever the reason, the brides of Europe were not interested in him.

'I would like to meet the most eligible daughters in your school' the Tsar continued quietly, and Lady Ramkinson's attention slid back to him. 'I can trust that you will keep these matters discreet?'

'Of course' she smiled. 'Would you care to dine with us this evening?'

'I would be delighted' he said with a smile.

The Tsar patted his whiskers once more with the napkin, dabbing stray crumbs of the shortbread biscuit from his richly decorated jacket. He eased forward in his seat and braced his feet on the floor, grimly shifting his weight onto them, and stood still for a minute to ease the pain in his lower back. Lady Ramkinson smiled and stood with him, reaching to take the hand of the elderly gentleman and drawing it through her elbow, before leading him towards the door.

'My girls dine punctually at seven every night Your Majesty; this routine ensures they are well trained to accept their husbands' observances' Lady Ramkinson said as she led him out of the parlour and through her elegant house to the front door.

Behind the automatic pleasantries she exchanged with the Tsar her mind was already picking over the girls in her school. Many of her former students had met and married wealthy and powerful men, one had even married an archduke, but no Crown Prince had ever come knocking – well, no Tsar had ever come looking on a Crown Prince's behalf, even if it was for a country so insignificant it was not on any of her maps.

Tsar Constantinovich's attaché, a lithe, elegant man who radiated decorum, was waiting in the front hall patiently. He stood from the carved chaise lounge when the door to the entrance hall opened, and bowed respectfully to his monarch and then to the lady leading him like an elegant sick-nurse. Quickly he gathered the thick coat from the rack and held it out for Tsar Constantinovich, his face betraying nothing of his thoughts.

The Tsar was old but not crippled, and this American woman had drawn his arm through hers, leading the Tsar through her boarding school. He wondered if this Lady Ramkinson, so highly recommended by their contacts in Boston, taught her students how to take the lead, and humble their husbands in doing so. An American bride, brash and bereft of feminine wiles would be scorned by Dalnerechensk's traditionalist population.

He said nothing as Lady Ramkinson took the coat from him, helping the old man dress, even buttoning the top two elegant brass disks to hold it closed. He handed the Tsar his hat wordlessly, it was not his place to say anything, although the Tsar would ask for his opinion while in his private suite at the hotel.

The attaché took Tsar Constantinovich's offered arm and helped him carefully down the sweeping stairs of the house, mindful his monarch's pride would have been wounded, but not quite willing to let him totter down them unescorted. Lady Ramkinson watched him open the door for the waiting carriage and help up the old Tsar. When he was seated the attaché climbed in and sat opposite him, nodding his head respectfully towards the headmistress.

She in turn dipped a small nod back, approving of his handsome features with a skilled and picky eye. Those silly girls had almost fawned over him while answering the door and their gossiping whispers had started even before the kitchen door had been shut. The attaché knocked twice on the roof then turned his attention to the Royal sitting opposite him.

The driver flicked his whip and the horses snorted, tossing their heads so the metal rings on their bridles jingled. The gravel of the wide, circular driveway crunched under the wheels as the carriage pulled away from the steps. Tsar Constantinovich nodded goodbye as they swung towards Boston, heading down the long avenue of trees that lined the school's driveway.

Lady Ramkinson waved then glided into her school to set the place in a fearsome uproar. Several younger girls were crowded at the far end of the front hall, hoping for a vain glimpse of the Royal who had visited their school, huddled together, terrified of being caught by Lady Ramkinson. When the Headmistress turned to step back into the school they scattered like a flock of frightened birds, flying through doors they slammed behind them.

Lady Ramkinson's lip curled in distaste. Fifty years ago the expansive home of the Ramkinsons had been converted into a boarding school; the west wing consisted entirely of bedrooms, one for each student. The large common room on the ground floor was furnished with a piano and a tasteful scattering of tables to play cards or write at, and practise other pursuits fitting of refined ladies. When girls enrolled in her school they were given modest, small rooms on the first floor. The older students had more comfortable bedrooms and a small dressing room each on the second floor. They also shared a small parlour where they entertained visiting guests or took tea with respective men who came to call seeking one of their hands, especially after the school's famous Debutante Balls.

Each Ball Season the tailors of Boston were kept busy for weeks constructing fabulous garments for the students who had reached the end of the education deemed appropriate for a lady. First Season Balls were held all over the city for daughters who had reached an age suitable to be introduced to prospective suitors, and first and best of all was the debut of Lady Ramkinson's girls.

Her distaste deepened when another door slammed somewhere in the house, probably behind the silly girls who were distancing themselves from their Headmistress so as not to be punished for forgetting how to act like a lady. Lady Ramkinson set her face in a frozen smile and opened the door to the large common room. Several girls were inside, going about their tasks; embroidering, singing, writing letters, playing the piano or conversing in French. While their outward appearance showed no signs of interest in anything but what they were doing, each and every ear was alert to the flutterings in the house.

The girls looked up from their embroidery and all but Margaret Thornton, seated at the piano forte and singing sweetly with her back to the common room door, stopped what they were doing to look at their mistress. Before she could speak the door from the servants' quarters was pushed open and Matilda appeared, carrying a silver tray with a china tea cup and pot of steaming liquid. She did not see Lady Ramkinson and headed straight towards the most beautiful girl in the room.

'You'll never guess Lady Crompton, he were a Tsar!' she blurted out, setting down the tray on the small round table beside the pretty blonde who had set aside her embroidery. 'And fancy, he were looking for -'

Lady Ramkinson did not carry the riding crop she normally did, having set it aside for her meeting with the Tsar of Dalnerechensk, but the thwack of her firm hand hitting the mahogany top of the sideboard near her reverberated in the room and stopped the wagging tongue of the maid in its tracks. Margaret's fingers stopped dancing over the ivory and she turned her neck elegantly to look.

'Enough, you stupid girl' Lady Ramkinson snapped, inspecting her hand and brushing at it irritably, as if she had felt something distasteful on the surface of the sideboard.

The maid shot Lady Crompton a quick, frightened look, and Lady Ramkinson knew the girl had bribed the maid for information. A small part of the Mistress approved, it was the lady of the house's job to know all that went on within its walls, but she despaired at her choice of informant. Matilda had no sense of decorum and was unmindful of her company. Lady Ramkinson dismissed her, sent to fold linen where she couldn't cause any more rumours.

Her gaze drifted over the girls in the common room. They sat like perfect dolls, their hands folded in their laps, their eyes lowered demurely, waiting politely, with just enough confidence befitting of a lady when meeting her betters, just as Lady Ramkinson had trained them. For a moment she thought of their glittering coming out party, a lavish, popular affair where the great ballroom sparkled with her graduating students and all the young, eligible bachelors of Boston society.

The party had been planned for the first week of October, and promised to be the most spectacular the school had ever seen. Each girl would descend down the sweeping staircase into the foyer below while the butler announced them to the crowd of admirers and prospective bachelors. And leading the girls down the stairs would be Margaret Thornton, the oldest girl to graduate.

Lady Ramkinson thought it fitting that the girls received honours in her school as they would in the family home. Margaret Thornton would be first to entertain gentlemen callers interested in pressing a suit with her, and first to accept invitations to other dinner parties of Boston's fashionable. It was only fitting that Margaret be introduced to the Tsar first at dinner that evening. Lady Ramkinson couldn't stop her distaste showing. Margaret was the oldest girl in the school, but she was not the wealthiest.

Her eyes drifted from the straight, proud back of Margaret to the peach-complexioned Belinda Crompton. One month younger than Margaret she was Lady Ramkinson's best pupil, gifted in language and music, witty, and the daughter of the most prestigious doctor in Boston. The Crompton family ruled Boston society and export markets, Lady Ramkinson had already booked her dance card with the most eligible young men in the city. She was a woman worthy of a principality.

The colour deepened in Belinda's cheeks, a triumphant smile playing on her pretty mouth. Margaret turned her head away and gathered the sheets of music together, aware that there would now be hours of schooling in etiquette to address the Tsar properly. That viper Belinda would again usurp her position as prefect in another of Lady Ramkinson's schemes to wed her wealthily for the benefit of the school.

*

At seven only ten of the prettiest and most eligible girls in the school stood in a line in the front hall, waiting for the late Tsar. A servant stood rock still, sweating beside the front door, waiting to be handed the coats from the Tsar and the handsome attaché.

All the girls were wearing brand new dresses and shoes and had spent the afternoon pampering themselves, perfecting ways to catch the eye of the Tsar. Lady Ramkinson strode up and down the corridor, the riding crop in her hand, her unforgiving eye lingering over each girl until they squirmed with discomfort.

'Stand still!' she commanded, her voice booming down the corridor. To prove her point she slapped the leg of the girl slowest to obey with the crop. The girl flinched but did not waver again.

At last the bell on the door jingled. Lady Ramkinson let the crop drop discreetly into the tasteful stand beside the door as she reached to answer it, the crop slipping behind the black folds of an umbrella. The Mistress smiled brilliantly, sweeping a curtsey to the men on the door step.

'Good evening Your Majesty' she smiled, stepping out into the chilly evening to draw his hand through her elbow and guide him across the threshold of her home.

The Tsar hesitated only briefly, uncomfortable at the etiquette reversal, but was too much of a gentleman to refuse a lady's wishes and stepped into the wide hall. The attaché followed and the servant darted forward, closing the door behind them before returning to her spot by the coat rack. Tsar Constantinovich removed his fur trimmed hat and coat. The Headmistress took them from him, letting her fingers surreptitiously slide along the exquisitely soft collar before reaching to take the attaché's coat and hat, handing them to the servant to hang up.

Despite his snowy-grey locks, the Tsar was still a figure of beauty and power in his elegant black evening jacket, gleaming with brass buttons, and the girls stood straighter, hoping the son had his father's looks. He stood tall and proud despite a lingering pain in his lower back, a powerful grace that the failing of his body had not quite eradicated from his poise and movement. He bowed courteously to his hostess as she glided forward, turning beside him and offering her elbow, smiling charmingly.

He smiled politely and took it, letting her lead him across the wide floor of the entrance hall to the line of waiting girls.

'Your Majesty, may I present the ladies of the school who will take dinner with us' Lady Ramkinson smiled as they walked, and the girls all swept perfect, deep curtsies. 'This is Margaret Thornton, of the Chicago Thorntons. She has a gift for music and art, but always has her head in the clouds I'm afraid' Lady Ramkinson said, stopping in front of the first girl.

One by one they coloured as Lady Ramkinson moved down the line, revealing their talents and their weaknesses to the gentleman king. They bid him a good evening with lowered, embarrassed eyes, offering a hand that received a whiskery kiss.

'This student will be sitting beside you during dinner, Lady Belinda Crom-'

The front door opened and two arrivals startled the small dinner party. They caught sight of the headmistress and her guests and stopped in shock, crashing into each other in their confusion. Tsar Constantinovich felt Lady Ramkinson's arm tighten in anger under his hand. He eyed the two girls in surprise.

Both were dressed simply, a plain travelling cape thrown about their shoulders. Their hair was loose and hung in disarray, and both looked horrified. They snapped to attention, dropping a quick curtsey, their heads lowered in embarrassment and fear.

'Good evening Lady Ramkinson, My Lord' one said, noting the decorations on the elderly man. She looked like she wanted to run off but knew she couldn't until dismissed.

The pretty dolls had gasped at their arrival and Tsar Constantinovich was surprised at the looks on their faces. He eyed the two girls carefully. The buxom blonde had not raised her face and had something of the peasant swagger about her. *A servant* he guessed. The other dark haired girl stood with her head turned just so, her eyes downcast, but a lift in her chin which could be described as defiant. He surmised she was one of the students and eyed the gleeful looks on the other girls' faces. They realised he was looking and quickly schooled their features back into attentive sweetness.

'Lady Belinda Crompton of the Boston Cromptons' Lady Ramkinson finished, her mouth tightening as she repressed her fury. 'Your Majesty please excuse me briefly; I must see to this matter. Belinda, show His Majesty our gardens, there are a few late blooms left, and a vigorous walk will greatly improve the appetite.'

'Of course Lady Ramkinson' she curtsied, then stepped forward and took the Tsar's elbow, gently leading him away, the other girls following like docile sheep.

They threw each other looks filled with petty spite and quiet horror. An uneasy titter swept through them and they whispered sidelong to each other, speculating on their classmate's fate. The attaché followed the girls at a quiet, discreet distance along the length of the entrance hall, past the foot of the grand, sweeping staircase and through the beautifully carved double oak doors behind the steps. Across the tasteful but barren ball room French doors opened onto a white terrace and steps led down into the garden beyond. Margaret shot the two girls one last look before closing the doors behind them.

As soon as the door shut Lady Ramkinson grabbed the arm of the student, bearing her along, up the grand staircase with the force of her fury till they reached the private corridors of the student's rooms in the west wing.

'You were sick were you *hmm*? *Resting in your rooms and not to be disturbed*, isn't that what you said this morning?' Lady Ramkinson seethed, dragging her into her room and slamming the door.

Her extended arm snapped round and caught her full across the cheek. She had been prepared for the blow but the force of it still staggered her back a step. Lady Ramkinson looked as delicate as a ballerina but had the strength of a prize boxer. The guilty pleasure of the Irish pub Clara had dragged her into on their way home from the circus flared momentarily; the heat of the room and the bodies pressed tight, shouting and waving money in a circle around two men, stripped to their waists and watching the other warily with raised fists; but this quailed before Lady Ramkinson's fury.

'*You impudent little wretch*! You have embarrassed me in front of the Tsar of Dalnerechensk and brought shame to the reputation of my school! How *dare* you!' she spluttered, livid. 'You will pack your bags and leave in the morning, back to that muck-hole in Texas. I told that stupid mother of yours when she enrolled you that money never has and never will make a lady out of the likes of you.' She stopped to catch her breath, snorting like a panicky horse in her fury.

'My colour is uneven Lady Ramkinson; would you be so kind as to slap the other cheek as well?' Laura said quietly.

There was a brief flicker in the proud lady's eyes.

'It does not matter *Miss* Asanton, you will not be joining us for dinner. You are hereby expelled from my school.'

She swept out of the room and slammed the door behind her. Laura's trembling knees gave way and she sat down with a bump, wiping her cheeks to calm herself. She had never seen the Headmistress quite so angry and thanked God silently the dreaded riding crop had not been in her grip. After a minute or two the trembling stopped and she got to her feet, discarding the thick and grubby cloak.

She rattled the door handle experimentally and was not surprised to find it locked against her. *There had only been ten dressed like perfect dolls*, she thought, and suspected the other plainer, poor or silly girls were locked in their rooms too. She knew Lady Ramkinson kept immaculate time; all girls had to be seated by seven for dinner in the formal dining room. Laura had been counting on the strict obedience of the rules to slip upstairs unnoticed like she had so many times before. To find the girls standing in the corridor with the Headmistress at half past seven had been a shock.

She wondered briefly about the men that stood in the hall too. No doubt if Belinda Crompton was there, in glittering array and outshining the other girls, it had to do with another advantageous marriage. *The Tsar of Dalnerechensk* Lady Ramkinson had called him. *Where was Dalnerechensk?* She felt a momentary stab of panic when she couldn't readily place it on a map and tried to remember those endless geography lessons. Try as she might she could not recall hearing the name before.

The moment of panic was pushed aside by the realisation that it didn't matter anymore. She didn't have to know where countries were, who was ruler, and how to catch their attention. She shuddered. *Imagine being married to a wrinkly old man!* She was no fool to think there would not be benefits from marrying a husband so past his prime. A kingdom of wealth and power made for attractive widows, especially if they still glowed with youth. No wonder Lady Ramkinson and her protégé were glittering like hard diamonds in the entrance hall, breaking a rule held for fifty years. Laura didn't doubt they would stand there till midnight if it meant they would find money, power or prestige in a husband.

Bitter disappointment had taught Laura that the students of Lady Ramkinson were to be nothing more than the dour doormats for egotistical husbands who wanted something pretty to hang off their arms and beget their heirs upon. Unseemly activities were actively discouraged and severely punished. The girls were forbidden to be seen making a spectacle of themselves, to be near places of ill-repute – they were even forbidden to go to town alone.

The school had been a rude shock for Laura, who had spent her youth running wild with hardened oil workers who sometimes forgot and cursed in front of her, to be shut away with books and lessons in etiquette. Lady Ramkinson's distaste for her spirit and untamed nature was obvious. She set about breaking her in just as she would a horse: with regiment, repetition, and regular beatings. Laura had learnt to conceal her feelings carefully, to accept Lady Ramkinson's iron will, but never let it break her.

She suddenly felt horrified to realise she was afraid of leaving this place. As a child she had dreamed of it constantly, but the finishing school had woken her social conscience and vanity. Her sense of failure was almost overwhelming and tears came close in her confusion; struggling between what she desperately wanted and what her father would think of her. She knew the way the girls talked about her, the vicious things they whispered, the looks they sent from Ladyship to Ladyship. It had been a bitter moment when Laura realised Lady Ramkinson was training these girls to send out into wider society. Boston was bigger than twenty-seven girls. She didn't know if she could live snubbed by Boston society.

Laura shut her eyes and got hold of herself. The excitement she had felt from her day at the circus was well and truly faded. She sighed and shrugged off the dirty cotton dress she had borrowed from Clara to wear out. A large pitcher of water sat on her chest of drawers and she poured a little into the basin on the chair, using a soft cloth to wash her body, pouring the water over her locks to wash out the sweaty, smoky smell of the pub.

Quickly she toweled her hair dry, pulling out a soft house dress in a stunning emerald green from her wardrobe. She ignored the corset Lady Ramkinson wanted all her girls to wear to encourage correct posture and shapely figures, and slipped the dress over her head then combed her hair till it shone faintly in the light. She opened her casement window, looking out over the beautiful gardens, turning her mind to the practicalities of her predicament.

No doubt when the Tsar had departed this evening Lady Ramkinson would return to her room, an encounter Laura was not looking forward to. She could endure no more: the constant terror of the riding crop, the girls that looked down their noses at her, the endless, endless lessons in French and etiquette. Her expulsion would not save her from this evening.

The desperate need to escape flared wildly in her. It overrode her sensibilities and she swung her leg over the sill, climbing down the trellis into the manicured garden below. At the bottom she paused, her heart thudding in her ears, her eyes darting round, searching for any locus of sound that meant she had been seen. Elation was flooding through her, and she wondered if she should head for the garden wall and climb over that too. She shut her eyes briefly, breathing deeply, the soothing scents of autumn flooding into her and easing her adrenalin away.

She could not leave, not like this. She had no money, no provisions, and she would have to walk all the way to town; a prospect that was no mean feat, and nowhere to go once she arrived. As much as she wanted to, she couldn't run away, she would have to swallow her pride and leave with the school sniggering behind their smiles at her. She felt her heart sink in her chest and shut her eyes again, trying to soothe her heart-wracking disappointment.

A bird sang to her left and she managed a sad smile, knowing she would miss the smell of roses, jasmine and gardenias in the summer; miss the humming of bees and the warm sun on her cheek as she sat under the droopy willow by the pond, miss tending her allotted garden bed. It had been the poorest patch of soil, a mockery of her lowly status, but she had tended it well and grown such vibrant blooms that even Lady Ramkinson had been impressed.

Laura glanced left and right quickly then set off through the garden to the small seat at the end of the formal area, placed exactly right so the people sitting on it could not be seen from the house. She picked a late flower, one of Belinda's, and sniffed carefully, shutting her eyes in quiet pleasure as she made her way along the path, sinking down onto the cool marble bench.

'I have not seen a lady escape a window before' said an amused voice beside her.

She jumped in surprise and scrabbled to her feet. The voice had rumbled out quietly, like distant thunder. The words were spoken precisely and the accent had rounded and filled the vowels. *Even his voice sounded rich* Laura thought and dropped a curtsey quickly to the Tsar, her eyes fluttering to the attaché behind him and away again demurely, as she'd been taught. He was young for his position of power and responsibility and his face was superbly blank of his thoughts. Laura wondered what rigorous training he had had to remain so impassive.

'Forgive me Your Majesty' she said hurriedly. 'I did not mean to intrude -'

'Bah' the Tsar said good-naturedly. 'I am just an old man, enjoying his pipe.' He puffed on it to emphasise his words and the smoke drifted lazily into the evening air. 'Sit and keep me company this evening.'

Laura swallowed her surprise and curtsied, shooting another look at the blank face of the attaché. She sat carefully beside the Tsar, folding her hands on her lap, wondering what she should say. Her quick mind blurred through the list of topics Lady Ramkinson had instructed was suitable for discussion, and in what situations to raise them. Nothing seemed suitable for a woman caught climbing out a window.

The Tsar eased back against the cool marble seat and puffed quietly in enjoyment, eyeing her open casement and chuckling. Laura wondered if she should talk to him first, she had seen him with his arm through Lady Ramkinson's, and was torn between doing so and having nothing intelligent to say.

The Tsar's chuckle rumbled deep in his chest again and Laura couldn't stop the smile that spread across her face. His eyes twinkled with a mischief and she dropped her eyes modestly, sniffing again at the stolen bloom. A comfortable silence settled between them and the Tsar tapped down the tobacco inside his pipe, sighing contentedly.

He wondered just what kind of woman his son wanted. There was no doubt the girls Lady Ramkinson had selected tonight were attractive, each in their own way. He had wandered away while they had discussed the flowers in the garden and whispered behind their hands with malicious glee, speculating on the girl's punishment, sneering that it served her right for trying to rise above her station, sighing it was about time Lady Ramkinson had realised money did not make breeding.

He had tired of them quickly. They had no modesty, they were young, silly girls backbiting and squabbling like chickens at a feed bucket, excitable and more interested in the latest gossip and scandal than their duty to entertain an ageing old man. He shut his eyes, wondering again why Aleksei wanted an American bride. The women here had not the decorum of the old families in Europe. He was dreading the evening ahead of him.

But the Prince had insisted. The Tsar had reasoned with him, had pleaded, to no avail. The Irish country lass of a wealthy land owner would be at home in Dalnerechensk but Aleksei had none of it. At last the old man had given up and made inquiries into the suitability of girls with an education and standing worthy of a principality.

A movement beside him brought his attention back to the fragrant garden. She had lifted the bloom to her nose again and breathed deeply, the red from the petals reflected in her cheeks, the dark fan of her eyelashes a smudge against the lily-white of her skin. She was attractive, with skin like blushing cream and a flourishing figure draped in spectacular emerald green that made her eyes glow with depth and warmth. There was something graceful in her movement, something elegant in the way she carried herself, a strength and stamina visible despite her delicate features.

He puffed deeply, rumbling disquietly in his chest as he breathed in the smells of the garden. Her name was Laura; he had heard them whispering it while Lady Crompton had prattled on about cultivation. The easy silence around them lingered, needing no words or pleasantries to fill the spaces between them, as if they were already old friends. He heard the distant voices of the students' rise, calling to him as they discovered he was gone. He tapped out the spent pipe on the edge of the seat at slipped it inside his elegant jacket.

'I have seen long years, and sometimes the young think that grey hairs mean deaf ears' he said, watching the way her eyes lifted to him; gentle, but with a careful intelligence reflected in them. 'Why do they whisper such things about you?'

Her smile turned sad and she closed her eyes briefly, folding her hands in her lap again. But when she spoke she looked at him again, an honesty tinged with pride and sadness in her face.

'My father is Luke Asanton Your Majesty. He discovered the richest oil well in Texas seven years ago and my mother decided to make a lady out of me. Though I am sure you are aware, money does not make one a lady. To them, I am no better than the stable boys that bring the oil for their new horseless carriages.'

'Ah' he said, brushing a spot of ash from his sleeve. 'A title does not make a lady either, does it Fedor?'

'No Your Majesty' the attaché answered, his voice as blank of opinion as his face. His timbre was quiet but clear, and carried his message unobtrusively to them. Laura found his manner fascinating.

Another silence fell, interrupted by the arrival of Belinda Crompton. She looked surprised and then her eyes hardened seeing one of her blooms in Laura's hands though she arranged her features carefully.

'There you are Your Majesty' she smiled sweetly. 'If you would be so kind, we are ready to eat.'

Tsar Constantinovich rumbled in his chest and eased forward onto his feet, heaving himself up onto them with as much dignity as he could. He brushed down the rumpled jacket as Fedor came forward then reached out a slightly trembling hand to Laura. Both girls could not conceal their surprise.

'Will you do me the honour of joining us for dinner?' he asked.

'If Your Majesty wishes it, I could not refuse' she answered with an uneasy smile, getting to her feet and avoiding Belinda's cold eyes.

He chuckled and drew her hand through his elbow. Laura slipped past Belinda, letting herself be led towards the wide balcony overlooking the garden. The French doors to the ballroom darkened with a silhouette and Laura knew Lady Ramkinson was watching them. Belinda swept on ahead and the Tsar faltered on the stairs, his face pinching in pain. Laura slipped her other hand under his elbow and gripped his arm firmly, lending her support while allowing him a little dignity. He smiled at her, grateful and pleased she had shown an initiative.

Fedor came along the other side of him and put a hand discreetly under his other elbow, helping him up the stairs. On the balcony he turned to look back over the fragrant gardens, using the moment of respite to recover from the exertion of climbing the stairs. Fedor retreated to a polite, unobtrusive distance and followed shadow-like as the Tsar led Laura into the barren ball room.

With gentle pressure on his arm Laura guided the Tsar through the heavy oak doors to the entrance hall then turned left down a corridor into the East Wing of Ramkinson Manor.

The corridor led away and disappeared into the gathering gloom at the end of the house but Laura shortly turned the Tsar into the large formal dining room.

Like every other room in the house it was elegantly understated and refined. Subtle brocades framed the windows like cloth waterfalls, and the high-backed rich mahogany chairs stood at uniform width from the table, a girl waiting demurely behind each. Three centrepieces arranged tastefully at carefully measured intervals sat on the long formal table, interspaced between lit candelabra. The flames caught in the silverware, burnishing it, while the crisp white table cloth was softened by a tinge of yellow.

A place for Laura had been set hurriedly at the far end of the table. Belinda swept the Tsar to the head of the table, prattling out the menu for the evening's meal to him, and Fedor followed them quietly. Laura took her place with her eyes downcast, feeling the cold fury in Lady Ramkinson's iron demeanor, and took her seat when the Tsar had eased down. There she remained; ignored for the better part of the evening, while the others kept up a lively conversation. She could hardly touch the exquisite meal, and thought of the poor girls in the kitchen, they had to have worked strenuously to have produced a meal such as this at short notice.

Clara eyed her barely touched plate as she cleared them from the table and hid it underneath Margaret's empty dish, but knew it was to no avail, Lady Ramkinson's quick eyes missed nothing, and Laura would be punished for being wasteful. They dared not look at each other and Clara bustled out to the kitchen, feeling that hard stare of the Mistress of the house thump her physically in the back before the door closed and protected her.

Laura folded her hands tightly in her lap and squeezed them to still the trembling. The cheeky hands on the clock were lagging and dragging, the tense seconds seeming to last forever while Lady Ramkinson's cold hatred grew, and then would skip ahead when she glanced away, bringing the evening too soon to a close.

Tsar Constantinovich set the delicate coffee cup back on the saucer and wiped his whiskers, patting carefully before folding the cloth on the table.
'An excellent meal, and fine hospitality Lady Ramkinson' he said, getting to his feet and bowing to the great lady. As he rose the ladies at the table rose automatically too. The Tsar straightened, his face catching at the pinch of pain in his lower back. His eyes drifted over the assembled beauties; silly, gossipy, fanciful girls, all who were shooting him looks from under their lashes, and boldest of them all was Lady Crompton, managing to keep her eyes on him with the way she dipped her head slightly to the left.
'Miss Asanton,' he said suddenly, his eyes drifting to where she stood pale at the end of the table, bringing her eyes back from the gilt clock on the mantelpiece. 'I would be pleased to have your company at noon tea tomorrow' he smiled at her.

Laura's eyes widened in surprise and shock, and she automatically dropped a curtsey, keeping her head bowed.
'If it pleases Your Majesty I could not refuse' she answered.
'Good, I shall send a coach for you at eleven.'

He bowed again and the table curtseyed, then he offered his elbow to Lady Ramkinson. She smiled and accepted, her manner that of a nurse indulging a willful invalid in her care, letting herself be led to the front door. The servant who had let them in hours earlier was still there, too terrified to move in case the fury of the Mistress turned to her. She quickly got down the hats and coats and offered them demurely to Lady Ramkinson, who helped the old Tsar into his coat.

They exchanged pleasantries for the night and Lady Ramkinson extracted a promise from the old man of another visit to spend time with Lady Crompton. The attaché guided Tsar Constantinovich down the stairs with a discreet hand under his elbow. At the bottom of the steps stood their waiting carriage and Tsar Constantinovich fussed briefly with his coat while he steeled himself to heave up into the plush interior, fighting through the pain in his lower back.

Fedor climbed in beside him, heaving himself up as the Tsar had then knocked on the roof for the driver. The girls waved them goodbye as the driver flicked the reins and Lady Crompton closed the door against the chill of the September evening. Lady Ramkinson's eyes were steel as she gripped Laura's arm hard, snatching the crop from the umbrella stand by the door.

2

She carefully eased herself down onto the hidden seat in the fragrant formal garden, wincing at the burning twinges in her skin and the shock of the cold marble against the backs of her legs, even through her dress. Lady Ramkinson had whipped her until she had drawn blood, but was no fool to think of sending her from the school now she had caught the attention of Tsar Constantinovich. Laura had spent the week since then agonised; standing all day and sleeping on her stomach, each simple movement pulling at her new healing skin and terrified the hesitations would draw more fury from the bite of the crop.

She had not cancelled her luncheon date with the Tsar, moving dream-like and cautiously, so much so that even a flicker had passed over Fedor's expressionless face. The kindly old Tsar had noticed her discomfort and asked, concerned by the pain he saw pinched in her eyes, but she had brushed it off with a tight smile and a wave of her hand. He had drawn her arm through his elbow then, and walked with her slowly along the streets nearest his sumptuous hotel suite, Fedor following as unobtrusive as their shadows.

Despite her discomfort that day Laura had noticed the Tsar seemed taken aback with the bustling, shouting throngs on Boston's streets; the carriages that whizzed past them, the smell of horse dung and industrial greasy smoke that hung over the city.

'Forgive me for being bold Your Majesty' she said. 'Is Dalnerechensk so very much different from Boston? I am curious.'

'It is a small Principality, somewhat -' he searched for the word '- sleepy. It is three valleys within the Ural Mountains of Russia. Let us take tea Miss Asanton, I wish to be at leisure.'

'Of course Your Majesty' she smiled, dreading sitting again.

The Tsar led her slowly into a hotel and Fedor held the chair for the Tsar to seat himself before graciously holding Laura's. She smiled tightly and sat, the skin on her back and legs protesting in red agony. She felt a hand on her arm and looked up into Fedor's face, realising she was leaning off balance.

'Miss Asanton?' the Tsar queried quietly.

'Forgive me, just a little moment of unbalance' she said, righting herself.

Fedor sat with them quietly; his face famously blank as the Tsar eased back in the chair and lit his pipe, disconcerted. Fearing he would soon inquire after her health, forcing her to come up with a suitable lie, Laura smiled softly and folded her trembling hands firmly in her lap. *If Lady Ramkinson could see me now she might just be moderately pleased* she thought wryly.

'Forgive me for speaking boldly' she said, 'you have teased me with but a glimpse of Dalnerechensk, I grow eager to know more.'

The Tsar chuckled at the girlishness in her voice and tucked the small oblong snuff box that held his tobacco back inside his elegant jacket.

'Well then, I could not appear so cruel, least no one marry my son for fear of a tyrant father-in-law' he chuckled. A ghost of a smile appeared on Fedor's face.

They ordered a pot of tea and Tsar Constantinovich took a sweetmeat from the cake stand, nibbling while Fedor poured the hot brew for them. Laura took a sip of her tea then set it down again as the tightness in her skin made it difficult to move gracefully and she was frightened of spilling the hot liquid on herself.

'Perhaps you have heard of Ivan Grozny?' the Tsar inquired. 'They call him Ivan the Terrible in English.'

'I do confess my knowledge is poorly lacking' she murmured demurely.

'A terrible, insane man; the first Tsar of Russia' Tsar Constantinovich said, tapping down the tobacco in his pipe to emphasise the words. 'He hated and feared the Boyars, the upper class; his madness thought they had poisoned his wife to death. In fifteen hundred sixty five he took the best land of Russia under his own personal control, the *Oprichnina* he called it, and his own personal guards, the *Oprichniki*: terrible black robed, riding black horses; *Tsar's Sobaki* they called them. They tortured and murdered all suspected of treason.

'Five years of terror followed; the crops failed, plague infected the people. The leader of the *Oprichniki*, Malyuta Skuratov, allowed the *Oprichniki* to grow murderous and massacre innocent nobles and peasants alike. We could not tolerate the persecution!' He took a deep breath, realising his voice had been rising as his passions stirred. He coughed apologetically and took another sip of tea, patting his whiskers with a folded napkin.

'One of the nobles, Vsevolod,' he continued, more sedately, 'realised we could no longer endure such conditions. He led fifty families from the *Oprichnina* and into the Ural Mountains to escape. As they fled more people joined them; peasants and nobility alike, all with horror stories upon their lips. The Tsar and Skuratov had led an army against the prosperous town of Novgorod, believing they were going to defect to Poland. They built a wall around the city to prevent anyone from leaving.

'Every day, for three weeks, a thousand people were brought before Ivan and his son, Feodor, and were tortured and murdered. Vsevolod saved those who managed to flee before the carnage and hid away in beautiful Liberty Valley. All the nobility with him were stripped of their lands and titles and declared criminals. But they were largely ignored; I do think Ivan forgot about us, he did have more pressing things on his mind.' A small smile tweaked at his lips.

'Vsevolod declared Liberty Valley and the two valleys that flanked her as Dalnerechensk, and the people declared him their Tsar and savior. He was a great man, Miss Asanton, humble and intelligent' he said, his voice glowing with admiration. 'A brilliant strategist, he first built Tcherepnin, the fortified village, mapping out the streets and the houses, and lived amongst his people, training an army from the followers.

'The years passed and Dalnerechensk grew. Vsevolod designed a new city in Liberty Valley, and built a castle where she could defend the citizens. After Ivan's death, his son Feodor, who had long resented us, claimed Russia's throne and brought his army against us.'

Tsar Constantinovich trembled with pride as he set down the cool tea, the half nibbled sweetmeat forgotten on his plate. Laura and Fedor were just as enrapt in the story.

'It was a terrible battle' the Tsar said softly. 'Many lives were lost. But Feodor was a weak Tsar and a weaker general, and the great Vsevolod forced back the invaders and saved Dalnerechensk!' He clasped a hand across his breast and burst into a few words of a song Laura was to learn later was the national anthem of the Principality.

'Bog spasi Dalnerechensk' Fedor added quietly. 'God save her.'

'What a daring place it sounds!' Laura said with admiration.

'Yes Miss Asanton' he smiled. 'We are small but a strong and proud people.'

He took a sip of the tea, pulling a small face when he realised it was cold. Fedor called for more and refreshed their cups, noticing how little Laura had eaten and drunk.

Now on the bench in the fragrant garden Laura recalled the conversation had then turned to Boston, and the grey pall that seemed to hang in the sky over the city. The Tsar confessed Dalnerechensk was not as technologically advanced as Aleksei would like, but the Tsar feared the valley would lose its beauty covered in thick, grey skies like Boston. Laura had then insisted the Tsar to come back to the school where the air was more fragrant, as Lady Ramkinson would be glad of another visit. The Tsar had agreed, and since then had visited the school every day, much to the delight of Lady Ramkinson and Belinda.

He had taken tea with Margaret Thornton and Belinda, and again with Laura in the small parlour on the second floor on the third visit since their lunch date, asking politely if his doctor would be of some service for the discomfort he still noticed in her movements. Laura had thanked him for his generosity and politely declined the offer, saying it wasn't necessary. It was not mentioned again.

She had accompanied the old man as he strolled through the autumn gardens twice more, always with one hand resting in the crook of his arm and the other under his elbow, Fedor an unobtrusive few paces behind them. They had talked more of the beauty of Dalnerechensk, the old Tsar burned with pride and Laura loved to hear the richness of his voice as he spoke. The medieval town sounded so daring and quaint at the same time, and she was fascinated.

She felt the warmth returning to the backs of her legs, drawing her back from her memories. The cold marble was no longer soothing and she braced her hands on the seat, raising herself while trying to remain rigidly bent and shuffled along so the cold marble once again relieved the painful welts on the backs of her legs. The chatter of the girls attending their garden beds floated to her on a breeze of rotting apricots and manure. She found the whole thing distasteful and wrinkled her nose, feeling a flash of horror when she realised Lady Ramkinson might see that and rearranged her features carefully.

She sighed and forced herself to focus on the problem at hand, trying to think of an eloquent way to word a telegraph to her father, to explain why she was coming home a year earlier than expected. Lady Ramkinson had allowed her by the grace of the Tsar to remain at the school until he had chosen a bride and departed, and Laura knew her time was running out.

Her father would be disappointed. She wondered if she should show him the scars she had on her back and legs, then was too embarrassed to raise the issue with herself again. After all, it was her fault, she had defied Lady Ramkinson, she had made a spectacle of herself, and twenty-seven horrendous gossips knew it. Her name would be smeared from Boston to Chicago, and she would be lucky if it didn't follow her as far south as Texas.

Her lip trembled as she swore silently, passionately, that she didn't care. Then she shut her eyes and relented, leaning back as far as she could without the twinges of pain in her legs, looking up into the branches of the tree she sat under. The leaves were rich shades of gold and red and she sighed, saddened to leave here, she had devoted seven years to Lady Ramkinson's snobbery to have it all come to nothing.

She had cared. Cared from that first instant when she had slipped out of her room the night she had arrived, her miserable tears stilled by the gaiety of the music and the noise of people; talking, laughing and dancing below in the huge ball room, light spilling out onto the lawn where couples walked like paintings come to life. She had knelt on the steps, peering down at the graduating girls at their glittering Debutante Ball, watching all the beautiful arriving dignitaries; how they walked and sparkled and laughed; and had been seduced by it all, wishing desperately, secretly, she would one day outshine them all.

It was all beyond her reach now. The backs of her legs twinged and she righted herself, knowing the cold marble was no longer soothing the ache of the cuts. Tsar Constantinovich was before her, still a pace or two away. Her moment of pain must have shown on her face as his was lined with worry. She smiled, pleased to see him, starting to get to her feet. He put out a hand to still her.

'May I join you?' he asked quietly, bowing stiffly.

'Of course Your Majesty' she smiled, bobbing a curtsey and moved over to allow him some room.

He eased himself down then felt in his pockets for hidden treasures, pulling out his pipe and some tobacco, filling the little chamber and clamping the stem between his teeth, slipping the small tin back into his jacket pocket. He struck a match and the smoke curled lazily into the air, weaving around the branches of the tree as it rose. Laura breathed deeply; the tobacco was the gift she had presented to the Tsar at their luncheon. It was the same brand her father smoked and the scent was soothing.

The comfortable silence fell around them again and she tried to ignore the hot lines of pain on the backs of her legs. The Tsar pulled out a large pocket watch from his waistcoat and clicked it open, studying the face in the watch before raising his eyes to the girl beside him.

'I wish to show you my son' he said, passing the watch to her. 'Crown Prince *Velikij Knjaz* Aleksei Stephanovich Vakhtangov, Regent of the Principality of Dalnerechensk and heir to the throne.'

Laura took the watch carefully. Inside was a miniature portrait of a handsome man in a decorated military uniform. His hair was thick and coal black, combed back from his face to reveal a high, broad forehead. His eyes looked kind, almost dreamy, and gave her the impression that they weren't looking out of the painting at her but past her, into some unseen future. His jaw was firm and strong, his lips soft and gentle. The sliming black of the uniform couldn't hide his wide shoulders and powerful body. She could not tell how tall he was but guessed him to be around six foot or more. She was surprised to find he was not young, estimating he was in his mid-thirties.

She studied the face, chewing her lip as she appraised the painting with an artist's eye.

'If I may be bold, he has something of the commoners and the nobility both' she said carefully. 'He appears a man that all men could respect. There is strength and gentleness about him; a goodness. He will be a fine husband to Lady Crompton.'

'Good heavens no, she would love her horse more than my son!' he exclaimed.

His bluntness startled her and she couldn't repress a giggle. His kind eyes smiled at her.

'My son gave me strict instructions to find a woman who would cope with the – peculiarities – of Dalnerechensk' the Tsar went on. 'He will not suffer a fool for a wife. I will confess, I was surprised he did not seek his bride in Europe, but he was adamant. I do wonder if this is the right choice, the people will not like his decision. He is in need of a bride who will be resolute against public hostility, and be charming enough to win their hearts.'

It went unsaid what he thought of the girls in Lady Ramkinson's school. Her eyes drifted back to the portrait; the soft mouth, the strong jaw, those dreamy, romantic eyes, and wondered why he appeared so disinterested in looking for a wife himself. She had been truthful in what she said to the Tsar. Crown Prince Aleksei did look like a man that everyone could relate to, he did not look pampered and indulged, yet he did not look uncouth and unrefined. He was a man that could relate to all, no matter what their walk of life. His eyes looked intelligent, somewhat visionary, and his wide, strong shoulders spoke of a man unafraid to lend a hand to see it built.

'Could one love a man such as he?' the Tsar mused quietly.

'He is appealing to the eye' she said, lowering her eyes, a pretty blush darkening her cheeks. 'One could like him well enough. Perhaps love is too presumptuous a word for a portrait, I know him not' she closed the pocket watch and handed it back to the Tsar. 'Yet, say he is but one tenth of the man you are, and yes, one could love a man such as he.'

He smiled, and lifted one of her hands for a whiskery kiss.

'I have come to bid you goodbye Miss Asanton' he said sadly. 'I leave on a ship bound to Constantinople in two days.'

Laura felt her heart sag. 'I will miss our walks together; I have so enjoyed them.'

She did not blame him for not finding a bride at the school, though she knew Lady Ramkinson and Belinda would take their disappointment out on unsuspecting servants and students alike. The Old Tsar was a welcome distraction from French irregular verbs and etiquette lessons, and she preferred to hear his rich voice tell her of Europe's histories and monarchies.

'I will miss our walks together too' he said quietly. 'We shall take our next stroll in my private gardens.'

'In Dalnerechensk?' she blurted out loudly, shocked.

'Of course' he smiled. 'I have seen you carry yourself Miss Asanton; I have seen your grace and your humility, your dedication and your wit. I have listened to your views on politics, philosophy and religion, all with care. I think you will find a lot in common with Aleksei.'

Laura closed her eyes tightly, feeling overwhelmed. She felt his trembly hand on her arm and thought she had swooned slightly again yet the soft fingers folded round hers and lifted her hand to his lips.

'Come to Dalnerechensk Miss Asanton, agreement is by no means a contract for marriage. Say yes, and I shall leave with a glad heart.'

Laura swallowed, her mouth felt dry, but she smiled and nodded carefully. The Tsar smiled then, kissing the back of her hand gently again. He took his watch from her and tucked it back into his pocket, smoothing down the soft bump in his waistcoat.

'Then I will leave with a glad heart, and I will give my blessing to my son to seek your hand. He will of course ask your father for your hand himself.'

He beckoned the unobtrusive Fedor forward and took from him a small card, handing it to Laura.

'Nikolai Ryzhkov is a trusted friend and advisor here in Boston, I have asked him to be at your disposal to answer any questions and to tend to your wishes. He will arrange passage for your family to come to Dalnerechensk and forward all of Aleksei's correspondence to you.'

Laura nodded, feeling numb and overwhelmed in the enormity of her decision. Tsar Constantinovich squeezed her hand gently to reassure her then let it go, shuffling forward on the seat to brace his feet before he stood, tapping out his pipe on the edge of the marble. Laura rose uncomfortably, feeling her skin pull tightly, but smiled as he frowned slightly, and clasped her shaking hands together in front of her. Tsar Constantinovich offered her his elbow and she slipped her hand into the crook of his warm arm, letting him lead her towards the stairs and the large, empty ballroom.

She felt a momentary twinge when she realised she would never sweep down the grand staircase to the tune of a Summer Waltz, never have admirers beg a space on her dance card, never walk in the fragrant summer garden, flushed with wine and company, never share a sweet kiss on the marble seat where no one in the house could see her.

'I do hope you will not be – distressed here, by – by this turn of events Miss Asanton' the Tsar began awkwardly, breaking into her thoughts, a worried look surfacing in his eyes. He was far too much of a gentleman to ask directly about the punishment she had received, but he knew it had been severe, despite her flippant dismissals. 'Do not hesitate to contact Nikolai if anything arises. He can be reached in the custom's building.'

He stopped at the top of the stairs to catch his breath, his faded blue eyes searching her face. She smiled gently, a strong, almost defiant look in her eyes and he smiled fondly at her, squeezing her hand.

'Farewell Laura Asanton, may the days pass quickly until we meet again. My son will grow as fond of you as I have' he leaned forward to kiss her gently on the cheek. 'Thank you for giving an old man his dignity' he whispered, his whiskers tickling her skin.

He bowed and turned from her, leaving her overlooking the beautiful autumn gardens. Fedor also bowed as he passed her, following the aging king into the Ramkinson's home. Laura put her hands on the concrete colonnade of the balcony, taking a deep breath. She was shaking with a flurry of whirlwind emotions inside her.

The Royal party crossed the wide, empty ballroom and Fedor opened the oak doors to the entrance hall. Lady Ramkinson and Lady Belinda Crompton were waiting expectantly by the front door, Belinda with the Tsar's coat over her arm, ready to help him into it. Fedor shut the door behind them carefully, his face characteristically blank of his thoughts and took the coat from Lady Belinda, helping the old Tsar into it.

Unfazed, Belinda retrieved the Tsar's hat from the rack and handed it to him, smiling coquettishly. The Tsar, ever the gentleman, bowed and then took Lady Ramkinson's hand, lifting it to his lips.

'My dear lady, I thank you for your hospitality and the generous time you have indulged me' he said, planting a whiskery kiss on the back of her glove, then straightened up, ignoring the twinge of pain in his lower back.

Lady Ramkinson dipped a pleased curtsey, letting go of his hand and watched Tsar Constantinovich take Lady Crompton's hand. She was flushing and glowing; triumphant, a woman expecting a proposal, and with a crown in her sight. The Tsar patted the back of her hand gently, then planted a kiss goodbye on her cheek.

'You are a jewel, Lady Crompton' he said. 'Your beauty and your singing are beyond compare. I have listened carefully to our conversations of theology, politics, philosophy and philanthropy all with care, and found them most informative. You will liven a man's life greatly, but I fear you will not find a suitable life in Dalnerechensk. I then, regretfully, cannot give my blessing to marry my son. I wish you all the happiness in finding a husband.'

Lady Crompton gasped, tears swimming up in her eyes. Her mouth dropped open and jerked a few times, speechless. The old man patted the back of her hand again then let her go and turned, letting Fedor take his arm as they stepped towards the front door.

'But why?' Belinda cried out, taking hold of the Tsar's sleeve, aware her crown was slipping away from her.

Fedor gently removed her hand from his master's arm, then opened the door, tucking his hand back into Tsar Constantinovich's elbow, stepping with him over the threshold of the school. Lady Crompton couldn't hold back her defeat and sobbed, hiding her face in her hands.

'Farewell Lady Ramkinson, may your school prosper for many years' Tsar Constantinovich said, placing his hat on his head, tipping it forward slightly in respect. Lady Ramkinson curtseyed politely again, but the Tsar had seen the hardness of her mouth at Belinda's spectacle. Fedor buttoned his coat and put on his hat, noticing how Lady Ramkinson stepped out onto the porch with them, closing the door discreetly on the sobbing girl.

'We would be grateful, Your Majesty, if you kept our school in mind when your granddaughter comes of age for suitable schooling abroad' she said boldly.

'Of course' he said, bowing again before beginning to amble slightly unsteadily down the stairs, the ever vigilant attaché beside him, supporting his arm.

At the bottom Fedor opened the door to the waiting carriage, holding it open to help his monarch into the luxuriously furnished cab. The old man shut his eyes in pain as he leaned back on the seat, waiting for his attaché to climb up beside him. Lady Ramkinson waved the coach goodbye cheerfully as it pulled away from the stairs, then turned back into the school and closed the door behind her.

Belinda still stood in the front hall, surrounded by girls trying to console her. When the Headmistress appeared they fluttered back nervously, standing in a straight line, shooting each other veiled looks, wondering whether the Lady's darling would taste the bite of the crop for failing to secure a principality for the school.

'Oh go and bawl in your room you stupid girl' she snapped at Lady Crompton.

Belinda picked up her skirts and fled up the grand staircase, the sound of her wailing floating down to them until the door to her room shut and muffled the sobs. Lady Ramkinson's eye distastefully slid over the girls gathered in the hall and all quailed before her gaze.

'You have a French test in one hour' she said to the dismayed company, the movement of the oak doors to the ballroom catching her eyes. Laura stepped into the room and stopped. 'And *you*,' Lady Ramkinson fumed, turning her attention to her, 'your bags are packed Miss Asanton, you are to leave immediately. You are hereby dismissed from my school.' She yanked her coat from the stand by the door and thrust it at her, as if she were holding something distasteful and wanting to be rid of the whole business.

A quiet, malicious gasp of shock and glee spread through the girls gathered. Laura's eyes widened, shocked that her grace had terminated while they could still hear the faint crunching of the carriage's hooves on the gravel driveway, but she smiled and took the coat, draping it over her arm.

'Matilda will bring your bags down. Wait outside' Lady Ramkinson said, not even looking at her.

The girls tittered at the Headmistress' rudeness. Laura pulled on her coat with as much dignity as she could muster, feeling shaky. Where was she to go? She had no money, not even for the fare of a carriage to town. *Surely she has called a carriage for me, she does not mean for me to walk all the way there*! she thought, but did not let the panic show in her face and movements.

Not one of the girls came forward to wish her well, not one was looking at her with sympathy, or even wistfulness that she had escaped the terror of the crop, or the much less torment of a French test in an hour's time. Spite had twisted all their faces into mocking smiles. Laura pitied all of them.

'Farewell all' she said, with more cheer than she felt. 'I shall send you a telegram when my husband and I have settled in our Dalnerechensk castle.'

The smiles fell from their faces. Laura glided out of the school and heard Lady Ramkinson slam the door with a horrible finality behind her.

The air was cool and she tucked her hands into her pockets, starting to think carefully about the predicament she found herself in. Her father was in Texas; he would not know she had been expelled. It would take three days to get a reply if she sent word immediately, and nearly a week before he could join her in Boston. She could not rent rooms with no money, and didn't want to think what might happen with nowhere to go. As worried as she was, she would not go begging to Lady Ramkinson for board.

Matilda struggled out with all her cases, setting them down quickly, trying to look like she hadn't dropped them, then curtseyed and disappeared back into the house, closing the door against the cold day. Laura sighed, gazing down the tree-lined drive, hoping for the sight or sound of an approaching coach. The cold feeling of dread began to swell in her stomach. *What if she had not called a coach? Would she be forced to knock on the door and beg the Headmistress to call for one?* Laura couldn't even stomach thinking about begging the cruel lady for a cab fare.

She could go to the servant's entrance and ask Clara to call the cab. Her friend would gladly do that for her. Laura knew the girl would even give her the fare to town and she shut her eyes, knowing she couldn't take it. Lady Ramkinson's favourite punishment for disobedient servants was the confiscation of their wages. What little Clara had would be stretched impossibly thin. She could not spare the money. Laura also knew she could not ask the other girls; she would be met with the same derision and possible refusal that she would receive from Lady Ramkinson.

In her pocket her fingers strayed against the edge of the business card still in her grip. She pulled it out and looked carefully.

Николай Рыжков

it read. She marveled at the strange letters, aware this was the language she would need to read, write and speak as Dalnerechensk's princess. Tsar Constantinovich had told her she could call on Nikolai should she be in need. She wondered if she could press it upon Nikolai to pay her cab fare if she arrived unannounced at the customs building. She would then need to press upon him board for a room in a hotel until her father arrived in Boston. She burned with embarrassment. No doubt her arrival as penniless as a pauper at the mercy of a custom's clerk would be reported to her intended and his court.

She sighed softly, tucking the card back into her pocket, watching her misty breath drift lazily along the deserted driveway. She could not arrive at the custom's building in that manner. Aleksei could still refuse to marry her, as disinterested as he may be. What a scandal that would cause then. She sighed again, rubbing her hands against the lining of her pockets to warm them.

She would take the cab to Jameson's offices. As much as she disliked the arrogant, officious little man, he was employed by her father to manage his affairs in Boston. She could instruct him to pay for the cab fare and rooms as a business expense. She could then send word to her father and compose herself carefully before he arrived.

Now that she had decided her spirits lifted once again. She had left the terrible school; she was free of the snobbery and prejudice of the other girls. She did not need Lady Ramkinson's Debutante Ball. There would always be men who wanted her father's oil and her hand, a businessman who could throw a party, a coming out party for her, and –

She stopped. She had just agreed to travel to Dalnerechensk, to marry a prince; there would be no coming out parties. No indication that she was available, no courting, flirting, dancing; no swapping of tokens and locks of hair, no kissing in the moonlight, no letters of love or whispered poems breathed through a racing heart; there would only be the wedding – and she smiled then. Smiled and began to dream.

She heard the faint crunch of wooden wheels on the gravel and looked up to see a small black coach turn down the tree-lined drive, sighing with relief. She pulled her hands out of her pockets and folded them in front of her, knowing it was important to be seen as a lady regardless of the situation. The carriage pulled closer to the steps where she stood and she eyed her luggage, wondering which case they had packed her gloves into.

The front door burst open and Clara rushed out, throwing her arms around her, hugging her tightly, ferociously.

'Lady Ramkinson will beat me for sure, but I couldn't let you go, not without saying tarah' she said, pressing Laura's hands tightly. 'Take care Miss Asanton, if you ever need me, you know where you can find me.' And then she was gone, the door closing behind her, leaving Laura to steel herself against the cold of her parting and the crisp autumn air.

The coach crunched to a stop at the foot of the stairs. The driver leapt down from his seat and opened the carriage door, extending his hand to help her in. Glad of the distraction Laura smiled, coming down the stairs, reaching to place her ungloved hand in his and lifting her skirts to step up into the coach.

She stopped, horribly surprised, one foot on the step. The carriage was not empty.

'Daddy!' she gasped, shocked.

Luke Asanton's ruggedly handsome face was sad and lined deeply, more deeply than she remembered. He looked drained and weary. Laura guessed he had been travelling as soon as he was able to leave the dig sites in Texas.

'Lady Ramkinson sent me a telegraph. I came as soon as I could' he answered.

She paused, feeling awkward, realising she was still holding the hand of the driver, one foot on the step, her free hand holding the gathered metres of her skirts and showing more of her bloomers than she should be. Her smile was sharper than she had meant it to be as she hoisted herself into the carriage. A flicker passed over Luke's face; for a moment she had resembled Emily in her last stages of pain wracked madness and he sat back, uncomfortably aware he didn't know his own daughter.

She sat carefully on the seat opposite her father, trying to judge the depth of his disappointment. The silence between them dragged, and the bumps and scrapes of her luggage being secured to the roof of the carriage seemed unnaturally loud and intrusive. Although she had written faithfully every week and thought of him constantly she had not seen her father since her mother's funeral five years ago.

It was a stranger that sat opposite her now, one with her father's face; somewhat more creased and care-worn than last she had seen it. She folded her hands in her lap, listening to the crunch of gravel as the driver walked to the front of the cab, climbing up to his seat where he wriggled into place comfortably before gathering the reins, waiting for the signal to go. Laura waited for a full minute before she broke seven years of social training and knocked on the roof herself.

The whip cracked and the carriage jerked, snapping Luke out of his reverie.

'Are you alright?' he asked quietly, eyeing her.

'Lady Ramkinson sent the telegram without my knowledge or consent' she said matter-of-factly.

Luke looked surprised. Seven years apart had estranged them, despite the fondness for each other. She seemed so cold, so commanding, and he wondered where his care-free daughter had gone. She sat so beautifully, so – *tamed* – that he hardly believed it was his daughter. Unsure what to do he wiped his mouth and nodded carefully.

She eyed him with downcast eyes, unsure of how to gauge his reactions. She was desperate to know what was written in the telegram, but knowing the Headmistress as she did it would have said the worst: That she had been thrown out of the school for conduct unseemly of a lady. She was aware Luke was watching her too, though not as subtly and guardedly as she had been taught to. Seven years of hiding her emotions and rigorous training in proper behaviour stopped her from throwing her arms around him and sobbing out everything.

The buildings of Boston came into view before they spoke again.

'So what is to be done father?' she asked, casually disinterested.

Luke's mouth worked up and down, then it clicked shut and he swallowed, unused to this coldness from her, and feeling stuffy and formal in its wake.

'I don't know' he said finally, helplessly.

He had been unready for his daughter's emergence into society next year, he had been completely confounded by the telegram he had received last week.

'Where are we going?' she asked.

'Jameson's Offices' he replied.

'That won't do' she said before leaning her head close to the window to call up to the driver. 'Cabbie? The Regent Hotel, thank you.'

'Right you are' he answered and cracked the whip, changing directions.

Luke eyed the elegant way she moved, the same graceful way Em had moved that caught his eye all those years ago. Laura was a woman now, and out of school. He had no idea what would make a fitting occupation for her, or where she would live.

'I suppose I'll have to wed you off' he said. It was a lame attempt at a joke, but Laura didn't laugh.

'We will take rooms at the Regent and wait for letters of correspondence from Prince Aleksei Vakhtangov' she said. 'Then we will both sail to Constantinople, presumably, and travel overland to Dalnerechensk where I suppose he will ask you for my hand.'

His melancholy gave way to shock.

'Suppose?' he gasped.

A pretty blush coloured her cheeks. 'Tsar Constantinovich was unclear exactly how the proposal would take place.'

'*Tsar*? *Prince*? Laura -' he stopped, flummoxed. 'Dal...'

'Dalnerechensk.' A smile played on her lips. 'In the Ural Mountains. It is a Principality.'

Luke blinked. 'A Principality? Lady Ramkinson's telegram did not mention that.'

'That is because the whorespawn was trying to secure the crown for Lady Crompton' she said.

'Laura!' he couldn't keep the shock out of his voice. Laura laughed with delight.

3

The rooms they had taken at the Regent Hotel were lavishly refined with subtle luxury. Upon entering her suite Laura had momentarily felt that Lady Ramkinson's far-reaching influence had followed her even to these rooms. Were it not for the formal impersonal feeling of the hotel suite she would have gone mad with anxiety. She had hardly left her rooms during the week, she had dared not go out, paranoid the society she craved knew she was the first woman to be expelled from Lady Ramkinson's finishing school.

Instead she had sent a telegram to Nikolai Ryzhkov informing him of where she could be contacted when Aleksei arrived in America. She had then kept herself busy with several embroidery projects, stitching all day long. Sometimes Luke would sit with her quietly, eyeing his grown daughter with gentle awe, or offer small pieces of information of the new drill bits and wells he'd found in Texas.

More often than not she found herself alone, the tricky stitches unable to keep her thoughts at bay. She finally set aside the hoop of material, examining herself carefully. She could recall the details of the small pocket watch portrait of Aleksei. He was handsome, that much she knew. But he was also many years older than herself, possibly as old as her father. Could she love a man who had lost the carefree indulgences of youth?

She knew she was fond of the Tsar. In the week she had known him he had grown dear to her. And she had been truthful, she could love Aleksei were he one tenth the man his father was. Would that love be passionate or dutiful, she could not say. It would be a high price to pay for duty, and fondness could not sustain a marriage, that she knew well.

What was it then that had bid her to agree? Some secret part of her knew it had been purely pride, to show she had bettered the snobbish girls that had tormented her for seven years. She could not deny revenge had played some part in her agreeing to marry the Prince. She sighed, aware that made her as spiteful and malicious as Lady Crompton, and rubbed her arms to get rid of the unpleasant sensation that stole over her.

She picked up her embroidery and eyed her neat work disheartedly. Her head swam with doubts; she had never heard of Dalnerechensk or the Vakhtangov Dynasty before the arrival of Tsar Constantinovich in America. Lady Ramkinson had verified the existence of the Principality, but was sketchy with the details. Laura thought it was because she too felt slightly perturbed, as if this was all an elabourate deception. For what purpose Laura couldn't guess.

A polite knock on the door interrupted her thoughts and she set aside her embroidery once more before bidding the person to enter. A young bellhop pushed open the door, a silver tray balanced on his white gloved hand.
'Begging your pardon Miss Asanton, but a letter has arrived for you' he bowed and

presented the tray.

Nestled in the centre was a thick parchment that had been folded and sealed with red wax. She lifted it slowly from the tray, trying to keep her shaky emotions from betraying themselves in her movements. The red seal was impressed with a coat of arms she guessed was the Royal Seal of Dalnerechensk.

The shield was flanked either side by a rearing lynx looking back over its shoulder. At the apex sat a plain coronet, unadorned with jewels. Laura supposed it was Vsevolod's crown. The lack of jewels and velvet adorning the piece spoke of a community too young in its existence to afford the luxuries of Royalty. It was also unassuming, fitting for a man who was not of pure royal blood to hold a throne. The shield itself was adorned by three cylindrical towers, linked by slightly curved walls, making the middle tower seem larger and more imposing. Beneath the towers and walls were two objects Laura could not make out.

'Will that be all Miss Asanton?' the bellhop asked, breaking into her study of the seal.

'Yes of course' she said, dismissing him hurriedly. He bowed and closed the door behind himself.

Laura's fingers caressed the seal of wax before reaching for a letter opener to slide under the seal. It broke open and she unfolded the oblong of parchment to read the short scrawled note.

> *Miss Asanton,*
> *You are requested to present*
> *yourself at the customs building*
> *at nine tomorrow morning.*
> *Respectfully yours,*
> *Nikolai Ryzhkov*

Her hands trembled as she read and re-read the short note. It was vague and blunt. She wondered if the engagement had been called off, and terror gripped her icily. She wondered if Aleksei was in America, and was going to ask for her hand tomorrow. She stood quickly, the letter tumbling from her numb fingers and flew into her dressing room, pulling open the large cabinet.

Her dresses were all elegant and made from rich fabrics, but suddenly none seemed worthy of a prince's gaze, especially not the man who's heart she was trying to win. She pulled out several dresses and held them up against herself in the full mirror, before dropping them all on the floor and heading to the door. Quickly she pulled on her coat and hat, tucking her purse chain over her wrist, closing the door behind her.

The elevator arrived and the operator opened the metal trellis for her, bowing as she stepped into the small compartment. She waited quietly while the box descended to the lobby and was greeted by the hotel manager as she made her way to reception.

'Good day Miss Asanton' he beamed. 'I trust everything has met your expectations?'

'Quite, Mr Wilson' she said, letting him take her hand for a kiss. 'Would you be so good as to hail a cab for me?'

He bowed and summoned a bellhop to see to a cab, drawing her arm through his elbow. As he walked her to the curb before the hotel Laura politely asked him to recommend a tailor to her, though she did not need to. Lady Ramkinson had ensured all her students knew who were the best tailors and suppliers in Boston. *It did not pay to run a household of excess* she had told the girls frequently. Mr Wilson recommended three tailors to her that specialised in particular garments. She smiled and thanked him, allowing him to help her up into the waiting cab. She hoped her father would understand her extravagances.

4

The customs building sat imposingly on a wide, dusty street near the port. Businessmen and laymen alike swarmed in and out the doors of the building, while outside on the street burly men carried sacks of goods on their shoulders to the store rooms, unloading crates and boxes from carts drawn by worn Clydesdales. Shouts and laughter filled the air, the street thrummed with activity and movement. It was echoed by the shouts and piercing rings of metal on metal of dock and wharf workers, busy repairing ships and loading goods onto the empty carts of the Clydesdales. Their bridles jangled with a heavy weariness and even their ponderous hoof beats on the street sounded tired.

The sight of this busy hive fascinated Laura. She had not slept for nervousness last night, spending the long hours trying greetings that would make her sound alluring, sophisticated and respectful, and could not decide between two expressions, hoping they didn't become mixed when she finally met Aleksei. She was laced tightly into a new corset and dress that had cost a phenomenal amount of money, feeling slightly uncomfortable.

Luke sat opposite her in the carriage. She had asked him to come in a fit of nervousness, worried she may need support if Nikolai was going to give her bad news. He watched her, aware of her beauty, worried about her tender heart. She was young, beautiful, and had never been in love before. She squinted through the carriage windows for a better look at the busy street, and almost fell off the seat when they jerked to a stop.

Luke alighted then reached up to help his daughter down. She was fluttering with nervousness, itching to know what news awaited her, or what man did. She shot him a small smile, tucking one hand in the crook of his arm and gathering the folds of her skirt to ascend the stairs.

A small, neat man stood on the front steps of the classically styled building, seemingly unaware of the bustle that parted and flowed around him, like a rock in a spring stream. Luke and Laura climbed the steps to where he stood waiting. He bowed deeply first to her and then to her father.

'I am Nikolai Ryzhkov, I am very pleased to meet you Miss Asanton, Mr Asanton' he said. Like Tsar Constantinovich his voice was rich and rounded with strange vowels. He offered Laura his elbow which she accepted, then gestured their way into the building, holding open the thick oak doors for them.

Inside the elegant building Nikolai swept them past the bustling lines of those waiting to pay customs duty on items they had imported, and up an impressive staircase to the quieter, comfortable offices of the bureaucrats. At the end of a short, wood paneled hallway Nikolai opened the door to an elegant office overlooking the bustling docks and escorted them in.

'May I take your coats? Please be seated' he offered, helping Laura out of hers and taking Luke's from him, hanging them on a mahogany stand by the door.

The office was large and comfortable. Opposite the door was a wide sash window, framed by rich brocade curtains. A grand mahogany desk sat at right angles to the window where the light fell full across the top, making it glow. Behind the desk the wall housed shelving filled with leather books and filing cases. Before the desk was a comfortable couch and a stately leather chair sat near a merrily burning fire in a marble enclave. The room was empty of any company.

Laura was slightly disappointed the Crown Prince of Dalnerechensk had not been standing in the room when Nikolai opened the door and hid her feelings carefully, worried that she might appear moody if he suddenly stepped into the room. Her heart leapt into her mouth at the quiet tap on the door but it was only an elderly woman with a silver tea set balanced on a tray. She placed it on a small table between the leather chair and couch.

'Tea Miss Asanton?' Nikolai offered.

'Yes please' she smiled, sitting beside her father on a couch that was more suited to a parlour than a customs office.

Luke accepted a cup as well and Nikolai poured carefully then sat in the leather chair, inquiring after their health. Laura smiled, not letting it tighten into one of displeasure as Lady Ramkinson's always had, and answered his questions. The brusqueness of his letter had been left behind, now he asked polite questions and discussed inane things like business and the port he was in charge of instead of Laura's upcoming nuptials. Laura was growing impatient. Every day since Tsar Constantinovich had left had been an endless drudgery of watching the clock and waiting for a message from Mr Wilson, the front desk clerk of the Regency, or from Nikolai Ryzhkov, to announce that Aleksei had arrived and was waiting; desperately anxious, nervously twining his hands together; to see her in the lobby.

Nikolai finished his tea and poured himself another cup, clearing his throat carefully.

'I have received two letters and instructions from His Royal Highness *Velikij Knjaz* Aleksei Vakhtangov' he started quietly. From inside his jacket pocket he pulled two envelopes, both sealed with imprinted wax. 'They carry the royal seal of the Principality of Dalnerechensk. His Royal Highness has asked me to present these letters to you.'

Laura smiled in relief and took hers. A quick glance at the imprinted seal told her it was indeed the same seal on the letter summoning her to Nikolai's offices. A small part of her wondered if the letter had been written by Aleksei or by Nikolai, which meant Nikolai had and was authorised to use the Royal seal of Dalnerechensk. Tired of too many questions without answers she broke the seal and opened out the thick parchment. Her brow creased in puzzlement seeing the strange script inside.

'I can't read the letter, it's in Russian' she said, dismayed, the letter falling to her lap dejectedly.

'What's the matter? Doesn't he speak English?' Luke asked testily.

Nikolai's expression could have cut steel. 'Oh quite eloquently sir, but Russian is the native tongue of Dalnerechensk. You would be wise to learn to read, write and speak Russian Miss Asanton. It will endear you towards the people. If you will permit me, I would read it to you.' Nikolai held out his hand.

Laura passed him the letter. Nikolai scanned it quickly, cleared his throat and read the letter out loud in Russian, translating each sentence as they went.

'My dear Miss Asanton,

Each day that passes waiting to see your sweet face seems an age of torment and cruelty. You may think it strange for me to speak such a way; as yet we have not met. I ache to do so, and yet I feel I have already known you. You live through my father's words as he describes you and you are constantly in my thoughts. He speaks highly of you, and endears me even more safely to you. The fondness in my heart for such a brave woman will only grow stronger to have you near to me. I understand what it is you have sacrificed for me when you but barely know me. I promise solemnly to care and cherish you all my long and happy life and will be grateful for your love till eternity runs dry. Please do me the honour and accept this mere token as a symbol of my commitment to your happiness.

May I be blessed by your grace,

Aleksei Stephanovich Vakhtangov.'

Nikolai finished reading and handed the letter to Laura again.

'They are some pretty words there' Luke said, seeing the effect they were having on his daughter. 'Perhaps they would be more sincere if he were here to speak them himself.'

'Daddy!' Laura hissed, chiding him. 'What does your letter say?'

Luke handed it unopened to Nikolai. The custom's officer broke the wax seal and unfolded the thick sheet of parchment.

'There is no need for me to translate, it is in English' he said, handing it back.

'Read it aloud daddy' Laura prompted, squeezing his arm.

'*Most respected sir,*' Luke started, scanning ahead with his eyes.

'*I have not come to rob you, yet I cannot help but feel like a thief. You possess a rare and vibrant treasure that I desire for my own. I have not enough tongues to express nor enough hands to write how dear this treasure has become to me* – he's asking for your hand in a letter?' Luke broke off, angry. 'Is this meant to insult me or my daughter?'

'I can assure you that it is not' Nikolai said icily. 'Aleksei runs a Principality; he cannot leave it for two months to chase a girl who can still refuse his proposal. Miss Asanton is not bound by any contract or oath till the wedding. His Royal Highness would not have it any other way.'

'I would still feel better seeing this man in person' Luke grumbled.

'I have booked passages for you both to Constantinople on board the *Queen of the Atlantic* Miss Asanton. I will arrange passages for any other family members you wish to have present at the wedding. You and your family are welcome to stay in Dalnerechensk, as long as you wish, as guests of the Royal Household. If His Royal Highness does not win your heart, you and your family will return to the New World at the time of your choosing.

'The ship bound for Constantinople sails in six weeks' he went on, a man used to organising large quantities of cargo. 'That will give you plenty of time to arrange matters.'

His gaze lingered briefly on Luke, one businessman to another, aware commerce did not simply stop for love. His gaze drifted on to the woman sitting stiffly in expensive silks on the couch. 'Perhaps you can find a tutor for some lessons in Russian Miss Asanton.'

'Yes of course' Laura answered.

'What is the token he is offering?' Luke suddenly queried, uncomfortable with the casual disregard for his wishes as a customs clerk arranged his life for him. It reminded him of his days as a youth, the flippant dismissals and casual rearrangement of affairs to suit the person with the most money. Since he had struck oil they had asked for his opinion, had expected him to rearrange their lives for them to suit his own whim. It had been a point of honour that he never did so. 'He promised her a token of his love' he clarified, noticing the way they were both looking at him.

'Yes quite' Nikolai sniffed.

He set aside his teacup and reached into a breast pocket inside his jacket, retrieving a small brass key. He stood and crossed to the desk that over looked the docks and unlocked a sturdy safe that stood near it, pulling out a small package. It was wrapped in brown paper and sealed with royal wax. He brushed at the package almost lovingly before presenting it to Laura.

She took it from him and pulled aside the paper. Inside was an oblong velvet box. She opened the small box carefully and gasped. Inside sat a glittering spectacle of emeralds, each cut with immaculate precision. They were mounted on a silver chain with diamond accents, arranged to drip elegantly down her throat. Laura's fingers strayed to the large gems, stroking them in wonder.

Lady Ramkinson had a fine collection of jewelry, pieces that had been handed down from mother to daughter for generations, and she had shown the girls how to value them accurately by size, cut and clarity of the jewels. The emeralds Alexei had presented her with were worth more than Lady Ramkinson's entire collection. Laura's hands trembled slightly while she pulled the necklace out of the box, fastening the cold jewels around her throat, wishing she had a mirror to see what they looked like glistening above her new dress.

'You look stunning' Nikolai said promptly, a man not used to giving compliments, but knew how they were to sound. "Does she not, Mr Asanton?'

'Positively regal' he murmured, aware of how heartbreakingly beautiful she was.

A pretty blush darkened her cheeks. As much as she wanted to she knew she could not wear them home. She unfastened them and laid them back in the box, wondering what performance was on at the theatre that evening, so she could wear the jewels then. Nikolai rewrapped the necklace for her in the brown paper, tying it with string.

'There is of course, the small matter of the dowry' he said quietly.

5

The accountant swallowed nervously, clutching the pile of paper to his chest protectively. It was late and the oil in the lamps had burned low. Luke sat in shadow in a leather chair, his sun-ravished skin like a flame in the uneasy light.

He had blown into Jameson's offices, his hair in disarray, his face like thunder, cursing and shouting at the top of his lungs. Jameson had not mentioned that he was expecting a visit from Luke before he had left for Chicago, and the profanity had drawn a crowd of worried faces out of offices. Luke continued to stride like the devil through the corridors, shouting Jameson's name, brandishing the portfolio he held like a sword.

The small accountant had cringed when Luke had spotted him, demanding to know where his father was. When Luke had been told Jameson was not there he had thrown the portfolio at him, demanding a full account of his net worth. Stammering, he had been pushed into his own office and Luke had followed, seating himself in a high backed chair and smoked furiously, watching Jameson Junior's every move.

Now black shadows twisted across Luke's face, his eyes glittering in the waning, red-tinged light. The accountant swallowed again and clutched the paper tighter, knowing he wasn't going to like his answer.

'It's the same' he said reluctantly.

'Not good enough, add it again!' he roared, kicking in frustration at a stack of thick legal books that sat beside the chair.

Jameson Junior swallowed and took a step backwards. He knew it was not the time to be reproachful for the treatment of his legal texts but could not keep the reprimand out of his voice.

'It's math Mr Asanton, not magic. Ten million dollars does not just appear. I've worked those figures four times.'

The silence stretched out into minutes, thick and unnerving. Jameson Junior fidgeted uncomfortably, unwilling to speak or move to draw attention to himself, as Luke's eyes were still smoldering in the dark. When he spoke again he sounded defeated, though he still looked dangerous.

'You included the rail shares?'

'Yes' he answered, amazed his voice still worked.

Luke was quiet, then asked: 'By how much can we increase the production of oil?'

'It's not advisable -'

'Then just what is?' Luke snapped, leaping to his feet.

Jameson Junior shrank back against the wall, wishing the paper in his arms was something more solid to protect him from his employer's fury. He swallowed hard and steeled himself.

'To raise that kind of money Mr Asanton, you'll have to sell it. Everything.'

Luke collapsed back in the chair, wiping his mouth, utterly defeated. The stuffy man shifted nervously and Luke ignored him, staring unseeingly at the swirling patterns on the silk rug. It was muted and indistinct in the gloom not penetrated by the stuttering oil lamps.

The shadows were dancing demonically, mockingly, in the dark whorls of the pattern.

Slowly, dream-like, he got to his feet and buttoned the coat he had not taken off all evening.

'Good night' he said quietly, pulling open the door.

'Would you like me to hail a cab?' Jameson Junior asked, relaxing his grip on the pile of paper. Several sheets fell to the floor in an avalanche of rustling.

'No' he said and left.

A chill wind was blowing in from the sea, stirring his coat, stealing away the sound of his steps on the cobbled street. He hunched his shoulders and pushed his fists deeper into his fur-lined pockets, glowering at the dark sidewalk.

In the seven years since he struck oil Luke had built his company painstakingly, nurturing it and strengthening it with profitable deals in several shipping companies and the newly established automobile company. He had strengthened it further with shares in many more companies, weaving an integral network of wealth and stability. It had paid for a luxurious house in Texas, nurses for Emily's illness and Laura's education. He had fought tooth and nail for its success, and now he had to give it up.

Velikij Knjaz Aleksei Vakhtangov wanted a ten million dollar dowry. If he agreed he lost everything; his company, his connections, his wealth, and his daughter to an isolated scrap of land in the Urals. He didn't want to think of her there alone, trapped with a man she didn't know, in a land she'd never heard of, surrounded by a language she couldn't speak. If something went wrong it would take him almost a month to know and do something about it. There were too many risks involved. He couldn't risk his daughter.

Aleksei's eloquent words couldn't sweeten the bitter taste in his mouth. He asked for the hand of his only daughter in a letter. He had sent his father to find a suitable wife for him. Luke clenched his hands tighter in his pockets, the rigidity in his body forcing him to stop walking. Laura had been chosen for her inheritance, for nothing more than money. As beautiful as she was, as capable of capturing a man's heart, however the old Tsar had taken to her; deep in his heart he knew he was selling his daughter.

Before him on the cobbles was a square of yellow light, thrown out of the Regency Hotel's window. Luke sighed, his eyes following the light into the dining room, alighting on a figure seated near the window. Laura sat alone at a table, sipping from a glass of red wine. Luke's breath caught in his throat. She was draped in a spectacular emerald dress; the neck cut square and low, her soft breasts pushed up in a seductive flash of flesh. Her new necklace sparkled at her throat in the guttering candlelight.

Luke had been so furious at Aleksei's letter he had forgotten to meet her for their evening meal. He didn't have to look at his pocket watch to know he had kept her waiting most of the night. Luke shut his eyes tightly, cursing himself, then eyed her again. Despite how elegant she looked her demeanor was heartbreakingly sad. Luke couldn't remember the last time he heard her laugh. He wondered if sending her away so young had broken her child's spirit, if Emily's fanatical desire to better her daughter and Lady Ramkinson's school had snuffed out the fire of carefree youth and innocent happiness.

He had not forgotten the look on her face when Nikolai had read the letter to her. She was ensnared by the flattery, by the romance of courtship. It would be cruel to snatch away that giddy feeling of first love from her. But he knew if he refused the dowry Aleksei would not marry her. *Would he gamble her happiness to save his livelihood?* Luke shut his eyes again. He could introduce her to society himself, throw her own Debutante Ball and invite the young sons of gentlemen who would treat her well, who would be deserving of her. *But could they ever offer her the security that a prince could?*

He pressed the heels of his hands tightly against his eyes, torn. The first time it had hurt like this was when he had held his new born daughter in his arms; that squalling, pink thing that shoved a fist into her mouth and eyed him, batting her lovely eyelashes from under a mop of chestnut hair. He had sworn then, sworn an oath to give up everything for her.

Luke didn't care about the money. He was not too old to start again, to fall on his feet with the old Asanton charm buoyanting him along. With the reputation he had now the banks would fall over themselves to finance another drill site in Texas. Or even in Pittsburgh. But he was not the only one who would lose everything this time. He now employed seven hundred men and they too would have to give up their security, their livelihoods, for a sixteen year old promise.

He would give her everything to make her happy, if only it would make her happy. He shivered in the cool Boston evening then pushed open the front door of the hotel, quickly heading to the dining room. Laura looked up in surprise; relief, confusion and doubt chasing each other on her face. Luke fell to his knees beside her, taking both her hands in his.
'Laura this is the most important decision you will ever make. I only want you to be happy. But will you be happy with this man?'

She was quiet for a long time, chewing her bottom lip absently as she thought, a habit that had earned her many a slap with the crop. Luke didn't need her to answer; he saw the doubt plainly on her face. He bowed his head to her hands and kissed them gently, resigned.
'I know what it is Aleksei is asking of you' she said quietly, squeezing his hands. 'Lady Ramkinson made sure we had arithmetic lessons to manage households when we were married. I know the dowry will bankrupt you -'
'It's nothing, I made you a promise sixteen years ago and I will honour it till the day I die' he interrupted earnestly. '*Will this make you happy*?'

She shut her eyes.
'I cannot say.'

6

A quiet, official knock on the door of her hotel room roused Laura from her embroidery. She kept her face blank but pleasant when Nikolai's eyes darted around for her maid when she opened the door for him.

'Mr Ryzhkov, to what do I owe this pleasure?' she asked sweetly.

'I hope you do not find me too forward' he answered, stepping into her hotel room. 'I have taken it upon myself to introduce you to Countess Ekaterina Ivanova of Dalnerechensk.'

He gestured to the open doorway. A young woman stepped into view. She was not much older than Laura, wearing a beautiful silk dress, her shoulders elegantly draped in a fur coat, her gloved hands holding a black purse before her. Laura automatically dropped a curtsey and invited her in, agog at her sense of style and sophistication. Countess Ivanova had the confidence and grace of the extremely attractive.

'Countess Ivanova's husband, Grigory Ivanov, is the Treasurer of Dalnerechensk' Nikolai continued. 'He works closely with His Royal Highness every day. He is a trusted advisor, and one of his closest friends.'

Ekaterina waved off Nikolai's talk, a gesture that had as much appeal as dismissal. Laura marveled at this woman who appeared so charming and appealing while in fact being quite rude. Nikolai bowed to her deeply, nodding in turn to Laura then excused himself from their company. Laura realised the lesser bow to her showed she still was not a princess yet. Nikolai took his leave and closed the door behind him, leaving the two alone.

'Would you care for some tea, Countess Ivanova?' Laura asked politely.

'If you insist my dear' she laughed, removing her coat and gloves. 'You and I shall see plenty of each other in Dalnerechensk Laura, as we are the only two beauties left in the Principality' she grinned, draping the coat and gloves on the stand beside the door. 'You must call me Ekaterina.'

'Of course, Ekaterina' Laura said, trying the name out, unable to help returning the Countess' smile.

Ekaterina flopped down gracefully in a chair, eyeing the hotel suite. Laura pulled a velvet rope in the corner to summon a maid then sat opposite the Countess near a small parlour table.

'I have taken it upon myself to educate you in the delicacies of the Principality's customs' Ekaterina went on. 'And I shall not teach you to read and write in Russian until you can swear like the soldiers in Tcherepnin.'

Laura looked shocked. Ekaterina laughed and clapped her hands in delight. She had a wonderful, flirtatious laugh and eyes that could make sailors blush. Laura should have felt scandalised; Ekaterina was the very model of the scandalous woman Lady Ramkinson had sneered about in her many lessons on etiquette. *You must avoid this woman at all costs* the Headmistress had warned the students. *Shameful gossip follows this woman, not least the gossip she herself starts. She will tarnish your reputation forever should you be long in her company.* Laura loved her.

A maid arrived with a brisk knock on the door. Laura excused herself and ordered refreshments for them. When she returned to her seat Ekaterina gave her a sly look and clearly enunciated a Russian word. Laura blushed, knowing the word was blue. She carefully copied the strange inflections of the word. Ekaterina laughed and said another, which Laura repeated again.

'You are a natural at languages' Ekaterina laughed. 'You sound as if you have been swearing in Russian your whole life. Aleksei is also a natural with languages' she said, changing tack in the conversation. 'He speaks English, French, Hungarian, Polish, Italian, Latin and Ancient Greek quite fluently.'

'You must tell me about him' Laura suddenly said impulsively. 'I hardly know him at all.'

'Of course' she smiled, interrupted by another knock on the door.

Laura excused herself again to let the maid and the tea trolley into the room. The small parlour table was quickly set and the maid poured tea before bobbing a curtsey and closing the door after her as she left, pushing the empty cart before her.

'Laura you must have a handmaiden' Ekaterina said a touch reproachfully. 'Dalnerechensk is a community entrenched in traditional customs, it will not do to have their royalty answering the door for servants.'

The Countess sipped her tea and sighed contentedly at the taste of the brew, setting the cup back on the thin china saucer then began to talk. Laura learned more about the man she was to marry as the day wore on; his likes and dislikes, his peculiar habits and mannerisms. In her mind a clearer picture of him began to emerge which endeared him to her, although she still didn't know if she could love him.

What was becoming clear as the Countess talked was she could be happy in Dalnerechensk with friends like Ekaterina and the old Tsar. In their short time together she had grown fond of the old Tsar, and was quickly developing a strong liking for the beautiful Countess. If the people of Dalnerechensk did not love her it would be no different to the spiteful girls in Lady Ramkinson's school.

As the day waned the conversation drifted from Aleksei to the community itself. Ekaterina and her husband were two of the nobility in the Principality, all of whom belonged to the Dalnerechensk court. Ekaterina herself had worked as a school teacher when she first came to Liberty Valley, and later as a foreign secretary for the Principality's administration. Both she and her husband made frequent trips to the New World to oversee their business connections.

Luke pushed open Laura's door with a knock then stopped in surprise.

'Daddy!' she smiled, rising to her feet. 'It pleases me to introduce you to Countess Ekaterina Ivanova from Dalnerechensk.'

Luke bowed low and took her hand, kissing it.

'Join us for tea' Laura gestured, casting her eyes around for another chair.

'Perhaps the Countess would care to join us for dinner?' Luke said instead.

Laura blinked in surprise then realised he was dressed in his formal dining jacket, and that the day was turning gloomy with dusk.

'Sadly I cannot' Ekaterina said, getting to her feet. 'Though I will call tomorrow Laura, we must find you a handmaiden and outfits befitting of all Dalnerechensk's occasions for you.'

Luke pulled down her coat from the stand by the door and helped her into it. She smiled graciously at him, glanced over his shoulder to Laura, uttered the foulest word she had taught her this afternoon and left, her laughter floating back along the hallway.

7

Laura tucked her hands tighter into the brand new fur muff she had been instructed to buy, leaning back against the leather seat of the carriage. Ekaterina had visited Laura every day, teaching her the customs of traditional Dalnerechensk and the language of the people. She delighted in her student and dragged her in and out of tailors, fabric stores and hat shops, dressing her in the finery expected of royalty.

A phenomenal amount of money had been charged to Luke's accountant for a new wardrobe; Laura had new luxurious garments for every activity, every occasion, every hour of her days. She had corsets made from whale bone and silk, bloomers made from Egyptian cotton so high in thread count it felt positively sinful against her skin. She had so many new scarves and ribbons for her hair that she had to buy a new suitcase just to transport them back to the Regent Hotel.

Opposite her in the carriage sat Luke, strained and white-faced. He had always ensured his daughter was well presented in the school but he had never seen her look so regal or beautiful as she did now. Her chestnut hair had been swept up into a fashionable coif, an elegant black hat pinned into place. Her fur-lined traveling cloak was fastened up to her neck but did not hide the curve of her figure, a new royal blue dress peeping out from under the thick folds of grey material.

They smelt the thick, salty oil smell of the docks before they reached them, the smell clinging to their nostrils as the carriage slowed to a walk, the driver negotiating the way through teams of Clydesdales and burly men carrying stock to the customs building. The driver reached the ship and pulled to a stop, jumping down from his seat. He opened the door and whipped his hat off his head, offering a hand to help Laura down.

She extended her hand gracefully, trying to hold onto the fur muff and lift the folds of her skirts and coat so she didn't step on them and trip herself, or rip the delicate materials. The driver took her hand, steadying her down and she eyed the large ship they stood beside.

The *Queen of the Atlantic* was by nature a cargo ship, as there was not a huge demand for passage to Constantinople from the New World. The decks were mostly bare of the trappings of passenger boats; instead they were stacked with large containers of raw materials and other goods desired by The Ottoman Empire. But there were a few comfortable private berths on board, and plenty of extra bunks in the sailors' quarters below deck for second and third class passengers. The wheelhouse rose above the deck of the ship and was backed onto by a large cabin in which crew and passengers would eat together. Above that the twin smoke stacks rose, puffing gently into the late November sky.

Luke stepped down from the carriage and she tucked an arm through his, looking for

Ekaterina. Unlike the lethargic month of waiting to hear from Aleksei, the six weeks till the sailing had passed in a blur of activity. The Countess had been Laura's constant companion and had invited her to dances and the theatre to show off her new gowns. She was grateful for the Countess' company, and was happy to know she was traveling with them to Constantinople. She could not see her, but the swarm of colours and faces, activity and dust made it difficult to be sure of definite features. She glanced at Luke, noticing the hardness in his jaw as he also scanned the docks.

'Don't fret father, you could use a holiday' she said, squeezing his arm to cheer him.

There was a sharp whistle from the deck of the *Queen* and the captain dressed immaculately in his blue uniform appeared at the top of the gangway. The carriage driver finished placing their luggage beside them on the ground then stood respectfully with his cap in his hands, awestruck at Laura's beauty and poise. Luke paid him for his fare and he bowed, convinced he had driven nobility of some kind to the docks that day.

A huge shadow fell across Laura and her father. Their eyes were drawn from the departing driver to the walking house before them. The seven foot man bobbed a fluid bow, sweeping up all their belongings into his arms as he did so. Laura had never seen a man so enormous, though he could not be more than twenty. The sun and salt air had leathered his skin into a membrane of mahogany and his sun-blonde hair, thickly plaited, hung down his back. His shirt was loose fitting and oddly tailored. Laura wondered if it had been sewn from a ship's sail, as she doubted he had the money to afford the material or the tailor to construct clothes for his huge frame.

'Mornin' Gentleman sir, me lady' he said. He had a strong cockney accent, and bowed slightly again. 'If you are pleased to follow me sir, I will see to it your belongings and yourselves are safely on board.' And he set off at a trot up the gangway which was difficult to keep up with.

Laura and Luke gripped the rails of the gangway, hoping the numerous packages in the sailor's arms would not go tumbling into the murky water of Boston Harbour. The captain greeted them cordially on the deck with a bow and a kiss on Laura's hand, welcoming them on board the *Queen of the Atlantic*. The seven-foot sailor waited patiently a few feet away, then led them into the first class cabins.

The hallways of the ship were plain; metal bulkheads were painted an off-white colour and pipes and wiring were left exposed, though neatly ordered, along the walls. The sailor stopped before a door to a private berth.

'Will sir be needin' all the luggage or would you be wantin' me to take some of it below?' he asked, opening the door to Luke's room.

'Leave it with me' Luke said quietly, stepping over the skirting lip of the door, surveying the small but tasteful cabin.

'Very good sir' the sailor said, setting down his bags. 'The captain wishes that you n' the miss join him for dinner this evening.' He bobbed a small nod at Laura. 'Pleased to be followin' me, me lady.'

Luke closed his door and followed the giant sailor and Laura to her room. Like her father's, her berth was elegant but cramped. A small round window to her left looked out onto the bustling docks. Under the window and built against the wall was a short padded bench seat, only wide enough to accommodate one. Opposite the seat sat a long chest of drawers, nailed to the wall. The top edge of the chest of drawers held small brass rings, and Laura saw the top had been cut into three sections. Grasping one ring and lifting the top she found a porcelain washbasin underneath.

'How clever' she smiled.

Opposite the door, running the width of the cabin was the bed, waist high and narrow, with a wooden lip to stop the sleeper falling out of bed in rough seas. A small shelf with sides and a rod to keep books from falling off and a mounted oil lamp were above the bed.

'Where is the bed pan?' Laura asked, trying not to flush.

'Ain't no bed pan me lady, gets messy in high seas' the sailor grinned, setting down her luggage then lifted one of the sections of the chest of drawers.

'Oh my' Laura murmured, embarrassed.

'The Countess gave me instruction to tell you she wants you to be on the deck as we set sail me lady' he said, bobbing a jaunty bow and turned almost sideways to fit out the door.

Luke's eyes followed the back of the sailor as he left, beginning to whistle a jaunty sailor's ditty. He then looked at his beautiful daughter, her cheeks flushed with embarrassment.

'Keep your door locked at night' he said quietly, then bowed to leave her and went back to his cabin to settle into his rooms.

Laura brushed at her cheeks to cool herself, then lifted one of her cases and placed it on the bed, rummaging in it for a bottle of rose water to freshen up. The foghorn blew overhead, startling her, and she heard the engines rumble to life somewhere below her in the bowels of the ship. She glanced into the small mirror, brushing back wisps of her hair before securing the door behind her and making her way up onto the deck.

Ekaterina waved her over to the railing, making room for her young apprentice.

'Now my dear, wave farewell to your old life, you're going on to find love in the green hills of Dalnerechensk' she laughed, waving at the dock workers.

The foghorn blew again, startling them both, and in the bow of the ship the seven-foot sailor cast off the thick mooring ropes as if they were shoelaces. People on the docks turned at the sound of the foghorn and began waving their handkerchiefs and calling bon voyage. The workers of the docks didn't look round at the horn, but a few managed a wave for the *Queen* as she began to ponderously move away from the wharf. Ekaterina spotted Nikolai standing on the docks while the workers swarmed around him and blew him a kiss. The corners of his mouth pulled in a way that might have been called a smile and the girls laughed, waving their handkerchiefs.

As the ship moved further away the gulf of water widened between them and the shore, making Laura feel as if her life as she knew it was now slipping away from her. She turned to eye her companion, who was still watching the diminishing shapes on the docks.

'What if I don't find love?' Laura asked, worried.

Ekaterina turned to her, her green eyes flashing with laughter and mischief. 'Then what an adventure you'd have.'

8

Laura felt weak and stiflingly hot. A crippling sea-sickness had taken her as soon as the docks of Boston had disappeared from view. She had not been able to keep her dinner appointment with her father and the Countess at the Captain's table, confining herself to her cabin for the next six days, violently ill. She had not eaten, drunk precious little, and now was running a fever that was sapping at the precious energy she had left.

The claustrophobic cabin seemed airless and Laura knelt on the seat, pressing her face into the open window for some relief. The air seemed cool on her face but her body was uncomfortably hot. Feeling ridiculous she got unsteadily to her feet and slung the woollen blanket from her bed around her, bracing herself against the tip and rock of the boat. She slipped out of the cabin and closed the door behind her, forgetting to lock it. She staggered up the short flight of steps to the deck, relishing the cold night air, feeling exhausted from her climb.

She let go of the bannister for the stairs and tottered on unstable legs to the rail of the ship. She was struggling to hold herself upright, and the swirling black sea below her was drifting in and out of focus. The world tilted and darkened. She suddenly felt light and off balance, as if she was falling.

A strong arm came round her, pulling her back from the rail.

'Careful now miss' said a familiar voice. 'You feelin' alright me lady?'

Laura shook her head. The seven-foot sailor swept her up in his arms like she was no more than a doll, carrying her to a seat. He set her down gently then sat beside her, tucking the woollen blanket tighter round her shoulders, keeping an arm around her in case she fainted off the seat.

'Alright now me lady, sit 'ere for a while, 'ave a whiff of this' he said cheerfully.

He produced a large flask from a pocket and unscrewed the cap, handing it to her. She took a swig and then coughed, spluttering at the heat and the foul taste of the alcohol. He swigged a large measure himself and then stowed the flask away again.

'Does this infernal swaying ever stop?' she grumbled, her stomach rolling over in discomfort.

'It's just Mama Ocean rocking her children to sleep me lady' he grinned.

'Well does she have to rock so hard?'

The sailor laughed, and Laura felt cheered by his easy nature. The alcohol was warming her stomach, finally settling her and the fresh cold air cooled her fever, dissipating the nausea with every breath. She pulled her feet up into the warmth of the blanket, folding her arms around her knees.

The sailor sat quietly beside her, his arm still around her. She looked at him carefully, wondering what his intentions were. Her notions of how men and women interacted were limited to what she had observed of the married couples that came to take tea with Lady Ramkinson. They had all been ex students of hers, or the parents of current pupils. There was a fondness and familiarity in their behaviour towards each other, but none had touched the other, as society dictated.

The arm around her shoulder was strong and warm. There was a friendliness to it, an unassuming casualness in the touch. It was very different to the courtly pretenses Lady Ramkinson had instructed them to give and accept. She should have felt shocked at this bold breach of etiquette and the unfamiliarity of a man's touch. Instead she felt strangely comforted. No one had ever held her like this before.

She eyed the contours of his face in the moonlight. He could not be more than twenty, though he had a self-confidence that belied his tender years. He was a gentle giant, self-assured, and with a poise that was uncanny in his class. He turned to look at her, aware of her eyes on him.

'What's your name?' she stammered, flustered that she was staring at him.

'Jonathan, but they call me Bal, on account of me being so big they could use me for ballast' he answered, grinning.

She giggled, feeling bold, and wondered exactly what was in Bal's flask, as wine had never made her feel like this. She snuggled deeper into her blanket, hitching it up round her, burying her nose in it. It left her feet exposed and Bal suddenly reached out and took hold of one, lifting it up for closer inspection. She gasped and batted away his hand.

'I ain't never seen feet so white n' small' he said by way of apology, letting her foot go.

She tucked it behind the other and dropped the blanket over them, unsure what to do, and realising that she should not be seen here with the arm of this sailor around her. She shifted away from him, forcing him to drop his arm.

'Come now me lady, a ship's deck in late November is a God-awful place to be' he said, unfazed by her behaviour. 'I'll help you below. Would there be anything else you'd be needin'?'

'Perhaps some water' she murmured, feeling suddenly exhausted.

Bal stood and slid his arm around her again as he guided her to her room. She yawned and Bal opened the door to her cabin and let her slip into the cabin alone. Laura clambered into bed, falling asleep as soon as her head touched the pillow. Bal bid her a quiet good night and closed the door behind him.

9

Laura woke when the first rays touched her cheek, glinting through the open window. She sat up, still feeling weak, but remarkably better and ravenously hungry. She swung her legs over the side of the bed, catching sight of her feet as she did. She suddenly grinned, extending a leg in admiration. Bal was right, she did have beautiful feet. She laughed, hoping her husband-to-be would think so as well.

The breeze had chased out most of the stuffy smell from her berth and a stoppered flagon of water sat in a wooden basket beside the door. Laura wiggled out of bed and poured a generous amount into the basin inside the chest of drawers, then drank thirstily from the bottle. She stripped quickly, washing her hair and body. Any fancies she had of her attractiveness vanished while she washed those livid purplish-pink scars on her back and thighs. Ashamed, she dressed quickly in a simple dress of soft cotton, and dabbed some rose water on her neck and ears.

As she closed her door behind her she wondered if anyone had seen her with Bal last night, seen him inspecting her feet. Although it had been completely innocent, and she had been ill, she realised that could not be an excuse. She was to marry a public figure and become a public wife. No matter how innocent, and what her state, she could never be seen to be in any situation that would smear her name or that of her husband. With this in mind she resolved herself to act impeccably at all times, as if Lady Ramkinson was there, breathing her disapproval. So strong was her mental admonishing that she glanced quickly behind her to ensure the dreaded lady was not actually there.

Chiding herself for her silliness, Laura headed to the large cabin attached to the wheel house where several tables had been set up to serve meals for crew and passengers alike. Luke and Ekaterina were dinning together at a table near the rear of the room. Ekaterina saw her first and gave a little cry, waving her over to them. Luke stood and grasped her arm as she joined them, his face lined with worry.

'Laura, you are so pale, we have not seen you for almost a week!' he said earnestly, looking her over carefully.

'The sea-sickness was horrible, but I'm faring much better now' she said.

'I'm glad to hear it' he smiled, holding her chair out for her.

Laura sat and was glad to see the table had been set for three. She had felt a small prick of alarm when she had seen them sitting together and laughing. The Asanton charm was legendary, and although there had been no one since the death of her mother, Laura was sure it was not for lack of willing replacements. Ekaterina was also the type of woman she had been constantly warned about in Lady Ramkinson's school. But she saw only concern for her in their faces and chided herself for her thoughts. She sat, draping the napkin over her lap and ordered a large breakfast.

Both Luke and Ekaterina were relieved to see the colour returning to her thin cheeks as she ate, and told her of the ways in which they had passed their time on board the ship. They too had also been ill, but only for the first night, and had not realised how much she had been suffering. Laura finally sat back from her plate, shutting her eyes over a steaming cup of tea, feeling her strength returning as a full belly soothed away the discomforting memories of rolling seas.

'Perhaps you would like to continue with our lessons this morning my dear; it is a fine day, if not a little cold' Ekaterina said, setting down her empty tea cup. 'Be sure to wear a shawl and I shall meet you on the foredeck in fifteen minutes.' She rose, excusing herself from the table.

Luke rose too, bowing as the Countess left, then sat, reaching across the table to affectionately squeeze Laura's arm. It was the first affectionate contact they had had in many years and Laura was touched by the concern she saw in his face. She took his hand, squeezing too.

'And what will you do this morning father?'

'I have been invited to a game of bridge with the first mate' he smiled.

Laura patted her lips with a napkin and rose, brushing crumbs from her dress. Luke stood and offered her his elbow, walking her back to her berth.

'The captain has asked after you' he said conversationally. 'We all disappointed his table the first night but he was kind enough to invite us again. We called at your cabin, but there was no reply. I shall tell him you are faring much better.'

He stopped at her door and bowed. Laura smiled.

'Of course, and that I would be delighted to dine with him.'

Luke promised to pass on the message. Laura unlocked her berth and stepped in, rummaging in her cases for a suitable warm shawl. She found one to compliment her dress and draped it around her shoulders, securing the door behind her again. She made her way to the deck and breathed deep, looking out across the ocean.

She didn't notice the rocking anymore, and the surface of the ocean twinkled with little wavelets that caught in the early morning sun. She inhaled deeply again, closing her eyes and turning her face up to the sun.

'That's a better colour in your cheeks miss' said a familiar voice, and a large shadow fell across her.

'Good morning Jonathan' she smiled, pleasant but reserved.

If he noticed the coldness in her he said nothing, stretching and expanding his great lungs with air in contentment. Laura found herself warming to him against her sensibilities; his easy good nature was uncomplicated by gossip and innuendo, making her envious of him, though he was so likeable the disgruntled feelings quickly dissipated.

But she excused herself, mindful that as innocent and honest as he was, she had to maintain absolute impunity in her actions and conversations. Ekaterina was walking on the deck, two books tucked into the crook of her arm. Laura joined her, linking her arm through the Countess'.

'Now my dear, let's see what you can remember' Ekaterina said with a mischievous wink.

10

Ship life passed quickly for Laura. Every day she, her father and the Countess took breakfast together, then Ekaterina would take her student by the arm and walk the decks or sit quietly, practising the strange pronunciation and the simple sentences they had learned. Sometimes Luke would join them, listening to his daughter at her lessons, other times he would spend his time playing bridge with the first mate or curling with the crew on the foredeck. Sometimes Bal would talk to her in his easy, carefree way, unfazed by her apparent coldness, or sometimes she would watch the water lapping quietly at the sides of the ship as it glided on towards Constantinople.

On the ninth day of sailing they passed through the Strait of Gibraltar and into the Mediterranean. Laura stood in awe at the huge rock marking the entrance, towering over the ship. Ekaterina tutted and ordered her back to her studies, giving her a book of poems to read aloud. At first she despaired, it was written in the Cyrillic script, but Ekaterina had been a thorough teacher, and she began to recognise the symbols for the sounds they represented. At first she stuttered, but as she had a talent for languages she soon was reading clearly, although she did not understand what she read.

Ekaterina leaned back on the deck chair, closing her eyes in contentment, correcting Laura's pronunciation. As she grew more confident with the text she fell into the rhythm of the poem, and Ekaterina sighed happily.

'My dear, even if you understood not a word Aleksei will enjoy your voice reading to him' Ekaterina said when she finished. 'Read me another.'

Laura did so, smiling at the effect the poetry had on her friend. Every now and then Ekaterina would correct her pronunciation, but for the most part she was left to recite unimpeded.

Ekaterina's lessons continued as the Mediterranean days warmed around them and they discarded their shawls as they walked about the decks, shading themselves from the hot sun with parasols. Islands sprang into view on the thirteenth day as the *Queen* passed Greece and headed towards the mouth of the Çanakkale Straight.

Ekaterina told Laura of the ships Menelaüs and Agamemnon had driven onto the shores of Troy, chasing the most beautiful woman in the world. Laura was familiar with the story, she had read widely from classical authors as the girls at Lady Ramkinson's school had been instructed to do; yet standing on the bow of a ship, steaming in the same direction, and seeing the islands she had no doubt Achilles had gazed on sent shivers of delight down her spine. She couldn't help but fall romantically in love with her own journey to chase love into the unpenetrated valleys of Dalnerechensk.

11

Laura and Ekaterina stood at the rails of the *Queen of the Atlantic*, watching the docks of Constantinople emerge from the hazy distance. The sky was punctured with the numerous minarets of the mosques, and above them all on the hill, the huge domes of the Blue Mosque and the Hagia Sophia rose into the air. Laura sighed, aware the idyllic, cocooned life on the ship was now coming to an end. As more and more of the docks emerged from the haze the sights and smells of the vibrant fish market became apparent. It reminded Laura of the docks in Boston and she felt a momentary pang of homesickness, though she couldn't identify what she longed for.

Luke joined them on the foredeck and they listened to the sailors and shipwrights call to each other in a foreign language. Huge mooring ropes were tossed to Bal who planted his feet on the decks and hauled, pulling the ship closer, securing the ropes around the *Queen*'s large metal capstans. The ship gave a small jolt as it bumped against the pier, then the engines cut and she bobbed gently, the bags of sand hung from her deck protecting the side of the ship from the wharf.

Men on the pier in long white dresses and cloth headdresses swarmed up to the ship, calling and waving to crew and passengers. The *Queen* gave another jolt when a gangway dropped into place and a strange mobile winching apparatus was pushed up to the side of the ship to unload the cargo from the decks.

Luke took Laura's arm, turning her away from the rail.
'It's time to go' he said quietly. 'We have a train to catch.'

Ekaterina followed them to the gangway. The captain stood waiting at the top to farewell them, and kissed each of the ladies' hands, bidding them good health for the remainder of their journey. They thanked him and wished him well, stepping onto the gangway. Ekaterina suddenly gave a cry and swept down to the docks, throwing her arms around an immaculately dressed man wearing a green and blue sash diagonally over his shoulder. Luke and Laura exchanged a glance and followed her down.
'Laura, come, you must meet my husband!' Ekaterina cried, taking her hand like an excited schoolgirl.

Laura smiled and let herself be presented to Grigory Ivanov. He was a small, neat man with an enormous moustache he had waxed to points. He was immaculately dressed in a black military uniform, buttons gleaming, as they had on the Tsar's uniform. Just seeing it again made Laura's heart skip a beat with excitement. He seemed embarrassed by the attention and uncomfortable in a full dress uniform. He was not the man Laura had envisioned Ekaterina falling in love with, but her affection for him was obvious.
'What's this husband? The sash?' Ekaterina asked in Russian.
'I am on official business' he replied in English. 'Ensuring some precious cargo arrives. Welcome to Constantinople Mr Asanton, Miss Asanton.' He bowed deeply before them. 'The Royal train is waiting at the station. We shall walk there, it's not far. Porter!' he snapped his fingers.

Bal's huge shadow fell across the group and he set down all their luggage together on the docks beside them, bobbing a quick bow to Laura.
'Goodbye me lady, it was a pleasure' he grinned, still innocent to his carefree attitude.
'Farewell Jonathan, I have enjoyed our talks together' Laura said graciously. 'I hope we can meet again. If you ever come to Dalnerechensk I shall be very pleased to see you.'
'Thank you me lady' he grinned. 'If you ever need help I will be glad to be of service.' He dipped a jaunty bow, grinning.
'You wouldn't be interested in a position as an attaché would you?' Laura suddenly ventured,

realising his strength, lightening reflexes and easy manner would make a perfect personal guard.

Bal looked surprised. 'I'm flattered me lady, but the sea is my mistress. I can't leave her, no matter how – tempted.' He gave her a wink.

Laura flushed at the sauciness in his look and wondered if she had misjudged his apparent innocent ease. She didn't have long to worry, Bal bounded away to help unload the cargo of the *Queen* and a skinny man in a long white shirt, pants and slippers had joined them, collecting up their bags and loading them onto an open cart, babbling away in an Ottoman tongue. To Laura's surprise Grigory answered in the same tongue, pointing towards a long pink building a short distance away from the docks. The man lifted the impossibly heavy cart with a strength that belied his size and called out to others who were rushing past with carts, jostling his way off the docks.

Laura slipped her arm through Luke's elbow, staying close as the small traveling party wove their way through the crowded pier. Men carrying fish and octopus and other strange creatures swarmed up to them, pushing the wares that were beginning to stink in the hot sun towards them, and babble away at them in their native tongue, with a mixture of odd English words thrown in as well. Laura shrank back against Luke, a little frightened at the insistence of these men and the repugnance of their wares.

Luke could feel Laura trembling against him and he folded his arm around her back, holding her close against him. He couldn't remember a time when Laura had ever felt as if she needed him to protect her; she had always been headstrong and confident. She had grown up with tough oil workers; men and landscapes that had given her an indomitable spirit. It was not for the first time he wondered if the education she had received had broken her.

There was no doubt she was refined and different to the young girl he had sent away at his wife's insistence. There was an air of gentleness about her, a delicateness; he didn't know whether it was part of her that had developed or mannerisms that had been imposed on her. He had watched her conversations with Bal, a man that despite his immense size reminded him in so many ways of an eager, excited child. She had struggled with herself, never quite comfortable with him, and even looking around once or twice to see who was watching her.

He had experienced firsthand the scandalous damage waging tongues of socialites could do. Emily's suffering in madness had been compounded by the slanders of titled rich. Luke even secretly blamed them for Emily's suicide that ended that suffering. He knew the demands that would be placed on his daughter, the common wife of European Royalty would far exceed those he and Emily had faced in Boston Society. He wondered if Laura's awkwardness had meant she realised too, and that the demands were too much for her.

The bustle of the busy dock drew his attention back from his dark musings. Keeping an arm around her firmly they dodged around a Turk pulling another cart loaded with cargo, his eyes darting back and forth for the Ivanovs, who he had momentarily lost sight of. They were a little ahead of them, deep in conversation, already across the road and heading towards the spice *souk*.

The air smelt of incense and dried herbs and Laura breathed deep to rid her of the smell of rotting fish. They followed the Dalnerechenskers past the spice *souk* and headed towards a long, pink building, catching up to the couple as they opened the door to the waiting room. Luke and Laura eyed the beautiful architecture of the Orient Express station; the exotic arches in the doorway, the beautiful tiles that made the station feel clammy with the steam from the engines.

'This is the station where the Orient Express connects Europe and China' Ekaterina said, noticing their amazement. 'This line joins Russia's Trans-Siberian line at Chelyabinsk, but that is where we will depart from the line and head north into the Urals. But, we are not traveling on the Orient Express, Dalnerechensk has her own railway' she continued. 'Dalnerechensk's tin is taken by railway to Chelyabinsk where it then makes its way to the factories of Russia. We only have Russia's permission to use the connecting track between Chelyabinsk and Dalnerechensk and this small section of line.'

Laura did not question the limited access Dalnerechensk had to the outside world. She was well aware of the legends of Vsevolod, and was no fool to think what an independent principality was to a proud Empire like Russia. It did not have to be said how fragile the Principality's relationship with her greater neighbour was.

'We shall leave shortly; it will take two nights to reach home' Ekaterina added, watching the porter struggle across the waiting room with their bags stacked about his person.

Grigory opened the door and they stepped through onto the sweaty, humid platforms, uncomfortable with the clinging wetness of hot steam. Standing before them on the rails was a hissing locomotive. Dalnerechensk's royal train consisted of three carriages, a coal cart and the gleaming iron and copper steam engine. Beside the engine stood two men, dressed in clean blue overalls, holding blue and green caps before them, their heads respectfully bowed. Beside them stood two women, both dressed in plain black cotton dresses and white pinafore smocks, their heads bowed too.

The porter staggered after them and dropped their bags at the end of the train, loading them into the last carriage. The younger of the two women's eyes sidled towards him, looking uncomfortable at his close proximity to the train. Grigory announced the Asanton's to the little group who bowed and dipped curtseys respectfully. Grigory climbed up into the first carriage then leaned down to help up his wife and Laura. Luke scrambled up after them and Grigory cleared his throat self-consciously, beginning a formal tour of the facilities.

The carriage in which they stood held the kitchen and an impressive dining table, furnished with exotic carpets and the royal standard of Dalnerechensk. It was a rectangle of cloth, half coloured blue, the other half green, and bore the seal of the Vakhtangov dynasty. Laura realised the objects underneath the walls and towers that she had been unable to distinguish from the wax seal were a pick-axe and a shovel, their handles crossed. Grigory explained the towers were the watchtowers of the fortified castle and the pick-axe and shovel represented the tin mines on which Dalnerechensk's economy was built.

The second carriage was a comfortable sitting room, including a bookshelf, a gramophone and a large table to play cards or write a letter at. Most of the décor and fabrics in the carriage were in the colours of the Royal house of Dalnerechensk; blue and green with trims of gold, and another royal standard hung from the wall. Laura guessed they would be spending most of their days here where Ekaterina would no doubt tease her with Russian lessons until her head spun.

The third carriage, where the porter was busily loading their baggage, held sleeping compartments. A narrow walkway stretched along the carriage between the right hand outer wall and the three custom-made sleeping compartments on the left, down to a heavy door at the end. Thick blue carpet muffled their footsteps and rich, dark wood paneling glowed in the midday sun.

One sleeping compartment was for the servants to share with the luggage and the others were lavish rooms for the guests. Laura wondered how secure the door at the end was, she could see no locks that would secure it against advantageous persons seeking to gain access to the royal train. She wondered if the respect the train carried inside Russian territory was deterrent enough, and made a mental note to ask Ekaterina.

The servant girl who had followed them through the train's compartments bobbed a curtsey in front of Laura and beckoned her to the heavy door at the end of the carriage. 'Please follow me' she said in thick English.

The door, it turned out, opened into the largest and most lavish of the compartments. An elegantly carved bed dominated most of the compartment, hung in fine green drapery, edged with gold trim and heaped with blue and green pillows. A large screen to dress behind was nailed to the wall to give it some stability, a comfortable brocaded chair sat near it, a small dressing table; and even a blue ceramic stove decorated with green tiles bearing inscribed coats of arms sat in the room.

Another heavy door opened onto a fully enclosed private balcony at the end of the train. Laura was glad to see a solid lock on this door which she turned to step out onto the balcony. A bench seat was nailed to the wall of the train so she could sit and watch the countryside as it faded behind the train. Now there was only the wet confine of the Orient train station. She heard the door to the carriage where the porter had been loading their cases slam shut. She turned and stepped back into her compartment, securing the door behind her.

'Are you hungry Miss Asanton? We will serve a midday meal soon' the girl asked, standing close to the brocade chair, her hands folded behind her back.

Laura realised she was to be her personal servant while on the train journey and would do everything under her watchful eye. She felt a slight despondency, wishing she could have some privacy, but resigned herself to the fact it was the first of much scrutiny she was going to endure.

'*Spasibo*' she replied in Russian, taking off her gloves.

The train whistle blew, startling her, then the carriage jerked and began to move. Laura bent to look out of the window, wondering if she should wave, but the only one watching the train leave was the porter, who was now sitting on the ground on the platform, picking his teeth with a grubby fingernail. She straightened again, eyeing the lavish room, finally laying her gloves on the small dressing table.

'Will there be anything else Miss Asanton?' the servant asked in her thick English.

'What is your name?' Laura asked suddenly.

The girl looked surprised. 'Olga, Miss Asanton.'

'Thank you Olga, that will be all for now' she said, dismissing her with a nod and a smile.

Olga smiled shyly, dipped a curtsey and left, closing the door after her.

12

'Laura, wake up. Quickly now, we are coming to Dalnerechensk' Ekaterina said, shaking her.

Laura rolled over, pushing her hair back from her face. It was not yet light and her room was cold, the ceramic stove had burned out of fuel during the night. The temperature had dropped and snow had started to fall as the train climbed into the Caucuses and had not stopped as they steamed towards the Urals on their two day journey. Ekaterina, already dressed, lit the oil lamp in her room and pulled the thick covers off her. The cold slapped her body and she shivered, pulling her knees up to her chin.

'Get up and wash, you don't want to greet the *Tsarevich* half asleep and looking tired, even if you don't marry him' Ekaterina teased.

Laura groaned and roused herself from the bed, trying to wrap her arms round herself and pick up her clothes at the same time. Her first instance of assisted dressing had been embarrassing and fraught with fear. Laura was terrified Olga, despite her amiable nature, was a spy for the Crown Prince – or worse, the Dalnerechensk court – where any perceived blemishes of character or body would be detrimental to her prospect of marriage. Laura had skirted the potentially damaging exposure of her scars by sending Olga for ribbons and dresses, and pulling on a soft chemise behind the dressing screen when she did so, allowing the girl to lace the corset over the top.

Now Ekaterina helped her into a corset over another soft chemise, lacing it tightly to accentuate her girlish curves. An emerald dress followed, cut low and tight in a style that suited her figure. Ekaterina, ever mindful of the impression she needed to make, unlocked the thick door to the private balcony and pulled Laura outside, combing her hair and pulling it into an elegant coif. By the time she was done the colour had come up in Laura's cheeks and her eyes were bright with moisture induced by the cold.

In the grey light of predawn Laura could see the shapes of houses and long low buildings lining the rails. The train passed under an arch in a strong wall and Laura noticed it had a portcullis before Ekaterina dragged her back inside. She crossed to the small dressing table, opened a jewelry box and pulled out the beautiful necklace Aleksei had presented to his bride-to-be, fastening it round Laura's throat.

The train passed through a short tunnel which darkened the carriage for an instant, like a large bird flying across the sun, and emerged inside the fortified city of Dalnerechensk. Atop a steep hill, against the lightening of the sky, Laura could see the three watchtowers of the castle wall, impressive and imposing against the grey sky. The train began to slow and Laura caught sight of the cluster of lights up ahead of the train. They were moving and dancing, looking like drunken fireflies as they jostled towards the place where the train was coming to a halt.

'We will depart from the middle carriage' Ekaterina said with a smile. 'Come now, Dalnerechensk has come to see you Laura.'

Dawn arrived at the hilltop castle first, peeping over the flanking hills to light the highest point in Liberty Valley. It warmed the stone walls, turning them first a soft pink and then a blazing amber. Laura snatched a quick glance up at the beautiful sight as she hurried across the gangway to the middle carriage. Grigory and Luke were already inside, sitting on the comfortable sofa, but stood as the women came into the room.

Olga and the cook stood nearby, hands folded demurely in front of them, though unable to hide their excitement as the train pulled to a stop at the station. Through the windows Laura could see a mass of people carrying candles waiting beyond a striking line of mounted men in dress uniform. Very few of the candles were still lit, and she wondered how long they had stood in the cold to catch a glimpse of her. She quickly fastened a blue cloak around her shoulders, patting self consciously at her hair.

The engineer leapt down from the now still locomotive and rushed to open the carriage door. There was a rippling murmur from the gathered crowd as they strained to see round the line of mounted military men that blocked their access to the railway platform. The engineer whipped his hat off his head, quickly wiping his hand clean before offering it to help down Grigory.

The light was slowly gliding down the hillside to the township below as they disembarked and the people called out greetings to their nobility. Ekaterina received a hearty welcome as she stepped out and she beamed radiantly at the people, calling a hello with a wave of her hand. Laura took a deep breath and took the hand of the engineer.

As she stepped out dawn arrived at the train station, accompanied by a gust of icy air. The sun hit her chestnut hair and made it glow, the gust blowing open her blue cloak. A loud cheer went up from the on-lookers; the effect of a beautiful figure draped in their royal colours hadn't gone amiss. Laura was surprised and pleased by the warm greeting and waved, calling hello and *how do you do* in her best Russian, her efforts rewarding her with another joyous cheer.

Ekaterina was smiling, waving to the crowd on the platform. Laura joined her, linking her arm through hers and Luke stepped out of the carriage, receiving a cheer as well. He managed a smile and a nod at the people, uncomfortable with the attention.

Grigory, stiff and uncomfortable, led them to a waiting carriage parked at the side of the station house. It was a stately black and gold affair, drawn by six horses. They had blue and green plumes on their bridles, as did the mounted guard. Laura smiled at those who called out to her, trying not to show how frightened she was by the sea of attentive faces and the strange tongue whirling around her. They pressed in close to the line of mounted guards, everyone trying to get a glimpse of their new Princess, and although there was no menace in the crowd Laura couldn't stop the feeling of fear, hoping it didn't show on her face.

Two men dressed in livery uniforms opened the waiting carriage, guiding the Ivanovs and the Asantons inside. The mounted guard broke from the restraining line to take up positions around them. The crowd swarmed onto the platform, still calling welcome and waving. When the horses were in place the two livery men climbed onto the driver's seat and gathered up the reins, calling to the front horse.

A sharp burgle note was sounded and the procession moved off from the small station, the crowd reluctant to part and allow them through, all still trying to gain a glimpse of the pretty American girl. Inside the carriage Ekaterina took Laura's hand and squeezed it tightly, satisfied.

'Well done Laura, they will love you now' she said, pleased, squeezing her hand to reassure her.

At last the leading horses managed to nudge people aside and the crowd parted, allowing the guard and carriage to pass through. They made a sharp turn from the platform onto a cobbled street that ran straight up the hill to the castle.

'This street is named after the gate we came through in the city wall' Ekaterina continued. 'It runs directly to the palace, as do most of the roads in Dalnerechensk, but this is the main road. At the new moon there is a market on this street, and at harvest time, a festival sees this street crowded with people. It is called Vsevolod's Way.'

Laura nodded, her head whirling with new information and trying not to stammer while the rest of her caught up. They were slowly making their way up the sloping street and Laura looked around at the city carefully. Vsevolod's Way was wide and the main commercial street in Dalnerechensk. Each shop had a metal sign with medieval symbols of their craft hanging above their doors. Though it was only dawn Vsevolod's Way was lined with people, calling out greetings, cheering as they caught sight of the magnificent procession, throwing fresh-cut alpine flowers on the road before the horses' hooves.

As the day lightened around them, Laura realised her first impression of the castle was wrong. She had thought it stood on an outcrop on the side of the hills that flanked Liberty Valley, but now she could see its three towers and thick stone walls sat at the top of a solitary hill, an ancient island carved millions of years ago by a long vanished glacier, slightly to the left of the centre of the valley.

Before they reached the gates of the huge castle wall the road narrowed and made a sharp S-bend. The guards at the gates had swung open the huge, thick wooden doors. Eight ornamental tin plates had been fixed to the gate, depicting scenes of life in Dalnerechensk, each of them extremely detailed. Laura wished she had time to see them properly but the carriage did not slow as it swept into the large, sunlit courtyard beyond.

The courtyard was paved with white gravel. The area extended from the castle's defensive wall to the steps of the medieval castle. The steps were flanked with dignitaries and servants of the Vakhtangov household, rising in rank from the bottom to the top. Right at the top of the stairs stood the old Tsar himself, and halfway down, surrounded by his court and household, waiting nervously, was Aleksei.

Laura recognised his powerful figure and she began to tremble, her breath coming short and hard in her throat, a fear crashing through her stomach, whirling butterflies round her middle. He was handsome, tall and strong, beautiful in the striking black uniform of Dalnerechensk's military. The carriage pulled to a stop and a page dressed in the livery of the royal household darted forward, dropping a step beneath the door and opening it, standing respectfully to the side with his hand outstretched to help down the people inside.

Grigory stepped out first and Aleksei called a warm welcome to him. Grigory bowed low to the Prince and then the Treasurer offered his hand to help down his wife. Aleksei and the rest of the court greeted her as warmly as the townsfolk had. Ekaterina was someone extremely beloved by the Principality, and anyone who was beloved by her held special affection from the people as well. Next Luke stepped out and Grigory announced him loudly to the assembled guests. Aleksei smiled.

'Welcome to Dalnerechensk My Lord' he called in English.

Luke nodded stiffly, respectfully, unused to pomp and ceremony and overwhelmed with the intense scrutiny of this royal meeting then turned to offer Laura his hand. He felt her fingers tremble as they slid into his and she appeared, glittering and glorious before the whole court of Dalnerechensk. There was a quiet gasp from the assembled court and a silence fell over them. Even the Crown Prince seemed startled by her youth and beauty. The uncomfortable moment stretched until Grigory took the initiative and spoke.

'Your Royal Highness I present Miss Laura Asanton.'

She let go of her father's hands and gathered her skirts, curtseying before them all. Aleksei came down the stairs to her. Flustered, her legs growing weak, Laura dropped to the ground kneeling before him, surprising him and making him stop.

'Come now, rise' he said softly, his voice rich and soothing like his father's. 'You are here at my honour. Look upon me.'

She trembled, then slowly raised her eyes to him.

The first thing she noticed was the painter of Tsar Constantinovich's watch had been kind. While he was still trim he was thicker than he had looked in the small likeness and his coal black hair had feathers of iron grey at his temples. He did not appear much older than the portrait, but there were deep lines round his eyes and he looked like a man with a heavy burden, lightened by his appreciation of a beautiful young bride-to-be, but burdened nonetheless.

He was also nervous and worried. Laura smiled tentatively, nervously, and Aleksei returned it. She rose as he took her hand and kissed it tenderly, his eyes still on her face. She smiled shyly, the colour rising in her cheeks and Aleksei's smile deepened. Then he gently drew her arm through his elbow, turning to face his court and his family. Laura's eyes were drawn back to Aleksei's face, his jaw was firm, and although there were strands of grey at his temples they did not detract from his air of vitality.

There was a sharp blast of trumpets, and a fanfare played while he led her slowly up the steps and into the castle. Laura tore her attention away, paying careful attention to where she put her feet, knowing she could not trip on the steps or the folds of her skirt. The steps had been swept clear of snow, and salted so that they did not slip but Laura didn't want to take any chances.

From Ekaterina's knowledgeable conversations Laura knew Dalnerechensk Castle had been built at the end of the Middle Ages by the small community seeking refuge in the Ural Mountains. At first they had lived simply, scratching a simple living grazing and farming the lush fields surrounding the central hill while they built the castle upon it. Upon its completion they had all lived inside the castle and built a protective high wall, with four watchtowers for defense. Only three of them could be seen at any one time from the valley below.

It was while they were quarrying the stone for the walls they had discovered large deposits of tin in the surrounding hills and the small community began to grow as more refugees and workers came to the valley in search of a better life. Aware that Dalnerechensk was now an attractive and prosperous place, the first Tsar Vsevolod had mapped out pretty streets and built fortified walls around the city of Dalnerechensk and the garrison village of Tcherepnin to protect the citizens trickling into the mountains to toil in the mines.

Dalnerechensk had the charm of a place forgotten by time, existing as it had for hundreds of years. The people were proud of its traditions, its history and its Prince. Laura swallowed nervously, eyeing the imposing façade of a castle built for defense. How could they love a child, a foreigner, who had come to sit on their throne and tell them how they would live their life? Their warm greeting would soon turn to bitter resentment. Laura had ignored the thirty-seven girls in Lady Ramkinson's school. She could not ignore a principality.

Aleksei noticed the tremble in her hand in the crook of his elbow and folded his over hers as the household followed them inside. The entrance hall was large and tastefully decorated with ancient silk tapestries hung from towering walls. The Crown Prince began a tour of his home, pointing out the features to the Asantons. To the left and the right of the hall were expansive wings of rooms designed to entertain guests and hold state functions. On the ground floor of the left wing was a magnificent throne room, decorated with bright mythic frescoes and dominated by an intricately carved throne. Directly beside the throne room was a large ballroom, crowned by a glittering chandelier.

In the right wing was a long dining hall. The tapestries that hung in this hall were of festive wedding scenes and celebrations depicting eating and drinking. The long oak table was polished to a high shine and surrounded by a hundred and twenty seats. In the middle of the table sat a large, high backed chair, presiding under a canopy of blue and green velvet, trimmed in gold. It was Vsevolod's original throne, Aleksei told them, an unassuming seat that was still such a potent symbol of state that it had not been removed when it was replaced by the current throne, and now served as the king's seat at meals.

He led them back to the entrance hall where an elegant, sweeping staircase led to the private rooms of the castle, where the business of running a principality was conducted in the maze of offices and store rooms on the first floor. There was also a huge Council Chamber where Dalnerechensk's ministers met and sat at a large, heavy table. It was not round, but Laura couldn't help but think she was looking at the relics and ideals of Camelot reinvented again in this small mountain principality.

She looked up at Aleksei again, wondering at this man who seemed so knowledgeable, so proud of his heritage, so aware of the ideals needed for good government. There were years between them, but she was finding herself more and more attracted to him, liking the deep timbre of his voice, the strength he felt in his arm, the intelligence and confidence he radiated. His cheek suddenly darkened slightly under her scrutiny. His voice did not falter in the commentary and she realised she was seeing an expert in diplomacy in action.

Back through the warren of rooms they went to the second floor which contained the rooms for the royal family and various guests. The second floor also housed a sewing room, a hunting room furnished with several mounted trophies and a billiard table, and a comfortable music room.

The third floor housed the sumptuous apartment for the Tsar of Dalnerechensk and richly decorated living quarters for honoured guests. It also held a vast library of leather books, maps, a giant marble fireplace and a beautiful oil portrait of a woman, the late Tsaritsa of Dalnerechensk.

'She is beautiful' Laura whispered, and felt Aleksei squeeze her hand in response.

To Luke's surprise both he and Laura were given majestic rooms on the third floor. Huge French windows in private sitting rooms commanded an impressive view of the farm dotted valley beneath them. Both had a magnificent bedchamber draped in luxuries of every kind; a small, private dressing room and a modest parlour to themselves. Their rooms were connected through a door between each parlour so they could meet in confidence if they wished.

In each room was a maid waiting for them. They curtsied low when they stepped into the room. Aleksei explained that the girls were employed to serve them only and would take care of any matter with the utmost discretion. As they talked a manservant carried in Laura's luggage and the girl set to work taking them to the dressing room, unpacking her clothes and hanging dresses in the closet.

As the tour had progressed the number of people following the Asantons and the Royals had decreased until they were almost alone in Laura's rooms. The court, having followed the visitors round the castle, had not crossed into the private rooms on the second floor, taking their leave from their Prince. Luke had been shown his rooms first and remained in them to unpack and freshen up while the Crown Prince and the Ivanovs led Laura to her private apartments. Almost alone the pressure of performing under the watchful eyes of a critical court melted away and Aleksei turned to Laura, suddenly awkward and embarrassed.

'You received my gift' he said uselessly, eyeing the necklace.

Laura had expected a comment about how she looked wearing it, a witty remark of a jewel wearing jewels, a romantic expression of how they did not shine as brightly as her, even a rhetoric of their origin, the cutter, the jeweler who had put it together. Instead he awkwardly turned, almost at a loss with what to say to her. Laura was surprised that a man so confident of himself in public could be so awkward. She wondered if it was her that tied his tongue, or because he was unrehearsed.

'You have not eaten yet, I will have the cook send up something for you both' he rushed on, filling the awkward silence.

He paused as if there was something else he wanted to say then he bowed and left her, closing the door behind him. The serving girl returned from the dressing room as Aleksei left, bobbing a curtsey in front of Laura.

'Will there be anything else My Lady?' she asked in English.

'What is your name?' Laura asked in Russian.

'Anna, my lady.'

'Well Anna, you must talk to me in Russian, I must practice as much as I can' Laura smiled, taking off her gloves and unpinning the blue cloak.

13

The snow fell against the French windows, making a faint hissing noise as it slid down the glass, almost inaudible over the crackling of the bright fire in her room. Laura sat on a thick rug combing her hair, relieved at last to be alone. Anna had gone to the attic to sleep and Ekaterina had finally departed, telling Laura where to find her room on the second landing should she need anything in the night. She set the comb beside her and gazed into the orange flames, feeling her eyelids droop wearily.

Aleksei had sent a meal to her room that she had eaten with restrained relish, aware Anna was still in her room. Ekaterina had joined her when she finished, instructing Laura to change out of her traveling dress and into another. She had pulled on a soft dress of virginal white, removed her hat and donned white elbow-length gloves. Ekaterina had smiled approvingly then led her down to the throne room where Luke had been waiting outside patiently.

He had looked taken aback at her finery then had offered her his hand. As honoured guests they had taken pride of place, entering the throne room first before Ekaterina had followed them in. It had been crowded with every dignitary and politician in Dalnerechensk. Aleksei had sat on the throne dressed in the regalia of state with the elderly Tsar on his left hand side. In deference to his health and the respect he still commanded in the Principality he had been seated, though slightly behind the line of the throne.

Laura and her father had come to the dais and stood on the right of the throne. Ekaterina had taken up station behind them, mindful they would need a translator. As they had stood each man in the room had come forward and kissed Laura's hand, introducing themselves and their titles, cordially asking after her health and well-being. Some had spoken hesitantly in thick English but most had spoken Russian. Ekaterina had quickly and quietly translated their well-wishings and Laura had smiled and nodded politely, feeling like her head was about to spin off her shoulders with the sheer volume of names and faces.

She had also noticed something that disturbed her a little though she had not let her thoughts show. While Aleksei and Grigory were by no means young men they were practically green compared to the Advisory Council of Dalnerechensk. Laura had never seen so many grey beards and white heads in one room. Her quick sensibilities had told her they were the Council of Tsar Constantinovich that Aleksei had kept on to advise him as they had advised his father. She wondered at the wisdom of an elderly body of men to advise a young Tsar.

The only elderly politician Laura had ever met before was Councilor Cabanel of Boston, a doddering old hunched up man who asked everyone where his false teeth were, despite having them in his mouth, and was forever mumbling to someone he thought was standing on his left regardless if anyone was or not. He had been kept on as an honourary member of the Council of Businessmen which her father dealt with every now and then, though the only decisions he had to make were whether he would have a biscuit or club sandwich with his tea.

Laura had felt a slight unease seeing so many gathered in Dalnerechensk's throne room. Most of them had served Tsar Constantinovich and had never been replaced, nor taken apprentices or protégés to train in the delicacies of politics. She wondered if the Prince was a man with deep respect for his father's administration and advisors, or too lazy to find himself new and younger ministers. She wondered, indeed, if there *were* younger men to take their places, or if they had left to find more prestigious positions in larger, more elabourate courts in Europe.

When most of Dalnerechensk had kissed her hand Aleksei had risen from the throne, causing the room to bow before them. He had smiled at Laura and offered his arm, and she had slid her hand inside the crook of his elbow. He had led them out of the throne room and the Dalnerechensk court had fallen in behind them, according to their prestige in the Principality, to the beautiful gardens. The topiary hedges and trees had been dusted with a soft crystal snow and the white gleaming lawn stretched down to the fortified wall, dominated by a watchtower. Here the Royal Guards had marched a perfect drill for their guests, churning up the soft powder under their feet. Luke and Laura had been impressed to see the drill was so perfect they had marched in each other's footsteps. To mark the climactic finish, the watchmen in the four towers had fired the cannons of Dalnerechensk.

Her ears had rung for a full minute afterwards and she had laughed and clapped her hands in appreciation. As full as their day had already been there followed a state lunch in the long dining hall and an afternoon of festivities; a delightful group of children that had sung the national anthem, a jester that had made jokes Laura didn't understand though the rest of the court had laughed, an amusing game of snow tennis, a joust, and even a re-enactment of the Battle of Dalnerechensk when Vsevolod had held off the approaching army of a Russian rebel who had wanted the mines for himself.

Despite her fatigue from the long day there had been hours of dinner and dancing. Laura and Ekaterina had changed quickly for dinner and had had their hair rearranged into a more elabourate coif decorated with small seed pearls. She and her father had been seated on the right hand of Aleksei, under the state canopy at the dining table and had done their best to answer questions and join in the conversations, grateful for Ekaterina's tireless translating.

And after the courses had been finished, when Aleksei had bowed to her and taken her hand the whole court had stopped to watch them dance. He moved well, and Laura felt herself smiling at him, enjoying the way his stride matched hers and the intricate and energetic steps of the dance. There was a flair and fervor in the way he moved, a joy in dancing she readily shared, ignoring the ache in her feet and legs.

They had danced in silence, and though he was confident and clever under the eye of his court and advisors, swaying their mood with a nod, a word or a jest; he was painfully awkward when he spoke to her, and as such he had barely spoken a word to her at dinner, and said nothing to her as they danced. She couldn't help but feel glad when the old Tsar had stepped down to the dance floor and bowed to her.

The small quartet of musicians had noticed and begun to play something less energetic so as not to embarrass the old man. Laura had accepted the dance with a curtsey and slid into his embrace, comfortable as a father and daughter. She had seen the eyes of the court on her as they danced, the ladies in waiting, the livery boys of the various nobility, the wives of ageing ministers and daughters that had come of age and been passed over by an eligible Prince, and knew what would be whispered in the days to come. The Tsar's affection for her was obvious. *He looks like he is the man engaged* they would whisper. *The Tsar is so fond the Tsarevich must take care he does not share her with him!*

The dance had ended and the Tsar had bowed deeply first to her and then to his son. 'With your blessing my son, I shall retire' he had said, his voice resonating round the room.

Aleksei had accepted and dismissed all the court then. The Tsar had shuffled to the staircase to retire to his rooms, aided by his attaché, and Aleksei, with Laura at his side, had stood on the steps of the castle to farewell each of the guests as they left, stable grooms and livery boys rushing to bring the correct horses and carriages to take the ministers home.

Aleksei had then walked Laura upstairs to her rooms and bid her good night with a kiss on her hand, then had left to escort her father to his rooms. Ekaterina, who had followed her to her rooms, had taken her hands excitedly, asking her a hundred questions until Laura had begged for peace, promising to answer all in the morning. Anna had then babbled excitedly away in Russian as she helped her prepare for bed and Laura had only half understood her. She had allowed the girl to unlace her corset, sighing as her body was finally free from its rigid prison, but had not allowed her to remove the chemise.

It was now well after midnight and Anna had turned down the bed and bid her a good night before she finally slipped up to the servants' quarters in the attic to sleep, leaving her completely alone for the first time since she had arrived in Dalnerechensk. Laura's feet were so sore even the prospect of the few steps to her bed was not appealing. Instead she had sunk down on the thick rug before the fire with her comb, dragging it through her thick locks then set it aside to massage her sore legs.

There was a quiet tap on her door. Without waiting for an answer it was pushed open and Aleksei stepped in, closing the door behind him quickly. He had taken off the stuffy dress jacket he had worn all day and the white shirt underneath was loose and rumpled. In the firelight he looked young, almost boyish; roguishly handsome. She gasped and scrabbled to her feet, wincing, dropping an awkward curtsey.

'I am not dressed to receive Your Royal Highness' she said weakly, folding her arms across her and bowing her head modestly so her hair covered her face.

'Will you receive a friend?' he asked quietly.

Laura hesitated then nodded, trembling at the pain in her feet. Aleksei came closer, cautiously, noticing how she shook.

'I am glad – pleased – at your strength today' he started awkwardly. 'Perhaps you will make a good princess. It is a hard thing to do, to be surrounded by people, and yet, terribly alone' his voice faded away.

'Is that how you feel Aleksei?' she asked, forgetting to call him by his title.

His eyes drifted to hers and then away again, a boyish flush darkening his cheeks. She didn't understand how this man could be so confident before his court and so awkward with her.

'You are very brave Laura, very brave' he said softly, almost to himself.

It was the first time he had called her by her name, and she loved the rich sound of her vowels on his tongue. It made her smile and take a step towards him, forgetting about the pain in her feet. She sucked her breath in sharply and Aleksei took her arms, worried.

'Forgive me, my feet hurt' she said, embarrassed, dropping her eyes.

Aleksei gently guided her to sit back on the thick rug and fetched a pillow from her bed, returning to sit with her. He placed the pillow before her then gently took her ankles and placed her legs upon it. A pretty blush stole into her cheeks at the warm feel of his fingers on her skin and she reached down, rubbing her leg, partly to ease the pain she felt there, and partly to still the strange butterflies in her stomach his touch had set fluttering.

'We have not had the time to talk to ourselves, privately' Aleksei said. 'I thought – perhaps you wondered – why I had not – I would not want you to marry me without knowing me' he stuttered, hardly able to look at her.

'Did you write that letter?' she blurted out, sick of protocol and unable to help herself.

He looked surprised and amused at her bluntness, which quickly turned to embarrassment.

'I did' he said, then confessed: 'It took me almost a week to write it. Everything I said made no sense, or sounded as if I didn't care, or sounded as if I spent my days sighing to a lute under a tree.'

Laura giggled then, and Aleksei smiled, a blush still strong in his cheek. He reached out suddenly and gently pressed the balls of his thumbs to her feet. She winced and groaned at the same time, watching the way his hands moved on her feet, his strong fingers brushing gently over her skin. The touch was wonderfully relaxing, but at the same time managed to knot her stomach with a tension she had not felt before. Despite this she couldn't stop the yawn and Aleksei looked up, surprised.

'Of course, it is late' he said, standing and bowing to her. 'Sleep well Miss Asanton, I shall see you again.'

He opened the door and checked the hallway outside before nodding once more to her and closing it soundlessly behind him, leaving her puzzled and alone.

14

Laura smiled softly, closing her eyes as she turned her face up to the sun, inclining her head just a little to listen for the bird song again. The heavy lexicon she carried was forgotten momentarily, as was the small leather book of Vsevolod's exploits she had been trying to read. The song and the sun were welcome distractions for the difficult script and she stopped in her walk of the gardens, sighing gently.

The day was cold and her breath puffed around her, glistening with tiny crystals. That morning after breakfast Luke, Laura, Aleksei and several members of the council had mounted on horseback and ridden out of the castle into the town of Dalnerechensk itself.

Aleksei had ridden beside Laura and Luke, pointing out the church, the hospital, the school and other buildings of interest. The streets at first had been quiet, then crowds began gathering, calling out greetings to the Americans. Laura had smiled and waved, calling hello to the people and Luke had uncomfortably copied her, struggling with the unfamiliar tongue.

They had then passed under the huge portcullis in Vsevolod's Gate, the iron shod horse hooves ringing on the railway tracks as they headed to Tcherepnin, the fortified village. Like Dalnerechensk, it was set out in neat rows round a large central parade ground. Aleksei had pointed out the long rows of barracks that encircled the parade ground, claiming proudly that they had hosted the victorious army of Vsevolod four hundred years ago, and now housed a mere tenth of highly trained garrison soldiers. Laura saw that some of the windows had flower boxes and some doors had been painted different colours and small ornaments that decorated the front paths and welcome mats and gathered that there were civilians living in the empty, unneeded barracks.

There was no flutter of nervousness and Aleksei had been confident and rehearsed in his rhetoric, even when he apologised for having to leave her on their return to the castle, disappearing into the Council Chambers with the rest of the Advisory Council. Laura and Luke had walked arm in arm up the ancient stone stairs to the third floor, laughing together. Laura had pulled a stern face, mimicking a particularly foreboding frown from an old oil painting.

'I wonder who they all are' Laura had mused, reaching out to touch the gilding on the bottom of the frame.

'I should think there would be something in the library' Luke had answered and Laura looked at him in surprise.

'Of course!' she laughed, dragging him up the hallway to the library.

They had slipped quietly into the room in case they disturbed anyone but found it quite empty. Luke was astounded at the sheer volume of books and manuscripts. The Vakhtangov Library rivaled that of Boston's University and both had quickly forgotten their original purpose for venturing in, lost amongst exciting discoveries in the large wooden bookshelves.

Before long Luke had a stack of books bearing English titles under his arm and staggered to a place to sit, greedily delving into the well turned pages.

Laura had found a thin, leather bound book with the simple title: *Всиболод*, seemingly handwritten. She pulled it out of the shelf and took it to the window to see the faded writing better. A flicker in the garden caught her eye, a flash of red that streaked across the white dusted mounds of the garden. She had smiled, slipping out of the library and out into the private gardens of Tsar Constantinovich.

Now a movement through the mist of her breath caught her eye again and she peered through it to the windows of the first floor of Dalnerechensk Castle. Aleksei was at the window of the room she guessed to be the Advisory Council, the piece of paper in his hand forgotten, looking as though his attention had just been caught by something in the garden.

A small smile played on her lips and she opened the small leather book again, trying to concentrate on the syllables of the text. A quick look told her Aleksei was doing the same, and sneaking quick looks at her. She took a few steps and bit her lip in an air of studious concentration, flashing a look at the window. Aleksei was still watching her, and she couldn't tell if there was a flush in his cheeks or not. She liked to think so, and it made her bold.

She had heard Belinda Crompton talking about the art of seduction to her giggling friends one night, instructing them to have dresses tailored with lace or ribbon or satin roses at the neckline. These fripperies would provide endless ways of attracting the eye of a calling gentleman to the curve of the breast, and to encourage that attention by unconsciously touching or playing with the trimmings. Laura flashed another look at the first story window then, encouraged by his gaze, reached up and began to play with the button on her thick coat.

It was hardly seductive in the big winter coat she had worn riding earlier, but Aleksei hadn't taken his eyes off her, and had forgotten to keep up the pretense of reading the paper he was clutching. Laura's smile deepened as she pulled off her glove to lick her finger gently to turn the page of the unread book. The cold made her instantly regret it and she tried to juggle the books and put her glove back on. She wasn't able to hang on to everything and the heavy lexicon took a tumble into a drift of snow, the soft powder puffing up as it landed.

There was a hearty laugh behind her and she turned, embarrassed, dropping a quick curtsey to the Tsar. She quickly retrieved the book from the drift, ashamed that it had been unceremoniously dumped on the ground and clutched it to her protectively.

'Ah my dear, what is it you disliked from my library so much you decided to bury it till next spring?' he chuckled, coming closer and taking the book from her. 'Ah, a dictionary! Very good.' he grinned, tossing the book to the ground flippantly. 'Terribly boring, such a poor plot.'

Laura laughed at his action, turning and slipping her arm into his elbow. Tsar Constantinovich chuckled again, his voice rumbling in the quiet afternoon. They walked in silence for a moment, Laura listening for the bird song again, enjoying the peace and tranquility in the frozen garden. She stole a quick look at the Tsar to see the smile still playing on his lips as well.

'I told you the next time we walked together would be in my private gardens' he smiled.

'Yes you did' she smiled. 'They're beautiful.'

'What other book displeased you in my library?' he asked, eyeing the small handwritten book in her hand.

'On the contrary, this one pleased me very much, only I was finding the script difficult to read.'

Tsar Constantinovich reached over and took the book.

'This is Natasha's account of Vsevolod's life' he said.

Laura knew from the many stories of Vsevolod she had listened to that Natasha had been his wife and Tsaritsa of Dalnerechensk.

'I have read about the two men I admire most in this garden' Tsar Constantinovich continued. 'Vsevolod, of course, and the son of Philip of Macedon: Alexander the Great.'

He reached inside his winter coat and pulled out a leather bound book from an inside pocket, handing it to Laura. She took the book from him and opened it, stealing a quick glance at the first floor window. It was empty, Aleksei had disappeared and she turned a page, trying to ignore the disappointment she felt. The book had been illustrated with beautiful colour drawings of battles.

'Such a leader…' Constantinovich said softly, reverently.

Laura read the title on the page out loud then carefully began to read the information on the page. Tsar Constantinovich walked with her, correcting her pronunciation, listening to her reading a familiar story. He smiled as the bird sang again, seeing it flash across the trimmed topiary hedges.

'You read well my dear' he said, interrupting her. 'Perhaps you should read to my son, he would enjoy that. Perhaps it would take his mind off things.'

'You named your son after Alexander didn't you' Laura suddenly said.

The Tsar swallowed. 'Yes I did' he said, a little strained. 'Please excuse me my dear, I think it is quite enough walking in the cold for one day.'

'Of course Your Majesty' she said, a little worried. 'Is there anything I can do?'

'Accompany me inside' he smiled gently.

She smiled and dipped a curtsey, rescuing the lexicon from the snow on the way past.

15

The man stood quietly on the elegant rug before the Council, smelling of cheap ale and tobacco. He was in his late thirties, grey at the temples though it was virtually indistinguishable in his sun-bleached locks. His body was lean and hard, with the wiry muscles of one used to physical labour, his hands hard and calloused, his skin burnished by hours of toil in the sun. Aleksei paced back and forward, eyeing him unhappily.

He didn't flinch under Aleksei's scrutiny, his hands hanging by his sides, shifting his weight to stand with one leg casually bent, easing it, waiting calmly for the Prince to give him an order.

'Is that all you have to say?' Aleksei finally demanded.

The man shrugged. 'The Prince should not marry a commoner, wealthy or not' he said.

He did not cower or drop his eyes on the floor but stood watching the Prince, gauging his reactions. His manner annoyed Aleksei who dismissed him, turning to the small group of advisors sitting at the long table in the Council Chambers when the door was securely shut behind him.

There was an uncomfortable minute of silence. The grey beards looked at their hands and the polished surface of the huge oak table – Vsevolod's dining table, relocated to the chambers when the court had grown too large to sit comfortably around it – and stared as if captivated by the sparkle of the sunlight in their glasses of water.

'He is right, you know' Grigory said first. 'She could win the people over as she is pretty and charming, but she will never quite be aristocratic enough.'

'So I make her a Countess' Aleksei shrugged flippantly, flopping down into a comfortable chair at the head of the table.

'That would not be advisable' said a grey head.

Aleksei's eyes narrowed, following the turning heads to gaze at the man who had spoken out. There was an uncertain pause and surreptitious eyes stole back to see the Prince's reaction.

'You cannot make her a Countess just to marry her. It will not endear you to the people' the grey head continued.

'I am in an intolerable situation!' Aleksei cried, slamming his palm down on the table. 'I can't title her but I can't marry a commoner! Perhaps I should abdicate then, will that make the people happy?'

'Don't be rash boy' the grey head said sternly. 'There is no other heir to the throne. It would cause chaos.'

The grey head was Nicholas Riminov, the oldest Councilman in Dalnerechensk. He had served Tsar Constantinovich for thirty years as his friend and favoured, and watched the *Tsarevich* grow into the man he was now. He was the only one in Dalnerechensk unwary of his place with Aleksei, the only man who could scold him still.

'There is one option open to us' he went on quietly.

'Well don't hold us in suspense man' Aleksei snapped.

'Appoint her father a baron.'

The advisors all began talking at once, shouting each other down and arguing amongst themselves, making the Prince wince and rub his tired temples. It seemed all his days were filled with arguments now.

Aleksei banged his fist down on the table for silence.

'It is a good suggestion, she will inherit the title then, and she will no longer be a commoner' one said enthusiastically.

'A mere baron is insulting!' another cried.

'Your Highness, you yourself said we can no longer afford to pay these salaries. Dalnerechensk was never able to support a large nobility or court' said another.

Aleksei looked at Grigory, wishing he would tell him something other than what he already knew.

'The salaries of the court are not the issue here' Grigory said, subdued. 'Dalnerechensk's wealth is slipping away from her, has been for decades. We could afford one more title, but the Principality teeters on the edge of financial ruin. The question here Aleksei, is if she does not agree to marry you, you cannot take away the title.'

'She is young and impressionable' scoffed another. 'Offering her father a title will ensure the silly girl marries you.'

'Mind your tongue' snapped Aleksei.

The Advisory Council collectively realised that his marriage was no longer a simple matter of duty to produce an heir to the throne. Aleksei had been taken by Laura's beauty and enchanted by her spirit. The way she had borne herself through hours of politics and festivities with charm and wit had impressed even the hardest members of the court. There was an urgency about this, and nothing was more desperate than a man in charge of fifteen thousand subjects on the edge of love and financial ruin.

'Forgive me, I meant no disrespect' the scoffer mumbled, apologetic.

'So how else to win her heart and secure the financial continuation of Dalnerechensk?' Aleksei asked bitterly. 'I do not want a young and impressionable thing to turn cold and resentful.'

The table fell quiet, thinking. Aleksei looked away, knowing they were turning over in their heads the same arguments they had voiced over the last five months. His eyes drifted to the window where delicate flakes of snow were drifting into the garden below them. A flash of blue at the end of the garden caught his eye and he stood, leaving his seat to lean against the cold stone surrounding the window, smiling as he watched Laura in her blue cloak pelt her father with another snowball, laughing as he returned the assault.

Alexei sighed to himself, listening to the way her musical laugh floated in the air here. There was a childish charm about her, and a strength that belied her young years. He now knew what his father had meant. She tucked herself into her father's arm again, but Alexei could imagine that mischievous look playing on her lips as she laughed again.

He watched as the two walked on slowly in the white dusted garden, brushing soft flakes off themselves absently and he strained, wishing he could hear what they were saying, wishing he could hear the strange way she talked. Her face suddenly turned up towards the window and he caught his breath, wondering if she had felt him watching her. But her eyes were closed, smiling as she tilted her face up to feel the flakes fall against her cheeks, a pretty colour in her skin.

He sighed gently. She made him feel young; he could forget the terrible problems of the Principality with her. She sparkled with life and wit, wonderfully aware of how to behave and yet charmingly able to break customs in a way that would have even the most rigid traditionalist smiling indulgently.

'If we give him the title, it cannot be for nothing' one finally said.

The solitary voice after such a long silence broke into his reverie. Unwilling to join the useless discussions again he stayed at the window, gazing down at Laura's graceful figure as she strolled towards the fortified castle walls.

'Nobility is always inherited; a new position must be justified to the people' the minister continued.

'Perhaps for making this financial contribution to Dalnerechensk?' another suggested tentatively and was shouted down immediately.

Ridiculous suggestions were made one after the other and were laughed at by the Council, small petty arguments breaking out at the validity of each suggestion. The arguments behind him built in volume and savagery and as Laura disappeared round the corner of the castle Aleksei lost his temper, turning on the squabbles and tempers behind him.

'Enough!' he roared.

The Council fell silent, watching him guardedly. Aleksei wiped his mouth, composing himself. These constant squabbles were wearing his patience very thin, none more so than the lack of feasible answers to alleviate their problems. He collapsed into the chair at the head of the table.

'You made the suggestion Nicholas, tell us how to make it possible' he snapped, eyeing the old man.

Nicholas was sitting tipped back in his chair, his hands folded on his portly stomach, his eyes closed and breathing slow, looking like he had nodded off in the heated discussion.

'It would need to be arranged' he suddenly said although he hadn't moved, startling the men. 'Orchestrated. It must be public and the people will beg you to honour him' he opened his eyes and righted his seat, sternly eyeing the other ministers of the cabinet. 'But he must do something worthy. He suspects the marriage, and your intentions Aleksei, it is clear he thinks so. She is his only child and he will not sell her for any price. Perhaps, though, if there was some act of heroism, a rescue -'

'Who here would move him enough to risk that?' one broke in.

There was silence, and they heard Laura's laugh float up, echoing off the castle defensive walls from the winter garden below them. There was a brief moment of shock before the Council once again erupted in loud argument. Several leapt to their feet, shouting and gesticulating wildly.

'You cannot put her in danger!' one shouted.

'He would question why the *Tsarevich* did nothing to help!' another cried.

'It was not her I meant' Nicholas snapped. There was a confused silence around the table. Nicholas sighed and folded his hands on the polished table top. 'What say you Your Highness?'

This time the outcry was unanimous. All the ministers were on their feet, protesting loudly, rebuking the oldest minister for a senile suggestion. There was no heir, no close relative, no one else to take the throne of Dalnerechensk, and yet they were to gamble the life of their Prince?

'We are already gambling a principality, a heart and a whim of a pretty lass; why not a life too?' Nicholas laughed. 'Of course there will be no real harm, only appear that way.'

Aleksei sat back, deep in thought. These measures were getting too desperate, too risky. He was brave but cautious in the face of adversity, carefully analyzing the options available to him before making a decision and now he would have to plunge headlong into whatever orchestrated danger the Council would come up with.

But he knew they were right. He had insisted on an American bride with American money to float the Dalnerechensk economy, modern money and a modern wife to pull the Principality out of the dark ages. They resented that, these people in love with their history; proud of their ancient traditions. If he titled her, they would resent her even more. If he titled her father without their approval they would blame him for one more aristocrat in a principality where too many were just managing to scrape by. But there was no other way. It was a gamble he had to take.

16

Laura knocked quietly on the door that gave her private access from her parlour to her father's then pushed it open. Luke was seated in a large comfortable chair, a book from the Tsar's personal library open in his hands. He smiled up at his pretty daughter, putting aside his book. He was getting used to seeing her in three dresses a day, one at breakfast, one for activities or state visits during the day, and an elegant affair in expensive silks for the lavish dinners and dancing in the evenings.

She had spent the morning with Aleksei touring the military barracks and fortifications of the village of Tcherepnin. Luke had not heard them return, but guessed Aleksei was in Council Chambers again. Nikolai's words came back to him, tinged with a deep seated unease. *The Prince is a very busy man.* He wondered what Laura's married life would be like if even his obvious affection was not enough to conduct a proper courtship.

'Hello father, it's market day' Laura said excitedly. 'I can see the stalls in the streets from my window, and I saw it briefly from the carriage as we returned from Tcherepnin. Ekaterina said we must experience it and I would very much like to go.'

Luke's smile deepened at her youthful enthusiasm.

'I'm sure I could spare a few hours from Dickens to accompany you' he teased, tapping out his pipe in the small bronze tray beside him.

He stood and pulled his heavy coat from the mahogany stand, fastening it in place. He then donned his scarf and hat and offered Laura his elbow. She took it, letting him lead her out of his room, closing the door behind them.

Their footsteps were muffled in the deep, rich carpet that lined the corridors of the third floor, and as they descended the stone steps of the stairs Laura eyed the formal portraits of the men and women that gazed imperiously down from gilded frames on the wall. They all had Aleksei's wide shouldered physique and coal black hair, strong lines of character in their faces, all with that quiet air of confidence about them. Even the women had similar but softer features.

As they reached the first floor Laura glanced along the corridor to the double doors of the council room seeing they were closed again, as they had been all day yesterday as well. She wondered what they talked about for so long, what would hide Aleksei's handsome face in a room all day. She wondered if she would only see him at meals when they were married. She realised a lot of planning went into the running of a household, Lady Ramkinson had ensured the girls knew what was involved. Laura knew running a country was a lot more complex than a household, but could not help feeling resentful that Aleksei spent so much time away from her.

At the bottom of the stairs Fedor was waiting quietly for them. He was the youngest member of all Dalnerechensk's Council and the accompanying body of secretaries. When his father had suddenly died he had taken his place, performing the duties with the same efficient discretion that had won his father the trust and friendship of the old Tsar. As such he had been appointed by the Tsar himself to guide and help them while they were guests in the Principality. The old king was fond of the American, and Fedor could see her charm and appeal, and had gladly taken the duty. He greeted them with a polite good morning and fell into step respectfully behind them.

Laura returned his greeting, stopping to gaze up at the giant tapestries that hung in the entrance hall of Vsevolod's ancient home. She had seen the swirling stitched material before, but had not had the time to stand and carefully take in the scenes depicted on them. She knew enough of Dalnerechensk's history now to gather a sense of what was happening in the tapestries. She stepped close to the first, taking in the detailed stitching of the silk panel.

It was a city besieged, surrounded by a dark and foreboding army, and frightened women, children and men fled from it, beckoned on by a noble savior, pointing the way into mountains. The fleeing people were pursued by black guards mounted on huge horses that looked somehow twisted and demonic.

'Tsar's *Sobaki*?' Fedor said. 'The Tsar's Dogs.'

Laura looked carefully at the stitched faces that somehow looked more animalistic than human and shivered. The terrible black robed figures of the *Oprichniki* certainly struck fear into the hearts of all who gazed at this tapestry, she couldn't imagine how terrifying they would have been in the flesh. *Sobaki* was a fitting name for them.

She then moved onto the next tapestry, noting the strikingly different mood. While the first was full of terror and darkness this one was filled with fruitfulness and productivity. The same heroic figure of Vsevolod stood with a hammer and a rolled scroll in his hands, masonry and timber at his feet, directing the construction of the castle. Around him the community in Liberty valley thrived, crops grew abundantly, miners sung as they pushed carts to work, women smiled as they sewed and children played. Soldiers also were there, helping to plan and build, while one kept careful watch, reminding Laura of the precarious existence they had.

The last tapestry swarmed with the twisted agonies of war, the bodies of those fallen, the inhuman faces on the retreating Russian army, the panic-stricken looks on the horses in the terror and confusion of noise and death. Within the solid stitched line of the city walls Dalnerechenskers wept for the dead, stood grimly with weapons and cheered victorious after their retreating foe. The heroic figure of Vsevolod was harder to find in this work, but he was there, fist raised defiantly at the Russian army, his other hand clutching an unbloodied white cloth pressed to his heart.

In one stance they had managed to capture his daring brilliance against a strong foe and his agony and humanity at the losses of his citizens. The smaller size of Vsevolod in this last tapestry also served as testament to the terrible nature of the battle and the brotherhood and nationhood it had fostered in each Dalnerechensk breast. Laura shut her eyes tightly for a moment then opened them again. It was no wonder Vsevolod was so revered by every soul in the Principality. Aleksei had large shoes to fill.

Luke led her down the front steps of the castle and across the wide white gravel courtyard. The guards at the castle gate that opened onto Vsevolod's Way snapped to attention when they saw them approaching. Laura smiled sweetly and called good morning to them, stopping to closely examine the detail of the tin panels on the gate. Fedor explained they had been commissioned by the Tsar's grandfather to celebrate the four hundred years since Vsevolod had won the Battle of Dalnerechensk. They were panels depicting the great principality Dalnerechensk had become, prosperous and bountiful.

Laura spoke to the guards as best as she could, Fedor translated for her when she did not understand or did not have the words to express herself in Russian. She recognised the guards from the drill that had been performed the day she arrived and complimented them on their precision marching. Both of them beamed and stood a little straighter, saluted a little smarter as the small party left.

The wide street of Vsevolod's Way twisted into a bottleneck S-bend before the adorned gates of the castle grounds. It was one of the many details of Vsevolod's skill that had kept the town from falling to the bigger army, as it prevented any attacking army from using a battering ram to knock down the gates in the narrow confines, and from standing more than four abreast in the street below. As the gate was thick and the wall above and around it well defended, the smaller army of Dalnerechensk could easily repel an attacking force.

Fedor called out and beckoned to four soldiers who stood waiting in the street outside the gate. They quickly stood to attention, came over and bowed before the Asantons. Fedor explained that they were to help keep the crowds at bay as they walked through the market. Laura greeted them in Russian and they bowed again, taking up positions behind the royal guests. Laura tucked herself into her father's arm as they rounded the bend.

The street before them was thronged with stalls and people, a visual feast of colour and movement, narrowing the wide main road to the castle. Through the crowds and the stalls three musicians dressed in brown lederhosen wound their way along, playing a merry tune on the accordion, tuba and trumpet. The stalls were covered with bright table cloths and laden with all manner of wares. Laura smiled, feeling happy in the gay atmosphere. The people recognised her and called out welcome to her, some dipping curtseys, while others who knew she was not royalty yet watched as the Americans and five escorts passed.

Soon Laura found a crowd had gathered around her, mostly children and young men who swarmed up to see her and talk to her, and the four soldiers were kept busy ensuring a respectable distance around them. As they made their way along the crowd followed a step or two behind them. Some of the children stuck their noses in the air and mimicked her walk behind her, but most waved and babbled a hello; two even took her hands while others held the folds of her skirts. Laura spoke to everyone she could, asking after their health and paying a compliment when her sharp eyes noticed.

She found no shortage of willing translators, helpers and admirers as they made their way along the street. Eager youths offered to buy the pretty girl trinkets, wanting to win her favours. She had to use all of Lady Ramkinson's skills to refuse diplomatically, even resorting to some of Ekaterina's dismissive gestures. From the smiles on their faces she knew her youth and charm had helped soothe their feelings of rejection.

Through the throngs of people came a farmer, pulling a cart laden with milk cans. The distraction of the cart to the procession gave Laura a brief moment to take clearer stock of where they were. To her surprise they had nearly walked the full length of Vsevolod's Way, she could see the small squat building that served as Dalnerechensk's railway and the towering fortified town wall. Just beyond the station she could see the arched gate through which the single track railway left. She could even see the thick, iron portcullis that could be rolled down to seal the wall.

Her wandering eyes alighted on someone familiar, a basket of vegetables on her arm and a worried look on her face.

'Hello Olga' Laura smiled, surprising the girl.

She looked stunned and then a pleased flush stole into her cheeks, dipping a quick curtsey.

'Good morning my lady' she smiled.

'Are you sad Olga?' she managed in Russian.

'It's my mother my lady, she's ill' Olga said, looking miserable.

Laura sympathised and squeezed her arm to comfort her.

'I'm sorry to hear, I shall say a prayer for her tonight.'

Olga burst into happy tears, kissing her hand and swearing her thanks.

There was suddenly a shout of warning. As one they looked up the hill to a terrible sight. The farmer had slipped or tripped and had instinctively put out his hands to break his fall. He was sitting helplessly, nursing a sore arm and watching his cart barreling down the street, already at a frightening speed and getting faster as it rumbled towards the crowd. They scattered, falling against the walls and into doorways, toppling the tables of the street stalls, scattering wares everywhere.

Laura was pulled to safety by Fedor, but Luke, left in the path of the cart, glanced quickly down the hill, realising to his horror there was an old woman directly in its path. She was nearly infirm, and could only shuffle her feet forward, leaning heavily on a stick, her wide eyes fixed on the wagon, hampered by a heavy basket of vegetables. Luke bent down, angling his body forward and cupping his hands between his knees to catch the bottom of the cart.

'Daddy!' Laura screamed, horrified.

The cart hit him hard. He grunted, his hands cupping under the bottom, leaning his weight forward and planting his toes on the cobbled street. The cart pushed him backwards but slowed, and he hung on grimly, planting his feet harder, leaning further into it. The wagon hit the corner of a building and spun sideways, stopping suddenly. The milk cans rattled alarmingly, swaying drunkenly, but did not spill. The sudden stop knocked Luke onto his back, the momentum carrying him over, coming to his feet facing the old woman he'd saved. He had lost his hat in the tumble but he popped a jaunty bow with a grin, the same Asanton charm Emily had fallen for all those years ago.

The lady cried out, throwing her hands in the air, clasping Luke's cheeks and kissing them. The crowd came running at a rush to congratulate Luke, to shake his hand, to cheer. Laura threw herself into his arms, relieved. The farmer came, tears in his eyes, partly from the pain in his wrist, and partly that not a single drop of milk had been spilt to ruin his livelihood. He knelt in front of Luke and swore to serve him and his daughter faithfully, Fedor translating his words.

'We thank you for your love' Laura managed in Russian.

He kissed Luke's hand and then Laura's, his eyes straying to the still cart. Luke understood at once, his arm was possibly fractured and there was no way he could pull that cart to the castle. He smiled and took the handles of the cart, unmindful of his own pain. At once the crowd rushed forward to lend a hand, pushing and pulling the cart to the gate,

Laura and the farmer walking together as he thanked her over and over.

The guards at the castle gate looked surprised and a little apprehensive to find a mob rushing towards them with a milk cart. Fedor called out to them and they relaxed slightly, still eyeing the mob apprehensively. There was a little bit of jostling as the four soldiers took over the pushing and pulling of the cart to drag it inside, as citizens were not permitted into the castle grounds. The two soldiers on gate duty let the cart into the courtyard then closed the gap behind them. When the cart was on level ground the four guards returned to the gate to hold back the crowds.

The citizens called after Laura, calling blessings and she smiled at them, waving goodbye. Fedor and Luke pulled the milk cart round to the service door, leaving her momentarily alone. The farmer fell on his knees again, cradling his injured arm and lifting the hem of Laura's gown, kissing it gratefully.

She wasn't quite sure what to do now and looked around for someone to help her in this strange situation. She spied the stables that were close by, the corner and two metres of the building poking out from behind the side of the castle. A man was sweeping the courtyard between the stables and the castle wall clear of stray sticks of hay, his back to them, seemingly unaware of the ruckus.

Laura called out then beckoned him over. He looked round from his work then set aside the broom, leaning it against the stable wall, walking closer and nodding to her before stopping to watch her. She was surprised but the farmer holding her skirts over-rode the groom's strange demeanor.

'What is your name?' she asked, feeling a little desperate.

'Olaf' he answered, and didn't add a respectful title.

'Arm hurt' she said, feeling like a child and flushing at her poor Russian, feeling strangely flustered with the farmer begging at her hem and the startlingly grey eyes of the groom. 'Get doctor for arm, take cart to home' she said, hoping her Russian was correct.

'He can leave it here, and send his son for it in the morning' Olaf answered.

His manner perplexed Laura. He looked boldly at her, though there was no disrespect in his gaze, only an openness that was refreshing and reminded her of Bal. She wondered if he was simple, but then realised his suggestion of leaving the cart here was a more intelligent course of action. Olaf took pity on her embarrassment and reached down, pulling the farmer to his feet and back to a respectable distance. With this distance Laura was able to regain some of her composure.

'Yes' she smiled, 'But please, a doctor for his arm.'

There was a flicker in Olaf's eyes and a pause, and then he nodded once. Fedor and Luke returned, rescuing her from the situation and escorted her away, leaving Olaf and the farmer in the courtyard.

17

Laura and Aleksei sat bundled together under thick firs on a sleigh, laughing at the speed of the horses and the rocking and bumping as they skimmed along the ground. Her eyes streamed with tears in the cold wind, making it difficult to see the snow covered valley in which they were riding and her cheeks were flushed red with exhilaration. She stole another glance at Aleksei, noting how his dark hair was boyishly poking out from under his thick cap, heartbreakingly handsome with his dreamy eyes sparkling and a high colour on his cheeks.

She felt deliriously happy here; exhilarated by the sleigh ride, happy with the popularity she received as the courted Princess. Ekaterina had shown her several editions of Dalnerechensk's newspaper; usually only a weekly publication, which was being printed daily in the Principality's insatiable want for information. Laura and Luke were invariably front cover news, especially when Luke had saved Natasha Riminova, wife of Nicholas Riminov, from the runaway milk cart, and the Prince himself three days later when they were hunting together in the hills around the valley.

As the Council had predicted the people had cried out for an honour, and Luke had been made a baron in a ceremony atop the west wall of the castle in full view of the town commons. Laura had stood beside him on the walls, choked with pride for her father's bravery and the fear of how close Aleksei had come to death, holding on to a tree trunk that grew out from the side of the gorge he had fallen into, clinging grimly above the deep, rock strewn bottom.

She was falling in love with Aleksei. He was gentle and caring and genuinely wanted to do right by his people. He had not touched her save for the courtesan lips on the back of a lady's hand, but she sometimes saw in his eyes the desire to, the want to take her into his arms. A shiver of delight would pass through her at the thought of his body pressed against hers, and sometimes it was cold terror, frightened of a wife's duty in the marriage bed. She found it strange that this man could be so confident under the watchful eye of his court and his Principality, and yet nervous and flustered with a sixteen-year-old girl.

Since arriving in the Principality her days had been filled with functions and parties, with walks with the Tsar in the gardens of the castle, with continuing lessons in reading and writing Russian with Ekaterina. Each evening the court had eaten dinner in the great hall and danced until she could barely stand. Since the first night Aleksei had waited three more days before returning to her chamber, letting himself in and sitting with her on the rug before the fire, talking quietly, often awkwardly, with her. They had not spoken of their feelings on those evenings, Aleksei was too awkward to express himself to her and she had not pressed him, unsure of the depth of her own love.

The horses were beginning to tire so Aleksei slowed them to a walk. At a slower pace the ride was smoother and Laura relaxed her grip on the sides, turning to steal another look at the Prince. Aleksei seemed younger than his thirty-four years; looking as he had the first night he had come to her room, handsomely roguish. He was a man who was handsome in state regalia, in military dress, in peasant garb no doubt. He smiled at her adoring scrutiny and leaned over to talk to her.

Laura kissed him. Aleksei was so surprised he let go of the reins and had to scramble desperately to get them back. Laura laughed then, and a boyish blush came into the Prince's cheeks. He didn't hesitate again, his gloved hand cupping her rosy cheek, his cold lips pressed against hers again. She gasped at the cold feel of the glove and the strange feel of his cold lips and hot mouth. Quickly he removed his glove and she gasped again at the hot feel of his hand on her skin.

'God save the *Tsarevich*!' someone cried out.

Aleksei remembered himself and pulled away, his lips tingling from the feel of her. Laura dropped her eyes, embarrassed at her impetuousness, but aware of how he had responded to her kiss. A warm knot was twining tighter inside her at the thought of marrying him, a thought that had hardly ever been out of her head since arriving in Dalnerechensk.

Aleksei turned the horses back to the fortified city, pulling his glove back on. As Vsevolod's Gate was not suitable for the runners of the sleigh he guided the horses round the city walls to Castle Street, the utility route to the castle. They passed the second gate in the city wall as they did so, the Tin Gate, bumping over the salted road that lead up the hill past Ladozhskoye to the pretty mining village of Macherna. He turned the sleigh at King's Gate and the snorting horses led themselves up Castle Street.

Aleksei relaxed his grip on the reins, looking down at his pretty companion that was chewing her lip distractedly, an action that was raising his desire to kiss them again. When they stopped he jumped down and reached up to her, catching her around her waist and holding her close when she stepped down. Laura shivered again.

'Laura, I must know' he whispered urgently, stepping harder against her. 'Before I ask your father for your hand, would you marry me?'

Instead of answering she burst into tears, shocking him.

'Nothing would make me happier' she sobbed. 'And nothing would make me unhappier.'

'What's this riddle child?' he asked, not unkindly.

'The dowry will bankrupt my father' she sobbed. 'I cannot accept, to see my father turned out will break my heart, and to refuse you will break my heart too.'

She dropped her face and pushed past him, running inside, ignoring the startled staff and locked herself in her room, leaving Aleksei distressed and alone in the stables.

18

Aleksei was reserved and grey faced at dinner. Laura sat on his left, her eyes downcast, and nervous whisperings and looks fluttered up and down the table. The whole Principality knew they had shared their first kiss that afternoon, and that Laura had fled crying into her rooms and refused to see anyone.

'Perhaps she is not to his taste after all' Tatiana Yegorovna whispered meanly to Natasha Chekhovna.

She barked with laughter, covering it with a cough and the comment was whispered up and down the table, titters following it. Laura heard it, but kept her face neutral, ignoring the barb. Ekaterina had warned her that of all the slander that would be whispered about her, most of it would come from Tatiana, as she was once considered by the Council as a bride for Aleksei. Many even suggested Tatiana had remained unmarried still because she was waiting for Aleksei to come to his senses.

Laura raised her eyes and looked at the faces of those gathered round the table, taking careful note of them. She had realised on her first day in Dalnerechensk that there were more grey heads than youth in the court. Now she looked carefully to see how very few at the table were in favour of her marriage to Aleksei. Those women still unmarried and young enough to be considered as possible brides whispered maliciously, and smiled simperingly at Aleksei; who, Laura was glad to see, didn't acknowledge them. Those who were married and disapproved of a non-traditional untitled bride passed on those slanderous whispers with as much relish as Tatiana.

The men were no better Laura decided. Each member of the Council owned businesses and shares in all aspects of Dalnerechensk, and all had their own personal interests they wanted to see preserved and patronised by the monarchy. None were openly hostile towards her yet, but she had no doubt that should her relationship with Aleksei sour further the ministers would not be so careful as to mind their tongues. She suddenly felt sorry for Aleksei, his job was not an easy one.

She reached over and laid her hand on his. He looked surprised and smiled, though his eyes were sad.

'Forgive me for my childish outburst this afternoon' she said quietly, dropping her eyes again.

'Of course' he soothed, his eyes softening, and he squeezed her fingers gently.

'I wish to dance for you' she said, a large blush tinting her cheeks.

Aleksei's smile deepened, pleasure rising and he called for the musicians. Laura's blush deepened as she rose, and called for a Mazur, beginning to move in the energetic steps of the traditional Polish dance. She was aware as she moved of the eyes that looked from her to the Prince and back to her surreptitiously, but Aleksei's eyes didn't leave her. She smiled, feeling desired, and curtsied low at the end, aware the table could see the curve of her breasts.

Aleksei was suddenly beside her, calling for another tune, and took her in his arms, his face heated. She smiled and accepted, letting him whirl her energetically round the floor, ignoring the looks on Tatiana's and Natasha's faces. The music ended again but before

Aleksei could call for another Tsar Constantinovich announced that the next course had arrived and waited for the Prince to sample it.

He remembered himself, breathing hard, and Laura knew it was only partly to do with the dance. She curtsied to him, turning her head in a way she'd seen Ekaterina do that looked appealing and Aleksei took her arm, walking her back to the table, his eyes never leaving her. The Tsar leaned over to whisper something to him but it went unheard, and his eyes didn't leave her for the rest of the evening.

*

Laura had expected a tap on her door that evening, she was surprised it came so early, while Anna was still in her room and people still moving throughout the castle. Aleksei stepped in, dismissing Anna, who bobbed a curtsey and flashed her mistress a look, closing the door behind her. Laura eyed the Prince, aware of his stirred passions. He flustered for a moment, struggling with words, then crossed the distance between them, taking her in his arms.

She sighed quietly, resting her head against his chest, feeling it hitch with his breath. He tightened his grip, almost fiercely and she tipped her head up to him, questions in her eyes. Aleksei's deep flush of desire darkened, and his lips closed against hers. She gasped and felt her knees tremble, putting her hand on his chest to steady herself.

Aleksei quickly helped her to sit on her chaise lounge, stroking her hair as he fell to kissing her again. Her innocent responses stirred him, his hand falling first to her breast then her thigh, where each touch merited a gasp and trembling responses. They were shaking away his resolve, and he began pulling up her skirts, cupping her knee. She gasped louder, whispering his name. That combined with the warm touch of silk under his fingers destroyed his composure.

Laura shuddered at the hot feel of his hand on her leg, she could feel the heat of him even through her stockings, aware that hand was creeping slowly up her leg. She trembled, wanting to feel his strong fingers brush her skin, wondering what new sensations the touch would stir in her. *He's going to find the scars* a small part of her warned. Her hand shot down, stopping him. Aleksei drew back, breathing hard.
'Are you innocent?' he asked, breathing heavily, concerned at how much she trembled.

Her response shocked him. With a gasp she pushed him away, righting her clothing and standing up angrily.
'A man should not sneak into a woman's chamber putting her good reputation at risk and then have the audacity to ask if she is innocent!' she stormed.

Aleksei's mouth fell open. Laura pulled open her door, turning her face away from him.
'Good night Your Royal Highness' she said.

Embarrassed and horrified he'd insulted her Aleksei capitulated, too awkward to even apologise as he slipped past her, still breathing hard from his roused passion.

19

Ekaterina and Grigory woke to a pounding on their door. It was well past midnight and all the members of the castle were in bed. Grigory stood and slipped on some warm shoes and a dressing gown, stepping out of his bedroom into the parlour. As he headed to the sitting room to answer the door he saw his sleepy and frightened maid Anya rush across from the small bedroom attached to the sitting room to the door.

Behind him Ekaterina stepped out of his room, wrapped elegantly in a robe.

'Who is there?' Grigory called.

Aleksei stepped into the sitting room, agitated and strangely quiet. The Ivanovs bobbed surprised bows and Anya closed the door against the dark interior of the castle, aware that others would have heard the knock on the door. Grigory sent her to heat some coffee in the kitchens and told her to bring it to the parlour when it was done. Anya left, her apron pulled hastily over her nightdress, her sleep-rumpled hair poking out from under her bonnet. He stepped into the sitting room, worried about his friend and guided Aleksei gently into the warm parlour, pushing him into a seat before turning to stir the embers in the fireplace, adding another log.

Ekaterina brought in a blanket to wrap around Aleksei's shoulders, noticing the mood he was in and shot her husband a worried look. Grigory thanked her and dismissed her, knowing she would wait in their room, sleepless, until Grigory had explained to her why Aleksei had arrived so mysteriously in their rooms.

Grigory sat in the chair opposite Aleksei, waiting until Anya had served them coffee, placed the tray with the half-full pot on a small table between them and left, closing the door behind her as she went back to bed. Aleksei had sunk into the high-backed, padded chair, staring into the flames that were starting to lick around the log in the fireplace. Grigory sipped his coffee and patted his mouth with a napkin.

'What troubles you, Your Highness?' he asked finally.

Aleksei continued to stare blankly into the flickering flames, his cup held in his hands but was never raised to his lips, virtually ignoring the company he was with.

'Aleksei' Grigory tried. 'We have been friends for many years now, but I am keeping a beautiful woman waiting. If you don't want to talk to me, I am going to bed.' He stood, putting the cup back on the tray.

'She is beautiful isn't she' Aleksei said quietly.

'Somehow I don't think you are talking about my wife' Grigory said, sitting down again, a small smile on his face.

Aleksei sighed and put down his untouched cup, his hands clenching and unclenching unconsciously, fluttering into several positions before picking up the cup again to keep them busy. Grigory noticed the insecurity in his friend and smiled inwardly.

'So, you are in love with this American child then' he said. 'And she is by all accounts amorous with you. Why then, are you waking me at this ungodly hour?'

'She won't marry me if I demand her dowry.'

The smile faded from Grigory's face.

'I see' he said quietly.

He knew Aleksei was now in an impossible situation, and was facing the very real prospect of having titled her father for nothing. Their gamble was spinning out of control; Aleksei had to choose between his Principality and his wife, his duty and his heart. The tormented look in his eyes and the helpless slump of his shoulders told Grigory it was a decision he couldn't make.

He wondered if his friend was heading for a breakdown. Other men had failed under the pressure of lesser decisions, and for the first time Grigory really understood what true burdens were involved in the running of a country, even one as small and insignificant as Dalnerechensk. The Principality would be plunged into civil unrest if Laura refused to wed, and economic ruin if the Prince waived the dowry.

'Perhaps he could pay annually' Grigory suggested. 'Although there is no guarantee he could continue to pay at the same rate every year, and Dalnerechensk needs the money now.'

'It will have to be less' Aleksei sighed. 'God help us all.'

20

Two days later Dalnerechensk woke before dawn to the loud tolling of the church bells and immediately began to rejoice. People flooded onto the streets, singing and dancing, making their way to the castle to call out their blessings to the Prince and future Princess. Soon the commons below the castle walls were thronged with people, and still more were coming, bringing bouquets of snow bells they tossed onto the walls, some landing on the fresh snow in the gardens beyond them.

Laura turned from the French windows in her room. She could see part of the commons and was surprised at the singing, swaying mass that had gathered at the announcement of their engagement. Ekaterina lay elegantly draped over a chaise lounge in her parlour, watching her with her teasing, happy eyes.

'Are they really so happy?' she asked. 'I did not expect so much joy.'

'It is a grand occasion Laura; the last royal wedding was almost fifty years ago when Tsar Constantinovich married the Polish Countess. The last state occasion was when they buried her nearly ten years to the day. The Vakhtangovs have suffered great tragedies, and Dalnerechensk has spent a decade mourning with them. They want to see them happy at last.'

She swung her legs off the seat and stood, clasping Laura's hands.

'I knew Aleksei would ask you, he is smitten. -'

'Yet he spends so much time away in his Council Chambers!' Laura interrupted, frustrated. 'What could they be talking about for so long?'

'Your title' said Ekaterina, uncomfortably.

'I am marrying a prince; doesn't that make me a princess?' Laura said, eyeing her.

'Russian society is much more complicated than that' she said, sitting again and patting the settee beside her. Obediently Laura sat. 'Russia has no formal peerage to speak of, only a collection of merchants, industrialists, courtiers and so on, with titles granted to them at the Tsar's discretion. Their title, roughly translated into English, is Prince or Princess. I am, technically, Princess Ivanova of Dalnerechensk, but cannot be called Royal Highness - at least I would be if I could claim birth in Dalnerechensk -' she stopped, seeing Laura's confused face.

'Oh dear, let's start at the top' she smiled. 'Tsar and Tsaritsa - though the English call her a Tsarina. Tsar is equivalent to Emperor, though Nicholas the Second calls himself Tsar and Emperor of all the Russias. Children of the Tsar are called *Tsarevich* if they are male and *Tsarevna* if they are female. It basically translates into "son of the Tsar" and "daughter of the Tsar." The eldest son of the Tsar is called *Tsesarevich*, or *Naslednik Tsesarevich*, which is the full title. It means Heir Apparent. Other sons of the Tsar, who are not the heir, are titled *Velikij Knjaz*, other daughters are titled *Velikaja Knjazhna*; Grand Prince or Duke, and Grand Princess or Duchess. They were styled as Grand Dukes because a Duke can beat a Royal Prince, and the Tsars wanted their children to have a higher station than the Dukes, understand?'

Laura nodded dumbly, trying to keep up with the titles and names.

'Alright. Dalnerechensk styles are slightly diferent from Russian styles. The Tsar is styled "Majesty" and his immediate family are styled "Royal Highness", his grandsons are *Knjaz* of Dalnerechensk and styled "Highness" - except for the eldest male grandchild, who is also a Grand Duke and styled "Royal Highness" as well. Great grandsons are also *Knjaz* of Dalnerechensk and styled "Highness." -'

'Would I not be simply called the wife of the *Tsesarevich*?' Laura interrupted. '*Tsesarevna*?'

'Possibly' Ekaterina said uneasily. 'You see, that is also the title for the female Heir Apparent, I'm not sure if they would title you that, you are not -' she stopped. 'You see, your marriage is morganatic, you do not hold an equal rank with Aleksei -'

'Well, what do they call foreign princesses?' Laura interrupted again, somewhat sniffily.

'*Princhessa*, but that would not work, you are not a princess in your own right' Ekaterina explained gently.

'The unequal marriage is what is causing the contention. Your father has been appointed a baron, yes, but it is the lowest rank of nobility, and usually they are German financiers. They could title you Countess with a surname associated with a place, perhaps Countess Dalnerechensk; or with a family: Countess Vakhtangova. But that ranks you lower than the entire court and it is the same title that can be given to any mistress of the Tsar.

'They could title you Princess Vakhtangovsky-Asanton, styled Serene Highness, as you are not royal, but from a respectable family - though some will argue against that -'

'My family is respectable!' Laura said hotly.

'Of course my dear' she smiled. 'It is not your honour that is in question, but your money. It is somewhat baffling to these old traditionalists who don't understand the concept of *nouveau riche*.' She took her hands, smiling. 'Whatever they call you, I shall still call you Laura' she laughed. 'I am glad we will not be parted. We will be the best of friends.'

Laura suddenly hugged her friend fiercely and Ekaterina laughed, returning the embrace. A tap on the door interrupted them. Anna opened the door and dropped a curtsey to Tsar Constantinovich. He beamed, seeing the young ladies happy together and stepped in, followed by two porters carrying a huge chest between them. They all bobbed curtseys then Laura offered the Tsar a seat and some tea.

He accepted and Laura sent Anna for a brewed pot. Both Ekaterina and Laura sat on the lounge opposite the Tsar and he smiled to see the two dark beauties together, Ekaterina regal in a plum dress and Laura positively angelic in a silver and cream. Anna returned with a tray she sat down on a small server near Laura. The royal-to-be served both her guests and poured one for herself, politely making conversation and trying not to eye the chest sitting on the floor between the two porters who stood to attention, trying to keep their eyes off the pretty Princess.

'I have come to ask you if you would honour me once more' Tsar Constantinovich said when he had taken a sip of the hot sweet liquid and wiped his whiskers.

With a nod from the Tsar the two porters bent down to unlock the chest then threw back the curved lid, taking hold of the garment and lifting it out of the box. Laura and Ekaterina gasped, getting to their feet, forgetting that the Tsar was still seated. It was a wedding dress, moon-white and almost glowing, embroidered with seed pearls and lace accents. The train was long and the veil made of the softest gossamer lace.

'It was my mother's wedding dress, and my wife wore it. I would be honoured if you would wear it too.'

Tears came into Laura's eyes and she dropped to her knees, taking the Tsar's old hand and kissing it.

'It's beautiful' she managed. 'Of course I will wear it.'

Tears came to the old man's eyes then too, and he placed his gnarled old hand on her head.

'God bless you *Tsarevna*' he said quietly.

A knock on the parlour door announced Luke's arrival and Anna hurried to open the door for him, bobbing a quick curtsey. The porters bobbed bows too, trying to be respectful and hold up the dress at the same time.

'Baron Asanton, excuse an old man his luxuries' Tsar Constantinovich said, remaining in his seat. Luke bowed and the Tsar nodded to him, one respectful man to another.

Anna brought over another chair for him to sit on and Laura poured him a cup of tea. Tsar Constantinovich finished his tea and set it aside, bracing his feet on her floor before maneuvering grimly onto them, the others getting to their feet too.

'The seamstress can make any repairs needed and ensure it fits you' the Tsar said and nodded to the porters to put the dress back in the box. 'Perhaps you can meet with her tomorrow.'

Laura curtseyed and the Tsar left, thanking her for the tea and the porters carried their heavy chest out after him. Anna closed the door behind them then wiped her eyes.

'Forgive me for speaking out of turn,' she said, turning to her mistress and clasping her hands together. 'The dress was beautiful; you will be a beautiful bride.'

'Thank you Anna' Laura smiled.

'I hear you have been given a beautiful stallion' Luke said, smiling at his daughter.

Laura smiled, a little embarrassed. Aleksei had come to her rooms the morning after she had thrown him out. Part of her had been frightened he would call the courtship off. Instead he had apologised somewhat stiffly, and presented her with a stunning necklace of sapphires and diamonds before taking her down to the stables, presenting her with the best stallion in his stud. Laura had forgiven him, apologising too that perhaps she had misunderstood his intentions.

'Perhaps you would like to come riding with me then' Luke continued.

Ekaterina smiled at Laura's delighted acceptance and excused herself from the parlour. Laura excused herself to change into her riding habit, a beautiful blue jacket she wore with a green dress, always mindful of her public appearance. Luke waited, sipping tea while she changed, standing when she stepped out of the dressing room, pulling on a pair of gloves. He offered her his elbow and hummed as he escorted her down the stairs.

Laura eyed him, noticing the good mood he was in and smiled. Luke had been strained and reserved ever since they had arrived in Constantinople, and she was relieved to see his familiar, easy charm had returned, and wondered what had brought the change on. It was not that Aleksei had gone down on bended knee yesterday and asked her for her hand in marriage, nor that Luke had been asked and given his blessing for the marriage. She wondered if her small display of tears in the stables two days ago had sent Aleksei running to her father to cancel the dowry.

As they crossed the entrance hall of the castle servants, Councilors and soldiers alike all called words of welcome to the Asantons. Laura had learnt enough to cope with every day pleasantries, and her quick mastery of the language had endeared her towards the citizens of Dalnerechensk. Even her mistakes endeared her as they were willing to help out, supplying her with words to plug her vocabulary which she would always repeat carefully and thank them for it.

Luke smiled as they stepped out onto the porch of the castle, quickly slipping down the steps and turning to walk the length of the castle, heading for the stables.

'Good morning Olaf' Laura called as they arrived.

The stable hand righted himself, leaning on the rake where he had been mucking out a stall. He didn't answer but nodded at them. By now Laura was used to his mannerisms. Anna had told her Olaf was a man of few words but meant everything he said. He was gruff and blunt but had a certain charm about him that made the court wink at his manner. Tsar Constantinovich especially had a fondness for his honest ways and the Councilors' fondness for the Tsar indulged Olaf's gruffness.

Laura disengaged herself from her father and went to the stall where the huge grey stood, letting him nuzzle her hand. He snorted then snickered softly as she stroked his nose, watching her with intelligent eyes. Luke quickly explained to Olaf that they wanted to go out riding, pointing at the bridles and saddles that gleamed along the rear wall near the stair case to the loft. Olaf set aside the rake and dusted his hands, retrieving the bridles for two horses.

He let himself into the stall, talking softly to the horse as he fitted the bridle over his head.

'He's beautiful' Laura said watching Olaf work. 'Will you come with us?' she suddenly asked him.

He looked surprised and turned to eye her frankly. Laura didn't flinch under his look, watching him back just as boldly.

'I do not ride with the court' he said quietly.

'We are not the court' she smiled. 'We don't know where to go. Come with us.'

He paused then nodded once. She smiled then, stroking the nose of the stallion and he turned gruffly away, saddling the horses then leading them out into the courtyard. Laura, well versed in how to behave with horses as equine training had been part of her education, walked the stallion in large circles, checking the way he moved. Olaf boosted her onto the horse and she arranged her skirts carefully over the side saddle, letting the horse prance in a circle.

Olaf watched her out of the corner of his eye as he boosted her father onto a brown mare. The stallion was huge and powerful, but wouldn't hurt a fly if she could control it. He knew of accidents in which strutting nobles had swaggered and tried to ride horses that had seen through the bravado with disastrous consequences. He could see however the royal-to-be could handle the horse and he mounted a smaller mare before nodding curtly to her.

She led the small procession down Castle Street to the main city entrance, the King's Gate. It faced north, up Liberty Valley into the recesses of the Ural Mountains and beyond, as the crow flies, to Moscow. Of the three gates that split the massive fortification walls of Dalnerechensk, King's Gate was the largest and closest to the narrow, winding path leading over the hills into Eastern Valley to the hamlet of Kalach, the most outlying settlement of the Principality. Between the two valleys rose a hunter's paradise of forested hills and it was into this frosted wonderland Laura led them.

The trees looked like ebony statues, coated in white mantles and dappled in the early sunlight. The wide path they rode in the valley basin was a pure carpet of crystal white, undisturbed except for the strange indented tracks here and there of an animal that had scurried across it. The footfalls of the horses' hooves were muffled by the thick fluffy blanket of snow and twice they startled a foraging animal as they headed into the forests, sending them scurrying, bleating in fear. Laura smiled and closed her eyes, turning her face up towards the weak sun.

The air smelt clean and fresh and her heart lifted so much she thought it might burst out the top of her head. Aleksei had proposed yesterday with a few flowery words, and despite how uncomfortable he had looked, it had still managed to be romantic. As Dalnerechensk custom dictated he had asked her father on his knees in the presence of his daughter, promising to love and support her till his last breath. Her father had blessed the union and Aleksei had then turned to her, asking for her hand. Laura agreed, and Ekaterina had explained the wedding would be very traditional; the ceremony would be planned by Fedor and ensured that her day met royal expectations. The only decisions she made were the style to wear her hair in and the dishes she preferred to be served at the banquet.

Fedor had met with her that afternoon and explained what would happen during her day, the ceremonies expected, the presentation on the castle walls above the commons, and the celebrations to follow during the day. He had told her the things that were non-negotiable, but had been flexible over the choice of dishes and decorations in the great hall.

She sighed happily and opened her eyes, dazzled briefly by the brilliant snow crystals decorating the tree branches. She blinked hard, looking at the tall and silent ghosts around her. Her wandering eyes drifted over Olaf who, unaware, had ridden up abreast of them in the forest instead of hanging back like he had in the valley. His hands were loose on the reins, his eyes closed, a gentle, sublime look on his face. So, she was not the only one enjoying this moment she smiled and she glanced at her father.

'You smile now' she said, maneuvering her horse to walk beside him. 'What burden has lifted off your shoulders?'

'Ah Laura' he sighed, smiling. 'You are in love, and engaged, and I am a baron. That was more than your mother ever hoped for.' He looked away. 'Through all she suffered Laura, I'm sure she would have liked to have been here.'

Laura shut her eyes. She barely remembered her mother now; she could not even recall the features of her face with precise detail. She only remembered the madness, and the look on her father's face when he came to tell her Emily had passed away. He had looked stunned and strained with the news. Laura remembered she had felt no emotion at all, just numb. She had cried because it was expected of her, but the woman they had buried was a stranger to Laura.

'I hardly knew her, at the end' Laura said sadly. 'She was not my mother, at the end.'

Luke reached over and took her hand, squeezing it gently.

'She still loved you, still wanted the best for you' he shut his eyes, fighting the lump in his throat. 'She would be so proud of the woman you've become. As am I.' he managed.

There was a moment of awkward affection, reminiscent of Aleksei's awkward fumblings with her. No matter how they had grown close since her expulsion from Lady Ramkinson's school there were still the lost years and Laura's rigorous training in social decorum. Even now she feared the crop, even now she schooled herself carefully in case someone saw moments of weakness and misconduct.

'Tell me Laura,' Luke said, clearing his throat of this awkward moment and changing the subject. 'How much did you have to do with a distraught Prince in my chambers renegotiating your dowry?'

She looked surprised, then her cheeks flushed a pleased pink. 'He does love me then.'

'And you him' Luke said quietly. 'I had hoped – selfishly – it would be a schoolgirl crush, but you have always known your own mind. I will only be sorry that we will be parted so far.'

Laura ducked under a snow-laden branch and felt it brush her back, sending a shiver of cold snow onto the backside of her stallion. It snorted and kicked a little jump. Laura reined him in tightly, aware Olaf had reached over to take control of her mount but stopped when he realised he didn't need to. She turned to face her father, brushing the snow off its back.

'Will you be alright father?' she asked quietly, looking for some sign he would not be in his eyes.

'I'll manage child; I won't be thrown onto the street at least. I would feel the distance between us even more acutely than before.'

'I will write every day to you' she promised, and knew she would faithfully, as she had composed a letter every week while at Lady Ramkinson's school for him.

At first they had been the tear-filled beggings of a frightened and angry little girl, and as the years went by they gradually cooled in their tone, informing her father of inane social gossip and respectable topics of conversation until they were flat, emotionless accounts of the routines of her life. She had hated the letters, there were so many things she had wanted to pour out in them, but she knew Lady Ramkinson read the letters and reprimanded them severely for every lack of judgment, indiscretion and unsuitable topic mentioned on the thin, delicate leaves of paper.

She dropped her eyes then, clicking her tongue for her horse to press on.

21

Laura hummed happily as she worked, her needle winking as it darted in and out of a length of silk. She was stitching the Dalnerechensk royal coat of arms onto a sash to replace Aleksei's fraying and faded one. She would present it to him the night before their wedding, and she hoped he would wear it during the ceremony. Anna was also sitting with Laura, winding silk thread for her and handing her the colours and needles she asked for.

She had met with the seamstress that afternoon and pulled on the yards of wedding dress, surprised at how heavy it was, despite how delicate it looked. It had been stored in excellent condition; there were almost no repairs to make, and barely any need for alteration. She had been shown her reflection in a full length mirror and marveled at how similar her stature was to the beautiful Polish Countess, whose portrait hung in the library, wearing the very same wedding dress. Laura wondered if she would have liked her, her face looked regal, but was softened with a gentle mouth and the dreamy eyes that were so romantic in Aleksei.

There was a heavy knock on the door, interrupting her reverie and Anna stood to open it, dropping a quick curtsey to Aleksei and the three members of the Advisory Council with him. Without waiting for Laura to welcome them in Aleksei dismissed Anna and closed the door behind her. The ministers looked grave and Aleksei looked strangely nervous. Laura carefully schooled her face, watching the Prince's agitated movements.

With him was Lev Dostoevski, a man she knew opposed the marriage as her commonness was not worthy of the great blood of Vsevolod in Aleksei's veins; Valatin Gogol and Maksim Yegorov, Tatiana's father. She suddenly felt very apprehensive at the outcome of this meeting. Before she could offer her visitors something to drink as Dalnerechensk customs dictated Aleksei spoke.

'Miss Asanton' he began, then stopped.

Laura and his ministers waited. Her heart was sinking, surely this could not be good. Aleksei clasped then unclasped his hands and started again, flustered and stuttering. Behind him the ministers looked grave, shooting each other looks they were trying to avoid giving.

'It has been rumoured – that is, said, - whether true or not -' he stopped again, embarrassed.
'It has come to our attention -' he faltered, desperately wishing he was elsewhere.
'Was your mother mad?' Maksim blurted out.

The silence crystallised around them. Laura turned her face away as if he'd slapped her. Indeed, she felt as if she had been slapped. She folded her hands in her lap, clutching them tightly to stop them shaking. She shut her eyes then spoke in English, knowing that only Aleksei had a good command of the language.

'My mother was ill' she said, swallowing against the lump in her throat. 'Ill for a long time, it ate away at her and she suffered greatly. It ended when she died, she fell from the balcony of our home.' She stopped talking, squeezing her eyes tighter. Her hands shook harder and she balled up some material of her dress.

'Leave' Aleksei told the ministers quietly, embarrassed and pained.

The ministers only half understood what Laura had said, but there was no mistake in their Prince's demeanor. He was seething with anger. Lev and Maksim shot each other a quiet look then bowed slightly, stiffly to Laura and made their way out of the room. Aleksei paused at the door, turning back to look at her, knowing he had insulted her again, and his awkwardness was hindering the deep regret he needed to express. She was still sitting, her face turned away, her neck elegantly displayed and he felt strongly stirred, despite the misery his fear and suspicion had caused.

Just as he turned to go she spoke again, just the whisper of his name, surprising him. He stopped, then carefully closed her door against the ears in the corridor.

'There is something you should know' she said quietly. 'Before our wedding. L-Lady Ramkinson would carry a riding crop...'

'Crop...?' he asked, confused.

She looked at him, tears falling down her cheeks. 'Um, stick. Whip.' she whispered.

Aleksei's eyes widened in horror when he realised what she was saying to him.

'*Moy Bog*' he said softly, wiping his mouth, tears welling up in his eyes. 'She *whip* you?!'

His distress was obvious in the loss of control of the English language. Laura nodded, more tears spilling down her cheeks. Aleksei suddenly crossed the distance between them and folded her into his arms. She sobbed, wiping her eyes on the balls of her fists, sniffing loudly. Aleksei stroked her hair and cheeks, whispering how sorry he was in Russian.

'Are you trying to find reasons not to marry me?' she asked, sitting back to look at him.

'*Nyet!*' he swore vehemently, wiping her tears. '*Nyet! Ya lyublyu tebya!*'

He stopped, surprising himself. Laura shut her eyes against the new wave of tears.

'You love me?' she whispered.

'*Da*' he said quietly, folding his arms round her and sighing gently.

They sat quietly for a few minutes, comforted by each other, wiping away their tears.

'Don't bring your ministers to me again Aleksei' she said softly.

'Never' he promised.

22

Laura rolled onto her stomach, resting her chin in her hands. She and Ekaterina were lying on the thick rug before the fire, blueprints of Dalnerechensk's only church before them, along with several accounts of Tsar Constantinovich's wedding to the late Tsaritsa. Fedor had left an hour ago with final details and preparations and Ekaterina had spent since then informing Laura of the rigorous ceremonies and celebrations to be held on her wedding day.

Each minute detail had been planned, how she was to walk, where she was to stand, where her family was to kneel in devotion to the Prince and the Principality. Laura felt like a spectator at her own wedding, and her heart sank to know it was only Luke who would kneel in devotion. Ekaterina had gladly accepted the role as Maid of Honour, but instead of unmarried sisters or close friends holding the train of her gown as symbols of chastity and fruitfulness it was to be servants as she swept down the long aisle of the church.

Invitations had already been sent to Aleksei's numerous relatives in Poland, Hungary and Russia. Ambassadors in foreign countries had been recalled for the wedding, as had relatives of court dignitaries and the Advisory Council. Laura had done her best to learn the complex family tree of connections and alliances, feeling terribly alone. She wondered if she would be more accepted by the court if she had been one of seven children, and had countless cousins and in-laws.

'Don't you ever feel lonely?' she suddenly blurted out.

Ekaterina stopped in her rhetoric of the wedding speech. She eyed her pretty friend, setting aside the account of the Tsaritsa's wedding speech she had been holding.

'Yes' she answered simply, but Laura heard no emotion behind the words, no timbre of longing or misery that meant they were sisters of suffering.

'How do you cope?' Laura demanded, sitting upright, despairing.

'We cope because we must' Ekaterina said, sitting up too. 'It is what is expected of us.'

She reached over and squeezed Laura's hand affectionately.

'My dear, you will come for tea in the village of Ladozhskoye. In all this time I don't believe I have shown you my home.'

Laura was surprised. Since arriving in Dalnerechensk Ekaterina and Grigory as well as several ministers of the court had lived in rooms on the second floor. It had not occurred to Laura that the castle was the sole residence of the Royal Family and ministers had stayed to support their patron while the marriage contract was negotiated.

She smiled and gladly accepted the invitation. Ekaterina got to her feet, pulling her friend up by her hands.

'Come then, we have studied these speeches long enough, dress and I shall meet you in the stables shortly.'

Laura rushed off to do as she was told, excited at the prospect of an outing. She quickly dressed warmly to ward off the cold of a Russian Winter and skipped down the stairs to the great entrance hall. Ekaterina was waiting in the warm stables, standing under the eaves already thick with snow. Olaf was stroking the noses of two roans as he hitched them to a small, handsome carriage. He then opened the door and helped the two inside.

Ekaterina thanked him with a girlish flirt and laughed, waving goodbye as a small boy scampered up to take the reins. The carriage left the snow dusted courtyard, heading down Castle Street before turning down Tin Way, trotting under the iron portcullis of Tin Gate. Ekaterina pointed to the clutch of buildings that clung to the side of Liberty Valley.

'First there was only one house here, the Ivanov home' she said, singling out the impressive stone walls. 'There were a group of buildings belonging to the estate, a game keeper's house, a servants' house, a separate kitchen and wash house, the stables and so on' she fluttered her hand expressively. 'The miners would come down past Ladozhskoye for the blacksmiths and the armory in Tcherepnin and Dalnerechensk, but they would stop and call in sometimes for produce and things from the servant quarters at the house.

'Eventually they built another armory and bakery on the slope of Liberty Valley, and some of the miners decided to build close to the mines so they could have a family, rather than living as they did in the shanty tents of Macherna. Of course, Macherna is now a self-contained village and Ladozhskoye has grown with families and farms to its current size.'

As they had talked they had driven up the slope of Liberty Valley and made their way to the stables of the Ivanov house. Ekaterina opened the door and slipped out of the carriage, turning to help down her friend. Laura thanked her and followed her to the warmth of the kitchen. Ekaterina called hello to her servants as they passed through, and they called a hearty welcome back to their mistress, bobbing curtsies when they saw the Princess-to-be with her, calling friendly greetings to her too.

The affection for the servants and their mistress was obvious and reminded Laura of Clara, the plucky maid left behind in Lady Ramkinson's house. She closed her eyes against the feeling of homesickness and fervently hoped she had not suffered severely for her forbidden friendship. But the moment passed when Ekaterina led her into the beautiful home.

As she led her room to room, pointing out features of the chattels and portraits on the walls Laura couldn't help but think the Ivanovs' wealth rivaled that of the Vakhtangovs. She wondered if all the ministers were as wealthy as the royal family, as till now she had always assumed they were not. Vanity burned her tongue to ask Ekaterina, but she resisted, not wanting to appear rude.

The Countess led her across the expansive ball room and opened one of the French doors, pulling Laura through onto the balcony beyond.

'This is my most favourite part of the house' she said dreamily.

Laura sighed. The Ivanov home sat high enough on the slopes of Liberty Valley to be almost level with the castle of Dalnerechensk. From this height the castle lost most of its foreboding dominance and became pretty, almost quaint. It sat like a sugar-dusted cake above the mound of brightly coloured confectionery houses of Dalnerechensk. The valley spread out below them, each detail picked out by the crystal white of the snow and sunlight, remote and somehow surreal.

'Oh Ekaterina, it's beautiful' she breathed softly.

'Had I not fallen in love with Grigory I would have married him for this view' she grinned.

'How wicked!' Laura laughed, and her breath puffed round her.

'Come inside for some warm wine my dear' Ekaterina said, reaching out to her. 'I can hardly see how Aleksei would ever forgive me if his bride caught her death standing outside on my balcony.'

Laura smiled and allowed herself to be led inside, glancing over her shoulder for one last look at Dalnerechensk Castle. Ekaterina led her to a cosy parlour where a fire was burning merrily. Anya, who had gone with the Ivanovs to Dalnerechensk Castle, made frequent trips back to the Ladozhskoye home to ensure it ran well and now served them wine heated with a poker before left them, curtsying to the Princess as she closed the door behind her. Ekaterina sipped her wine and stretched out her toes to the warm fire.

'You must join me here again on Tuesday Laura' she suddenly said, bringing the girl's attention back from the crackling flames. 'I will invite a few ladies who are not concerned with the idle maliciousness of court, or at least have decorous tongues.'

Laura smiled, grateful. She was acutely aware of how few friends she really had, and how heavily she relied on Ekaterina. A chance to make friends didn't come along so easily in a place where traditions were jealously guarded against foreigners. And even if they didn't welcome her it was still a chance to talk with others. Ekaterina smiled and sipped again, stretching her toes closer to the fire.

23

Dalnerechensk buzzed with excited preparations. The wedding date was set and the Principality was scrubbing and scouring in feverish anticipation. The houses had been washed and now glowed when the sun hit them, like glazed sweet buns. Street sweepers had scoured every cobble stone in Dalnerechensk and no speck of dirt drifted in any street, commons or garden. Festive blue and green ribbons had been strung across the streets from the eaves of houses and the lamps were decorated with posies of snowbells and alpine flowers.

Inside the houses they were spring cleaning rooms, dusting hearths and polishing silverware. The Principality sparkled with newness and cleanliness the length and breadth of the three valleys. The children made giant prince and princess snowmen in their yards, skipping higher, laughing louder, caught up in the infectious enthusiasm. The old sat by the fires at the home hearth or in the taverns and talked about the wedding nearly a half century ago, arguing about how handsome the Tsar had looked, how beautiful the Countess had been, how much like his father Aleksei was.

In the castle the preparations had reached fever pitch in anticipation of the arriving dignitaries. Doors to rooms Laura didn't even know existed were flung open and aired, the livery staff and servants were frantically scrubbing, polishing, dusting and washing every fixture in every room. Grigory, Ekaterina and the other ministers who had taken up temporary residence on the second floor of the castle moved back to their stately homes dotted in Dalnerechensk, Tcherepnin, Ladozhskoye and Macherna in order to offer rooms to the families who could not be housed in the overflowing castle.

The larder was full with game and vegetables brought from the hamlets and villages and the fires of the kitchen burned long into the night. Wineries unearthed their vintage stock and sent them in cartloads of barrels to the castle. A confectioner had been hired from France to make the desserts and sweetmeats for the feasts and Laura and Ekaterina had taken delight in sampling the wares to be served at the receptions.

Most affected was Laura, who could barely sleep with the manic fervor in her. She busied herself with directing servants, by inspecting rooms, by learning hundreds of steps for new dances, by pacing back and forward with nervous energy as she carefully enunciated her words for the wedding speech. Luke would take her walking in the castle grounds in an effort to keep her occupied but even he could not curtail the excitement in her.

She looked up from the Cyrillic script in her hand at the blast of a trumpet and rushed to the window, peering down into the streets of Dalnerechensk. A procession of six immaculate carriages, each pulled by a team of six magnificent black horses was making its way up Vsevolod's Way towards the castle. Anna burst into her room, crying that she must hurry as Aleksei's cousins were nearly here. Laura tore her eyes away from the procession and quickly donned a coat, slipping quickly down the stairs.

The Vakhtangov household turned when she pushed open the door, eyeing her with disapproval. Laura ignored them, slipping down to Aleksei, standing on tip-toe to kiss him girlishly on the cheek. He smiled indulgently at her, liking the sparkle in her eyes and the flush on her cheeks. She lowered her eyes and composed herself on the step beside him, watching the procession pour through the gates like a black tide and pull to a stop, lining the snow dusted driveway.

Olaf jumped down from the leading carriage, uncomfortable in livery uniform and opened the door, placing a step before the door and stepping back to help down those inside. A tall and unforgiving man stepped out, ignoring Olaf. He had iron grey hair and a face carved in granite. Laura almost shivered. He was a cold, steelish man, she imagined his slow purposeful movements was like watching a fast moving glacier, and fancied she could hear him crackle as he moved.

Aleksei welcomed Count Norwid, who bowed stiffly then turned to help down the slender woman within. Laura smiled at her, noting the way the aging, frosty beauty carried herself. Count and Countess Norwid were the late Tsaritsa's family, a wealthy and pedigree nobility from Poland, related by blood or marriage to almost every royal family in Europe. The Countess did not return Laura's smile and ignored her, directing all her conversation towards Aleksei, and all in Polish.

Laura's smile didn't falter at the slander and she felt the chill of hundreds of years of diplomacy and breeding pass by her as Fedor guided them into the castle, leading them to their rooms on the second floor. The doors to the other carriages were opened and Olaf raised his hand to help out a dashing beauty, every bit as frosty as her mother. Ekaterina leaned forward and murmured softly in Laura's ear.

'Her name is Linka, she was also one Aleksei once considered marrying. Be wary of her and her sister Róza, they will not be pleasant.'

Aleksei smiled and welcomed his pretty cousins as Róza stepped out of the carriage, steadying herself on Olaf's strong arm. Both sisters were beautiful, but Laura could not see any resemblance to the soft, passionate features of Tsar Constantinovich's wife in her sister's children. Both were as cold as arctic wind and Laura could feel the sneer radiating out of them. She felt her heart sinking. She kept the smile on her face, but knew she would stand on this step many more times in the week to come, greeting her wedding guests from Poland, Russia, Prussia and the Austro-Hungarian Empire, all of whom she didn't know, and all of whom would sneer behind their fans over Aleksei's choice of bride.

From the other coaches tumbled an assortment of officials and advisors to the Norwid family who all bowed to the royal couple in respect, their faces blank of opinion. Livery boys and servants scrambled over the now empty carriages, unloading the baggage and stacking it neatly to be carried into the castle. Aleksei himself escorted his pretty cousins to their rooms and laughed and joked with them in Polish while Laura was left to trail in their wake with the rest of the court, feeling like an unwanted handmaiden.

Part of her wanted to scold Aleksei for forgetting her like this, after all, she was to be titled *Velikaja Knjaginja*, the title for the wife of a *Velikij Knjaz*, she was above the ranks of Linka and her sister, but knew an outburst would be childish and embarrassing. Part of her wanted to slap those smug smiles from their faces, but she kept her features soft and her hands gentle as she slipped herself into Aleksei's arm. He smiled down at her, his eyes warming in pleasure.

'Come, we will go to the garden' he said, folding his hand over hers. 'I should like to walk before dinner.'

'Of course My Lord' Laura replied, turning her back on his cousins to snub them.

24

Castle Dalnerechensk's dining room was stuffy with the press of bodies. A second consignment of the Vakhtangov family had arrived that afternoon, cousins Aleksei had not seen since his teens. Laura had marveled at the change that came over Aleksei as they sat recounting their carefree days, laughing and joking in Aleksei's sitting room. Laura had sat with them too, smiling at the jokes, answering questions put to her, graciously filling wine goblets as they were emptied.

The ruckus and laughter had not stopped all afternoon and now swirled around the dining hall. Russian and Polish and Hungarian tongues called to each other and shouted each other down in a cacophony of noise. Fans fluttered incessantly to cool the lavishly dressed beauties and wine served poured over goblets of snow did nothing to stop the flushes appearing in the cheeks of all there.

Aleksei sat under the canopy on Vsevolod's throne, Laura in a place of honour on his left, Tsar Constantinovich on his right. Linka and Róza sat beside their uncle, and leaned around him to talk to Aleksei, flashing looks at Laura.

'How terribly sudden' Linka exclaimed in Russian while Aleksei had been recounting their brief courtship. 'Of course these matters are always delicate, but one must always insist they simply do not – settle.'

Aleksei's flush darkened a little and his awkwardness in expressing his feelings for Laura made him falter in his reply.

'Of course' Laura smiled. 'Though one must have many offers before one could say settled.'

The teeth in Linka's smile could have cut diamonds. Laura stared down her bold slight, Linka was beautiful, but aging, and as attractive as her families' wealth was there was no offer of marriage for her. Not even Aleksei's interest had blossomed into a proposal. Róza nudged Linka, who picked up her melting snow goblet to hide her smirk. Laura waited, knowing her offence would not go unanswered. The sisters had been whispering together, sending each other secret and knowing looks all evening.

'Tell me Laura,' Linka started. 'Have you no brothers and sisters?'

The cacophony at the table dropped a decibel as people strained to hear her reply whilst appearing carry on their own conversations. It was too late to regret her slight, Linka was insulted and determined to have the last say. Laura knew she had chosen the one thing that worried the Advisors more than anything. She had seen the looks on the faces of Aleksei's ministers when it was announced that only Luke would kneel in devotion to Aleksei at their wedding. One man was laughable. One man was almost an insult. It had quickly been decided Luke would kneel as representative of the business connections that Dalnerechensk could make with America. An unofficial ambassador would save everyone from humiliation.

But the swearing of devotion to Aleksei was not the only issue. Russians and Dalnerechenskers loved family and children. Ekaterina had even told Laura a saying the Dalnerechenskers had: *Mnogo sinovey porozhdaut mnogo sinovey;* many sons beget many sons. The Vakhtangov family was large, but she was an only child from only children. If her common blood, small dowry and mad mother were not deterrents for her marriage the lack of heirs certainly would be, and Linka knew it.

'No I have not' she answered.

There was a ripple of whispering as her words were passed down the tables.

'Have you no cousins? No Aunts? Uncles?' she went on; aware her words were being passed on by malicious tongues. 'No relatives at all? Not even a mother?' The cloying smile on her face was sickening.

Aleksei had grown pale under the flush of wine, and two dark spots were fermenting on his cheeks. His stiffness and awkwardness was beginning to make him look like a pantomime puppet at his own banquet. His mouth opened then clicked shut again, jerking in wine fuzzed fury. Laura laid her hand on his, folding her fingers around his, trying to soothe his embarrassment and anger. A malicious little notion was forming in her mind, one that would need careful execution for her final insult.

'Linka there is no need to inquire so much, just ask' Laura started, smiling with false pleasure.

'Ask what?' she looked surprised.

'Your modesty is flattering, but do not be embarrassed' Laura went on.

'About what?' she said, looking round the table nervously.

'It is so kind of you to think of such things, I have had my head in the clouds for weeks, it had simply slipped my mind! I would be greatly honoured to have you to hold my train, you and your sister' she said sweetly.

The smiles fell from their faces. Ekaterina gave Laura a wink and raised her glass to her. The horror of the Norwid family was lost in the rumble of approval round the tables. Linka and Róza flashed each other miserable looks.

'Of course' Linka said unhappily, aware she had been outwitted.

Aleksei leaned down close to Laura's ear, aware how her fingers trembled in anger on his. 'Oh yes Laura, you will make a perfect princess' he whispered, smiling.

25

Olaf rose in the early hours of the morning, slipping down from the stable loft to the stalls, stretching and breathing in deep the smell of fresh hay. The stables were warm and horses whickered quietly, already awake and aware of the excitement in the air. Olenka purruped a welcome and rubbed against his leg. Olaf leaned down and scratched her behind the ears, noting with some satisfaction that her hair now clung to the pant leg of the black livery uniform. He left the stuffy jacket hanging over one of the stable doors and gave Olenka one more pat before shooing her out of the road.

Today was going to be a long day for the horses and the Princess-to-be. Olaf stretched one more time then trotted down to the end of the stables where dozens of harnesses and bridles had been oiled, polished and hung. He talked to the horses quietly as he worked, pulling on bridles and harnesses, making sure the blue, green and gold plumes stood erectly and properly from their heads.

He heard the crunch of gravel outside and slipped out of the stables, opening the door of the carriage, offering his hand to the Ivanovs as they alighted. Ekaterina tipped her face up to the still dark sky, breathing in deep.

'What say you Olaf? Fine weather today?' she asked.

'Da' he answered, closing the door and taking the reins of the horses.

Ekaterina smiled then slipped her arm through her husband's as they made their way to the steps of Dalnerechensk Castle.

Olaf clicked his tongue and led the horses over to the side of the stables where they could shelter. He disappeared briefly to retrieve blankets which he draped over their backs and left them hitched to the carriage, slipping back into the stables to finish readying the horses.

He wondered if the Countess was going to help the young Princess dress for her wedding. Rumours abounded in the castle that the American had not let anyone see her undressed since she had arrived, she had refused to have a maid assist her at bathing or dressing. Ugly gossip had whispered that the girl was a hermaphrodite, or disfigured. Olaf felt sorry for her. She had probably been horribly embarrassed at what was expected of her, still so young and unready. He wondered if anyone had explained what was going to happen to her tonight.

His private thoughts were interrupted by the arrival of one of the pages. Olaf disliked anyone in his sanctuary of the stables but knew he would need help today. Still, he couldn't keep the curtness out of his voice as he sent him to shovel out the horse night soil from the stalls and tugged the heavy carriage out by himself, liking the feel of his muscles limbering under the strain.

The day was slowly lightening and he could see what he was doing without straining his eyes now. One by one he led the horses out of their stalls and hitched a team of four to the carriage. It had been scrubbed, polished and newly painted and sat gleaming in the pre-dawn light. Olaf talked quietly, stroking the noses of the horses as he maneuvered them into the harnesses, letting a small smile play on his face at the thought of horse hair joining Olenka's on the stuffy uniform. He sighed contentedly, looking up at the grey sky. It was going to be a warm day.

The page came back and Olaf set him to work cleaning the horses' hooves, watching another stately carriage roll into the castle grounds. It belonged to *Episcop* Vasily, the Bishop of Dalnerechensk. No doubt he was here to bless the girl's womb till Aleksei only had to look at her to impregnate her. He said nothing, opening the door and extending his hand for the man inside. Four jeweled fingers grasped his sleeve before the fat Father heaved himself out of the carriage, standing breathing hard in the cold morning air.

Olaf wanted to shake his arm free but stood silently, Vasily was famous for shrill rants and shrieking sermons. Olaf did not want to incur Aleksei's wrath for offending the minister on his wedding day. Vasily gave him a pompous command to see to the horses before hitching up the lengths of his robe and waddling to the castle steps where he had to pause to catch his breath again.

Olaf hid his smirk and turned away, leading the carriage out of the way. By the time midmorning arrived, when the royal household was due to leave for church, the entire courtyard was full of carriages and horses. Pages and soldiers had congregated in the stables, stacking crates for tables and chairs at which to play cards until Olaf lost his temper and threw them all out.

'Come Olaf, no harsh words today' said a voice behind him.

Olaf turned to angrily eye Aleksei but swallowed and dropped his gaze to the ground. The Crown Prince stood with his court in all the regalia of state, wearing his crown and thick ermine mantle, which he had wrapped over his arm to stop it dragging on the ground. His black boots gleamed with a high polish and the jewels in the sword hilt hanging from his belt caught in the sun as he moved. The new sash stood out proudly against the smart black of his military uniform, the one that Laura had stitched for him as a wedding present.

'No blessing for your Regent on his wedding day?' Aleksei teased, knowing full well Olaf was uncomfortable with pomp and ceremony.

'God bless His Royal Highness' Olaf said promptly, making the old Tsar laugh.

'Put your jacket on my boy' he said indulgently, smiling.

Olaf dipped a respectful nod then went to do as he was told, shifting his shoulders uncomfortably in the stiff material. Pages and livery men swarmed over the stables, fetching, adjusting, fussing over the procession and the court. Olaf eyed them all miserably, wishing the day was over. Peter Kaminin, the Captain of the Guard, shouted orders at the soldiers, watching them fall into line, kicking the livery and page men who were slow to obey the order too.

Olaf opened the door to the open carriage, holding out his hand to help the fat *Episcop* in. The bishop heaved himself up, breathing hard and rearranging his robes. He then leaned over and ruffled Olaf's hair, more amiable now that he had had his customary three goblets of wine with breakfast, blessing Olaf for his hard work and dedication. Olaf thanked him and closed the carriage door, wondering when he was going to be stripped of his office.

The *Episcop*'s carriage would lead the procession through Dalnerechensk to the church, followed by members of the Vakhtangov family in enclosed carriages, culminating in those of Tsar Constantinovich and Aleksei, who would ride separately in their own carriages. Once all the members had alighted the procession had to return to bring the bridal party to the church. Olaf eyed the swarms of people in his stable courtyard unhappily, bit down an angry yell and clambered up onto the driver's seat of the open carriage, watching Peter and his second in command bring their mounts to the head of the column.

A page came forward to brush away Olenka's fur from his pants and he kicked him away roughly, relieved to hear the sharp fanfare that announced the procession was leaving the castle grounds. The trumpets were greeted with an enormous cheer outside the walls and the bells at the church began to ring joyously. The huge ornamental gates to Vsevolod's Way were thrown open and Olaf flicked the reins gently, listening to *Episcop* Vasily begin to call the blessings.

Vsevolod's Way was crowded. Men, women and children stood in tightly packed throngs craning their necks for a glimpse of the procession. Some stood inside the shops, pressing up to the window glass to see out. Others flung open windows from the rooms above the shops and leaned out them dangerously, calling to each other if they could see the Prince yet. The noise and the press of faces were overwhelming.

Olaf guided the carriage to the commons in front of the church. It was already crowded with people waiting to call blessings to the royal couple, and he knew when the bridal procession had passed those lining Vsevolod's Way would flood to the Church commons for the service. He stopped the coach and leapt down, opening the door for the minister. Vasily stepped out and Olaf leapt back up to the seat, flicking the reins to take the carriage back to the castle, aware that the procession behind him would have to stop every time the occupants alighted at the steps.

Dalnerechensk's other streets were deserted, and Olaf made a quick return to the castle along the utility street, aware that his moments alone would be brief before the other liveries trotted up Castle Street. He wondered if he would arrive to see the end of the procession had still not left but was pleased to see the stables virtually deserted. He walked the open carriage to the front of the stables, knowing he would need it for the Prince and Princess' procession through the valleys once the wedding was complete.

He shrugged his shoulders uncomfortably in his jacket and wondered if he could take it off. Eagerly he reached to pull them open but as he did the second carriage rolled into the courtyard and he sighed, knowing his respite was over. Peter and the mounted officers began returning, remaining on horseback to take up positions around the bridal party. Bitter bickering announced the arrival of Linka and Róza in the courtyard, their beautiful faces sour. Countess Ivanova was with them, as was another of Aleksei's pretty unwed cousins.

Olaf turned his face away. They were dressed in beautiful silks, two in green, two in blue, all trimmed with gold. All four wore white gloves and gold beads in their hair. Only the Countess looked happy, and wore a dreamy look on her face. Olaf opened the door to Vasily's stately carriage and held out his hand to help up the four women, closing the door behind them. Just as the fanfare had announced the groom's procession the trumpets blasted another series of notes from the wall above the ornate gates to Vsevolod's Way. The carriage left, and an even bigger roar from the crowds greeted them.

Luke joined the soldiers in the courtyard, terribly uncomfortable in his stiff and formal attire. He was unused to wearing a sword, and kept knocking the hilt with his elbow, cursing under his breath and shrugging his shoulders uncomfortably. Olaf caught him doing it, and a sheepish understanding look passed between the two. Olaf reached over and tugged the sword hilt into the proper position so Luke wouldn't knock it every time he moved, then opened the door to an enclosed carriage, stepping back to help him up.

'You drive my daughter carefully' he said, then realised Olaf probably didn't understand him. 'Laura' he said pointing to the carriage. '*Carefully.*'

Olaf hesitated then nodded, his face blank. Luke patted his arm resigned, then swung up into the carriage. Olaf closed the door and watched it pull out of the courtyard, surrounded by a guard of honour. He shut his eyes, knowing from the quiet gasps that Laura had stepped out of the castle, not wanting to turn around.

'Good morning Olaf' she said quietly, her voice shaking.

He hesitated then turned reluctantly. His eyes swept up from the hem of the dress to her face. She was so beautiful it winded him and he shut his eyes, realising too late that he had let it buckle him. He sighed inwardly and bent forward even more, an awkward, hesitant bow for her. She carried a beautiful bouquet of lilies, white iris and jasmine, and there were tiny mountain daisies in her hair, the national flower of Dalnerechensk.

He wondered how on earth they had found fresh flowers for her in the heart of a Russian winter, then realised they had frozen them in the cold larder months ago. He forced himself to stand upright, his eyes settling only briefly on her happy, nervous face before looking away again. *The poor child* he thought as he turned away and fussed with the plumes of the bridle on a horse. *She will never have any say again, not when she is Aleksei's property.*

He then turned back to her, shifting his shoulders uncomfortably as he reached out to her, feeling how her hand trembled as she stepped up into the carriage, the yards of her train and dress folded numerous times over her arm so it didn't drag on the ground. She sat then arranged her skirts carefully, holding the flowers in her lap and wiping her cheeks to clear them of her nerves.

Olaf closed the door and leapt up onto the seat, waiting till the guards had formed around the carriage before flicking the reins gently. The trumpet blasts from the top of Vsevolod's Way's gate were drowned in the roar from the expectant crowd. Their virginal Princess glowed in the Tsaritsa's dress and she waved while they called blessings to her, throwing flowers beneath the horse's hooves.

Olaf drove slowly through the streets of Dalnerechensk, listening to her strange voice call blessings to the children as she had been instructed to do, to bring many children of her own to the royal nursery. The overwhelming press of the crowd was so dense, and the noise so loud he doubted anyone save him could hear the blessings. Yet still she called, all the way from the castle grounds to the Principality's only cathedral, where kings had been crowned and wed, and mass took place every day.

Olaf stopped the coach at the steps to the church and waited for the mounted guard to move off into new positions to keep the crowd from surging forward at the sight of their new Princess. Luke and the bridesmaids were waiting at the top of the steps. They swept down to greet them and Olaf jumped down, opening the door to help Laura out of the carriage.

There was a loud gasp, but only Ekaterina told her how beautiful she looked. Laura let the folds of her train slip to the ground, aware she was now the centre of Dalnerechensk's attention. The four women quickly brushed out the wrinkles in her gown and arranged her veil over her face before reaching down to pick up the train, brushing the dirt and the wrinkles out of that too.

Behind them Olaf clicked his tongue and the carriage moved off, allowing the crowds to catch the first full glimpse of her. A joyous cheer rang out and Laura turned to them, waving and calling blessings to the children, watching as the crowds that had lined Vsevolod's Way flood down the street and onto the church commons, pressing against the line of mounted horsemen and jostling good-naturedly for a better look.

Linka said something in Polish under her breath to her sister and they both tittered. Laura ignored them and turned to her father, who was glowing with pride and emotion. He offered his elbow and she slipped into his arm, letting him lead her up the steps, holding her dress so as not to step on it and rip it or trip.

The guardsmen at the huge double doors bowed deeply to her then threw open the doors. Inside the assembled guests turned as one to look at her then swept deep bows. There were muffled gasps and whispers in the silence then the organist started the wedding march.

Laura knew she couldn't gawp round her at the magnificent architecture of the church and was glad Ekaterina had suggested a visit before she was married to take in the wondrous sights. She knew she couldn't even look to her left and right to see who was in the pews paying homage to her. She kept her eyes on the magnificent altar piece, on *Episcop* Vasily who stood before it, dressed in vestments embroidered with gold thread, on Aleksei, who waited for her at the top of the aisle.

'I'm so proud of you' Luke whispered as they walked up the aisle, trying to hold back his emotion.

Laura bit the inside of her lip firmly to keep the tears in check and squeezed his arm gently. She knew he had despaired of her behaviour sometimes, and despite the distance she had felt from him she did still love him, and he her. Her eyes drifted from the priest to Aleksei, distracting herself so she wouldn't cry.

He was dressed in the long white mantle of state, arranged so it cascaded behind him down the steps of the altar. He had turned mostly towards her to watch her progress down the aisle. He was dressed in the beautiful black military uniform, though it was highly decorated as fitting the Commander-in-Chief of Dalnerechensk. An ornamental sword hung from his belt, so jewel encrusted Laura wondered if there was a sword under them at all. The crown he wore was quite sparse by comparison, a wide band of gold with simple points, a ring of mounted rubies at the base.

Each step brought her closer and closer to him, till she could see the desire in his gaze at the sight of her glowing with youth and beauty in the silken dress. She could see he even looked winded, breathless, the look of a man gazing at the most beautiful thing he had ever seen. Carefully she lifted her skirt to climb the steps, not wanting to trip on the delicate fabric.

Luke let her slip out of his arm as he had been instructed to do and Ekaterina, Linka, Róza and Aleksei's other cousin arranged the folds of her train to cascade down the steps as Laura mounted them alone. She turned quickly to smile at Luke as he released her, then gave her bouquet to Ekaterina to hold as they took up their positions at the base of the stairs. The priest began the service in Latin and Laura smiled shyly at Aleksei, who had not been able to take his eyes off her.

They both knelt for Vasily to bless them and to bless their union, then stood again for the service. Aleksei swore to value her as his most treasured property in a lovely speech reminiscent of the beautiful letter he had written to her in Boston. Both he and Laura blushed at the sentiment in the words and several women sighed, either in approval or defeat. Laura swore to relinquish all her worldly possessions and her desires to Aleksei as his property, to be provided for and cherished by him alone. Somehow she made it through her Russian vows faultlessly and the women again had sighed when she promised to serve the Prince and Principality equally with her love and devotion.

Aleksei pushed a band of exquisitely engraved gold onto her finger, and Laura could feel how much he was shaking. She then slid a band of gold onto his finger, biting her lip in concentration, as her own hands were shaking just as much. Aleksei raised her veil and kissed her gently, sealing the vows before God and the court of Dalnerechensk.

The church cheered, and the people standing in the street before the church cheered too, knowing they had a new Princess. Aleksei and Laura turned at the altar to face the full cathedral, and Aleksei held his hand out, palm down. Laura placed her arm on his and Vasily tied their hands together with a wide red ribbon, a symbol of unity, love and faithfulness. The assembled guests cheered again, and Aleksei called a blessing over his people and his lands.

Luke stepped forward, looking emotional and worried. He knelt before his daughter and her new husband, knocking his elbow on the hilt of his sword. A long silence followed and someone coughed nervously in the crowd. Finally Luke began to talk, in English, as he couldn't remember the words of the speech Fedor had prepared for him. His voice was quiet, his head bowed, and most of the words were lost in the thick lump in his throat.

At the end he raised his head, and Laura was moved to see tears on his cheeks. There was a moment of unsure silence then the entire court knelt, swearing an oath of allegiance and duty to the crown, the same oath used four hundred years ago when the crown was offered to Vsevolod. Aleksei blessed them all again and the crowds cheered, echoed again by those waiting outside to get a glimpse of their new Princess, then he led his bride out into the sun-lit winter day.

Olaf was waiting for them with an open carriage at the foot of the stairs, still uncomfortable in his uniform. The crowds roared when they appeared, surging against the line of horses that blocked their access to the royal couple. Peter and a mounted guard had taken up positions around the empty carriage, glowing in the midday sun. Aleksei led Laura down the stairs to the carriage then boosted her up first as she was struggling with yards of her dress and only one hand. She quickly pulled the material out of the way so Aleksei, still joined to her with the red ribbon, could climb into the carriage behind her.

Ekaterina and Aleksei's page tucked the train of the mantle and the dress into the carriage with them. They sat, placing their joined hands on a pillow that sat between them on the seat. The crowds cheered as the happy couple waved. Ekaterina and the page stepped back, letting Olaf shut the door before climbing back into the driver's seat of the carriage, taking up the reins again. A fanfare sounded from the castle walls, and Laura wondered if they were watching with a spy glass to ensure the timing was right. The crowd cheered and Laura tossed the bouquet she was still holding, which Linka caught, then blew a kiss to the court as the carriage started the bridal tour.

On the pillow placed on the seat between them Laura linked her fingers between Aleksei's, and felt him squeeze her hand gently in response. The crowds cheered when they saw their joined arms and linked fingers, calling blessings to them and tossing flowers into the carriage until they were almost buried.

Peter, mounted at the head of the bridal party, led the procession three times round the fortified city and then under King's Gate, taking the road that led up the valley to Ladozhskoye. Laura was very glad of the pillow between them as her arm was getting tired, and would never have been able to hold her arm up for the entire procession. Aleksei's thumb gently caressed the back of her hand, sending delighted tingles up her arm and she blushed deeply, remembering the sensations of his touch on her thigh the night she had danced for him.

As the bridal party circled Ladozhskoye Laura glimpsed Dalnerechensk and the hilltop castle far below them. She gazed down at the lazy river meandering through the valley floor and the run-off from the natural spring in Tcherepnin that joined it, watching the way the sunlight rode over the little ripples in the water, sighing happily. They circled Ladozhskoye and Grigory Ivanov's stately home in its commanding position above the village three times, noticing it was like a ghost town as all of the inhabitants had crowded onto the streets of Dalnerechensk to see their new Princess.

They then rejoined Miner's Way, the road that lead past Ladozhskoye into the forests adorning the western slopes of Liberty Valley, climbing the steep hills to the pretty village of Macherna. It was nestled in a clearing atop the Western Ridge, surrounded by tall pines that scented the warm day. The houses for the miners and their families who dug the tin from Dalnerechensk's earth were set out in rows very similar to the military barracks of Tcherepnin. They rode three times through columns of burly, hardened men and women who cheered for their pretty Princess with strained faces and before watching them ride westward into the neighbouring valley, to the outpost hamlet of Davostok.

The Western-most settlement of the Principality was no more than a cluster of three homes, a mill and a low stone wall that marked the boundary of the Principality. The wall ran north and south, and Laura believed it encircled all of Dalnerechensk's territory. Here at Davostok the wall was broken to allow Miner's Way to pass out of Dalnerechensk and into Russia, heading towards the Austro-Hungarian Empire. The road was snowy, and Laura imagined since the invention of the steam engine and the railway to Dalnerechensk from Chelyabinsk that the use of this road had declined. Still, it was a border crossing, and there was a small guardhouse beside the road, opposite a huge iron bell hung from thick wooden beams. The bell was sheathed in ice and a lone, cold guard stood beside it. He snapped a stiff salute as his Commander and Prince swept by, then grabbed the bell rope and yanked firmly, swinging down with all his weight.

Laura turned back to watch the ponderous bell rise into the air then crash down in a violent arc when he let it go. The toll of the bell was so loud it shattered the ice coating and boomed around them, scaring birds from the trees as far as the eye could see. No doubt the tolls could be heard in Dalnerechensk, and if not, the clouds of birds that rose shrieking from the trees would be warning enough.

With her ears ringing loudly, she began to understand why Dalnerechensk had so few soldiers on her borders and so many concentrated in the valley itself. The outlying provinces had a system of bells to alert Liberty Valley and the populous therein should the Principality ever be invaded. Perhaps it would have been very effective four hundred years ago, but Laura wondered what would happen to Dalnerechensk if it ever had to fight a modern war.

From Davostok they turned south, following the low stone wall along West Valley before turning with the wall to slip through a pretty pass into Liberty Valley again. They emerged a long way south of the garrison village of Tcherepnin into a valley dotted with the patchwork of cultivated farms. Hundreds of years of peace and a treasury that could not afford a standing army save for the royal guards had seen Tcherepnin transformed into a farming community. Nevertheless, most of the guards were still stationed inside the garrison, as the village blocked the valley from attacking armies coming from the sprawling Ottoman Empire.

The royal train had traveled through the garrison village on the Asanton's arrival into Dalnerechensk, unbeknown to Laura, who was struggling into her clothes at the time. Both gates that let the trains through Tcherepnin could be shut with portcullis and thick fire-hardened doors to block any troops coming through, or if they had already reached the village, to force them to break down two sets of defenses before they even reached Dalnerechensk, as both gates could be secured with the heavy cross beam protected behind the lowered portcullis. The engine of Dalnerechensk's only train could also be protected here by sealing it inside the village.

Laura could see why Vsevolod was such a revered leader in Dalnerechensk. He was a brilliant military strategist, architect and statesman and the fruits of his labour were ever present in the proud community. It was easy to forget the precariousness of the Principality when one viewed all the magnificence they had achieved.

At the south end of Liberty Valley stood another guard house beside the railroad tracks and opposite another ponderous bell. As in Davostok the wall and gate was poorly defended with one lone guard on duty. Laura thought it strange to have so little force on the borders and so many in the valley itself. But her thoughts turned from the guards as Aleksei rubbed his thumb across the back of her hand again, rubbing some warmth into it.

She looked at him shyly again, blushing a little. He smiled at her responses and lifted her exposed hand to his mouth, blowing warmly on her fingers. Her blush deepened and she looked away to compose herself, trying to ignore the feel of his hot breath misting on her fingers. She noticed the mounted guard at the head of the bridal party had turned back up Liberty Valley to Tcherepnin, as the terrain was too uneven to follow the border wall into the East Valley. Soldiers on the walls of Tcherepnin waved and called blessings and the small church inside the village rang her bells as they passed. Aleksei lowered her hand back to the pillow between them, conscious that the military frowned on Commanders seen nibbling on the hands of beautiful women, even if they were husband and wife.

The mounted guard then picked up the pace of the tour, leading the carriage at a trot onto the forest road between Tcherepnin and the tiny hamlet of Kalach on the eastern border, owned and farmed by one family. The bell tolled the bridal party's passing and they galloped north through East Valley, then the party slowed again at Hunter's Pass, the main route through the private forests and hunting ground of the Royal Family, arriving back in Liberty Valley, close to the Northern Border.

Laura noticed that the walls were unbroken, as they had been in Kalach. The ponderous bell in Kalach had been rung, but here at the Northern boundary of the Principality there was no guard house, or bell, or any road. The absence gave her a slight feeling of unease, she turned to look at Dalnerechensk, at whether the bells were needed here. The procession turned towards King's Gate, and Laura put the thought of the city behind her, she had a speech to give on the walls of Dalnerechensk Castle.

She swallowed nervously, only half aware that the Cathedral bells were ringing and so were large bells in the watchtowers of the Castle walls. The loud rapport of cannon fire made her jump and Aleksei squeezed her hand gently, soothing her. The procession passed by thongs of cheering crowds who threw even more flowers into the open carriage before arriving back in the courtyard of the castle.

Olaf leapt down from the driver's seat and opened the door. An avalanche of flowers came tumbling out as Laura stood, as if she were Persephone herself rising from a bed of petals. Olaf dropped his eyes and reached up, taking Laura round her waist, seeing she was encumbered with the yards of her gown wrapped round her arm and the red ribbon. She stepped forward as he lifted her, setting her down on the cobblestones before reaching up to help Aleksei down. Laura thanked him for his gentleness and Aleksei plucked one of the small white daisies from her hair, giving it to the stable hand. Olaf dropped his head and curled his fingers round the flower, protecting it, or hiding it, mumbling a soft thank you into his chest.

Aleksei then led his bride from the stables to the East Wall of the castle defenses. Here a set of steps led up the side of the wall to the ramparts, overlooking the commons below. It was crowded with people, all of them straining to get a glimpse of their Princess. Laura climbed the steps carefully, aware there was no rail on the side to protect them from a fall into the castle grounds. Aleksei had gallantly wrapped the yards of material round their joined hands and slid it round her to help her feel secure as they climbed together, still awkwardly tied. The bridesmaids and the groom's party followed them to the gangway.

Laura looked down into the sea of faces and felt fear swim over her. The roar of the crowd's greeting was loud and her carefully practised speech disappeared from her head. She stood there awkwardly, trying to remember the words. Ekaterina whispered the beginning to her but Linka coughed loudly, masking the help. Ekaterina tried again and Linka coughed even more loudly than before. A hush began to fall and Laura could hear them murmuring restlessly. She was not going to make a good impression if she stood without addressing them, nor would she if she could only stutter through a half remembered rhetoric. Even Aleksei was looking at her to start. Finally she pressed their joined hands to her heart and started the only thing she could remember. She sang their national anthem.

The crowd gasped and then as one they joined in, pressing their hands to their hearts too. The court joined her and when it was over they cheered for her, and Laura waved and called blessings, leaving the wall and knowing one song had endeared her better than her carefully practised speech.

26

Laura was nervous. Finally free of the awkward symbols of matrimony back inside the castle Laura had tied the red ribbon that had bound their hands together elegantly around her neck where it glowed against the paleness of her dress and skin. The reception had gone on long into the night, scores of dignitaries coming forward to offer their congratulations, blessings for their marriage and offering gifts, each more splendid than the last. Linka and her sister gave her beautiful dresses, sewn with gold and silver thread, though it rose their gall to do so. Even Anna had given her a present, blushing before the court, and offered her a plain handkerchief, embroidered with her initials. Laura thanked her and praised her needlework and Anna had scurried back to the throng of other servants who stood in the great hall, her face burning with pride.

The food at the reception meal had been sumptuous and Laura was praised for her choice of dishes and confectioneries. She and Aleksei had sat proud as husband and wife under the canopy of state, and Laura had hardly touched anything for fear her shaking hands would drop food down the beautiful dress. The court did not notice her frugality, distracted by the merry dancers and musicians who entertained them with popular Dalnerechensk songs and well known music from famous composers. There was even a Troubadour who sang French love songs for a delighted Laura.

The court had danced and drank, merry and sure of the love between their new royals, as they had not taken their eyes off the other. Aleksei had held her close as they danced their bridal waltz, gallantly holding the end of her train wrapped over his arm and did not dance with anyone else that evening, only letting her go to dance with her father or Tsar Constantinovich.

Laura was tired but knew the evening was not over yet, they still had the Putting To Bed Ceremony. It sounded wonderful, as she had been awake for nearly twenty hours but still she smiled winningly, and danced lightly, and laughed at ever more silly, wine-inspired jokes from the court. Finally Aleksei took her hand, dismissing the court in a loud voice. They cheered, falling in behind their royal couple as Aleksei led his bride up the stairs to his chambers.

She had never been here, and her gaze swept round the room, trying to take in all the details and intricate patterns without looking like she was staring. The large, four poster bed dominated the room. It was hung with thick brocaded curtains and the covers turned down to reveal silk sheets a muted yellow in the candle light. On each side of the bed was a large dressing screen, Anna stood before one, and Aleksei's page Mikhail stood before the other. A marble fireplace dominated the wall opposite the bed, flanked by two windows, their green velvet curtains drawn.

In the middle of the room was a row of joined colonnades, separating the room into two halves, on one half the bed, dressing screens and two matching chests of drawers placed to the left and right of the bed, in front of the dressing screens; on the other half: the fireplace and two double doors at each end of the room, one set leading to the corridor, the other to Aleksei's private dressing rooms.

She heard talking and laughing behind her and was surprised to see the court had followed them into Aleksei's bedroom; all the ministers, the wives, the daughters, the chilly Norwid family. Laura flushed a deep red and Aleksei stroked her cheek with the back of his fingers gently. Mikhail came forward and opened a hidden latch on the colonnade, swinging open a door and stood back.

Aleksei swept Laura up in his arms and carried her across the barrier, setting her down inside the sanctuary of his room. Mikhail closed and latched the colonnade closed again. The court crowded into the small space between the two sets of double doors and stood watching. Aleksei squeezed her hand then let it go, disappearing with Mikhail behind the dressing screen. Anna came forward and took her hands, leading her behind the other dressing screen.

Part of her was afraid that Aleksei would be able to see her undressing, even if the court did not. She was relieved to see that it was angled so she was hidden from the court and Aleksei. Anna quickly set to work freeing her from the hundreds of buttons on the ancient dress, letting it fall to the thick rug on Aleksei's floor. Laura let her three petticoats follow suit till she stood in a sea of expensive material. Her cheeks flushed hotter to think only a thin screen separated the court from seeing her in her corset and bloomers, and even hotter to think her father was among them.

Anna slipped behind her and began to unlace the corset, pulling it down over her hips to sit with the other folds of her clothes. A quiet murmur from the court told her that Aleksei had stepped out from the screen and she was now keeping him waiting. She and Anna looked at each other carefully, knowing her aversion to being seen undressed by anyone. Laura shut her eyes then took hold of her short chemise and pulled it over her head. Anna averted her eyes from her mistresses' body and grabbed the silk nightdress, helping her into it.

Laura's cheeks were dark with embarrassment. Anna quickly unpinned her hair and Laura took a deep breath, hesitating at the verge of the screen. In the room Mikhail flipped back the silk sheets of the bed and Aleksei, dressed in a long nightshirt, sat on the edge, swiveling his legs onto the bed. Mikhail reached across him and pulled the covers over his lap. Anna gave Laura a little push and a blessing in her ear. Another murmur went through the court at her arrival and she bowed her head in embarrassment.

Anna slipped out from behind the screen and flung back the sheets of the bed. Laura hesitated, unsure what to do. Her eyes flicked nervously to the crowded room then back to Aleksei. He too was embarrassed, and Laura slipped to the bed, letting Anna fold the sheets over her. Laura grabbed for Aleksei's hand, squeezing tight in fear. A lone flower still in her hair fell onto the sheets between them. Aleksei saw it and picked it up, sniffing it carefully.

Anna undid the curtains on Laura's side while Mikhail undid the curtains on Aleksei's side. Laura stole a frightened look at Aleksei.

'Are they to watch all of this?' she whispered, hardly able to look at him.

'I am sorry for this' he answered, embarrassed too.

He turned to his court and bid them a good night, and they called a hearty good night back, then Anna and Mikhail closed the curtains, blocking them from view. Aleksei sighed, sinking back on the pillows and shutting his eyes. Laura stayed sitting upright, holding her breath and listening to the muffled sounds of footsteps on the wooden floors until she was sure the court was leaving the room. She heard a soft click of the door closing and pushed back the covers of the bed.

Aleksei watched her crawl down to the end where she pushed one finger through the gap between the curtains and surreptitiously pull it open, relieved to discover the bedroom was empty. She sighed softly, relaxing a little, then turned back to look at her husband. He smiled, sitting up to watch her.

'Are you nervous?' he asked in English, playing with the flower that had fallen from her hair.

She nodded, folding one arm to her chest to partially cover her.

'Don't be' he whispered before sliding closer to her, taking her hand away from her neck and rubbing his thumb across her skin. 'You did not finish undressing' he said, eyeing her silk stockings.

'Forgive me, I didn't want to keep you waiting.'

She quickly reached down to pull off her stockings. Aleksei stopped her, taking over the job himself, tossing the stockings over his shoulder. He reached out and took an end of the red ribbon still fastened round her throat and pulled the knot out gently, brushing his fingers on her throat as he slipped it under the loops of the ribbon, pulling it off her. She swallowed nervously, watching him work. By Dalnerechensk law she was now the property of this man, this Prince before her. She shivered and resisted the urge to pull away from him, to hide her face, and wished desperately that she knew what to do. Aleksei pulled the ribbon from behind her hair, a sensation that caused her to shiver.

'Are you frightened of me my tender bride?' he asked softly.

'No Aleksei, not of you, never of you. Just of my duty' she whispered, dropping her face in shame.

Aleksei stroked her hair back from her face, tilting her head up to him. She blushed but reached out to stroke his cheek gently. Aleksei kissed her, pulling her close to him.

'Don't hide from me' he said, letting his hand slide onto her leg.

She gasped, letting herself respond to his touches, though frightened of where these emotions would take her. Aleksei drew back and pulled his long night dress off him, then took her hands and placed them on his chest. She smiled, embarrassed and he crawled closer to her, pulling undone the laces at the throat of her night dress.

His hand slid inside her nightdress, stroking her young breast as he fell to kissing her again, pushing her back on his pillows. She felt his weight press on her chest, his hand slipping from her breast to pull up her night dress. His fingers brushed her bloomers and he sat back to pull them off. Laura flushed, catching a glimpse of his nakedness and shut her eyes. He leaned against her again, sliding his hand up her thigh.

She gasped, aware that his fingers had brushed a scar and that he had gone still above her. She shut her eyes tighter, feeling him explore the back of her leg gently, silent as he was holding his breath.

'*Moy Bog*' he whispered, breathing out at long last, wiping his mouth.

'I'm sorry' she whispered, trying to hold back her tears.

'You have nothing to be sorry about' he said fiercely.

He managed a smile for her, and reached out, tracing his gentle fingers along her cheek and down her front, making her gasp as they brushed over a soft breast. Her fear and anxiety melted from her and she folded her arms around him as he lay against her again, feeling a hunger rise in her as he kissed her, moving on top of her and nestling between her knees. And later, as she moaned softly under his caresses and felt him shudder in spent passion she sighed contentedly, safe in a loving embrace.

27

Laura woke, drifting out of a gentle dream, aware she was being watched. Something moved on her back and she opened her eyes, looking round carefully. Aleksei was lying beside her, propped up on one elbow, his free hand tracing the fading scars on her back and thighs. He saw she had woken and brushed back her hair from her face.

'Good morning' he smiled, brushing her cheek with the back of his fingers.

Laura sat up, pulling up the covers of the bed as she did so, a little embarrassed. Aleksei smiled then covered a yawn with his hand. He caught the look of horror on her face and pulled back the covers to see what had caught her attention. There was a patch of dried blood on the sheets. Embarrassed, Aleksei soothed her, explaining that it was normal and would not hurt so much in future couplings. Laura flushed again, not sure what to think.

Instead she reached out and stroked Aleksei's rough cheek, enjoying the intimacy between the two of them now, away from the court and the eyes and gossip and slander. Aleksei kissed the palm of her hand, smiling warmly.

'Are you to go into the Council Chambers today?' she asked.

'On my honeymoon?' he asked, surprised.

'I had hoped not, but you spent time there during our courtship. I know a Principality does not stop for romance -'

'It stops today for romance' he said, then flushed at his words.

Laura smiled and shifted closer, resting her head on his shoulder, aware that blood had also crusted on her legs. Aleksei folded his arms around her, kissing the top of her head.

'Are you happy?' he asked awkwardly.

'Yes' she smiled, shutting her eyes contentedly.

Aleksei took up a lock of her hair and let it slide like silk through his fingers. There was a quiet tap on the door and Laura stiffened, holding her breath. The door opened, and the sounds of someone stoking the fire could be heard. Aleksei disengaged himself from Laura and sat up, pulling on his nightshirt, then pushing open the curtains of the bed.

'Good morning Mikhail' he said, twitching the curtains closed behind him, smiling at the embarrassed scrabbling as Laura hunted for her nightdress.

Mikhail came forward and helped Aleksei into a robe, then turned and twitched open the velvet curtains of the windows, flooding the room with light. Aleksei strode into his dressing room and Mikhail followed, leaving Laura sitting in the confines of the poster bed. She heard splashing water, and the soft scraping of Aleksei's shave. She then heard the soft rustle of starched cloth being pulled into position about the body and wondered if Mikhail ever saw Aleksei naked.

The curtains of the bed twitched open, giving her a fright and Aleksei poked his head in, fully dressed.

'I shall send for Anna' he said. 'Mikhail is running the water into a bath for you.' He caught the look on her face and added quickly: 'He will leave when Anna arrives.'

'Where are you going?' Laura asked, confused.

'To breakfast' he said. 'Join me when you're ready. It will be just a few of us, the court will not eat with us today.'

He leaned in and planted a kiss on her head then twitched the curtains shut again, heading downstairs.

Laura listened to the sound of Mikhail pouring water and heating it over the newly stoked fire in the room. Laura wondered if she should talk to him, wondered what to say. A knock on the door announced the arrival of Anna. She and Mikhail called shy good mornings to each other and Mikhail took his leave, closing the door behind him.

Anna knocked timidly on the wooden post of the bed. Laura pushed back the curtain and peeped out, equally timid.

'Good morning Your Highness' Anna smiled. 'The bath has been run, please follow me.'

Laura slipped out of the curtains and gasped. The room had been full of ministers and dark shadows last night, but in the morning light she saw how truly magnificent the room was. The walls glowed with rich wood panels that did not reach the ceiling and beautiful pastoral scenes had been painted on the walls above them. The ceiling was painted as if a window had opened in heaven, and several seraphim and putti had stopped to glance down into the room. Laura was glad of the brocade cover of Aleksei's bed, she didn't know how she would have felt under his body and looking at angels watching her.

Anna held open the door of Aleksei's dressing room and Laura stepped through, eyeing the surroundings. The room was large and housed a magnificent wardrobe, intricately carved. A blue silk couch sat near it, embroidered with richly coloured peacocks. In the middle of the room, filled with steaming water sat a claw foot bathtub. Anna closed the door and Laura, feeling bold now she had been through the secret initiations of her marriage bed, let the night dress slip to the floor to step into the tub.

The gasp behind her told her that Anna hadn't left the room as she thought. She turned, clasping her hands before her to cover her downy hair. Anna had dropped her eyes and turned her head, frightened of the reprisal she might receive. It was a horrible moment of embarrassment, Laura exposed and naked, her secret shame now known.

'You can't tell anyone' she said hurriedly.

'But my lady -'

'No! Anna you must promise me you won't tell anyone!' Laura begged, taking hold of her shoulders. 'If you tell I will have you fired! You will have to go and work in the mines!'

Anna's terrified eyes met Laura's.

'I won't tell' she promised. 'I swear on Vsevolod's grave.'

Laura let her go, relenting from her passionate outburst. She smiled, a little shamefacedly, and Anna managed a small one in return. Laura turned back to the bath, aware Anna was now looking at the scars, and stepped into the steaming water.

'Would you like me to wash your hair?' Anna suddenly asked.

Laura looked surprised, then realised since Anna had now seen her she had nothing more to fear. She smiled then beckoned her closer, lying back in the warm water and liked the feel of it trickling over her scalp as Anna scooped it up in a small pail. Laura rubbed away the blood on her legs, wondering if all married women felt as she had felt, knew what she now knew.

'Are you married Anna?' she asked suddenly.

'No my lady' she answered, smiling. 'But I want to be.'

Laura was quiet, a small smile playing on her lips.

*

Aleksei smiled when she stepped into the dining hall, dressed in blue iridescent silk that flashed hues of green as she moved. The dining room was crowded with the wedding guests and the Vakhtangov family. Laura thought this was hardly a 'few' but she smiled and sat beside him, answering questions posed to her and returning greetings from the guests.

She saw that most had finished eating, but knew custom dictated they could not leave the table until their royals left and Laura sipped daintily and slowly, aware that Tatiana and Linka were whispering uncomfortably together. Laura called one of the pages to bring her some more bread. She was not hungry, but liked the thought of making those snobbish cows wait on her whim pleased her enough to drag out her meal.

Maksim Yegorov made an embarrassed comment about the marriage bed improving the appetite and the dining hall laughed politely. Laura patted her mouth with a napkin and put it down, then folded her hand over Aleksei's, smiling shyly at him. His smile deepened and his cheeks reddened, aware the hall was watching them. Laura girlishly kissed the back of his hand and laughed.

Aleksei stood and helped her to her feet, the dining hall following suit. Aleksei tucked her hand through his arm and led her back up to the second floor of the castle. Laura thought for a fleeting moment they were returning to his chambers and wondered if he would take her back to his bed again. She flushed a little hotly at that, but was thankful the court wasn't following them this time.

'I want you to have these rooms' he said, opening a set of double doors opposite his.

The rooms beyond were musty and the furniture covered with dust cloths. The room was dark as the velvet curtains were still pulled, protecting the colours of the tapestries and paintings on the walls from the fading effects of the sun. Despite the gloom Laura could see the rooms were tasteful and feminine.

'These are the Tsaritsa's rooms, they were my mother's rooms' he said softly, crossing to the window where he slid back the curtains lovingly, the dust motes winked and danced in the light as they were disturbed. He turned his back, looking out the window. 'These rooms need another woman in them.'

Laura looked surprised and felt a flicker of cold crawl down her spine.

'Am I not to share your rooms with you?'

Aleksei turned back, surprised, which quickly turned to embarrassment.

'No' he said, burning. 'You would be alone most of the day, here you can have people visit when you wanted to.'

'I could not have them visit me in your rooms?' She tried, feeling unsure.

'A wife needs her own rooms' he said, feeling swamped with having to justify years of tradition to a sixteen-year-old girl.

Laura swallowed and looked around the dusty rooms, feeling a gap between them. This was not the marriage she had envisioned. She took another step into the room, looking around carefully. They were not ugly rooms, and she would like a place she could make her own inside the castle. She touched a dust cloth gently, trying to remember what she knew about royal marriages. Romantic stories she had read ended at weddings with a dissatisfactory "happily ever after", and she couldn't remember any story that told her about the loneliness queens felt in their own rooms.

She glanced into one of the other rooms and stopped, another cold fear slithering down her spine.

'There is a bed here, am I expected to sleep here?' she asked, her voice a little too loud.

'Yes' Aleksei said, confused at her behaviour.

'Then how are we to -' she stopped, flushing.

Aleksei's embarrassment deepened further as well.

'I will send for you' he stuttered.

Laura shut her eyes, the callousness hurt her, that they would not go to bed together at night unless he sent for her like a servant. *A servant can refuse and be fired* a small part of her said. *You are worse than a servant, you are property.*

'Can I not come to you?' she asked, feeling despondent.

Aleksei laughed.

'If you wish' he grinned, coming to her and taking her hand, slipping it through his elbow. 'Come now, the rooms will be aired for you, come riding with me.'

Laura managed a smile, masking the unhappiness she felt and let him lead her down to the stables. Aleksei called to Olaf to saddle his horse and Laura wondered if she should call out for her stallion, or whether Aleksei would do that for her. She was terribly confused. But Aleksei didn't call for her stallion and she stayed quiet.

Olaf led the magnificent horse over to them, his eyes averted from them and gruffly nodded to present the horse to them. Aleksei boosted himself up then reached down to lift Laura onto the saddle before him. She smiled shyly and he smiled back, sliding his arms around her to take the reins. Her smiled deepened, liking the feel of his arms around her.

Aleksei clicked his tongue and guided the horse out of the castle grounds, heading out to show his Principality his beautiful wife.

28

Laura had let Aleksei lead her up to the Tsaritsa's rooms and bid her good night, kissing her hand gently. She had slipped into her room where Anna had a merry fire burning, her nightclothes spread before the flames to warm up. Having someone see her naked still felt strange to Laura, and she still was hesitant to take off her chemise before her servant. Anna said nothing but brought her the warm night dress and slipped it over her head.

The pile of discarded clothes was gathered up and Anna bid her mistress a good night as she took her leave for the evening, slipping down the steps to the laundry room in the cellar before climbing the steps again to crawl tiredly into bed. Laura listened to the sounds of the castle as it settled to sleep; the closing doors, the muffled goodnights and the heavy silence that descended. She breathed deeply, eyeing the door to the Tsaritsa's bed chamber then turned and opened her landing door, slipping across the corridor.

She tapped quietly on the door then pushed it open, slipping into Aleksei's rooms. He stepped out of his dressing room, stripped to his waist, Mikhail shadowing him. Laura clasped her hands in front of her, bowing her head a little.

'The rooms still smell musty' she said softly, embarrassed, then rushed on: 'I want to be with you.'

Aleksei dismissed Mikhail and he slipped past them, closing the door to the landing behind him as he left. Laura raised her eyes shyly to look at her husband.

'Forgive me' she said, upset. 'I want to be a good wife, but I want to go to bed with you each night' she stopped, biting her lip to calm herself. 'I didn't know what to expect' she finally blurted out, despairing.

'Forgive me, I am at fault' he said gently. 'I should have explained this more.'

'Do you despise my body?'

'No' he interrupted, coming closer and taking her hand. 'I do not.'

Laura reached up and pulled undone the ties at her throat, letting her nightgown slide to the floor. Aleksei's cheeks darkened with desire and he slid his arms around her, planting a kiss on her forehead.

'Come then my bold little flower' he whispered, leading her back towards his bed.

Laura followed willingly and lay down beneath him when he guided her back onto his pillows. His warm hands stroked her curves and woke in her a trembling feeling that anxiety had smothered in her the night before. She wondered if all wives felt like this, if every woman covered a small smile of satisfaction knowing the mysteries of the marriage bed. She gasped when Aleksei's fingers brushed her, seeking entrance to her.

There was an awkwardness to their love making, as Aleksei found it difficult to express his emotions to her, and she was inexperienced and unsure of what to do. They made love in silence, Aleksei's experienced hands rousing pleasure in their secret unions, his gentleness and patience rewarded with her loud gasp and the shuddering release of desire.

They lay together quietly, Laura listening to the thud of his heart and the roaring of his breath in his chest. Emotions swam in her, dizzying her. She was the property of this man, for him to choose when and if to make love to her. He could have easily sent her back to her own rooms tonight at his whim. A small, wild part of her loathed being someone's property, yet she could not deny her attraction to Aleksei. She wondered if this is what love felt like; the desire to be with another, to wish to make him happy.

'Aleksei?' she whispered, stirring against him.

He mumbled sleepily, tightening his arm momentarily.

'I love you Aleksei' she whispered, shutting her eyes.

29

When Laura woke Aleksei was already up, Mikhail helping him into his starched white shirt. Aleksei smiled when he saw her stir and called out a good morning to her.

'My cousins leave today, see to it that you dress for their farewell' he said, slipping down to breakfast.

Laura wasn't exactly sure what their farewell entailed, and was glad to see Anna, who let herself in after a quiet knock, with warm clothes for her mistress. Mikhail bid them a soft farewell and excused himself, closing the doors behind him.

'Which cousins are leaving?' Laura mused out loud as she slipped out of bed, sitting naked on the edge so Anna could brush her hair.

'Count Norwid and his horrid daughters' Anna promptly answered. 'Begging your pardon Your Highness but there was more friendliness in an arctic fox.'

Laura tried hard not to giggle. Anna's gossip continued as she worked, telling Laura how many bottles of wine had been consumed by Aleksei's boyhood friends over the last few days. Laura was shocked, she had heard tales of excess, but never had had the facts presented to her before. Anna stopped brushing her hair and grabbed a pair of bloomers and a short chemise that she gave to Laura.

She pulled them on and stood, letting Anna lace her into the corset and fasten a petticoat round her waist. Mindful that she had kept the court waiting yesterday Laura finished dressing quickly and slipped down to the dining hall, taking her place between Aleksei and Tsar Constantinovich.

She saw the hall was not as full as it had been the day before, and wondered who was not there, and why. No one had left from the wedding party, she still could see all the familiar strangers' faces in the room. She realised she could not see the Ivanovs, and as she looked more carefully, her father was not there either.

'Where is my father?' she asked.

'He is packing and sends his apologies' Aleksei answered, biting into a slice of bread.

'Excuse me' Laura said, leaping to her feet and running upstairs to Luke's room.

She did not wait for decorum and pushed open his door, finding him standing at the foot of his bed near an open trunk, folding items carefully into it. He eyed her sadly but did not say anything. Laura closed the door behind her, trying to stop that hollow whirling inside her. They had not spoken much since the Putting To Bed Ceremony, they were deeply embarrassed at the performance and had lost the ease that had been growing steadily between them.

'Were you to leave without saying goodbye?' she asked quietly.

'No Laura' he soothed, then looked away. 'How do I say goodbye? I feel I have said it to you twice now.' He wiped his mouth and dumped a shirt into his trunk. 'I shall miss you.'

'And I you father, but I will write every day.'

'I know' he smiled sadly.

Laura shut her eyes, knowing that the letters she had written to him had done nothing to build their relationship over those missing years. At first they had been filled with the tears of an angry and homesick young girl who blamed her father for sending her to a horrid school, but over the years they had cooled in tone.

She bit the inside of her lip, holding back the tears. Luke finished packing and pulled on his coat, buttoning it to his throat. Laura hugged him fiercely, then fled out of the room to fetch her coat and handkerchief. Luke had already gone from his rooms so she hastened down the stairs and out into the cold morning.

Several grand carriages were parked at the foot of the castle stairs, Olaf and livery men swarming over them as they loaded trunks and passengers while Aleksei and Tsar Constantinovich stood on the steps and exchanged farewells with their leaving relatives. The Norwid family and their entourage climbed into the carriages, waving farewell as they departed, calling goodbye in Polish and ignoring Aleksei's common bride.

Aleksei and Laura then climbed into the remaining carriage with Luke, and Olaf drove them down to the station. The short drive was in silence, Luke and Laura too miserable to say anything and Aleksei too uncomfortable to. Olaf leapt down and opened the door, offering his hand to help down the occupants. Laura spied another handsome carriage and stopped in surprise, her hand still in Olaf's.

'Ekaterina and Grigory are here!' she blurted out. 'Are they leaving too?'

Olaf's face was blank and she remembered herself, letting go of his hand. The small party joined the Ivanovs on the station platform next to a hissing, gleaming engine. Laura hugged her teary friend, finding out from quick enquiries that Ekaterina was not leaving though Grigory was, to see to their affairs in the Mediterranean. A few of Aleksei's Slavic relatives were also on the platform, transferring from the train in Chelyabinsk to destinations in Russia, Romania and the Balkans.

Olaf loaded Luke's luggage into the train then gave the small Ivanov groom a hand as he was struggling with the larger of Grigory's cases. Grigory and Ekaterina bid each other a teary goodbye then he and Luke climbed onto the train. Laura fought the urge to climb onto the train after them, raising her damp handkerchief to wave them goodbye, feeling Ekaterina's arm link through hers.

The train whistle blew, making them jump, then the carriages clunked and jostled as the engine slowly rolled out of Vsevolod's Gate. Laura bit her lip to stop herself from sobbing and pressed her handkerchief to her face to catch the tears. Olaf and Aleksei waited patiently for Laura and Ekaterina to finish watching the train disappear then the Prince climbed back into his carriage.

'Countess, soothe her sore heart as best you can, I have pressing matters in the Advisory Council' he said, knocking on the roof for Olaf to take him back to the castle.

Laura couldn't help but feel part of him was pleased not to have to deal with the awkwardness of a weeping woman. She had married a man of many contrasts it seemed. Ekaterina comforted her young friend as best as she could as they watched the carriage pull away from the station but knew Aleksei had condemned his American Sweetheart to a lonely life of malicious scorn from his noble and entitled family. She did not voice her opinion and squeezed her friend's arm again.

Laura gazed after the carriage sadly, knowing she had married a man in charge of a principality, knowing his work would take him from her side for most of her days, but wished, just for a second, that he would put aside signing documents and reading treaties – or whatever else he did locked in that room with his advisors – to spend some time with her, if only for the morning, or an afternoon. She sniffed and dabbed her eyes again.

Ekaterina called out to her young groom, telling him to take the carriage back to Ladozhskoye as she was to spend the day in Dalnerechensk with the Princess. The boy bobbed a bow and scrambled up onto the seat, flicking the reins gently.

'Come my dear, a walk by the river will do us good' Ekaterina said, leading Laura out Vsevolod's Gate.

The train had already reached Tcherepnin, it was hidden inside the village by the buildings though they could see it passing through by the wandering smoke that snaked its way above the roofs. Ekaterina diplomatically turned Laura away from the fortified village, leading her to the pretty stone bridge that crossed the river. Peasants called out and waved to them as they passed and Laura and Ekaterina were both gracious despite their misery.

They walked on in silence for a while till Laura asked:

'Do you not fear for your safety?'

'In Dalnerechensk?' Ekaterina asked, stopping to look at her friend. 'Never. The people are honest and simple; they respect each other, not just the nobility. They bear you no grudge, they will not try to hurt you' she laughed.

Laura managed a smile and squeezed her friends arm, grateful for her company.

'Tsar Constantinovich tells me you're bored with his library already' Ekaterina teased. Laura blushed. 'He tells me you read very well too.'

'If I do it's credit to you' Laura said, smiling.

'Of course' Ekaterina said with mock vanity, making Laura laugh.

They walked on in a more amiable silence, enjoying the company of each other and greeting the peasants that called out to them.

*

The blonde man stood on the rug before the Advisory Council again, one leg casually bent, work calloused hands hanging by his sides in an air of confidence. His news had not been good, but he didn't cower, watching the Prince for his reaction, aware of the looks on the faces on the other members of the council.

'Am I to even be denied my honeymoon?' Aleksei snapped.

'His children and his wife were threatened' the man answered. 'The only reason why there wasn't a riot was because he gave them all his bread then closed his shop and barricaded himself inside. His storerooms were ransacked; he has nothing left to sell let alone bake.'

'Why was the theft not reported?' Maksim asked.

'No one blames a man for stealing food to feed his starving family' the man said. 'Especially if the young or old are sick.'

Aleksei ran his hands over his face wishing there was something he could do.

'Send what food is left from the wedding feast out for the people' he said finally.

'That won't solve anything -' Maksim started.

'I know!' Aleksei exploded, rounding on his ministers. 'But it might stop them dying tonight.'

An uncomfortable silence fell in the chambers. Aleksei dismissed the man and waited till the door was shut behind him.

'Gentlemen we must do something about the pension' he sighed.

30

Laura paused, startled by the sound in the other chair. She looked up from the Cyrillic script in the book she had been reading aloud to Tsar Constantinovich and glanced across at the old man. She smiled gently; he had fallen asleep before the warm fire, his hands folded on his stomach, drifting off while she had read aloud to him. Her smile faded when she realised that she had read uninterrupted for the last thirty minutes not because her pronunciation was better but because the Tsar had been asleep.

She sighed, dropping her eyes to the page and stroking the paper gently. Her head swam from the strange syllables that had poured off her tongue. She could read well, recognising the sounds the Cyrillic symbols represented but she barely knew any of the words she read. The ones she did recognise were too few and far between to get any real sense of what she was talking about. She closed the book, knowing there was no sense in her putting in the gold ribbon to mark her place as she would have to read some of it again when the Tsar woke up.

She settled back in the chair, casting her eyes to the merry fire they sat beside. This was not how she envisioned her life as a princess, waiting for an old man to wake up again so she could finish her story. She felt like a nursemaid, or a servant, and sighed unhappily. Aleksei had dismissed the court early last night, but instead of retiring with her to his rooms he had excused himself and disappeared into the Council Chambers, leaving Laura to climb the stairs alone.

She had gone straight into his rooms and changed into her nightdress, but had fallen asleep in his bed waiting for him to return. He had not roused her when he had finally come to bed and they had not made love. He had planted a kiss on her forehead in the morning, and greeted her tenderly, but had disappeared back into the Council Chambers after breakfast.

Laura knew Ekaterina had returned to Ladozhskoye, but was surprised to find more empty seats at the table in the dining hall. The youths that had kept the meals boisterous with their talk and banter were missing, and Laura suspected they had only come to the castle for the wedding festivities and inane social gossip. The thought made her glad that the viper Tatiana might too soon depart, but also made her sad that all those in her age group whom she could have turned to for friendship were slipping quietly away, as unwilling to be her friend as the girls in Lady Ramkinson's school.

Deciding she was not going to play sick-nurse, even as fond of the old Tsar as she was, she stood and placed the book on her chair and slipped quietly out of the room, descending the stone steps to the main hall. She didn't know where or how, but by the time she had reached the stables Fedor had joined her, following her surreptitiously. Laura looked, feeling as if she should explain herself.

'I thought perhaps to ride in the forest' she said, wondering why she felt like a naughty child.

'I will join you' he answered.

It was not a request. Laura wanted to be alone, but realised it would be silly for her to ride off alone into a forest she didn't know. Besides, Fedor was an expert at fooling people into thinking he wasn't there. It was all the solitude she was allowed. Laura thanked him then called Olaf for their horses. He brought her stallion over and boosted her onto its back, noticing she wasn't wearing her riding habit. He didn't say anything and Fedor quickly mounted too.

Laura clicked her tongue and led him down Castle Street, listening to the sound of the horses' hooves as they crossed under King's Gate. Laura then turned her stallion towards Hunter's Pass. She liked the cold smell of the forest as it closed in around her and she breathed deeply, watching as her breath puffed out around her.

A movement through the trees caught her eye and she turned to see a magnificent stag standing close to the road, chewing bark as he watched them, seemingly unafraid. Laura watched back, wondering how old it was as its antlers were large and spread like the branches of a gnarled tree.

'Fedor?' she called back to him. He rode up beside her, waiting for her question. 'Do the court still hunt in these forests?'

'No Your Highness' he replied, eyeing the deer whose ear had flicked when she had spoken but not run away.

'Does the court ride at all?'

'Very rarely Your Highness' he answered.

The court is too old to ride a small part of her said. *And there are no youth here to go hunting in their place* a deeper, darker part of her said.

They rode on in silence, Laura listening to the sounds of the forest, wondering if she would see any more deer. It was easy to forget Fedor's presence, he dropped back enough to leave her with a sense of privacy, but not so far back he wouldn't hear her if she called out to him again. Laura smiled softly, it was no wonder Tsar Constantinovich liked his company.

As the day waned the forest began to grow gloomy around them, which suited Laura's mood. She could see the lights of the small hamlet of Kalach wink in the distance ahead. She shivered in the deepening chill of the night and behind her Fedor called out that they should return to the castle. She was unwilling to do so but agreed, as she knew the court would be sitting down to dinner soon.

They rode quickly back to the castle and dismounted in the stables. Laura ran up to the queen's rooms quickly to freshen up with rose water and change her dress before slipping back down to the dining hall. Those that remained of the court and Advisory Council were already seated though Aleksei's chair was empty. Laura masked her surprise and took her place at the table.

'Forgive me gentlemen, I was so enchanted with the forests that time quite got away from me.'

There was a murmur of agreement, annoyance and reluctant amiability. Laura noticed Tsar Constantinovich was also not present and several glasses by ministers' elbows had dregs of wine in them. She wondered just how long they had been waiting. Anna stepped forward to pour Laura a glass of wine, whispering to her:

'They are waiting for you to call for the meal to begin.'

'Thank you Anna' Laura said then raised her glass to the table. 'To your health gentlemen.'

There was another murmur and some fumbling for wine glasses. Several looked flushed with the effects of the wine already. She wondered if the old Tsar was still sleeping in the armchair in his library, and if Aleksei was still in the Council Chambers.

'Where is my husband?' she asked.

At once Tatiana's fan came out and fluttered to hide her vicious slander to Natasha, who grabbed her fan to hide her spiteful laugh. The ministers didn't look surprised at Aleksei's absence and Lev Dostoevski quickly informed her that Aleksei did sometimes take his evening meal in the Council Chambers to better understand the affairs of Dalnerechensk.

'What luck that I've married a man with such care and dedication to his subjects!' she smiled warmly, pleased, and thanked God they couldn't see that sinking feeling in her.

Instead she called for the first course and kept up a light banter with those sitting closest to her, and then for musicians when the meal was finished, trying to keep up a gaiety she didn't feel.

31

Ekaterina knocked on the door to the queen's rooms, letting herself inside. Laura looked up from her embroidery, very pleased of the distraction.

'Good morning Your Highness' she grinned, flopping down onto the couch beside her. 'If you can bear the thought of tearing yourself away from this solitude I should like very much of your company in Ladozhskoye today.'

'Of course!' Laura laughed, dropping her work on the seat beside her. 'I have been lonely.'

'I know, but you have also been very naughty' Ekaterina chided. 'You have neglected your lessons!'

Laura laughed and stood, fetching a pair of gloves and a hat from her dressing room, pulling on her thick winter coat. Ekaterina waited till she had finished dressing before standing and hooking her arm through Laura's, leading her down to the stables, pointing out items that caught her eye and saying the Russian name, which Laura dutifully copied. Olaf, sweaty and dirty from raking the hay in the stalls, nodded a curt greeting to the ladies when they arrived. Ekaterina ordered her horse and Laura's stallion to be saddled and continued with her lesson while he worked.

'Seno' she said, pointing to the hay. 'Sedlo' she pointed to the saddle, and Laura copied her dutifully.

'Khui' she pointed beneath Laura's saddled stallion.

Olaf burst out laughing and Laura looked up in surprise, her cheeks darkening when she realised the word was probably crass and anatomical. Olaf gave the reins of a pretty mare to Ekaterina and said something fondly that Laura didn't quite understand. She eyed Olaf carefully, noticing how transformed he was when he smiled. Ekaterina's eyes flashed wickedly.

'Zherebets' she said, pointing at Olaf, making him laugh again.

Laura's flush deepened, knowing that was the word for stallion, and dropped her eyes in embarrassment. Ekaterina laughed, boosting herself up on her horse. Olaf came forward, still chuckling to himself and held the reins, offering Laura a steady hand while she climbed up.

'Farewell Olaf!' Ekaterina called teasingly over her shoulder. 'You may tell His Royal Highness that if he has tired of his bride already I will take her as my own, and I shall be very reluctant to give her up!'

Laura laughed and clicked her tongue, guiding her stallion after Ekaterina's mare. The guards at the gate to Castle Street saluted their Highness as she left the grounds and she smiled and waved to them. Ekaterina rode beside her friend, and Dalnerechensk called out blessings to the prettiest girls in the Principality, waving as they passed.

Laura smiled, and waved at the peasants in the fields between Dalnerechensk and Ladozhskoye, nodding at the old men sitting outside the village tavern on a bench seat. They watched them quietly but then took the pipes out of their mouths and raised it to them in greeting. Ekaterina giggled and led the way to her stately home, greeting the guard on duty at the gate.

He opened it and bowed his head respectfully as they passed, shutting the gate behind them. Ekaterina dismounted and gave the reins to her young stable groom, waiting for Laura to slip to the ground and follow her hostess into the magnificent home.

'Come Laura, you are still expected to converse in Russian, and perhaps Polish as well' she said, pulling off her gloves. 'Aleksei's cousins will not think to insult you to your face again should you speak enough to tell them where they could shove their fans.'

She opened the door to her beautiful sitting room and ushered the Princess in.

'You will come to me for lessons every day, I should be glad of your company' Ekaterina said as she closed the door behind them.

Anya entered and Ekaterina ordered a pot of tea and a light brunch for them. Anya left and was quickly back with refreshments, setting them on the small table between the two couches. Ekaterina poured tea for Laura then handed her a book of poems.

Laura dutifully took the book and began to read out loud. Ekaterina listened carefully, interrupting occasionally to correct her pronunciation.

'What good does this do?' Laura suddenly asked. 'I read well, yes, but the sounds are nearly meaningless, I recognise words here and there but I do not understand what I am reading!'

'Have patience my dear' Ekaterina soothed, putting down her tea cup and taking her hand affectionately. 'It is frustrating to learn any language I know, but perseverance is a virtue.'

Laura shut her eyes, trying not to feel despondent.

'There's so much I don't know!' she wailed.

Ekaterina squeezed her hand in sympathy then her dark eyes flashed.

'Come, I have an idea.'

At once she leapt up, pulling Laura to her feet and dragging her after her, letting her go in her lavish bed chamber to retrieve a book laid neatly on the bed covers.

'We must simply read this, Aristophanes' *Wasps*. It is a play, we can take turns reading, *Annnd...*' she stressed, turning around and seizing the large puff that sat on a jar of powder, whumping it down on her head so the powder puffed out, turning her dark locks grey. 'We can dress up!'

Laura laughed, she was familiar with the play and Ekaterina looked ridiculous.

'You don't look much like a fat old man' she giggled, covering her mouth with her hand.

'You're right!' Ekaterina exclaimed, and disappeared into a small room Laura guessed to be her dressing room, re-emerging in Grigory's pants and a white shirt, comically throwing up her hands. Laura laughed hysterically, holding onto her corsets to save from splitting them. Ekaterina grabbed a pillow and pushed it under the shirt, swaning around with a portly pouch like a gouty old man.

Laura doubled over in hysterics.

'Come come Xanthias, do not keep an old man waiting!' she croaked, patting her new portliness.

Within half an hour Laura was stripped to her corset and bloomers, hair piled with powder and a fire poker as a sword, brandishing it on Ekaterina's bed and crying for the vote, her sides sore from laughing, her cheeks wet with tears.

There was an official rap on the door and it was pushed open by Fedor. He took one look at the sight within and stopped in amazement, his jaw falling open. Laura fell to her knees, snatching up the bedclothes to hide her undergarments from him.

'You are interrupting my lesson!' Ekaterina croaked and slammed the door.

Laura screamed with laughter, burying her mirth in the bedclothes while Ekaterina flopped beside her on the bed, holding her portly pillow. They were uncontrollable for a few moments until Laura finally stretched back beside her friend, sighing contentedly. Fedor knocked timidly on the door.

'Your Highness?' he called.

Laura sighed. 'I expect he is calling me as they cannot eat unless I tell them to' she grinned, then the smile faded. 'Help me dress and brush out this powder.'

Ekaterina smiled and fetched her own hair brush, dutifully brushing it out and then fetched several items of Laura's attire scattered round her room. Once she was more presentable she opened the door and tried to look regal. Ekaterina grabbed her skirt like an avaricious old man, claiming she was the best she'd ever had.

Laura's composure failed and she laughed, running down the stairs, claiming that Ekaterina would be the rack and ruin of any reputation she had left. Fedor followed at a discreet distance and Laura didn't look back for fear of what she might see on his usually blank face.

The small stable groom handed Laura the reins of her stallion and Fedor helped her up into the saddle, mounting lithely onto his own mare. Laura snuck a quick look at him as he did so, relieved to see his face still characteristically blank of opinion and thought. She smiled gently and turned her mount towards Dalnerechensk, letting Fedor trail behind her.

Fedor was glad for the dark and that Laura didn't look back so she would never know of the ghost smile he wore for the ride home.

32

Life settled into a comfortable pattern for Laura. Every morning after breakfast she travelled to Ladozhskoye for Russian lessons with Ekaterina and took lunch with her on the balcony overlooking the valley and the sun-lit, hilltop castle. In the afternoons she walked with the old Tsar and talked with him in the snow-covered garden, or sat embroidering in her rooms while Anna gossiped unashamedly.

Laura was glad to have seen the last of the wedding guests leave, but had been disappointed with how few of the court remained behind. Their numbers had dwindled to a handful, till it was almost ludicrous to sit around the long tables in the dining hall for their meals. Aleksei bid her a good day every morning and disappeared into the Council Chambers with his advisors, emerging at sunset looking drained and withdrawn, their conversations turning from treaties and law to hunting and other idle pleasures more fitting for their gentler company.

Laura busied herself with a myriad of distractions, none of which could make her forget Aleksei was spending more and more time locked away in his Council Chambers. He began to call for the midday meal to be delivered to the chambers and Laura virtually dined alone in the great hall, ignoring the whispers of the servants that seemed so much louder in the echoes.

As the days turned into weeks Aleksei called more frequently for the meals in the council rooms and Laura began to notice the sad, pinched look in his eyes when he emerged at sunset. Though he would smile at her, his eyes lighting up in warm pleasure, she could see he was distracted by something weighing heavily on his mind.

Concerned she had asked him what troubled him, and he had smiled sadly, saying simply they were just matters of state, and did not elabourate. And so she spent her days in idleness, while Aleksei disappeared every day, emerging every night drained and troubled. Laura tried her best to liven the despondent moods Aleksei fell into; telling witty jokes, singing sweetly or dancing for him till he smiled again, and when the court was dismissed for the evening he would take her by the hand to his bedchamber and stroke her body gently till she could weep for desire before making love to her.

But as the winter weeks drew on it grew harder and harder to lift his spirits. Even Tsar Constantinovich noticed and his old face was lined deeply with sorrow and pain. When Aleksei called more frequently for his evening meals to be sent to him where he sat alone in the Council Chambers a gloom began to descend on the court. The infrequent evenings when he did eat with his bride in the great hall were marred by Aleksei's steady drinking, the wine and exhaustion making his temper and composure brittle.

Even his affections had changed, he would emerge from the chambers and climb exhaustedly to his bed chamber, mounting Laura quickly, not bothering with intimacy and then roll off to sleep, or if the hour had grown so late and his eyes so heavy he would manage no more than a kiss on her forehead before collapsing exhausted beside her. One night he failed to come to bed at all and Laura had cried herself to sleep alone in the Tsaritsa's bed the next night, waiting for him to send for her. It was the first night she had slept there and her confusion and hurt had cut her deeply.

Constant exhaustion and wine frayed the Prince, making him irritable and argumentative. He grew tired of his advisors and after a particularly unproductive and heated argument he dismissed them all, locking himself away in an office alone, pouring over treaties and old documents, muttering to himself. Dark rumours began to circulate in the Principality, whispers the Prince had become disillusioned by the floundering economy, with his young, inexperienced wife. And there were darker rumours, ones conveyed with winks and nods and whispers, alluded to but never spoken out loud. *It's happening again.*

Left to her own devices for most of the time Laura's quick mind turned to mischief. The cold winds blowing from Siberia were keeping the castle's inhabitants inside, tucked up with warm wine and cherry fires. Too listless to join the Tsar in his library, and far too listless for the studies Ekaterina set for her, Laura had decided to explore every nook and cranny of the castle she was mistress of.

She decided to start at the bottom and headed down the steps she had seen servants take from the dining hall, startling the servants in the kitchen, who whipped their hands behind their backs and dropped respectful curtseys, bowing their cloth-covered heads. Laura's eyes breezed over them as she called a cordial greeting, looking around the room.

It was incredibly hot down here near the furnaces and several blackened pots hung from a spit over the enormous fire. Beside the fire was a large pile of wood for keeping the fires stoked. A faint sheen came up on her brow from the stuffy heat and she fought the urge to wipe at her forehead with her hands. She knew there was a cellar here, beyond the heat of the castle kitchens, as they had managed to keep a bouquet of summer flowers fresh till her wedding day.

She spied in the dark recess in the kitchen a staircase that led down and she headed for it, relieved to be away from that airless stifle. At the top of the stairs the air smelt cool and musty and Laura put her hand on the wall as she descended, not wanting to tumble down the stone steps worn smooth with many pairs of feet. The steps seemed to descend into the centre of the earth, and the room beneath the castle was cold. It had a fine layer of snowy grit on the floor, and a largish hump where snow was falling through a grate in the ceiling.

Large barrels of wine and beer lined the walls of the room and in the centre stood large racks holding hundreds of wine and spirit bottles. A few were very dusty and old looking. She reached out and selected a bottle, turning the label up so she could peer at the strange writing. It was hand written and difficult to make the Cyrillic script out.

'Can I help Your Highness?' asked a nervous kitchen girl, perched on the bottom stair to the cellar. 'I can send the wine to your room.'

'I have no need for wine at this hour' she said, dropping the wine back into the rack, wiping her finger through the dust that had collected on several more bottles.

The girls stepped nervously off the stair, throwing a glance over her shoulder back up to the kitchen, and Laura could imagine the curious members of the staff who were peering down, wondering what was going on. Laura wondered if this cellar used to be a dungeon when it was first dug. It was deep enough, and might be the cause of the servant's anxiety.

'Are you looking for a particular wine?' the nervous girl tried as Laura pulled another bottle from the rack, and couldn't stop herself glancing backwards.

'What does this label say?' Laura asked, showing her the strange script.

The girl bobbed a curtsey. 'I can't read Your Highness' she answered. 'But that is a chardonnay, I know the picture.'

'Why can you not read?' Laura asked, surprised. 'Do you not go to school?'

'My family needs the money I earn' the girl said simply.

Laura placed the wine back on the rack, astounded by the girl's frankness. She walked once more round the racks of wine, surreptitiously looking for any more hidden rooms or passages leading out but realised there were none, and headed back to the kitchens above. Her emergence from the cellar caused another ripple of staff fastening their hands behind their backs and a wave of bowing respectful heads.

'Send the chardonnay up with the evening's meal' she said to the room, before sweeping out and closing the door behind her.

Laura blew her cheeks out in the small corridor off the main entrance hall of the castle, steadying herself. Her first encounters in her exploration had been disastrously embarrassing, but her resolve had not crumbled. She quickly passed a hand over her face and hair to make sure she was still presentable then continued on her search of the castle, bypassing the doors to the rooms she knew and turning the handles to the rooms she didn't.

Many times she was disappointed by the rooms behind the doors, which were either barren or were draped with white dust cloths. She made her way aimlessly along the second floor, startling maids making beds and dusting rooms vacated by the wedding guests. She wondered if the castle was going to turn into a pretty prison for her, and her mind turned to ways to escape it.

She soon began to realise as she made her way along the second floor corridor that admiration and servants weren't everything. Since she had first stepped foot in Lady Ramkinson's school Laura had secretly desired the admiration and awe that had followed the nobility around. She had not realised how meaningless it was without the love and affection of those who knew and loved her the best.

She climbed the stairs to the third floor, knowing she was running out of places to look for secrets, treasures and wonder. She glided past the doors to Tsar Constantinovich's private rooms, past the rooms Luke had kept, wandering into the recesses of the third floor.

She had never been this way before, and after having thought she had seen everything on the top floor she was delighted to see three more doors presented to her. She reached out and grasped the handle of one door. There was an almighty crash behind her. She jumped and whirled around, her heart leaping into her mouth and pounding hard against her throat. The head of staff was standing behind her, a horrified look on her face, a dropped tray dusted with broken pieces of crockery at her feet.

'You cannot go in that room!' she gasped.

'I am *Velikaja Knjaginja* Laura Aleksa Stephanovna Vakhtangova' she snapped, trying to recover from her start and relishing the power the name had, the feminine version of Aleksei's and daughter by marriage to Tsar Constantinovich. 'I will go where I want.'

The old lady fell on her knees then, tearing at her hair and wailing.

'You must not Your Highness, I beg of you!' she cried, distressed. 'For the love of God do not!'

Laura eyed the door, feeling unease wash over her. She demanded to know what was hidden behind the door but the old woman wailed louder, almost incoherent. Bewildered now Laura took a step away from the door, promising reluctantly she wouldn't go into the room. The woman that ran the staff in the Vakhtangov household sniffled loudly, pulling out a large white handkerchief and dabbed her eyes with it, blowing her nose noisily.

Somewhat appeased she collected the broken pieces of crockery together and stacked them on the tray before heaving herself awkwardly to her feet. She dusted off her knees with wide swipes of the handkerchief, and wiped her face again, before picking up the tray.

'Your Highness, it is not a room you can enter, it will bring a grave misfortune' she said, more tears running down onto her cheeks. 'You must swear not to enter there.'

Laura relented, feeling alarmed and curious, but sent the distressed woman down to the kitchen for something strong to steady her nerves. She then reluctantly headed away from the mysterious rooms, shooting a wistful look over her shoulder. She desperately wanted to know what was hidden in the rooms but knew she had no friends in Dalnerechensk save for the Tsar and Ekaterina. She did not want to find herself even more isolated by offending the Vakhtangov household.

She reached her rooms and closed the doors behind her to hide away from the eyes and ears of the castle, flopping backwards onto her chaise. She could see the grandfather clock from where she lay and sighed miserably to think it was not even three o'clock yet.

*

Laura sat beside her husband's empty chair, dressed in her prettiest lace and the beautiful sapphires Aleksei had given to her. She had hoped that her lace and jewels would distract Aleksei from whatever it was that made him look pinched and tired. She had waited, not calling for the meal though she had accepted the chardonnay that the serving girls brought up to the dining hall. Now five empty bottles of the chardonnay lay scattered on the table and the grumbling from hungry ministers had gotten louder.

Tsar Constantinovich leaned over to Laura, noticing the sadness in the young Princess' face, whispering that she should call for the food. She agreed and announced the court could eat, though she herself could barely manage anything in her disappointment. The Tsar watched her, concerned, though she masked it well behind pleasant conversation. There were only a handful of the court left taking tea at the castle and as Ekaterina had retired early to Ladozhskoye complaining of a headache Laura directed most of her conversation at the Tsar.

After dinner there was dancing, but the mood was forced and miserable and the musicians were the most jovial in the room. Laura called an end to the evening only half an hour later, feeling completely alone as she climbed the stairs to the second floor. She paused, undecided between heading into her rooms or into Aleksei's bedchamber. Her hand fluttered to her throat where the jewels lay, terribly torn.

She heard a soft sound behind her and knew Tsar Constantinovich was making his way up the stairs labouriously. Unwilling to see the pain in his eyes for his stiff lower back or the pain for her solitary nights Laura quickly opened the door to her apartment and slipped inside. Anna looked round from where she was stoking the fire.
'Good evening Your Highness' she said, sliding the poker back into the stand by the fire then dusted her hands on her apron.

Laura sat down at the dressing table and unfastened the string of jewels from round her throat, feeling Anna unpin her hair and brush it out gently. She was getting used to someone else being with her when she dressed and undressed. Sitting at the dressing table feeling her hair being brushed reminded Laura of when she was a little girl and Emily had brushed her hair, often humming while she worked out the knots. She shut her eyes, sighing softly.

Anna put the brush on the dresser and Laura stood, letting her undo the buttons on the lace dress and untie the silk petticoats. Laura pulled on her fire-warmed nightdress then stood indecisively on the rug before the fire, eyeing the Tsaritsa's bed chamber. She wondered if Aleksei would come to her rooms, wondered if a king ever slept in queen's rooms. She wondered if he would knock and beckon her across to his chambers, if he would send Mikhail for her.

Anna slipped into the bedroom and turned down the sheets, slipping out and bidding her good night as she closed the door behind her. Laura's musing turned darker now she was not in danger of being observed. She wondered if he *did* come, red eyed and exhausted, would he mount her quickly, his passion spent in minutes, and fall into a deep, restless sleep beside her; or would he only plant the soft kiss on her forehead before slipping under the covers and shutting his eyes, letting sleep have him instead?

She shut her eyes tightly, pressing the heels of her hands against them. She despaired that her husband would never take his time with her again. Only a few short weeks ago every instant with him had broken desire over her, she did not want to think those moments would only be fleeting memories. She did not want to have been woken to such passionate desires only to have her husband forget them so soon, and banish her to a life of spinsterhood in her marriage bed.

She pressed her lips together, forcing back the tears for what she had lost. She wiped her hands over her face firmly, pushing away the pain, then decided to bring her husband to her bed herself. Having made up her mind she threw a gown around her shoulders and took a lamp, letting herself out of her rooms and padded down the stairs to the first floor.

The castle was quiet, her footsteps silent on the stone steps. She glanced quickly around on the landing to the first floor, hoping no one would catch her wandering the halls of the castle in her night shirt. The corridors were empty and silent and Laura folded her gown tighter around her, glancing back over her shoulder as she made her way along the dark corridor.

The doors to the Advisory Council stood open and it was empty and dark. Laura padded past it quietly, stopping by a door labeled "Study of State". It was closed over, almost fully shut and she reached out timidly, pushing it open. It creaked faintly, but the sumptuous study behind it was dark and empty. Laura turned and continued down the corridor, noticing a small glow from one of the rooms.

Aleksei was seated at a desk in Grigory's office, his jacket open and his hair tousled, his eyes red rimmed and raw. The glow came from a dying fire and the room was growing cold, though Aleksei did not seem to notice. He was surrounded by piles of books and paper; some thick parchment sheets, some thin letters, all of them piled up in stacks on the desk, on the bookcase, even on the floor. Aleksei sat amongst them, consulting one document after another.

As she watched him from the darkened hallway he suddenly snatched up a piece of parchment and furiously began flicking through a stack by his elbow, muttering furiously, a manic expression of determination on his face. He seized a sheet and leapt to his feet, scanning it, his breath snorting through his nose in excitement. There was a terrible moment when his face sagged, unbearable agony flooding from his eyes down his features and he slumped, collapsing back into his seat.

He hung his head, tired and beaten, letting the parchment slip from his fingers, almost uncaring where it landed. Laura's heart went out to him. She didn't know what it was that kept him from her side and her marriage bed, what troubles the Principality faced, but knew as she watched him rest his elbows on the desk and cradle his weary head in his hands that Aleksei was doing all he could to meet them. His agony moved her and she sniffed, buffing at her tears quickly.

The movement caught his eye and he looked up in surprise at the sound of her tears, suddenly aware just how late it was. She smiled at him despite her misery, slipping into the office with him, setting the lamp down on the desk.

'Why are you crying?' Aleksei asked, trying not to feel unkind.

'Because of you' she smiled gently. 'I miss you Aleksei, and yet as I have watched you now, your agony has moved me. I know you care for them. You exhaust yourself my love.' She laid her hand tenderly on his cheek.

'They don't understand' Aleksei said hopelessly. 'They don't realise what I'm trying to do for them.'

Laura slipped behind him and reached out, stroking his shoulders, massaging out the tension she felt there. Aleksei groaned and again when he felt her lips graze the top of his head. She rested her cheek on the spot she had just kissed and breathed in deep the scent of his hair, still easing the tension she felt in his shoulders.

'Tell me what ails you' she said softly.

'It's politics' he shrugged, sighing. 'It's nothing to trouble a woman's brain.'

'I could help ease your mind' she said, rubbing his back. 'One man cannot carry the weight of the world on his shoulders.'

Aleksei turned to smile at her.

'Ah Laura, your innocence is a God-send sometimes.' He stood and took her hand, raising the lamp from the desk. 'Let's to bed.'

33

The days wore on in the Principality. Laura grew tired of her lessons, tired of holding her own at court, tired of thinking of reasons and excuses for Aleksei's continued absence, aware of the whispers, the looks, the slander behind her back from the few who remained at court, the chidings for a prince who had married a child, not the woman he needed in his bed. Aleksei would send for her less and less, and she grew tired of waiting for him alone in his bed.

Rumours were circulating, and while Laura heard some whispered at the dining table Anna's ear for gossip and tongue for spreading it kept her informed of the latest piece of maliciousness. Laura would have given anything not to have to see the looks on the faces of the servants and the wives and daughters of the court today. She had dressed hurriedly in her riding habit after breakfast and slipped down to the stables.

She pulled on her gloves and hat as she left the castle, picking her way carefully over the snowy cobbles of the courtyard, keeping her balance and her poise. Inside Olaf was talking soothingly to the horses as he spread new hay on the floors of their warm stalls, unaware of the Princess' presence. Laura stopped to watch him, almost wistful of his simple life, where deception and decorum were not needed.

'Your Highness?' Fedor asked quietly.

Laura turned to eye him in surprise. She was so used to him following her silently on her many rides into the forest that she hardly noticed him at all anymore, and knew his sudden quiet voice would not be a good thing.

'I regret I cannot go riding with you today, I have an errand for His Royal Highness to run' he said quietly then bowed before her.

'Of course' she said unhappily, watching him turn and trot away.

She wondered darkly if Aleksei had called him away deliberately to prevent her from riding off into the forest, jealous of the time she spent with a livery man. She shook herself for her stupidity and gazed sadly after Fedor. She looked wistfully at the castle, reluctant to return, then turned back to the horses and the stable groom.

'Saddle two horses and ride with me today' she said suddenly, eyeing Olaf.

There was a tiny hesitant pause as Olaf stroked the coat of a rusty mare, dusting her down.

'I do not ride with the court' he said quietly, then turned to look at her.

'There is no court, only me' Laura pointed out.

'As you wish *Tsesarevna*' he answered, turning back to the horse.

Laura didn't know what to make of his words; his tone was not derogatory, and he had called her the *Tsesarevich's* wife, not by her title. She decided to be offended by his strange manner and swept pompously up into the saddle when he brought over the stallion, not even glancing backwards to see if he had finished saddling his mare before she commanded her stallion down Castle Street, letting it find its own way into the Hunter's Pass.

She heard the hooves of Olaf's mare approaching quickly, and slow to a walk while still behind her, keeping pace easily. She relented and smiled then, breathing deep, turning her horse off the wide cart track and into the seclusion of the forest.

Laura liked the serene solitude of the Tsar's forest. Once hunting in the evergreen hills had been the preferred pastime of the Dalnerechensk court and Royal hunting parties had sent the creatures of the forest fleeing in panic every day from the loud baying of hounds and thunderous rapports of gunfire. Many trophies from these numerous occasions were mounted in Tsar Constantinovich's private library, and one prize buck with antlers like an uprooted tree hung mounted in the dining hall.

But the old Tsar was too weak to ride now, content to sit in his chair with warm wine and relive his glory days through the pages of his leather bound books, and Aleksei kept the ageing court at arm's length while he locked himself away with his Advisory Council in the cloistered comfort of Council Chambers. The animals of the forest forgot the fear of the hunt and once again ventured out to chatter noisily to each other while scampering about their foraging for food.

Laura would hear them as she rode her grey stallion in the peaceful hills around Dalnerechensk, escorted only by Fedor. Out alone in the forest Laura felt free to be herself again and would often sing, especially when she forgot that Fedor followed her.

Now alone in the forests again Laura sighed contentedly, feeling the warm sun on her cheek. She was noticing the signs of spring around her, the snow was beginning to melt and trickle away in tiny dripping rivulets. Ahead of her she saw the sun had broken through the trees and beamed down in a line of glowing warmth. She guided her stallion into it and shut her eyes, turning her face up to the light.

A strange wave of dizziness passed over her and she felt off balance. She opened her eyes quickly and was surprised by a hard jolt on her backside. Her stallion stepped over her then stopped, waiting for his mistress. Laura felt uneasy to realise she was on the ground and checked herself quickly, wondering why she felt no pain. Olaf dismounted quickly and knelt beside her.

'*Tsesarevna*, are you hurt?' he asked, taking hold of her arms.

'No...' she said, confused, her voice trailing off.

'Are you *beremennaya*?' he asked bluntly.

Laura didn't know the word and blinked at him, not understanding. Olaf repeated it, pretending to clasp his hands under a swollen belly, then rocked his cradled arms to remove all doubt.

'No' she said, then blinked, looking at him. 'I'm pregnant?'

She struggled a little unsteadily to her feet. Olaf eyed her carefully then gripped her waist and sat her on his horse, whistling over the grey stallion and gathered his reins.

'We will return, the mare is better than a stallion to ride' he said, and began to walk, leading both horses.

Laura clung to the saddle till she realised that she was not going to faint again then relaxed a little, looking around her carefully.

'Come Olaf, I have taken your horse, you must ride mine' she said.

'You are kind *Tsesarevna*, but I will not' he answered.

Olaf didn't speak again and Laura stopped trying to make him, wondering what had brought on that sudden dizziness, wondering if she was pregnant. That would make Aleksei happy. He would love a son. *He would love seven sons* she smiled. *Seventy-seven sons.* Her hand fell to her stomach, rubbing it gently, asking herself if she was ready for motherhood.

Instead of feeling happy a great sadness fell over her. She was not even seventeen, and not ready to settle down. She had pictured herself at parties and adored by society, not riding a mare with the stable groom walking in front, alone while her husband locked himself away and the court whispered about them, and she became nothing more than the girl who had a child.

She doubted whether she would even see her son, the raising of an heir was too important a job to leave to an inexperienced girl. She had often overheard the girls in the finishing school talking about the nannies that had raised them, and the indifferent way they regarded their mothers. Laura felt her heart wrench inside her chest. She didn't want to face this awful burden of motherhood alone, to have her husband desert her for his treaties, and her child taken from her to be raised by a wet nurse, her duty as property of the Prince of a Principality fulfilled.

She sobbed then, putting a gloved hand over her mouth to stifle the noise. Olaf looked round once then ignored her, leading the horses resolutely back to the warmth of the stables. All Laura could hear now were the chitters of the animals in the forest, her muffled gasps and the crunch of the icy crust on the ground under Olaf's feet and the hooves of the horses.

The north wall of Dalnerechensk and the valley at the end of Hunter's Pass was now visible and she composed herself, wiping her cheeks quickly and sat up straighter in the saddle, plastering a smile on her face. She tried to look radiant although she felt miserable, and she could see from the concerned looks in people's eyes she had not hidden her feelings well enough. She shut her eyes briefly, guessing she made a strange sight in a muddied dress, returning to the castle mounted on a horse other than the one she had left on. Still she smiled and called hello and Olaf said nothing, and didn't look at her.

In the stables Olaf quickly tethered the two horses then reached up, sliding her off his horse. She mumbled a thank you and turned away so he wouldn't see her tears, spying a brush she picked up, gently combing the mane and tail of the rusty mare to give her time to compose herself. She heard Olaf move further into the stables, talking softly to the stallion.

I'm not ready for this, she thought desperately. She had no release, no idle or wicked pleasure to compensate for the dreary, lonely monotony of her day. She suddenly spied a sharp pair of scissors hanging on a nail and shot a quick look at Olaf's distant back before she grabbed them, snipping off the tail of the mare. She had been grateful for Clara's friendship and her long blonde hair she had unselfishly snipped off for her friend, and Laura had sewn a clever wig to disguise herself, slipping out once a month to a bar in a secret rebellion of her sheltered and lonely life.

She needed this wicked release. Quickly she hid the snipped tail inside the warm coat she was wearing and dropped the scissors back over the nail hammered into the wall, leaving the stables at a trot. She slipped once on the icy courtyard as she made her way to the castle and forced herself to slow down before she had an accident.

The horse hair tickled her, burned at her, she was sure everyone knew, and had to stop herself from throwing open her coat, exposing the hair to check that the tips didn't poke out beneath the hem. She was breathing hard by the time she slipped up the stairs to her rooms, shutting the door behind her.

Ekaterina was in her rooms, embroidering a piece of lace. Laura stopped in surprise and fear.

'There you are Laura, I thought you might be absent all day again' Ekaterina smiled, then her face changed. 'What has happened? You're white!'

'I'm not sure' she said, feeling flabbergasted. 'I felt dizzy while I was riding.'

At once Ekaterina stood, sending Anna scurrying out of the room for a doctor. Laura tried to protest but Ekaterina would have none of it, taking her arm and pulling her to sit down on the couch, before wetting a handkerchief in a pitcher of water, dabbing her head with it.

'I am fine Ekaterina!' she protested, flimsily swatting at her attentions. 'I don't know what brought on the dizziness. Perhaps I shouldn't have been looking up at the sun!'

'Stop this silly protest, you are too important to Aleksei' Ekaterina said firmly.

Only because I can have a son a small part of her said, but all the same her heart did a little flip. She managed to take off her coat and conceal the tail in it carefully while Ekaterina was stoking the fire and dropped the coat on a chair. The doctor arrived with Aleksei close behind, a wake of ministers and court gossips following him. At once Ekaterina shut the door on the court and Aleksei dropped to his knees beside her, taking her hand.

'Are you ill?' he asked, and Laura could have wept for the concern she saw there.

'No my love, just a moment of silliness, I looked up at the sun while riding.'

Aleksei wiped his mouth, the relief clear on his face. He stood, dusting off his knees then stroked her hair.

'You are pale' he said. 'Perhaps you should not ride in the forest so many times.'

'If that pleases you' she said softly, feeling her heart sink.

Aleksei excused himself and left again, and Laura heard his voice in the corridor giving some diplomatic excuse for the fluttering of excitement in the castle. The crowd laughed, and Laura couldn't help but feel it had been at her expense. She shut her eyes and sighed, letting the doctor examine her carefully.

34

Laura looked up from her reading, marking her place in the large leather bound book. The old man looked troubled in the light of the flames from the huge marble fireplace. The orange light crawled across the deep furrows of his face and his chin had sunk deep onto his chest, his breathing deep and slow. Laura thought he would have seemed asleep, but the fire had caught in glints in his dark eyes. Unnerved she glanced to the expensive Persian rugs where his gaze seemed to be directed, wondering what had disturbed him so.

There was nothing there, and the silence filled with the crackling flames and the hiss of snow against the windows seemed intrusively loud. Laura wondered if he was growing tired of her presence in his private rooms; he often retired to the library when it snowed or he felt poorly, climbing the stairs with his face pinched in pain, steadfastly ignoring Aleksei's attempts to install an elevator for him, and ease himself into the library's comfy leather chairs by the fire, rumbling contentedly.

The Princess would often accompany him, bored with no friends and limited distractions within the castle walls, and read to him from his collections of books while the Tsar sipped warm brandy and wiggled his toes before the cherry flames. As at first with Ekaterina's poetry, she could read the phonetic Cyrillic script well but could only recognise a few isolated words. Yet as the evenings passed she recognised the story as one she knew, and the strange words began to make more sense.

But the Tsar had not interrupted her, and had hardly spoken this evening, despite the story being one of his favourites on Alexander the Great. He seemed lost in some private torment, the fire drawing devils in his eyes.
'Your Majesty?' Laura asked softly.

He did not respond. Gently she reached out and lay a hand on his arm.
'What troubles you Your Majesty?' she asked, a little louder.

As if a spell had been broken he snapped awake, his skin taking on a friendlier, warm glow.
'I'm sorry my dear, I was not listening' he apologised, a little sheepishly.
She smiled kindly. 'What ails you?' she asked again.
'My son' he sighed. 'He has not come to you for weeks has he.'

It was not a question. He knew she was sleeping alone at nights now.

Laura coloured, dropping her eyes in shame, wondering if Lady Ramkinson had been right, wondering if she would be blamed for her husband's disinterest in her. She tried to think of how to explain this and act like a princess, while wanting to throw herself on the floor and sob that it was not her fault, that she was only a child, that she didn't know what a man wanted from his wife, or how to make him want her again. But Tsar Constantinovich went on without waiting for her to explain herself.
'Every night he spends there, in Grigory's office, pouring over the numbers; the documents, the accounts. He hardly eats, if he sleeps it's at the desk from complete exhaustion, he gets

no fresh air save for what blows in with a messenger bringing *more* documents, *more* accounts -' he broke off, shutting his eyes.

'I know what it is I have asked of him' he continued quietly, somehow drained now, an old man hunching closer to the fire to warm himself. 'This Principality exists purely at the whim of its neighbour. There is nothing – nothing. And my son, my poor dear son, was never meant to rule this.'

Laura stared at the old man, frail and small in the leather chair, reduced in his misery and torment to a figure half of what he had been in Lady Ramkinson's garden. He looked withered and defeated.

'Forgive me' he said tightly. 'I shall retire now.'

Before she could collect herself the Tsar had maneuvered awkwardly out of his seat and was stiffly walking towards the door. She watched him go, her thoughts whirling inside her. *What did he mean? Was there something wrong with the Principality? Was Aleksei not meant to rule at all?* She stood and dampened down the fire, her thoughts whirling and troubling her. She didn't want to be in the room on her own, the fire was still casting demonic shapes on the Persian rug so she slipped out into the corridor, leaving the book on her seat and closing the door behind her.

She stood for a long time in the hallway, eyeing the secret, silent surrounds of the castle, wondering what she had not been told. A sudden sense of fear gripped her, and she couldn't placate it. Doubt nagged at her. *If Aleksei was never meant to rule there must have been someone else. What had happened to him? Was this the tragedy Ekaterina had eluded to the day her engagement had been announced to the Principality? Or if he had not died where was he and why was he not ruling Dalnerechensk? Would or could Aleksei lose the throne?*

She decided to confront her husband. Regardless of whether or not she was his property she was still a Royal of this Principality, and should her worst fears be confirmed she had the right to be forewarned. She hitched up her skirts as she marched determinedly along the corridor to the stairs. She wondered if she should be letting her passions rule her like this, if she should burst into these offices and demand the truth from her husband. He could send her away in disgrace, he could even have her flogged if he felt suitably humiliated by her outburst.

The thought made some of her anger dissipate, but did not dissuade her from her course and she slipped along the corridors to Grigory's office. The door was open and Aleksei was sitting inside, feverishly pouring through documents and charters, the candles burning low beside him. He did not seem to notice how low the light had become, or how hard he was peering at the documents. He was writing quick notes as he worked, scratching some out and muttering aloud, pinching the bridge of his nose as he forced himself to come up with a different conclusion.

Laura's anger and fear melted and she managed to smile softly to herself. Aleksei was dedicated to his lands and loved his country; anyone could see that. *Anyone standing* here *could see that* she thought suddenly, and glanced to her left and right in the dark corridor, realising just how alone they both were. She tapped lightly on the door and stepped in.

'Laura' he said quietly, surprised.

'I have come to ask you to bed' she whispered tenderly.

'Just a little longer, there is something I need to do' he answered, dismissing her, turning back to the documents in his grip.

Refusing to be dismissed she took his hands, firmly but lovingly. 'Aleksei, the Principality's problems will still be there in the morning. You need -'

'They don't have to be!' he cried, interrupting her, snatching his hands away in frustration. 'There must be something – *something* – here in all this mess!'

'My love, you are just one man -' Laura pleaded, trying to soothe him.

'I am responsible!' he shouted, his temper erupting. 'Me! I am the *Tsesarevich*, Regent of Dalnerechensk! My father couldn't do it, *he* couldn't do it, it's up to me to find a way to make this work!'

Laura had an uneasy feeling that 'he' referred to someone other than the Tsar. She felt suddenly sick, wondering if her wild thoughts earlier had any grains of truth hidden in them. Her confusion doubled tenfold, as she didn't know what the truth was yet. Aleksei thought the stricken look on her face was because of his outburst, that he had frightened his beautiful bride and his rage imploded, and he collapsed back in his chair, utterly exhausted, wiping his mouth firmly.

Laura bit her lip, unsure how to stop this man from killing himself with the stress of his office. She saw it now, how thin and strained his composure was, how old and haggard he was beginning to look. She didn't know what troubles kept him from her every day, what was so terrible he fell asleep in the embrace of treaties and documents instead of his wife's.

He wiped his mouth again, ashamed, unwilling to meet her eye. Laura could see him struggling with his feelings, trying to think of a sincere apology that would still allow him some dignity. Her heart went out to him, this man who seemed so burdened with worry. If only she had some good news for him. Suddenly she realised she did, and gently she took his hands again and pressed it to her belly, folding hers over the top.

'Aleksei, I do not want to see you work yourself to an early grave' she said softly, 'nor see your son grow up without you.'

Light dawned in his eyes and his whole face lit up, the years of worry falling off him in his joy.

'You are pregnant?!' he cried, suddenly deliriously happy. 'Are you sure?' he leapt to his feet, taking hold of her arms, his eyes drawn to her stomach to read the truth there, and then back to her face for any trace of a lie.

'I was dizzy while riding two weeks ago and the doctor thought it was too soon to tell. But my course is late. I am pregnant.' She flushed.

Aleksei cried out in joy, throwing his arms around her and kissing her with passion, lifting her up against him. She folded her arms around his neck, feeling her blood rise as he kissed her, liking the way his hand rested on her belly. She brushed back stray strands of his greying locks and he broke from her, stroking her cheek gently.

'Laura, you have made me the happiest man alive!' he whispered gently, glowing with happiness.

'Come to bed Aleksei' she said softly.

35

The court was very surprised when Aleksei suddenly cancelled all his appointments, retreating to his personal chambers. Laura also cancelled her Russian lessons with the Countess and sent Anna out for the day, cloistering herself with her husband. The Council was left to its own devices, wandering about aimlessly in the entrance hall and the offices on the first floor, asking themselves if the Royal couple had fallen ill, wondering out loud if they had eaten anything the rest of the court had not also eaten, and could not agree, small arguments breaking out among them.

Tempers were soured by the bickering and the uncertainty, and Tsar Constantinovich, disturbed and roused from his library, bellowed at them from the staircase, sending them to inspect the towers and the walls of the castle. Many grumbled at the menial task, especially when the light dusting of snow began to fall, but were secretly glad of something to take their minds from the worry of an ill monarchy.

They dared not think of Dalnerechensk without a ruler. The American girl was young and strong, and the people loved her, but she was innocent of their problems. Aleksei was growing old; no one could deny it. His hair was steadily greying, and the months of sleeplessness was taking its toll on him, wearing him down until he began to resemble his father in age as Tsar Constantinovich had resembled Aleksei in his youth.

The Principality was teetering on the edge of instability. If Aleksei took ill now, even with the flu, especially if Laura took ill with him, it would plunge the three valleys into complete chaos. The rife rumours had already upset the delicate balance. The Principality would not survive a crisis like uncertain succession to the throne.

Maksim and Lev had even dared to climb the stairs to the second floor but found the doors to Aleksei's chamber barred by two armed guards with strict instructions that the royal couple should not be disturbed. They had inquired and pried, threatened and demanded, all to no avail. The guards were resolute in their responses and the ministers feared disturbing Aleksei if he really was ill, and retreated back down the stairs, bickering irritably.

But at dinner that night the royal couple appeared, healthy and robust, tender towards one another. Laura glowed in a cream gown with peach underskirts, while Aleksei was attentive and smiling, his day away from his advisors remarkably improving the colour of his skin. The court shot each other confused and weighty looks, whispering over wine goblets and behind fans. Aleksei waved away delicate inquiries about his health and sat, calling for the first course.

The court sat, and new rumours flew up and down the banquet table, rumours that hinted the rift between the couple had closed after a day reconciliation and of passionate love making, that Aleksei had taken the time to teach his child bride a few tricks in the marriage bed that every wife should know, or that her glow could be attributed to the already blessed and blossoming state of motherhood.

They watched as the two ate together, noting the shared secret looks and smiles, the closeness and gentleness as they talked to each other. They waited with baited anticipation, reading into their body language, analyzing their speech, watching for any hidden or overt messages in their exchanges. Any minister who broached the subject of the agenda they hadn't covered in the Council Chambers that day was waved off with an amiable reproach.

Fans fluttered frantically and servants were sent to find more people who could shed any light on the situation. Aleksei called for music after dinner and they smiled across fans and wine glasses when the three musicians were forbidden to play anything fast or exerting. They watched them move together, watched the way he seemed to avoid stepping close to her body though still holding her warmly. The rumours grew even more when Aleksei announced an early evening, and suspended the Council for a week, declaring he wished to spend more time with his family. It was all but said that Laura was expecting.

For two nights they appeared together at dinner; glowing, tender, in love for all the world to see. Wives and daughters eyed the Princess and discussed the lines of her stomach, arguing whether it was curved or flat, some even imagining it growing before their very eyes. No one in the Principality could have pointed to a happier, more in love pair than the Prince and Princess, and the court breathed sighs of relief to think of a gurgling nursery, and stability in the Principality again.

The ministers grumbled good naturedly about their Prince's absence from the Council, unable to meet without him. *The break was doing him good*, they said, and each breakfast they waited with baited breath, each evening they wondered when Aleksei would announce what the whole Principality knew anyway. But on the third night Aleksei appeared alone, white faced and drawn. He drank heavily and waved away questions, ignoring the bewildered looks.

Ekaterina watched Aleksei guardedly, the brittleness of his temperament had become almost legendary in the last month, and she wondered if his anger had gotten the better of him. As soon as she could slip away she excused herself and climbed the staircase to the second floor, knocking on the door to the Queen's Apartments. A white-faced Anna opened the door a fraction to tell her to go away. Ekaterina pushed open the door, ignoring the servant and eyed Laura, alarmed.

She was sobbing on the floor, stripped down to her corset and bloomers, the expensive carpets rolled back, a strip of bloody linen beside her.

'What has happened?!' she cried, pulling her into her arms, kneeling beside her young friend who was beside herself with misery.

'It's her courses, My Lady' Anna said, distressed. 'It's come. She's been like this all day. I can't soothe her.'

Ekaterina thanked God quietly her slanderous thoughts against Aleksei had been unfounded then quietly sent Anna to prepare Laura's bed before dismissing her for the evening. Laura sobbed still, uncomforted, and Ekaterina stayed silent until Anna had left the room and shut the door behind her. As much trust as Laura put in her faithful servant another pair of ears and a tongue for gossip was a recipe for trouble.

'Oh Laura, my darling' she soothed, stroking her hair and rocking her. 'Don't cry. You are young, fertile and randy, you'll soon find yourself staggering under a swollen belly.'

'He all but told you all I was pregnant, and now I will have to tell them I have failed because I have not produced an heir.'

'Nonsense Laura, the people love you, you're their American darling' Ekaterina soothed, stroking her hair and planting a loving kiss on her temple. 'It does not matter you are not pregnant yet, you are young. -'

'He hasn't touched me for almost a month' Laura blurted out, too miserable to be embarrassed. 'You saw his face when he thought I was with his child. He loved me then, and I would give anything to feel like that again. But all he does is spend his time with old men and stupid bits of paper, too tired to come to me at the end of the day! He loves his country but he married me! I cannot grow a child if he will not -' she stopped, her eyes darting to the locked door, afraid she had said too much, afraid Lady Ramkinson would burst through the door, the dreaded crop raised high, ready to thrash it across her back.

She flinched, the thought too strong for her in this fragile state and Ekaterina tightened her embrace, soothing her again. Laura glanced again at the door, assured now that Lady Ramkinson was not going to burst through it, but terribly conscious that the door was a thin piece of wood against the prying eyes and ears of the castle.

'What am I to do Ekaterina?' she whispered, despairing.

Ekaterina told her. Laura's eyes grew very large.

36

In the last days of March Laura noticed that the sun was growing warmer as the days lengthened, dancing merrily on the dripping tree branches and the new bubbling brooks in the hills in the Hunting Forest. Once or twice when Fedor had been indisposed Olaf had ridden into the forest with her, hardly bothering to protest. Laura guessed it was because he enjoyed riding, as she had often caught a small smile on his lips when he thought she wasn't paying attention.

The snow was melting, trickling in rivulets of liquid cold down the valleys, dripping from lengthening icicles into the river that cut along Liberty Valley, the crisp powder disappearing slowly day by day, and although snowfall was still quite frequent it steadily retreated to reveal a lush new green that Laura had never known. It was her first spring in Dalnerechensk.

The first lamb born in the Principality was dressed in blue, green and gold ribbons and carried through the streets of Dalnerechensk while people blessed it for a bountiful harvest. It was then brought to the Castle kitchens where it was slaughtered and the court feasted on a succulent dish of lamb. Laura had tried her best to be lively at the Spring Feast, but knew the lamb was blessed enough to fertilise her womb by eating it, and Tatiana and Natasha were still whispering behind their fans, finding malignant satisfaction in the latest rumours concerning her empty womb.

Aleksei had sent for her once or twice since her false pregnancy but their love making had been quick and dispassionate. Laura despaired, wondering if she had hurt him so deeply, vowing next time she would not tell him until her belly was huge and her labours had come. By then it would be safe enough to know for sure. She sighed, and rubbed her eyes, relenting. Ekaterina was right, she would be pregnant soon enough, she should be thankful for the small mercy of time yet to be admired.

She wondered if she should slip into his room and undress before him as Ekaterina had told her, wondered about the words she had been instructed to say, wondered – she stopped, flushing madly at even the thought of that. Ekaterina's knowledge of carnal pleasure had shocked Laura, but as time wore on Laura grew willing to give anything a try.

She was glad that Aleksei had suspended meeting with his advisors today, and glad that they were going on a rare outing together to Ladozhskoye where the Ivanov's had graciously opened their expansive grounds to the court to celebrate their eighth wedding anniversary. Grigory had returned from Constantinople the night before, and Laura was glad that Aleksei and his friend would have a chance to talk and make merry together. She suspected it had been a while since Dalnerechensk's last party.

Aleksei smiled at her when they reached the grounds, stepping out of the carriage then reached back, offering his hand for her. She took it and stepped down, smoothing out the wrinkles from her emerald dress, liking the way his cheeks darkened when the sunlight caught her skin and made it glow. Grigory called a greeting and Aleksei tucked Laura's arm through his elbow, returning the greeting.

Ekaterina gave Laura a wink as she kissed her cheek, and led them to the rich lawns where a canvas pavilion had been set up. Underneath was a long table draped with white cloth and set with a place for every member of the court. Most of the ministers were here already, and greeted their royals with more cheer than they had that morning at breakfast.

Laura noticed with a little disappointment that Tatiana and Natasha were also on the Ivanov's lawn, talking behind their fans and shooting the royals looks and smiles. She wished Ekaterina had not invited them, but knew her friend was the wiser of them both. Dalnerechensk was too small to snub those you did not like, and both were daughters of men who held powerful positions in the Advisory Council, second only to Aleksei and Grigory.

Laura sighed resignedly, and let Aleksei go when he excused himself to talk to Grigory. Ekaterina waved to the six men who were carrying musical instruments, directing them where to set up. She then tucked herself tighter against her friend, flashing her a look.

'You do not look happier my dear' she said, looking askance at her friend. 'Did he not like them?'

Laura didn't answer. Ekaterina stopped, facing her.

'You did not do them?'

'He has not called for me' Laura admitted, desperately wishing to avoid this conversation.

Ekaterina laughed. 'My dear, you cannot wait forever for him. You must make the first move, whisper to him, rub him like I told you to -'

Laura suddenly spied Aleksei talking to Tatiana, his hand casually on her arm, and saw the inviting smile on her lips. She stopped suddenly, turning her back to them. Ekaterina thought she had pressed too far with her young friend then saw her obvious distress in not wanting to look at her husband. She smiled sadly and squeezed her hands sympathetically.

'Are you sure it will work?' Laura asked, miserable and desperate.

'Yes' Ekaterina smiled. 'Come, dry your eyes my dear, and smile radiantly, I know it is not easy.'

Laura wiped them as discreetly as she could and managed to smile, letting her friend walk her to another group of women and talk politely with them while service was laid out on the table. Grigory then called them to the table, sharing a joke about the place of honour.

'By all means Grigory, I would not deprive a man of his head' he laughed, sitting in the chair beside the middle of the table, unwittingly sitting in the place Ekaterina had guided Laura to. 'But it seems he will deprive a woman of her seat!' Ekaterina laughed, pulling the seat next to his out in a show of mock chivalry.

'He has had my seat many times, and shall always have my seat, as I have promised him' Laura suddenly said.

There was surprise, then Aleksei's cheeks flushed at the innuendo, but he burst into a hearty laugh. The ministers laughed too, then took their places around the table. Laura sat beside Aleksei, reveling at her boldness and lowered her eyes to take a careful look at her husband. He did not seem angry with her, and although his cheeks were dark he didn't seem humiliated, and wondered if Ekaterina had been right. She decided she would like to find out.

The feast started and the conversation was lively, the focus on the Ivanovs, sitting in the seats of honour usually reserved for the king alone. Even the fans of Tatiana and Natasha were beside their plates as they talked flirtatiously with Ivan Gogol, the Headmaster of Dalnerechensk's school who had recently been appointed as secretary to the Advisory Council. Laura was glad of their distraction from malicious gossip and allowed herself to relax and enjoy the company.

During dessert after a few whispered phrases Ekaterina had instructed her to say Laura dropped her hand to her lap then surreptitiously slid it over Aleksei's thigh. He jerked visibly, and his cheeks darkened with heated blood. Laura could hear him breathing loudly, intensely, and wondered if his heart was racing as much as hers was, though knew hers was racing in fear. He didn't make a sound, and he didn't stop her, so she let her fingers brush against him again.

The musicians suddenly burst into song, startling them both. Aleksei stood then and bowed to his wife, offering a hand that trembled to her. She smiled, slipping her fingers into his and let him lead her out onto the lawn. They were joined by the court, and the press of bodies forced couples to dance more closely than custom dictated. Laura didn't mind and flashed Aleksei a look, letting her body brush against his as they danced. It reddened his cheeks further, but she could now see the desire in his eyes as he held her, and smiled at the hunger there.

The song ended and the musicians struck up a lively Dalnerechensk folk dance. The crowd cheered and swung round their partners, clapping and calling out as they excused themselves from standing on toes and knocking the elbows of the person they danced next to. Laura laughed as she swung through the partners, stepping hard against Aleksei so he rubbed against her, laughing as she was swung away.

Before she could greet her next partner she was pulled away, Aleksei hurrying her away from the crowd of people, stealing with her into the arches of the Ivanov's gazebo where the fear of discovery had made their love making quick, passionate and so carnal Laura had wanted to scream, to sob, to tear at her lover as he took her on a bed of moss under the warm sun. It was all she could do to stop herself crying out at her climax.

It was not until some time later the party noticed their royals were missing. Before they could worry about their whereabouts they slipped back into the crowds of dancers, the heat between them making the young ones wink at each other and flutter their fans, making the greybeards sigh and shake their heads resignedly; but all of them, all there on that wide lawn with the spring sun glowing above them, knew that a new life could not be far away.

37

Laura sighed, a sound of happiness tinged with just a little wistfulness. Aleksei had kissed her forehead tenderly as he left her that morning, but she could see the strain of his office piling back on him again, the joy of the Ivanov's feast fading quickly. She had dressed in a light riding habit and slipped down to the stables, casting one eye back along the first floor landing, noticing the Chamber doors were closed again.

As disappointed as she was to see him locked away again she was pleased to know the rift with his Council had closed and he had allowed them back into the chambers to advise him. She didn't pause on the steps and slipped down to the stables, greeting Olaf and Fedor who was waiting for her.

She boosted herself up onto the stallion and waited till Fedor had also mounted before turning her horse down Castle Street. Her spirits were still high so she let the horse walk slowly, calling greetings to the people she saw. They turned and bowed or dipped curtseys, some calling back politely. Suddenly a man stepped in front of her horse, making it snort and toss his head up. The man grabbed the reins, stilling the animal, but preventing them from riding on.

At once Fedor rode up beside her.

'Forgive me Your Highness' the man said, his earnest eyes fixed on Laura. 'I have come to beseech you -'

'Let go of the horse' Fedor instructed.

The man ignored him, gripping the reins tighter, fishing in a pocket for something.

'We implore you -'

'Let go of the horse' Fedor said again, loudly.

The man's eyes flicked to him, but again he ignored the command, drawing out a crumpled piece of paper from his pocket.

'A petition, for the Tsar!' he tried desperately, pushing the paper at Laura.

Fedor neatly plucked it from his hands and slipped it inside his jacket. The man made a move as if to grab at him to retrieve the paper, but then relented and let the reins go. The stallion tossed his head again, pleased to be free of the nervous grip. Fedor rode forward a little, forcing the man to step back to the side or risk being trodden on under the horse's iron hooves.

'I will make sure my husband gets it' Laura promised the man, whose wild eyes had unnerved her a little.

Her promise didn't seem to satisfy him, but he relented and watched them ride off down Castle Street, trotting out into the royal forest of Hunter's Pass. As if sensing the Princess would not be satisfied until she had answers Fedor rode silently beside her, waiting patiently.

'What did he want?' she asked, turning to look at him.

'I expect the petition will be for higher wages for mine workers' he answered. 'It is usually what the petitions are for.'

'Oh' Laura said, unsure what else to say.

They rode on in silence, Laura mulling over the strange event and Fedor's words. *How often were petitions sent to the castle?* she wondered. She didn't think they asked out of greed, there had been desperation rather than arrogance in his eyes. *Are the wages really so poor?* She suddenly felt guilty for threatening to send Anna to work in the mines for exposing her deformities.

But the guilt didn't last long. The warm sun was bathing her, and the birds bickering in the trees, and she forgot all about the piece of paper inside Fedor's jacket when she saw the Ivanov carriage roll out of Ladozhskoye and head up the valley to Macherna. She wondered if they were going out together, wondered what interest they would have in the Western Valley or the village of Davostok. She smiled, thinking of the spring feast, and felt her cheeks get hot.

She had been embarrassed, terrified of being exposed in such an intimate act, but after whispering the words she had been taught into Aleksei's ear, and stroking the front of his breaches as they danced together, feeling his blood respond to her, there was nothing she wouldn't have done that day.

38

Spring was warming, and Aleksei was beginning to despair. The months of arguments with his Council had come to nothing but frayed tempers and the complexion of an old man that glowered back at him from his mirror. Dalnerechensk teetered on the edge of financial collapse and there was no way to ease the Principality's growing economic depression. There was unrest, someone had even torn down the royal standard from the common's flagpole, leaving it to blow around on the muddy ground. Three more petitions had been sent to the castle in one week, demanding to lower the price of grain, lower the taxes and to raise the wages of the miners.

Aleksei couldn't act on any of them. Just to buy another month of grace before the Principality toppled into spiraling inflation would mean another tax on the already high crops. The situation was desperate. His people would be hungry in the bountiful days of summer; they would begin to die when the snows of next winter covered the ground.

He had considered borrowing money, knowing he could never pay it back, knowing the terms Russia would put on the loan would be impossible to keep. The money Russia paid for the tin scraped from the rock in Dalnerechensk was not enough to keep the economy afloat. As the price of tin had fallen, more workers had been employed in the mines to meet demands and then the wages had to be lowered because the treasury could not afford so many. It was a vicious cycle.

He had known Dalnerechensk was teetering on the edge of collapse for eight years. Tin was almost worthless, and the Principality only had subsistence agriculture to fall back on. His attempts to modernise the country had been met with resistance and reluctance, and in the end he had to concede that Dalnerechensk had neither the skills nor the inclination to become technologically advanced.

His anger flared again, knowing that if the economy collapsed the Principality would have to exist on what they could grow themselves, and the royals would have to work in the fields too. It meant he would have to sack every member of his household staff, and the army as well. He knew they could not grow enough food to support the population. Vsevolod's proud castle would fall into ruin with no one to look after it, and the people would quietly pack up and slip across the border to Russia, looking for work and money.

Money! We need money!

He stopped and squeezed the bridge of his nose, trying to keep his emotions in check. For an instant he regretted his insistence he marry an American. Luke Asanton's daughter had appealed because of the mining connections but Aleksei had realised as soon as the child stepped out of the carriage that she knew nothing of technology or industrialisation, and his hopes to save his country had fallen away.

But when he looked at her again all his bitterness melted away. She was beautiful, beautiful, beautiful. He cursed himself sometimes, that he couldn't tell her how he felt. He forgot all else while she was there, and desperately wanted to forget his duty to this place as well. Four hundred years after Vsevolod defied Russia, Aleksei would be the monarch that saw his city crumble and be swallowed up by the nation they had escaped.

He looked around him, at the sea of parchment and paper that covered the desk, the walls, even the floor of Grigory's office and sighed, admitting defeat, his soul sagging within him. He swallowed against the bitter lump in his throat and reached for a quill and ink, penning a letter to Tsar Nicholas Romanov.

Hesitation made large splodges of ink fall onto the paper, and he crossed several words out before scrunching it in his fist angrily, starting again, twice, unhappy, and tried not to think of the outcomes of their meeting. He knew he was offering Vsevolod's crown to Russia.

Finally it was done, and he held it before him, staring without seeing the words. He knew he should blow on the ink to dry it, but the longer he waited the more it dried on its own, till there was nothing for him to do but fold the parchment and make it official with his seal. Just before he was about to stamp the melted wax on the letter Grigory knocked on the door of his own office, rushing in excitedly.

Aleksei paused, knowing the wax was solidifying without his seal, but Grigory's excitement on his return from Moscow stayed his hand.

'I have news Your Highness' he said, his words tumbling over themselves. 'As you suspected, I was not permitted to review documents in the Russian Treasury, but I have with me a telegram received this morning. With your permission, it says: *Knjaz* Nikita Rurik, Ambassador to the Royal Romanov household, will arrive shortly in Dalnerechensk and requests that his needs be met for the duration of his stay.'

'An Ambassador?' Aleksei asked, surprised. 'Read on, what does he want?'

'Forgive me, that is all the telegram says' Grigory answered.

Aleksei was confused at the ambiguous nature of the telegram, but then he caught the gleam in Grigory's eye. A Russian Ambassador could only mean one thing. The Treaty of Dalnerechensk would be invoked, one way or another. If the terms were to be renegotiated the Principality's economic problems could be eased. If it was to be absorbed back into Russian Territory Aleksei had been spared the humiliation of begging for charity from Tsar Nicholas.

A weight slid off his heart and a repressed chortle of laughter burst out of his mouth. He leapt to his feet, throwing the letter into the fire, feeling refreshed and vital again, laughing loudly, striding out into the corridor. He bellowed orders at servants he saw, sending them scurrying off to meet his requests, the castle flying into an uproar of activity. Grigory was ordered to send a telegram back to Russia, expecting the Prince's arrival.

The guest rooms on the third floor were thrown open to air again, the dust covers removed from all the furniture, and the beds to be fluffed and larders stocked again in anticipation of his arrival. Ekaterina, sitting with Laura in her parlour, paused in her lesson, then sent Anna to enquire what was going on. Upon learning the reason for this fervour she noted with some glee the Russian was getting the same treatment Laura's wedding had.

Aleksei burst into her room, looking more vibrant than he had in weeks. He dismissed Ekaterina and instructed Laura to put on her riding habit, that he would race her to Hunter's Pass. She accepted with delight, pleased to see him casting off his duties to spend time with her.

She slipped into her dressing room to don her habit and when she emerged Aleksei was already gone, bellowing somewhere in the castle below her for food and wine. *A picnic!* A pleased part of her said, and she snatched up the thick rug at the end of her bed to spread on the ground for them to sit on, grinning at Ekaterina's laugh as she fled down the stairs.

Aleksei was already mounted, and called teasingly over his shoulder that she would have to do better if she expected to beat him in a race, then kicked the flanks of his horse, the satchel of food and drink rattling on his back as he headed at break-neck speed out of the castle grounds. Laura cursed then threw the blanket over the stallion. He was not saddled but Olaf boosted her quickly up and she grabbed the reins, heading off at a gallop.

Aleksei glanced back as he ducked under the portcullis, surprised to see her following so quickly. He spurred his horse again, turning it towards the pass, hearing the stallion's hoof-beats come closer behind him. He was surprised at how close the race was as they thundered into the pass, his gelding ahead by a nose. He threw up his hands in victory, then turned to eye Laura, who was flushed with excitement and breathing hard.

'You are a magnificent horsewoman' he said.

'And you are a frightful cheat!' she exclaimed hotly, laughing.

Aleksei laughed and turned his horse off the road, leading her to a pretty waterfall in a glen. Laura gasped when they entered into the secluded clearing, marveling at the fresh greenness of the trees, and wet rainbows that glistened in the spray. In the winter this waterfall and small lake would ice completely over, and still now hung thick from the rocks and clung to the shores of the lake, despite the warmth of the sun.

Aleksei dismounted and looped the reins of his horse round a tree branch, reaching up to help Laura down. She looped her stallion's reins beside the gelding's and took the blanket from his back, shaking it out before spreading it on the ground for them. Aleksei sat, pulling out bottles and food wrapped in cloths that Laura was surprised to see were still whole.

She sat close to him, thanking him for the bread he passed her, liking the rusticness of the meal. They ate in good natured silence, smiling at the other, then Aleksei stretched back on the blanket, sighing contentedly. Laura lay beside him, resting her head on his chest and felt his arms fold round her, felt his chest expand as he sighed happily.

'Good news today, my love?' she asked him, tilting her face up to see his reply.

'An Ambassador is coming to Dalnerechensk' he said, then sat up, pushing her back to look at her. 'We must do everything in our power to appease him Laura' he said seriously, searching her face for any reluctance. 'I cannot stress how vital his goodwill is for the future of Dalnerechensk.'

'Of course my love, whatever you ask of me I will do it.' She took his hand and kissed it. 'Now, should you not claim your prize?'

She laughed and lay back, pulling him above her, her hands snaking down to the front of his breeches. Aleksei groaned.

39

Laura woke early, aware that the castle was rustling with excited nerves. She planted a kiss on Aleksei's chest as he stirred and let him slip out from her embrace, hunting for her night dress under the covers. Aleksei slipped out and greeted Mikhail quietly, watching him stoke the fire in his cold room. Mikhail returned the greeting and followed his master to the dressing room, helping him pull on the cold material.

Anna slipped into the room, bringing in beautiful dresses of Laura's for her to decide which to wear. She bid Mikhail a shy good morning as the manservant and Aleksei headed down to the state rooms to see if everything was ready to receive their guest. Laura slipped out of the bed, standing close to the fire to warm herself. Anna held up the three dresses and Laura decided on the blue with the low neckline, knowing she could wear her green velvet coat with it as she stood on the steps to greet the Russian.

A small part of her felt apprehensive, that the Prince would be as hostile and sneering as the Counts she had greeted on the steps nearly five months ago, and wondered if she could stand another noble's disapproval. She didn't have long to wonder, there was a shout from the south wall that a carriage had reached Tcherepnin and was heading through the sleepy village. Laura quickly struggled into her corset and dress, racing down the stone steps of the castle, pulling on her coat as she reached the door.

Tsar Constantinovich stood at the head of the steps, dressed in the black military uniform with all the trimming for the highest office of state. Before him on the steps stood Aleksei and Grigory, both wearing the uniform as well, with the royal standard sash across their middles. Ekaterina stood beside her husband and Laura quickly slipped down to stand beside Aleksei, slipping her hand through his elbow. He smiled at her, a smile strained with hope and anxiety.

Across the courtyard the guards at the gate to Vsevolod's Way saluted and a beautiful carriage turned into the castle grounds, pulled by dusty and sweat-stained horses. The driver quickly jammed on the brake and jumped down from his open seat, retrieving a small stool he placed before the carriage then opened the door, bowing low to the dark interior.

A graceful hand emerged from within and gripped the door firmly before he stepped into view. Quickly Laura took in his appearance, hoping she wasn't staring. He wore an elegant black suit and a lemon ruffle at his throat, a brown coat folded over his arm. His dark hair was long and combed back to brush at his shoulders, a few boyish strands blowing into his eyes. His nose was straight and his mouth full but firm, and his eyes flashed the same mischievous way that Ekaterina's did.

She was looking at a man who could barely be in his twenties, and the most handsome man she had ever set eyes on. He carried himself with perfect grace and poise as he stepped out of the coach, letting go of the door and adjusting the brown coat that hung over his arm, those mischievous eyes darting around him quickly, alighting on the two women that glowed like two flanking gems.

'Welcome *Knjaz* Nikita Rurik!' Aleksei called, raising his arm in greeting.

Nikita folded his hand onto his heart and bowed respectfully then came up the stairs towards them.

'You did not tell me Dalnerechensk was heaven, Your Royal Highness' he said.

Laura noticed his voice was almost musical, and purred with sophistication and breeding. Aleksei looked surprised. 'No?'

'Surely it must be, or else angels walk the earth. How did you convince these heavenly beauties to greet me?' he flashed Laura and Ekaterina a smile that would have melted tar.

Aleksei shifted, embarrassed and awkward.

'I present my wife, *Velikaja Knjaginja* Laura Vakhtangova and Countess Ekaterina Ivanova' he said.

'Delighted' Nikita said, kissing their hands almost seductively. '*Enchanté.*'

'We have prepared rooms for you, you can refresh until dinner' Aleksei said, trying to move along this awkward meeting. The young, handsome dandy was not what he was expecting.

Nikita bowed again and offered his elbow to Ekaterina, smiling at Laura. The Countess accepted Nikita's arm, letting herself be led into the castle. Laura felt her heart do a little flip at his smile and dropped her eyes modestly.

She was relieved *Knjaz* Rurik was warm and pleasant, she had been prepared for chilly disdain, the kind words from a handsome man had nearly sent her into giddy stammers, and was glad Aleksei was doing all the talking, though he seemed nearly as flummoxed as her. *Knjaz* Rurik had impressed her immensely, speaking confidently with the flattering, flowery tongue Aleksei's letter to her had been filled with. He was appealing and did not shy with embarrassment from speaking his mind and his feelings like her husband did.

She had begun to wonder if Aleksei had written that letter to her at all, and wondered which of his advisors had penned it for him. She wanted to be flattered, wanted to know she was attractive and desired. Tsar Constantinovich shut the doors of the castle against the cold and the company shrugged off their winter coats, draping them over the arms of waiting servants.

Aleksei explained that *Knjaz* Rurik had all the honours as befitting a member of the royal household and could go where he pleased at whim. He was given a maid and page to see to his needs and no request would be turned down. Nikita tossed his coat flippantly at his maid, flashing Laura a look from under his long lashes as he did so. She flushed, aware of how her body looked in her blue dress and felt a heat grow in her stomach. She was looking forward to his company.

40

Laura sat at her small dressing table in the queen's rooms, feeling Anna brush her hair into a fashionable coif, listening to her babble excitedly about the Russian.

'So handsome Your Highness!' she sighed dreamily. 'Anastasia said his wardrobe is all velvet and silk, the most expensive she'd ever seen, begging your pardon Miss! And she said that he slept all of today too!'

Laura smiled, eyeing her reflection in the mirror. Anna had pinned her hair with little seed pearl pins and she looked very elegant. She thanked her servant then stood, slipping into her ivory gown, liking the way it made her skin glow. Anna sighed wistfully at her mistress' beauty, and told her how angelic and heavenly she looked then picked up the delicate lace fan and gave it to her. Laura thanked her absently, turning this way and that to see her reflection in the mirror.

Satisfied, Laura smiled then closed the door behind her and slipped down the stairs to the banquet hall. It was filling with members of the court, and she was surprised to see those that had dwindled away from the castle after her wedding were back, eyeing the Prince, murmuring over brandy glasses and behind fans.

There was a flurry of movement out of the corner of her eye. Nikita had leapt to his feet when he saw her, and Aleksei, whom he was seated next to, had no choice but to rise too. She smiled at them and they both dropped low bows. The rest of the court had noticed this display with some interest, but no one else had risen. Laura made her way to the canopy where the royals sat, stopping beside Nikita.

'Good evening *Knjaz* Rurik, I trust you are refreshed from your journey?' she said, slightly amused.

'Revived as if I had drunk the very elixir of life!' he claimed, taking her hand and kissing it gently. 'But then I should expect no less when tended to by angels in heaven.'

Laura smiled and wished him good appetite then excused herself and took her place between Ekaterina and her husband, whispering a good evening and planting a kiss on his cheek. He smiled and sat, calling for the first dish.

There was much laughter and bantering at dinner that night. Ekaterina translated the few pieces of conversation Laura didn't understand, watching as Nikita charmed the Dalnerechensk court, his wit and intellect entertaining the men, his flattery and grace courting the ladies. She shot a quick glance at her student and knew she too was marveling at how such a young man could say just the right thing in just the right way every time.

The musicians struck up a lively tune and the court stood, following Aleksei and his young Princess to the dance floor. They smiled together as they turned and swung partners, liking the fun of a traditional dance. Laura was watching Nikita dance out of the corner of her eye. She liked watching the way he moved, he was graceful and energetic, giving himself to the joy of the movement.

Aleksei swung her around and she lost sight of him, laughing as Aleksei led her ducked through the raised arms of the others on the dance floor, swinging arms and changing partners at the end of the festive salute. Aleksei bowed to Ekaterina as she became his new partner and Laura curtseyed to Grigory, twirling round the floor. She changed partners again and suddenly found herself in Nikita's arms.

'You are so light on your feet, how winsome!' he smiled. 'Would you do me the honour of accompanying me one afternoon? I should so like to see your beautiful valley.'

She flushed and explained that she did not wish to appear rude but she had not understood him completely. Nikita smiled then tried Hungarian, then German, then French. Her eyes lit up at the last language, she was fluent in the tongue and happily accepted, the innuendo lost after several translations, and swung away to join a new partner.

The dance finished and Nikita begged three more dances with her before she retired to sit with Aleksei and Ekaterina, laughing and clapping at Nikita's antics as the court danced. He smiled and flattered, turning this way and that. It was like watching a swan in water; he was powerful, elegant, and ultimately in his prime.

'Aha!' Ekaterina said, catching Laura's gaze again. 'He is a cad is he not?' she winked. 'He shall certainly set this court's tongues wagging. I shall be very sorry to miss this.'

Laura looked surprised, then horrified.

'You are leaving?' she cried, a little too loudly.

'Alas my dear, I must' she said, taking her hand. 'Aleksei will need Grigory here, but we have other interests that need attending to in the New World. I am going back.'

'Will you be long?' Laura implored. 'Oh I wish you wouldn't go!'

'I will be gone two months; it is the least I can spare. I do wish I wasn't leaving you, but perhaps the *Knjaz* can continue your lessons, he does share your gift for languages.' She gave her a sly look.

Laura couldn't think of a more appealing tutor and agreed, trying not to show how excited she was at the prospect. Her eyes darted back to the dance, finding Nikita easily in the crowd. She wondered how it was that she knew where he was, even without searching for him. He smiled at her, shooting her a veiled look through lowered lashes. She smiled and dropped her eyes, turning her attention back to Ekaterina.

As attractive as her new friend was, it could not lift her sorrow at losing her closest friend. Ekaterina was her shoulder to cry on, her friend and her confidante. Nikita caught her eye again and her stomach turned over, a strange heat starting in her. *Knjaz* Rurik made her feel like a rambling schoolgirl in the craze of her first crush. She could quickly see herself getting in over her head, the perpetrator of her own scandal. It would hurt Aleksei so; her awkward, unemotional bureaucrat, locked away in an office, unaware of the needs of a young woman. Laura didn't doubt for a second Nikita knew exactly what they were. The thought made her tingle.

41

Anna bid her mistress a quiet goodnight and blew out the lamp, smiling at the Princess' sweet face in the moonlit room. She sighed with envy at her perfect skin and whispered a blessing over her sleeping friend then shut the door quietly behind her, holding the latch so it wouldn't click loudly and disturb her. Laura kept still, keeping her breathing even as she listened to her footsteps fading along the corridor, her heart thudding hard in her chest. Keeping her exterior calm while her insides were jumping and twisting about was the first trick Laura had learnt in Lady Ramkinson's school.

She waited till she couldn't hear any sounds in the castle then sat up, lighting a lamp and turning the flame up. She took it to her chaise lounge in her parlour and pulled the sewing box to her, lifting out her tray of bobbins and the scraps of linen underneath. She found her looped locks of the horse's tail and pulled them out, lifting out the secret sewing project.

Quickly she threaded a needle and began to make quick, neat stitches in the fabric, pulling her lamp closer to her work. Every now and then her nervous eyes would dart to the door, imagining footsteps on the carpet outside, wondering if Aleksei was going to send for her tonight, wondering why he had looked at her all evening with that sad look in his eyes, that inner torment.

Nikita had agreed with delight to be her tutor while Ekaterina was away and had arranged their first lesson to take place the next day. Laura tried to defer till Ekaterina left but the Prince had insisted, and Aleksei had agreed, if not a little sadly. Ekaterina had laughed and said she would have to think of other reasons to get Laura to Ladozhskoye if her lessons were not enough. It had been in jest, but Laura had seen the sadness there too.

She sighed gently and stitched faster, her needle blurring along the fabric. Every now and then she would pause to eye the garment, or to pull on a lock of horse's hair. She sewed until the oil in the lamp began to burn too low, the light fading and flickering across her work. Laura stopped and eyed it carefully. It was nearly finished, she wondered who she could show it to, wondering if she should show it to someone.

Sadly she realised she was alone here, she knew these people clung fervently to their traditions, even Anna and Ekaterina, and no one would recognise what her new garment meant to her. Carefully she buried the sewing and the horse's tail at the bottom of the sewing box, putting it back in place and carried the lamp with her to bed. She slid under the cold covers and cupped her hand round the lamp, blowing quickly onto the wick and shutting her eyes in the sudden dark.

42

Laura looked flusteredly at Fedor, a slate and a piece of chalk in her hands. She had been standing outside Nikita's rooms for ten minutes and there had been no replies to her persistent knocking.

'Am I to wait all day for *Knjaz* Rurik to answer the door?' she finally blurted out.

Fedor knocked with a bang loud enough to wake the dead and opened the door to Nikita's chambers, ushering the Princess inside. He then bowed low and stroke across to the bedchamber door, knocking loudly on that too. Without waiting for an answer he pushed open the door and disappeared into the darkened room beyond. Laura averted her eyes but found she couldn't help listening intently to the sounds from inside.

There was a sleepy sound, a pronounced intake of breath, as if Nikita had been fast asleep until the rude intrusion into his chamber.

'Forgive me Highness, but Her Highness is waiting for you to deliver your lessons for the day' Fedor announced.

Laura could just imagine Nikita wincing from the wine he had drunk last night and the bed creaked.

'Very well. Bring the bowl of water here and give my apologies to Her Highness for keeping her waiting' came Nikita's muffled reply.

Fedor stepped out of the room and bowed to Laura. Before he could say anything to her Nikita called out from the bedroom:

'Send up a breakfast tray, and some tea, it would not do to have Her Highness so frightfully parched during my lesson.'

'As you wish, Highness' Fedor said, bowing to the door, even though Nikita could not see him. 'Excuse me Your Highness' he said, letting himself out of the guest apartment. He did not approve of Nikita's behaviour, but Aleksei had made it clear what would become of his staff who refused the Russian Prince.

Laura spied a high-backed, padded chair next to a small, round table in Nikita's sitting room and sat down, resting the slate and chalk on the rich mahogany surface, folding her hands in her lap. She could hear Nikita splashing his face to revive himself, and the gasped exclamations at the temperature of the water. She found herself straining towards the sounds and quickly composed herself, dropping her eyes to her hands and rubbed at the chalk dust on them.

A tap on the door interrupted her thoughts and a serving maid brought in a tray with two cups, a pot of tea and a selection of breads and cold cuts of meat. Laura moved her slate and instructed the girl to put the tray on the table, and to pour two cups of the freshly brewed tea. There was no sound from the bedroom now, and Laura strained to hear what Nikita was doing.

The maid curtseyed and left and Laura lifted her cup, sipping the hot liquid. She wondered how much longer Nikita was going to make her wait. Aleksei had impressed upon her the utmost importance of pandering to the Russian Prince's whims, whatever they may be, to ensure good relations with their powerful neighbour, and a positive environment in which to invoke the Treaty of Dalnerechensk.

Laura knew the history as well as any Dalnerechensker now. After the defeat of the Russian Rebel's Army, Vsevolod had forced Russia to sign the Treaty of Dalnerechensk, which compelled Russia to recognise the tiny Principality as an independent state. Dalnerechensk had been rich with tin, and Russia had swallowed her embarrassment and signed, on the condition that Vsevolod sold all the ore to Russia.

For four hundred years the Treaty had dictated Dalnerechensk foreign policy and relations, and cocooned Dalnerechensk from the changes taking place in Europe. Laura thought she was very naïve in some ways, and when she thought about the Principality's peculiarities, she felt almost worldly. She set down the cup of tea and sighed quietly, glancing at the clock.

Nikita blew into the room and flopped down onto the chaise lounge, naked to his waist, propping his boots up casually on the seat. Laura gawped at him, hardly able to tear her eyes away. Nikita took a cup of tea, ignoring her schoolgirl gawp and sipped, exhaling noisily in pleasure. He then took a slice of bread and munched on it, obviously relishing his breakfast.

'*Knjaz* Rurik!' Laura gasped, finding her voice at last. 'Your attire is most unbecoming!'

'You insisted, Your Highness, that I was keeping you waiting' he shrugged, tossing a book to her. 'The Tsar tells me you read well in Russian, read aloud to me.'

She shifted uncomfortably, feeling hot and flustered, opening the book at a page marked for her, beginning to read carefully. She knew precious little of the words and she began to feel stupid and incompetent. She tried to ignore Nikita's attire and concentrate on the difficult phonetic script, the sexually explicit word sliding off her tongue before she realised what the word had been.

She gasped and looked up. Nikita was watching her from under his lashes, one elegant hand stretched out along the back of the lounge he reclined on, the fingers of the other touching his chest delicately. Laura slammed the book and held it out as if it disgusted her.

'What have you had me read?' she demanded.

'Perhaps I shall not have to teach you so much after all' he smiled.

Laura banged the book on the table and stood, fuming with him, clutching the book so hard her knuckles went white.

'Perhaps you would feel it fitting to hold the lessons in the afternoon when you have recovered somewhat from the debauchery of the previous night and manage to remember how to dress yourself properly *Knjaz* Rurik' she snapped and swept out of the room.

She stamped along the corridor like a child in a tantrum and thumped down the stairs, wishing they weren't made of stone so the whole castle would hear her indignation. She wondered what Aleksei would do if he knew what Nikita had given her.

She stopped, suddenly afraid he would be terribly angry with her for insulting him. *But he insulted me first!* she thought helplessly, terribly confused. *Am I not a royal of this household? Do I not have any rights at all?* She made up her mind not to bring the matter up with Aleksei just now. If he was angry with her he could order her back to Nikita's rooms, and suffer the humiliation. Instead she quickly went down to the stable and ordered Olaf to saddle her stallion.

He noticed her foul mood but said nothing, boosting her up onto the horse when he had finished. She quickly sped down the hill to the valley, heading at a quick trot to Ladozhskoye. The stable boy came forward and took the reins of her horse and she slipped to the ground, heading to the Ivanov front door. She rapped hard, ignoring the smart in her knuckles and waited impatiently for it to be opened.

Ekaterina's maid peeped out then dropped a curtsey quickly.

'The Countess is dressing Your Highness' she said, explaining the delay, letting her into the house.

Laura said nothing and followed the serving girl to Ekaterina's chambers. The Countess was standing wearing only a corset and her petticoats, only half laced into the constricting garments. Ekaterina nodded respectfully to Laura, readjusting her grip on the poster of her bed, and the maid began to tug the ties firmly, squeezing Ekaterina into a shapely hourglass.

Laura waited with barely concealed impatience, fidgeting irritably. Ekaterina looked amused and dismissed her maid, both of them waiting until the door had shut behind her.

'Look what he had me read out loud!' Laura exclaimed, thrusting the book at Ekaterina.

She took it, flicking through the pages and grinned at the young Princess.

'I see I am not the only one to play tricks on you' she laughed, then translated the words for her. 'Come Laura, do not blush like a silly girl, you are married!' Ekaterina teased. 'You have done much more than read of these things.'

'It was not appropriate for Nikita to make me read such things, I believe he quite enjoyed my ignorance!'

'I'm sure he would quite enjoy your participation!' Ekaterina laughed, tossing the book over her shoulder so it landed on her bed, and gathered the miles of material of her dress before easing it over her head, tugging it down into place. 'But you are right Laura, it was not appropriate for him to give you such a book. Perhaps you should ask your husband if he wants you to pander to *every* whim of his.'

Laura dropped her eyes, gazing at the red leather cover of the book of erotic poems. She enjoyed the secret unions with Aleksei, and wished they were not so infrequent now, unsure how to demand more satisfaction from him when she was only his property, his to decide how and when she would be used to fill the nursery. Then Laura realised he could order her to *Knjaz* Rurik's bed for the better of the Principality if the whim so took him.

She looked away, torn between duty and desire. If he ordered her, would she be willing? Would she refuse because she had promised to be none other than his? *If he forbade her*, a darker part of her wondered, *would she go anyway?*

'I do not envy you my dear' Ekaterina said sadly, breaking into her thoughts and taking her hands gently. 'But come, do not think of him, bid me farewell at the station, I am leaving soon.'

Laura felt the loss wrench in her chest and her lip trembled.

'I shall miss you so horribly Ekaterina' she said.

'Hold your head high Laura, you are still a princess remember' the Countess chided her softly, then called to her maid to fetch a porter to carry her trunks to the courtyard.

Laura forlornly followed Ekaterina to her courtyard. The stable boy and a porter were stacking the trunks onto the roof of the carriage and tiny flakes were falling, melting on impact with the ground. It was the last snow of a vanished winter and the day was grey and cold around them. Ekaterina linked her arm through Laura's then pushed her hand back into the fur muff.

The porter secured the load with a strong rope and jumped down, dusting his hands before opening the door and helping the Princess and Countess into the carriage, shutting the door behind them. He then disappeared into the warm castle and the stable boy climbed aboard the driver's seat, flicking the reins gently. The carriage jerked and rolled out of the courtyard.

Laura and Ekaterina sat in silence during the short trip, listening to the horse's hooves on the cobbles. When they reached the station they sighed quietly, finding each other's hand and squeezing gently. Laura noticed one of the carriages from the castle was also at the station, and fear gripped her icily, thinking Nikita had been so offended by her comments he was leaving. She gasped and squeezed Ekaterina's hand miserably. Their carriage rocked as the stable boy jumped down from the driver's seat and he opened the door.

Olaf came forward from the castle's carriage, and Laura saw it was not Nikita but Grigory waiting at the station.

'The train has not yet arrived *Tsesarevna*, Countess' Olaf said before offering a hand to help them down.

'We shall wait for it in the station where it is warmer' Laura said, relief flooding through her.

Ekaterina quickly slipped out and ran to her husband, tucking herself into the crook of his arm. He smiled fondly at her and kissed her temple, then called a good morning to the Princess. She returned his greeting, noticing the puzzled look on his face. Ekaterina quickly whispered to her husband and the look on his face changed. Laura said nothing and headed to the station house. Olaf opened the door for her and she noticed he too was scrutinising her face and body language.

Inside the small waiting room was a glowing potbelly stove and long bench seats that lined the walls. The stationmaster and ticket clerk stood rigidly at attention behind a small desk and three middle-aged women clutched shawls and baskets to them as they stood in dour silence. Olaf closed the door behind Ekaterina and Grigory and hunched his coat up round his ears, preferring the cold to company, and talked quietly to the horses, stroking their velvety noses gently.

Laura smiled at her people, cringing inwardly at having to uphold a public image when she felt like crying. As one they swept deep curtseys and bows but did not call out or try to talk to her. Ekaterina nudged her elbow and the three took a seat on the bench close to the potbelly. The others in the room sat then, and an odd silence fell.

The Princess didn't notice, she was lost in inward misery and torment.

'I shall be lost without you dear Ekaterina' she finally said softly.

Ekaterina hadn't heard. Her head was inclined towards Grigory, listening intently. Laura sighed then heard the faint chug of the approaching engine. She left the Count and Countess and slipped out into the cold, leaning off the platform to watch the approach of the steaming train.

The stationmaster and ticket clerk rushed out to the platform behind her and began to blow distinctive calls on their whistles. Somewhere to her left, obscured by several carriages sitting on extra tracks, were answering whistles and the ring of metal on metal. The train passed under Vsevolod's Gate on her right, the brakes squealing loudly as it approached the station, pressurised steam hissing out and enveloping those on the platform.

The engineers leapt down from the locomotive and dragged a dripping hose over to the train, swearing at each other as they tried to man the pump fast enough so half the water wasn't wasted as they filled the engine. It hissed and roared disgruntledly, and sacks of coal were dumped into the open bin coupled behind the locomotive.

Once the supplies of coal and water had been replenished the engineers and the ticket clerk quickly scrambled aboard and eased off the brakes, letting the pressure build in the engine again, and the train slowly began to roll out of the station further into the train yard. There was a distant whistle, and the stationmaster answered with a short blast of his own. Laura followed the tracks with her eyes until she could see no further, wondering what was happening to the train. There was another whistle and an answering one from the platform, and the engine steamed back into view.

The locomotive had been turned around, and coupled to ten carts that Laura guessed held refined tin from Macherna inside them. Between the tin carts and the open coal bin were two carriages: the black dining carriage from the royal train and a passenger car. The engine hissed to a stop at the station again and the three middle-aged women who had been waiting inside with the Ivanovs climbed into the passenger car. Grigory and Ekaterina joined Laura on the platform, whispering quietly together, exchanging words of affection and love. Laura averted her eyes, their feelings for each other were clear, and she tried not to feel jealous.

Ekaterina and Grigory shared a parting kiss while Olaf loaded her baggage into the carriage and then they bid each other a soft farewell. Ekaterina then turned her attention to the Princess she had ignored for almost ten minutes, folding her in her arms.

'Be flattered Laura, and desired by *Knjaz* Rurik' she said softly. 'But remember sex is power and power is politics. Do not give your heart away, no matter what the body asks of you. God guide and give you strength' she blessed her, then stepped into the carriage, waving goodbye to them both.

The train blew a sharp whistle and the platform hissed with steam then it began to ponderously move out of the station, picking up speed as it went. Grigory and Laura watched until the carriages disappeared from view before turning away, blowing on their cold fingers.

'Will you be returning to the castle?' Laura asked quietly.

'No, I will come this evening though' he said, and bowed to her as he took his leave, climbing into his waiting carriage.

Laura waved him goodbye then accepted Olaf's hand to help her into the castle carriage. Olaf shut the door then leapt up to the driver's seat, flicking the reins gently before heading towards the castle.

43

Laura tried to concentrate at dinner, but her mind was turned inward, Ekaterina's comments tumbling over and over inside her head. She had been cloistered away from men in Lady Ramkinson's school, and before her marriage the only knowledge she had of sex had been the bawdy jokes and innuendo of the women in the bars Clara had taken her to. She had not understood them, and had been too embarrassed to ask for an explanation.

She found herself beginning to understand now; Ekaterina's words were truthful, even from Laura's inexperience. When she had whispered in Aleksei's ear, when she had rubbed him gently through his trousers and felt him respond, the power she had felt was intoxicating, that she could command his desire so. And when he had looked at her, with that longing, that raw want, there was nothing he could not have commanded her to do.

Nikita desired her. She could see it in his eyes, even veiled through his long lashes, and Laura did not think for an instant she was the only one to have noticed it. She began to wonder, to entertain the notion of using the flirting, the attraction to help her husband. She could lie back on a chaise lounge and watch Nikita through her lashes too, could flirt and hint at forbidden pleasures if it would help Aleksei achieve the results he wanted from invoking the Treaty of Dalnerechensk. She smiled to think she might even enjoy politics.

The smile faded and she dropped her eyes. She was a child, she had not yet begun to fathom the power sex had. Nikita was only a few years older than her, and yet she knew his knowledge of such power was far greater than hers. Part of her was forced to admit the Russian Prince already held power over her, and knew how to wield it.

She trembled then, realising the Prince could manipulate her into an agreement that would see Dalnerechensk suffer at the hands of their powerful neighbour, all because she had desired carnal pleasure. She felt an ache inside her then. Aleksei had made her weep in desire and then had abandoned her. If Nikita propositioned her, even though she knew it was manipulation, would she agree? She shut her eyes, trying to avoid answering that.

Her thoughts were interrupted when the musicians struck up a lively tune. The court stood, bowing to partners and began to dance. Aleksei did not rise, and Laura stayed with him, wondering if he was not feeling well. He too had been quiet through dinner, and she had feared that he was angry with her, or angry with Nikita. She reached out to take his hand, to look at him searchingly.

'Go and dance' he said softly.

Laura felt Nikita's eyes on her and she leaned closer to Aleksei, whispering in his ear.

'Forgive me my lord, I do not feel like dancing tonight.'

'You cannot disappoint the court Laura' he chided softly. 'You are a princess; it does not matter what you feel like.'

'*Knjaz* Rurik wishes to dance' she said quietly, dropping her eyes.

'So dance' he snapped, becoming impatient.

'As you command' she said quietly.

Nikita approached and bowed low, asking for her hand. Laura shot one more look at her husband then took his proffered hand, letting him lead her down to the dance floor.

To her surprise he held her formally in the waltz, keeping a diplomatic distance from her. She eyed him, astonished, and he cleared his throat, aware of her scrutiny.

'Forgive me for my attire and behaviour this morning' he said formally. 'I was ignorant and arrogant and I humbly beg your forgiveness.'

'Of course' she said, feeling stiff and formal too.

He did not speak to her again, except to ask her for another dance when it had finished. She agreed, hot and uncomfortable with this formal pomp. She took his cool hand again, and then remarked casually:

'You certainly have changed *Knjaz* Rurik.'

'I have been wracked with guilt all day thinking of how I had offended you' he said, and Laura felt the flush spread through her belly as well as her cheeks.

'You do not strike me as a man concerned with the thoughts of others' she said, smiling.

'Only yours, Your Highness' he said, and flashed her a quick look through veiled lashes.

Laura laughed at the butterflies the look stirred, and decided to encourage Nikita's flirting again. She hated to think of him becoming stiff and restrained like the Dalnerechensk court. She wondered how Ekaterina could resist it for so long.

She smiled at him, and let herself sparkle in the arms of the Prince, always demure and restrained but responsive to his attentions. As she danced and turned she could see the faces of the court; the smiling, encouraging looks of those ministers like Valentin Gogol and Lev Dostoevski who upheld Aleksei's view of pandering to the Russian's every whim, she could see the fluttering fans of Tatiana and Natasha as they whispered together and eyed her, mean smiles on their faces. She sighed to think even more rumours would fly through the castle about her, when she was only doing as her husband had told her to. She saw Aleksei's face once and dared not look again, unable to explain the feeling that surged though her at the strange look in his hazel eyes.

She finished the dance then excused herself from Nikita's company, sitting next to her husband. He managed a smile that did not reach his eyes and he laid his hand on hers, a rare show of public affection for her. She smiled radiantly at him and whispered she loved him, leaning close to press a sweet, girlish kiss on his cheek. He smiled then, his affection melting his resentment of his inability to express his feelings with her.

She shifted closer, and leaned forward to whisper in his ear again.

'Aleksei, I should enjoy the boyish rogue who slips into a woman's chamber, afraid of being caught by the staff and his father, should he wish to talk on the rug before the fire again. Or if words fail us, perhaps actions may speak louder' she said, squeezing his hand gently.

The flush stole into his cheeks at the thought of her sprawled naked on the rug before the fire but he quickly swallowed down his desire.

'We will not leave until *Knjaz* Rurik does' he said quietly.

Laura dropped her eyes, crestfallen. 'As you wish my lord' she whispered.

Her disappointment increased when the court retired to their rooms and Aleksei sent her to sleep alone in her bed. She didn't know what to think, and was terrified she had insulted him in some way. Confused beyond words she slipped beneath her covers and cried herself to sleep.

44

'Good morning, most beautiful of all the angels' said a silky voice behind her.

Laura composed herself as best she could and turned to greet the Prince cordially. His eyes drank in the sight of her emerald dress and he bowed, kissing her hand gently.

'Ah, still so repulsed by me then?' he asked in French, looking wounded, and as Laura stuttered to correct him a teasing smile spread across his lips. 'Well then I must be given grace to win back your affections' he kissed the back of her hands again. 'Guide me today around your Principality, you will see how perfectly well behaved I can be.'

Laura accepted and arranged to meet him in the stables shortly. The butterflies were tickling her insides and she splashed her face quickly with water to bring her back to her senses. She dressed warmly and demurely, slipping down to the stables. Nikita was not there, so she called a greeting to Olaf and ordered the open carriage to be hitched to two horses.

'I need you to drive *Knjaz* Rurik and me around Dalnerechensk today' she said.

Olaf didn't answer, his eyes flicking to Nikita as he arrived and stepped beside her, offering his elbow to her. She accepted cordially and waited while Olaf worked, taking his hand to step up into the carriage. Nikita scrambled up behind her and Olaf climbed onto the driver's seat, flicking the reins carefully.

*

Aleksei paced nervously in his Council's chambers, fishing his pocket watch out of his inner jacket pocket and clicked it open, eyeing the late hour. The advisors were watching him as if he were a hawk stalking a rabbit's burrow, wondering when he was going to pounce. At mid-morning Fedor knocked politely on the door in the manner of a man about to deliver bad news.

'Forgive my intrusion' he said, bowing low before the Prince. '*Knjaz* Rurik has gone driving for the day with the Princess.'

Aleksei's face was like thunder. He had seen the looks he had shot Laura since he had arrived, and seen the silly, moonfaced gawps and smiles she had shot him. He was not the only one to have noticed their indiscreet flirting and his temper frayed at the whispering of his ministers.

'Has he come to talk about the treaty or to seduce my wife?' he roared, making his Council cringe.

Nobody answered.

*

Laura sat composed in the open carriage, not quite trusting herself in Nikita's company. He looked radiant in an ebony-blue coat and black trousers, a thick fur muff round his hands, and she tried to stop thinking about how good he looked with the brisk wind blowing those boyish strands across his forehead. It was getting harder and harder to resist the urge to reach across and tuck them back behind his ear. The only thing that stopped her was the fear of her indiscretions being reported to Lady Ramkinson, and even now she feared the crop.

In French, Laura explained the layout of the fortified city and the story of Vsevolod's repel of the Russian Rebel. She told him of Dalnerechensk's customs and the villages and hamlets that made up the Principality, pointing out sights of interest as they meandered through the city. Olaf sat above them, hunched in a thick coat, and drove through all the streets of Dalnerechensk's town then headed out into the forests between Liberty and East Valley in complete silence.

Nikita stretched, groaning in pleasure and lay back comfortably in the carriage when they rumbled into Hunter's Pass, away from the eyes of the Principality. Laura resisted the urge to do the same and Nikita eyed her.

'Relax' he teased, tugging on a fold of her skirts.

'A Princess cannot go lounging about so in a carriage' she retorted, brushing his hand away.

'You are also a woman' he grinned. 'Sitting so straight over the bumps hurts your back does it not?'

'I do not complain' she answered stoically.

'Oh Laura! There is no one to see you in the forest!' he chided. 'Unless you think the bee will buzz in your husband's ear, or the trees will whisper it to the wind, or perhaps if he comes to the stable he will hear it straight from the horses' mouth!'

'Oh stop!' she scolded, laughing. 'Is it your intention to scandalise me *Knjaz* Rurik?'

'I could not dare whisper words that would make one think ill of you' he said, suddenly serious. 'But come, rest your back against a pillow, it is only your comfort I am thinking of. I shall tell the horse not to look.'

She snorted, unlady-like, then slid a pillow behind her and reclined, easing the pressure on her back. They were quiet for a while and Laura closed her eyes, soaking in the warm sun and the wet, green smell of the forest growing around her.

'Tell me Laura, what does an American girl do for fun in Dalnerechensk?' Nikita said quietly. 'There is no opera, no theatre, no -'

'The Ivanov's party was fun' she said, smiling, dreamy, the colour coming up on her cheeks.

'Only that?' Nikita asked after a pause.

'And the spring feast' she added, trying to think of what else she had enjoyed.

'This is not a young court,' Nikita interrupted. 'Why does your husband not employ youngsters to liven the company? The Countess and you sparkle alone, like forgotten diamonds.'

She thought it prudent not to answer that, shutting her eyes again. Nikita let the silence drag out, eyeing the curves of her body from under his long lashes. Finally he blurted out:

'Come Laura, don't rest on decorum. Have you ever not wished you were free of this place?'

'No' she smiled. 'I am in love with Dalnerechensk. I love the hills, the people, the sky, the air -' she stopped, aware Nikita was laughing at her. 'Dalnerechensk is my heaven.'

'Does not the huge responsibility wear you down? You shine with youthful exuberance, and yet I fear it will soon crush out your spirit dear girl.'

Laura was quiet for a while, then said carefully: 'I am responsible for the emotions of these people, how they perceive the monarchy. But I am not responsible for the management of the Principality, the business side of it, if you please. My husband does not believe the council room is a place for his wife. He does not discuss the Principality with me. So I have no responsibility.'

'For a modern man he has fairly archaic ideals' Nikita scoffed.

Laura wanted to agree, but could feel herself being manipulated by this handsome stranger. Nikita was playing games with her, and soon she feared he would have turned her completely from her husband. She decided to risk insulting him again.

'I must remind you *Knjaz* Rurik you are as a guest here in Dalnerechensk. It would not do to insult my husband' she said coldly, sitting up straight again.

'Forgive me, I did not mean to insult him, but does he not realise your intellect? What you could offer his court besides an heir? –'

'It is not my place to say and nor is it yours *Knjaz* Rurik' she snapped.

They fell silent. The carriage rolled on through the green of the forest and Laura ignored the bumps in her back.

45

Laura kept her composure cool with the Prince for two days, refusing to accompany him on any more excursions, even refusing to dance with him, complaining of a sore ankle, which was miraculously cured when Aleksei led her to the dance floor. Thus snubbed, Nikita retired to his rooms complaining of an illness that racked his head and chest, despite the Vakhtangov doctor diagnosing a clean bill of health for him.

The court had fluttered nervously, bickering, blaming the Princess, blaming each other, no one quite brave enough to blame the Prince's disgraceful consumption of wine. After three days of Nikita's absence Aleksei paid him a visit, concerned for his guest's wellbeing, with his young wife in tow at his insistence.

Nikita lay stretched out on a chaise lounge, his loose, white shirt open at the neck, his face and throat covered in a damp sheen, his hair hanging in wet clumps on the pillow. He propped himself up as best as he could and nodded a respectful welcome. Laura couldn't help but feel that a small smile was playing in the corners of his mouth.

'How fares you *Knjaz* Rurik?' Aleksei asked, worried for reasons other than genuine care for his guest.

'The same still Your Royal Highness' he said quietly, as if it pained him to talk.

'I am sorry for your ill health' he said. 'Perhaps a drive in the fresh air will help to revive you?'

He looked hopeful, hoping he didn't sound too eager, wishing that his ties with Russia were secure, not knowing how they might be hurt by Laura's actions. He had lost many a sleepless night worried about Nikita and Laura and the Treaty of Dalnerechensk.

Nikita looked like he was considering the offer.

'I would need a guide' he said finally, faintly.

'Excellent! I'm sure my father could spare Fedor for a few hours.'

'I had hoped, Your Royal Highness, that you would send me with someone possessing all the sweetness of a nursing mother, and the carefree casualness of a young woman to lift my spirits. Princess, would you do me the honour?'

'You will find beneath Fedor's formal countenance a heart of gold, he is very attentive when Tsar Constantinovich feels poorly' Laura said sweetly. 'You will be in good hands *Knjaz* Rurik.'

'I doubt he could turn my mind from my misery as easily as you' he answered.

'Of course my wife will go' Aleksei said shortly.

Laura swallowed her temper and conceded stiffly to her husband's demands, excusing herself so she could change into the most unbecoming outfit she could find.

Anna brought her dress after dress, holding each up against her in the mirror. It was no good; Laura's wardrobe was designed and made by Boston's most prestigious tailors, she owned nothing that would not compliment her figure and colour. She sighed, dressed warmly, and slipped down to the stables where Nikita was already waiting. The colour had begun to return to his cheeks and she hoped the outing would not be long.

It was not that she had found Nikita's remarks particularly insulting, she was finding herself thinking more and more about him as the week progressed, his dark good looks, his easy flattery; the way he moved when he danced and walked. She could feel hot heat in her stomach and deep within her when she was with him, and it took an act of will power to put him from her thoughts.

She had not questioned her marriage once in six months, whatever difficulties she had faced were directly linked to Aleksei's struggle to manage a Principality. She had supported him as best as she could and looked past this trial in their relationship to their future together. Nikita was a distraction at a crucial moment. She didn't dare let him turn her head, but it was so difficult not to, she was a neglected woman, and Nikita was young and attractive.

Olaf had rigged up an open carriage to two stallions in the courtyard before the stables. He nodded in greeting to Laura and offered a roughened hand to help her into the carriage. Nikita was helped up beside her and the door latched shut. Before Olaf had even stepped back to climb up to the driver's seat, Nikita suddenly leapt onto a horse's back and flicked the reins firmly against its flanks.

The fierce slap startled them both and they bolted, knocking Olaf onto his back in the gravel, throwing Laura back in the seat with a short scream. The carriage bounced out of the castle, almost knocking down the two guards on duty. Her heart leapt into her mouth and she clung to the sides of the carriage, too terrified to even beg him to stop.

Nikita laughed wildly, watching scared people scramble out of the way, scattering children and dogs alike. Soon they were thundering along the muddy path of the Hunting Forest, climbing wildly up and down hills with no regard for the cut road. Laura feared an axle would break and send her flying to her doom.

And as suddenly as he had spurred their wild escape Nikita pulled on the reins and slowed the panicked and snorting horses. He turned back to grin at her and her palm caught him full against the cheek. He tumbled from the horse's back, managing to grab her and pulled her off balance, both of them landing in the soft mud. Laura slapped him again and Nikita pinned her arms to her chest.

'You vile rogue!' she yelled. 'You could've gotten us killed!'

'Oh come now Laura, have you not ever been reckless?' he laughed. 'Did the fear of being caught or death not make these moments of your life more exhilarating?'

She pushed him away and struggled to her feet. Nikita grabbed at her again and she slapped him a third time, raining blows on his chest. At once he seized her, pushing her bodily against the side of the carriage. She shut her eyes but couldn't stop the tears that overflowed, standing there crying miserably with shock and fear. She felt him relent, and lay a hot hand against her cheek. She twisted away, not wanting to see what she might find in his eyes.

Nikita sighed and composed himself, reaching into his jacket pocket for a handkerchief and wiped away the mud from his face and clothing. He eyed the trembling, upset Princess and held out his handkerchief to her. She ignored it. Nikita swiped at his jacket twice more then tucked the handkerchief back into his pocket, eyeing the Princess.

'Forgive me Laura' he said with sincere regret. 'I did not mean to scare you so, only I wished us to talk without eyes and ears.'

'Olaf cannot see out the back of his head and he does not speak French' she snapped, rounding on him. 'That's deaf and dumb as far as we're concerned.'

Nikita laughed at her indignity then reached into another pocket and pulled out a small velvet box.

'Peace be with us Laura; I have something for you.'

He opened the box and pulled out the sparkling arrangement of sapphires and diamonds. He held it out to her. Her eyes widened at the gems, knowing the necklace cost more than the emeralds Aleksei had sent to her. In this lonely patch of forest she suddenly felt very vulnerable.

'And is this to buy my forgiveness and affection?' she said, trying to sound cold.

'How you do suspect me!' he cried. 'Cannot the royal ambassador, member of the Russian Romanov household, not give his hostess a token of his appreciation of her generosity?'

'Not here like this' she said, feeling uneasy, and casting her eyes around for any eyes to see them. 'You may present this to me before the court and you will receive my public thanks' she said. 'I cannot accept it here like this.'

She turned away from him again, leaving him holding the gems with nothing to do but put them back in their velvet box. The horses snorted again and stamped in the soft mud, still terrified, their eyes rolling. She began to whisper to them the way she had seen Olaf do to soothe them, stepping closer and stroking their necks. They quietened while she talked softly, and felt her own heart ease its frantic beating.

The adrenalin was fading, and she had run the gauntlet of fear and relief, leaving only anger. Nikita was behaving like a spoilt child; he had terrified her and the horses, and had tried to give her a present worth thousands of dollars in secret, like he was courting her. He had made no secret of the fact he found her attractive, and though his flattery and mischievousness was winked at like Ekaterina's was by the court, Laura knew they were whispering behind their hands.

He was too attractive, too full of passion, and Laura vowed she would not leave with him unescorted again.

'The fresh air seems to have revived you *Knjaz* Rurik' she snapped. 'I am returning to Dalnerechensk; you can please yourself.'

And she started back towards Dalnerechensk on foot. Nikita called after her, trying to turn the horses round, then left them and grabbed her arm, stilling her gently, turning her to face him. Laura wanted to resist but her resolve crumbled. She had been frightened, and wanted nothing more than to be pulled into loving arms and soothed. She kept her eyes lowered and chewed her lip, trying to keep in control of herself. Nikita stepped closer, stroking away a mud fleck on her cheek.

'Forgive an impudent man Laura' he said softly. 'You must think me crass and reckless, my only defense is that I am young and spoilt, and have been surrounded by young and spoilt friends. Court is no place to find integrity. You have proved me wrong, and I don't know how to act' he shrugged helplessly. 'I do so wish for this friendship to blossom.'

Laura shut her eyes, chewing harder on her lip, fighting her tears. Nikita whispered her name again and she dared to look at him, flicking a quick peek and then away again. For once she found them honest and frank, not veiled with his lashes and she believed him, wanting to believe him, not wanting to be taken as a fool by this sophisticated man.

'I have you at your word you mean no dishonour to myself or my husband?' she asked quietly.

'At my word Your Highness' he swore.

Laura heard her name being called through the trees, accompanied by several of her titles from various others in the search party. She called back and they turned towards her, Fedor and Olaf heading the search party on horseback. Fedor dismounted, asking if she was hurt, taking in their muddied attire. Laura shook her head, wiping away her tears. It was clear from the looks on their faces what they thought had happened between them. By the end of the night Dalnerechensk would believe it too.

46

Laura sat on her chaise lounge, staring at her embroidery without seeing it. Since Nikita's miraculous recovery she had dutifully gone for lessons with him in the Tsar's library, glad that someone always came in under the pretense of finding a book. When her lessons were over she excused herself from his company and hid in her rooms, trying desperately to put him from her thoughts. But it was no good, Nikita's words were echoing in her head, and had taken up a constant repetition the past three days. *Oh come now Laura, have you not ever been reckless?* She shut her eyes tiredly. *Yes* she wanted to tell him. *And I still want to be.*

She was tired of being a princess. She had been tired of pretending to be a lady in Boston. She hated all those eyes on her; she didn't know how Ekaterina could do it. The stress of constant scrutiny and Lady Ramkinson's riding crop had reduced her to tears more than once. She knew what was being whispered behind the fans every time she stepped into a room, and Aleksei had grown cold and distant from her; he had not sent for her at all.

She had not been ready for this, a husband who hardly came to the marriage bed anymore, barely a title and little wealth; and a huge, insurmountable barrier between herself and everyone else who smiled politely and bowed, respectfully asking questions dictated by protocol and not by friendship. It had nearly destroyed her, that cold distance in Lady Ramkinson's school, and would have, had it not been for the plucky Irish servant.

She had been thankful for Clara's friendship. Those rare evenings had been her ray of hope that had helped her through the boring repetition Lady Ramkinson had made of her life. Laura had wanted more than social parties and a rich, titled husband. It was not to say she hadn't wanted those things; she had wanted that and more. She had dreamed of a rich adventurous husband, who stared death in the face laughing as he decoded the pyramid walls and discovered wild new civilisations, winning fame and glory with his wife at his side.

Knjaz Rurik; bold, daring *Knjaz* Rurik had hardly been from her thoughts, though Laura had deliberately kept herself from his eyes. She knew how he looked at her. She knew how he could whisper, how he would recklessly flatter and flirt, how the looks from under his lashes were breaking down her resolve and making her desperately wish she were no longer a married woman.

Had she regretted marrying her prince? Laura didn't know. She had not even been introduced to Boston Society; only the graduates were paraded before the fashionable, eligible men as willing, tame and eager future brides. She had not known love, she had not courted anyone; she had not really known what it was like to be desired by someone, so much so that he would risk damnation for her.

She wanted to be reckless, she wanted to flirt and feel his hands on her, wanted him to give her what his eyes promised from behind their silky veil, wanted to risk everything for passion and pleasure.

And yet she loved Aleksei. Awkward, unemotional, embarrassed Aleksei. However he covered his feelings with decorum and protocol she knew letting Nikita broach her would deeply wound him, and that was something she couldn't bring herself to do. She didn't want to hurt Aleksei, she just needed a release, an evening with no eyes on her, a night with no whispers and slanders.

She stood suddenly, her embroidery falling to the ground. Anna looked up from where she was darning a pair of socks and asked if she was alright, a shadow of concern falling over her.

'Help me undress, I will go to bed' she said quietly. 'I don't feel well and am not to be disturbed, not for *any* reason' she looked at Anna firmly.

Anna was frightened, knowing that meant she would have to tell Aleksei he couldn't have his wife if he sent for her. She dropped her eyes then, knowing it was highly unlikely that he would send for her, especially now the rumours were circulating that she was an unfaithful wife. She put aside her mending carefully and stood, helping her friend through into her room, noticing how fever-bright her eyes were.

Laura said nothing as she undressed with Anna's help, not even embarrassed by her nudity anymore. Anna asked once if Laura wanted her to send for the doctor, or for something to drink and she declined both offers, crawling into the covers of her bed. Anna tucked her in and wished her a good sleep, hoping she would have recovered in the morning. Laura thanked her quietly, feeling guilty for deceiving her friend, but dared not risk exposure.

She lay still and listened for the soft click of her parlour door that meant she was now alone. When she heard it she pushed back the covers and padded quietly over to her dressing room. It had been hard to hide clothing when she knew Anna knew all her wardrobe, but she had managed it, and now pulled out the pair of boots, trousers, shirt and worker's cloak she had taken from the laundry secretly.

She quickly changed and pulled the thick cloak around her, pulling it low over her eyes, eyeing her reflection in her mirror. She chided herself quietly, thinking she had chosen too small a pair of pants that didn't do much to hide the shapely curve of her thigh, but the shirt did well to hide the swell of her breasts. She drew the cloak around her more carefully and thought that the way it hung by her legs would have to do.

She carefully retrieved and folded a precious object from her sewing box and pushed it deep into a pocket, wondering if she should use it, or wait till she was out of the castle grounds. She wondered if she could slip out of the castle unnoticed, there were more people who would recognise her, more people whose job it was to take notice of her. She couldn't hesitate now; she had planned this outing for two days.

She took a deep breath and peeked out of the door. The sun was going down and the Advisory Council was leaving, as were the day servants. Who would notice a small, cloaked figure leaving the castle grounds in the midst of all these people? Laura quickly slipped in behind them, shuffling along and keeping her head bowed. The guards at Vsevolod's Way didn't even blink as they left the castle grounds and headed down the hill into the fortified town.

Laura could have laughed at how easy it was and she ducked into a gloomy alleyway, hunkering down in the deepest shadows she could find. From her pocket she retrieved the precious object and unfolded it.

She had decided Dalnerechensk was small enough to know all her fallen women and a new face that somehow looked familiar would certainly set alarm bells ringing. She had not sewn a wig from the horse's tail like she had with Clara's blonde hair. Instead she had sewn a linen cap with strips that caressed her cheeks and chin and had attached the hair, creating a convincing rusty crop of hair, beard and moustache.

Quickly she smeared her face with a little dirt and pulled the hair cap on, arranging the hood again then stepped out onto the street. She swaggered the way Clara had taught her, her steps deliberate and firm like a man's, her thumbs pushed into her belt loops. To her disappointment there was hardly anyone on the street, and suddenly she felt a little apprehensive. She would hate to have sneaked out only to be arrested for loitering. What an embarrassing scandal that would make then!

She slipped down a narrow side street and followed the curving cobbles along, nodding curtly to an old man who sat in a doorway, smoking his pipe. He eyed her with suspicion but nodded back, puffing at his pipe. Laura had to force herself not to skip that her disguise had fooled him. She kept her footfalls heavy and deliberate though she didn't know where she was going. She kept walking, knowing that if she faltered or looked out of place she would be stopped and questioned.

The darkness deepened around her and she began to relax a little, knowing the night would make it more difficult to identify her. It also made her more aware of things around her and she listened carefully for sounds close to her, trying to identify what they were and where they came from. A sudden cheer turned her attention to an alleyway leading away from the street.

It was gloomy and the shadows were pregnant with suspicion. She could see the murky outline of a door in the dusky shadows created in this corridor of tall buildings and instantly her curiosity was pricked. She took a deep breath and walked towards the sound of the cheering, opening the door and slipping inside.

The small room was crowded and stank of sweat and cheap ale. Laura wrinkled her nose, detecting vomit and urine in the fetid mix of air and closed the door, breathing through her mouth, trying to accustom herself to the smell. The burly men that packed the pub paid no attention to the small waif that joined them, their eyes were on a small, stocky man standing on the bar top. Laura found herself a seat next to an old man at the back of the room and sat quietly, nodding curtly when the waitress offered her a small glass of vodka.

Thinking this was some sort of entertainment she sat in the shadows and watched quietly, wondering what this man was doing to make so many burly men cheer him on. He wasn't smiling. In fact he looked angry, and stalked back and forward on the bar, knocking off the drinks that were not moved in time, splashing the closest patrons.

'Aleksei has forgotten his Principality!' he suddenly shouted and the men cheered again, raising their glasses and fists into the air. 'He sits up there in his old castle, entertaining the – *Russian*,' he nearly spat the word in his distaste, 'while men - *good* men - are dying in the mines, dying on stale bread and rotten crops!'

Laura suddenly felt cold. This crowd was angry, bitter and drunk. A disagreement could turn into a brawl, a brawl into a riot, a riot into a revolution. Her hand tightened round her glass, her knuckles white with fear, wondering how to slip out without calling attention to herself now.

'For years we have suffered while His Royal Highness sits and forgets what it means to rule properly!' the man on the bar yelled, his eyes sweeping the crowd. 'He has forgotten us! His loyal subjects! *We*, who have given our taxes, our sweat, our blood and even our very *lives*, to watch him piss it away! Who here has not lost a father, a brother, a *child* in those terrible hell holes?'

The crowd cheered, stamping their feet and banging on the benches in approval. Laura made a half-hearted attempt to fit in, hoping desperately to avoid being detected here. The man pulled out a rolled document and made a show of opening it for the crowd.

'I have here the latest wisdom of our esteemed leader!' he snarled. 'By *Royal Decree -*' Laura heard the suffocating sneer in "royal decree", thick and distasteful, and it made her embarrassed to be sitting in this room. But the man wasn't finished. '- His Royal Highness *Velikij Knjaz* Aleksei Vakhtangov has proclaimed the falling price of tin warrants a measured fall in the wages paid to the miners who pull it from the ground. *Twenty rubles a week!*' he hollered. 'Your lives are now only worth twenty rubles a week! He has broken the back of his people!' he screamed and the crowd cheered. 'He has turned against us and ground us into poverty! He has sold you into slavery! He has condemned you to a hole in the ground where you rip worthless metal from cold soil and forget the light of day; starve under rotting soil and return home to watch your children die! Your wives die! This will not do! This will not do!'

The crowd cheered and leapt to their feet, chanting *this will not do* over and over, stamping their feet in time to their chant. Just when Laura feared they would all rush out for their torches and pitchforks and swarm to the castle in rage-filled revolution the man held up his hands and called for silence. It took some doing, but finally all were waiting, simmering with rage and impatient for action.

'My friends,' he started again, quietly, making them lean forward to hear him, shushing others. 'The winds of change are blowing through Liberty Valley. I am a patriot and I love my country; but I love her too much to see her brought to her knees to beg at the feet of a Russian.' There was utter silence. He spread his arms hopelessly. 'I have lost faith!' he moaned. 'I have lost faith in my Tsar, in my Royal household. I do not believe the Vakhtangovs are the right people to lead this nation.'

There was a hushed intake of breath at the treasonous statement. Burly men looked at each other carefully, wondering who agreed, wondering who didn't, and there was a dangerous feeling of fear and hate in the room. Laura dared not meet anyone's eyes, her breath seemed loud in her ears, so loud it drowned out the sounds in the room, and she couldn't shake the feeling that someone was looking at her, and *knew*.

There was a cough then someone yelled:

'The Princess could lead us!'

'The Princess is American, and God bless her, no more than a child herself' the man smiled. 'What would she know of mines? Of politics? Of evil Russian devils? She is innocent!'

'She could rule until a son could -' started another and a disapproving sound interrupted him.

'She is an only child from an only child! She has been married nearly six months and is not growing any rounder!' someone yelled.

'And how are we to know the boy is not a Rurik bastard?' cried another.

A sudden scuffle broke out, an angry drunk lunging at the last speaker.

'You take that back, how dare you call her a whore?!' screamed the attacker, and several others stepped in, separating the fighters, holding them at bay. Laura held her breath, her chest so tight she wondered if her lungs would be crushed and she would faint or fall dead here. The fight could start them racing for torches and pitchforks again.

But the bar quickly subdued them and the attacker found himself unable to move for the press of restraining bodies around him. He held his hands up.

'The Princess is innocent of all of this!' he appealed to the man on the bar, stopping his struggling. The men let him go cautiously, but he didn't lunge again.

'*Da*, my friend' the man agreed quietly. 'She is an innocent, she is not responsible for Aleksei's actions. She will not share his retribution.'

'She is kind hearted, and the people love her' said another. 'Perhaps if we petitioned her, asked her to intervene with her husband for us -'

'It's no good my friend,' the man sighed dejectedly. 'She has no power over him. She cannot command him to his own bed, she cannot command him in this.'

'She can command *me* to her bed!' someone shouted bawdily and the room roared with laughter. 'I will sire a score of bastards for the throne, every one of them patriots and Dalnerechenskers!'

Laura scrabbled to her feet, knocking over a chair as she tried to climb out of the room, her head whirling from the revolutionary talk and the heightened fear of discovery. A few men looked round at her and she kept her head down and crashed into another person, heading the wrong way in her desperation to be free of the place. She was cursed but she spied the way out and headed for it.

Someone grabbed her arm, inches from the door and she growled a course swearword, demanding to be let go, her fear making her voice squeak a little.

'You are far too young for a full beard' said a voice then the face leaned closer. '*Tsesarevna*' he added in a whisper.

Laura stiffened then began to tremble, feeling cold dread slide up her spine. Her horror-filled eyes snapped up to find those of her captor.

It was Olaf. She didn't know whether to be relieved or shocked. He roughly took her upper arm, yanking her out with him, saying loudly:

'Off you go young rascal! This is a place for men, not skinny boys!'

The door swung shut behind them and cold fresh air rushed around them. Laura's knees went weak, making her stumble. Olaf dragged her up by her arm, pulling her along, twisting and turning around a few streets, looking over his shoulder and quickening his pace. Laura was desperately frightened, so much so she was nauseous, her heart racing unnaturally fast, her skin sweaty with cold terror, making her shiver in the chill spring night.

Olaf didn't stop and soon she was hopelessly lost, dragged along alleyways and side-streets in a confused warren of darkness and cobblestones. At the end of one alley the shadows widened and spilled out into a dark courtyard. Three tall walls created by the backs of the three buildings rose up around the yard, flanking them and secluding the area from the rest of the world. Terrified, Laura wondered if she should scream, wondered would someone come or would they shut their windows tighter and hide from the murder in their back yard? A quick glance confirmed her worst nightmare. No windows looked out over this courtyard.

Olaf let her go suddenly and she backed away, her eyes darting round for ways of escape. But the stable groom blocked the only way out.

'Forgive me if I hurt you *Tsesarevna*' he said quietly. 'It was a dangerous place for you to be.'

'You listen to that talk Olaf?' she snapped, her fright making her loud and angry. 'Just where do your loyalties lie?'

'With you' he said simply.

Her anger imploded and the tears spilled over. She crumpled, her knees folding till she was sitting hunched on the ground, sobbing into her hands. Olaf knelt beside her, making her flinch as if she expected a blow, her eyes searching his for any sign of threat.

'Don't think ill of me *Tsesarevna*' he said quietly, reaching into a pocket and retrieving a white handkerchief. 'I am loyal to Dalnerechensk.'

'You were there, in that room...' she trailed off, frightened and not sure what to think.

'*Da*' he said. 'I spy, because no one knows the stable's groom. I spy and tell His Highness.'

Laura sniffed loudly then suddenly tore the wig off her, throwing it into the dirt, her secrets worming themselves free in the darkness.

'I just wanted to get away from the eyes, to feel like no one was watching, to be reckless and not have it become a consequence for me, a shame on my reputation, or Aleksei's. I didn't expect to be so in danger, to feel so frightened...' she stopped, pressing the handkerchief hard against her mouth and eyes, trying to stop the misery. 'I don't know how to get home' she whimpered. 'I didn't think.'

Olaf said nothing then picked up the wig, turning it over in his rough hands. He recognised the horse's tail at once; he had known the Princess had taken it after her dizzy spell. He had thought at the time she had taken it to a witch or mixed it in a potion to help make her fertile and now shut his eyes in shame for thinking of her like that.

He turned it over, holding it closer to his eyes, squinting in the dark, marveling at the tiny stitches. It had been so well made that it looked real; it had only been the graceful way she moved and her eyes that had given her away in the tavern.

Laura sniffed loudly and mopped her face with the handkerchief, her eyes red and her cheeks a mess of tear-streaked dirt; hardly a princess at all anymore. Olaf felt sorry for her then. She was no more than a girl, caught up in politics and a burgeoning revolution that could see her dethroned at the least and dead at the worst. He looked at her sadly, knowing the revolt would go easy on her if they knew she was with child. His eyes strayed to the gentle swell of her breasts then dropped lower, noticing the way her legs looked in men's trousers. He felt his blood rise at the sight of her and quickly looked away.

Despite the promising shape of her body Olaf knew she was still a child. *She is too young to bear children* he thought.

He stood then gently held his hand out to her, helping her to her feet. She wiped her messy face and pulled the cloak around her tightly, ashamed of her attire and shivering in the cold. Olaf shrugged off his jacket and wrapped it round her shoulders, leading her through the deserted streets, winding their way up to the castle. Laura composed herself as they walked, her quick mind turning to the problems of getting back in to the castle grounds.

There was no way she could slip in unnoticed, and could think of no plausible reason as to why she would be outside the castle this late at night, or why the guards had not known of her leaving. That in itself was a problem. She could not present herself at the gates and claim they had not seen her leave. They would have to report her arriving, and at the late hour. As they had not noticed her leave they could both be hung. The thought made her shiver.

At the end of another alley they turned and Laura saw they were on Vsevolod's Way, close to the castle. She could see the dull shapes of the guards at the gate two hundred metres away and panicked, not wanting to cause their hangings, her step faltering. Olaf suddenly pushed her against a building, stepping close to her. She gasped but he leaned closer, stilling her.

'Say nothing. Do exactly as I say' he hissed quietly, then pulled her away and folded his arm around her, walking boldly up to the gates.

'Who goes there?' one of the guards challenged.

'The stable groom and his bride for the night' Olaf answered. 'The castle hay is the softest in the world, everyone knows that.'

The guards laughed quietly and Laura burned with embarrassment.

'She must be special' the other guard said, amused.

'Very' Olaf slapped her bottom.

She gasped, shocked, and the guards laughed, waving them through. Laura was stunned but Olaf pushed her in, keeping his arm round her till they got to the stables. Olaf checked quickly over his shoulder then led her to the rear door for the kitchen and opened it, ushering her inside. The fires of the stove had been banked down for the night and cast a low light over them, but the room was still warm and Laura felt safe for the first time that evening.

She rounded on Olaf, rubbing at the hurt.

'You slapped me!' she said, stupefied.

'It was no less than you deserved' he smiled, taking his jacket off her then turned to go. 'Goodnight *Tsesarevna*.'

'Olaf…' she said softly, stopping him in his tracks.

He turned back to her, seeing she was struggling with the right words.

'You spy?' she managed finally.

'*Da*' he answered, closing the door again and turning back to her.

She twisted her hands together, ashamed and distraught. 'You won't tell Aleksei will you?' she managed.

'*Nyet Tsesarevna*' he promised, noticing the way she seemed to sag with relief. 'Would Your Highness care for something for her nerves?' he said, spying the decanter of alcohol on the sideboard, feeling clumsy.

She nodded and he poured her a brandy, handing it over with a nod then turned to go again.

'Have you ever been to the mines? Are they as bad as he said they were?' she whispered, feeling terribly wicked for threatening Anna now.

'I don't know' he said awkwardly.

'Will you take me there tomorrow?' she asked.

He paused then nodded, closing the door behind him, leaving her to finish her drink alone.

47

Laura opened her eyes again, noticing the room had become more distinct in the grey pre-dawn. She sighed and rubbed her face, knowing it was useless to try and sleep now. Her thoughts had whirled round and round her head all night, giving her no peace at all. The talk in the bar last night had frightened her, even more so that Aleksei had not spoken to her of this before. She now understood why he had locked himself away and sweated over old treaties. He was kind hearted, and desperately wanted the best for his people. He would not have deliberately pushed his Principality into poverty.

The castle was still silent and she pushed back the covers of her bed, slipping over to the large French windows of her room. If the talk last night was any indication of the general feel of the population then Dalnerechensk was in trouble, yet Aleksei insisted on keeping her in the dark. *What did Nikita mean to the Principality? Did he cause the fall in the wages? Is he going to buy the mines?* Laura could have screamed with frustration. She was a royal, if Aleksei died this place was hers to rule. Why did they insist that politics was none of her business? What could she do if Aleksei suddenly fell ill and died? It was a real possibility when he pushed himself so hard.

She could see his temper and his composure fraying away as the days continued to pass without Nikita setting a foot in the Council Chambers. The Russian Prince had gone hunting, dragging a tight-lipped Aleksei and the younger members of the greying Council with him, and had spent his days in idle pleasures, reading or gossiping with the minister's wives, flirting openly with all ladies of the court, especially the young Princess.

Nikita was trying Aleksei's patience. Whatever he was here to discuss was of significant importance that Aleksei swallowed his pride, did nothing to silence the rumours, pandered to Nikita's tastes and sent his wife to do the Russian's bidding. Aleksei's pride was hurt but he had to continue to endure this outrage. Laura felt sorry for him, caught in a desperate situation.

His people were bitter, angry – *murderous*. She had felt it, in that room, that simmering undercurrent of hate and revolution. She had only wanted to be reckless, but not *that* reckless. She had never felt fear like that when she had been with Clara. She shivered and rubbed her arms, wincing at the flare of pain in one. She pushed up her sleeve and eyed the five bruises left by Olaf's fingers, distinctive even in this half light.

Thinking of him made her flush, and she rubbed at her backside again. She was shocked that he dared to lay a hand on her like that, and astounded that the guards had let them through without checking her identity. The thought made her feel cold. How many times did this happen? Who else could they have let in unwittingly? Thieves? Revolutionaries? *Assassins*?

She shivered again, squeezing her arms, then winced at the bruises. She needed to know what made those men angry enough to revolt, to want to kill.

She was interrupted with a soft click behind her. Anna had stepped into the sitting room, and she heard her stoking the fire, pushing back the velvet curtains on their rods to let in the early rays of summer. Laura inspected her bruise one last time then pushed down her sleeve, turning as Anna opened her door. She looked surprised to see her awake.

'Good morning Your Highness, are you feeling better?'

'A little, thank you' she answered, the lie rolling off her tongue easily.

'Did you not sleep well?' Anna asked, noticing the rumpled and tossed state of her bed.

'I have a troubled head' she answered softly, glad she could tell the truth again.

'I'll run you a bath' Anna smiled, disappearing into her dressing room.

Laura waited till she re-emerged, hanging three pots of water on the fire to heat.

'Send Peter Kaminin to me' she instructed. 'And do so *with haste.*'

Anna bobbed a curtsey and scuttled out the door. Laura eyed the cold pots of water on her fire then quickly dressed in a simple yellow gown, sighing with a little regret as she would have liked to have soaked for an hour in warm water, but could not greet the Captain of the Guard naked in her bathroom. There were enough rumours as it was. A guilty part of her also was pleased Anna would not see her bruises, and she would not have to explain where they came from.

She was nervous about this meeting, but by the time Peter was ushered into her sitting room she was composed and had thought of what to say, even having time to check the right words in the lexicon she kept in her rooms. Peter bowed deeply to her and Anna shut the door behind him, then took the boiling water off the fire, pouring it into the bath tub.

'Good morning Your Highness' Peter said, his face betraying nothing of his surprise.

'Last night, when I was ill and couldn't sleep, I saw two people moving about in the castle grounds. I don't believe either of them had a reason to do so.' Peter looked shocked but she went on. 'I do, however, think it not a crime what they were doing in the stables -' she coloured '- but must insist that care be taken in knowing exactly who is on the castle grounds and for what purpose.'

'What time was this, Your Highness?' Peter asked.

Laura had been ready for this. If he knew what time he knew which guards to punish for their breach of duty.

'I do not remember' she said, and saw his thoughts flash across his face. She knew he couldn't punish the entire night watch, though he was sorely tempted. 'I do not think this a matter to trouble my husband, nor it a matter of punishment, but a reason to be vigilant. Who knows who could be let in if faces are not checked.'

Peter paused then conceded, bowing to her again.

'As you wish Your Highness.'

Laura dismissed him and watched him walk away, hoping he would be discreet in his inquiries. A small part of her wondered whether she should confess it was her then decided against it, she had already hinted that the two were lovers. She did not want another rumour of unfaithfulness circulating in the Principality.

Peter shut the door quietly, slipping out of the castle. He could not call in on Aleksei as he would want to know why he was in the castle. He could not confess how serious the breach of security had been last night. There was only one it could have been slipping into the stables, as the groom was infamous for his dislike of others in his realm. He was coming out of the kitchens with his breakfast when Peter arrived at the stables.

'Who was she?' he snapped.

Olaf stopped and eyed him, his face blank.

'You were seen last night, by the *Velikaja Knjaginja* no less. She fair blushed to tell me' Peter continued.

Olaf dropped his eyes, his cheeks darkening.

'It won't happen again' he said.

'See to it that it doesn't. It's only by her good grace that no one is being flogged for this' he swung himself up onto his horse and kicked its flanks, riding back to Tcherepnin.

*

Laura sat at the dining table. It was virtually deserted at this early hour but she didn't notice. Guilt was making it hard for her to chew and swallow. *I am eating well and my people are starving* she kept thinking, and she quickly lost her appetite. Then the thought that she had wasted this food made her feel even guiltier and she forced herself to eat some more, the vicious cycle repeating on her.

A hand lay on her shoulder, making her jump.

'My dear, are you not well?' Tsar Constantinovich asked, sitting beside her, concerned at the little she had put on her plate, and even less that she had eaten.

'Yes, I mean no, I mean -' she stopped, folding her hands in her lap. 'Perhaps just some fresh air might revive me' she murmured.

She stood before he could ask any more questions and quickly slipped outside, ignoring the briskness of the morning. Grigory was coming up the stairs and bid her a cherry good morning, surprised to see her so early. She returned his greeting as he passed then suddenly turned, calling out his name. He stopped and turned back to her.

'I mean to send some money to my father, for a present for his oil partner' she lied, her quick mind in overdrive. 'What would twenty rubles be?'

'Hardly worth sending' Grigory answered. 'It would only be about one American dollar.'

'I see' she answered. 'Thank you.'

Grigory bowed and disappeared into the castle. Laura slipped down the stairs and made her way to the stables.

Olaf was seated on the old stump of a tree used for a chopping block outside the stables, eating a bread roll stuffed with cheese and pork. He looked surprised to see her so early and began to fold away his breakfast, dusting his hands on his rough trousers. Quickly Laura insisted he finish and sat beside him on the block, calling a pleasant greeting to Nicholas Riminov as he arrived for another day in the Advisory Council with Aleksei. He bowed to her, his gaze sweeping over Olaf sitting beside her and eating but said nothing.

Olaf stood, cramming his breakfast in his mouth and pulled open the large stable doors, dragging out a royal carriage, afraid of the repercussions from the lack of protocol despite his fondness for indulging the Princess. He stamped to the stalls and bridled two stallions, talking to them quietly, fondly, as he led them into the courtyard and backed them into the harness. Quickly he hitched the carriage to the horses then opened the door and helped Laura in.

Nikita burst out of the castle, his clothing untidy, his sleep rumpled hair flapping in the breeze.

'I did not realise we were leaving so early this morning' he said, clambering into the carriage beside her.

'I'm sorry *Knjaz* Rurik; I am leaving on another matter. I am going to inspect the tin mines today' Laura said quietly, excusing herself from his presence.

'Excellent!' he exclaimed, sitting back comfortably, tucking himself in and making himself more presentable.

Laura hesitated, unsure what she was going to see and realised it probably was not suitable for a visiting dignitary to see. Then again, if Nikita were here to discuss diplomatic relations with her husband, as he had yet to do, a visit to the mines would keep him fully informed of the stakes involved in selling tin ore to Russia.

'Your Highness?' Olaf asked quietly, watching her carefully.

'Thank you Olaf, we shall go' she said.

'*Tres bon*!' Nikita laughed, patting her hand affectionately.

Olaf said nothing and swung into the driver's seat, released the brake and flicked the reins. The carriage rolled out of the courtyard and down Castle Street to Tin Gate, trotting onto Miner's Way, by-passing Ladozhskoye and heading straight up the hills on the East of Liberty Valley to Macherna, nestled on top of the wide, forested ridge.

Nikita inhaled the scent of pine deeply and sighed contentedly, eyeing the forest out the carriage window.

'It is beautiful here Laura, I understand now why Dalnerechensk is your heaven. I may decide to settle on some land here, perhaps overlooking the ridge where I could mine.'

'Is that your business here in Dalnerechensk? Purchasing some land for mining?' she asked, her quick mind working.

'I could not, Dalnerechensk's greatest jewel is already married' he laughed. 'Let's not talk of business now Laura, tell me about the flowers, I do so like to hear you talk.'

Laura didn't reply, she could see they were approaching Macherna.

The village had grown from a mining camp two hundred years ago and with the exception of one or two families it was still populated only by the miners who walked a kilometre to the mines every day. The children of the village who climbed the oldest and tallest tree could look down into both valleys, clinging tightly and calling out with glee to the guards in Davostok and Ladozhskoye, despite them being too far away to hear.

Macherna was the prettiest village in Dalnerechensk, surrounded by evergreen trees and wide, well set out streets. At first glance it looked like other sleepy villages, but on closer inspection one would notice the large presence of castle guards and a well-worn track disappearing into the trees, caution and restricted signs nailed to their trunks. Olaf guided the horses along this path, startling the guards who saluted smartly, looking at each other apprehensively.

The wide, packed dirt path meandered through the trees for a kilometre then opened into a large, flat area of rock; grey and dusty with constant use. On one side of the bare clearing sat a cluster of miners on felled tree logs, eating from metal pails balanced on their knees. On the other sat a small cottage, smoke rising lazily from the brick chimney, three guards armed with rifles standing on the veranda. Between the miners and the cottage rose a towering face of bare rock. It was punctured by a cavernous maw, great and black.

Laura shivered to look at it.

Olaf directed the horses towards the cottage, calling a halt and jamming on the brake. The door of the cottage burst open and the overseer ran out. He had recognised the royal carriage through his window as he was sitting down to breakfast and the napkin was still tucked in his shirtfront. He swept a low bow at the carriage, tearing the napkin away as he did so, stuffing it in his pocket where a cheeky tail peeked out.

Olaf leapt down from the driver's seat and opened the carriage door then stepped back, offering his hand to Laura as she stepped down. The miners leapt to their feet, their meal pails scattering, spilling food all over the ground but no one dared pick it up. As one, like mechanical puppets, they all bowed low, holding half eaten hunks of bread behind their backs. Nikita slid out of the carriage and the overseer bowed again.

'Good morning Your Highness, *Knjaz* Rurik' the overseer said, looking nervous.

'Ah, I see my reputation precedes me' Nikita laughed.

'Forgive me, I did not receive a telegram to tell me to expect you' the overseer stuttered.

'I did not send one' Laura said quietly, slipping her arm through Nikita's. For some reason this made the overseer even more nervous.

'May I ask why you have humbly graced us with this visit?' he swallowed.

'I am to see the conditions of the mines, the tin that is produced and some of the men that work here.'

The overseer's eyes darted nervously round the small party.

'Right now?' he sounded shocked. 'Would Your Highness prefer to return another day?'

'Are you refusing your sovereign admittance?' Nikita asked suddenly.

'No no, of course not' he said desperately. 'The mines are cold and dark Your Highness, if we had known, we would have brought in more light' he explained.

'It is my intention to experience firsthand the conditions of these mines. I warrant no special lights' Laura said.

The overseer gave in and bowed miserably, taking two helmets from the miners who were still standing and gave them to the guests.

'Please wear these' he begged. 'Follow me.'

Olaf waited with the horses while Nikita and Laura followed the sweating man into the yawning maw of the mine. Laura kept her face carefully composed and only Nikita, feeling her nails dig in and her hand tremble on his arm, knew how scared she really was. Within four steps they were in complete darkness and the overseer switched on their headlamps for them, explaining how the tin was cut out of the rocks and what happened to it once removed.

He led them to a cage that was winched up and down through the shaft to the belly of the world and opened the door, waiting for them to step into the hanging basket.

'How deep is the tunnel?' Laura asked quietly.

'Two hundred feet' he replied.

'Oh' she said faintly, stepping into the cage, her nails digging deeper into Nikita's arm.

She shut her eyes on the slow, deep descent into the earth, thanking God when it was over. The lower levels of the mines were indeed cold and she shivered, stepping closer to Nikita, thinking this was a horrible place to work in; the dark, the cold, the groaning press of tonnes of rock above them, bearing down on them in silent threat, the deafening ringing of picks on stone.

A new appreciation of her father's work was growing in her heart. He had spent many nights ensuring the safety of his workers and had cried bitterly at Carlton's funeral when his oldest friend had been killed in a mining accident in Texas. She was beginning to understand the fury and the bitterness in the room the other night.

The lights of the miner's hats in the gloom before them flickered and bobbed like industrial glow worms, seeming to rhythmically dance in time to the rings of picks on rock. Faces loomed suddenly bright in the beam of her headlamp and were gone again, men's faces, all streaked with sweat and grime, ghoulish in the light and then vanishing in the black hell of the mine.

She tried to pay attention, but the faces that flashed so brightly before her lamplight were startling her, breaking her concentration. She was beginning to realise, with growing horror, that many of the men were so old they were bent double under the weight of their pick axes, their white whiskers stained with black grime, the dust settling into the creases in their faces and necks.

But there were more slight and scurrying creatures in the dark. One bumped into her and doffed the miner's cap.

'Beg pardon Your Highness' the voice squeaked and then disappeared again, fading into the unnatural night.

'There are children in here!' she cried out loud.

The tour party stopped, turning to face her. The overseer looked sickly in the lamp's light.

'*Children*!' she cried, her voice echoing down the tunnel.

'*Da* Your Highness' the overseer said, unable to think of anything else to say.

Laura stared at him, wondering what kind of a man employed children to scramble around in the dank, dark bowels of the earth. Another child brushed by her and cheerfully begged for forgiveness, whistling as he faded into the gloom of the tunnel. *It was only one dollar a week, to feed a whole family*, her mind whispered to her. *A starving child would scrounge in the dark for his living.*

'I think I've seen enough' she said quietly. 'I want to leave.'

'As you wish Your Highness' the overseer said, leading them back the way they had come.

She shut her eyes in the cage, hating the rocking motion of it, counting the seconds until she would be free. There was a sudden grinding and the cage gave a shudder. Laura gripped Nikita's arm tightly.

'What was that?' she whispered.

The overseer looked just as shaken and turned his face upwards, watching the approaching platform. Before he had reached it he opened the door and leapt up, reaching down for Laura, pulling her out roughly, Nikita taking the initiative and leaping clear himself. There was a loud crack like a rifle shot that reverberated in the narrow space.

Laura was horrified, her mind turning to the armed guards outside and she wondered if someone had been shot. The daylight outside was blinding, and she could see nothing beyond the mouth. There was another loud crack and a chunk of the roof fell in, grazing Laura's arm and making her yelp in pain, throwing her hands over her head.

There were cries of alarm and pain deep inside the mine shafts, a terrifying roar and a shivering, straining tremble in the walls and ceiling. Nikita dragged her out into the open, rushing past miners that stood at the mouth of the mine and called frantically for others to hurry.

There was a deafening crash and thick clouds of dust billowed out of the mine, a blast of air knocking them onto their backs. The silence descended instantly, the miners stopping their calls, the whisper of the settling dust the only noise on the ridge.

'No!' Laura screamed. 'The children!'

She leapt to her feet and ran back towards the dusty hole. One of the miners stepped in front of her, holding her back.

'*There are children in there!*' she screamed, trying to twist her way out of his grip.

'It is not safe' he said, fighting to keep her out. 'It is *not* safe; it is *not safe!*'

Laura sobbed and wrung her hands, pacing back and forward. Nikita took her arm and she shook him off irritably, surprised at the pain it caused.

'You're hurt' Nikita said, eyeing her arm where the falling rock had ripped her sleeve and gashed open her arm.

He dragged her over to the carriage where Olaf stood, watching the men dash into the dusty tunnel with bits of strong wood, dragging out rocks and debris.

'See to her arm' Nikita commanded, pulling out a handkerchief and flicking at the dust on his jacket.

Olaf tore his eyes away and pushed Laura back on the carriage step, seeing she was making another bolt for the mine.

'Olaf the *children*!' She moaned, distressed. 'Who is in the mines? Who hasn't come out?'

'They have to make it safe before anyone goes back in' he answered, hooking his rough fingers into the hole in her sleeve and tore it wider.

Laura winced then shivered when he poured the cup of cold water over her arm to clean it. The graze was not deep but he caught sight of the five distinct bruises on her arm and shut his eyes briefly.

'I'm sorry if I had hurt you' he said softly, binding her arm with a clean handkerchief.

Men began emerging from the mouth of the mine, slate grey with dust, some bloodied, some not. Laura darted forward, asking each if they were hurt, calling for help if they were. They staggered out in pairs and threes, helping each other, carrying the young and the elderly. She checked one grizzled old man who was coughing and struggling for breath, giving him some water to drink. When she turned back to the mine she saw something that tore open her heart.

A child was brought up from the depths and laid gently on the ground to the side of the clearing, near the felled tree logs. She rushed over calling for a doctor, falling to her knees beside him. The boy was struggling to breathe, coughing up blood. She slid her arms around him and lifted him into her lap, looking wildly around for help. The men she cried out to took their hats from their heads and bowed them, turning away.

Laura screamed hysterically for help then realised the boy's body was broken beyond repair. He was dying. His small, frightened face looked up at her, tears washing down his cheeks.

'I don't want to die!' he sobbed, blood bubbles flecking onto his lips.

'Shh' she said softly, stroking his hair back from his face. 'Don't be frightened my dearest boy.'

The boy coughed again, struggling for breath, crying out for his mother in fear. Laura stroked his hair, holding him close to her, her yellow dress soaking up his blood. The boy struggled again and then lay still and Laura sobbed, rocking his frail body back and forward.

The news of the cave-in had reached Macherna and worried families were streaming to the site, some joining the rescue effort, helping out the injured and the dead, others calling anxiously for those that had not appeared. There was a sharp scream of a wounded animal and suddenly the boy was pulled from her arms, the distraught father breaking down over the body of his dead son.

'I'm sorry' Laura said, tears washing rivers of dust and grime away from her face. 'I'm so sorry.'

The look he shot her was one of infinite grief and despair and hatred all mixed together; but the hate faded fast and he sobbed, cradling the small body in his huge miner's hands, burying his face in the crushed chest.

Nikita pulled her up off the ground and led her away.

'What was his name?' she asked no one in particular. 'What was his name?'

Nikita led her back to the carriage and sat her on the step. She struggled and protested against his insistence but he held her firmly in place. She gave up and sat limply, tears streaming down her face as they lay the bodies beside each other, children, old men and sturdy alike, pitiful broken and grime covered mounds of humanity.

'We need to leave' Nikita said softly.

'No!' Laura looked at him horrified.

'There is nothing we can do Laura' Nikita said softly. 'We must go, before they start looking for someone to blame.'

She looked shocked but realised he spoke the truth.

'Forgive me, I'm so sorry' she wept and allowed herself to be pushed into the carriage.

Nikita climbed up into the driver's seat and flicked the reins, guiding the carriage past the ambulance wagons and the undertaker's cart.

The shock and pain congealed in her into a deep, red anger. Her blood was singing in her ears, a roaring rushing anger pulsating round her body. Nikita stopped the coach in the stable yard but before he could leap down Laura slammed open the door and slid out, stamping her way into the castle.

*

Aleksei rubbed his eyes tiredly. They were gritty with the dust of parchment paper and his throat was clogged as well. Yet although he felt mentally drained he was enormously satisfied. He placed his hands on the tabletop and eyed the men in the Council Chambers. They all looked tired and at the limits of their intellectual abilities, but satisfied as well. Maksim Yegorov stretched back in his seat, his bones creaking as he settled more comfortably.

In light of Nikita's absences, the Advisory Council had decided to press ahead and draw up a list of their recommendations for the Treaty they hoped to amend. The Council had been divided evenly over the issue of the price of tin. Aleksei wanted the price to increase by at least two hundred and fifty percent. Vasilievich Chekhov and several others of the Council had feared this price was too much and would risk Russia's wrath. For nearly four hundred years they had co-existed uneasily surrounded by the greater nation. They did not want to risk another war with their neighbour.

Aleksei had argued and threatened, ranting and raving at his ministers but finally had to settle for a price only increased by a hundred and fifty percent. It was not enough to stop Dalnerechensk's descent into poverty, but it would slow it enough to buy the Prince enough time to find another method for increasing the Principality's wealth. The arguments had gone back and forth for two long weeks but at last it was done. Aleksei's satisfaction and accomplishment was marred only by the fact that Nikita Rurik had refused to take part in the discussions.

The doors of the council room suddenly slammed open and Laura stepped in, covered in grime and drying blood, her hair in disarray, the sleeve of her dress torn and a bloodied handkerchief wrapped round her arm. Tears had washed streaks down her cheeks and there was an angry fire in her eyes. She slammed shut the doors and turned to face a stunned cluster of old men.

'Laura! Are you hurt? What has happened?' Aleksei cried.

'There were children!' she said, looking aghast.

Aleksei took her arms but she shook him off suddenly furious.

'There was an accident, and people died! They were children! *Why are their children in the mines?!*' she cried, shaking so much she had to lean against the wall to stay upright. 'Have you been to those mines Aleksei? Have you seen how they work? *How could you only pay them twenty rubles?!*'

'Lev, make sure the *Velikaja Knjaginja* reaches her chambers, have the doctor look at her arm and soothe her hysteria' Aleksei commanded.

The round advisor came forward, his normally ruddy face drained of colour. He took her arm, despite her attempts to shake him off and firmly guided her out of the Council Chambers. Unmitigated tears washed down Laura's cheeks, too stunned to do anything else but be obedient.

The castle was in an uproar, several servants had seen Laura and had screamed, bringing more to the large hall. Several members of the court came flying out of the dining room, asking what the matter was, calling out to each other and heading up the stairs. Lev screeched for a doctor, dragging the bloodstained Princess up to her rooms. The women and the servants screamed again, and even Tatiana was struck dumb with horror. The men swore and Tsar Constantinovich bellowed from his study, demanding to know what was going on. Lev barged into the queen's apartments, screeching for the doctor, almost as hysterical as Laura was.

Anna dropped the fire poker with a crash, crying out when she saw her bloodstained and disheveled appearance. Lev hovered at the door and Anna leapt forward, folding her arms around the sobbing Princess, guiding her carefully to the chaise lounge. Lev shut the door, bellowing again for the doctor, and the castle was full of shouting and questions and fear.

There was a scuffle outside the door then Fedor burst into the room, his eyes widening in horror.

'Your Highness! The blood!' was all he managed in his shock.

'It's not mine' she said, shaking.

Fedor opened the door, eyeing Lev. 'Brandy, water, sharp scissors, towels' he barked then shut it again.

Lev was only too glad to have something new to yell and other voices echoed his. A sharp tap on the door announced the arrival of the doctor and the items. Fedor pulled it open, ushering him in and took the brandy and towels from Lev, shutting the door against those who were craning their necks round it to see what was going on. He blew his cheeks out, wondering where the hell Aleksei was.

'It's not mine' Laura was still whimpering.

Anna had stripped her out of her stained yellow dress. The blood had soaked into her petticoats and corset and Anna stripped her mistress out of her underskirts, exposing her bloomers. Fedor couldn't stop his eyes dropping to the shape of Laura's legs. Anna wrenched on Laura's corset strings and Fedor remembered himself, turning his back hurriedly, trying to forget the sensual sight of her in her underwear and remember that she may be gravely injured.

There was the sound of material being dropped to the ground and a relieved gasp. Anna swept the throw rug from the chaise lounge round Laura, leaving her arm exposed for the doctor to clean. She winced and Fedor turned back, eyeing her carefully. She looked pale and drained, holding the covers around her with one hand while the doctor cleaned away the blood from the gash on her exposed arm, asking a barrage of questions.

'It does not need stitches Your Highness' he said finally, bandaging her arm carefully.

Fedor came forward when he was done and handed her the full brandy. She swallowed it all, coughing afterwards. Anna picked up the fire poker she had dropped, putting it back in the stand. The doctor collected his things together and packed them into his leather bag, giving Anna instructions on how Laura needed to be cared for this evening, shutting his bag with a click.

He looked quietly at Fedor and an unspoken understanding passed between them, then they opened the door, pushing the crush of people back, shutting it behind them. They were mainly the servants of the household that stood before the door, their faces were all pinched in worry and fear; and Lev, who was waiting for word to take back to Aleksei in his Advisory Chambers.

'I can confirm,' Fedor started, 'That Her Highness and *Knjaz* Rurik were present when there was a cave in at the mines. Her Highness escaped with only a gash to her upper arm. While we are thankful for her safety, our thoughts and prayers are with those who did not survive.'

Fedor and the doctor pushed them away, making their way through the throngs of people, heading separately for Tsar Constantinovich's private rooms and the Advisory Chambers to give the Royals the news.

48

Olaf squinted against the fading, flickering light of the oil lamp, buffing polish labouriously onto a tall riding boot. He had moved a small box into an empty stall to serve as a table and sat on the scarred stump on which he cut wood for the castle fires. It was warm in the stalls and the smells of the hay and horses were reassuring. It made the task of his menial chores endurable.

He sighed and put the boot on the table, lighting a match that he touched to the polish, letting it melt before he dropped the tin lid onto it, smothering the flames. He rubbed his eyes, tired. It had been a long day, and he did not want to deal with any more chores this evening. He took off the lid and swiped a soft cloth in the liquid polish, buffing at the boot again, vowing this would be the last chore he would do tonight. God knew there would be plenty of time tomorrow.

He heard a soft sound and looked up in surprise. Laura was standing in the stables, pale and drained, looking like a haunted ghost. She was dressed in a warm, dark traveling cloak, her hair pinned up in a simple bun, which made her complexion almost translucent and her eyes bottomless. Olaf stood quickly, his knee knocking the makeshift table and setting the liquid polish rocking wildly, sloshing. He grabbed it to steady it, eyeing the table to see if much had been wasted by the accident. It hadn't, and when he looked back up the Princess was beside him, waiting quietly.

'His name was Ari' he said softly.

She shut her eyes in an effort to keep the pain out, biting her bottom lip hard. She looked hollow and exhausted, as if she were just a shell, or a graceful puppet. He wondered if she had slept at all, it was well past midnight, and the events of the day had taken even the strength out of him.

'Saddle a horse for me Olaf' she said quietly. 'I cannot rest until I have seen Grigory Ivanov.'

The request surprised him and he eyed her worriedly. She looked as fragile as glass, and he thought of suggesting the coach, which would at least afford her some protection from the cold night. But glass was sharp too and he held his tongue, saddling both the grey stallion and the rusty mare with the re-growing tail. She swung herself gracefully into the saddle and looked surprised to see him mounting too.

'I cannot let you ride out into the night alone Your Highness' he said quietly, and clicked his tongue for the horse to start forward.

As they passed out of the castle gates onto Castle Street Olaf leaned down from the saddle and murmured to one of the guards, letting them know the Princess had left the castle grounds and was proceeding to Ladozhskoye and the home of Grigory Ivanov. Laura did not hear, or if she had she ignored it, and the only sound that night was the clop of the horses' hooves on the cobbled street.

Olaf breathed in deep, exhaling through his nose in a long sigh. Dalnerechensk was still and cold and the half moon shone like polished silver above them, lighting the landscape with a gentle bluish glow. *She still did not act like a princess* he thought quietly. *She acted like an impulsive, impetuous girl. Once it was known by the court she had ridden a horse in the dark to Ladozhskoye on a whim her reputation would be permanently damaged. Her actions would ally Valentin Gogol's fears she had inherited her mother's madness and would surely doom the throne.*

He sighed again and eyed her back as she rode ahead of him towards the village on the slopes of the hills of Liberty Valley. No matter what the reason for her midnight visit to the Ivanov Estate it would not be viewed positively by Dalnerechensk. He wished passionately she would realise this before it was too late, wished passionately that Aleksei had not married a child.

His hands tightened on the reins in anger but he held his tongue, and they rode quietly into the grounds of the estate. Olaf dismounted in the courtyard then reached up to the Princess, helping her down from her horse. She seemed distant and light, and Olaf wondered if her ordeal this morning had broken something inside her. She stepped away from him and she dropped her eyes demurely.

'Stable the horses and come inside out of the cold, I could be a while' she said softly.

She turned away from him suddenly, and for the briefest moment Olaf wondered if she was having an affair. It was no secret she slept alone in her own chambers now, but Grigory Ivanov was not the man he would have thought could draw Laura to his bed, not when Nikita Rurik's attentions had been so clear. He dismissed those thoughts quickly with shame for thinking ill of her and led both horses into the stable, rousing the young groom with a kick to his backside, handing over the reins and instructions to care for them properly.

He slipped back outside, strangely relieved to see her still waiting for him then followed her to the majestic front doors. She paused and he lifted his fist, knocking loudly on the cold wood. A startled maid opened the door two minutes later and dropped a quick curtsey before letting the Princess into the house. Grigory stood on the landing, sleep rumpled and surprised to see her, a robe thrown over his nightshirt.

'Your Highness!' he said, astounded. 'What brings you here at this hour? What has happened at the castle?'

'How bad is it really Grigory?' she asked softly. Her voice had barely been above a whisper but he heard her and dropped his eyes.

'Your Highness, you've had a fright -'

'Grigory...'

There's that sharp edge Olaf thought and hid his smile. Grigory relented, hearing that soft warning on the fringes of her voice.

'Come to the study Your Highness. Anya, heat some wine for us, and see to the stable groom.'

Laura grasped the bannister, seeming to waver off balance as she started up the steps. Olaf put up his hands, wondering if he should dare climb the Ivanov stairs. Grigory came down them and slipped his arm around her waist, helping her up the stairs.

He was very much surprised and concerned at the Princess' late night appearance, aware of the rumours it would cause. But he couldn't help but feel sorry for her and indulge her. She was young and alone in Dalnerechensk, and God alone knew what her strained marriage and Nikita were doing to her nerves.

He escorted her into the study and led her to one of his high backed chairs, turning to bank the fire and light a lamp in the room. He took his seat opposite her, eyeing the way she seemed sunk in herself, and had pulled her knees up to her chin, her hand resting gently on the bandage hidden under her coat, heating the hurt she felt there. Grigory couldn't help remembering another evening, not too long ago, when Aleksei had come to him with the same look in his eye, and he wondered what he should tell her.

Anya knocked on the door and brought in two goblets of wine heated with a hot poker. She offered one to the Princess then the other to her master, curtseying before closing the door behind her. Grigory thanked her quietly. Laura stirred from where she had been staring at the flames and sipped the wine carefully, being careful not to burn her mouth.

'I am *Velikaja Knjaginja* Laura Aleksa Stephanovna Vakhtangova of Dalnerechensk,' she said quietly, 'I know nothing of my country. Aleksei is no longer a young man Grigory, and -' she shut her eyes, her face strained. 'Any son of mine will not be fit to rule for some time yet. You must tell me what I should know.'

Grigory drained his wine and placed the goblet on an ornate table beside his chair.

'Very well' he said softly. 'I'll begin with the terms of the Treaty of Dalnerechensk.'

*

Olaf stretched his legs uncomfortably, crossing his right on top of his outstretched left, shifting awkwardly in the horsehair chair in the entrance hall. He thanked the Princess for her forethought, it was cold in the foyer, he would have been in grave trouble if he had had to wait outside for her. The morning light gently began to pick out the colour and the details of the rug in the foyer, on which his mud-caked boots were resting.

He cursed quietly, knowing he had a full day's work ahead of him, and no sleep to aide him. He was stiff and sore from his long wait, and wondered how much longer she was going to be. As if in answer there was a soft click from the landing and he looked up. The house had already begun to stir, servants shutting doors as they descended for their days' work, but he knew this click was the Princess's.

She stood at the top of the staircase, her hands clasped in front of her; looking so forlorn it was heartbreaking. She began to descend with all the strength and movement of a ghost and Olaf stood, a twinge of warning in his mind. *She's going to fall.* He bounded forward, coming up the stairs towards her and ignoring the pain in his back and legs from sitting still so long.

He reached the step below her and her unfocused eyes drifted to him. She reached out curiously, as if to see if he was real before her knees crumpled. Olaf caught her and held her up in his arms, calling for help.

'I'm alright Olaf, just tired' she said faintly.

He ignored her words and called again, sweeping her up in his arms. Grigory stepped out on the landing, instructing Anya to send a page for the Vakhtangov doctor.

'Bring her up to a room Olaf' he commanded.

He obeyed, carrying her up the stairs and along to a room a maid opened for him, gently lying her on a large guest bed, noticing how white she looked against the sheets. Grigory followed them into the room and lay his hand on Laura's forehead, checking for fever, then took her wrist, checking how fast her pulse was, counting carefully while looking intently at his gold fob watch.

Olaf stepped back, knowing it was no longer his place to be here. He turned to go, placing his hand on the door, stepping aside to let Anya into the room.

'Olaf is a faithful servant' Laura suddenly said and Olaf stopped, looking back.

The Princess's eyes were on Grigory.

'He has waited through the night and has not slept' she went on. 'Give him a bed here, and take your own groom to replace him at the castle for the day. Olaf will see to his duties here, and return at evening.'

'As you wish Your Highness' Grigory bowed and gave Anya some instructions to ready a bed for the groom.

Anya gave Olaf a saucy look.

'I'm sure I could find a bed for him' she said under her breath, giving Olaf a sly look, then said loudly 'Yes My Lord,' and gestured for Olaf to follow her.

He shot one more look at the pale Princess on the large bed, and followed Anya upstairs to her narrow cot.

49

The loud knocking on her door roused her and she started awake in fear, swearing. For a moment she couldn't remember where she was then it all came crashing back in around her. The doctor had given her something to help her sleep and she was lying in a guest bed in the Ivanov home. Her head hurt from the tears she had cried and the information she had been given last night, the full realisation of the Principality's dire need. She had no wish to be disturbed now.

The insistent knocking sounded again. Without waiting for an answer the door was pushed open and Nikita strode into the bedchamber, Anya fluttering nervously after him.

'Forgive me Your Highness, I could not stop him' Anya said, horrified.

Nikita strode straight to the window and flicked open the curtains, flooding the room with light. Laura grumbled, throwing the bedcovers over her head, not sure if she was wearing a dress or a nightdress.

'Go away!' she snapped, muffled by the covers.

'Come Laura, I have been entrusted with your education; you are doing me a disservice disappearing in the middle of the night' Nikita said haughtily.

In a rage she sat up, throwing back the covers.

'You were there Nikita; you saw how many children died!' she shouted.

Anya crossed herself quickly at the mention of the children. Laura was too wild to care.

'And I am here, seeing how you have deserted your marriage bed, riding off to seek comfort in the arms of another man' Nikita answered, flicking open the other pair of drapes in her room. 'That will be all Anya, shut the door behind you.'

Anya shot Laura a look, unwilling to leave the two of them alone in a bedroom.

Beside herself with anger Laura flew off the bed, her fingers hooked like claws to tear into Nikita, but he was ready for her. He seized her arms and twisted them behind her back, pinning her body with his up against the poster of the bed.

'Well now, my passion flower, still so frustrated?' he laughed.

'*How dare you*!' Laura screamed, spluttering with rage. 'How *dare* you insult me with these accusations -'

'Oh come now, do not act so ingenuously. I am merely repeating what your entire court is saying' he said flippantly, giving her a little shake.

She gasped with rage and horror, feeling her body press against Nikita's, realising he was standing too close to her. But he wasn't finished.

'Your court is wondering why you rushed to the bed of your best friend and ignored such a handsome Russian on your own doorstep.'

Laura twisted her arms savagely, trying to free herself so she could strike him, but he held her too firmly. The twisting hurt the gash on her arm and she cried out, falling into miserable tears, relenting in her struggle.

'That will be all Anya' Nikita said again, a softly dangerous note in his voice.

Helpless she dipped a curtsey and left, closing the door behind her.

'You have much to learn of how a princess acts Laura' Nikita chided, letting her go and moving away to look out her window. 'Count Ivanov was good enough to explain you were resting at Ladozhskoye after your ordeal because you enjoyed the view there' he said distastefully, eyeing the trees that were the view from her window. 'So perhaps you'd better dress and join me on the balcony where there is a view to speak of.'

He strode across her room and shut the doors behind him, leaving Laura with nothing but to scramble to do his bidding. She was shaking, confusion whirling in her. Nikita had burst into her bedroom, she, a married woman and a princess no less, and yet he had left her feeling ashamed and guilty, as if she were the reproachable party.

She shut her eyes, letting herself cry two more tears and sob aloud once before wiping them away and composing herself. She was glad to notice she was still dressed in the gown she had worn to travel to Ladozhskoye the night before so she had not fought so passionately with Nikita dressed only in a nightdress. She brushed out the wrinkles and wrapped herself warmly in a blanket she folded as a shawl, walking quietly to the balcony, trying to compose herself.

The small table outside had been set with a silver tea service for two. Nikita was seated and had already begun to eat. He flicked his napkin free of crumbs when she joined him but did not stand to greet her as he should have done. She ignored him and walked to the colonnade of the balcony, gazing down into the courtyard below, watching Olaf sweep the cobblestones.

There was something soothing and reassuring about him that made Laura appreciate his presence. She wondered if Anya had thought to send for him to protect her when Nikita had forced himself into her bedroom, or whether he had been aware at all of the danger. She turned back to Nikita, eyeing him.

'Why have you come?' she asked quietly.

Nikita patted his lips with the napkin and dropped it back on the table before answering her.

'I was concerned for you' he said with a sniff.

Laura scraped back the chair and sat, eyeing him across the teapot and silver milk jug.

'You can see *Knjaz* Rurik that I am well, and you needn't concern yourself anymore' she said firmly.

'Don't be ignorant Laura' he snapped. 'You have caused yourself irreparable damage to your good name and that of your husband's and Count Ivanov's because you behave like a silly child.'

'Don't speak to me so!' she cried, adamant he was not going to make her feel at fault again.

Nikita banged his fist down on the table, making her jump.

'You are no longer permitted to be an ignorant common girl' he snapped. 'You are a princess and all the eyes of Europe are on you, not just your court. You must be above reproach for any word or action! You must be perfect Laura. Perfect and nothing less.'

'I cannot be these things!' she cried, tears spilling down her cheeks, feeling terribly inadequate.

'You must' he answered simply, taking a handkerchief from his breast pocket and holding it out to her to dab at her tears. 'Dry your eyes, take your tea, and read me this' he said, handing over a book bound in red leather.

Rage exploded in her again and she seized it, throwing it off the balcony, leaping to her feet.

'You dare to play this game with me?!' she yelled. 'You tell me to be above reproach and yet you hand me a book where many words would certainly be reproachable! If you have only come to Ladozhskoye to upbraid, confuse or seduce me I should like you to leave. I am in mourning for my children.'

She turned away from him, hearing his chair scrape back angrily behind her. Out of the corner of her eye she saw Olaf arrive at the top of the stairs from the courtyard below, but hesitate, not coming onto the balcony. Nikita grabbed her arms from behind, hissing in her ear:

'Oh you are hot, passion flower. That unemotional pill box had no idea what he got when he married you.'

This time he was not strong enough to stop her fury and it caught him full across his lip, forcing him to let her go. She then retreated to the house, turning once to eye him again. 'Do not come here again' she yelled.

'As you command, Your Highness' he snapped stiffly, and stamped away from the balcony.

50

Laura sat in the high-backed chair in the Tsar's library, gazing without seeing at the Cyrillic script of the book opened in her lap. She had spent the day in tears at Ladozhskoye, glad that no one had been around and the staff had not disturbed her. She had slept too, though she didn't know what time she had drifted off, only that the sun was setting when she woke. Feeling drained she had summoned Olaf and returned to the castle as the sun dipped below the horizon.

Olaf had barely said anything to her, and she knew what he was thinking: that she was indeed having an affair with Nikita, his arrival in Ladozhskoye was proof enough, and he had seen the way he had grabbed her on the balcony. She doubted he had heard his words, or if he had, was thankful that he had not understood them, as they had been in French. But the tone and his actions had been clear enough.

The court was just sitting down to dinner when she arrived, so she had gone to her room to wash and change, taking her place beside Aleksei. He had eyed her, a look filled with worry and suspicion but had not spoken to her. Dinner was sombre and quiet, but the tragedy was still not enough to stop the rumours skipping from fan to fan. By now they all knew she had been at the cave in, but the blood that had soaked her bodice and skirts still kept the word *miscarriage* floating along the tables.

Nikita had looked sour throughout dinner and snubbed the Princess by talking to all but her. Aleksei noticed, and his eyes narrowed to think of all the things she had done now to offend the Prince. *Did she not know how important this was?*

There had been no dancing after dinner in light of the tragedy the day before, and Aleksei had dismissed the court early then taken her aside and rebuked her for offending the Russian so grievously.

'I will not pander to his every whim!' she had raged, rounding on Aleksei. 'I will not debase my vows for his amusement and pleasure!'

Aleksei had shut his eyes, struggling with words and his emotions but stopped short of ordering her. A small part of her had rejoiced, knowing that he knew of Nikita's desires and was not wanting to share her with him, but it was lost in the hurt and pain between them.

'How could you not have told me?' Laura had moaned. 'Those children -'

'It is not your place' Aleksei had answered, diplomatically cold.

'Don't be so ignorant!' she had cried. 'If anything happens to you Aleksei what would I have done?'

'My ministers would have managed' he had said coldly. 'Now come Laura, your nerves are still raw. Go to bed and get some sleep.'

'Will you send for me?' she had asked, holding her breath.

He hadn't answered, and she had felt her misery well up again.

'Why don't you love me anymore?!' she had cried out in anguish.

'Laura don't!' he had cried, tormented too. 'It is not a question of that, not a question of us! There are more important things than us!'

Laura had turned, too angry to listen anymore, wanting to throw spitefully over her shoulder that she hoped those other things helped him get an heir.

Tsar Constantinovich reached over and touched Laura's hand, breaking into her reverie. She looked up, surprised.

'You have not spoken one word tonight' he rumbled quietly. 'What ails you *tsarevna*?'

Laura tried to think of a way to tell him in a composed manner and completely failed, tears washing unmitigated down her face. She dropped to her knees and buried her face in his stout stomach, weeping her sorrows to him. The Tsar was surprised and then his gnarled old hand began stroking her silky locks to soothe her.

She told him of her fear in the mines, the horror at finding the old and the young in those tunnels, the terror of the cave-in, the thoughts she had while waiting for them to clear the debris away and pull out the survivors. She told of her anger that the poor price of tin had forced children to work or starve with the rest of their family.

She told of her bitter disappointment that Dalnerechensk was on the verge of financial collapse and how useless she felt being in a position to do something about it and not even knowing of the problem, and of her guilt; that she had manipulated Aleksei into halving her dowry to save her father from ruin and condemned a principality to the poorhouse. She spoke of the jewels that Aleksei had sent her, and how she now owned the net worth of Dalnerechensk on a pretty string in her jewelry box.

She spoke of her love for Aleksei and her bewilderment at finding his affections for her had cooled, long before Nikita had arrived although his constant attention and flattery hadn't helped matters. She cried lonely tears for her father and Ekaterina, loved ones that were not there in her time of need, of the pressure of having to do the right thing and not knowing what that was, of the strain of public scrutiny and confessed how many times Lady Ramkinson had scarred her with the riding crop in her temper, making her terrified of making a mistake.

She cried and cried because she needed the release, and when her tears were spent and her knees were aching she stayed curled against the old king because she had not been held by a father since she was six years old. The Tsar stroked her hair gently, whispering soothing words to her, moved by her misery and abuse. He had suspected she had suffered some kind of rebuke at the finishing school, and he had noticed the way her eyes had tightened in pain and the stiff interruptions in the graceful way she moved but was now sickened to know the true extent of her sufferings.

His eyes watered and his hands trembled in anger. He knew what loneliness it was that she endured. Dalnerechensk was an isolated community, with none of Boston's or even Moscow's sophistication. There was no theatre, no opera and no outdoor recreation areas, save for the town commons. Dalnerechensk was a simple, poor farming and mining principality, with a small population. It was run by an aging group of frightened conservatives and the minister's daughters and granddaughters were too busy jealously whispering spite behind their fans to befriend a lonely foreigner.

He and Aleksei had made mistakes. He had admired her strength and endurance in Lady Ramkinson's school, but he had forgotten she was still a child, and had forgotten how much she needed those her own age around her. He made a silent promise to her as he stroked her hair, listening to her tears, to bring her those she needed most.

Finally she sat back and wiped her eyes, sniffing loudly.
'Thank you' she snuffled, composing herself, rearranging her limbs to ease her aching knees.

A knock on the door interrupted them and Aleksei stepped into the room, a worried look on his face. He sat on the floor beside her and took her arm, gently placing a warm hand over the dull ache of her cut.
'Is your wound hurting you?' he asked, stroking her cheek.

Laura was touched by his tender affection for her, shutting her eyes at the warmth of his hands on her. He was still so tender, so gentle and concerned, and her heart moved to think that he still loved her. But his affection and concern on the floor before his father couldn't alter the fact it was the first time he had touched her with any emotion for weeks now. The bitterness rose in her and she swallowed hard to suppress it, feeling the lump in her throat tighten. She shook her head and took his hand, kissing his knuckles.
'I don't think I would know what to do with myself if I didn't have you' he said suddenly.
'You would find yourself another treaty to write' she said.

Her spite surprised her, and Aleksei pulled away, wounded. Laura instantly regretted it; her words hung heavy and thick between them. She wanted to take them back, to stop them from hurting, but it was also the truth. She resented the hours and days that took him away from her, but she hadn't known his absence from her also hurt him deeply.

His eyes were filled with pain and suffering and a frightening longing. Laura relented, dropping her eyes.
'I'm sorry Aleksei,' she said quietly. 'I'm tired, and I've felt alone for too long.'
'You seem to have found yourself company in Nikita's arms' he snapped.

The insult stung her, bringing tears to her eyes as if he'd slapped her. She stood, drawing herself together.
'At least he was there with me. Your people want to know where their *Naslednik Tsesarevich* is' she said and stamped out of the room. 'You're their flesh and blood Aleksei, I just married you' she threw over her shoulder then slammed the door.

51

Laura barely touched her breakfast the next day, and slipped out to the stables, instructing Olaf to saddle her stallion. He did so curtly, refusing to talk to her. Laura ignored him and mounted, heading down Vsevolod's Way to the small hospital.

A nurse at the desk looked very surprised to see her and dipped a curtsey, asking if she was ill.

'No, I am here to see the children' she answered.

It did not have to be said which children she meant. The nurse glanced around for the rest of the diplomatic party, worried that it was only the Princess.

'Your Highness' said a voice behind her and she turned to see Doctor Pushkin, the Vakhtangov physician. 'Is your arm troubling you?'

'No, thank you' she answered. 'I am here to see the children.'

'Perhaps you would allow me to escort you?' he asked, offering his elbow to her.

'Yes, that would be most kind' she said, managing a smile, slipping her hand into the crook of his arm.

Instead of taking her straight to the ward Pushkin started a tour of the hospital, leading her through the laundry and kitchens, through a theatre room and a rehabilitation centre, keeping up a running commentary on the rooms. She was shown the Royal Suite, a lavish room where royals had been born and died in for generations. A room in which she was expected to birth the next king.

She listened politely as he talked, asking questions she was only half interested in hearing the answer to. At last he led her to the wards, making sure she understood what she was going to see.

The room was lined with beds, all of them occupied by a small body. Here and there, beside the bed, sat a grandmother, a mother, or a sister; holding the hands and talking to the child, or working: sewing or darning torn and patched clothing. The room was large and white with iron grey bedsteads. There was no colour, save for a small section at the end of the room where a few books and puzzles sat on a low, child sized table.

Laura stopped by each of the beds where Doctor Pushkin told her their names and their condition. Most had severe fractures or concussions, one had a broken back, one's legs were oddly flat beneath the sheet he lay under, and leached blood and ooze into the sheet that covered him. She greeted all of them, squeezing their hands or stroking their brows, asking them how they felt.

One of the children suddenly piped up, asking to be read a story, and was shushed by his mother.

'I would be happy to read to you' Laura smiled, and crossed to the small table, picking up a story and hoping her command of the language didn't fail her now.

Some of the children got out of bed and sat near her, wrapped in their blankets, while others stayed in their beds but turned their faces towards the small table and chair at the back of the room. Laura selected a brightly coloured book and began to read. Doctor Pushkin faded away to see to other patients and Laura was left alone in the ward.

As she read the adults drifted together into clumps, inspecting each other's work, whispering to each other, shooting her veiled looks. Laura could hear the whispers in the large, echoing room. *What was she doing in the mines?* They whispered. *She didn't know* was whispered back. *Well now she does, now she's as guilty as him.*

Laura kept on reading, her voice unwavering though she felt the tears well up in her eyes. She sniffed then closed the book carefully when she reached the end.

'Your Highness? It's a *happy* book' one of the children explained, worried.

'Yes my dear, it was' she said, smiling for him, then quickly stood, putting the book back on the table, wiping her eyes.

She thanked them all for their time then excused herself, quickly heading for the door. The mothers jerked mechanical puppet bows as she walked past, and Laura knew it was only because that was what tradition and custom dictated, not out of any real respect for her or her authority. She sped out of the hospital, not hearing those who called out to her, and leapt up onto the back of her waiting stallion.

The hospital was close to Vsevolod's Gate, and in her desperate desire to be away from people she turned the stallion out the gate and galloped along the valley between Dalnerechensk and the rising slopes of East Valley. Tears blurred her eyes, making her misjudge the turn into Hunter's Pass and her stallion snorted at the uncomfortable movement. She apologised, but did not relent, pushing the horse hard until she reached the secluded glen with the waterfall.

She dismounted quickly and threw herself down on the grass, sobbing hard, trying to block out the sights and sounds of the hospital.

*

Olaf heard them calling out for the Princess, heard the approaching hooves on the cobblestones. It was growing dark, and he was angry she had been gone all day and had made up his mind to tell her off, that the horses needed rest each day. He turned and stopped in shock.

The horse was riderless. The stallion pawed at the ground and whickered. He called out to two of the guards who were coming off duty, crying that the Princess was in trouble, then swung up onto the stallion and spurred it back into the forest. Behind him he could hear the cry of alarm being taken up, and before him on the road several townsfolk were heading into the forest, some with lanterns, but most without. Olaf cursed for not thinking of bringing a lantern. The forest was already gloomy, and would be dark before long.

He took a lantern from one of the peasants and rode on into the forest, heading straight for the ravine, hoping she was not broken and dead at the bottom. He lay on his belly and hung the light over the side, calling her name and peering deeper, waving the light around. He considered dropping the lantern, but knew if she was not there he would have wasted the kerosene.

The Prince suddenly joined him, calling down into the ravine frantically.

'I don't think she's there' Olaf said.

Aleksei raced back to the horse and swung himself up. It was unsaddled and unbridled, and at any other time Olaf would have been impressed with his command of the horse.

'Head towards East Valley, I'll double back from here' Aleksei commanded and wheeled the horse around, galloping into the night.

Olaf cast a final glance at the ravine then swung up on the stallion, listening to the voices of soldiers, servants, peasants and ministers alike calling for the Princess.

*

Laura woke. It was dark and she was lying face down in the grass. He had woken her, calling her name in a tone that stirred her heart. She rolled over and threw her arms round his neck, feeling his arms snake across her back, holding her tightly. He smelt of sweat and fear and she couldn't suppress the happy sob.

'Aleksei...' she sighed, the name sounding like Alex. 'Have me, now! Have me!'

There was a tiny hesitation.

'*Tsesarevna*' he said.

Laura stopped, letting go. There was only one person who called her that. He kept one arm round her firmly, the other doing a quick brush down of her limbs, checking for broken bones.

'Are you hurt? Your horse came back without you' he explained, gently cupping her skull with his hand, checking for head wounds.

'Olaf...' she said quietly, sitting up.

He turned his head to yell he'd found her, that she was unhurt.

'I fell asleep in the sun' she said quietly, pushing his arm gently away from her. 'Thank you for your concern.'

Olaf leaned back then stood and pulled her to her feet. She could hear people calling her name and answered them, carefully picking her way over the ground so she didn't trip in the dark. A horse and rider burst into the clearing and Aleksei dismounted, calling out to her, thanking God she was alright. She slid her arms around him, apologising for making him worry and he soothed her with a sweet kiss on her forehead.

He gave his horse to Olaf then mounted the saddled stallion, lifting her up and seating her before him, folding his arms around her. He ordered Olaf to see to the other horse and to let everyone know that the Princess was safe, then clicked his tongue, guiding the horse back to the stables.

Laura slid her arms around him as they rode in silence, nuzzling at his neck and chest.

'I was worried' he said quietly.

'I know, my love' she answered, planting a kiss in the middle of his chest.

His breath quickened and he tightened his arms around her, spurring the horse on again. Laura was amused, but eager too, wondering if the scare had roused Aleksei enough to want to make love to her. It certainly felt like it. He rode the horse straight into a stall in the stables then dismounted, reaching up to lift her down gently.

'You're very pale' he whispered, concerned. 'I want the doctor to look at you before -' he stopped.

Laura could have sung for joy and hugged him fiercely. He laughed quietly, a sound full of amusement and desire and he kept his arm around her, leading her up to her rooms.

Anna was missing, and Laura wondered if she was out looking for her, her heart warming

191

in appreciation of her friend. Aleksei stoked the fire in her bedchamber and told her to change for bed, watching with amusement and desire as she boldly shed her clothing in front of him and let her hair down, standing naked on the rug before the fire.

In an effort to control himself he collected her nightdress from where it was laid out on the end of her bed and gathered the material from the hem, slipping it over her head, unable to help noticing the way her breasts moved when she raised her arms. He let the material go but she had stepped close to him, stopping the fall of the material, her hands snaking down to the hardness in his breaches.

He groaned and said nothing, there were no words to say. A tap on the door interrupted them and Aleksei stepped away, the material falling down and covering her nakedness. Doctor Pushkin opened the door and set his medical bag on the end of her bed, snapping open the catches. Laura sat on the bed and let herself be examined, watching Aleksei, who stood with his back to her, staring intensely into the flames of the fire.

Doctor Pushkin stepped back, folding his stethoscope back into his bag.
'You must eat and you must rest Your Highness' he said, snapping the bag shut with a click.
'I am prescribing two days of bed rest for you, and you are not to be excited in any way.'
'What if I lie still?' Laura asked, and Aleksei covered his explosive snigger.
'Certainly not' Doctor Pushkin said. 'Complete and utter rest for two days.'

He bowed then shut the door behind him. Aleksei turned to eye her, amused and sad.
'Sleep well, and get better soon' he said, hardly trusting himself to kiss her goodnight.

Laura sighed, grumbling, and snuggled into the covers, shutting her eyes tightly.

52

Laura woke at the quiet tap on the door, the kind where they weren't sure if the knock would be heard, but not wanting to wake the person inside. She smiled, sitting up and brushing down her hair with her hands so she looked presentable.
'Come in' she called.

Anna opened the door and ushered in Tsar Constantinovich. He smiled, thanking Anna.
'Good morning my dear, how are you feeling?' he asked.
'Relaxed' she said, smiling.

It was the truth, two days of enforced bed rest away from Nikita and the court had done wonders for her state of mind, and the tears had helped ease her feelings of guilt, so much so that she had taken two extra days as well. She was only disappointed that Aleksei had not come to her, and tried not to listen to her mind mock her with Nikita's words: *Still so frustrated, passion flower?*
'I'm glad to hear it' he said. 'Would you care to join us for breakfast this morning? I have a

surprise for you.'

At once Laura's curiosity was pricked and she smiled, promising to join the court for breakfast. He smiled and took his leave of her, shutting the door behind him. Anna came forward and opened the curtains, pushing open one of the windows to let a fresh breeze into the room.

Laura slipped out of bed, and padded into her dressing room. Anna had run her a bath already, and she had planned to soak for an hour until she was almost pickled and then slink back to bed to sleep some more. Now she stepped in quickly and let Anna wash her hair, drying and dressing in a soft cream gown. Anna combed her hair and rubbed it dry, pinning it up into a plain coil.

Laura then opened her door, slipping down to the dining hall. To her surprise Aleksei, Nikita and Tsar Constantinovich were standing near the door, talking to a group of ten youngsters. The three men were dressed in Polish officer uniforms and looked to be about eighteen or nineteen years old. They stood with seven girls, four who were dressed lavishly in dresses cut from heavy, expensive fabric, and ranged in age from sixteen to twenty. Three younger girls stood with them, about twelve years of age and dressed in bright muslins.

Aleksei saw her and smiled, beckoning her over to the group. Tsar Constantinovich turned and smiled, taking her hand and drawing her in close.

'Ah, you are up and well, I am glad' he smiled, then gestured to the group of teens. '*Velikaja Knjaginja* Laura Vakhtangova, these are my great nieces Hannah and Saskia, their brother Franz, and their friends.'

Laura greeted them politely, knowing they had been invited to keep her company because of her fit of tears in Tsar Constantinovich's library and couldn't help but feel a little ashamed, the blush coming up in her cheeks. The three relatives of Aleksei's came forward, greeting her and introducing their friends.

Franz, as awkward as his uncle, kissed her hand ceremoniously, and introduced the other two officers as Sven and Filip. All three looked dashing in their uniforms but the other two outshone Franz with their easy confidence. One of the young girls too impatient to wait her turn shook her hand, introducing herself as Saskia and her two giggling friends as Izydor and Zofia. Laura laughed, welcoming them to Dalnerechensk, amused at the curtsies the three dipped to her.

'*Dzień dobry*' Hannah said, taking her hand. 'These are my friends Lana, Rebecca and Elzbieta. Everyone we have met speaks so highly of you. We shall all get along splendidly' she smiled.

Nikita then took Laura's hand and kissed it gently.

'I'm glad to see you have recovered Laura' he smiled. 'May I escort you to the table?'

'Of course' she answered, letting go of Aleksei and slipping her hand into his elbow.

Aleksei and Tsar Constantinovich followed with their relatives, taking their seats around the table.

Laura's appetite had improved and she ate a full breakfast, to the delight of the old Tsar, who had really begun to worry about the little she ate. Nikita flirted with the four older girls unashamedly, and the banter was light and fun.

When the meal was finished the guests retired to their rooms to see to the unpacking of their belongings and the second floor of the castle was filled with laughter and noise and excited opening and closing of doors as the siblings and friends explored their new surroundings. Laura had retired to her rooms briefly, but had been drawn out by the laughter, wanting to go and see what all the fuss was about, but afraid to as well.

The laughter of the other students at Lady Ramkinson's school was either at her expense or a cruel reminder that she was not accepted by the bourgeois and the nobility. It had also meant that she was excluded from any games that were played in the evenings she had desperately wanted join in with. The other girls ignored her, or snubbed her spitefully, and Laura had finally stopped trying, spending long evenings alone in her room perfecting her embroidering skills, producing garment after garment of exquisite detail.

She stood on the second floor landing, wondering if she should wander past their rooms and inquire what they were doing to make so much noise, when one of the doors flew open and Hannah and another tumbled out, laughing. Laura turned suddenly, feeling like she should run away least the laughter turn on her. They saw Laura and cried out a greeting, coming to take hold of her hands.

'There you are Laura!' Hannah cried, tugging her along the landing to her room. 'You must uphold our feminine honour!'

'We are playing cards and we have been losing most horribly!' Lana added, equally as flushed and happy.

'Franz has won almost all of the games we have played -'

'He's a frightful cheat!'

'And we simply must have you on our team!' Hannah giggled, dragging Laura into the room.

The siblings, their friends and Nikita were sitting on the floor, cards and pieces from games scattered around them, laughing, their faces flushed with fun.

'Aha Franz, you will not dare cheat now!' Hannah cried, sitting in a swirl of skirts beside her brother.

Franz leapt to his feet and brought a cushion from the chaise lounge for the Princess to sit on, smiling shyly at her and flushing. She thanked him and the teens took it in turn to explain the game to Laura, their words and laughter tumbling over each other.

Laura agreed to uphold feminine honour and Sven shuffled the cards, making a great show of it. Hannah, Lana and Laura closed ranks, comparing cards and soundly won the first game. Cheered by her win and the laughter of the others Laura smiled. They were all wildly impetuous and Laura found herself liked and respected by her peers for the first time in her life.

They played all afternoon, laughing and joking together, and Laura was glad that Nikita had four more attractive women to flirt with, not just with her. Even Saskia and her giggling friends were not spared his attentions, though Laura was relieved to see that he did not use his more risqué flirtations with them. Sven and Filip, encouraged by Nikita, told ever more wild jokes while Franz burned with embarrassment and tried to dissuade them for the sake of his young sister and her friends.

Saskia and her friends screamed, running out of the room with their hands over their ears, laughing as they headed down to the music room. Soon the soft strains of a piano being badly played were heard and the company of older teens drew in closer, playing game after game until Fedor came to collect them for dinner.

There was a flurry of activity as they all retreated to their dressing rooms, to comb their hair, dress and dabble on rosewater before descending the stone staircase to the dining hall. Laura dressed in a magnificent red gown, the short sleeves exposing her still bandaged arm then slipped out to join the teens on the second landing.

There were a few looks at the bandage, but Nikita turned his head to them and Laura knew he was whispering of the cave in at the mines. She didn't let the smile fall from her lips and slipped her hand into Filip's elbow when he offered it to her. He smiled and Laura led the way down the steps, surprised to find the dining hall filled with the sons and daughters of the ministers dressed in their best and warmly calling a greeting to their guests.

She realised the ten teens must be the talk of the town and the curious court had come to see what all the fuss was about. She would have been annoyed with their transpositions were she not so happy.

Filip let her go with a bow and Laura swept to her place beside Aleksei, dropping a kiss on Tsar Constantinovich's cheek as she passed him, whispering words of thanks in his ear. He smiled at her as she took her place and Aleksei called for the servants to bring in the meal.

Laura sipped her soup delicately, marveling at the change in the behaviour of the Dalnerechensk court. Those young that had slipped away during the weeks following her wedding were back, introducing themselves to the Poles and flirting shamelessly. A small smile played on her lips, knowing that those girls still single and hadn't been able to secure Aleksei's love were now turning their attentions to the young officers in the hope of still marrying well.

Nikita, Tatiana, Natasha and a group of snobbish friends sat near the Polish nobles, their fans beside them on the table, laughing and flirting. The dinner was fun and Laura glowed with a happiness she hadn't felt since the heady romantic days before her wedding. She smiled, thinking she would ask the Poles to come again as soon as they left, and when Ekaterina was back, they would spend a wonderful summer together.

A sudden cry from Hannah brought the attention of the court to the laughing party.

'Oh Laura, we simply must have a riding party!' Hannah cried. 'A most excellent suggestion Tatiana!'

'Do lets!' cried the rest of the group.

'Of course' Laura smiled, noticing how Tatiana's smile looked like a twisted pout.

53

Laura drifted out of sleep, her heart light and her body feeling as if it was filled with a buoyant cloud. She could barely wait for Anna to arrive to carefully check her gashed arm. It was healing nicely thanks to her care and attention. She pushed back the covers and slipped out of bed, humming, too eager for the day to begin to wait patiently for Anna. Her step was light as she headed to her dressing room, and although she was too old to skip she did let one childish hop escape her and grinned.

She poured a little of the chilly water in the ewer into a bowl and splashed her face so her cheeks shone with roses. She heard her parlour door click and greeted Anna as she came into the room, unable to hide her pleasure or her smile. Anna smiled back, glad to see the Princess so happy again and helped her dress in a green gown that did wonders for her complexion.

Laura found it hard to sit still while Anna brushed and pinned her hair up carefully, but at last she was done and Laura blew out the door excitedly, running along the corridor to meet up with her friends. Tsar Constantinovich was on the stairs, heading down to breakfast. She kissed his cheek as she skipped past, calling good morning over her shoulder as she bounded along the second floor.

His chuckle followed her and he called a greeting too, but she was already halfway along the landing, knocking on the door to Hannah's room. She opened the door and pulled Laura in, laughing excitedly. Her three friends were already dressed for the outing and waiting in Hannah's room, anxious to start.

Laura called a warm good morning to them and led them down to the ground floor, passing Tsar Constantinovich again on the stairs. Laura giggled and pressed another kiss on his cheek, as did Hannah. Not to be left out, Lana, Rebecca and Elzbieta also kissed his cheek and their giggles ran after them, chased by the Tsar's hearty laugh.

They took their places round the large dining table, and Laura was pleased to see Aleksei was dressed for the outing too, looking happy. She kissed him warmly on the cheek, greeting his nephew and his two friends. They smiled back, greeting her by her name, and she was secretly glad that none of the children had called her Aunt Laura. The Tsar joined them, still chuckling, and greeted his son warmly, sitting with a sigh of relief in a chair under the canopy.

Laura eyed the people gathered for breakfast as she ate, glad to see that most of the chairs around the table were filled, and the people seemed to be happy and talkative. Perhaps she too was not the only one disillusioned by an aging court. Perhaps if she arranged a party like the Ivanov's had, perhaps if she invited them and was a diligent and gracious host they might stay, they might warm to her.

Ekaterina sometimes had Laura for tea, and had also invited two other women to tea with them. They had been polite and had shared jokes and laughed and chatted, but Laura had felt that thin barrier between the charade and true friendship. She could do more to break it down she thought. A laugh from the ladies clustered around Nikita broke into her reverie and she smiled, finishing her breakfast quickly.

Aleksei dismissed them from the meal and Laura ran quickly upstairs to fetch her riding habit, fastening her jacket in place as she descended the stairs again. She stepped out into the wide courtyard and stopped in surprise. It was filled with people and horses, livery boys and Olaf, and there was an excited festive air about them all. Many of the people were sons and daughters of the ministers, some she had not seen since her wedding. Some were on horseback or preparing to mount, or milling about talking and laughing with people as if they hadn't seen each other since the wedding too.

It was probably true, as she well knew life in Dalnerechensk without her friends was lonely. Better to be at a school in Russia or Switzerland where she could make more friends than stay alone in the Principality. She suddenly found she no longer begrudged the youth of the Principality for slipping away, and was only saddened that she could not do the same, and hoped that they might stay for the summer.

Olaf rushed past her with a saddle, and two livery boys helped women onto the saddled horses, shouting instructions at each other. It was a noisy, lively chaos and Laura smiled, feeling her heart expand even more in her chest. Aleksei stood in the middle of the chaos, dressed in a habit and laughing, a crop tucked casually under his arm. He boosted Saskia onto her horse and handed her the crop, directing her on the finer points of riding. Laura made her way over to them, smiling up at Saskia. Her guilt and sadness at the Principality's dire trouble was melting away from her to see her husband full of life again. She stood on tip-toe to kiss his cheek then whispered:

'A race to the glen, my love?'

Aleksei tucked her into his elbow, planting a kiss on her temple then let her go to boost Izydor and Zofia onto some of the smaller and more docile mares in his stable. Laura could have burst into song at her happiness and squeezed her hands tightly to control herself. There was a soft snort behind her then large nostrils nudged her in greeting. She turned and stroked the nose of her stallion, whispering a soft hello. Olaf greeted her curtly, fond of her but irritated at the swarm of people in his stables.

'Should you be riding in your condition Your Highness?' Tatiana asked loudly as Olaf bent to boost her onto her horse.

Laura stopped, shutting her eyes to help her mask her emotion then turned to face her, knowing it was a deliberate jibe, daring her to disclose her state of expectancy. Tatiana's face was pleasant, but Laura could see malice and jealousy twisting under her skin, and knew Tatiana would say anything to make her stay behind or humiliate her in the company of her friends.

'Come Tatiana, you know a good horsewoman can ride well whatever the conditions may be' she said sweetly, and was glad to see that those who had overheard laugh and turn away, busying themselves with mounting horses.

Tatiana's eyes narrowed and she walked her horse closer, confronting Laura. 'And you still mount the stallion?' she continued cloyingly, a softly dangerous yet smug note in her voice as she looked down on the Princess from her saddle.

Laura felt herself grow very still, and white noise was singing in her ears. She knew it was common knowledge in the castle that she slept alone at night now, but it hurt to hear it come from Tatiana, jealous malicious Tatiana, who undoubtedly prayed for her demise every night so she might wed the widowed Prince. She trembled with anger but also pitied her, dropping her voice so only Tatiana could hear her.

'At least I have mounted the stallion' she said triumphantly.

Tatiana's teeth smiled. 'My dear, you are not the only one to claim that' she said then slapped the rump of her horse with the crop, heading out of the courtyard.

Laura flinched at the sound, her eyes flicking to Aleksei, unable to hide the questions in her look. But he was already mounted, his back to her, talking with Grigory and pointing out their route in the Hunting Forest. Tatiana cantered past them, saying something that made them both laugh.

Laura shut her eyes, feeling her stomach stretch coldly, finding new depths of misery. She had known Tatiana had been considered as a bride for Aleksei, she had not thought they had slept together. Had they been lovers? Were they *still* lovers? *Had he slept with her while she had been ill?* That agony twisted through her maliciously. She had seen the way Aleksei had touched her arm in the Ivanov gardens that day. Is that why he had been so reckless and carnal with her? *Did he love Tatiana? Why had he not married her?*

She bit her lip, trying hard to put these questions out of her mind. The entire court knew she slept alone. Did they know Aleksei had taken a mistress to warm his bed? She bit her lip harder, trying to force the tears back. She had no desire to be riding with the court today. *That's what she wants* a dark part of her said. *And you won't give her that victory, no matter what it costs you.*

'Your Highness?' Olaf asked quietly.

She wiped her eyes quickly, mentally shaking herself then let him boost her up onto the horse, taking the reins. Tatiana's words had deeply wounded her, but she was determined not to let it get the best of her. A small, cruel part of her whispered that she should even the hurt by taking her own concubine, she now had four attractive men to choose from.

As if beckoned by her thoughts Filip and Sven rode up to her, complimenting her on her handling of the stallion and Nikita joined them, flashing Laura a look while greeting them all.

She smiled at them and greeted the four older girls as they joined them, turning their mounts out of the courtyard as the procession started down Castle Street. Aleksei rode at the head of the column with Grigory and Saskia, her two giggling friends riding a neck-length behind. Laura was glad to see Tatiana was nowhere near her husband, but didn't look around to see exactly where she was.

Nikita, Hannah, her brother and their friends rode beside Laura, laughing and teasing each other. Laura joined in the banter somewhat reservedly, watching how they drew the court around them, like moths to a flame. Those youths of Dalnerechensk that had been stiffly polite to her since she had arrived, only doing so much as protocol dictated, began to warm to her and join in the light banter. It had taken almost six months, but finally the ice between Laura and the elitist, traditionalist court was beginning to break. She could have wept for happiness, and the smile she had forced to her lips after Tatiana's words became genuine.

Ivan Gogol rode beside Laura, asking questions about her life in Boston, attentive and responsive to her comments. It was the first time anyone in the court had shown an interest in her and Laura smiled at him, gratefully. Nikita teased her about the boring nature of her life in the school and declared she should have run away for evenings of enjoyment and pleasure. Laura hid her secret smile.

'You ride very well, Your Highness' Ivan said, noting the way her stallion pawed at the ground but she kept it in check.

'That she does, though I dare say she does not ride so well as officers of the Polish Cavalry' Nikita broke in, teasing still.

'Imagine, *Knjaz* Rurik, that I ride every bit as well!' Laura boasted.

'A race! A race!' cried Hannah, laughing.

'Very well!' Filip cried. 'And what should be our prize?'

'A kiss from the Princess!' Nikita laughed.

'That is hardly incentive for me to win then is it?' Laura retorted, laughing.

'A hundred rubles then' Ivan laughed. 'Will that be incentive enough Your Highness?'

'Generously so!' she laughed. 'A race to the Eastern Border then My Lords, you cannot miss the low stone wall past the farm in Kalach.'

Nikita suddenly spurred his horse forward, claiming he would have his kiss and the others broke into a gallop behind him. Laura easily overtook Ivan and Sven, and the sound of their crops against the flanks of their horses filled her with a nervous panic of Lady Ramkinson behind her, quickly gaining ground. That panic infected her horse, spurring it faster towards the Eastern Valley. She overtook Franz as they thundered out of the pass and could see Nikita and Filip neck in neck ahead of her.

She spurred the stallion faster, gaining on the riders slowly. Kalach was rapidly approaching as she reached them. Nikita laughed and thwacked his crop against his mare but could not go faster, cursing as Laura edged ahead of him. Filip glanced at her and urged his stallion faster as the three flew past the farm. The wall was rapidly approaching, and Filip glanced at Laura again, knowing the first one that slowed would lose the race.

Laura wasn't slowing, and urged her horse faster. Filip glanced again at the wall, knowing they were running out of time to turn the horses. Behind them Nikita reined in the mare, cursing loudly. Filip glanced at Laura one last time then swore, yanking the reins to the right, feeling the stones of the wall graze his boot, gouging them deeply. Laura and her mount sailed over the wall then turned to eye him triumphantly, breathing hard.

She could see the four girls pouring out of the pass, the rest of the riding party behind them. Franz threw up his hands and applauded her, graceful in defeat, and Ivan joined in, awed by her ability.

'Magnificent' Nikita said, watching her through his lashes.

Laura bowed her head and patted her stallion's neck, a pleased glow in her cheeks. She then wheeled her mount and leapt back over the wall, trotting back to her friends happily. The five beaten riders handed over twenty rubles each with much laughter and banter. The rest of the party joined them, congratulating Laura on winning the race and she flushed with happiness.

54

Aleksei slipped across the corridor and let himself into Laura's apartments, closing the door behind him. Part of him had hoped to see her sitting on the rug before the fire, waiting for him, and he was disappointed to see the sitting room was empty. He couldn't understand why she didn't come to his bed anymore, why she looked at him with such hurt in her eyes now, although a small part of him whispered it had been because he had taken her so carnally in the Ivanov's garden. She had become so reserved, so — *old*, she didn't act like the girl he had fallen in love with.

Ah, but he had seen it again, that glow of girlish enthusiasm as the Poles had challenged her to race to the Eastern Border. His pulse had quickened at the sight of her flying past and he had caught his breath, watching her figure disappear into the trees of the Hunting Forest, remembering that same glow he had seen as she had sat beside him in the carriage on their wedding day.

The young company was bringing back her girlish sparkle, and his chest tightened painfully to think of Tatiana's snubs and the cold aloofness of the rest of the youth that remained at court. Quickly Aleksei crossed the room to her bedroom, pushing open the door.

She was alone in bed, and Aleksei couldn't stop that surge of relief that flooded though him. He slipped across to her bed and pulled back the covers, joining her.
'Laura' he whispered, stroking back her hair.

She was awake, lying quietly on her back. Aleksei lay beside her, stroking her stomach, wondering why she was so unresponsive to his touches. He kissed her lips but she did not respond and he wondered what had happened to change her attitude so drastically from when she had suggested a race to the glen that morning. They had not had the opportunity to slip away from the riding party, and Laura had spent her time with his niece and her friends.

His hand dropped to the plump curve at the end of her body but she didn't even gasp, lying as still as the dead beside him. He withdrew then, rolling onto his side, his back to her, frustrated and feeling sulky. He waited to see if she would apologise, waited to see if she would say anything at all. Sleep was sneaking up on him but he resisted it, trying to stay awake, and stay angry.

He heard a soft snuffling sound behind him and wondered briefly if she was crying. But he was fooling himself; Laura was asleep. Aleksei waited to make sure, and called her name out softly, but there was no response. He slipped out of bed and left her.

55

Laura stretched back, sighing. The day was warm and she had taken refuge under one of the tall trees that grew near the banks of the river in Liberty Valley. The ten teens and Nikita were sprawled around her, talking quietly, picking early, bitter blackberries, laughing at the bawdy jokes.

Laura eyed the towering castle. It was golden in the afternoon sun, and looked very pretty. The river meandered through the valley before her, ducking under a quaint stone bridge, reappearing on the other side, burbling happily. She sighed blissfully again, thinking how pretty this place was, how glad she was here. She would hold many picnics here in summer, and would bring her children here to play, and watch Aleksei teach them to fish from the old stone bridge.

She shut her eyes at that thought, chiding herself for her behaviour last night. Aleksei had never come to her bed before, and she had lain still, unable to stop herself from wondering if he had gone to Tatiana's bed, if he had touched her like that. He had turned away from her, angry, and she had said nothing, for fear it start an argument. She squeezed her eyes tighter then pushed away the thoughts; this warm, picturesque river bank with handsome friends was not a place for sad thoughts.

Hannah's giggle drew her attention to the small group, where Nikita was theatrically tying a white handkerchief around his eyes. She smiled, amused, thinking they were too old to be playing Blind Man's Bluff, and wondered whether this was the result of the bawdiness and silliness of the afternoon.

Nikita finished tying the handkerchief in place then leapt to his feet, charging through the group of girls, scattering them with screams of laughter. He lunged at the laughs but missed the girls by a whisker, the silks of their skirts brushing his fingers so fleetingly he wasn't able to grip it. He lunged once or twice more before his outstretched arms found Saskia.
'Aha!' he cried. 'And who do I have here? Long hair, small stature, giggly... Franz?' he inquired.

There was a hoot of scornful laughter from the slighted officer and Saskia fell into helpless hysterics, twisting away from Nikita. He was not able to keep a grip on her and he threw up his hands in mock despair, grinning.
'And as slippery as an eel!' he cried out. 'I shall have to find a new little fly in my web!'

He spread his arms wide and tottered unsteadily around the river bank. Hannah laughed rushed past him, falling to her knees beside Laura and grabbing her hands, laughing. Nikita heard them and gave chase. Hannah laughed and pulled Laura to her feet, tugging her away from the tree. Laura laughed, breaking away from Hannah, slipping past Nikita's outstretched arms. Nikita spun in a circle, trying to track their movements.

The teens laughed and ran past Nikita, confusing him. He made several wild grabs at the footsteps and the swish of skirts, missing each time. Laura retreated to the tree on the banks of the river, watching their antics, amused. Nikita had his back to her, his searching hands waving in front of him. He made wild grabs at thin air while Lana and Rebecca laughed and danced past him, always just out of reach. His fumblings, twisting this way and that, were herding him towards her, and he was too close. She stepped away from the tree to avoid being caught. A twig snapped under her boot and Nikita whirled around, lunging.

He grabbed her, his hand sliding across her breast, cupping it, before sliding down the curve of her body. He seized her thigh and lifted her against him, crying out:
'I have a nymph! Let me ravish her before she runs away!' and rubbed himself against her firmly.

Laura slapped him hard. Nikita let her go, staggering back a pace or two. His hand cupped the hurt cheek then he smiled and threw up his hands.
'Ah, so sweet a promise, and so harsh a rebuke, I must have caught the Princess!' he said loudly. He tossed one hand in the air then flung it across his stomach, bowing low, his movements exaggerated and jerky, as if he were a puppet. 'Forgive me Your Highness, I meant no disrespect' he grinned.
'You are too easily deterred *Knjaz* Rurik' she teased.

Nikita's smile deepened and he lunged at her. She sidestepped and heard his cry of surprise as the ground disappeared under his feet, and the splash a split-second later. Nikita surfaced, pushing up the blindfold, only to see the company laughing and running across the stone bridge, racing back to Dalnerechensk. Sven stopped and turned back, calling to Nikita:
'Give me the blindfold, I want to try my luck for a nymph!'

The girls screamed with laughter and swept into the city, leaving Nikita to get himself out of the river.

56

Laura placed her empty wine goblet on the table, feeling reckless and happy. The colours of the ball room were swirling around her and she quickly found a seat, fanning herself with a pretty lace fan Franz had presented to her. The music was lively and the court was as drunk as they had been on her wedding night. They were shuffling through dances unsteadily, unable to lift their feet anymore. Nikita flopped down onto a seat beside her, suddenly grabbing her hand and pointing to Hannah and Rebecca who were trying to teach a few of the court a traditional Polish dance, laughing at their antics. Nikita and Laura laughed too, they were all frightfully drunk and loud with laughter.

Nikita's hand fell to his side then stole into the folds of her dress where it could not be seen. Laura's breath hitched in her chest as he stroked her thigh gently, seductively, his fingers stinging heat into her. His boldness terrified her, it thrilled her, all her senses tuned and straining for the feel of his hand there. She paused, her eyes daring to meet his. They were red from the wine and pipe tobacco, but they were no longer veiled by his long lashes. He was looking at her with a raw desire, his breath panting quickly.

'*Knjaz* Rurik, you must not -'

'To hell with must and must not!' he said passionately.

'The market is on tomorrow, you must come, if only to say you have been!' Laura said, desperately trying to turn the conversation. She looked away, her eyes swishing over the crowd of people, wondering who knew, wondering who was watching.

'I will not be so easily deterred' Nikita murmured, and Laura cursed herself for her flirt that afternoon. 'How much longer are you going to deny yourself?' he whispered urgently, and she shut her eyes, longing rising to the surface.

'Enough!' Aleksei suddenly bellowed, leaping from his seat where he was watching the dancers.

The musicians stopped and a hush quickly fell over the crowd in the great hall. Laura gazed at him, frightened that she had been caught, feeling as though she was displayed with her skirts over her head and Nikita's hand snaking inside her undergarments for all to see. Aleksei looked as if he had swallowed a tornado, a red and black mood was twisting across his face and the air crackled with static electricity around him.

'*Knjaz* Rurik I will see you in the chambers, now. And my wife. Court is dismissed.'

At once Tatiana's and Natasha Chekhovna's fans came out, fluttering frantically. Laura shot Nikita a guarded, frightened look then rose and followed Aleksei to the Council Chambers, dreading the confrontation, wondering what she was going to say. Nikita trailed them, wondering if the Prince had seen what he was doing. He was certainly angry enough. He sniffed, an argument was going to ruin his mood.

Aleksei was nearly frothing at the mouth, his hands clenched by his side in fury, anger radiating out of the stiff way he held his back as he walked. Laura shot Nikita a quick look. He was unabashed, as if Aleksei had summoned him for a brandy, as if he had been no more than discussing the weather instead of instigating an affair with her. She felt suddenly abandoned, as if she were the one in the wrong, and wondered how many jealous husbands Nikita had faced over his indiscretions.

Aleksei thrust open his door and stalked into the room, leaving Laura to close it behind herself and Nikita. Both of them stood on the rug before the Prince like naughty children while he paced back and forward, his fists clenching and unclenching. He was so angry for once he acted out of emotion, setting aside decorum and formality.

'*What is the meaning of this*?!' he nearly screamed. 'Every morning you sleep late and then disappear with my wife while the rest of the court is left to speculate on your indiscretions!'

'I am part of the Royal Romanov household; I don't take kindly to this insult -' Nikita started arrogantly.

'*Don't trifle with me boy*!' Aleksei thundered, rounding on him.

The violence of his words shocked Laura, she had never seen Aleksei so moved by his passions before.

'Husband please -' Laura started, trying to soothe him.

'Husband?' he mocked. 'You would do well to remember that my dear. The people think you have forgotten.'

'Your wife's reputation is unstained; you have my word on it' Nikita swore gallantly.

'That does not account for much' Aleksei snapped. 'You have been deliberately vague these past fifty such days and my hospitality is wearing thin. State why you have sent an imperial telegram if your manner here is purely recreational, or, if not, explain why you have delayed matters of state so long.' He stopped, his chest hitching as if he had been running instead of yelling.

'Very well' Nikita sniffed. 'I am here with an official offer from his Imperial Majesty Tsar Nicholas the Second. As I can see you are angry with me I can but humbly beg your forgiveness. The time I have spent in Dalnerechensk has made me loathe to leave her lush valleys and I unwisely tested your patience by dragging my heels to deliver my message. Again forgive me Your Royal Highness, I will deliver my message in full tomorrow morning before your assembled council, I swear on it.'

'See that you do *Knjaz* Rurik or I will have you dragged there no matter what state the guards may find you in. Leave us.' He waved him away.

Nikita's eyes narrowed in annoyance at the flippant dismissal but he bowed, bidding them both good night, letting his lips linger on the back of Laura's hand before stepping out of the Council Chambers and closing the door behind him.

'I am sorry if I have caused you embarrassment or pain' Laura started quietly.

Aleksei made a sound of disapproval and looked ready to stalk from the room on his heel.

'I am young, and without friends in this court' she said quickly. Aleksei stopped, relenting. Laura bit her lip hard and continued. 'I do not begrudge you this, my love, I accepted you and your Principality as my own as it stood and I do not regret it. But I did not think I would feel as lonely as I do, as I had few friends at Lady Ramkinson's school, you have seen how much I was despised there on my back.'

Aleksei shut his eyes, pained at the abuse she had suffered. Laura bit her lip harder, trying to force the tears back.

'I *am* lonely' she said quietly, clasping her hands in front of her and squeezing her knuckles hard. 'I miss Ekaterina, she is fun and spirited. *Knjaz* Rurik agreed to take over my Russian lessons while she was away. I accepted because sometimes he reminds me of Ekaterina, and I could not neglect my lessons. I don't understand yet, I want so much to understand.'

She brushed at her tears and sniffed loudly, like a child. Aleksei softened and took her arms, kissing her forehead and sighed gently.

'Alright Laura' he said quietly. 'I am sorry I was so angry with you. Go to bed, we will forget this now.'

Laura wiped her tears, composing herself carefully. She wanted to ask him if he was coming to her bed that night, but didn't want to hear him refuse. Instead she set her features carefully then opened the door, closing it after her with a soft click.

Hannah, her friends, Franz, the Polish officers and Nikita were waiting in a huddle in the corridor, and only the Russian seemed unfazed by the sudden dismissal of the court.

'Laura,' Hannah started quietly, unasked questions in her eyes.

Laura didn't drop her gaze for a second.

'Tomorrow is the new moon, and there is a street market on Vsevolod's Way. You must come with me' she said quietly. 'Perhaps you could join us once you have finished delivering your message to the court *Knjaz* Rurik.'

'Of course' he said flippantly, sniffing.

'I confess we have been too reckless with the wine tonight, if you will excuse me I will retire for the evening. Could I escort you to your rooms?'

They agreed demurely, following her along the first floor corridor to the stairs, bidding her an answering good night as she saw each of the guests to their doors. One by one they shut the doors behind them, questions on their lips but pride and decorum forbidding them to ask. Laura soon found herself alone with Nikita in a dark, cloistered section of the second floor; the narrow window at the end of the corridor opening onto a moonless night. The corridor had turned at a right angle from the stairs and they were both hidden from the eyes of the castle.

He stepped towards her but she escaped quickly, walking determinedly to the stairs, hoping to leave him behind. There were several quick steps and Nikita caught up to her as she rounded the corner, walking in silence up to his rooms on the third floor. She bid him goodnight and turned to leave, glad she had avoided another confrontation that night.

Quick as a flash Nikita grabbed her arm, pulled her into his room and shut the door. Laura found herself pressed up against the back of the door, Nikita's hands firmly on either side of her shoulders stopping her escape, his handsome face inches from hers. She gasped, afraid, wondering if she was in danger. Nikita's eyes looked wild, and only partly so from passion.

'What did he ask you?' he hissed.

'Nothing' she squeaked, trying to escape.

Nikita grabbed her arms, pushing her up against the door again, stepping against her to keep her in place. She gasped, closing her eyes, a tear sliding down her cheek.

'What has he told you?' he demanded, his voice hissing through his teeth.

'That you are important, and your every whim must be seen to' she whimpered, trying to look everywhere but in his fierce eyes.

He reached up and stroked her soft, chestnut chair, twining a lock round his finger. She turned her face away, desperate not to see that raw hunger for her in his eyes and felt his lips close on her throat.

'And what if my whim is to have you?' he said huskily, his voice layered with thick desire.

'I am Aleksei's property, I am his to command' she answered, another tear sliding down her cheek.

This time he was not quick enough to stop her as she pushed him away and she fled from his room, throwing herself miserably into her bed to dream of his fierce, desire-filled eyes.

57

The glass smashed, waking Laura. A loud voice, bitter and drunk shouted something she couldn't quite understand, intrusive in the quiet of the night. She sat up, pulling the covers up around her, frightened, her senses straining. Another glass smashed and her eyes were drawn to the window. The noise was outside, at the walls of the castle. More glass smashed, and more loud voices shouted. Laura slipped out of bed, and rushed to the window, peering out into the darkness beyond the castle.

She could see one of the four watch towers from her bedroom windows, the North Eastern corner of the walls. It was dark and silent, giving her no hint of the reason for or the location of the commotion. There was suddenly a loud grinding sound and a rattle to her left, hidden from her sight. She realised it was the rattle of the Castle Street portcullis being lowered. There was a solid metallic thunk as it met the cobblestones, then the sound of running feet crossed the courtyard beneath her window.

Laura pressed her face against the glass, trying to see round the corner but it was no good. Something glass smashed again, and there were more yells. Frightened she flew across her sitting room, swirling on her robe as she did and yanked open the landing door, raising her fist to knock on Aleksei's door.

What if he's not in there? a small part of her said. *What if he* is, *and he's not alone?* Her fist stopped and she turned away, knowing Nikita could catch her hesitating in the corridor, and that was something she hoped to avoid. Instead she quickly padded down the stairs to the ground floor. People were awake, stirring through the castle, asking each other in loud whispers what was going on. Franz, Filip and Sven rushed down the stairs before her, half dressed, boots untied, their jackets open, swords in their hands.

Laura paused, frightened. Elzbieta saw her and called out to her but Laura didn't stay to comfort them, slipping down the stairs and out of the castle. The cold concrete of the stairs hurt her feet and she gasped quietly, looking around her to see what was happening. The watchtower before her had been lit with a bright brand and she heard an alarm ring far away. She guessed the fire in the watch tower was to signal the garrisons in Tcherepnin, and she could hear distant shouts and barking dogs as the troops mobilised. The gate to Vsevolod's Way was blocked by three guards, and two more stood atop the wall walk, their hands on the windlass to drop the portcullis into place should they need to. The three Poles stood at the foot of the castle stairs, swords at the ready, their eyes searching the dark courtyard before them.

Filip looked round at her gasp and ordered her back into the castle. She ignored him, breathing short in fear, trying to see into all the dark nooks and crannies of the yard. Behind her livery men and male servants were flooding out of the castle into the courtyard. Some were carrying lanterns and they quickly rushed to light the area, beginning to fan out and patrol the castle grounds.

The shouts outside the wall hadn't stopped but there were new voices, and the sounds of scuffling. There was one last smash of something glass and Laura jumped, reaching out to touch Filip's arm, glad he folded it round her for some comfort. She could feel he was just as nervous as she was. They could hear the sound of approaching feet, and Laura held her breath, unsure if the boots belonged to friend or foe.

'What is it?' Hannah whispered from the stairs, Lana, Rebecca and Elzbieta holding on to their friend, frightened.

The line of guards at the gate parted and four rushed in, carrying horizontally between them a struggling, yelling drunk by his arms and legs. He cursed to the ground, and the soldiers marched him smartly to one of the watch towers and disappeared inside.

The silence descended onto the streets of Dalnerechensk again. The barking dog in Tcherepnin was silenced and the boots of the approaching guards halted inside the courtyard, their breath steaming above their heads. Peter Kaminin softly gave them orders, his voice carrying easily in the darkness. Some headed back down Vsevolod's Way, returning to the garrisons while others fanned out, helping the servants search the grounds for anything amiss.

Carefully Filip lowered his sword, checking the Princess with a quick, careful look, relaxing. Beside him Franz and Sven relaxed too, and Sven sheathed his sword, rubbing his cold hands together, hugging his jacket around him.

'Come inside Laura, before you catch your death' Filip said, guiding her inside.

'It is alright, it is just a drunk causing trouble' Franz soothed his sister and her friends, blushing with awkwardness when he saw they were all still in their nightshirts and not one had put a robe on.

Laura let herself be led inside, wondering if the drunk had been in a bar, in a particular bar where revolution found fertile ground in anger and alcohol. She shivered and Filip gallantly shrugged off his jacket, slipping it around her shoulders. They shut the door against the cold of the spring night and Laura gave back Filip's jacket, thanking him for his thoughtfulness.

Aleksei stood at the top of the stairs, Saskia, Izydor and Zofia standing with their thin, girlish arms around him, peeping down at them from around his body. Aleksei's sword was still raised, partly from unknowing, partly to avoid cutting his niece or her friends with the edge.

'It is just a drunk throwing bottles at the walls Uncle' Franz said. 'He was brought to one of the towers.'

'To bed then children' he said to his niece and her friends, shooing them before him back up the stairs to their rooms.

Laura turned to the Poles, managing a weak smile.

'Would anyone care to join me for some tea or warm wine?' she asked, aware there was a waver in her voice.

They all agreed, glad for company after the rude awakening, none more so than Laura. They followed her to the queen's apartments, sitting on the assortment of couches and chairs she had. Anna had been sitting in the rooms, worried about where her mistress was, and hurriedly went to do her bidding, glad Laura was alright.

They sat quietly, and laughed nervously estranged titters of relief. Anna returned with a pot of tea and poker heated wine, setting the tray she carried on a small card table, serving all the guests and her mistress their choice of drink. Laura then sent her to bed and they sipped at the hot drinks quietly.

No one was quite willing to talk about the strange events that night, and Laura eyed the teens over her tea surreptitiously, wondering if they knew about the Principality's desperate trouble, wondering if they knew they tottered on the edge of Revolution. *The boys looked at each other with a quiet sense of understanding* she thought, and realised even if they didn't know about the troubles they were aware things were not as they seemed.

Outside a light suddenly went on in the watch tower she could see from her window. She watched it curiously, wondering if the prisoner was being held in that tower, and shuddered to think that the drunk could see into her rooms. As if to confirm her fears the shouts sounded again, from inside the tower. The Pole's heads turned, looking out the window.

Black shadows leapt into the light thrown out of the window and the shouts were cut off suddenly. Sven reached over and carefully, deliberately pulled the drapes of her room shut. He knew the drunk would now be beaten into submission or unconsciousness.

'Never a dull moment is it?' Filip said, and the company laughed with nervousness rather than amusement.

Sven drained his spiced wine with a flourish and dropped the mug onto the tray with a loud clink.

'Excuse me now Laura' he said, bowing slightly unsteadily. 'Now that I have drunk even more wine I will be buying a witch's larder of herbs and potions tomorrow to cure a wretched hangover if I do not get any sleep' he grinned.

Lana laughed and agreed, the Poles bidding her goodnight and slipping out of her room, leaving her with nothing to do but climb into bed and hope sleep would still come.

58

Olaf stretched, feeling the muscles in his back pull, feeling a twinge of discomfort between his shoulders. He splashed his face quickly in the well water, dressing hurriedly to ward off the chill of the spring morning. He ate standing at the window of his room above the stable, watching the castle while he chewed thoughtfully. Today he was taking a year-old foal out on its first run. He had been training her all winter and now she was strong enough to bear his weight he would test all his handling skills.

She was a pretty mare, sired by the Princess's stallion and birthed by the best mare in the stable. If she responded well to his command she would fetch a good price in the Russian market. He finished eating and wiped his mouth free of crumbs, a movement in one of the castle windows catching his eye.

The pretty Poles were awake already, Hannah, Rebecca, Lana and Elzbieta were dressed and cavorting around the room, their faces flushed with fun. He smiled, imagining he could hear their giggly, teasing tongues as they ribbed each other good-naturedly. Their heads suddenly turned and Olaf knew someone had knocked at the door. Lana went to answer it and came back, dragging the Princess after her.

Olaf dropped his eyes. She was dressed in white, and even this far away he knew she looked radiantly beautiful. All of Dalnerechensk was talking of her sparkle, and women sighed with envy as they discussed her figure and hair. He too had noticed the change in her, and seen the way the eyes of the court followed her, relentlessly ravenous.

He had heard Tatiana's poisonous words to Laura in the courtyard, had seen her tremble as she had tried to recover from that cutting piece of information. The poor girl hadn't known the Prince had taken lovers, hadn't known the law said he could take as many as he liked. As soon as she had had a son the Prince was entitled to banish her if he chose. Whatever education she had received in America would never protect her from thousands of years of snobbery and politics in Dalnerechensk.

He wondered if she had heard the drunk yelling last night, wondered if any of them had. The gagged prisoner had been removed from the tower before dawn and thrown out onto the streets a few blocks from the castle with warnings that if he came back he would be re-arrested and charged with treason. Olaf sighed. The Principality was restless, dangerous; he wondered if the Princess still feared for her life.

Another movement from the castle caught his eye, interrupting his thoughts, and he looked up to see all five girls at the window giggling as they gazed at him. Hannah and Elzbieta waved while Lana blew a kiss then they threw back their heads and laughed, scrambling to hide behind the curtains and peep back at him, teasing each other and laughing. He smiled and turned away, a spring in his step as he descended into the stables.

He bridled and saddled the foal, talking to it soothingly as he led it out of the stall. It snorted in the cold morning and he soothed it, swinging up onto its back. It shied, prancing uncomfortably, but Olaf leaned forward and offered it a few sugar cubes from his pocket. It ate, snorted once, then stood still, waiting.

Olaf smiled, nudging its flanks gently, walking it first to the left and then to the right. The horse responded, and Olaf's smile deepened. He clicked his tongue, kicking its flanks again, gently directing it down Castle Street, avoiding the noisy crush of market day in Vsevolod's Way.

The horse responded to all his gentle instructions and he delighted in realising the horse loved to run almost as much as he liked to ride at full gallop. He would be sorry to see the horse sold; it had trained well, and didn't protest when he turned it up a hill in a canter. He ducked under a low branch, urging the horse faster, feeling his blood pound in time to the horse's hooves.

At the top of the ridge he slowed the horse and sat back, listening to the mare snort under him, feeling his own breath pant in and out of his lungs. The forest smelt good and he sighed deeply, trying to avoid remembering his menial tasks still waiting to be done in the stables. He patted the neck of the horse, knowing it was not exhausted yet and was tempted to push it further.

Instead he clicked his tongue again, walking the mare to keep her blood warm. She flicked her tail and trotted along, tossing her head prettily. Olaf smiled again, keeping a tight rein on her, stopping her from sprinting, giving in to the joy of the run, though he was sorely tempted to let her.

'You shall be called Light Dancer' he said, patting her neck again.

They rode on through the morning, feeling the sun warm them. Olaf knew he should be heading back but didn't want this feeling of freedom to end. He wondered if the infectious flirting and fun of the young company had gotten even to him. He certainly felt reckless enough to risk Aleksei's wrath.

'What do you say Light Dancer? To the northern wall then?'

The horse snorted and Olaf nudged her on, keeping her bridle tight.

The border wall was not as well maintained in the forest as it was in the valleys. Olaf knew it was because it was difficult to get to, and also because no one had been paid to maintain the forest wall for nearly thirty years. The wall was covered with moss and some of the stones had fallen away. It was less than a foot high in places now, and Olaf's mare stepped nonchalantly over it, meandering on their way into Russia.

He did not fear the Russians, nor Dalnerechenskers. No one came to the forest anymore, not the aging court, and Dalnerechensk peasants were forbidden in the king's private hunting forest. Even the Princess had not been this far before. It was isolated, and he couldn't help but smile to think that Russia would never know about this small Dalnerechensk invasion.

The laugh surprised him and he reined in the mare quickly, listening carefully. It had been faint and distant, but distinct nonetheless. *What are the gypsies doing in the Urals so early, and so close to Dalnerechensk?* he wondered. Even though the snows had melted he knew a late storm could block the passes and freeze horses. He slid to the ground, looping the reins round a tree branch and headed deeper into Russia, trying to glimpse the caravans through the trees.

He could hear voices, and turned towards them moving through the trees carefully, becoming aware of other alien sounds in the forest. It sounded like a lot of people were camped together, and he bent low to the ground, trying to stay out of sight. The sun reflecting on metal caught his eye and he peered through the trees, seeing a flash of gold and navy blue in the distance.

He stopped, turning quickly, then mounted the mare again and spurred it back to the castle.

*

Nikita leaned forward in his chair and folded his hands on the top of the table, his eyes drifting languidly over the treaty parchment before him. Aleksei's council of advisors sat watching him nervously. They had outlined the conditions they wanted in the amended treaty and were waiting for his answer. He was sure Aleksei was holding his breath. He had been surprised at his forethought, and if Nicholas Romanov's message had been any different, if he had been entrusted with any power to make decisions, Nikita just might have considered the revised treaty.

Instead he smiled, his eyes drifting from the parchment to the grey, wrinkled faces of the Advisory Council.

'Gentlemen' he started pleasantly. 'I commend you on your thorough and painstaking efforts to amend a treaty so as not to offend Russia's good grace. I must, however, sadly inform you that your efforts were in vain. It is not worth Russia's trouble to renegotiate the treaty; the price of tin is too low.

'Instead, His Imperial Majesty Tsar Nicholas the Second proposes to buy the mines outright for the sum of a hundred thousand rubles. You will find these terms quite generous' he smiled like a snake. 'If you feel these terms are unreasonable you may offer a counter. The Tsar will consider any satisfactory offer.'

He stopped and sat back in the chair. Aleksei's face was like a purple hurricane; his grey eyes two smoldering pinpoints of hate. The others in the room looked white and stunned. Nikita almost laughed at their naïvety. How could they have not even considered Russia vying for control over the mines after they had been accepting her deflated prices for so long? The Russian aristocracy was right; they really were backward children.

He was almost sorry his time in Dalnerechensk was at a close. Toying with Aleksei and the feeble old ministers was almost as fun as toying with the Princess. When Dalnerechensk was part of Russia again, he would ask the Tsar for the fortified castle as his own. It really was pretty here.

'I can see you have plenty to talk about' Nikita said. 'I shall retire to my rooms. Summon me when you have reached an agreement.'

He stood, bowed flippantly and left, closing the door behind him. For a terrible moment no one in the chamber moved, the sick and hollow feeling settling in the pits of their stomachs. Aleksei seized the crystal decanter of water near his elbow and flung it at the door, shattering it into a thousand pieces. The delicate rock tinkled onto the wooden floor, scattering and winking in the sunlight, seeming to mock the Prince even more. The water dripped and ran down the door, staining the wood darker and collected in a puddle.

Unsatisfied Aleksei seized the small serving tray on the table and sent it crashing into the oak door, scarring it with deep gouges. Broken bits of crockery and glass rained onto the floor and cold cuts of meat and cheese thumped squelchily into the water, splashing the puddles. Ministers ducked, avoiding the flying mess, and no one dared reproach him.

'We are ruined if we sell the mines!' Aleksei cried. 'There will be nothing of worth in Dalnerechensk. The people will trickle away for better jobs and lives in Russia and abandon Vsevolod's proud history. Dalnerechensk will become a ghost principality!'

'We cannot refuse Russia' someone said. 'If we anger Russia we incur the wrath of her army.'

'An army we had defeated once before!' Maksim swore passionately. 'The castle is unbreachable, we all know that. Let Russia bring her army' he sat back with a triumphant huff.

'And her machines, and her cannons' Nicholas Riminov said quietly.

'And what of our cannons?' Maksim snapped. 'We will return everything they throw at us, and if it comes to it, the palace guards will -'

'The palace guards are too few and have not seen fighting for four hundred years! They know nothing of warfare, only of marching and parades!' Valentin Gogol cried, leaping to his feet, his chair tipping over with a crash. 'We would not stand a chance. Dalnerechensk would be razed.'

'But we cannot accept this!' Aleksei cried, Grigory and Lev Dostoevski agreeing with him.

'We would have no choice but to concede to Russia! Become part of Russia! They would persecute us again! It is why we left all those years ago.'

He seized the amended treaty and tore it in half, throwing away the crumpled pieces in anger. One piece fluttered down and landed at the feet of Vasilievich Chekhov. He reached down and picked it up, gently smoothing the crumpled title. They had worked so hard on the treaty, had argued and bickered and almost come to blows more than once, but they had achieved something great in this room.

'Perhaps this is not all for nothing' he said. He shifted nervously when he felt the eyes of the Council turn on him, some filled with outrage. 'We wrote a good treaty' he swore, waving the ripped half in front of them. 'We know we cannot accept the purchase of the mines. *Knjaz* Rurik said Tsar Nicholas will consider any satisfactory offer.' He waved the paper at them to emphasise his point. '*This* is a satisfactory offer.'

A knock on the door interrupted them. Olaf pushed it open, glancing down in surprise at the mess of food, water, and broken dishes the door ground out of the way. He guessed their deliberations were not going well. The Councilors sniffed, he was covered in mud and stank of sweat. He ignored them, eyeing the enraged Prince.

'What?' Aleksei snapped.

'*Knjaz* Nikita Rurik is a Commander of a company in the Imperialist Army' he said shortly.

'So what of that? Many princes have lead men in war' Aleksei said irritably, pushing back his hair from his face and wishing Olaf would drop his eyes respectfully. He had no desire to be reminded of Nikita now. He had suspected the dandy was wasting his time, spinning out a visit that should have only taken three days to almost two months.

'There is a company of Imperial soldiers camped on our Northern Border' Olaf answered.

There was deathly silence and the colour drained from every face in the room. Aleksei sank slowly into his chair, gripping the arms tight.

'So it has begun' he said softly.

*

Hannah and Rebecca took Laura's arms, calling *dzień dobry* to the castle guards at Vsevolod's Way and giving them a sultry wink as they swept past, giggling. It wasn't just the court enjoying the refreshing youthfulness and the guards saluted smartly, puffing out their chests as the pretty girls went by. Peter Kaminin, Fedor and four other guards fell into step with them, accompanying them through the chaos of the market. Laura knew the unrest was getting worse and looked round her carefully, trying to remember to smile at her subjects.

The stallholders were calling out their wares and bantering with passerbys. The street was full of colour and smells, children and dogs. One cheeky terrier had stolen a sausage from somewhere and was delightedly gorging itself under a table selling jam jars. Chickens in small cages squabbled irritably with the geese in the cages beside them, and wind chimes tinged lazily in the gentle breeze. The group of visiting Poles gasped and commented how quaint it was, how adorable and traditional.

Laura found herself surrounded by a great number of the court again, and was surprised to find them warm and talkative, bantering with the Poles and the Princess good-naturedly. Ivan Gogol walked with them, talking quietly with Laura. Laura suddenly stopped, turning to him.

'Ivan, I am finding myself without a tutor for Russian again, would you do me the honour?' she asked, watching him carefully.

He was surprised, and then he smiled and agreed.

'Laura!' Lana scolded. 'You cannot possibly think of books and lessons on a day like this! Come Ivan, I must drag you away before she forces you to set up a school in the jam jar stall!' she giggled, dragging him away.

The group began to split up, drifting away as various colours and items at stalls caught their eye, turning to shout back at the group in their excitement or to move on to the next stall, like fascinated bees in an exotic garden. Laura soon found herself shadowed only by Fedor as she walked down the hill, calling hello to some and accepting bouquets of fresh flowers from the children. She greeted Olga and her mother and they both beamed, dropping curtseys to her.

While the people in the markets were loud and welcoming; Laura couldn't help but think they did not shout so loudly, or as welcoming, as they had when she had walked with her father several months ago. *If it were not for the purses the visitors and she carried would they call out at all?* she wondered. She needed to know what the people now thought of her, of the monarchy since the cave in, and made up her mind to ask Olaf to report his findings to her as well as to her husband.

She couldn't stop her eyes from darting round all the faces in the crowd, peering at them all carefully, wondering if any had been in the bar. A small shiver went down her spine. Her searching eyes were caught by a bright twinkle and she made her way towards the table, curious.

Near the wall of the fortified city, almost obscured behind the stationmasters building, stood a small table bedecked with sparkling wares. Laura wondered how it was the people here could afford to buy and fashion silverware, but as she drew closer to the table she realised it wasn't silver at all but tin; cast, polished and shining in the warming sun.

The old woman behind the stall was watching her with her head respectfully bowed, shaking nervously. Laura greeted her, eyeing the trinkets that were scattered on the table. She picked up a small figurine of a cat and marveled at its simple beauty, its incredibly fine detail.

'Did you carve these?' Laura asked. 'They are beautiful!'

'Nay, my husband' the woman answered. 'I have not the steady hand for this.'

Laura suddenly spotted another figure and picked it up, turning it round in her hand with wonder.

'Look Fedor, it's me!' she smiled.

The figure was four inches tall and carved with the most intricate detail. It was her wedding dress, the long folds of the train wrapped around one arm, the edge of her skirt plucked between the fingers of the other hand, her face radiantly happy, the skirts swirling as if she were captured in the middle of a dance. Laura wondered: If she looked that beautiful and graceful in tin, how had she looked in the flesh on her wedding day?

She did recall it was the only time Olaf had ever bowed properly to her.

'I've never had a statue of me carved before' she smiled. 'Your husband is a gifted and talented man.'

The old woman flushed to the roots of her hair, pleased.

'I shall tell him you said so' she said, curtseying. 'I give you the figure, as a gift.'

'I could not accept such a fine piece of work without giving something in return' Laura gasped.

'You remembered my grandson, Ari, that is return enough' she said, and bowed low.

Laura stared at her, the image of the boy dying in her arms rocketing into her thoughts, realising the woman had lost much more than the price for a piece of tin. Hannah and Rebecca suddenly joined her, interrupting the mood.

'We found you! And what have you got there Laura?' Hannah asked, then turned to the lagging group. 'Come and look what Laura's found!'

They rushed forward, exclaiming at the quality of the statues, squabbling good-naturedly over the pieces that had caught their eye. Laura took a step back, eyeing the beautiful statue then turned to look at Fedor.

'They cannot afford to give this away can they' she demanded quietly.

'No Your Highness' he answered.

She was quiet for a minute, thinking. The Poles selected a statue each and handed over a few coins for their treasure. Fedor waited patiently, and Laura smiled suddenly.

'Two men brought a hog to the kitchen this morning, take it and give it to the family. I'm sure the court could do without it.'

Fedor smiled and bowed.

'As you wish, Your Highness.'

59

She set the little tin princess on the table in front of her so it caught the light and shone, smiling as she twisted it this way and that, like it was dancing, remembering how she had danced at her wedding with Aleksei. They had returned to the castle not long after buying the tin statues, and now Laura could see the game of croquet the court and the teen guests were playing on the lawn through her window, their laughter floating around the garden on a summer breeze.

Anna poured two cups of tea for Laura, before asking for permission and picking up the figurine.

'It's beautiful Your Highness' she smiled. 'You looked just like that on the day, everyone who was not married wanted to be when they saw you, and those that were married were jealous they were not as happy as you' she said grinning.

Laura sipped her tea carefully, thinking ruefully that they were probably having the last laugh now.

There was a hesitant knock on the door. Anna put the tin ornament back on the table and opened the door, letting Olaf into the room.

'Thank you Anna, that will be all' Laura smiled, and Anna curtsied, shutting the door behind her.

Olaf glanced round him uncomfortably, dusting his hands against the other, trying to eye the finery of the room but unwilling to as well. His awkwardness and uneasiness made the smile fade from her face. She had seen the same look on the ministers' faces as they had returned, and the castle was full of nervous flutterings.

'Please sit Olaf, have some tea' Laura said, gesturing to the chair opposite her, half expecting him to refuse.

Olaf looked around him again then crossed over to the chair, perching on the edge and dusted his hands, uncomfortable. Laura sipped her tea, watching him over the rim, wondering if she had made a mistake. He caught her eye and picked up the delicate teacup poured for him, feeling awkward and clumsy.

Laura set down her tea cup, folding her hands in her lap, dropping her eyes.

'Today I went to the market' she started quietly. 'Fedor, Peter and four guards went with us, and as I smiled at the people, and took flowers from the children, I couldn't help but think as I looked at all their faces: *Were you in the bar that night?* And I felt unsafe -'

'Don't' Olaf interrupted. 'The people love you *Tsesarevna*. You have nothing to fear.'

'Don't be so naïve Olaf' she whispered quietly. 'I am the monarchy, of course I have to fear, if not for myself then for my husband' she stopped and dropped her eyes. 'Anna is a good friend, she has an ear for rumours and a tongue for gossip, but we both know women have no place or power. I need to know what the men are thinking of me, of my husband. I want you to bring any information you learned from your spying to me as well as to my husband.'

'As you wish, Your Highness' he said abruptly, putting down the teacup. 'Will that be all?'

Laura concealed her surprise. 'What are you not telling me Olaf?' she said, eyeing him carefully. 'There are worried ministers and court members fluttering all over the castle. What is going on?'

Olaf shut his eyes, the desire to hold his tongue evident on his face, but he relented.

'There are Russian soldiers camped on our Northern Border' he said quietly. 'They are most probably the company *Knjaz* Rurik commands.'

Laura's hands shook and she clenched them tightly together in her lap.

'Are we going to be invaded?' she whispered, not daring to meet his eyes.

'Perhaps you should ask the Prince that' Olaf said curtly.

He stood and left her, without asking permission, without a bow, without closing the door behind him.

Laura sat still, trembling in fear. Olaf was angry with her, it was clear from the tone of his voice he believed her to be his lover. She doubted he would tell her what snippets of information he had found out.

There was a Russian army on our Northern Border. The thought terrified her. Not only were they in danger of tearing the Principality apart from inside they were surrounded by a powerful neighbour who was humiliated by the very existence of the country. *What was Nikita doing?* she screamed silently. He had not joined them in the markets, and was not playing croquet with the Poles. *What had he said in the Advisory Council today?*

She stood quickly, her chair rattling back and marched out of her rooms, along the corridor on the third floor to Nikita's apartments. She knocked smartly then pushed open the door without waiting for an answer.

Nikita's shirt was open at his throat and he was seated on one of the couches in his room. The maid leapt out of his embrace, crying out in shock and shame, running out of the room, hiding her face and apologising to the Princess as she left. Laura eyed Nikita coldly.

'Oh come now, all men have needs' he snapped, sprawling back on the chaise lounge. 'Except, of course, your husband.'

'Do not insult me *Knjaz* Rurik' she snapped.

'Why did you burst into my rooms unannounced and flush so hotly to see another woman in my arms?' he asked, flashing her a look from under his long lashes.

'Do you know anything about the company of soldiers camped on the Northern Border?' she demanded, her hands clenching angrily.

'Of course I do' he sighed, as if talking to a child. 'I am their commanding officer. Russia is at war with Japan, and expanding her borders in the East. No company can be without their commissioned officer.'

'Except yours these past two months it seems' she said haughtily.

'They are but two hours away' he snapped, and Laura heard the veiled threat in the words. 'Come Princess, did you think I was going to invade? Did you come to extract the information from me or did you come for another service?' he smiled, his elegant fingers touching his chest delicately.

She turned on her heel and stamped to the door. Nikita flew off the couch and shut it as she pulled it open, turning her roughly round so she was pressed up against the door. She shut her eyes, avoiding looking in his eyes, aware how close he was to her.

'Men are not the only ones with needs' he said. 'I know why you have come Laura.'

'You forget yourself *Knjaz* Rurik' she said, trying to escape from him.

He pushed her back, stepping closer, watching the way her breasts heaved inside the virginal white of her dress.

'I know how your body begs for release' he whispered, his lips grazing her throat, his hand cupping her breast and felt her intake of breath. 'I know the needs of your body.'

'I swore my body to my husband' she said.

'He does not want it' he whispered urgently, huskily, stepping hard against her.

Laura fought him off, pushing him back a step firmly.

'*Tres bon* Nikita, I almost believed you' she said.

She opened the door and left him, stamping back to her rooms.

60

Laura pulled the hood down over her eyes, slipping into the crowd of day servants that were leaving the castle. The castle guards were paying more attention to who left, but did not stop any of them. Laura had used the nervous fluttering in the castle as an excuse to go to bed early, giving Anna instructions that no one was to disturb her. She had then dressed in a looser pair of pants, shirt and cloak, cursing that she no longer had her carefully sewn wig.

Ahead of her she spied Olaf and knew that he was heading for the tavern again. A small part of her was scared, wondering what would happen if they discovered her in their mix, discovered her with a spy? The anger and the bitterness had been real. She shivered and lost sight of Olaf, realising he had turned down a side street. She quickened her pace and slipped down the street, seeing him already a good way ahead of her.

She quickened her pace again, watching the way he twisted and turned down different lanes and alleyways, hoping she wouldn't lose him in the warren of buildings. She was surprised at the quick pace he kept easily and knew she was falling further and further behind. She rounded a corner and saw an empty street before her. She paused for a second, frightened she had lost him, then rushed on, breaking into a trot to try and make up lost ground.

A body burst out of a dark doorway, pushing her bodily up against a wall, a forearm pinning her chin back.

'Stop following -' Olaf stopped, realising who he had and let her go, stepping back quickly from her. 'What are you doing here *Tsesarevna*?' he asked, eyeing her.

'You weren't going to tell me, I was going back to the tavern, I knew you would be going there.'

'You cannot do this -'

'If you do not tell me what little choice do I have?'

'This is foolish!' he snapped.

'I am going Olaf' she said quietly, then turned and headed further along the street.

There was silence, then she was relieved to hear his footsteps behind her. She folded the cloak around her tighter and pulled her hood further down, looking around her carefully. Olaf turned down another side street and Laura followed him. He stopped before a door and hesitated, then opened it and ushered her inside.

Men looked around at them, and the mood in the room was tangibly different from the last time Laura had been in the pub. There was the strong smell of something dead, and the air was rank with blood and fear. Something lay on the bar top, covered with a blanket. Laura felt Olaf step closer to her. She stayed with her head bowed, eyeing the thing on the bar top, hoping it wasn't someone killed in the unrest.

The blanket was suddenly twitched back, exposing the bloody and butchered deer carcass. Laura suppressed her gasp of shock and repulsion. The deer smelt bad, the meat was beginning to spoil, and had been dead at least a day. It had been poached from the Hunting Forest. Laura didn't blame them for killing the deer to feed their starving families but she was frightened, the penalty for poaching was flogging. It was probably why the meat was spoiling, the deer would have had to have been moved to the city after dark.

A man quickly set to work, hacking a hunk of flesh from the carcass. A patron in the bar stood near them and when the hunk of meat was severed from the body he took it, wrapped it in a grubby handkerchief and quickly slipped out of the bar. Another stepped up to the carcass, announcing his name to the carver. The carver half turned, repeating it to the man who sat behind him, writing the names down, almost obscured behind the carcass.

They're taking names Laura thought, starting to feel frightened.

'We can't take the meat' she said to Olaf, her voice low and barely audible.

Olaf bent down in the pretense of scratching his knee.

'If you don't take the meat they will kill us' he answered.

The blood cooled in her body, her stomach icy and thick with fear.

'Go. Say your name is Lavrov' he said. 'Keep your voice low.'

Laura stepped forward, aware that the eyes were drifting towards her. She said the name, her voice struggling past the thick fear in her throat. The eyes stopped, and all of them avoided looking at her. There was a hesitation then the carver sliced a small hunk of meat and held it out to her, almost turning away.

Laura took it quickly, hiding the meat inside her cloak and turned away, slipping out the pub door, Olaf following her. Outside he quickly took over, leading her along several streets, putting distance between her and the dangerous undercurrent he had sensed in the bar. Laura held onto the lump of meat, feeling slightly sick, trotting after Olaf dutifully.

He stopped and turned to Laura, gently taking the meat from her and wiping her fingers with a handkerchief, wrapping the meat in it. Laura wiped her fingers on her trouser legs, looking around them carefully.

'Lavrov?' she asked, eyeing Olaf.

'Her son was killed in the mines yesterday. She has no family left' he answered.

Laura bit her lip, forcing back the memories of the mines, forcing back her sympathy for Lavrov. Olaf knocked quietly on a door they stood next to. They waited silently, Laura wondering what they were doing here, wondering where *here* was. At last a latch slid back and the door was opened a fraction, a face so swollen and miserable, so cloaked in shadow and dark bags it was hardly recognizable appeared. Olaf handed over the meat.

'If they ask, you were in the pub' he said.

There was no sound, no motion of consent. The door closed, leaving them alone on the street. Laura began to walk, wanting to run away from the misery she had seen. In two quick steps Olaf was beside her, keeping pace easily.

'And, *Tsesarevna?* You know you can't sneak back in, they lower the portcullis and check all faces since I took my lover to the stables' there was a touch of reproach in his voice.

'I didn't plan to' she answered quietly. 'I would go in the same way I left, with the day staff.'

Olaf shot her a look.

'What were you to do? Wander the streets until dawn?'

'No' she answered, but didn't explain.

Olaf eyed her, watching her as she made her way back to Vsevolod's Way then turned away from the castle, heading down the hill. Laura checked around them carefully then slipped up the stairs to the church, pushing open the door and disappeared inside. Olaf followed her, eyeing the deserted pews. *It was inside, but cold, and the pews would make an uncomfortable bed.*

Laura headed to one side of the nave, her soft footfalls echoing in the large building. Olaf paused, wondering if she was going to confessional, then wondered if she were going to throw herself on *Episcop* Vasily's mercy. He nearly called out to her, nearly shouted out warning and hurried after her, reaching to grab her arm.

She stepped into a small chapel and sat on a stone bench with a swirl of her coat. Olaf hesitated then stepped in, closing the chapel door behind him. The small room was warm and pleasantly decorated. He sat beside the Princess and leaned back, surprised to find the seat and the wall were warm.

'*Episcop* Vasily was very proud of telling me about his huge fire place, pointing out where it was between the church's chapels and his luxurious apartments' Laura said. 'We will be warm and safe here tonight, and I dare say comfortable' she managed a small smile.

Olaf smiled too, rubbing his shoulders back into the warm stone. He was surprised to feel Laura lie her head on his shoulder and after a brief hesitation he lifted his arm around her to hold her comfortably. She sighed softly, thanking him. They sat in silence for a while, listening to the emptiness of the church, their eyes drooping tiredly.

'Do not do this again, *Velikaja Knjaginja*' Olaf finally said.

Laura felt a twin flush of pleasure and fear go through her. It was the first time he had called her by her title, out of respect for her. She realised for him to do so the situation must be terribly dire. She nodded then, rubbing her cheek against his shoulder.

'You will come and tell me?' she asked plaintively, trying not to feel too hopeful.

'Yes' he answered. 'You would be wise to visit the hospital again, see more of the children. It will be good for you.'

Laura leaned back to eye him carefully, but Olaf stayed looking straight ahead, not meeting her gaze. The look reminded her of her father, arm around her, trying to comfort her but not knowing how to, unable to look at her as he told her of Emily's death. She shuddered at the memory and Olaf looked at her, breaking the mood.

'What is it?' he asked quietly.

'You'll think me silly' she flushed.

'I will not' he insisted, smiling.

'Just now, when you didn't look at me, it reminded me of my father' she said, burning. 'You remind me of my father. Not now,' she explained quickly, 'not as he is now, we have grown estranged over the years, but you remind me of the father I knew, when I was a little girl. I dare say I loved him then' she sighed.

'He held me, but did not look at me when he told me of my mother's death. We were two strangers almost, all those years of decorum, of being told how I should act and feel about men, about my father, they confused me, confused him too I suspect.'

She stopped sadly, then stole a look at him. His face was unreadable.

'I can see why Tsar Constantinovich indulges you Olaf' she smiled, leaning her head back on his shoulder. 'You are roguish, but charming. Comforting' she sighed, shutting her eyes with a yawn.

Olaf chuckled quietly, shutting his eyes and leaning his head back against the wall.

*

The chapel was cold when they woke, the chilliness peeling back the layers of comfort. They sat up, rearranging their limbs carefully, stretching out sore muscles.

'It is still early *Tsesarevna*, no one will be heading to the castle yet' Olaf said quietly.

Laura stood, arching her back and stretching out her arms, yawning deeply. She swayed with the light-headed rush of blood through her then turned to eye Olaf, her body tingling with waking nerves.

'You should not tell my husband of the deer' she said. 'People will be flogged, and they will guess there is a spy. It would be most unwise.'

'And what shall I tell him *Tsesarevna*?' he asked, a hint of sarcasm in his voice.

'Nothing' she answered simply.

'And what if he sent me? He will want to know where I was all night.'

'Tell him the truth: In church.'

'With his wife?' he challenged.

'And what will you say when he asked you what you were doing? Just talking? He will not believe you. I have made half the Principality my paramours you know' she said bitterly.

'*Tsesarevna* -'

'What will you say Olaf? That you had me in your embrace all night?' she smiled as his cheeks darkened. 'You might even tell him I sighed once or twice. But you know what he will do. I will be whipped and you will be hanged. I know you cannot tell him you were with me' she smiled triumphantly.

Olaf's anger rose, conscious that she was more manipulative than he had realised. He had thought her innocent, caught up in politics and scandal over her head but saw in her now calculation and cunning he had not known about before. Perhaps she deserved everything she got.

She turned, opening the door of the chapel and slipped out, leaving the warm confines behind. Olaf followed, knowing there was nothing else he could do.

Laura slipped in behind a small cluster of people as they neared the castle gate on Vsevolod's Way, aware that Olaf was no longer behind her. It was a wise act on his part, to not be seen with her entering the castle, but she couldn't help but feel a little alone. She had sensed he was angry with her this morning but shook herself, making herself concentrate on the last little deception she faced.

The guards on duty glanced over the small group with a disinterested but careful eye. A small shadow of puzzlement passed over one's face, as if he had seen her before but couldn't quite put his finger on it. But he didn't stop her or call out and Laura slipped into the castle, relief flooding into her veins. Quickly she slipped upstairs, shutting herself in her room.

She rested back against the door, shutting her eyes in relief and pleasure. But she didn't stay there long and quickly crossed to her dressing room, peeping in carefully to make sure Anna was not inside. The room was empty so Laura stepped in, closing the door after her then stripped and washed. She bundled the shoes and clothes and hid them in a small space behind a chest of drawers.

She dressed in a simple green dress then stood at the windows and flung them open, letting the cold morning air slap every nerve in her awake. She then closed the windows and slipped down to the dining hall for breakfast.

Aleksei's chair was empty and she sat beside it quietly, greeting the members of the court as they joined her, helping themselves to the cold cuts and hot saveloys that had been laid out for breakfast. Nikita and the Poles joined them, calling a cheerful good morning to all there, the Poles asking after their absent uncle.

'I expect he is sleeping or dressing, he has not had decent bed rest for quite some time' Laura said, and the court laughed at the unintended sexual nature of her comment.

She decided to ignore the malicious thoughts about who had exhausted him that the mean side of her was parading through her head and instead ate quickly, being pleasant with all those seated there. When the meal was done she dismissed the court and slipped upstairs to change for her outing.

Anna was in her room, a feather duster in her hand, swiping the same patch of the mantelpiece over and over, a dreamy look on her face, her fingers lightly resting on her lips. Laura recognised the look and the touch immediately: Anna was in love, and had shared a kiss with her beloved very recently. She smiled though her heart wrenched in her chest. She had forgotten how long it had been since she had been caught touching her lips and smiling at nothing. Her fingers fell to the little tin princess sitting on her table and she stroked the statue gently.

'Good morning Anna' she said lightly, trying to force away her own unhappiness.

Anna looked round a little shamefacedly, realising what she was doing, and greeted the Princess.

'Dress me in something dignified but plain Anna' Laura said. 'I am going for Russian lessons with Ivan Gogol, and then I am going to the hospital to see the children again.'

Anna crossed herself and Laura did the same, knowing the God-fearing community liked to think she believed as they did. Anna slipped into Laura's dressing room and came back with an elegantly simple blue dress. Laura approved of her choice and turned her back, letting Anna unbutton her dress.

61

Laura sat on Hannah's bed, pulling out clothes as quickly as Hannah put them in. The Poles were laughing at their antics till finally Elzbieta and Lana dragged the Princess away so Hannah could pack in peace.

'You can unpack my clothes all you want my dear, it does not change the fact we have to leave tomorrow' Hannah chided.

'I know' Laura said. 'It doesn't change that I wish you wouldn't.'

'I know, my dear' Hannah soothed.

There was a knock on the door and Franz, Sven, Filip and Nikita stepped into the room, all a little flushed with wine already. They greeted the girls boisterously, spilling in and amusing themselves by lifting up items, pointing to others, teasing the girls.

'What? Not dressed for dinner?' Sven laughed, pulling out one of Hannah's gowns and holding it up, pressing it to him and holding one sleeve, dancing round the room as if with a partner. 'I must ask your thin friend to marry me, she is wonderfully light on her feet!'

Hannah laughed and tore the dress away from him, folding it up again.

'If that is how you treat your friends it is no wonder the Princess has sent you packing!' he teased.

'Imagine! I was just to ask you all again!' Laura laughed. 'Come back in a few weeks, I have so enjoyed your company and we should have a wonderful summer together.'

There was a tiny, almost imperceptible hesitation. Laura noticed the look the three Polish officers shot each other. *They are no fools* Laura thought. *Their Russian is better than mine, they know what that drunk was shouting, they know the Principality is in trouble.* The moment was lost in the girl's delighted cry of acceptance. Hannah and Elzbieta threw their arms around Laura, starting a quick capering dance around the room.

'Quick! Dress for dinner and meet us downstairs' Filip laughed, pushing out the rest of the men before him.

Hannah raced to her trunks and began throwing out items to find something to wear. Laura laughed and slipped along to her rooms, dressing in a gown that made her look heartbreakingly beautiful. She hesitated, somewhat ruefully, then fastened Nikita's necklace round her neck.

Anna, still dreamy, pinned up her hair with pretty seed pearl clips then dabbed a beautiful perfume Hannah had given the Princess on her throat and ears. Laura stood, eyeing herself in the mirror, then grabbed Franz's fan, slipping down to the dining room.

Tsar Constantinovich sat under the canopy in the middle of the great table, beside Aleksei's chair. The Prince Regent had joined the court for dinner and was brooding, staring at nothing. The Poles and Nikita were already seated a little further down the table and the Polish officers smiled at the Princess, waving her over to their seats.

Laura glanced at Aleksei for permission and he waved her on without even looking at her. The flippant dismissal hurt her, he hadn't even looked to see what she was wearing, but she smiled at her friends and sat beside Franz, noticing how he smiled at her shyly. Nikita, enjoying some secret joke, leaned over and poured a large measure of wine for her. She would be sorry to see them all leave tomorrow, and apprehensive too, they had all become wildly roguish with their flirting and their teasing, and when the train departed Nikita would be left alone with her. She didn't want to think about that.

She glanced away from the company, looking round the rest of the dining room. There was a tangible fear in the room, and the conversation of the ministers was flat and forced, the laughter loud and hollow. *It is Nikita's soldiers that have got them so worried* she thought quietly. *How had they not known of the company before now? What had happened when Nikita had met with the Advisory Council? He had not joined them at the Market on Vsevolod's Way as he had promised, and she had known from snippets of gossip that he had spent all day in his rooms.*

She looked at him carefully, not sure if she trusted him. He appeared to be enjoying himself immensely at the thought of their fear of his soldiers and he was even more arrogant and open with his flirting. She suddenly hoped Nikita would leave soon. There was something about him that told her he could be sadistic and enjoy it, and if things got any worse in Dalnerechensk they just might see it.

'Why do you stare at me so openly wearing my jewels tonight?' he asked suddenly, the smile curving his words, his delicate fingers brushing her throat on the pretense of inspecting her necklace.

'I was wondering when you were going to leave us Nikita' she answered, dropping her gaze.

'Never fear Laura, I have not done yet' he smiled, and there were fangs in that look. 'Your Royal Highness!' he suddenly called to Aleksei, silencing the court. 'Send your wife to me tomorrow, I have heard she spends quite some time riding in the Hunting Forest, I should like to have a trophy to take to Tsar Nicholas.'

There was a held breath silence at the deliberate taunt. Laura gasped, horrified. Nikita was commanding her husband, and he could not refuse or he would anger Russia, and could not agree, or he would be humiliated before his entire court. And Nikita knew it. A savage look twisted across Aleksei's face, dark and passionate.

'My wife and I will be delighted to accompany you on a hunt' he answered tightly.

There was silence, and Aleksei called for more wine. The uncomfortable mood was fractured, and several glasses were refilled, the conversations starting again, even more forced than before. The Poles looked from one another to their uncle and back to Nikita and Laura, questions in their looks but decorum keeping their tongues still. Filip broke the mood by telling a joke and the Poles laughed, calling for more wine.

Anna and two other servants kept their glasses full as the evening wore on and Laura felt herself growing reckless. Nikita was sitting close to her, closer than he needed to. His thigh was pressed against hers, and as he moved it brushed against her. It was no good, she had tried to avoid him as much as possible, but she was infatuated, and as the butterflies stirred maddeningly at the touch of his thigh and she began to think about the feel of them chafing the insides of her thighs as he lay atop her, as she guessed the touch was designed to do.

Sven leant his head forward and in a conspirator's whisper told an especially explicit joke. Laura looked at Nikita who was snickering beside her, not understanding. Nikita lowered his eyelids and turned his face into her neck, whispering the explanation of Sven's bawdy joke into her ear, his hot breath misting on her neck and making her flush inside again. She gasped at the crudeness, chastising him for his words, aware Nikita's lips were still very close to her neck.

'Your perfume is enticing' he murmured, almost turning into her, his hand pressing against the flat of her stomach, his fingers straying low against her body, his lips nearly closing on her throat in a seductive kiss.

There was suddenly an almighty crash from the middle of the table and the court jumped, turning to look, falling silent. Aleksei was on his feet in a rage, the serving platter clattering to the ground beside a terrified cook, food flying everywhere.

'Where is the hog?' he demanded. 'It was brought here two nights ago and still it is not served! Are even my servants stealing from me now?' he snapped bitterly.

'It is gone Your Royal Highness' The cook said, quaking in her shoes.

Aleksei threw a wine glass at her. The red liquid soaked her apron, the glass bouncing off her arm, shattering on the floor. Laura felt her stomach drop away and she rose to her feet, feeling as terrified as the cook and took a deep breath.

'My Lord I had the hog sent away' she said.

All the eyes of the court swung onto her. Aleksei looked stupefied at her words.

'*What?!*' he roared.

Laura paled, she had never seen him so angry. Hannah reached out and found Laura's hand, squeezing gently. Laura squeezed it hard, trying to stop the tremble. She took another deep breath then calmly explained why she gave away the hog, trembling visibly. Aleksei gave a short bark of mad laughter, throwing up his arms in mock despair. It did nothing to ease the tension in the court.

'A whole hog for tin?' he sneered. 'You must have paid for his skills then. Bring me the statue' he snapped at the gaggle of serving girls.

Anna shot her mistress a frightened look then bowed her head and went to retrieve it from her room. The court waited tensely, knowing whatever the outcome of this confrontation was, it wouldn't be good. Anna returned and presented the statue to the Prince, her frightened eyes flicking to Laura. Aleksei took it and turned it over in his hands, eyeing it with meticulous critique.

'It seems my wife's tender heart got the better of her judgment' he said to the assembled court.

'I am sorry that I have angered you' she said, her cheeks burning with shame. 'I can only beg your forgiveness -'

'A princess never begs for anything' he snapped. 'I am not running a charity I am running a principality!' his words echoed in the silence of the dining hall. 'Fedor,' he snapped at Tsar Constantinovich's servant. 'Go to the house and retrieve the hog. If it is finished take it out of the hide of every man woman and child that ate it.'

There was a gasp from all in the room. Laura stared at him, horrified.

'Surely you could not mean -'

'They have poached from the Hunting Forest!' he thundered. 'The penalty for that is flogging!'

'Aleksei please! Your hunters killed the hog, and brought it here, I sent it away, as a gift! The blame is mine, not theirs!' she cried desperately.

'*Do not dare defy me!*' he thundered.

'Remember yourself Aleksei' the old Tsar snapped as the Prince slammed back his chair.

But Aleksei didn't listen. The chair toppled over with the force of his shove. He ignored it, striding down to Laura with all the fury of a hurricane, seizing his wife by the arm, dragging her after him as he left the hall.

'Court is dismissed!' he roared over his shoulder.

He dragged Laura up to his room, slamming the door behind them. Laura was too frightened to protest or cry out for help, knowing she had never seen Aleksei like this before.

He struck her, stunning her, and made her lip bleed. He threw the little tin princess into the fire that Mikhail had banked in his bedchamber. She screamed and reached to retrieve it but the flames were too hot and Aleksei grabbed her, pulling her against his lips.

She struggled, her lips hurt from the strike and his kisses were mashing them back against her teeth. His arms came round her, trying to still her struggling, grabbing at the hundreds of buttons on the back of her dress. He tore it open, yanking it from her then lifted her up, half carrying, half dragging her to his bed. She tried to resist him, frightened by his sudden, violent attention and grabbed at the canopy curtains.

They tore, pulling away from the bed, the material at the top splitting open and sagging into the bed. Aleksei grabbed at the front of her corset, trying to tear it off her, shaking her violently in the process.

'Aleksei don't! Please!' she cried out, rattled by the attack.

He ignored her but let go of the corset, reaching down to tear open her petticoat. There was another underneath and he tore that too, the materials tangling. He stood and tore them from her, grabbing her leg as she tried to get away, climbing back onto the bed. He pressed furious kissed against lips that were swelling from the slap, tearing the remainder of her undergarments from her.

Laura cried out in shock, unprepared for the violent act her forced on her. She tried to accommodate him, he was her husband and they had not slept together for months. But Aleksei had always ensured his child bride was aroused and ready for his attentions, she had never been made love to like this. The shock and pain of it tore her into a confusion of feelings for this man. The tears came, rolling down her cheeks, and soaked into the pillows long after he had left her.

62

It was dark and cold when she woke. The fire had died out some time ago as she had slept and the curtains were still drawn firmly. Something was brushing at her back. She sat up and grabbed at it violently, pushing it away from her. The torn canopy ripped completely and fell into a bedraggled heap at the foot of the bed. The room was empty.

She got to her feet slowly, aware of the painful sensations as she moved. The sheets where she lay were dark and she knew they were soaked with her blood. She reached behind her and undid the corset strings, tugging the material gently off her, dropping it on the floor. She felt dream-like and detached, as if she were somehow removed from all of this.

She crossed into his dressing room, pushing open the door cautiously in case Aleksei was inside. But the room was dark and cold and empty. She slipped into the room and lifted the pitcher of water from the dressing stand, pouring a small amount into the cast iron claw-foot bathtub. Carefully she climbed in and sat, unaware of the cold. She dipped her cupped hand into the water and poured the palmfull over her skin, scrubbing manically at the blood on her thighs.

She washed all of her body in the cold water, and tried to rub some feeling into her numb limbs, feeling nothing as the water slid down her skin and pooled in the shallow basin. Finally she rose and stood in front of his mirror, looking at the bruise that had come up on the side of her mouth, ignoring the rivulets that dripped onto the floor and the cold prickles on her skin. Her lips were dark with hot blood, trembling and tender. The bruise was faint, no more than a shadow, and she stroked it gently, wincing at the flare of pain.

She turned from her reflection in his mirror and stepped back into the abandoned bedchamber. The room looked a frightful mess. She knew Mikhail and the maid who came to dust would see the room in this state and more rumours would begin. She didn't care anymore, and shivered, aware she was still naked. She reached down, avoiding the stained sheets, and gently pulled a thick brocaded throw rug from the end of the bed, pulling it up around her shoulders and holding it fast with one hand, folding the layers round her.

A dull flash of something glinting in the fireplace caught her eye. She stepped over the colonnade, wincing slightly, and bent down, using a finger to push away cold embers of the long dead fire. The tears started again as she pulled out the little lump of tin, wiping the soot away from it. It had melted, and drooped into an unrecognisable tangle of droplets and solidified leaching. She rubbed it clean on the corner of the throw rug she was wrapped in and held it tight in her hand.

She sniffed loudly, buffing at the tears with the throw rug then opened the door a crack and stared out into the hallway for several minutes, watching the empty castle cautiously. It was silent; no one was stirring. She dropped her eyes and stepped out of the room. Instead of crossing to her chambers, Laura took a cautious step towards the stairs, using her free hand against the stone wall for support. She was fearful that Aleksei was sleeping in her bed, and didn't want to see him now. At every step she listened for the footfall of someone close to her, and her breathing was loud in her ears.

She lifted one candle from a holder on a table that stood close to the stairs on the deserted first floor of the castle and lit it from a guttering oil lamp at the foot of the grand staircase, holding it up under the huge, official royal marriage portrait that hung in the entrance hall. The light danced across the images of her and Aleksei, across the dress and flowers and his eyes.

She had never thought Aleksei could have been so cruel; he had always been kind and shy of displaying any kind of emotion.

She shut her eyes, remembering the shy almost boyish man sitting on the rug before the fire, telling her of his hopes and dreams, remembering the lover that had pressed open her virginity and whispered how much she had meant to him, the man that had been delighted with her body in the warm sun at the spring dance, remembering how he had held her in his strong arms and thanked God she was his.

He had hurt her, but at the same time, had tried not to. He was frustrated and aroused and insecure of her love for him. Laura sniffed and gazed up at the handsome face in the marriage portrait. She did love him.

But she also suspected him. In his youth Aleksei would have been a handsome and sort-after catch, despite the isolation or the failing of the Principality. *Perhaps he had bedded Tatiana, her and a hundred other girls, he had not been some shy, clumsy boy in their marriage bed. It was inconceivable that Aleksei would still be chaste at thirty years of age. But why he had not married before now? And why he had sent his father for a bride in America? What else didn't she know? What else was there?*

Perhaps father had been right to suspect him, she thought, though at the time she had thought he was only being prudish and old fashioned. She felt a sort of supernatural tug from behind her at the thought of her father and she turned to eye the huge, thick double doors of the castle. Frightened that even the candle might be watching this monumental indecision she blew it out, feeling the silence settle over her.

The door was whispering to her, and something pulled deep inside her. *She could walk out now, go back to Boston, and send Aleksei the divorce papers, starting again with a coming out party to introduce herself to high society. After all, she had been a princess. Everyone would be clamoring to be her friend.*

She eyed the doors through the gloom of the entrance hall. On the other side were night watch guards charged with keeping the castle secure, and Laura knew they would not let her leave unescorted. *There was more than one way to leave a house, and the front door was not always the best option* she reminded herself. She eyed the door, then turned and looked back at the painting, at her radiant happy face, at Aleksei's dreamy contentment.

She shut her eyes then. *I can't leave him* she thought. *Not like a thief, not slipping out in the middle of the night.* He owed her an explanation for his sudden lack of control, and although he had struck her and made her bleed at his breach it hurt no more than the night she had surrendered her virginity, and he had held her tightly but not sadistically.

She put her hand out on the wall, making her way labouriously back upstairs. She put the candle back in the holder, torn with where to go. She could not go to her friends, Aleksei was their uncle, and blood ran deeper than friendship. She could not go to Nikita, she would fall into his arms and his kisses, and let him have her despite the pain she had already endured. She could not go back into her rooms, frightened to think Aleksei was sleeping in her bed, and she could not to go his rooms.

She slipped along to the Library, closing the door behind her. A few embers were still glowing in the fire place. Laura stoked it with moss and kindling then added a few logs to the fire, sitting deep in one of the leather chairs and folded her naked limbs back up into the throw rug, waiting for the dawn.

63

Laura had dressed carefully, alone, and was sitting on the chaise lounge in her parlour, glad Anna had not arrived yet. She had heard the maid gasp across the hallway when Aleksei's door had been opened and had shut her eyes. The Prince had come to her room, apologising without emotion, as stiff and awkward as a bureaucratic puppet, hardly able to look at her. She had said something dully, unsure what it was, and he had left again.

Laura had no desire to eat anything and had stayed up in her rooms, but knew she couldn't stay here forever. The Poles were leaving soon, and she had to farewell them at the station. She stood and pulled on her coat, slipping down to the stables being politely automatic with anyone that looked at her.

Olaf glared at her angrily when he heard her approach. The look on his face changed and he eyed her curiously. She knew he was looking at her bruise and turned her face away, ordering him to hitch two carriages to take the Poles to the station. He turned away, saying nothing and Laura was glad that he hadn't asked any questions, half fearing that he might.

The livery boys carried out trunks and the Poles joined her in the stables. Hannah took her hands, eyeing her carefully. Laura managed a small, sad smile for her. Hannah hugged her, pressing a kiss on her cheek. Nikita joined them, yawning at the early hour, flirting with Lana and Rebecca. Fedor helped load the trunks onto the roof of the carriages before climbing up to the driver's seat.

Sven, Filip, Franz, Nikita, Izydor and Zofia climbed into one carriage, the remaining girls climbing into the other. Olaf clambered up to the driver's seat and flicked the reins. The carriages rumbled out of the castle grounds. The short trip to the station was in silence.

Laura was surprised to see how many of the Principality had turned out to farewell the Poles. Many of them were members of the Advisory Council. Laura knew they were supposed to be in chambers, and wondered how many were using the Poles' departure as an excuse not to be with Aleksei today; wondered how many of them knew what he had done to her.

She bit her lip hard, forcing the tears back. The carriage stopped and Olaf jumped down, holding his hand up to help them all down. Laura winced slightly, the distance uncomfortable for her, her hand tightening on Olaf's. She stepped aside, eyeing the ministers surreptitiously as Fedor helped out Franz and his friends from the other carriage.

The train whistle blew, startling her, and her friends threw their arms around her, promising to return for the summer, promising all sorts of wild parties. Laura smiled but said nothing, wishing they would not go. She could bear just about anything with friends.

Their trunks were loaded into the train and one by one they slipped aboard, leaning out the windows to wave goodbye. Laura let the tears run down her cheeks but stopped herself from sobbing, waving her own handkerchief. The whistle blew again and a great cloud of steam puffed onto the platform. Laura waved until the train disappeared through Vsevolod's Gate then turned and took Olaf's hand to climb back into the carriage.

She felt it rock and was surprised to think Olaf had climbed in behind her, but it was Nikita. He sat down and ordered Olaf to drive them into the Hunting Forest. Laura said nothing and sat quietly, folding her hands in her lap, wishing for the world that she was anywhere but here. Olaf climbed up to the driver's seat, telling Fedor to return the other carriage and unhitch the horses, that he would do the rest when he had been dismissed.

Laura listened to the clop of the horses' hooves on the cobble stones, her face turned away from looking at Nikita, staring without seeing at the plush covers of the seat beside her. She heard the cobble stones give way to grass, felt Nikita reach out to her as he spoke her name.

'Don't touch me I cannot bear it!' she cried out in English, turning to push his arms away.

'My God what has he done?' he breathed softly, fighting to keep his arms around her. 'Sweetheart -'

'Say nothing!' she begged, sobbing. 'Say nothing, just hold me.'

*

Aleksei squeezed the bridge of his nose, his elbows resting on the table in Council Chambers. He was the only one seated at the huge table, and only Grigory, Lev Dostoevski, and Vasilievich Chekhov stood in the room with him. All of his ministers had found one excuse or another not to be in the room with him today, most were at the station farewelling his Polish relatives and making them promise to return again soon.

He shut his eyes miserably, cursing himself for his actions last night. She had sparkled so much, laughed so gaily, shone like Venus herself that he had ached for her, almost in a state of constant arousal for a month. What he had done was inexcusable, that fire of want and lust had mingled with anger and boiled over, blurring his thoughts and vision until his white passion had poured out of him, draining away all his lust and want and heat until he was cold, and sickened, his beautiful wife trembling and weeping under him.

He couldn't think of the words he needed to express how she had made him feel, how much he had desired her until all else disappeared, how his reason had fled, how his constant humiliation at the hands of Nikita belittled and demeaned him, and his embarrassment at the missing hog from the palace kitchens had been the final straw that had broken his control of himself.

His stiff, formal apology in the morning had done nothing to change the look in her eyes when he had brought his own to meet hers. Laura had been hurt by his attack, and he abused himself in private all the more for having lost control. She was still a child, she knew nothing of commanding a court, of why some things were better not to know, why he had kept information from her before she had married him.

Part of him had been too scared to tell her the things he knew, had worried that she would decline to give her hand in marriage and return to America. He had hoped she would sparkle no matter what, and a new admiration of Ekaterina grew in his heart. His court was ageing, and their daughters and granddaughters were in schools in Switzerland or clinging desperately to the malicious thought that he had married beneath the Principality and would come to his senses sooner or later.

He knew the wishes of his court. His marriage to the American girl for half her dowry had been against the advice of all of his ministers. They had wanted him to marry the Hungarian, ten years older than Laura and of good breeding. But her elegance and her intelligence couldn't compare to Laura's smile, and her charm, or her fresh good looks. He was madly in love with Laura; he couldn't put her aside for the Hungarian, not even now. He wouldn't know what to do if she left him now.

Embarrassed and ashamed he had retreated into the council room and had accepted the apologies sent by the members to excuse their absences, thinking the less there were the better. He knew what they would be whispering after his display last night. *His blood was mad.* He did not want to think about that, let alone whether any offspring of his marriage would suffer fits of madness.

He sighed heavily, screwing his eyes shut in misery. He doubted if he would have children now. He wondered if it would be for the best, there would be no Principality by the time they could come to the throne.

Gently he extended his hand and laid it on the redrawn Treaty of Dalnerechensk, as lovingly as if he were placing his hand on the sunny head of his own son, watching the way the warm sun streaming through the windows turned his weathered skin the colour of bronzed gold. He had turned the possibilities of Tsar Nicholas the Second's proposal over and over in his head. If they refused, Russia would invade. If they sent this new treaty, and they had asked too high a price, Russia would invade. If they accepted the hundred thousand rubles for the mines they would lose the only revenue in Dalnerechensk, and Russia would, inevitably, invade.

Dalnerechensk was dying. With any luck Aleksei would become an honoured member of Romanov household, but he would be prince in name only. He would never rule again.

He suddenly laughed, wondering what it would be like to be a prince with no country to rule, a man with all the privileges and none of the responsibility. His head whirled at the prospect of no responsibility, after eight years of constant stress. None of it would be his worry, his responsibility to feed and pay his subjects; he would be free to spend his time on himself instead of wasting it away at Vsevolod's table. His laugh grew in his throat and he leaned back in his chair, letting the sound bubble out of him.

'Your Royal Highness?' Lev asked carefully, shooting Vasilievich and Grigory a look.

Aleksei's laugh suddenly turned into a chortle of pain. He winced, his gut twisting violently inside him and he vomited, blood spraying across the table. There was a shocked gasp from the men in the room. Aleksei wiped his mouth, looking in surprise at his red stained fingers.

I've been murdered he thought, tasting the warm, metallic tang of blood. He folded his hands over his stomach, wondering which one of the doddering old men had put poison in his tea, or stabbed the letter opener into his gut. He was surprised to find no wound on him though the pain flared sharply again. Someone called for the doctor and the council doors were flung open, the call echoing down the stairs.

Another twist of pain made him double up, eyeing his minister's suspiciously. Lev Dostoevski had vehemently opposed his marriage, believing Laura was an inappropriate choice because of her age, her breeding and her family history of mental illness. Vasilievich was too conservative to anger Russia; he was the only council member to seriously consider the sale of the mines to Russia to appease their greater neighbour. Aleksei knew that Laura had slipped out of the castle and gone to Ladozhskoye in the middle of the night, staying there till dawn with his best friend. Grigory had married the woman he had once been interested in, and he had no doubt each of these ministers had a motive for killing him.

Doctor Pushkin arrived, hurrying in the door and set down the medical bag beside him, flicking open the catches. The bag gaped open on its hinges and he pulled open Aleksei's shirt, eyeing his abdomen. There was no outward sign of trauma and he eyed the blood dripping from his lips, barking questions at the three remaining Councilmen, wanting to know what Aleksei had eaten and drunk during the morning.

Dismissing poison and a wound as the source of the bleeding, he began to tap on various places on his abdomen. Aleksei suddenly screamed, shoving him away roughly with a curse. 'You have a stomach ulcer' Pushkin said grimly. 'I am not surprised; you have worked yourself too hard the last few months Your Royal Highness. You must retire to your bed immediately.'

Aleksei started to protest but the pain flared again, making him grimace and double over. Grigory came forward and helped Aleksei to his feet, shouldering his weight, taking a firm grip on his side and guided him out into the hallway.

Frightened or curious of all the shouting in the castle, servants and livery boys alike were standing around, some in the middle of their chores, a stack of plates or a mop in their hands, watching the Prince staggering out of the Council Chambers like a drunkard. Anna gasped and called for her mistress to come quickly. Aleksei shut his eyes, not wanting to see what would be mirrored in Laura's eyes, if she came at all.

Grigory shouldered him carefully up the flight of stairs to his rooms, the doctor opening the doors for them. Aleksei limped to his bed and Grigory helped to lay him down carefully. Aleksei wiped the blood away from his lips. Pushkin retrieved his stethoscope from his bag, listening to the Prince's chest carefully.

He turned and measured out a dose of laudanum for Aleksei, who swallowed it quickly, pulling a face at the bitter taste, the creases of pain disappearing from his forehead as it began to work. Pushkin then listened through his stethoscope gravely, pushing carefully at his stomach, wary of another violent reaction from Aleksei.

Finally he took off the stethoscope and folded it into his battered bag carefully, folding his hands in front of himself as he did when delivering his medical opinion. 'Fortunately it does not appear to have done much damage. I will prescribe regular doses of laudanum for the pain, and your meals must be chosen carefully to avoid aggravating the digestive acids in your stomach. You must rest until it has healed, and there must be absolutely no aggravation to your person. I'm ordering you, in the best interests of your health, to stay in bed for a month.'

Aleksei shut his eyes tightly against his frustrated tears, gritting his teeth in anger.
'I will make the announcement' Grigory said, bowing as he turned to leave.
'Are you insane?' Aleksei cried, sitting up. Pushkin pushed him back down firmly. Aleksei resisted it, turning to eye his friend angrily. 'If you tell them I am ill it will send the Principality into total chaos!'
'Lie down! You are aggravating your condition!' Pushkin snapped.

Grigory, Lev and Vasilievich looked carefully at each other, not wanting to meet the other's eye. Aleksei was right; if they made any kind of announcement it would cause panic and they feared what the outcome would be. Their worst fear was unfolding before them in this room, their ageing Prince had fallen ill and the succession to the throne was in jeopardy. There was a strained silence, awkward and miserable.

They were interrupted by a knock on the door and Fedor opened it, announcing Tsar Constantinovich to the assembled company. The ministers and Pushkin bowed respectfully. 'What is going on?' Tsar Constantinovich asked, worried and alarmed.

The doctor repeated his diagnosis and prescribed remedy to the retired ruler. The Tsar nodded, strained and pained.

Aleksei groaned and rested his head back on the pillows, shutting his eyes at the effects of the drugs. The doctor quietly shooed out the three ministers with a firm word that Aleksei was not to be disturbed unless it was a dire emergency. They bowed and the doctor closed the door behind them, leaving the Royals alone in the room.

'I am old my son, but I will accept the burden again if you so desire' Tsar Constantinovich rumbled softly.

Aleksei opened one eye and watched his father suspiciously. Tsar Constantinovich was surprised to see the distrust in the look and wondered if his ulcer inflammation had narrowly staved off a breakdown. There was no doubt he had been acting strangely these past few days.

He feared for his son then, desperate to see him well again. He was well aware of the rumours that were keeping tongues wagging throughout the three valleys.

'Aleksei, you must appoint someone to take the mantle of the monarchy -'

'And have them give my throne to Russia?' he spat, his distrust of the Advisory Council evident.

Tsar Constantinovich looked shocked, he had not realised the rift between Aleksei and the Council had grown so large. He had known Aleksei had sent them away on several occasions, and sometimes the arguments nearly turned violent, but Aleksei had never replaced them with younger or more agreeable men.

'Leave me' Aleksei sighed, lying back on the pillows, tired.

The old Tsar looked at his son, trying to think of the right words, then finally bowed and left silently, shutting the door behind him. He trod along the corridor to his rooms, burdened and worried.

Fedor was waiting by the large fireplace with the glass of brandy on a small tray the Tsar had ordered before the yelling had erupted in the castle.

'Where is Laura?' he asked quietly.

'She has gone riding in the Hunting Forest with *Knjaz* Rurik and Olaf' Fedor answered.

'Take a horse and go after them. She must return to the castle immediately' Tsar Constantinovich instructed, taking the brandy and swallowing it all.

Fedor bowed and slipped out of the room.

*

'Laura…' her name was whispered seductively.

He had held her for an hour, his hand stroking her hair and arm, his lips falling to her crown and temple, pressing sweet kisses there, he had called her sweetheart and darling and she had sobbed into his chest for an hour, uncaring where they were and who saw her. His body was radiating heat; his breathing had quickened.

She sat back, keeping her eyes lowered. Nikita cupped her chin, tilting her face up to him, his thumb stroking over her lip. She winced and pulled away.

'How rough of me,' he murmured huskily, slipping his arm round her and knotting his fingers in her hair, tilting her head back further. 'Is a kiss more gentle?'

'They are too tender even for that' she said, then gasped as his lips closed on her throat, the thumb that had hurt her lips falling to her breast where his hand cupped it firmly, the ball of his thumb exciting her nipple.

'That's better, isn't it?' he asked, the laugh hiding in his words.

Hot blood rushed into her loins, heightening the sensitivity of the raw parts of her. The pain flared again and she pushed him away, moving herself away from him. She took a shaky breath, wiping her eyes free of the tears that had consumed her for their ride.

Her name was called and Olaf stopped the carriage. Laura leaned out the window, eyeing Fedor as he approached on horseback.

'What is it?' she called.

Fedor reined his horse in quickly.

'Your Highness, you must return to the castle at once' he said. 'Tsar Constantinovich sent me for you.'

Laura eyed Nikita.

'It seems our drive must be cut short, *Knjaz* Rurik' she said quietly.

'Perhaps another time then' he sniffed, sitting back on the seat.

Fedor turned the horse and galloped back to the castle. Olaf turned the horses on the wide road and soon was following the distant Fedor back to the city. Laura sat in silence, wondering what she was being called for. She prayed it had nothing to do with his son's conduct with her.

The ride back was in silence. She could sense Nikita's bitterness and sullen disappointment but she did not look at him. Part of her was scornful that she could confess her painful abuse to him and he would expect her to offer her body to him only a few short hours later. She said nothing, and stood quickly when the carriage stopped in the castle courtyard.

She flung open the door, and hopped down from the carriage before Olaf could help her and ran into the castle. Fedor was on the stairs and beckoned her up to the third floor. She burst into the Tsar's rooms, looking around, alarmed.

Tsar Constantinovich was seated in one of his leather chairs, an empty brandy glass in his hand. Nothing seemed amiss and she eyed the old Tsar quietly.

'Forgive me for alarming you my dear' Tsar Constantinovich said. 'Sit, please. Another Fedor' he waved the brandy tumbler at him.

Fedor took the glass and poured the Tsar another drink, pouring Laura one as well and bowed deeply before offering the small tumbler to her. She thanked him quietly, sitting on the chaise lounge, still disquiet. Tsar Constantinovich raised his glass to his nose, sniffing the brew deeply.

As they sat in silence he watched the Princess carefully. She had developed a sparkle while the young Poles had been there and it had not yet slipped away from the roses in her cheeks. He could appreciate as much as any man the shape of her body. He sipped at the brandy and wiped his whiskers.

'He is ill, my dear' he said softly. 'He has an ulcer, in his stomach. Doctor Pushkin has ordered him to bed for a month.'

Laura was silent, digesting that information, a hundred thoughts and emotions flooding through her.

'Dalnerechensk is autocratic' he continued, watching her sip at her brandy and lick her lips absently. 'There is only one who can make decisions for the Principality.'

'Aleksei' Laura said quietly.

'The monarchy' Tsar Constantinovich corrected gently. 'I am old Laura, and I retired from this years ago. All my life left me when my wife died, and when -' he stopped suddenly, eyeing her. 'A man with no heart is not the man to be running a country' he continued. 'Aleksei is Regent, but he is in no condition to be making decisions, especially decisions that will cause him much anxiety.' He suddenly stopped and swallowed, his eyes swimming with emotion.

He coughed and swallowed the rest of his brandy, wiping his whiskers with a shaking hand. He shut his eyes, controlling his breathing to check his emotions, and when he looked at her again his eyes were warm and kind.

'The boy Olaf tells me you want to know more than what you have been told of the Principality' he said, and Laura smiled to think of Olaf as a boy, he was grey at the temples though his blonde hair hid it well and she knew he was thirty-seven years old. 'You still have heart Laura, and I believe you might have some of your questions answered should you sit in Council Chambers.'

'Me?' she gasped.

'They cannot meet without the monarchy present' he said, setting his brandy tumbler on the tray Fedor held out to him. 'Aleksei cannot go, and he has forbidden anyone to hint at his illness. If his charade is to be believed the Council must meet every day.'

Laura paused then accepted apprehensively. The Tsar smiled and sat back in his seat, the happiness fading from his face.

'How – how fares you Laura?' he asked, feeling awkward. He was fond of this girl and they had grown close over the months, and he did not want to think of what Aleksei had done to her. The tales the maid who cleaned his son's bedchamber had rattled off her tongue had painted a horrible picture of brutality; he didn't want to think his son could have inflicted that abuse on her.

Laura looked tragic and torn between conflicting feelings.

'My husband is ill, that is my only concern' she said softly.

The Tsar was a little surprised at her answer then nodded, knowing there was a careful layering of truths and emotions, of politics of the heart. She was beginning to learn the true meaning of being monarchy in the eyes of society; but also knew that she still loved him, though her trust and security had been battered.

'Is he in pain?' she asked quietly.

'Some' Tsar Constantinovich said. 'Doctor Pushkin has prescribed laudanum. If he is not aggravated the pain should not trouble him.'

She nodded quietly, putting her brandy tumbler on the small table beside the chair she sat in then excused herself from Tsar Constantinovich's company.

She slipped along the corridor then tip-toed into Aleksei's rooms, knowing that if his charade was to be believed his mistress would not be in his rooms. She closed the door carefully behind her.

The fire was lit in his room, and everything was lit by the light of the flames. The torn canopy of his bed was removed and the carved poles stood bare around Aleksei. He lay asleep on the bed, one arm resting on his stomach, pressing away the hurt, the other thrown out across his empty bed, as if inviting her to join him. She turned away, the conflicting feelings threatening to tear her apart. She stared into the flames, but couldn't force back the memory of the little melting princess.

She shut her eyes, trying to get control of herself. He was ill, he was suffering, and her duty was to see him well again. It did not mean she forgave him for his loss of control, for the terror he had put her through. But his words came back to her, swelling thick in the silent air. *There are more important things than us.* This was Dalnerechensk's worst nightmare, an ill Prince, no blood heir, a naïve, young Princess and a Principality about to collapse. He had to get well again.

She forced herself to look at him again, at the bed that had caused her much pleasure and much pain. His arm was still flung across the empty, clean sheets. She took a step towards him, but could not bring herself to lie beside him, to lie in his arms. Instead she took up the throw rug again, wrapping it around her. She sat on the window seat, pushing open the curtain to let in the weak moonlight, settling down to wait out another sleepless night.

64

Laura took a deep breath before opening the doors of the Advisory Council. It was richly decorated with lavish tapestries that she had barely noticed when she had burst into the chambers the day of the mining accident. The room itself was of a moderate size; spacious enough to house a full cabinet of ministers, yet cloistered enough to feel secretive and congruent. It was filled with worried looking ministers, who turned in surprise at the intrusion, the conversation falling silent. They bowed respectfully but watched her as she walked to Aleksei's council chair, seating herself quietly. The ministers took their cue and sat around the oak table, watching her expectantly.

'As you know His Royal Highness is recovering from a stomach ulcer and cannot be with us. He wishes that you are to continue as normal, however, the monarchy must be present for Council to meet. I am here at your service gentlemen.'

'Thank you Your Highness for your time and consideration' Nicholas Riminov said.

There was an uneasy pause, then Grigory cleared his throat and read aloud the minutes of the yesterday's meeting. After every point that was meant to be raised for discussion he announced 'unamended'; then set aside the piece of paper, folding his hands on the table top and looked hard at some of the ministers.

There was a nervous shuffling then someone spoke and an amicable debate ensued, a caucus of ministers agreeing with a point and they amended a bylaw, noting it down in the minutes that Ivan Gogol was meticulously keeping. Laura watched them quietly, for the better part of the discussion ignored or forgotten. She wondered if they would dare turn their backs if it were Aleksei sitting in this chair, then wondered if they *did*, and that was why he despised these men so much.

A second bylaw was agreed to with a majority against a proposal submitted to them and Laura thought they were making astounding progress. *The ministers were coping well without Aleksei in the room* she thought. *Perhaps it is he that confounds these issues*. She chided herself severely for thinking ill of her husband. She had seen how he had ruined his health for a better life for his people. *It could very well be the dislike between the Prince and his advisors that caused this inability to come to decisions*, she mused, deciding this was probably the most likely answer, until Valentin Gogol raised the issue of the pension for retired persons.

There were groans from some of the ministers, and an argument immediately broke out between Maksim and Ivan Gogol. Before long they were on their feet, nose to nose and shouting at each other, their hands clenched at their sides, while Valentin tried in vain to pacify and defend his son. At once the room was a hot bed of tempers and stubborn egos, of men yelling for a fight and others yelling to calm them down.

'The payments are too high!' Maksim cried.

'Idiot! They can barely afford the necessities!' Ivan countered, red faced and snorting with emotion.

'That money could be better spent elsewhere!'

'There is no more money!' Valentin exploded, silencing the argument. 'God knows what he was thinking when he passed this act.'

'How many pensioners are there?' Laura asked, interrupting them.

They turned to look at her, surprised, and a little embarrassed at their behaviour. They looked at each other, then Grigory cleared his throat.

'Approximately ten percent of the population qualifies for the pension His Highness decreed seven months ago' he said. 'He was aware of the hardships of the elderly, but our advice was not to implement this policy as Dalnerechensk could not afford it.'

'Your Highness there is something you should know' Maksim Yegorov said suddenly.

'Her Highness is aware of the issues' Grigory interrupted.

'She does not know of the -'

'I know the Principality is bankrupt' Laura interrupted. 'I know that my diminished dowry of five million dollars did nothing to alleviate the problems here. I know that *Knjaz* Rurik's company of Imperial soldiers is camped on our Northern Border and that there is a very real danger of the Principality being torn apart by revolution. Are these the issues I need to know of?'

Maksim bit back his rebuff. 'Yes, Your Highness.'

'Perhaps we should then discuss the matters raised and not concern ourselves with things past that I cannot change' she said firmly.

There was a quiet, disgruntled acceptance and the ministers sat, waiting for her to continue. Laura was quiet for a minute, thinking. She guessed Aleksei had introduced the pension because families in Dalnerechensk could ill afford to feed themselves, let alone any extended, dependent relatives, as dear as they may be. She had seen herself that many of the men in their twilight years worked in the mines for a poor wage, and when she had confronted Aleksei in the chambers he didn't seem surprised at her revelation. She wondered if he already knew, and had passed the act as a desperate measure to alleviate the problem.

She felt her heart start to melt then, he was desperate to see the lives of his subjects enriched, so much so he turned against the advice of his ministers and threw money in an area where he knew there was a dire need. She paused, knowing the ministers were waiting for her to say something, and Maksim was finding it hard to hide his smirk at her silence.

'Economic depression is reversed by the spending of money. Dalnerechensk has use of a printing press, with which she prints her own currency?' she suddenly asked. 'Why could we not simply print more money?'

'That possibility was raised before Your Highness' Grigory answered. 'I fear if we flood the economy with more currency it would render the ruble almost completely worthless, and cartloads of bills would be needed to afford the basic necessities.'

Laura fell silent, thinking again. They had to spend money, but they had to have something of worth to spend money on. If inflation spiraled out of control the price of food would be unaffordable, and many more people would risk flogging to kill royal deer – she stopped, a myriad of confusing thoughts and feelings flooding into her, and the beginnings of a plan.

'Your Highness,' Maksim started, 'Dalnerechensk cannot afford this pension -'

'Your Highness,' Ivan interrupted, 'the elderly are suffering because they do not have even the basic necessities.'

'You are both right Gentlemen' she said gently. The Councilors looked surprised. 'But perhaps there is a way to reduce the pension, cover the basic necessities and perhaps have a little left over.'

Someone scoffed and hid it behind a cough, clearing his throat uncomfortably.

'A little left over?' Maksim said scornfully. 'Your Highness, they are retired and no longer contributing to society! Why would they need money left over?'

Laura swallowed her anger, thinking of the grizzled old men in the black tunnels of the mines, breaking their frail bodies to keep Dalnerechensk's export economy alive. *Several of you would qualify for the pension, and many of you were no longer contributing to society either* she thought meanly.

'My Lords, Dalnerechensk has no retired persons, I have seen them all in the mines, in the markets, selling baubles and darning clothes for pennies. Dalnerechensk has no retired persons.'

Nicholas Riminov agreed heartily, impressed at the Princess's wit. Other ministers looked embarrassed, and several exchanged a quiet glance.

'Grigory, how much does each person qualifying for the pension receive per week?' Laura wanted to know, not to be put off by Maksim's scowl.

'Ten rubles' he answered.

Laura looked surprised. It was a large amount by Dalnerechensk standards, it was no wonder it was causing such contention. Her quick mind set to work crunching numbers, jotting down notes for herself on a sheet of paper. The greybeards were sitting quietly again, looking towards her, waiting till she asked another question or offered an answer, beginning to take her presence in the Council Chambers seriously.

'Of those who qualify for the pension gentlemen, approximately how many of them have dire circumstances?' she asked.

Several ministers put their heads together and consulted figures and quoted case studies amongst themselves until they reached an agreement and Grigory answered:

'We believe that about thirty percent who qualify have dire circumstances.'

She fell into thought again, and the ministers watched her, waiting with genuine interest to see what remedy she would prescribe. She knew they were judging her, testing her ability to rule wisely. Her words would have to be chosen carefully so her meaning would be clear. Part of the reason why she took so long to answer the Councilors was because she was trying to recall all the Russian words she had learnt, phrasing her ideas like an acrobat walking across a high wire. She took a deep breath then spoke.

'The pension, though well intended, is unsustainable in its current form. Therefore, the only logical outcome is to lower the amount to a sum of around three rubles a week. This will not cover basic necessities for those in dire circumstances, so I propose that the lowered pension is supplemented.'

'With what Your Highness?' Nicholas asked.

'With care and moderation, the meat from an entire deer carcass will feed a family of six for nearly a month. Perhaps the pension could be supported by a meat ration for those who have dire circumstances. I believe a total of twelve deer a month would be needed. Can Dalnerechensk's forests support this amount?'

The ministers looked at each other carefully. Poaching had been strictly forbidden in Dalnerechensk and the court had aged too much to keep up the annual hunt they had enjoyed in their youth. A few deer were kept penned for the castle table and every year at least one or two were released from this stock into the wild, but no one really knew how many animals roamed the forests anymore.

'It is possible, but we do not know for certain' Lev Dostoevski finally answered, and the greybeards nodded in agreement.

Laura smiled then. The feeling of growing admiration and respect for her was clear on their faces.

'Perhaps I could suggest a census of deer to be gathered this afternoon?' she said. 'Once we know more definitely we can decide if this is a viable option for Dalnerechensk.'

As one they agreed, and Laura's smile deepened.

'Thank you gentlemen. If there is nothing else, perhaps we should to lunch.'

'There is something else' Maksim said.

The ministers looked at him blankly.

'What say you to these charges of Adultery?' Maksim said.

His words hit her like a slap. She clenched her hands together in her lap, squeezing her fingers so tight her knuckles turned white and bit her lip, knowing this was a challenge.

'Where is Peter Kaminin?' she asked.

'What has this to do with -' Maksim started.

'I see no guards, and only Peter Kaminin has the authority to incarcerate royalty. Are these charges to be laid before or after I am arrested?' she asked, refusing to be cowed by Maksim.

'Rumours, rather than accusations' Grigory said, trying to defuse the dangerous political minefield.

'My Lords, I do not think we should amuse ourselves with idle gossip -'

'It concerns the succession to the throne, it is not idle' Lev spoke up.

Laura eyed them all carefully. Some, like Grigory, were clearly embarrassed by the confrontation, but all were waiting for her answer.

'I have not taken any lover' she said defiantly. 'What I have done I have done only as I was ordered by my husband. I was instructed to see to every whim of *Knjaz* Rurik's and I did so. But he told me his whim is to have me, and I will not indulge him as I refuse to debase my matrimonial vows. I *will not* unless Aleksei orders me to his bed and *only then* I will do so because -' she stopped, taking a breath and biting her lip, controlling herself. '- because that is what a dutiful wife does.' She stopped and eyed them all coldly. 'If we are quite done with this interrogation we shall go to lunch. We will not meet this afternoon.'

They were quiet, eyeing each other, some a little shamefacedly.

'*Knjaz* Rurik has delivered Tsar Nicholas' message' Nicholas Riminov said quietly. 'He proposes to buy the mines for a hundred thousand rubles. He said he would consider any reasonable alternative.'

'Reasonable to whom?' Laura asked. 'Sale of the mines is out of the question.'

'We know' Grigory said quietly.

'Do we have any reasonable alternatives?' Laura asked.

The ministers looked at each other carefully.

'We don't know' Grigory finally said.

Laura nodded, feeling her emotions twist in her. *That snake!* she seethed. *What fun he has been having!* She stood, watching the ministers rise before her.

'This is indeed grave news' she said. 'I must think and talk to Aleksei. To lunch!' she dismissed them.

They bowed deeply to her and began to file out of the room. She followed, her sense of accomplishment for her suggested remedy to the pension lost in the anger of Nikita's message and she vowed to avoid him completely, even at the risk of Russia's wrath.

65

Laura sat, trying to force herself to concentrate on Tsar Constantinovich's words as they talked through the meal. She had barely eaten anything; too angry at the ministers, too angry at Tsar Nicholas and his Royal Ambassador Nikita, and a little excited at the prospect that she could contribute in meaningful way to the Principality. She pushed the food around on her plate with her fork, unaware of Tsar Constantinovich's look as she sat beside him in the middle of the table, and Nikita shot her a veiled look from where he was seated with Tatiana further down the table.

Laura quickly looked away. *I must avoid him!* she thought desperately. She was infatuated with the Russian Prince, and knew if she were alone with him again, pressed against the back of the door and trying to look everywhere but in his fierce eyes she would gladly give herself to him.

She dropped her eyes, finishing her glass of wine, noticing that the numbers of the court were beginning to dwindle again. She sighed quietly to herself; she had expected that, though she was pleased to note the numbers had not dwindled as much or as quickly as she had thought they would. She dismissed the court, hardly aware of what Tsar Constantinovich had said to her. The servants began clearing away the table and Laura slipped up to her rooms, changing quickly into a riding habit, darting out to the stables as quickly as a princess should.

'Olaf!' she called sweetly, stepping into the stables.

He looked up from where he was mucking out a stall with a pitchfork, turning the muck into a barrow while the occupant of the stall was tethered to a post a few feet away, chewing contentedly inside its oat bag. He started to smile at her sweetness but then he stopped himself and looked away, turning the pitchfork onto the barrow heap, mopping his forehead on the arm of his shirt.

Laura's enthusiasm for her outing dampened then, and she composed herself so she sounded cold and authoritative.

'Saddle two horses, you are to come with me into the forest this afternoon, I have a task for you.'

'As you command' he said, dusting his hands then went to the far wall where bridles and stirrups hung from nails and well-oiled and pretty saddles sat lined up on a shelf above the straps. He chose two bridles and slung them over his shoulder, heading to the stallion's stable.

He whispered softly to it, his affection for the animal obvious. The stallion nuzzled him then allowed the bridle to be pulled over his muzzle, and the bit to be pushed behind his teeth. At another soft word Olaf opened the stable door and the horse stepped out, trotting to the shelf where he tethered him and placed a blanket on his back before strapping the saddle to him and threading the stirrups on.

Laura watched him work quietly, and when both horses were saddled Olaf led her stallion to her and boosted her up. She stroked the horse's neck gently while Olaf mounted, and then led him out of the castle grounds, passing under the thick iron portcullis that was now lowered at sun down, sealing the ancient stronghold from Castle Street. She guided her mount round the narrow S-bend and let it meander down the utility road.

They rode in silence through the city and King's Gate, heading east into the Hunting Forest. Laura wondered at Olaf's behaviour, surprised at his sudden change of mood towards her the morning after their sleep in the church's chapel. Since then he had been even more aloof and uncommunicative than usual. She suddenly turned the stallion, bringing him to a halt in the path of Olaf's mare.

'Have I said something to anger you Olaf?' she asked quietly.

He stilled his mare with a gentle word, gathering the reins in one hand casually.

'No Your Highness' he said quietly.

She nodded, dropping her eyes at the use of her title, then couldn't help herself from blurting out:

'Then I must have offended you in some way -'

'*Tsesarevna*,' he said softly. 'You should not concern yourself with the thoughts of your people -'

'That would be a very foolish mistake Olaf and I didn't ask if I had offended my people, I asked if I had offended you.'

'I am no one -' he started then stopped at the fleeting, haunted look on her face. He took a breath then said quietly: 'Why do you care what I think of you *Tsesarevna*?'

'I am without friends and those I feel I can trust in Dalnerechensk' she said, dropping her eyes. 'The malicious things that are said about me, that are *believed*...' she trailed off, biting her lip hard. 'They accused me this morning. Accused me of being the whore of Dalnerechensk.'

'*Tsesarevna*' he said, pained.

Laura buffed at her tears furiously. 'Everything I have done is because I was ordered to! I have taken no lovers; I cannot even make a lover of my husband!'

'You should not be telling me this' he said.

To hell with should and should not Nikita whispered passionately to her again. Laura bit her lip hard, shutting her eyes against the tears, knowing he spoke the truth. She took a few moments to compose herself, even managing a smile at her behaviour.

'I am very foolish' she chided herself quietly. 'Come, we are to find deer and count them. It is a lot of meat that can be put to better use.'

'If you have no qualms of poaching from Russia Your Highness, you will find approximately two thousand deer and half that of pigs in and around the Principality of Dalnerechensk' he answered.

Laura blinked then laughed, astounded at his answer. The number of deer was more than she had been hoping for, and would comfortably support the families struggling to care for the elderly. She wondered how accurate Olaf's figures were, and if asking him how he knew would offend him, and then chided herself that he had no reason to lie to her.

'Why Olaf, your knowledge astounds me' she smiled.

'You will find, Your Highness, that I am quite knowledgeable' he said quietly, and Laura wasn't sure if the comment had been a shy boast or a gentle rebuke.

'I should like that very much Olaf' she smiled, wiping at her wet cheeks again, sighing softly, spying a deer walking close to where they stood. 'We should not waste this beautiful afternoon' she said. 'Tell me of the trees that grow here, I should like to know.'

He smiled then, and reached up to an overhanging branch, picking a spring of fragrant, needle-like leaves. He held it up to his nose and breathed deeply, shutting his eyes at the simple pleasure before holding it out to the Princess. She smiled, taking it from him, and shut her eyes in simple pleasure too.

66

Aleksei blinked slowly, roused by the sound of someone singing softly and sweetly in his chambers. His unfocused, sleep-blurred gaze wandered through the distortion of his room, alighting on the figure by the window. At once his vision became crystal sharp and Laura was there, sitting on the window box, the late sun streaming through and bathing her chestnut hair in gold and red, making it glow. She was embroidering, singing softly to herself as she worked, the tiny needle flashing and winking as it danced through the fabric.

He dropped his lids and watched her through his lashes so she would think he was asleep if she looked at him. He wondered why she was here, what she was thinking. Perhaps she was waiting for him to die, ensuring that she would never have to suffer him again, but her soft song was at odds with any malicious thoughts. He wondered if she was waiting for him to wake up to talk to him, and he dreaded what she was going to say, but again her song was at odds with that confrontation.

A small part of him wondered if she *was* happy to be with him, but he couldn't bring himself to think that after he had treated her so abhorrently. He shut his eyes tightly then. He was just so tired of thinking, and it was always fruitless! He couldn't second guess people any more, he couldn't second guess Russia. Eight years with dry and dusty parchment, deliberating and contemplating, dreaming and scheming for some way to make the Principality work had led to dead-ends and looped back on itself, twisting and turning around like a nest of vipers, slowly leaking venom that confused, burned, and distempered him, until he began to loathe the very walls around him.

He stopped and took a deep breath. He was becoming worked up, and he didn't want to aggravate the ulcer. He slowly let his breath out, squeezing it out of him until his lungs were completely empty and begging for oxygen. This method had always prevented him from making a hasty decision or from losing his temper in his hotheaded youth. It felt good to do it again, it reminded him of the days when his father held the responsibility of the Principality and he was carefree and beloved by his people.

Despite the deep, complete breath making him feel light headed and his lungs ache he did it again, feeling his years of worry strip away from him. He had become as dry and dusty as some of the papers he worked with in his time in office; a cautious old man. In his youth he had not been afraid. Some things had worked and some had not, but at least he could say he had not been afraid to take the chance that it might.

What he resented most about the cabinet of advisors he had inherited from his father was how much they had influenced him, how much they had turned him into a doddering, cautious, ineffective old man. He had lost his youth in their hands, it had slipped away unnoticed until he had woken one morning with grey temples and a sparkling young bride who preferred to sit with his nephews and nieces and that damn Russian flirt.

He was losing control of the country, of his wife and himself. Olaf kept a steady stream of information flowing to him concerning the thoughts and feelings of his people and he knew how desperate the situation was becoming. His illness would dangerously prevent any progress being made to resolve Dalnerechensk's problems, and yet at the same time it provided a moment of reflection at a critical point.

Dalnerechensk needed a change. It was time to look for other means of revenue that would strengthen the economy and form strong ties with other countries that could be counted on to protect the tiny Principality from Russian aggression. Countries like America.

Aleksei still believed ties with the New World was the only way to resolve their economic depression. An American bride was the start of those relationships, but he had hoped she would come with a larger dowry than what he had been left with. He needed more money to pour into the Principality, and a large army to protect her interests.

No, not an army, he suddenly thought, *just the life savings of a few very prominent businessmen from America, France and Prussia, or the newly formed nation of Germany. Nurturing a large portion of America's gross national profit wouldn't hurt either. Russia would not dare attack the Principality if she risked war with so many other powerful countries. Dalnerechensk could even afford to lose the mines then. She could modernise as a centre of commerce, or of tax-free bank accounts for the wealthy American businessmen.*

We could compete with Switzerland, we could! he thought excitedly, rolling onto his back to think clearer. The Swiss were the managers of European funds, but America was a new, vastly untapped market, especially with oil being discovered in Pennsylvania and Texas. He would get Grigory to send a telegram to Nikolai Ryzhkov, authorising him to market Dalnerechensk as a tax haven for the wealthy, and match interest rates to those offered by Swiss banks.

It was a gamble, he knew that. The ministers would advise against it. A dark thought flashed across Aleksei's mind. The ministers were old, feeble and scared; hoping the Principality would not descend into total chaos until after they had met their makers. Many of them were old enough to retire; Nicholas Riminov was eighty-two years old!

He needed a new cabinet of advisors, men who were young, who were not afraid to take risks, men who had an all-or-nothing attitude; men like the friends he used to have in his youth. He shut his eyes, pained suddenly. *Had it really been over a decade since I'd last seen them?* He had known they had slipped away over the years, finding themselves at various Universities, in various countries, and they had lost touch.

He wondered about them now, only Grigory had stayed with him, accepting the position of Treasurer of Dalnerechensk after Maksim's father had died. He remembered the hell they all had used to raise together, galloping wildly through the cobbled streets of Dalnerechensk, hunting illegally in Russia, climbing trees or leaping over the narrow but steep gully in the Hunting Forest, listening to Tatiana and the others giggle behind their fans.

He remembered the day they had found the gully, the same gully Luke Asanton had rescued him from to earn his title of Baron of Dalnerechensk. It had been Alexander's twenty-first birthday, and they were drunk and reckless. Dmitry Zametov and Semyon Turgenev had challenged their drunken party to a horse race through the Hunting Forest, and cajoled by a thirteen-year-old Tatiana, Alexander had accepted, cheered on by Anton and Aleksei.

They had drained their glasses and mounted their horses, laughing and teasing each other. Sofya Vlasyevna promised a kiss to the winner, and at the drop of her silk handkerchief they sped out of the castle courtyard, the iron shoes on the horse's hooves sparking against the cobbles. The course was not planned, nor was it agreed upon, and the light was beginning to fade as black thunderclouds threatened the sky, yet the intoxicated riders followed loyally after the leaders, regardless of how many times they changed directions.

Alexander and Dmitry Zametov had quickly taken the lead, followed hotly by Anton and Semyon Turgenev. Aleksei was trailing Dmitry's brother Leo, but managed to overtake him at the bend in the road, and Matvy Luzhin cursed him as he passed him a few minutes later. Anton's horse threw a shoe and had to pull out of the race, and Aleksei managed to edge past Semyon fifteen minutes later, his horse snorting in exhaustion, his stride shortening as it reached the limit of its stamina.

He could see Dmitry then, and he urged his horse on, bringing it alongside the black beauty the older boy rode. He saw him and kicked his horse's flanks, keeping pace with the Prince. Try as he might Aleksei could not get ahead of him and cursed him. The boy laughed and turned his attention back to the road, ducking under a low branch.

They could see Alexander ahead of them, the rump of the magnificent stallion that had been a gift from Tsar Constantinovich glowing in the gathering gloom, the long white tail streaming behind it. Aleksei knew his and Dmitry's horses were at their very limits of speed and endurance, and still Alexander was pulling away from them.

Suddenly the white horse screamed and stopped. Alexander tumbled over the neck, yelling out in fear and surprise. There was a loud, sickening crack, and Alexander disappeared. Aleksei and Dmitry looked at each other and quickly reined in their horses, dismounting and running to where the white stallion was snorting and panting, its reins hanging forward over its face.

There was a narrow chasm in the ground, Aleksei estimated its width at only two and a half to three metres, but it plunged down at least ten. He called Alexander's name, dropping to his knees to peer over the edge. He was hanging from a horizontal tree trunk, his left elbow hooked over it, his right arm crooked and held protectively to his chest, his legs pistoning over an empty, steep drop. He looked white-faced and scared sober.

'Give me your hand!' Dmitry had cried, and Alexander reached up with a crooked forearm. Dmitry hesitated; eyeing the break, then took his hand. Alexander screamed in pain and Dmitry let him go, apologising.

'Hold my legs and lower me over' Aleksei said, wriggling forward over the drop.

Dmitry fixed a strong grip on him and Aleksei held his breath as he was lowered down to Alexander. He clasped him firmly round the chest and he let go of the tree trunk. There was a horrible moment, a sensation of sliding forward, and they both realised their combined weight was too much for Dmitry to pull to safety, and indeed was pulling him closer towards the lip of the gully. The day nearly ended in disaster, with three broken bodies at the bottom of the gully, had it not been for the arrival of Semyon and Leo, who pulled them to safety.

They had remounted quietly and ridden home at a more sedate pace, quite shaken and sober for the experience. They had looked quite a sorry sight when they returned to the castle, soaked through to the skin because of the rain that had started to fall heavily when they left the forest, and streaked with mud and forest debris.

How they had been scolded for their actions! Aleksei smiled to think of his mother's sharp rebuke, made even more poignant because it had been the last time she had been truly angry with him. Before the week had been out they were back at the gully, hanging by the tree branch, daring each other, seeing who could hold on the longest, while young Tatiana and Lizaveta Gurovna giggled and whispered behind their fans and Sofya Vlasyevna promised a kiss to the winner.

Aleksei smiled to himself, sighing. At Harvestmoon Alexander, Dmitry and Leo had returned to the University in Moscow, Anton and Semyon to Prague University and Matvy Luzhin married Arina Lesnitzkaya and returned to his officer's post in the Prussian Army, while he and Grigory Ivanov started their last year of schooling in Dalnerechensk. If he had known that within six years Alexander would be gone, his mother would be dead and his father would have stepped aside and crowned him Regent of Dalnerechensk at twenty-four, Aleksei would have savored the fear of knowing his sweaty palms were slipping on the tree bark and Sofya's kisses more.

He sighed again, folding his hands behind his head. Matvy Luzhin now had five daughters and two sons, and Aleksei doubted he would leave his position as a Lieutenant Major in the Prussian Army to take the position of Commander of the Dalnerechensk Army. For one, he would not be able to match the Prussian salary, at least not at first, and secondly there was no Army yet, only the palace guard and a scattering of garrison soldiers throughout the rest of the three valleys, mostly in the fortified village of Tcherepnin where the old barracks were.

Anton had studied commerce at Prague University and now managed customs goods in Pilsen, Bohemia. He might accept the position of Minister of Customs and Trade if it were offered to him. Semyon had studied Law and had a small practice in Kazan. He also might accept a ministerial position in Dalnerechensk. Aleksei scratched the stubble on his chin and tried to remember what had happened to the Zametov Brothers, Dmitry and Leo. He vaguely remembered Dmitry taking lessons in Swedish, and wondered if he was working in foreign affairs.

He was suddenly aware of the silence in his room. Laura had stopped singing. A match flared brightly near him and she lit an oil lamp with the long taper, turning the flame up. She glanced at him carefully but surreptitiously, and Aleksei thought she was wondering if he was awake or not. She reached out and stroked back a lock of his greying hair. He was surprised at the tender gesture, but forced himself not to respond.

A quiet knock on the door announced Anna with a silver tray of his evening's meal. Aleksei inwardly groaned, hoping it was not more of the tasteless, saltless, seasonless mush they had brought him for lunch. Laura's maid set the tray on the server and wheeled it closer to the bed, removing the lid from the steaming plate.

'His Majesty Tsar Constantinovich requests you join him in the dining hall Your Highness' she said to her mistress.

'Thank you Anna' she said softly, eyeing her husband sadly. 'Let him sleep, he is exhausted. Leave the food for twenty minutes, then check to see if he has woken. If not, take it back to the kitchen.'

'*Da* Your Highness' Anna curtseyed, and left, closing the door gently behind her.

Laura kissed her fingers gently them pressed them to the middle of his forehead, stroking back another lock of his hair then left, whispering a short prayer to heal quickly as she did.

67

Laura jerked awake, trembling, gasping out loud. She sat up, patting her bed frantically to see if there was anyone in it with her. She was alone, but she threw back the curtains of her bed, checking her room to make sure.

It was empty. She shuddered, shaking herself free of her dream. Her lips and loins where hot with blood, roused and still painful from Aleksei's assault. She had dreamed of Nikita's dark eyes, his smile, the way he looked at her through the silky veil of his lashes that did nothing to hide his intentions. In her dream she had watched him, watched the swan-like grace of his lithe body when he moved. She had listened to his musical voice demand things of her, felt his hot breath on her skin, felt his body grow and arch into hers, wracking wave after wave of pleasure on her.

She shuddered again, sore and angry, hating herself for feeling this way. The tears welled up in her and overflowed. She put her face in her hands, letting herself have this release. She knew the pleasures of sex and missed the joy she had experienced with Aleksei. He was stiff and reserved, but once he had been roused, once he had surrendered to his senses, he had whispered things in the solitude of their bedchamber that she knew he would never repeat to another living soul.

She didn't care that Aleksei had bedded Tatiana, didn't care that she was not the only woman he had ever been intimate with. He may even have whispered things to Tatiana in the solitude of his room, *but he had not married her*. Tatiana was wealthy, of good breading and he had cared about her, but had not married her. Laura had to take comfort in that.

She was glad to see the dream's pleasure was fading from her. She loved Aleksei. She was the only woman for him. She had no such illusions with the Russian Prince. Fickle, spoilt

Nikita would take dozens of mistresses into his bed, or put her aside for another, or encourage her to forsake her vows with other lovers when he no longer desired her. She knew what her fate would be with him, but that didn't stop her from wanting him whenever he looked at her like that.

She sniffed loudly, wiping her eyes then slipped out of bed, padding across her silent sitting room. Carefully she opened her door then flitted across the silent corridor to Aleksei's room, pushing open his door just enough to let her through and closed it silently behind her.

Aleksei was sleeping restlessly on his side, both arms folded over his stomach, his knees drawn up. Laura added another log to his fire then sat on the edge of his bed, stroking back his greying, boyish strands. His eyes fluttered open, his forehead creasing in pain. He looked surprised to see her.

'Laura…' he whispered, his voice edged with pain.

'Do you hurt my love?' she said, then sniffed, then looked away, buffing at her tears.

She spied the bottle of laudanum and the glass on his bedside table and quickly poured him a liberal dose. Aleksei took it from her and swallowed it all, pulling a face at the bitter taste again. He groaned at the drug's effect, his grip on the glass loosening. Laura took it from him, putting it back on the bedside table, sniffing and buffing at more tears.

Aleksei groaned again, rubbing his temples with one hand, rubbing his stomach with the other, eyeing her as she sniffed again, wiping her tears. He didn't dare ask the reason for her misery, didn't know how to comfort her, didn't know if he should. The pain suddenly let go and he groaned in relief.

Laura sobbed, putting her face in her hands then sniffed loudly, mopping her face on the sleeve of her nightgown. Gently she crawled closer to him, stretching out beside him on his bed, resting her head on his shoulder. Aleksei sighed quietly, hesitantly, awkwardly folding his arm round her, his hand resting on her shoulder.

'Laura -'

'Don't talk' she whispered. 'Just sleep, you need to get well.'

Aleksei said nothing, shutting his eyes, trying to block out everything till sleep claimed him again.

68

A new pattern of life began to emerge for the young Princess in the days following the announcement of the revised Pension for Retired Persons Act. In the mornings when she woke Anna would bring letters of correspondence from businessmen in the Principality which she would read while she took breakfast in her sitting room. Then she would wash and dress and descend to the Council Chambers where she was respectfully welcomed, and spent the mornings with the ministers; arguing and negotiating, juggling needs and finance to improve Dalnerechensk's well-being.

Grigory sought her advice and patiently explained the situation, outlining any new developments to her, and was often surprised by her answers that displayed a maturity and soundness that belied her tender years. She began to realise that the Councilors were starting to look to her for direction while Aleksei was ill and she found both a newfound freedom and responsibility, all but ruling in his stead.

She had read and re-read the redrawn treaty, comparing it to the original she read with some difficulty, and sighed deeply each time, trying to guess what Russia's reaction to it might be. She knew that any answer to the proposed sale of the mines was linked directly to Nikita's length of stay in Dalnerechensk. She also knew that asking for a raise in the price of tin would not be acceptable to Russia, and the sale of the mines was unacceptable to Dalnerechensk. For now, all they could agree to was to do nothing for the mean time. It was not a satisfactory outcome for any of them.

Laura had no desire to spend all her day arguing in chambers with old men and refused to enter the rooms after lunch, knowing the Advisory Council could not meet without her presence. Instead she spent her afternoons with Ivan Gogol, studiously concentrating on her Russian lessons. She proved herself to be an apt and industrious pupil and Ivan took great pleasure in their lessons, and was genuinely sorry when she called short the afternoon to spend time with Tsar Constantinovich or to go riding in the forest.

The old Tsar would offer his elbow to her and they would walk together quietly in the fragrant gardens. Sometimes he would tell her in his quiet, rumbling voice how proud he was of her efforts in the Council Chambers, sometimes they would talk of her lessons she was taking with Ivan, sometimes of Aleksei's slow recovery and their desire to see him well and strong again; but mostly they walked in silence, enjoying each other's company.

In the evenings Laura would visit her husband, and sing quietly while she embroidered, or would read aloud to him. Sometimes they would talk, but they would always avoid any subject of intimacy, and Aleksei refused to talk about her presence in the Council Chambers, though he knew of it and her accomplishments there. Often he was bitter, frustrated and short with her, sending her from him to spend their nights alone.

Once she had accompanied the hunters who the shot dear and boar for the pension plan. They shot the animals with a bow and arrow so as not to scare away the animals and ensuring future successful hunts. She praised them for their skills, and they protested embarrassedly, pleased smiles on their flushed faces. They had gathered the carcasses, and Laura had returned with them to town, watching the castle butchers carve up the bodies, watching the large presence of troops keep a nervous order as the food was dished out to waiting families.

But it was the times she spent on horseback in the forest that she loved the most. She slipped away frequently into the forest on her stallion with Olaf for a guide until she knew all the trees and plants that grew in Dalnerechensk's hills. She enjoyed her afternoons alone with him, and he eventually warmed to her again, enough to smile and speak almost pleasantly.

While scrambling up steep embankments following deer tracks Olaf would tell her any news he had learnt from his visits to the pub, and she would tell him of the oranges from the castle orchard she took to the children in the hospital, and the time she spent sitting and reading to them quietly. Sometimes they would spot a dear and Olaf would tell her if it was male or female, of its species, of how old it was until she could tell these things for herself.

It was after returning from an outing in the forest one afternoon that Laura found herself cornered in the stables by Nikita. He looked angry, fierce and passionate and determined to have words with her. She looked around desperately for Olaf, wanting to avoid this confrontation, but she was alone.

She backed into the stall, away from him until she was pressed against the wall, trying to think of ways to explain why she had avoided him, to explain why she had snubbed him for the last few days but couldn't think of any, and the look on his face made her want to burst into frightened and sad tears.

Nikita held up the telegram he had received, following her into the stall.

'I have been summoned to Vladivostok' he said. 'I must leave immediately.'

At once her head was filled with whirling emotions and thoughts. She would miss him terribly, despite her avoiding him she was still infatuated, and thought of him constantly. Unless Aleksei had secretly sold the mines or delivered another message to Nikita, Tsar Nicholas' offer was unanswered. Doubt and insecurity swarmed close. *Why was he leaving? Had he been reassigned because the invasion had been called off? Because it had not gone ahead? What was happening in Vladivostok that would suddenly uproot him and place him at the other end of Russia?* She opened her mouth to say something, so confused she could only stammer when the Prince broke in:

'Come with me Laura.'

Her heart tore in half in her chest. She shut her eyes, fighting the desire to agree, to take his hand and leave this tiny country behind her. Nikita kissed her, pushing her up against the wall, his hands falling to her breasts. She sobbed, trying to fend him off, trying to arch so he could reach more of her.

'For God's sake Laura, can you not see how I desire you?' he cried, his hand slipping down into the folds of her skirts. 'I must leave! Your husband does not want you! Come with me, be my mistress, I will teach you pleasure you never dreamed of!'

She shut her eyes tightly and pushed him away. She guessed what had happened to make him so angry. Aleksei had received the telegram, and he would have taken great pleasure in giving Nikita his marching orders. Nikita's attraction for her was only physical; he wanted her because she belonged to another, and he had been toying with her as much as he had toyed with her husband. He did not love her; he would have her then discard her. She could not leave with this man.

He tried once more to kiss her but she held him off, breathing hard.

'What's this Princess?' he said, suddenly turning cold. 'Are you actually refusing me?'

'I am a married woman -'

'An unhappily married woman' he snarled, suddenly ugly. 'You have panted after me like a common whore, and everyone knows it. I'll roll you in the hay like a milk maid and Dalnerechensk will hear their Princess squeal -'

'Have you told my husband you are leaving?' she interrupted, sickened by his cruelty and lust for revenge.

Nikita's face hardened. 'You will regret this' he swore.

He turned on his heel and stalked out of the stables. Laura stayed propped against the wall, shaking miserably, feeling her heart tear itself into tiny pieces. She had been a fool, a childish flirt who had disgraced her husband with her indiscretions. It was no wonder he was so angry with her, so frustrated and hostile when he talked to her now.

Her knees gave in and she crumpled, folding into a small huddle, burying her face in the sweet smelling hay as she sobbed. She was still suspected of adultery. Anna had told her on her knees in tears, and swore vehemently she had defended her mistress' honour; but it didn't matter. Tatiana had spread poison about her to anyone who would listen, and Aleksei had done nothing to quell the rumours. The Monarchy of Dalnerechensk was only allowed to marry once, but could take as many mistresses as they desired.

She knew Aleksei would now put her aside, an unwanted piece of furniture, for a mistress such as Tatiana, or any other, and she would live scorned in her forgotten rooms, dismissed by a Principality that mourned their Prince's folly in choosing an American child for his marriage bed and praised him for his mistresses. His sons would all be bastards, and no bastard could come to the throne, and he would drag her, crazed by frustration and lust into his bed again, and tear her clothing off her for his duty to have an heir.

She doubled over, pushing her face hard into the hay, heartbroken and miserable, terrified of the fate left for her in Dalnerechensk. She did not want to be the forgotten wife, didn't want to be suspected and spurned. *How will I win back my good name?* she wept. She suddenly felt hands on her back and thought Nikita had returned. She whipped over, ready to fight him off and Olaf took a surprised step back.

'Are you hurt?' he asked quietly, concerned at her tears.

'M-my ankle' she said, thinking quickly. 'I twisted it.'

'I will get the doctor.'

'No!' she said, then realised she didn't have a good reason for not wanting to see him. She shut he eyes helplessly.

'Perhaps this is a hurt that is better when left to heal for itself' he said quietly.

Laura nodded, sniffing. Olaf pulled out a slightly grubby handkerchief and gave it to her then retreated to give her some privacy. She pressed the handkerchief to her eyes and buried her face back in the hay, sobbing until all her tears were spent and the hay under her was damp. Through her silent tears she heard Olaf moving around in the stables once, and wondered if he was hitching the Prince's carriage to his horses, farewelling him on his long trip. She didn't much care why he was urgently required in the far reaches of Russia, only that she was glad he was gone, despite how heartbroken she felt.

She sighed and shuddered as the last tear rolled down her cheek, feeling oddly comforted now her emotional dam had broken. She felt peaceful and closed her eyes to breathe in deep the smell of fresh hay.

There was something soothing and safe about the scent of fresh cut hay. It spoke to her of honest, hardworking men like her father, like Olaf, men who sang as they scythed hay from the fields, bundling it into stacks for the threshing machine. She had seen hundreds of workers in the fields as her family had traveled into the yellow south of Texas, many of the workers with skin like polished charcoal.

A sudden summer storm had forced them to shelter in a barn that stood beside the road and the smell of cut hay had been strong and soothing. She remembered her father had stretched out in the hay, a piece of straw between his lips, teasing her and her mother in a yokel accent, pulling Laura's pigtails gently and tickling her. She had squealed happily, and tickled back, finding herself wrapped in a close and comforting bear hug. She had sighed contentedly and rested her head on his chest, listening to his heart while she watched her pretty mother sing softly and comb her wet hair with her fingers.

Laura sighed softly. It was a good memory to have of Emily Asanton; her face was still blurred and indistinct but she looked happy and content. Laura could hardly remember the times when her mother had been happy; all she remembered was how angry and miserable she became in the last stages of her madness, until Laura had avoided coming home to see her mother despite how hated Lady Ramkinson's school was.

There was suddenly a quiet scrabbling beside her and her eyes flew open, hoping it wasn't a rat. The three kittens jumped and hissed, their tails puffing up, their backs arching. Laura laughed, relieved, and sat up. Olaf smiled, kneeling beside her and set down the forth kitten on the edge of her dress.

'They are old enough to leave their mother now' he said with a shy smile.

She smiled gently, picking up one and eyeing it against the orange light of late afternoon. 'Olaf! Did you drop these kittens in ink? They're blue!'

'*Da Tsesarevna*. They're Russian Blues, it is their natural colour' he laughed, stroking one gently.

It meowed and purred, nuzzling its head against Olaf's calloused palm. Laura smiled and stroked the kitten's soft fur, feeling its tummy spasm under her fingertips in pleasure. She smiled and reached to smooth down the puffed fur of the other kittens, listening to them mewl and purr.

'Bring me some water to wash my face' she said quietly.

Olaf dipped his head characteristically and slipped out of the stall. Laura sniffed and wiped her eyes with his handkerchief, feeling something rough scrape her skin. She leaned back to examine it carefully. The roughness was stitching; embroidered letters in the corner of the material. The handkerchief itself was very fine, and Laura knew that a high thread count for the material coupled with the Cyrillic initials A B meant it could only have once belonged to Aleksei Vakhtangov.

Olaf returned with a metal bowl filled with cold water for her. She thanked him quietly and took it, dipping the corner of the handkerchief into the bowl, washing her face with it carefully. When she was done she handed it back to the stable groom and he tucked it into his pocket still damp. She smiled sadly and tidied her hair carefully, smoothing back the strands that had escaped from her elaborate bun.

'Thank you Olaf. What will you do with the kittens?'

'I give them to you, *Tsesarevna*' he said, dropping his eyes with a smile.

'The only Russians I'm allowed to love huh?' she smiled, stroking their soft fur.

69

Laura sat at the small writing table in her rooms, trying to think of something to write to her father about. She was terribly homesick when she thought of him, and although she loved Dalnerechensk and the people, she had heard more shouting in the streets last night, a drunken party of complainers of the Monarchy protesting at the castle walls, brawling with the palace guards who hurried out of the gates to arrest them. They were taken to the cells in the west tower of the fortress walls where they had continued to shout their complaints from the barred window until a guard had gone to quiet them. Laura was thankful they hadn't been placed in the east tower where they could see into her rooms.

She wanted to tell her father she was beginning to fear her personal safety was in jeopardy, to tell him of Aleksei's loss of control and her confusion of feelings for him but she couldn't; he never even knew of the riding crop scars she had received. Most of all she wanted to tell him of Nikita, of the Polish relatives that should have called her aunt when she was young enough to have called them siblings.

So she sat staring miserably at the end of the pen, of the swelling beads of ink that threatened to splatter onto the unmarked parchment paper, and she almost missed the pretty hurricane that flung open her door until it was in her rooms, pulling off soft gloves and chattering happily, throwing her arms around her.

'Ekaterina!' Laura gasped, hardly able to talk she was so overwhelmed at seeing her friend again.

She threw her arms around her and held on tight, as if frightened she would disappear again, unable to stop herself sobbing with relief and happiness. The Countess stepped back and held her arms, looking intently into her face.

'And you are not happy to see me?' she asked, amazed at the change in her. 'What has happened?'

Laura sobbed, incoherent, and Ekaterina guided her to sit on the chaise lounge as she blurted out everything; the people that had been hurt in the mines, the loneliness she had felt since Aleksei's nieces and nephew had returned to Poland, his frightening lack of control and the ulcer that wracked him every day, leaving him groaning in pain alone in his rooms bitter and distempered, Nikita's rash flirting and desperate urges to run away with him.

'I had no one to turn to!' she wailed, miserable. 'What would you have done?'

'Nothing different' she soothed gently, stroking her hair. Then she added with a devilish grin: 'I would have exhausted him, and left him begging for me again.'

Laura gasped, shocked, then burst into helpless laughter. Ekaterina joined in, holding her sides in merriment. Laura laughed until she was crying again, overjoyed at Ekaterina's return. Dalnerechensk was indeed a lonely place to be without youth and vitality. She decided her letter to her father could wait; she would pen one to her Polish relatives as soon as she had a spare moment.

At last she sighed quietly, her bout of emotion over, comforted by Ekaterina's embrace. Two of the kittens meowed at her, and she picked them up gently, setting them in her lap before wiping away her tears. Ekaterina reached over and stroked the soft ears of a kitten, eyeing the other two that pounced and jumped around the rug at their feet, toying with a furry mouse Laura had sewn for them.

'Nikita was a rash impudent boy; I am sorry he broke your heart' Ekaterina said finally. 'But come, I have good news. My sister is finally getting married, and you will come with me to the wedding.'

'I haven't heard of a wedding, and I have heard of everything that will happen in Dalnerechensk for the next month!' Laura exclaimed, surprised. 'I didn't even know you had a sister!'

'I am Hungarian, my dear' she smiled. 'You and I are foreign jewels in Dalnerechensk.'

'Ahh...' Laura said, trailing off. 'How did you come to marry Grigory?'

'Ah, now that is a tale of true love' Ekaterina smiled, turning dreamy. She leaned back on the couch, her hand falling on the golden locket she was wearing at her throat.

It was one of the few pieces of jewelry the Countess wore, and Laura could hardly remember a day when she had not been without it.

'Eight years ago Aleksei came to Hungary to find a wife and for a while he courted Marie, my sister. Of course who could love a plain woman with a little sister such as me?' she flirted, pulling the kitten's ears gently in fun. 'Aleksei did think to court me for a wife, but he had brought with him a friend to judge for him a fit match. Grigory decided Aleksei should not marry a horse, and younger sisters were for younger men.

'Grigory asked me to marry him and I agreed. My family was outraged because we consummated the marriage without their blessing. We ran away to Dalnerechensk, and I have lived here ever since.' She stopped, smiling at the look on Laura's face. 'You do not think I could love a man enough to run away from all that I knew without him looking like Adonis?' she giggled, then opened her locket for Laura, showing her the portrait inside. 'You did not know him in his youth!'

Laura's eyes widened at the stunningly handsome face in the locket. Though he looked very different now, it was Grigory nonetheless. She had known Aleksei had been handsome in his youth, she had not thought Grigory had been too. He hid it well behind his huge moustache and bashful demureness, but Laura could now understand why Ekaterina had forsaken everything for him.

'I love him still, because of the man he is, and I remember what his looks once were' she sighed gently, and Laura felt her fingers itch to stray into her drawstring purse where the little lump of melted tin was hidden. Ekaterina smiled softly and folded away her locket, letting it fall back at the base of her throat.

Her friend was a romantic run away Laura thought, amused. *What a scandal it must have been!*

'Have they forgiven you or am I to be your strength there?' Laura asked carefully, wondering if Ekaterina had invited her to the wedding because she needed at least one person to talk to her.

'They forgave me when I had my son' Ekaterina shrugged.

'You have a *child*?!' Laura cried. 'Ekaterina! Why have I not met him?'

'He was dead when he came into this world Laura. I buried him almost seven years ago now' she looked sad for a moment, and Laura admired Ekaterina all the more for her strength and vitality. 'Come,' Ekaterina said, her mischievous sparkle returning. 'We are to be bridesmaids, and we will outshine the bride! Marie is a spiteful old hag; her fiancé must be very ambitious indeed!' she laughed gleefully.

The kittens sitting in Laura's lap pounced down onto the furry mouse their sisters were batting on the floor, startling them. All four puffed up, spitting in fright at each other. Ekaterina laughed then shot Laura a sly look.

'Tell me *Tsesarevna*,' she teased, using the word Olaf used to address her. 'Are these not a litter of kittens from Olaf's Blue?'

'Yes' she said, puzzled at Ekaterina's innuendo. 'He gave them to me.'

'He did? Ah! I think you have quite impressed the man, a present of his beloved animals is a cherished gift indeed!'

'It was only because you were away!' she giggled, teasing Ekaterina.

'Oh you!' she laughed, and embraced her friend warmly.

70

Grigory had excused himself from the Advisory Council the next morning and Laura couldn't help but feel jealous as she granted his leave with a smile, knowing she would rather be with her love than with a number of stuffy old men arguing and bickering. She admired the Count and Countess for their love for one another, and sighed to think of her own empty marriage bed. Grigory closed the door and Laura shook herself mentally, trying to focus on the tasks at hand.

'Gentlemen, Countess Ivanova has graciously invited me to Hungary for two weeks for the marriage of her sister, Marie. Is there any here who would oppose the adjournment of meetings for that period?'

'What reason would Aleksei have for the sudden dismissal of his advisors?' Maksim asked, unimpressed.

'What reason did he have before?' Laura answered, watching him levelly.

Maksim scowled but did not answer. There was a quiet pause while ministers weighed up the pros and cons of the suggestion. Ivan cleared his throat, managing a small smile when the Princess looked at him.

'I would advise against the adjournment Your Highness' he started. 'It is our duty to uphold the reputation of the monarchy as well as to govern wisely. A sudden dismissal of his Council and his wife sent to Hungary, regardless of the intention, will not bode well given the current feeling of the populous' he stopped, dropping his eyes, skirting as close as he dared to the latest damaging rumours.

Laura shut her eyes, sad, knowing he was right. She could only imagine what was being said about her and Aleksei now Nikita had left the Principality. She made up her mind to ask Olaf when they went riding this afternoon.

'So the Council must meet' Grigory said, breaking into the silence.

'Yes' Laura answered. 'Tsar Constantinovich will be asked to join you while I am gone, though I fear, gentlemen, he will not want to be involved in any decisions, he has told me as much already.'

'So we must meet but must not be of any use' Lev said, as unimpressed as Maksim.

'Advise me then gentlemen, am I to disappoint my only friend in Dalnerechensk and snub the Varennikov family by refusing to attend as bridesmaid at the wedding?' Laura asked.

Maksim banged a hand on the table in frustration but did not answer. The Councilors looked away, unwilling to start another argument.

'I am sure, gentlemen, that a break from policies will do us all good, there must be other things you can talk about while sitting here, not being of any use' she shot Lev a look. 'I also must press upon you that Aleksei cannot be disturbed unless it is a dire emergency. If it is not dire, it can wait two weeks.'

'There is one pressing issue I fear will not wait two weeks' Nicholas Riminov said, his hands folded on his portly stomach, tipped back in his chair, for all the world looking as if he were asleep, and had he not spoken Laura would have thought he was. 'Do we send the revised Treaty of Dalnerechensk to Tsar Nicholas the Second or not?'

There was quiet, and all eyes in the room slid to Laura. She held up the old newspapers she had requested from Dalnerechensk's printers, showing them the large headline. *Russia Declares War!* it shouted.

'You are all aware of this fact gentlemen' she said quietly. 'Russia has been in skirmishes for a while, but now it is outright hostility. But I am not of a military mind, so I have asked Peter Kaminin here for his opinion on the state of our great neighbour. Grigory ask him to come in please.'

Grigory stood and opened the scarred door. Peter Kaminin was standing in the hallway, his hat tucked under his arm, his back to the chambers. He turned when called and strode into the chambers, unable to hide his surprise at seeing the Princess in the room. He saluted the cabinet of ministers then bowed low to Laura, his face arranging itself into schooled discipline.

'You have been asked here to give your opinion on the progress of Russia's war with Japan and her territorial achievements in the East' Laura said.

'That opinion is limited by what news Russia sends us' Peter said, setting his hat on the table. 'And that news is carefully guarded.'

'Of course' Laura said. 'Please continue.'

Peter quickly outlined the geography of the battle grounds in the east and in the body of water between Russia and Japan then recited the numbers and figures of the Russian Imperial fleet and those of the Japanese they faced.

'I cannot say how accurate they are' he said. 'It is as much propaganda as it is information.'

He cleared his throat and went on to outline the limited information they had received about the progress of the war.

'Is there still a company of Imperial soldiers camped on our Northern Border?' Laura asked when he was finished.

'No Your Highness, there is no company within a twenty mile radius of any of our borders' he answered, and felt the tension in the room ease, the ministers shooting each other nervous smiles.

'In your opinion as a military man Peter, what could this mean?'

Peter paused, considering his words carefully.

'From the limited information about the positive progress of the war, and the little that is printed is worded so ambiguously, and the sudden recall of a possible invasion force leads me to believe that Russia is experiencing embarrassing setbacks or that she has bogged down with poor planning, underestimation of her enemy or underestimation of the resources needed to capture and hold her new territories.'

'Thank you Peter' Laura said. 'I need not remind you that any matter in this chamber need not be discussed with anyone again.'

Peter saluted, bowed to the Princess then left, closing the door behind him. The ministers looked at each other carefully. Laura had guessed there was something happening in Vladivostok, at the far reaches of the Russian empire; and Peter had confirmed her thoughts as much as he was able to.

'More troops mobilised and a distinct lack of concrete information' Laura mused.

'We cannot know for sure' Grigory said.

'No' Laura agreed. 'But I do not want to provoke a forceful and violent confrontation with her. If this even ends in delay or worse, stalemate, her pride will be wounded and she will look for other, easier victories. As unsatisfactory as it sounds, I think we should wait.'

'That is unsatisfactory' Maksim said. 'How much longer will the Principality endure?'

'Maksim, Russia was on the brink of invading anyway. Or at least, threatening invasion to force the sale of the mines. Let her be distracted by her problems in the east. Let her forget about us for a while. We will endure while we do not concern her.'

'And what about our own issues?' Nicholas said, sitting upright again, watching her curiously.

'There have been drunks shouting at the walls and brawling with guards, but I have heard no reports of riots, civil disobedience or break down of law. While I am not downplaying the seriousness of our situation I do not believe it is critical yet. The pension plan has been received positively?' she asked, eyeing them.

They looked at each other and agreed reluctantly that so far it appeared to have been.

'But they are not the only ones with dire needs' Laura went on. 'There are families like Lavrov, people who have lost all male relatives and face eviction and destitution. They must not be forgotten. Increase the deer cull from twelve to sixteen a month and see to it that these families are afforded some help.'

'You cannot hand out free food indiscriminately' Valentin Gogol said. 'If they do not spend money on food they will not spend at all and the economy will collapse.'

'I assure you it is most discriminatory' Laura countered. 'It applies only to those families who have lost all male relatives and have no means to support themselves independently, and those who have been evicted from their homes. These families will receive a generous cut of meat that they can use themselves or sell part or all thereof and thereby encourage spending. The remaining meat must be given to the church, not for the *Episcop's* groaning table but for the needy that turn to the church for help. Vasily has those in his employment to ensure fair and even distribution.'

The ministers sat silently, considering her words. She knew the last decision was received well, and boded better than *wait*. At least the problems were being addressed. She could see them turning arguments over in their heads, thinking of ways to bring up the Treaty again, and she dismissed them quickly, tired of the arguments, understanding Aleksei's frustration with them.

The ministers looked unhappy but they stood and bowed, retreating from the chamber. Laura slipped out of chambers and headed up to the second floor, peeking in on Aleksei. He was asleep, and the torn canopy of his bed had been replaced. Laura decided against going in and turned to her own rooms, stepping in.

Anna was in a flurry of activity, packing trunks and making arrangements for her to leave. She greeted her mistress cheerfully, folding dresses and pulling kittens off the curtains, sighing as they mewled and steadfastly climbed back up. Laura discovered her riding habit had already been packed away, so she dressed in a summery white cotton and dabbed on the delightful perfume that Hannah had given her to freshen up. She waved goodbye to Anna and trotted down to the kitchens for a light picnic lunch to take with her, wanting to avoid all members of the court, so much so that she declined to eat with them today. *Tsar Constantinovich will have to tell them they can eat* she thought.

Olaf already had her stallion saddled in anticipation of their outing, and Laura smiled to think he enjoyed his time in the forest as much as her, that he too liked to get away from duty and decorum. She watched him as he finished adjusting the straps on the saddle of the brown mare, nuzzling and talking to her softly and lovingly under his breath.

Ekaterina's words came back to her; Olaf's animals were certainly beloved. There was a tenderness behind his gruffness, a tenderness of duty and affection. He smiled absently, petting the stallion's neck affectionately before unlooping the reins and leading the horse to her. She gave him the rucksack of food and he boosted her up onto her mount, handing her the reins.

Laura clicked her tongue, watching Olaf shrug the rucksack onto his wide shoulders then mount the mare, noticing that for a large awkward man there was a grace to the way he moved. She flushed a little at that thought and turned her mount down Castle Street, keeping him reined tightly. Olaf followed and she smiled at her people, calling hello to them, watching the way they dipped automatic curtsies but only one or two called back.

Laura was glad to be rid of the city and turned into the Hunter's Pass. She did not speak until they were safely cloistered in the hills of the Hunting Forest, and Laura dropped back beside Olaf so they were close enough to talk quietly. Once or twice their knees brushed as they rode.

'The unrest is spreading, isn't it' she said softly.

'Yes' he answered simply.

She looked away, shutting her eyes for a moment. *What more could they want from her?* she stormed, her cheeks flushing with an angry pink before the colour and warmth drained away from her skin.

'What will they do to me?' she whispered.

The reins creaked as Olaf's grip tightened on them.

'I don't know' he answered.

Laura could guess at what happened when men were flushed with jealousy and rage and desire for another man's possessions. Her hands tightened on the saddle, reeling from the graphic depictions of her fate that lurched through her thoughts; butchery, public execution, rape –

'You will not come to harm while I can help you' Olaf said, breaking into her thoughts.

She looked at him; surprised he had spoken out of turn. He was staring diplomatically ahead. *So he did feel loyalty for her* she smiled. *And more, he cared about her too.* She reached over and lay her hand on his forearm, squeezing it gently.

'Thank you Olaf. It comforts me greatly to know that.'

His cheeks darkened a little and he swallowed. She smiled, removing her hand and saw his mare paw at the ground as they walked.

'Let's race!' she suddenly cried and spurred her stallion forward.

A small smile twitched at Olaf's lips and he spurred the horse after her, watching the way she rose in the stirrups and leaned into the gait of the stallion. She was a magnificent horsewoman, and he was impressed by her skills. She shot him a laughing look as she ducked under a tree branch, checking to see how far behind he was and spurred the stallion faster, pulling away from him.

The path narrowed and he was forced to ride behind her, not minding so much as he watched her graceful back in her white dress. She suddenly veered off course, and Olaf was both surprised and amused. He turned the mare after her, making up the lost ground easily, and came alongside her again, aware of the effect the rough ride was having on her breasts inside her tightly bound corset.

She glanced at him then suddenly changed tack again, turning her horse in front of his. He was forced to rein in the mare sharply, and he laughed out loud at her trick, forgetting himself. The mare whinnied and pranced, and he soothed her, looking up to watch the Princess ride off into the trees.

'Stop!' he suddenly cried, realising where she was heading.

As if sensing the danger, the stallion whinnied and skidded to a halt. Laura was leaning too far forward, and she somersaulted over the horse's head. No ground rushed up to jar her to a stop and she realised she was tumbling into a steep narrow gully. Her shoulders suddenly wrenched painfully, the bridle she was hanging on to had stopped her from falling to her death. She screamed from pain and shock, her legs flailing over empty air.

Olaf dismounted at a run, grabbing the stallion's reins and throwing his strong arm round the terrified Princess, dragging her up to safety. They fell back, the Princess landing in his arms, shaking with relief. They were both breathing hard with the adrenalin of the moment, their hearts racing. Olaf folded his arms around her gently to comfort her. She shut her eyes thankfully, listening to his heart pound in his chest, his breath rush in and out of his lungs.

His strong hand fell to her shoulders, checking her carefully for torn muscles and broken bone. Instead of feeling indignant that he was checking her like he would one of his horses she was slightly amused. His skin was rough from hard labour but his touch was light, almost delicate. She shuddered again and felt him sigh with relief, and was glad to know she wasn't seriously hurt.

Olaf's heart had slowed in his chest and she realised how soothing he was, sitting here with her. He had some quiet, pleasant strength like the old Tsar. He suddenly turned his head towards her a little and breathed deeply. *He's sniffing my perfume* she smiled, amused, glad he was so much more discreet than Nikita had been. She sighed and shuddered, tilting her face up to look at him. He absently brushed at a speck of dirt on her cheek, then shrugged the satchel off his back, rummaging in it for wine, keeping his arms around her. He uncorked it, feeling the way he unintentionally squeezed her to him as he struggled with the stopper, then gave it to her for her nerves.

She drank deeply then offered it back to him. He drank then stoppered the wine again, setting it aside. She sighed and sat up, shifting her shoulders carefully, wincing a little.
'Are you in much pain?' he asked quietly.
'Not so much' she answered. 'That is the gully my father rescued Aleksei from, isn't it' she asked quietly, shivering. 'That is twice now you have saved my life Olaf' she said. 'Or perhaps it is more? You deserve a reward.'

He coloured.
'I want nothing' he said, embarrassed.
'Nothing at all?' She asked, surprised. 'But ask Olaf, and it is yours.'
'I want you safe' he blurted out then turned away, busying himself with laying out the table cloth and the wrapped slices of bread and cheese for lunch, angry with himself.
'That's very admirable of you Olaf' she said quietly, laying a hand on his arm to soothe him.
He shut his eyes. 'Go to the wedding *Tsesarevna*' he said dully.

She paused and her hand trembled. *If she were not in the country for the revolution it was the only way her safety could be completely assured.*
'Will it be so soon?' she whispered.
'It's possible, but unlikely' he sighed, wishing he could tell her to leave her marriage.
Laura sighed, sitting back.
'We must not talk of such things here again Olaf, it ruins such pleasant places and company' she said.

He laughed suddenly.
'There are few who consider me pleasant company' he grinned.
Laura shrugged. 'What would I know?' she said, making him laugh again.

Olaf's admiration for her was growing. He hadn't known what to make of the pretty child Aleksei had brought from the Americas to marry, but he was discovering a resolve and spirit as strong as teak inside her. He found two glasses in the rucksack and sat them beside each other, pouring a liberal dose of wine into each. She ignored the glass and took the bottle from him, settling back against the trunk of a tree. Olaf let a small smile tug at the corner of his mouth and he drained one glass then sat back opposite her with the second.
'So Olaf' she said quietly, reaching for the apple in his hand before he had time to put it on the tablecloth. 'Tell me something no one else knows.'

'But then you would need to tell me what everyone else knows *Tsesarevna*' he smiled.

She laughed, amused at his jest.

'I do not need to because I know what it is no man knows' she said. 'You Olaf. Tell me about you.'

'There is nothing to tell Your Highness' he said, dropping his eyes. 'I live in the stables at the Castle of Dalnerechensk, where I tend to the horses, occasionally spy for His Royal Highness and Her Highness, and have been known to take long horse rides in the Hunting Forest with the *Tsesarevna*.'

Laura laughed again, leaning back with a sigh against the tree, shutting her eyes and sighing contentedly. Olaf peeled an orange and ate silently. Laura smiled, liking the tang of the citrus smell. She opened an eye and looked at him carefully.

'There is nothing I can reward you with?' she asked, still incredulous. 'A house? A raise? A pardon? A kiss?'

Olaf flushed at that.

'I want nothing' he insisted.

Laura sighed wistfully. 'You must tell me what it is that makes a man want nothing, that can make a man happy' she said softly.

Olaf paused then said: 'I understand the horses and I give them what they need; sometimes I give them what they want.'

She sighed sadly then, rubbing her shoulder gently, and looked away, back across the gully.

71

Laura opened her eyes in the dark of her room, knowing sleep would not come. Olaf had been whispering *I give them what they want* to her incessantly since she had changed in her room and slipped into bed. She sat up and pushed back the covers.

She had gone to Aleksei's room when she and Olaf had returned to the castle late in the day. Their afternoon had been very pleasant and Laura had returned in good spirits. Aleksei had been awake and she had read to him for an hour, talking pleasantly when he interrupted her, correcting her pronunciation or blurting out a small snippets of cordial information that ultimately meant nothing other than they were growing civil with each other.

She had tenderly brushed back his hair, kissed his forehead as she had bid him good night, and she had felt his hand brush her arm gently as she had done so. The touch had sent a shiver through her and she had smiled as she slipped across the corridor to her room. But sleep had not come for her. *I know what he wants* she thought, lighting a lone candle on her bedside table. *He wants an heir.*

She stood and lifted the holder, slipping her finger through the gilded circle and padded through her silent sitting room. Her breath frosted around her in the cold night. She did not pause, but slipped directly into Aleksei's chamber and set the candle on the table beside his bed.

He looked thin and drawn on his pillows in the light of the candle and the dampened flames from his fireplace. She could see he was losing weight, had lost the paunch that made his pants too tight. In the dark room the grey in his hair was not even visible. He looked young again, like the boyish man who had slipped into her chambers some nights before they were married.

She reached down and folded back the thick covers of his bed, joining him in the warmth between the sheets. He slept on as she rested her head on his shoulder, listening to him breathing. She remembered lying against him as he slept on their wedding night, her head resting on his shoulder after their lovemaking, a turmoil of emotions inside her.

She had been so embarrassed by the Putting To Bed Ceremony, by Anna seeing her breasts, being naked with Aleksei and seeing his nakedness too. She had been frightened by him, by the strange situation she found herself in, by the weight of him and the initial pain of his body inside hers. She had been surprised as well as scared at the depths of feelings he had stirred in her as they made love, frightened that a man, an act, could provoke so much from her. She had lain feeling guilty at her enjoyment, and anticipating the next time he would take her in his arms and breach her body with his.

Now she lay against him again with the same emotions, but for different reasons. He swallowed and sighed in his sleep, turning his head towards her, a hand folding over his stomach. It was a gesture she had seen him do many a time as the laudanum began to wear off. She eyed his hand, watching the way the orange glow from the fireplace turned his skin a burnished copper colour.

She reached out and touched the long fingers resting on his stomach. She admired his hands; they were fine and regal, but at the same time strong and hardworking. They had been so tender with her those times he had loved his bride, and so commanding on the reins of his horse, strong and masterful, and yet restrained as well as powerful. She had felt that in his touch too, in those first nervous couplings with him, and she had trusted him.

She let her touch stray from his long, strong fingers onto the warm skin of his stomach, thinking of the ulcer that ate at him inside. She was miserable at seeing him suffer, knowing the stress of his position had given this to him, and there was no way to alleviate the stress, the Principality was in dire trouble. *This job will kill him* she thought, and felt a deep wrench in her chest at the thought. *I'm afraid to lose him* she realised. She loved him still, she couldn't deny that. She didn't know how she would cope in Dalnerechensk on her own.

She turned her face into his neck, breathing in deep the scent of his skin, her fingers straying to his limp manhood. Aleksei woke with a start, seizing her wrist and pushing her roughly from him.

'I'm sorry' Laura said quietly, retreating from him. 'I just wanted to make you happy.'

She slipped out of bed, hurt at his reactions and ran out of his room, across to hers, cursing herself for being so foolish.

Her husband had washed his hands of her, that much was certain. Alone in her rooms she burst into sobs. *So she was spurned, the rejected property of the Crown Prince*, she wailed silently. Deeply wounded by her indiscretions with Nikita, her cuckolded husband suspected her, believing she had cuckolded him in his own Advisory Council as well, and he would not love her again, subjecting her only to his rage induced passions for an heir.

The soft click of her door opening startled her, and she turned quickly to see Aleksei slipping into her room, shutting the door after him, as if we were afraid of being caught with her. The sight! reminded her of the boyish rogue she had fallen in love with before they were married, and the thought stirred her compassion, the tears sliding down her cheeks.

'Laura?' he whispered quietly.

There was curiosity in his voice, which rumbled across the silence between them like his father's did, a voice that could fill up spaces in a room with authority and power, even when spoken in a whisper. But Laura also heard the aching longing in it, and she shut her eyes tight, hardly daring to breathe.

'Why did you come to me?' he asked softly, almost afraid of her answer.

'I love you' she said sobbed. 'I miss you.'

He closed the distance between them and clasped her to him, kissing her firmly. She sobbed, sliding her arms round his neck, molding against the kisses he pressed on her lips, firm and tender.

'You must go to bed' she said, reluctant to let him go.

He pulled her harder against him, lifting her up against him, breaking from her lips to kiss her eyes and cheeks and neck.

'How can you love me, when I treated you so abhorrently?' he moaned quietly, his voice thick. 'I was so certain that you hated me, that you would leave with Nikita.'

Laura's breath hitched. 'I thought you were so disappointed in me because I didn't give you a child,' she sobbed, and Aleksei tightened his arms, covering her hair with kisses. 'I was never unfaithful my love, never, and I thought you would take Tatiana back to your bed again.'

He faltered in his kisses. Laura drew back from him, watching the way he couldn't look at her, a chasm of hurt opening in her. *He has bedded her again* she realised. A wail escaped her and she let him go, turning away, her grief wracking her.

'Laura…' he moaned, helpless to stop her pain.

'How dare you!' she sobbed, aching. 'How dare you let them all call me Dalnerechensk's whore and debase the vows you swore to me!'

'I'm sorry' he said, wanting to comfort her but unsure what to do, not even knowing if he could comfort her.

'What will you do now Aleksei? Put aside your unwanted property, and take whomever you choose to your bed?'

'Laura don't!' he cried. 'I came here to – that is – you're not unwanted – I came to make love to you!' he said, burning, struggling with his emotions.

Laura wiped her eyes, pushing the pain deep down in her, trying to separate herself from her hurt.

'As you wish My Lord' she said in a dull, flat voice.

Aleksei stopped, horrified at the change in her.

'Laura, please listen -' he begged.

'Don't' she said dully. 'You don't have to explain yourself. It is the law. I am your property to use as you will.'

'I did not marry you to make you my property!' he snapped, angry now.

'You married me for my dowry' she said.

'If I had done so,' he hissed evenly through his teeth, 'I would not have bargained for you.'

He turned and slammed the door behind him, leaving Laura cold and alone in her room.

72

Laura opened her eyes, rolling onto her back. She had not slept but she had been unable to cry, too drained to feel anything anymore. She pushed back the covers of her bed and padded over to her mirror, eyeing herself carefully.

Her skin was tired, and the shadows under her eyes seemed darker today. Her tears and heartaches were taking its toll on her. She pinched her cheeks to make a red glow come up in them, smoothing her forehead of the crease that seemed to have developed there. *I am a tired, haggard old wife at sixteen* she thought miserably.

She turned away from her mirror and greeted Anna quietly as the maid stepped into the room. Anna smiled and called good morning though she looked miserable, and pulled out a warm woollen dress from Laura's wardrobe. Anna sniffed loudly as she helped Laura dress.

'Why are you crying Anna?'

'I will miss you' she said, sniffing loudly.

'Thank you Anna' Laura smiled. 'I will miss you too.'

She sat at the dressing table and Anna pinned her hair up into a simple bun then went to answer the quiet knock on the sitting room door. Laura stood and donned a grey traveling cloak, listening to Anna direct the livery boys to the stack of trunks containing the Princess's clothes. They quickly lifted the trunks and carried them out of the room, bent under the weight of the boxes.

Laura stepped out of the dressing room and embraced Anna then collected her gloves, shutting her eyes as she glanced across the corridor to Aleksei's door, knowing she would have to tell him she was leaving. She sighed then stepped out of her room, surprised by the loud voices inside the room.

'You don't make that kind of decision!' Aleksei yelled. 'I am Regent of Dalnerechensk, not you!'

Laura pushed open the doors, stepping into the room. Olaf stood on the rug before Aleksei's huge bed, and Laura realised she had interrupted the stable groom's espionage report. Olaf's face didn't change but a flicker of annoyance creased Aleksei's face though it was gone quickly. He wiped his mouth and dropped his eyes.

'I have come to say goodbye' she said quietly. 'Your father has kindly offered to sit in the Advisory Council till you are strong enough or I return. When you have been dismissed Olaf please see to the carriage.'

The stable groom nodded curtly, and Laura turned to go.

'Why did you not leave with Nikita?' Aleksei suddenly asked.

Laura stopped, afraid this confrontation would come. She was surprised he had dismissed decorum and confronted her while the groom was still present.

'I will see to the horses' Olaf said diplomatically and left, closing the door behind him.

She turned to look at her husband, lying propped up on a mound of pillows on his bed, the covers pushed down his body, and shut her eyes. *He didn't love me* she wanted to say, but wondered if Aleksei would laugh at her for her folly. Her heart was still tender; she had been hurt by his flirting and callous manner. She thought to say *I am your wife and I love you*, but couldn't bring herself to say it. She was bitter, knowing Aleksei had made love to Tatiana, and she had not submitted to Nikita because she had known how much it would hurt him. *I wish I had left with him* she thought to snap spitefully, but couldn't bring herself to say that either.

He was watching her, so she answered:

'It took me a long time to see the man he was Aleksei. He came to Dalnerechensk to take everything away from you; your Principality, your dignity and your wife. You are a good man Aleksei, I don't believe you should lose everything.'

He looked shocked at her words. She dropped her eyes and left, slipping down to the castle courtyard where the carriage was waiting for her.

Their luggage had been loaded onto the roof of the carriage, and Ekaterina stood waiting patiently beside the two harnessed stallions, stunningly brilliant in a red traveling cloak, her hands buried deep in a black fur muff. She greeted Laura, smiling as Tsar Constantinovich and Grigory stepped out of the castle, coming down the stairs to kiss them warmly on the cheeks.

'Travel well, and safe' the old Tsar said, kissing Laura's cheek.

She thanked him quietly, taking Olaf's hand when he opened the carriage door and climbed up into the carriage. Olaf helped up her charming companion then leapt up to the driver's seat, flicking the reins gently.

Anna, the livery boys, the old Tsar and Grigory waved goodbye from the castle steps and Laura was disappointed that not more had turned out to see them off. She wondered if she would have a chance to talk to Olaf alone before they boarded the train.

'Fret not Laura' Ekaterina smiled. 'The Tsar will not let the Principality fall to ruin before you get back. Then you can play with it some more' she teased.

Laura flushed hotly. 'I do not play with such things!' she cried, embarrassed.

'Hush now, I'm only teasing you, and Grigory does speak very highly of your ability.'

'He does?' she asked, her flush now a pleased one.

'And he is not alone in his praise. They say you have a wise head on your pretty shoulders. My dear, I do believe you are melting the old hearts of the Principality.'

Laura laughed, and pulled on her traveling gloves as the carriage drew to a halt at the steam-engulfed station. The porter rushed over and began to unload the carriage. Olaf leapt down from his seat and opened the door, standing to the side, holding out his hand to help them down.

The train hissed at the platform and Laura eyed it, thanking Olaf unconsciously. It was not the royal train that she had arrived on. Behind the engine and the coal cart was the dining car from the royal train. Their trunks were being loaded into this car by the Stationmaster. Laura guessed this would be where she and Ekaterina would spend the short trip to the Russian station of Chelyabinsk where the Dalnerechensk Line ended.

Behind the dining car was a passenger car, and one man was pushing his meagre belongings into the luggage compartment at the back of the carriage. Inside the carriage sat two hunched shapes, one a woman, the other a little girl who waved out the window at the Princess. Laura smiled and waved back, a small part of her wondering if the family was leaving Dalnerechensk for a better life. Behind the passenger car was a long line of cars containing the tin that was being transported to Russia.

The Stationmaster finished loading their trunks and stood by the doors, offering a hand to help Laura and Ekaterina up into the train. Laura thanked him and climbed up, noting that the tile stove was lit and the carriage was warm. It would be a comfortable trip to Chelyabinsk and she hoped when they changed trains for the journey through the Urals to Western Russia that the carriages would be just as comfortable. They would only be travelling as far as Samara before changing onto another for the long trip to Debrecen so they would not have long to endure if it was not.

The Stationmaster closed the carriage doors then blew his whistle, and the engineer answered it with a whistle of his own, releasing the brakes for the mighty steam engine. Laura and Ekaterina pushed open the windows to wave goodbye to Dalnerechensk. Olaf was the only one standing on the station to see them off and he waved uncharacteristically as the fully loaded steam engine began to chug through Vsevolod's Gate down to Tcherepnin. Laura waved back, blowing him a kiss as the train disappeared from view.

'Ah, so you have even melted Olaf's heart' Ekaterina smiled.

'Tsar Constantinovich seems to have quite an affection for him, despite his curtness and refusal to grovel before royalty' Laura answered, grinning with mischief.

'I have heard the maids sigh he is gifted like a stallion' Ekaterina laughed. 'No wonder you like to take so many rides with him!'

'Shame on you!' Laura cried, her ears burning.

'Come my pretty pupil, I have much to teach you of Hungary!' Ekaterina laughed.

73

The berth in the first class carriage train from Samara to Debrecen was comfortable and elegant and they were glad of it after the uncomfortable ride on the Russian Line from Chelyabinsk. It had been almost ten in the evening before they bordered the train in Samara and once their trunks had been loaded into the berth they had dressed quickly for dinner and trotted across the swaying bridge to the dining car. Despite how long they had been travelling that day the two Dalnerechenskers sparkled with charm and beauty and people had fallen over themselves to be hospitable to them.

An elderly French Marquis had been introduced to them by the Conductor at dinner, shocked to discover they were traveling unescorted, and gallantly offered to chaperone them. The two girls had been delighted, and spent the evening dining together while the Marquis regaled them with tales from his involvement in the Franco-Prussian War.

It was after midnight before he chivalrously escorted them to their berth where Ekaterina and Laura bid him adieu, promising to join him again for breakfast. Ekaterina had then locked the door and they had changed for bed, sharing the same room like sisters.

The Countess had turned off the lamps and proceeded to terrify Laura with horrible tales of peasant superstition from the Transylvanian land they traveled to. Laura had listened with spine tingling horror and spent a terrified night awake in her bed, sleep banished by thoughts of walking corpses sucking blood from her neck and screaming, hissing bats tangling through her hair. Ekaterina had slept on peacefully, completely oblivious to her friend's distress.

The days had stretched on endlessly as the train steamed towards Marie's wedding. Despite the charming company of the old Marquis, Laura and Ekaterina had grown restless and bored and Laura hadn't missed the sad looks on her friend's face. Ekaterina had smiled sadly when asked and changed the subject, telling Laura stories of Marie until she had to fold her hands over her stomach for fear she'd split her corset laughing.

In spite of Ekaterina's gift for telling tales Laura was glad when the train pulled into the station at Debrecen. The busy hive of activity caught Laura off-guard; she had grown accustomed to the sleepy, twice a week run of the tin and passenger trains to Chelyabinsk. The thriving, mass of people and goods made her think of the ports at Boston, and the customs building where she had met Nikolai Ryzhkov, and been given the net worth of Dalnerechensk on a pretty chain around her neck.

But the over-powering, oily salt smell of the Boston Docks was missing, and Laura felt neither homesick nor nostalgic at the sight of the bustling station. Her spirits began to rise as the busy nature of the city thrilled her. She hadn't realised how much she had missed the noise of people in Dalnerechensk until the train hissed to a stop in Austria-Hungary.

The carriage doors were thrown open and smart porters in glowing uniforms darted forward to the carriage, bowing low bobs in front of them. Ekaterina directed them to their trunks and smiled prettily at the teenagers. Laura laughed at her friend's coquettishness and pulled on her traveling cloak to exit the carriage. The porters fell over themselves to take her hand and guide her down the stairs. She smiled sweetly at all of them and stepped lightly to the ground, stopping suddenly with shock.

A huge and frighteningly grand black carriage was waiting for them. Her nightmares had not painted such a vivid image of the coach that loomed in front of her. The tall gaunt groom stood beside the coach, his hands folded in front of him. He moved with a quickness that was almost startling; he was a blur of efficiency as he came forward, so fast that Laura could hardly follow his person as he darted forward, black coat flapping, taking trunks two at a time in his immense hands back to the coach.

The young porter who was helping her down asked her something in a language she didn't understand. Laura realised she was trembling, and had gripped the hand that had helped her down tightly. She managed a small smile and let go carefully, feeling vulnerable and scared.

'Come *Velikaja Knjaginja*, Count Dracul is not my family's groom' Ekaterina laughed, stepping down beside her, slipping her arm through hers.

Laura smiled at her friend nervously, but couldn't help feel reluctant as the Countess led her towards the huge black carriage, drawn by a team of black horses as still as statues as they stood hitched together in the cool morning air. The groom towered above her, and offered a hand that felt cold and powdery to help Laura to step up into the carriage.

The interior was grand and luxurious but steeped in shadows. Laura wondered how on earth she would manage to sleep for two weeks in this bleak, superstitious land. Ekaterina sat opposite her, draped in velvet black shadows, and Laura shuddered involuntarily. The carriage jerked and the horses sprung into a gallop, their hooves sparking, the grand procession rolling out into the city itself.

They flew along the cobblestones; faces, buildings and streets passing in a blur out the windows. It made Laura's head ache to try and watch them, but the shadows and the speed of the carriage frightened her, and she desperately tried to think of other things.

Her fears were not placated when Varennikov Castle, the Holy Roman fortress, came into view. Behind a huge imposing wall and locked with heavy, baroque iron gates, the once towering building was now a ramshackle hulk of disrepair. As the family and the grandeur of their titles had grown, the large fortress had been extended with massive wings that were now sagging. Parts of the castle had tumbled into ruin and the west wing was now completely uninhabitable. The roof over the west wing had lost its shingles and the attic gaped open to the deepening purple of the sky.

The coach suddenly jerked to a stop and Laura nearly tumbled off the seat. The door was pulled open before she had time to right herself and she fell out into the arms of the groom. Ekaterina laughed gaily and the groom set Laura on her feet, bowing low and leaping up to unload the baggage. She patted her cheeks and hair quickly, disturbed by the unnaturally quick movements of the groom.

There was no one on the stairs to greet them save a single servant. Ekaterina alighted beside Laura and tucked her arm through hers, giving orders to the groom over her shoulder. The servant came down the stairs and set to work organising their luggage, leaving the two women completely alone. It was not the reception Laura had expected at Varennikov Castle.

Determinedly Ekaterina propelled Laura up the stairs to the imposing porch, her hand trembling on Laura's arm. Laura squeezed her friend's hand, knowing she was not the only one frightened of this place. Ekaterina reached out and opened the doors of the castle.

Laura stepped into the wide, dark foyer, eyeing the black stairs that lead up into the heart of the castle and felt a shiver go through her. The tapestries hung around the entrance were decaying and fraying, stained with centuries of soot and dirt, and did nothing to lift the gloom and disrepair of the home. It was no wonder Ekaterina had eloped with a Dalnerechensker Count. Laura was surprised that a woman who sparkled as much as her friend could have come from a place such as this.

Her eyes wandered from the gem in the red traveling cloak round the bleak walls of the castle again. She felt oppressed and ill in this place, and hoped her room would not be as depressing as this was.

There was someone on the stairs. Laura hadn't heard her approach and her presence startled her, making her grip Ekaterina's arm tightly in alarm. The woman was dressed in a simple, black silk dress, her mousy-brown hair loose and combed to hang over one shoulder. She was tall, and so thin she was gangly, her hands too big and her face long. Laura thought with her hair combed over one shoulder like a mane Marie did indeed look like a horse and tried not to burst out laughing.

Ekaterina's eyes drifted up the stairs to her sister and greeted her formally in their native tongue. Marie's face did not change and she did not unfold her arms. She looked like her body was caught between shivering and stroking her arms sensuously.
'You have an accent Catherine; it is most unbecoming' she said in perfect Russian. 'And you have brought your own servant, how perfectly charming.'
'This is *Velikaja Knjaginja* Laura Vakhtangova, Aleksei's wife' Ekaterina said in Hungarian.

Laura had expected a curtsey or a nod of recognition from the bride-to-be. Marie didn't move.
'I knew she was coming, I didn't expect to find her so – common' she said in Russian, sniffing.
'Well I did tell her to expect a rude horse in a dress' Ekaterina retorted happily, switching to Russian so Laura would understand.

A door to their left suddenly flew open. A handsome middle-aged man stepped into view, his face lit with recognition.
'Papa!' Ekaterina cried, rushing to throw her arms around him.

He laughed and kissed his daughter warmly, his words tumbling over themselves happily. Ekaterina laughed and broke in, introducing Laura. Count Varennikov bowed deeply, taking her hand and kissing it. Laura tipped her head forward in respect, and couldn't stop her eyes from drifting up to the staircase, wondering what the horse-bride would make of her father's display. Marie had vanished.

The Count and Ekaterina babbled happily together, their faces flushed with pleasure and affection. Laura watched them, smiling quietly, wondering how anyone could stay mad with her for long. Ekaterina took her hand and smiled, switching to Russian, telling her father how Laura had twisted a snub from Aleksei's cousins into an embarrassment for them, making them her bridesmaids. The Count laughed heartily, slapping himself on the knee as he bent double in amusement. It was a gesture Laura would see frequently in the days to follow.

'Ah, how charming *Velikaja Knjaginja*!' he laughed. 'A woman with the same mischievous heart as my own dear daughter. Is it any wonder how you are fast friends?'

'I would have been quite lonely if not for her company' Laura smiled.

'Ah yes' the Count said, looking sad. 'Yes indeed.' He reached out and gently squeezed Ekaterina's arm. 'You are tired from your journey. Catherine will take you to her rooms, we do hope that you will be refreshed enough to join us for dinner.'

Ekaterina kissed her father's cheek then led the way up the stairs, promising to be there for dinner. Two long corridors stretched away from the top of the stairs, wide and gloomy. Hundreds of imposing counts glared and frowned from the walls. A string of livery boys followed them, carrying trunks up the stairs as Ekaterina led Laura deep into the right wing of the house.

The rooms Ekaterina had as a child were modest and plain. Cold, grey stone walls were dressed with bright tapestries of romantic pastoral scenes. Laura was beginning to understand where her friend got her romantic notions to sparkle like a heroine and run away with a young, handsome Dalnerechensk Count. Ekaterina pushed back the drapes from the windows and opened the shutter. Weak sunlight filtered in through the medieval arrow-slit cut in the stone and set the dust motes dancing in the air.

The livery boys stacked their trunks in the room and bowed, taking their leave of them. Ekaterina stood by the window, gazing out, reminiscing, so Laura glanced around the furnishings of the room. The large sitting room was still scattered with pieces of childish furniture though there was a table and a settee that looked far too expensive to be placed where it could be damaged by rough or wanton play. Two bedrooms opened into the sitting room, and neither had windows. Laura thought it would be dreadful to sleep there, like sleeping in a tomb. She wondered if the second room belonged to Marie, but decided Ekaterina's nurse had probably used them, as Marie didn't look the least bit romantically inclined.

'This was our family home long before Charlemagne' Ekaterina sighed quietly. 'It cost us too much to repair and Marie has let it fall further into ruin with the money she insisted was spent on her. When she is married she will leave our father's home, and we have no brothers. When my father and mother die Varennikov Castle will be abandoned, if it is not sold beforehand' she looked sad for a moment, touching the stone, then grimaced at the slimy feel of it, wiping her fingers on a drape.

'Grigory and I did talk about moving here once, but I hate this place, and we have not the money to make the changes I would like. Perhaps we could have the stone recut...' she mused thoughtfully.

'Shame on you Ekaterina' Laura suddenly said. Her friend turned round in surprise. 'You filled me full of horror stories of Vampires and such, but all along it was to poke fun at your sister.'

Ekaterina grinned. 'I'm sorry if I frightened you my dear. Come now, you must be famished. We'll freshen and dress for dinner.'

Ekaterina unfastened her huge trunk and pulled out a stunning red gown, stripping down to her petticoats. Laura helped pull the volumes of material over Ekaterina's head and laced it tight against her body. Ekaterina brushed down the skirts and smoothed the firm bodice against herself, squeezing in her corset tighter. Laura finished lacing and stepped back to look at her friend.

'Am I going to break Marie's heart tonight?' she asked, twirling sensuously.

'No' Laura smiled. 'Marie has a heart of stone; it is difficult to break stone with a dress.'

Ekaterina laughed. 'How I do so cherish you!' she cried, taking hold of Laura's arm affectionately.

The Countess laughed at her sudden rush of emotion, and dragged the Princess over to a traveling trunk. Laura laughed too, and they scrabbled and clawed at her trunk like children on Christmas morning. Ekaterina flung it open, pulling out dresses and tossing them over her shoulder until she found one she liked. Laura laughed at her, caught up in the spirit of the moment, and quickly pulled off her thick traveling cloak and dress. Ekaterina tutted approvingly, helping her into a soft cream and silver gown, then stepped back to eye the effect the colour had on Laura's figure, on her skin.

'Ah, but you my dear…' she whispered softly, 'I'm sure a goddess could break stone.'

Laura giggled, and sat on one of the chaise lounges in the sitting room while she brushed her hair carefully. Ekaterina sat beside her, combing her own hair quietly. She suddenly turned towards her friend, her face serious.

'I am truly glad you came with me Laura. I would feel very lonely here if not for you.'

Laura smiled gently at her friend. She had not asked the reason why Grigory had not traveled to Debrecen with them for the wedding of his only sister-in-law. She wondered if they had forgiven Grigory for taking their precious daughter away from them. It was clear Ekaterina was the favourite of the two. While their wayward daughter may have been forgiven perhaps their stuffy son-in-law was not.

They twisted their hair into elabourate coifs, pinning pretty jewels into their hair and fastening them round their necks. Laura slipped on the string of sapphires and diamonds Nikita had given her, and dabbing on Hannah's perfume she shared with Ekaterina, before pulling on gloves and clutching fans, descending the black staircase to the long banquet hall.

Ekaterina weaved her way through the labyrinth of corridors and hallways and Laura was hopelessly lost in a very short space of time. The dining hall was entered into through a stone archway three feet long. Inside the dining hall, next to the lavish stone archway, stood a doorman dressed stiffly in a coattail who announced their names to the assembled guests.

Marie's wedding party was almost three times the size of Dalnerechensk's court and they all turned to see Count Varennikov's returned daughter, and the young American Princess she traveled with. Laura was unmindful of the fluttering fans, awed by the grandeur of the room.

Long tables followed three of the walls, leaving a wide space for the dance floor and one wall bare, where dozens of servants and scullery maids stood waiting on the whims of their guests. Count and Countess Varennikov sat in the centre of the bridal table, proud beside their unattractive daughter and future son-in-law. Two of the white gloved servants came over to Laura and Ekaterina, offering their elbows to escort them to seats. Count Varennikov waved Ekaterina over to the spare seat saved for her on his left; and she smiled radiantly, squeezing Laura's arm in parting before taking her place of honour in the middle of the table.

Laura smiled and looked around for a spare seat. They were the last to arrive, and the three tables were almost full. A handsome blonde man leapt to his feet a few places down from the bridal party and beckoned the servant over to a seat beside him. Laura smiled sweetly and allowed herself to be led to the seat.

The blonde stayed on his feet as she joined him. The group of men he was seated with stood to greet her, smiling and bowing deeply to her. The servant let her go and bowed, leaving her there, babbling something she didn't understand. The blonde man who had called her over offered his hand for hers and when she presented it to him he kissed the back of it, asking something in Hungarian.

Laura blushed winningly and said the only phrase she's learnt off by heart on the train journey: *Please forgive me, I don't understand. Do you speak Russian?*

The group shook their heads, looking a little crestfallen.

'*François?*' she tried.

'*Oui*' they all smiled, and the blonde introduced himself as Baron Fredrik von Schmidt from Bayern.

Across the table from where Fredrik and she stood was his older brother Karl, twenty years old, blonde, blue-eyed and a titled Count. He reached across the table and kissed her hand, telling her she was beautiful. Laura smiled and thanked him winningly.

Beside Karl stood Gustav; a brooding, dark-featured youth, approximately fourteen years old. He did not have the same colouring as his two older brothers, nor did he have their titles. Although he was trying to be polite and friendly in such pleasing company as a pretty, royal princess, his face kept rearranging itself back into a predominantly moody scowl. He kissed her hand because it was expected but looked like he wished he was elsewhere.

On the other side of Count Karl von Schmidt, across the table from Laura stood Kurt, the youngest von Schmidt brother, who reminded her of Saskia. He too took her hand and kissed it as his older brothers had done. The last man of the group, standing beside Laura was Burgrave Axel von Schmidt, uncle to the four brothers, though she didn't think he could be more than twenty-five years old.

He kissed her hand and they sat. Servants rushed forward and set delicate china bowls of soup on their plates. The bowls were so thin she could see the shadows of her fingers through them as she delicately touched the rim to test how hot it was. The five young men were watching her politely, waiting for her to begin to eat before they did. She smiled, and her eyes flicked to Marie and her bridal party.

If she was annoyed that her guests were taking their cue from the Princess and not from the bride she didn't show it, delicately dipping the silver spoon into the broth and sipping daintily. Laura then dipped her own spoon into the soup and the men copied her, sipping quietly. Conversation dwindled while they ate, and a relative silence filled the banquet hall.

Laura studied the five men demurely through her eyelashes as she ate, and a small smile played on her lips to think that they were also studying her with quick, veiled looks and demure eyes. Fredrik von Schmidt was the handsomest of the men seated around her. His blonde hair and blue eyes seemed to catch the candle light and glow warmly. Although he was not the oldest it was clear the others looked to him with respect. His manner was cultured and refined, and he sparkled with youthful exuberance but had none of Nikita's rash impudence and arrogance.

Karl was as handsome as his younger brother, but he had a silly, simpering look sometimes, his eyes turned in inward reflection. Laura wondered if he was in love, it was clear they did not have any partners with them at the wedding. The looks she got from the youngest, Kurt, made her smile. He idolised his brother and tried desperately to emulate Fredrik's grace and poise as he drank and ate. His eyes would only stray from his adored brother to alight briefly on the Princess then flush and look away again, hoping he had not committed some social faux pas.

Suddenly someone broke into pearls of laughter, startling the silence. All the heads turned to see Ekaterina, sparkling and beautiful, laughing gaily at some whispered comment from her father. Her laugh was sweet and musical and Count Varennikov guffawed loudly, slapping himself on the knee in merriment, pleased he had amused his daughter.

Laura smiled at the brothers and politely inquired after the health of the men and their families. She learned that none had any family of their own, though Karl was indeed in love and engaged to a Swiss Baronet's daughter, pining for his absent sweetheart. Burgrave Axel von Schmidt was a cousin of Marie and Ekaterina. The four brothers and Axel had grown up under the same roof, and looked upon each other as siblings, unmindful of the generation between them.

Axel politely asked after her husband and none of the men at the table missed her sad pause, or the way her eyes lowered while she lied and said he was well. To move the conversation past the awkwardness she asked the Burgrave of the general feeling in the newly formed Germany.

At once they erupted in enthusiastic patriotism; full of praise for the charismatic Bismarck and Kaiser Wilhelm.
'Germany is booming' Karl said. 'Our factories grow every day; my fortunes have tripled in one year' he boasted.

Fredrik's and Axel's wealth had also tripled in the economic boom, the factories they owned were at the height of their production lines and demand still rising for their products, while the shares Kurt and Gustav had in other factories had made them comfortably wealthy. Laura listened sweetly, asking intelligent questions that had the brothers falling in love with her wit and charm as well as her looks. They were boastful of Germany's achievements, and the newly unified country had achieved so much in such a short space of time she couldn't tell if the brothers were exaggerating the power of the nation or not.
'The Krupp Steel Factory has prospered enormously under Bismarck and Kaiser Wilhelm' Fredrik explained, smiling at Laura. 'Germany is now a massive industrial state. The Unification was a most ingenious plan. The navy has grown rapidly and the demand for raw material is high.'
'Is there such a demand for steel?' she asked, surprised.
'Yes of course' Karl said, enthusiastic. 'It is strong, we can build higher buildings, longer bridges, and when it is coated in tin it does not corrode. There is nothing it can't do. -'
'Tin?' Laura interrupted, surprised. 'It must be in demand then.'
'Very much so, steel's one weakness is corrosion' Karl said.

If it is in demand it must be valuable Laura thought, feeling disquiet when she thought about the poor price for tin at home.

'But enough' Fredrik smiled. 'We must have bored you with talk of factories. Tell us about your life, *Velikaja Knjaginja* Laura of Dalnerechensk.'

'Yes tell us Laura' Marie spoke up, listening with jaded ears, her French pronunciation perfect. 'How does one not get frightfully bored in Dalnerechensk? Oh, but excuse me, I forget, the haystacks must just remind you of home' she tittered.

Some of the table laughed too, and Laura could feel herself growing hotter and the old scars from Lady Ramkinson's riding crop began to itch.

'But tell us Laura, are you *still* without child?' Marie went on, smiling in her spiteful jest. 'The court must be getting worried that you cannot produce an heir. What is wrong with you? They say Aleksei was incredibly virile.'

'Come now Marie' Ekaterina said reproachfully. 'What a daunting thought for your husband on the verge of his wedding.'

The table roared with laughter, Count Varennikov slapping his knee as he guffawed. Laura swallowed, she had never been attacked so publicly or so maliciously before, and the jests smarted more than the wounds from the riding crop. Marie's eyes narrowed.

'But of course, it is your mother' Marie went on. Laura froze. 'Did your mother not go mad before she died? Did she not throw herself off the roof of your home in the grip of this madness?'

There was silence as they looked at Laura. Axel and Fredrik both looked horrified and uncomfortable. Laura's pretty face was strained and she dropped her eyes, biting her lip and struggling with her emotions, unable to respond with dignity to Marie. But she wasn't finished, enjoying the moment.

'He must be too terrified to bed you; madness runs in his blood. If you ever were to have a child it would be an imbecile! By all accounts Aleksei is going mad like his brother. It's such a shame.'

Laura's mouth dropped open in shock, her eyes flicking to Marie, her composure completely lost.

'His brother?' she blurted out.

Marie feigned shock. 'They have not told you?' she cried, looking smugly round her assembled guests. 'How could you not know when they knew your mother was insane?'

'She was ill; her death was an accident' Laura said quietly.

'Of course' she simpered, patronising her.

Ekaterina gripped her sister's arm hard, turning her face to Marie's ear, snapping something in Hungarian only she could hear. Marie ignored her, her face twisting in a smile poisoned with satisfied malice.

'Ten years ago when the Tsaritsa died Alexander Andrei went mad and disappeared. Aleksei was crowed Prince Regent not long after.'

Laura chewed her lip, her eyes shut tightly against the pain. She knew all the eyes of Europe were on her, and she had never felt more like a child. She wanted to scream, to slap that bitch Marie, to give her a lovely black eye for her wedding portrait, to burst into tears and sob into her hands. She clenched her hands tighter in her lap, aware Lady Ramkinson would have whipped her for the lack of composure.

She had not known about their mad blood. But now as she sat here, with the silence dragging out, and the eyes of Europe on her, things that had always troubled her began to make sense. *So Aleksei had been the younger son and was not meant to rule Dalnerechensk. That was why they informally called him Tsarevich, not Tsesarevich. Where was Alexander Andrei? Was he dead?* Tsar Constantinovich's reaction to her comment about the naming of his son made sense now. He had named *both* his sons after Alexander the Great.

Someone coughed and they all desperately looked elsewhere for conversation.

'I can assure you Marie they are both completely mad' Ekaterina said.

Laura gasped, looking at her friend in surprised hurt.

'I never saw two people who were madder about the other than Laura and Aleksei' Ekaterina continued. 'Sometimes when they are sitting together at dinner the wine begins to boil, and when they dance it is all he can do to stop from having her right there on the floor!'

'Yes well, Aleksei always did like pretty whores' Marie sniffed.

'And not a pretty horse?' Ekaterina laughed.

The table roared with laughter. Laura shut her eyes tightly and willed herself not to cry. She was grateful for the distraction that Ekaterina had provided, though she wished that the words had been true. Marie's information had been devastating, and Laura was reeling from the pain and humiliation of it all.

Marie, angry that Ekaterina had made all her guests laugh at her, called for musicians who struck up a tune. Marie's future husband led his horse-bride down to the dance floor and Laura hid her smirk to think Marie was ungainly on her feet as well.

'The dance tutor finally despaired of her I'm afraid' Ekaterina said to Laura. 'I believe her words were: *I'm going to hitch you to the carriage and teach the horse the Maxima, I might have better luck*!'

The table roared with laughter again. *She is not popular* Laura realised. *It was difficult to be liked when you were a spiteful, bitter old hag.* She stole a quick look at the company she sat with. Gustav was scowling absently, Kurt was studiously copying the painfully embarrassed and disapproving look that Fredrik wore. Laura sighed softly, reaching for her wine glass and drinking deeply.

Her movement stirred responses from the others. Fredrik stood and bowed to Laura.

'May I have this dance?' he asked, extending his hand.

'Forgive me Baron von Schmidt, I should very much like to dance with your brother Gustav' she said, managing a smile at the surprised look on Gustav's pouty face. 'Perhaps you would permit me the next dance.'

'Of course' he smiled. 'But you will allow me to escort you round the table to the dance floor?'

She accepted and took the hand offered to her, letting him draw her hand through his elbow, walking in silence, aware of the fans and the looks from those seated around the table. Laura kept her head up and pretended not to see them.

'Allow me to extend my deepest and sincerest apologies on behalf of my second cousin' Fredrik said suddenly. 'That was intolerably cruel.'

Laura smiled sadly. 'That is most kind of you Baron von Schmidt.'

They reached the other side of the table and he presented her to his brother. Laura took the automatically presented hand and Gustav led her to the dancers. She curtseyed to him and he bowed, and as they talked and danced he forgot himself and smiled, his fair complexion lighting up. Laura told him when he smiled he looked more handsome than his brothers. Gustav's grin nearly split his face.

74

Ekaterina pushed open the door to her room and peeked inside carefully. Her expression didn't change when she saw Laura sitting on the chaise lounge in her nightdress, a shawl around her shoulders and a blanket over her lap. She closed the door carefully behind her, saying quietly:

'You are still up then.'

Laura was angry, she had been waiting for nearly three hours for Ekaterina to come to bed. It was well after midnight, and the dinner had long since ended. When Marie had called an end to the festivities Ekaterina had excused herself from Laura's company, preferring to spend some more time with her father. Laura had given her blessing, but knew it was partly an excuse to avoid the confrontation she knew was coming.

Fredrik, Axel and Karl had gallantly escorted Laura to her rooms and had asked her to join them for a drive in the city. She had accepted graciously, pleased that she was not going to be snubbed for her lack of composure, and had slipped into her room alone, dressing for bed and waiting, knowing Ekaterina could not avoid her forever. As she had waited her anger had grown, and her demeanor as she came through the door only served to inflame her accusation.

Laura's anger spilled out in hopeless, frustrated tears.

'Did you know?' she begged her friend. 'Did you know of Alexander Andrei? Why did you not tell me?'

Ekaterina came to her friend and folded her arms around her. Laura fought her off, angry, then fled into the comfort of her embrace. Ekaterina stroked her hair gently and kissed the top of her head.

'No one talks of him, in Dalnerechensk' she said softly. 'He has disappeared Laura, I believe he is dead. I believe that Tsar Constantinovich thinks he is dead as well. I never knew him; it has been ten years since he disappeared. He is the phantom prince, the forgotten royal.'

'Why was I not told?' she wailed. '*Why did I have to learn of their madness from Marie?!*'

'Oh Laura' Ekaterina sighed softly. 'I am sorry my dear, I truly am.'

'Aleksei no longer loves me' she sobbed, clinging to her friend for comfort. 'He took Tatiana to his bed.'

'That is the law' Ekaterina said quietly. 'Aleksei is entitled to have who he wants. It is no comfort to you Laura I know. But he does love you -'

'It's not fair!' Laura cried. 'How dare he break my heart and excuse it with the sanctity of the law! I had half a mind to fuck Nikita for that!'

'Shh!' Ekaterina chided. 'You are his property Laura; all women are property of their husbands. But you are a princess, and they must know their heir is legitimate.'

'He already suspects me of unfaithfulness and his ministers accused me of such!' she burst out, sitting upright in anger.

'It is an uncertain life for the husband of a beautiful woman Laura' Ekaterina said softly. 'His jealousies plague him; he is in torment of uncertainty and suspicion every waking moment. Sometimes that makes him angry, sometimes that makes him sulky. He will never be certain of your love for him, and that will drive him to do stupid things.'

Laura looked at her friend carefully, wondering if the Countess, the beautiful jewel of Dalnerechensk, was telling her from her own bitter experience. *Had Grigory bedded another woman? Is that why he did not come?* She could not believe he would do so. Ekaterina smiled sadly and patted her hand affectionately.

'Take what little comfort I offer you Laura' she said gently. 'Come. It has been a long night, and I have drunk far too much. Go to bed my dear.'

75

Laura had surprised herself by sleeping soundly in her large, crypt-like room, and was woken when a maid knocked on the door to the sitting room, bringing in a tray for their breakfast. She heard Ekaterina thank the maid and realised she was already up and dressed. Laura's stomach growled and she quickly stood and dressed herself, joined Ekaterina at the table in the sitting room, eating ravenously. Ekaterina laughed at her, warning she'd split her corset. Laura sighed and corrected herself. Trying to act like a princess was hard work, even alone with her best friend.

'Do not mind Marie' Ekaterina said finally, setting down her empty tea cup. 'She is a spiteful girl with a spiteful tongue. I learned long ago you must not react to her words, no matter how it wounds you. She hates that. And think Laura, of her poor husband to be, he is getting a horse and a fishwife all in one!'

Laura burst out laughing, covering her mouth with her hand. 'That poor man!' she giggled.

A knock on their chamber door interrupted them. Ekaterina bid them to enter and Fredrik pushed open the door, stepping into the room.

'Good morning Your Highness, Countess' he smiled, bowing to each in turn. 'I hope I am not interrupting?'

'Not at all' Laura smiled. 'We have just finished. Please sit *Euer Hochwohlgeboren*, whilst I dress for our outing.' She addressed him by the style Ekaterina had taught her last night.

He bowed and thanked her for her kindness and Laura slipped into her bedchamber to dress in a stunning green gown and pulled on a warm grey traveling cloak, pinning her hair up elegantly. Fredrik stood again when she emerged and offered his elbow to her, smiling. She slipped her hand inside and bid farewell to Ekaterina as she was lead out of the room.

'Your Highness, you look beautiful' he said, a slight blush coming up in his cheeks as he led her along the corridor.

She smiled demurely, blushing at his praise, knowing it was sincerer flattery than Nikita's had been. They descended the grand stair case in a pleased silence. Karl and Axel were waiting in the wide, bleak entrance hall to Varennikov Castle. Both bowed as they joined them.

'I must commend your charm Your Highness' Axel said, taking her hand to kiss it gently. 'My gloomy nephew has had nothing but sunshine and rainbows on his face since you snubbed his brother to dance with him.'

Laura smiled sweetly. 'You must tell your gloomy nephew *Euer Hochgeboren* that scowling will not win him a wife and when he smiles he is more handsome than his brother' she laughed, slipping her hand into the elbow of the head of the family.

If Fredrik was disappointed his uncle took precedence with her it didn't show and he opened the door for them, escorting her out into the cool Debrecen morning. The groom suddenly strode in and Laura gasped, startled, her hand tightening on Axel's arm, trembling as the tall, eerie man glided quickly past them.

He looked at her in surprise. 'Your Highness?' he asked quietly.

Laura realised how tightly she had gripped him, how close she had stepped to him and forced herself to become composed again, looking around her in fear of the groom and Lady Ramkinson.

'Forgive me, Countess Ivanova terrified me with stories of Count Dracul. I do believe she was mischievously describing her groom when she described that hideous fiend!'

Axel laughed then folded his hand fatherly over hers, petting away her fears.

A small, grand carriage sat waiting at the bottom of the stairs. To Laura's relief a groom already sat on the driver's board and she gladly took Fredrik's hand when he offered it to her, holding open the door for her. The von Schmidt family climbed in behind her and Axel knocked on the roof to instruct the driver to go.

As the carriage turned in the wide drive they gazed out the window at the ruins of the West Wing of the extended fortress. Axel tsked quietly under his breath.

'*Scharde*' he said softly. 'It is such a shame that the castle has been left to fall into such a condition. I hear tell it was very beautiful when first built.'

'Countess Ivanova said it is very expensive to keep' Laura said, eyeing the gaping, sagging holes in the roof where the blackened and rotting walls of the attic and first floor were clearly visible by the early light of day.

'Still,' Karl smiled, 'it is a fitting haunt for the Grey Ghost.'

'The Grey Ghost?' Laura asked, puzzled. 'Varennikov Castle is haunted?'

'Very much so Your Highness' Fredrik smiled. 'It is said that Varennikov Castle has at least ten ghosts, of whom the most famous is the Grey Ghost.'

'Legend tells that the ghost is the unearthly remains of Fenitchka Raskolnikova, A Russian bride for one of the younger Varennikov Counts during Charlemagne's reign' Axel said. 'It was said she was very beautiful, but unconscionably cold, she rejected all of her husband's advances. After years of frustration and in a fit of rage the young Count set her dress alight and embraced her, crying the fire would soon warm her.'

'That's horrible!' Laura cried.

'The fire destroyed part of the West Wing of the house, and it was bordered up for many years' Karl explained, embellishing his uncle's story.

'Once the fire was finally out they found the body of the Count. His arms were encircled, as if he were embracing someone, but of her there was no trace' Axel continued. 'Even in death she refused to lay with him, and while he rests in the family's crypt she roams the empty halls of the West Wing, as pale as the ash she was reduced to.'

'How perfectly horrible *Euer Hochgeboren*!' Laura cried, her hands clasped tightly in her lap. 'I declare I shall never sleep in Varennikov Castle again!'

'They are but silly stories' Fredrik said soothingly, chiding his uncle with a look. 'And I'm sure you will sleep again Your Highness, Countess Varennikovna has planned several exhausting nights of festivities that will have us all asleep on our feet!' He took her hand and was surprised at how cold and trembling they were.

At once he fished his own gloves out of his pocket, presenting them to her.

'Here, Your Highness, I regret they look indelicate, but they will keep your hands warm' he said, helping her to pull them on.

Laura smiled, blushing prettily and sat back, looking out the window, strange onion-domed architecture catching her eye.

'Pray tell me *Euer Hochgeboren*, what is that building there?' she asked, turning to look at Axel. 'Alas, I don't know' he answered. 'However, I do know we are on *Piacz Utca*, Market Street, and our destination is the beautiful City Centre Park.'

The carriage rumbled to a stop and Axel opened the door, alighting on the cobbled street, offering his hand to help Laura down. She smiled and accepted then slipped her hand into his elbow.

Fredrik paid the cab driver and they strolled through the park together, discussing history and theology, enjoying each other's company. Laura was glad of the education she had received in Lady Ramkinson's school, despite what it had cost her and she felt herself smiling, laughing in their company.

Pleased that the Germans had found such an agreeable person to spend their time with they invited her out again with the young Countess, *if*, they teased, *she could be prised away from her family*. Laura laughed and accepted for the both of them.

76

Marie led her guests down the long, rich lawns to the tall hedge maze at the bottom of the garden. The party had been enjoying a fine lunch on the wide terrace and the wine had been flowing freely. Laura had sat with the von Schmidt family, and many of Marie's guests had stopped to talk to her, uttering condolences on behalf of Marie, and she had thanked them all graciously. Someone had made a comment about being unable to find their way back to their rooms to sleep off the excess of lunch, to which Ekaterina had clapped her hands delightedly and announced they should all run the maze.

Cheered by her enthusiasm and delight, the party agreed, and Ekaterina clapped her hands excitedly. Those less enthused about willingly losing themselves for hours in the leafy maze were roused when Ekaterina cried:

'A prize then!' and held aloft the pretty rubies, warm from where they had hung round her own throat. 'The person who finds these jewels may keep them!'

Marie could only smile tightly as her younger sister like a bright brand in her ruby dress flew down the steps and across the lawn, disappearing into the maze. The minutes passed, and some of the guests began to drift down the lawn to the hedge maze, eager to begin. Marie and the remainder of her guests had followed, waiting till Ekaterina appeared, laughing, her hands empty and her throat bare.

Fredrik bowed to the Princess and asked if she would help him look for the necklace. She smiled and agreed, slipping her hand into his arm.

'I fear we shall have to postpone our excursion this afternoon' he said, smiling.

'It seems so *Euer Hochwohlgeboren*, although I think I will have better luck persuading the Countess to accompany us for an outing tomorrow' she answered sweetly, and Ekaterina laughed, promising to join them.

With that Fredrik laughed and hurried into the maze, following several others as they twisted and turned round the paths. Although the avenue between the leafy walls were wide enough for two to walk comfortably side by side, the ground was uneven and hard, and soon they were forced from their quick pace to a more leisurely stroll for the conditions.

The baron and the Princess were soon lost, and listened to others who found themselves in a similar predicament, calling out to each other in the hopes of finding their way out. Every now and then they would see someone run past where their lane intersected with another, or would call out to someone walking the same lane, inquiring if they had found Ekaterina's jewels.

Each time the answer had been no, and Laura wondered if her spirited friend was playing a trick on them, having hidden the necklace somewhere on her person before emerging from the maze. She laughed and told Fredrik, who agreed, but did not suggest they return to ask her. Laura's smile deepened, she enjoyed the German baron's company, and was delighted by the maze she was walking. She decided she would very much like to create one in the town commons in Dalnerechensk, or outside the city, if the Advisory Council and Aleksei permitted her to do so.

Laura suddenly felt an unexplainable feeling of unease and she faltered in her step.

Fredrik looked at her curiously.

'What is it Your Highness?' he asked.

She felt a curious sensation that someone was watching her, and she turned quickly, only to see an empty, gloomy lane behind her. She noticed how quiet it had become, and how dark with the deepening evening shadows. They had entered the maze after midday, and the tall walls cast twilight across the path.

'I suddenly feel most unnerved *Euer Hochwohlgeboren*' she said softly. 'Forgive me for my flight of fancy, but I would like to leave now.'

'Of course Your Highness' he said gently, noticing the way her hand had tightened on his arm and the nervous looks she shot over her shoulder.

Fredrik too then noticed how quiet it was, and wondered if they were alone in the maze, if the others had managed to find their way out of the tall jungle. He called out but no one answered him. They turned back the way they had come, hopelessly lost, calling out to the silence around them. Laura wondered if they were alone, she sometimes thought she heard a foot fall and would look around them, growing more frightened.

The shadows began to lengthen and deepen into a purple bruise. The avenues between the hedges turned dark, and the air around them grew cold. They began to hurry, twisting and turning around the maze, and Laura was sure they was being followed.

They turned a corner and were blinded by the bright glare of the setting sun. Laura stumbled on the uneven ground, tripping on something that snaked across the path. Fredrik was too slow to stop her fall and she landed heavily.

'*Mein Gott!*' Fredrik swore, reaching down to help her up. 'Your Highness, I'm so sorry…'

Quickly he knelt beside her, reaching out his hand to her. She turned her head to look for his hand and saw a bright flash out of the corner of her eye. Under the hedge, displayed prettily and winking in the setting sun were Ekaterina's jewels, and beyond them, in the next row, the unmistakable coloured silk of Marie's skirts. *Why are you following us, you spiteful hag?* she thought meanly. Quickly she thrust out her hand and grabbed the necklace, holding it up triumphantly.

'What luck to trip here *Euer Hochwohlgeboren!*' she laughed, showing him the jewels.

'Bravo!' he laughed. 'Forgive my slow reactions Your Highness, I was dazed by the light.'

'As was I' she smiled, undoing the clasp of the necklace.

'Allow me' Fredrik said, taking it from her and fastening it around her neck gently. She shivered at the cold touch of the gems at her throat and his warm fingers on the back of her neck. 'They quite become you Your Highness' he smiled, sitting back to eye her. 'You must tell me if you are hurt. I should feel most guilty if you are.'

'Not at all' she smiled. 'Kindly offer me your hand again *Euer Hochwohlgeboren.*'

He stood and helped her to her feet, drawing her hand through his elbow to lead her out of the maze. They twisted and turned round the leafy walls, aware that the light was now fading fast. Laura began to shiver, and Fredrik gallantly shrugged off his fine coat, fastening it around her shoulders. She thanked him, but as their wanderings led them into one dead end after another he too began to shiver, and asked permission to fold his arms around her to stay warm.

Laura feared they were truly lost, and considered calling out for Marie's help, wondering why she did not respond to Fredrik's calls, though she must be as cold as they were. They turned another corner and found themselves confronted by a small boy. They stopped in surprise, eyeing the boy who stood there, as if waiting for them. He said something to them, beckoning to them.

'He says we are lost and to follow him' Fredrik said quietly to Laura, then asked the boy a question.

He didn't answer, but beckoned for them to follow him. Fredrik stopped, looking around carefully.

'Here, that twisted root, I remember it. I believe it was near the entrance and that is the wrong way Your Highness' Fredrik said, indicating the way the boy had pointed. 'Wait here, I will be back shortly.' He then gave the same command to the small boy before heading down the row of trees.

Laura felt abandoned and alone while she watched his back disappear into the gloom. The boy suddenly grabbed her hand in a strong grip, babbling something she couldn't understand. She gasped, pulling her hand free in shock, forgetting herself, alarmed with how cold he was.

'You poor thing! You're frozen!' she cried in Russian, pulling off Fredrik's jacket and holding it out to help the boy into it.

'Your Highness!' Fredrik suddenly called to her. 'I have found the way out!'

Relief washed over her and she turned to the boy, wondering how to tell him to come with them. He was gone, she stood holding a jacket out to empty air. She turned around quickly, wondering if he had darted deeper into the maze. Fredrik suddenly appeared beside her, taking her elbow.

'Come Your Highness, you are frozen.'

'He's gone! He was so cold!'

Ekaterina suddenly appeared, leading a rush of servants and concerned party guests to her.

'Laura! We were beginning to worry!' she said, throwing the shawl around her shoulders. 'Oh! And you found the necklace! Well done!' she applauded.

A warm blanket was produced for Fredrik and Axel folded his arm around his nephew, insisting on a warm brandy for them both when they reached the house.

'The boy!' Laura said. 'He is still in the maze -'

'Hush' Ekaterina said firmly. 'The boy had been in the maze for seventy years now. I am afraid you have just met one of Varennikov's ghosts. He froze to death in the maze and is mostly seen in wintertime. But it is a cold night tonight. Come dear; do not trouble yourself with him. He is mischievous, but not harmful.'

'I do not know how you live in such a place Ekaterina!' she cried, trembling.

'I grew up here, they are not strange to me' she smiled gently. 'Come,' she said as they entered the warm castle. 'Sit here by the fire, both of you, and there is something on the sideboard to warm you with.'

She did as she was told and they found themselves curiously alone after such a rush of people to find them. Laura carefully looked at Fredrik to see if he was as shaken by the experience as she was, noticing his trousers had dirty marks where he had knelt in the avenue to help her up. A quick look told her she had the same marks on her dress and sighed. She took a deep breath then stood, holding out her hands to the open fire to warm, trying to settle her nerves again.

The door opened and the two younger Schmidts burst into the room, dressed for dinner, seating themselves on the floor at the feet of their adored brother.

'Did you see the ghost?' they asked, tumbling over each other in their desire to know. 'You truly saw it?'

Fredrik laughed and eyed Laura.

'*Oui*' he smiled, 'but the *Princessin* touched him!'

Both boys turned to look at her, their eyes wide and full of questions.

'You touched him? *Princessin* how brave!' they cried, each daring the other to hunt out the ghost, to spend the night in the maze, to rush daringly into the West Wing tapping on the walls to rouse the Grey Ghost.

'*Genug Kinder!*' Fredrik suddenly said. '*Loss mit dem fragen! Raus jetzt.*'

The brothers looked disappointed, and stood, bowing to the Princess before leaving, promising to save places for them at dinner, closing the door behind them. Fredrik apologised to Laura on behalf of his brothers and stood to pour her a strong brandy from the crystal decanter on the sideboard, returning to her with a tumbler for them both.

She smiled then, and thanked him for the drink, sipping at it quietly. They stood together at the fireside, not talking, allowing the other the solitude of their thoughts. Laura shivered involuntarily again. *What would Aleksei have done if she had frozen to death in the maze?* she wondered. *Would he marry Tatiana?* The thought made her miserable and she shut her eyes.

'Your Highness?' Fredrik asked softly, suddenly. 'Your tears move me, what can cause such distress in you?'

She looked away, buffing her tears with her thumb. Quickly Fredrik pulled out his pocket corner and offered it to her.

'I am most distressed to see you so unhappy' he said. 'What has hurt you so?'

'I was wondering who would mourn me if I had died' she said, pressing the fine cloth to her tears.

'Surely not!' he breathed. 'Permit me to comfort you, it is intolerable to see this distress!'

Laura sighed, letting him draw her into his arms. She could smell the light scent of cologne and the warmth of his body. She sniffed, wiping her eyes on his handkerchief.

'Is your marriage so int-'

'Don't' she interrupted, opening her eyes.

The flash of Marie's skirts reflected in the silverware resting on the mantelpiece startled her and she turned, eyeing the spot at the door where she had vanished. Slowly she stepped away from Fredrik, composing herself carefully.

'Forgive me for my indiscretion' Fredrik said.

'Of course' she answered, managing a smile. 'Your concern is appreciated more than I can tell you.'

She folded his pocket corner and gave it back to him. He took it and tucked it back into his jacket.

'Please excuse me while I dress for dinner' she said.

'Of course' he bowed, watching her leave.

Laura pushed open the door, half expecting to find Marie huddled in the shadows of the corridor, her eyes glittering with malignant glee. The image of the demonic pleasure on her face caused Laura to shudder and she quickly ran upstairs, opening the door to Ekaterina's rooms.

Her arm was seized and she was pushed in roughly. For a terrifying moment Laura thought Lady Ramkinson was going to thrash her for allowing Fredrik to hold her.

'So you had him on your knees did you, you little whore' Marie hissed spitefully in her ear.

Laura's fright turned to anger and she rounded on Marie, petty and hurtful.

'Tell me Marie, how much will your husband have to drink on your wedding night before he is convinced he is not bedding a horse?'

Marie slapped her and stormed out of the room. Laura rubbed at the hurt then went to dress for dinner, pulling on the most beautiful gown she had.

77

Kurt knocked on the door and dropped a polite but impatient bow before the Countess and Princess.

'Your Highness, my brother has sent me to present you and the Countess with this present' he said, bowing again as he presented the gilt edged cards to her.

Laura shot Ekaterina a smile and took the tickets from the boy.

'They are tickets to Mozart's *Marriage of Figaro*' she said. 'And box seats no less, for the both of us tonight. Should we be inclined to accept Countess? After all, Marie has planned a night of festivities for us.'

'Of course we would accept' Ekaterina scoffed.

Laura smiled at the mischievous look in Ekaterina's eye.

'Tell His *Hochwohlgeboren* we shall be happy to accept' she answered, placing the tickets on the small table beside the chaise lounge she sat on.

The young boy bowed to her and scampered out of the room, turning to bow at the door again before shutting it behind him. Laura giggled and looked at Ekaterina, the laughter fading when she saw the look on her face.

'What is it?'

'Tell me Laura, what was it that caused you and the young baron to take so long in the maze yesterday?'

'What?' she laughed in disbelief. 'Do you suspect me now too? We were lost, that's all.'

'You are going to break his heart Laura' she said quietly. 'He is trying desperately to remember that you have a husband.'

'My husband no longer cares for me' she snapped, suddenly angry. 'He has spurned me for an old lover and done nothing to silence the rumours that I am unfaithful. Good God Ekaterina he told me to flatter the *Knjaz*, to see to his whims, he made it so easy being handsome and reckless! I admit I was foolish and I shamed my name and that of my husband's but I never, *ever* was unfaithful! And you know why Ekaterina? Because I knew what pain it would cause Aleksei. I knew he loved me. I knew it would break his heart.

'I desired Nikita, God knows I did. But I did not have him.' She turned away from her friend, chewing her lip hard so she would not cry. 'Why in God's name do I want to protect his heart after the pain he has caused mine?'

She stopped then, taking control of herself, setting her shoulders straight and wiping away her tears.

'I still have the right to be a woman Ekaterina, to be desired, to be loved and to be honoured by my husband. For everything I will give him that was all I asked in return. It is not much, and yet it is everything.'

She looked away then smoothed down the folds of her dress. Ekaterina was silent. Laura picked up the book she had been reading and turned to the door, calling over her shoulder that she would read on the sunny terrace for a while.

'Laura,' Ekaterina called softly, finding her voice again. 'Do not be angry with me my friend. It is only you I am thinking of. Were you not married my cousin's nephew would make a warm, sincere and most loving husband for you. But you are married, and there it is.'

'There it is' Laura repeated softly.

'Come, we must have new dresses for the opera tonight' Ekaterina said.

She managed a small smile, and Laura managed one too.

78

The carriage swept along the wide entrance to Csokonai Theatre and Laura eyed the two storied romantic building as the horses pulled up shortly, their hooves kicking on the cobbled street. Large, Roman inspired arches decorated the building and the front was ornate with statues of women. Laura thought they were probably allegorical figures of some kind, while Ekaterina explained the six statues arranged at even intervals before the magnificent building were great poets who were honoured in Debrecen.

The Countess had excelled herself as they had combed Debrecen's tailors for suitable dresses for the evening, finding a vibrant blue silk dress cut in a flattering shape. *It was no wonder she was so despised by her unhandsome sister and called the Jewel of Dalnerechensk by the peasants* Laura thought as she eyed her. She glowed and sparkled like the sapphires she wore at her throat, laughing at the moonfaced gawp on several of the theatre attendants as they exited from the coach.

Several of them came forward at a rush to escort them into the theatre. There were gasps from the patrons inside and Laura and Ekaterina left their fur stoles with the coat check girl. The attendants slunk away to gossip together, boastful and jealous. Ekaterina slipped her hand into Laura's arm, leading her towards the stairs for the boxes.

The manager of the theatre himself was waiting at the bottom of the stairs. Laura passed their tickets to him. He bowed deeply.

'Please follow me' he said softly, trying to be respectful but unable to stop staring.

Ekaterina winked at Laura and followed the kindly gentleman up the stairs to a box seat near the stage. The von Schmidt family was already seated inside, Gustav and Kurt were reading the programme for the performance and teasing each other unceasingly in their native tongue while Karl, Axel and Fredrik nodded in polite acknowledgement to others in the theatre.

The manager cleared his throat politely and announced the guests to the box party. At once they stood and turned, and Fredrik couldn't stop his breath catching in his throat before he bowed deeply to them, his uncle and brothers copying him automatically.

Laura was glad Ekaterina had talked her into buying the pure white dress. She had been afraid that the neck was so wide and scooped it was in danger of falling off but it had hugged at every curve and the delicate hints of lace drew the eyes around her body. She had worn Ekaterina's ruby necklace and pretty seed pearls in her hair. It was clear from everyone's reaction to her that evening that she looked heartbreakingly beautiful in her new dress.

'Mein Gott...' Fredrik swallowed.

He held out his hand to her, and she noticed how gentle and tender his grip was, how it trembled as he guided her to a chair next to him in the front row of the box.

Axel bowed and kissed Ekaterina's hand before he led her to the spare seat between his and Laura's and waited till the women had been seated before sitting himself. Laura noticed the upturned faces in the gallery below them, fans fluttering frantically while women turned to each other, shooting her veiled looks. She snapped open the white lace fan she carried and waved it seductively. The movement stirred a response from Fredrik.

'Your Highness,' he breathed softly. 'You are as beautiful as the angels in heaven.'

'You are too kind' she smiled, dropping her eyes demurely. 'Who is it that looks so intently at me?'

Fredrik tore his eyes away from her to look across the theatre to the boxes opposite them.

'In the box directly opposite us are the Marquis Louis de Valleret and his wife Antoinette' Fredrik said, leaning close to Laura to talk to her. 'He is one of the most powerful men in France.'

Laura smiled at them, dipping her head forward in acknowledgement. They returned the greeting, de Valleret inclining his head to his wife to say something. Fredrik leaned closer, telling her that the patron of the theatre was sitting in the box beside the de Vallerets. She smiled to think he was inhaling her perfume and thought she really must ask Hannah where she had gotten the fragrance from, she would buy enough to bathe in it. She smiled at her wasteful, erotic thought and let Fredrik move closer, introducing her to all the powerful persons in the opera house.

She turned her face into his neck, aware of the clean smell of his hair and skin, and the light scent of his cologne.

'You must abuse me horribly if I ever buy a hat like that!' Laura said, laughing at one of the women seated below them in the gallery. 'She looks like a partridge!'

Fredrik's skin deepened in colour and she knew he was smiling, caught between wanting to laugh out loud and maintain his impeccable manners. Laura sat back in her seat, folding her fan away in her lap as the light dimmed in the theatre and an expectant hush fell over the audience. Fredrik sat back in his seat, but Laura noticed he still leaned towards her. She wondered if he was paying any attention to the opera and smiled to herself as she thought to tease him with questions later that evening.

She laughed at the antics of Cherubino on the stage, watching the way he leapt around to avoid being caught by the Count while the Countess and Susannah laughed at his amorous attention. She leaned forward, putting her hand down to brace herself forward so she could see the whole orchestra playing beneath them then realised she had put her hand on Fredrik's thigh. She removed her hand, flushing and apologising for her touch.

The lights came on for intermission soon after and Laura shot Fredrik a look.

'Are you enjoying the performance?' she asked, teasing. 'Did you think the choice of soprano was right for Cherubino or should the soprano playing Susannah sing his part?'

Fredrik blinked, his cheeks darkening, aware she was teasing his inattention. He was saved the embarrassment of answering by the arrival of the manager at the door, bowing low and inquiring if the Princess was enjoying the performance. She smiled and said the singing was beautiful, Ekaterina translating her words.

'You are most gracious Your Highness' he said, pleased, bowing again. 'The Marquis de Valleret bid me to extend this invitation to you Your Highness. He would be most grateful if you and Countess Ivanova would join his wife and he at their hotel after the performance.'

'For the love of God do not accept' Ekaterina added in English to the end of her translation.

'Why ever not?' Laura asked quietly.

'He may be the most powerful man in France, but he is also one of the most perverse' Fredrik said in English, his accent thick and charming. Laura looked at him, liking the sound of her mother tongue on his lips.

'It is instant ruin of a reputation' Karl said in English too.

The manager, not understanding, was still waiting patiently for an answer. Laura smiled and opened her mouth to reply when de Valleret appeared behind him at the entrance to their box. The Marquis dismissed the manager, who bowed deeply before moving off. Ever the gentleman, Fredrik stood, dipping a courteous nod of the head to de Valleret, and introduced the Princess, Countess Ivanova and his family to him.

De Valleret took Laura's hand to kiss it but did not let it go again, and she was instantly repulsed by the lecherous way he looked at her. She opened her fan, not to flirt, but to hide her breasts from his gaze.

'It is not often one meets a woman so enchanting as you Your Highness' he said in French. 'What say you to my invitation?'

'You are most kind, Marquis de Valleret, but I am here at the invitation of Baron von

Schmidt, I could not be so rude as to -'

'But of course he and his family will come with us' he interrupted, slightly impatiently. 'All of them.' His eye passed disinterestedly over them, but lingered on young Kurt's golden features.

'That is most thoughtful Marquis' Laura said, shooting Ekaterina a veiled look. Her friend smiled tightly, unhappily.

'You would not accept another invitation after mine?' a new voice said in thick, accented French.

They all turned to look at the handsome, fatherly man in a crimson military uniform. At once the Schmidt family leapt to their feet, bowing low.

'*Ihr Majestät*,' Axel said softly.

'His Royal Majesty *Prinz* Sebastian of Bayern' his valet announced to the box.

Ekaterina and Laura rose to their feet, glad to be able to pull her hand away from de Valleret's grip to hold her skirts to curtsey. De Valleret bowed stiffly. *Prinz* Sebastian offered his hand and Laura placed hers in his strong grip. He kissed it firmly then kissed Ekaterina's, with none of the emotion and all of the ceremonial resoluteness of a man performing a military maneuver.

'No Your Majesty' Laura said, grateful he had come to their rescue but was not quite sure what to make of this blunt man. 'I was just about to tell the Marquis so.'

De Valleret sniffed. The German Prince's frosty eyes fell to the Marquis, his disapproval radiating out of him. The corner of de Valleret's mouth pulled in the ghost of a sneer then he bowed again and excused himself, stalking away from the box. The Prince's eyes lost their ferocity as they roamed over his subjects and their pretty guests, bidding them to sit.

Laura and Ekaterina did so, but the men remained standing, knowing they could not sit until the Prince did, or took his leave of them.

'Thank you, Your Majesty' Laura said. 'It was a most uncomfortable situation.'

He bowed slightly. 'Angels should not have their reputations sullied' he answered brusquely.

Laura tried not to be shocked with his conduct. He was not spiteful or trying to be rude but spoke his mind simply and forthrightly. She wondered if de Valleret had heard his last comment.

'I will send a carriage for you after the performance' *Prinz* Sebastian continued. 'Enjoy Act Three Your Highness, there is a particularly beautiful aria.'

'I'm sure that I will Your Majesty' she smiled.

He nodded then turned, speaking to his valet as he left their box, making arrangements for the von Schmidts and their consorts to join them. No sooner had he left then the lights began to dim again in the theatre. The von Schmidts hurriedly took their seats again. Laura noticed Fredrik still sat close to her, and hundreds of fans were fluttering in the theatre. She wondered if anyone at all was paying any attention to the opera.

79

Laura rose to find Ekaterina's rooms empty. A cold pot of tea and a serving tray of cut meat had been left for her on the small table in the sitting room. She sat in a chair, placing a napkin on her lap. Ekaterina had been accosted to participate in Marie's wedding rehearsal, Laura excluded because of her frightful slander. In fact Marie had not even acknowledged her since her disgraceful comment. Laura felt suitably ashamed of it, but was glad Marie's silence meant she was not subjected to her spite.

Laura buttered a thick slice of bread, pleased to have these brief moments to herself. Last night as they had danced at *Prinz* Sebastian's party Fredrik had held her gently as if she had been delicate, fragile china; close and attentive to her, his hand held behind her to support her as they moved in case she crumpled. *Prinz* Sebastian, smiling and kind, had noticed and commented on Fredrik's feelings for her.

She had thanked Fredrik for his care and attention, and he had dropped his eyes, fighting against wine induced passions to say what he knew he could not. She sighed softly, patting the crumbs from her breakfast away from her lips with her napkin. Fredrik was handsome and gentle but she was not free to encourage him. *My heart still belongs to Aleksei* she sighed gently.

Her eyes wandered round the room, looking for a maid or a bell chord to summon one and could find neither. Instead her eyes alighted on a small collection of stacked newspapers on the chaise lounge. Curious she stood and made her way over to them, realising the papers were in Russian and one was in French. She smiled delightedly and sat down on the chaise lounge to read them. At first she found the Cyrillic script difficult but she read aloud quietly and listened to the words for their meaning.

The newspapers were not recent, and only served to clarify what she knew already: Russia was struggling with her conquests in the east and frustrated with her involvement in the Balkans. There was no mention of her mobilisation to invade Dalnerechensk, not even in the anti-Imperialist pamphlet she found in the pile, and she concluded that none had known about Nikita's troops on their doorstep. She wondered what Nikita would have done. *Would he have caused international outrage by taking it upon himself to seize the mines by force?* she wondered. He was certainly rash enough to risk it.

The French newspaper was easier to understand and Laura was surprised to read of riots in St Petersburg and Moscow. *So Russia was as plagued with internal strife as Dalnerechensk was.* The thought gave her no comfort. *Desperate times make us all desperate* she chided herself ruefully, turning the page of the newspaper. The next article was of the Nationalist movement in Serbia and the unrest it was causing throughout the Austro-Hungary Empire. It spoke of Russia's support for the movement, and that the newly formed Germany, so recently created from over three hundred individual principalities and states, opposed it.

The world is changing, and is full of unrest Laura thought, reading on to discover that the new German state itself had not wanted to unify, that the Southern states had banded together against the unifying North, and it had only been through what amounted to diplomatic trickery under a brilliant Otto von Bismarck that saw them join as one country for the

Franco-Prussian War. After the initial resentment the defeat of France and the acquisition of Alsace-Loraine, economic boom of a quickly industrialising workforce, growing navy and wealthy citizens helped foster a growing sense of national identity.

She smiled, thinking of the von Schmidt's enthusiasm for their new nation, and she had no doubt they were not alone in their praise. *If her wealth had tripled over night she too would praise those that made it happen.*

The smile faded from her face and she folded the French paper carefully, putting the paper back into the stack and smoothing her hand across them absently. *What did this mean for Dalnerechensk?* she wondered. *These were uncertain times for Europe, how was a principality as small as Dalnerechensk to survive?*

She stood, deep in thought and went back to the small table, sitting again and popping small morsels into her mouth as she pondered. *Steel was important to an industrialising nation* she mused. *And tin was important to keep it from corroding, therefore tin must be valuable.* Laura poured herself a cold cup of tea, popping another cold cut into her mouth, chewing thoughtfully. *Russia must not be paying enough for our tin* she concluded, and couldn't stop the feeling of outrage that grew at that thought. *How dare they do this to my people!*

Laura began to think, tapping her fingers on her lip, furrowing it with her teeth. *Was Russia industrialising?* she didn't know. *Even if she wasn't, she would still need steel for her armies.* She made up her mind to tell the advisors to send the redrawn Treaty of Dalnerechensk to Tsar Nicholas the Second. *Perhaps we should draw it again, and raise the increase to two hundred percent* she thought.

What if Russia refused? the pessimistic side of her wondered. *We can withhold the tin* a reckless part said. But Laura knew that was no good. Russia would simply invade, whether she could spare the man power or not. She needed the tin. The more cunning part of her came to life. *What if we didn't simply withhold it, what if we sold it to another?* Laura paused, letting the dangerous thoughts run their course. *To who? Germany! What would Russia do if they sold the tin to Germany? There was no doubt Germany would mobilise to protect any threat to their interests. Would she risk a war with Germany by invading? A war on two fronts?*

It was a sudden, powerful bargaining point in a dangerous, precarious position. *Suppose it worked...*

Laura sipped her tea, disgusted to remember too late that it was cold. She spat the tea back into the cup and dropped the cup on the saucer, wiping her mouth with her napkin, chewing a morsel of cheese to rid her mouth of the taste. *What a Godsend it would be if it worked* she thought. *All that stress would be lifted off Aleksei, he would heal and he wouldn't be* —

She stopped, biting her lip harder, torn between her feelings for him. *Was he mad?* She had seen his looks of desire, had felt the desperate way he had hungered after her in the Ivanov's garden, felt the enjoyment that had washed over her in waves in his responsive, tender lovemaking.

But she had also felt his cold decorum, the distance and the animosity towards her, his anger and frustration that she was not the bride he had wanted. She was not yet seventeen, she didn't want to spend her life hidden inside the castle of a failing Principality, to learn to fear the footsteps outside her door that meant her husband was coming, drunk and enraged, to spill his mad seed in her for the heir his country demanded, while he whispered words of love in his mistresses' ears.

She stood quickly, upsetting the table, the lid of the teapot rattling, shutting her eyes against the pain.

He had loved her once. She knew it. She had felt there was hope the last time she talked to him. *I will not be the forgotten wife* she vowed. She would win his heart back from Tatiana, from the suspicion he harboured towards her. Aleksei was a good man. She would be a good wife for him.

She wiped her cheeks with her fingers to cool her flush of emotion, patting her hair gently to soothe herself. She was frustrated with the pomp and ceremony of Marie's wedding feasts and the endless snide comments about everyone and everything from the spiteful bride. *Really! How did anyone ever put up with her?!* she thought, feeling sorry for her friend that had grown up with this maliciousness. In four days the train would leave Debrecen Station for Chelyabinsk. Laura itched to return to Aleksei and Dalnerechensk. Four days was plenty long enough.

Gently she touched the now quiet lid of the teapot absently, leaving the napkin crumpled by her tight fist beside her plate. Again she looked around for the bell pull and sighed, leaving the dishes where they were.

She smoothed down her silk bodice, liking the way the blue cornsilk colour caught the sunlight and shone, deciding to explore the huge Varennikov Castle, unwilling to be part of Marie's planned festivities today. The verge of one marriage had reminded her of her own and she was listless to be with Aleksei again.

She opened the door and made her way along the corridor, admiring the ancient, elabourately shaped furniture that was scattered in the hallway: the carved high-backed chair, the elegant hall piece with a mirror, a small table on which sat a pretty Swiss clock, chiming the hours merrily. She stopped before each grand portrait that glared down at her from the walls, wondering who each man was, and why they looked so grim and unhappy.

Every now and then the face staring sternly out of the cracked portrait was that of a woman, and Laura often had to blink and peer carefully to determine the sex, as the faces of the women lacked any soft feminine qualities, and were rather plain and mousy like Marie. Laura almost began to believe her friend was an illegitimate child, as she did not resemble anyone in those bleak paintings.

Slowly Laura descended the grand staircase, one hand resting gently on the polished wooden rail. It had been stained with oil and years of use until it looked black and she could see sunlight from the high arrow slits reflecting on the bannister.

A sudden flicker of movement in the reflection made her heart leap into her mouth. She stopped and looked back the way she had come, but the curve of the grand staircase hid the cause of the shadow from her. She looked at the shining bannister again, holding her breath, listening for the sound of footsteps on the stone steps. There was no movement, no noise at all. *Is Marie following me again? Or is it the Grey Ghost?*

She gulped quietly, feeling fluttery with scared butterflies and descended the rest of the stairs. Once or twice she heard a muffled step behind her, but didn't see the shadow of the person glide across the sunlight on the bannister. She paused briefly at the bottom of the stairs, then turned and opened the door Count Varennikov had come through the day she and Ekaterina had arrived, eyeing the lavish corridor beyond.

Yet more grim portraits glared down from the walls, but their countenance was lifted somewhat by the warm sunlight drifting lazily in through large windows. She stepped into the corridor, leaving the door ajar, but gave it a slight push so it slowly creaked closed behind her. She listened carefully as she continued on, her heart loud in her ears, and heard the creak stop halfway.

So she was being followed. She stopped and turned, wondering who it was that was following her, and why they had not called out to her. The corridor behind her was empty, the door standing ajar and stopped. She chided herself for being silly; the shadow she saw in the bannister was just a maid or a livery boy going about their mundane business. Ekaterina's tales of peasant superstition was playing silly tricks on her mind, as was the encounter with the ghost in the maze.

But she found it difficult for thoughts of ghosts to stay long in her head as she stood in this finely decorated corridor, while warm and strong sunlight streamed in through the large windows, making the dust motes wink. She clasped her hands behind her back and strolled contentedly, eyeing the polished ornaments and occasional pieces of rich furniture.

Rooms opened off the large corridor, all of them lavish and tastefully decorated. Laura looked in through the open doors, liking the majesty of forgotten ages. This castle had been designed both to defend and to impress by the wealthy, powerful Varennikovs and Laura couldn't help but feel sad that this great house would be deserted in another fifty years. *Maybe even in twenty.*

The corridor ended with double doors. They were closed and Laura reached to pull them open.

'Your Highness!'

It was Fredrik. Laura stopped, turning in surprise to eye him as he stepped out of one of the rooms.

'Do you often follow young women like this *Euer Hochwohlgeboren*?' she asked, teasing him.

He coloured. 'I was curious to know what you were doing' he said, embarrassed.

'Had you asked me, I would have told you' she said reproachfully, but unable to hide her smile at his discomfort.

'Of course' he said shamefully. 'Please forgive my foolishness.'

'I could not stay mad with you long *Euer Hochwohlgeboren*' she smiled. 'So now that we are acquainted with each other's presence perhaps you would like to accompany me? I am enjoying losing myself in Varennikov Castle.'

'I suspected you did not know where you were' he said, reaching to grasp the door handles. 'Behold the haunt of the Grey Ghost.'

He pulled open the doors, revealing the charred remains of the West Wing. Fire had gutted the corridor, painting it all in soot and ash. All the furniture stood as it had in Charlemagne's reign, twisted and bubbled by the heat of the fire. Laura laughed at Fredrik.

'I declare you have as much a taste for theatrics as Ekaterina!' she grinned.

'And I that you take the same delight as she in your teasing of me' he said.

'Come now *Euer Hochwohlgeboren*, you protest too loudly' she teased. 'I think you are not as opposed to my sport as you say!'

'Guilty' he grinned, looking down into the ruined West Wing. 'Tis a fitting haunt for the Grey Ghost' he said, and was surprised to see Laura step past him into the wing.

'Come *Euer Hochwohlgeboren*, think of how much more young Kurt will adore you if you tell him you rescued me from the Grey Ghost!'

He smiled and stepped into the room in the manner of someone testing the denseness of the ice over a frozen pond. Laura smiled, amused, and slipped her hand into his elbow. They walked in pleasant silence, enjoying each other's company, half listening for ghostly moans or strange footsteps.

The voices surprised them. They appeared to be ahead of them, where the corridor turned at right angles. Laura looked at Fredrik curiously then crept closer determinedly. Fredrik followed her. The voices were low but angry. One of them belonged to Ekaterina, and Laura guessed the other belonged to Marie. She peaked quickly around the corner and saw them standing in a wide room together. They were talking in Hungarian, and neither looked happy.

Laura turned her face to Fredrik, raising herself on tip-toe to whisper in his ear.

'What are they saying?'

'They are arguing' he said, trying to be discreet.

'What about?' Laura pressed.

'About money, I believe' he answered, uncomfortable.

'Translate what they are saying' Laura suddenly said. Fredrik paused. 'Please *Euer Hochwohlgeboren*, she is my friend!' she whispered urgently.

Fredrik sighed softly then stepped close to her, cocking his head so he could hear better, whispering softly in her ear, his warm breath tickling her neck.

'You have bled the fortune dry' Ekaterina said, their argument coming to life on Fredrik's tongue. 'You have ruined the castle.'

'Not everyone wanted to get married in the -' Fredrik stopped, painfully embarrassed. Laura squeezed his arm, urging him on. 'Not everyone wanted to get married in the pig sties of Dalnerechensk' he finished, ashamed.

'I wonder Marie,' Ekaterina said after a moment of silence. 'What will your husband do when he realises that you have no money? At least I am beloved -'

'Beloved?' Marie scoffed. 'You were just a -' Fredrik stopped again. 'I will not translate that word' he said, deeply embarrassed.

Laura's ears had pricked at the mention of Aleksei's name.

'Please! The rest!' she urged desperately.

'You stole Aleksei from me!' Marie had said. 'You were always flirting with him -'

'So you do still love him, no wonder you were so spiteful' Ekaterina said.

'You dared to show up at my wedding and dared to bring his pretty ___ as well!' Marie stormed, rounding on her sister.

Laura guessed the word Fredrik had left out was not *wife*.

'Were it not for Laura and I you would have no one to hold your train Marie' Ekaterina said reproachfully. 'No one likes you enough to even want the place of honour at your wedding.'

'You made them all dislike me!' Marie yelled, her hands clenching in anger.

'Yes of course, it has nothing to do with the way you abuse everyone around you' Ekaterina snapped.

'You have done this for years!' Marie went on, too enraged to listen. 'All the men that came here, you smiled at them all and spread poison about me and no matter what I did I could never be as charming or as graceful or as good as you at sucking their -' Fredrik gasped, horrified. 'Your Highness, please, this is too distressing!'

'Please Fredrik, *please*!' she whispered as Ekaterina replied.

Marie was seized with rage at her words and slapped her hard, storming off towards them. Quickly Laura pushed Fredrik ahead of her and they slipped into one of the rooms that lead off the fire ruined corridor. The room was only a closet but there was no time to find another. They slipped in, pressed tightly together and shut the door, holding their breath as they heard Marie stamp past them.

'What did she say?' Laura whispered.

Fredrik sighed.

'She said: *There are always men willing to marry swine for pearls, thank God you have found a man who lusts after your money enough to save you dying a shriveled up old spinster.*'

Laura sighed sadly. 'Poor Ekaterina' she said. 'How horrible to have a sister like Marie.' She was silent then added 'Poor Marie, how terrible to be ungainly unhandsome and have a sister like Ekaterina.'

'That does not excuse her despicable conduct and language' Fredrik said. 'Although I could not disappoint your request Your Highness it was terribly unpleasant.'

'I know. I'm sorry *Euer Hochwohlgeboren*. Please forgive me.'

He sighed gently. 'I could forgive you anything' he said quietly.

Afraid that he had said too much he reached for the door knob to step back out into the corridor. Laura stopped him.

'Ekaterina' she said warningly.

A floor board creaked in the room and Fredrik shut the door again. They stayed quietly pressed together, listening to the sounds Ekaterina was making. She was moving around the room, but had not left it. Laura shifted uncomfortably, trying to ease the pins and needles that were making her limbs ache.

'I fear she is not leaving the room' Fredrik said uselessly. 'Perhaps we should attempt to leave?'

He reached for the door again, but as he did Laura heard Ekaterina finally begin to move towards them. She grabbed his hand and pulled it back, holding her breath tightly, aware Fredrik had done the same. Ekaterina's steps passed by them and faded away. When they heard the quiet click of the door to the corridor closing after her they let out their held breaths, laughing quietly together.

Fredrik reached for the door a third time and they stepped out into the blackened corridor, closing the door to the cupboard behind them. Laura checked her dress carefully, wondering if it had been dirtied by the sooty corridor, wondering if Marie would see soot on her back and accuse her of having had Fredrik pushed against the walls of the West Wing, or sprawled on the ruined floors. The thought made her flush a little.

Having satisfied herself that neither she nor Fredrik were covered in soot to start gossip she offered him her hand which he drew through his elbow, his cheeks still dark with embarrassment.

'Please escort me out of the West Wing *Euer Hochwohlgeboren*' she said quietly. 'I think I have satisfied my desire to see ghosts.'

80

Laura waved her fan, cooling herself on the wide terrace. Behind her the ballroom throbbed with the steps of the dancers, and hot waves of sweaty air pulsed out onto the terrace where she stood. Laura finished her glass of wine and set it on the colonnade, fanning herself harder.

It was no good, the air steaming out of the ballroom felt like the clammy air of a train station and she itched to be returning to Dalnerechensk. She smoothed down the soft silk of her dress and stepped off the terrace, slipping down alone into the garden, relishing her escape from Marie's festivities. She found her more insidious as the days passed, as each moment passed. Even Tatiana was not as evil as Ekaterina's sister. She wondered if she should say something to Ekaterina of what they had overheard, but knew it would embarrass her.

She sighed, slipping along the lawn, letting the cool of the night envelop her, smiling gently. The garden was fragrant with early blooms and she shut her eyes as she breathed deeply. She loved the smell of flowering fruitful gardens. She gripped her fan behind her and walked through the gardens quietly, enjoying being on her own.

All the time I wanted to be surrounded by people admiring me and the times I most enjoy are when I am alone she smiled ruefully. *Or as alone as I can be in Dalnerechensk.* She sighed again, singing softly as she passed the herb garden, picking a sprig of mint and rosemary, sniffing them as she inhaled between the lines of her song, smiling gently.

She glanced once back at the castle, at the ground floor lit brightly and the two hulking wings dark and shadowy. She turned, making her way down to the lake, slipping under the trailing leaves of a weeping willow and sitting on a stone bench, sighing happily. The lake shone in the moonlight and she eyed the sleeping swans that floated in the water, their elegant necks stretched back over their bodies.

She shut her eyes, sniffing deep the scent of the herbs, smiling.

A soft, unsubtle cough interrupted her moment of solitude and she looked up. Fredrik pushed aside a few tendrils of the weeping willow, smiling as he joined her, bowing.

'All alone here Your Highness?' he smiled. 'Surely you could not be waiting here for someone?'

'Perhaps I was, but you will scare off your brother Gustav' she laughed.

Fredrik laughed at her jest, taking a step closer to her.

'I could not with all good conscience leave you alone here' he said. 'May I walk with you in the gardens?'

'You may' she consented, smiling. 'Since you have scared off my paramour it is your duty to attend me.'

Fredrik laughed again, coming forward to take her hand. She stood and slipped her hand into his elbow, pushing aside the leaves of the weeping willow as they continued along the side of the lake together. She sniffed the sprig again, smiling gently. The silence settled comfortably between them and they walked to the far edge of the lake, stepping into a pretty gazebo to look back at Varennikov Castle, listening to the music floating across the water to them.

'What a beautiful evening' Laura sighed, resting her cheek against one of the carved posts of the gazebo.

'You have looked more beautiful each day' Fredrik said behind her, taking her hand and turning her to face him. 'Laura, I must say -'

'Don't forget yourself' she interrupted shutting her eyes.

'Please, I insist on spilling what my heart has carried these past days -' he cried urgently.

'You could only make a whore of me' she said, interrupting him. Fredrik stopped.

'I assure you I would never -'

'*Euer Hochwohlgeboren*, you are kind, handsome and impeccable but I must unkindly say that my heart does not feel like yours, though it would be intolerably cruel to do so' she said.

'I see' he said quietly.

'Do not be angry with me *Euer Hochwohlgeboren*. I have made solemn vows and I must uphold them' she shut her eyes. 'Please don't be cold or awkward with me because of this' she begged. 'It has been such a long time since I've felt such kindness.'

'It is only you who could endear me more to you after such rejection' he said, taking her hand.

Laura slipped it back into his elbow.

'I'm a little cold *Euer Hochwohlgeboren*. Kindly walk me back to the castle' she said, looking away from him.

81

Laura shifted uncomfortably. The dark morning was creeping closer to Marie's wedding. She was tired and had been unable to sleep in the tomb-like bedroom so she had finally dragged the covers from the bed and stretched out on the chaise lounge in the sitting room, pushing back the thick drapes to let in the cool night air. The couch was not comfortable and her conscience had not let her rest.

Fredrik had looked so crestfallen when she had told him she didn't feel anything for him. It had been a lie, she was attracted to him, but she knew she could not encourage him. He had courted her, attentive to her, walked with her in the fragrant moonlit gardens like paintings come to life. It was just as she had imagined it to be as she had sat on the stairs of Lady Ramkinson's home, watching that first Debutante Ball. *How terrible it was all too late for her!*

She shut her eyes tiredly, turning over on the chaise lounge. *There was no reason why Aleksei and she could not walk in the moonlight in their own gardens* she thought. *There was no reason why they could not continue to act as if they were courting.* She smiled to think she would enjoy winning his heart back.

She turned over again, sore and cramped. Ekaterina had told her what would happen during the wedding today. She couldn't help but feel this was the second wedding that she was a mere spectator in.

The dawn peeped through the arrow slit windows and she sat up, returning to her room to wash her face in a basin of water she poured from a porcelain jug. Behind her was a knock on the door of the sitting room and a maid brought in the dresses she and Ekaterina were to wear as bridesmaids, leaving them draped over the back of the chaise where she had tried to sleep.

Laura stepped out of her room, wondering if it was another form of insult Marie had devised that no maid ever stayed to wait on them in their rooms. She eyed the dresses. They were of some dark maroon shade that was almost black and cut in an unbecoming style. Laura quickly pulled one on over her night dress and held her arms out, looking down at the material. *It looks like a tent!* she thought and burst into Ekaterina's bedchamber and showed her the horrible dress.

'Is it supposed to be a wedding or a funeral?' she demanded.

Ekaterina rolled over and stretched lazily.

'Perhaps it is the groom's funeral' she laughed, eyeing the dress. 'It is a very old custom that the bride's family dress in mourning before her wedding because they are losing a daughter. But on the wedding day it is a joyous celebration because they have gained a son. Marie has some nerve, she is not that loved, and like everything else about her it is twisted. Perhaps if everyone else looks miserable and ugly she might have a chance of being marginally attractive.'

She pushed back the covers of her bed and sat up, stretching.

'The young baron came back to the party looking miserable' she said eyeing Laura. 'I knew you would break his heart. Did you do it gently?'

'I lied to him, but did it as gently as possible' Laura answered, dropping her eyes.

'I am glad and I am sorry' Ekaterina said. 'Come, you cannot wear your nightdress under that. Go and lace your corset as shapely as you dare bear it.'

She smiled devilishly and pushed Laura out of her room, closing it so she could wash and dress. Laura went to do as she was told, stepping out wearing a firm corset, two petticoats and the ugly shapeless dress. Ekaterina looked round, tugging the maroon dress down into place over her corset and petticoat.

'They are hideous aren't they' Ekaterina said.

She turned and crossed to a large box that sat on a table against the wall. Laura had thought the box was a toy chest, a relic from Ekaterina's childhood. The Countess lifted the lid and pulled out a handful of brightly coloured ribbons, pulling out several long black ones. She brought them back to the chaise lounge and sat, pulling Laura to sit beside her.

'My mother used to wind ribbons through my hair when I was a little girl. She would wind some fantastic works of art in our hair. There was a ribbon for every occasion' she said absently, combing her hair.

She reached out and turned Laura so she could comb her locks, beginning to prepare it for an elegant coif.

'Let's see if I can do it...' Ekaterina mused quietly.

'Should we not ask your mother?' Laura asked.

'She has not forgiven me' Ekaterina said matter-of-factly, twisting her hair up.

Laura did not respond, sitting silently while Ekaterina pinned it in place, decorating her coif with seed pearls and pretty rubies. When she was finished Laura admired the elegant creation, watching Ekaterina twist a long black silk ribbon through her own locks.

'Ekaterina, they're beautiful, you have great skill' Laura said, watching the Countess pin seed pearls and rubies into her finished coif.

Ekaterina stood, dusting down the ugly dress. Laura thought with their hair pulled up they looked quite handsome in the colour as their skin glowed whitely around it, and wished it was not so shapeless. She retrieved her ruby necklace from her room and fastened it round her throat, noticing that Ekaterina had also found a ruby necklace to wear.

'Come my dear, let's see what can be done with this ugly thing' Ekaterina said, pulling long ribbons out of the pile she had placed on the chaise lounge.

Ekaterina fastened one firmly under Laura's breasts, beginning to wind it around her body, gathering the material close to her stomach and hips. She tied the ends or the ribbon behind her and stepped back to eye her work then gestured for Laura to see her reflection. The gown had been transformed into something quite elegant and resembled a Greek chiton, accentuating her figure. Laura smiled at Ekaterina.

When they were both dressed and wound with latticed silk from under the breasts to the hips, their hair coiffed and dark gems shining at their throats, Laura decided they looked very exotic and mysterious indeed. A servant arrived with their bouquets of lilies, gasping as she saw them. Ekaterina took the flowers and Laura smiled approvingly, the white flower looked stunning against their dark dresses.

Ekaterina ushered Laura downstairs, catching sight of Marie as she stood in the wide entrance hall, surrounded by fussing servants. The maids gasped when they saw them on the stairs, and the bride was almost completely forgotten. Laura felt sorry for her. Marie was not a woman that could ever be called pretty, not even on her wedding day with a becoming dress and a delicate pleased flush in her cheeks.

The flush darkened with rage when she saw the two of them.

'What have you done to the dresses!' she hissed, angry. 'You have ruined them!'

'Shouldn't you be pulling the carriage?' Ekaterina answered, arching her eyebrow.

Marie turned on her heel and stamped out of the castle.

'And don't pout, it's most unbecoming!' she called after her.

Marie swept out of the castle and slammed her carriage door, so mad a tail of her train was left poking out. One of the livery men opened the door again, pushing in the dress quickly then shut the door to avoid a spiteful comment from Marie. Laura and Ekaterina came down the stairs, watching as Marie's carriage pulled away from the steps. Quickly another carriage was brought to the foot of the stairs and livery men helped Laura and Ekaterina into the plush interior.

They sat in silence during the drive to the church, both lost in their own thoughts. They reached the church before Marie did and stood quietly on the steps, waiting with Count Varennikov. He looked proud of his beautiful daughter and frequently patted the hand that was tucked into his elbow. Countess Varennikova peeked out once, noticing that there was only one carriage and no sign of Marie. She sniffed, disapproving, and disappeared back inside.

Marie finally arrived and Laura eyed her quietly, trying to see if her delay had been due to tears. There was no trace of them, and though she was pale she still managed to keep some semblance of the blush in her cheeks. Count Varennikov opened the door and helped out his daughter, kissing her cheek warmly. Laura and Ekaterina busied themselves with Marie's train, shaking out the wrinkles in it and holding it elegantly.

Count Varennikov offered Marie his elbow and she smiled, tucking her hand into his arm, letting herself be lead up the stairs to the cathedral. Laura listened to the strains of the wedding organ and let her eyes drift surreptitiously round the magnificent interior, lingering on the guests, spotting Fredrik in the pews.

His face was deep and his eyes lowered, a man losing the battle with his emotions. He lifted his eyes as they passed and Laura saw how he was unable to bring himself to look at her, bowing slightly deeper as they passed him. She dropped her eyes too, looking away, noticing the way Axel's eyes had drifted over the exchange between them.

Marie reached the top of the aisle and Ekaterina and Laura dropped her train, moving quietly to the side of the steps. Laura sat when the congregation did, listening to the service she did not understand. Marie and her new husband sealed their vows with an awkward kiss. Laura wondered if it was the first time they actually had kissed. *Of course not, who marries a man they have never kissed?* she chided herself.

They turned at the top of the aisle and Ekaterina and Laura gathered up the train again, carrying it as the groom led his new wife out of the lavish church.

On the steps leading down to the waiting carriage Marie turned and snatched the train from them.

'Go back to the castle, both of you. You are not welcome at the reception' she snapped.

She turned from them, stepping into the carriage. Her husband climbed in behind her and she reached back, slamming the door against them. Laura was stunned but Ekaterina took her arm, escorting her down the church steps to another waiting carriage.

'Why did she invite you if she didn't want you here?' Laura asked, confused.

'She didn't. My father did' Ekaterina smiled. 'Marie can have her day; I have no wish to look at her hapless husband when he realises what he has gotten himself into. Come, we will go and take tea to celebrate being excluded. And later perhaps we will go to the opera.'

They were suddenly joined by *Prinz* Sebastian, who overheard the last comment.

'You are not dressed appropriately to take tea' he said bluntly. Both girls hid their smiles and curtsied to him. 'Return to Varennikov Castle and change, I will meet you for tea in one hour' he continued, then named a popular coffee house.

'Yes Your Majesty' Ekaterina said, a smile playing on her lips. 'It is so refreshing for a man to be so commanding!' she said to Laura as he took his leave of them, knowing he could hear them still.

He laughed as he walked away, and Laura and Ekaterina scrambled into their carriage, hurrying to do his bidding.

82

Prinz Sebastian was late and Laura sat quietly, her eyes drifting around the décor of the room. Beside them a waiter was clearing an empty table, folding up a newspaper that had been left on the chair. Laura glanced at it then gasped.

'Ekaterina, ask him for the paper!' she whispered, pointing to the sheets of newsprint on the verge of disappearing under other bits of disposable waste.

She did, and the waiter bowed deeply before handing it over, noticing what Laura had seen. It was in English. Laura was delighted to find something in her mother tongue as she had not read her language since she had left Boston, and was shocked at what she read in the headline.

'Russia's navy has been all but destroyed!' she whispered, aghast, noticing Ekaterina looked equally surprised. A quick check of the date told her that the paper was also not recent, but more recent than the papers that she had read in her room. Laura began to read the article out loud.

'War between Russia and Japan was inevitable as they had conflicting interests of territory in China and the Asian mainland. Outright hostilities began when the Imperial fleet of Japan launched a surprise attack on the Eastern Fleet of Russia's navy stationed in Port Arthur. The Baltic fleet was quickly disengaged to meet the threat. As much as this traversing of the world is admirable the fleet was not without their misadventures.

'The Battle of the Tsushima Straits was fought between the opposing fleets on March twenty eighth. During the confrontation the Russian fleet was virtually annihilated by the Japanese high explosive rounds which were far superior to Russia's out dated and ineffective armor piercing rounds. Several ships of the Russian fleet were able to break away from the battle but were slowed by fouled ship bottoms.

'The Japanese fleet gave chase during the night of the twenty eighth and ninth, spotting the remaining Russian ships who were scanning the waters with search lights. Only a few ships made it to the safety of Vladivostok. Russia was forced to concede victory to Japan in the Treaty of Portsmouth.

'Many have been surprised by Tsar Nicholas the Second's impervious indifference to the onset of the hostilities and the many defeats she suffered. As a result Russia's esteem has received a crushing blow and the Imperial government is rocked by the strain. A collapse of the government seems inevitable.'

Laura put the paper down, eyeing Ekaterina, trembling with the new information.

'It is worse than I thought' she said. 'Is there nothing more recent than this? Ekaterina, ask for a newspaper, please!'

Ekaterina waved over a waiter and ordered more tea, asking for a paper as well. The waiter bowed and left. Laura folded the paper over, reading the next article in silence commenting on what she read.

'There was a rebellion of some sort, a demonstration in January led by Father Gapon, some sort of socialist priest. Oh!' she cried out in shock. 'They shot at him! And his followers! Nearly a hundred dead and six hundred wounded. No wonder the headline calls it Bloody Sunday!'

She looked up from the paper, seeing the waiter return with a recent copy he presented to Ekaterina then poured fresh cups of tea for them. Ekaterina thanked him absently and unfolded the paper, scanning the article quickly, her expression of shock deepening.

'What does it say?' Laura begged her, frightened by the look.

'It is very grim indeed' Ekaterina said softly. 'It mentions the demonstrators who were shot in front of the Winter Palace in St Petersburg and goes on to say Grand Duke Sergei was killed by a revolutionary bomb in Moscow as he left the Kremlin. He is Tsar Nicholas' uncle' she explained to Laura.

'My God' she whispered, horrified.

Ekaterina gasped. 'It is much worse!' she said. 'The Black Sea fleet of the Imperial Navy has mutinied. There was a railway strike, but it has developed further, and now Russia is virtually paralysed by a general strike in schools and factories. The unrest it is causing has erupted in violence several times and policemen have been murdered.'

She dropped the paper, equally shocked and frightened as Laura. Their hands reached out across the table and found the other, squeezing tightly, noticing how much the other was trembling.

'My God, she is desperate, and dangerous' Laura said. 'So that is why Nikita left in such a hurry, and took his company with him.'

'What?' Ekaterina said.

'Nikita commanded a company of Imperial Troops. They were camped on the Northern Border of Dalnerechensk all the while he was there. I doubt very much it was for his own personal protection.'

Laura felt Ekaterina's hands tremble harder and clutched at them firmly, trying to press down her own fear. Ekaterina shut her eyes tightly.

'Are we going to be invaded?' she whispered in a frightened hush.

Instead of answering she let her hands go, throwing open the financial section of the paper still spread before her on the table. *How desperate was Russia for tin now she needed to rebuild a navy? How much was it worth?*

'Tin!' she said to Ekaterina. 'Check the price of tin!'

She found what she needed and gasped, blurting out the price. Ekaterina's more recent paper had an even higher value. Laura cried out in shock, her face twisting into a rage.

'That is a strange look for a pretty face' *Prinz* Sebastian said, joining them.

Ekaterina and Laura looked up at him, shocked and forgetting themselves. Quickly they rose and dipped curtsies, Laura struggling to swallow her anger as she would struggle trying to swallow a hurricane.

'Forgive my lateness, I was unavoidably detained' *Prinz* Sebastian continued, watching the two women before him. 'Have I interrupted something?'

Laura grabbed the paper Ekaterina had been reading and showed it to him, pointing in the general area she had seen Ekaterina reading.

'Is this correct Your Majesty? The price of tin, is it correct?'

'Of course. Why would it not be?' he asked, eyeing them, curious.

Laura shut her eyes, balling her fists tightly to keep control of herself, feeling light headed under the strain. *Prinz* Sebastian caught her as she swayed and sat her down, instructing the nearby waiter for a brandy. Ekaterina fanned her with the English newspaper, explaining to *Prinz* Sebastian the reason for her swoon. Laura could feel herself shaking with a strange tense humming and took a deep breath, surprised it came out in a sob. Instantly she took control of herself again, biting her lip hard, wincing.

The waiter arrived with the brandy and Laura took it, sipping carefully.

'I'm alright' she said softly. 'Please sit Your Majesty, your care is most appreciated.'

He sat and Ekaterina did too, putting the newspaper on the table, but where she could reach it should she need to. Laura sipped her brandy again, a malicious thought forming in her head.

'Tell me, Your Majesty, how do you suppose Kaiser Wilhelm the Second would appreciate the sale of Dalnerechensk's tin to Germany?'

Beside her Ekaterina gasped in shock.

'Laura you cannot!' she gasped in Russian. 'Aleksei would never agree -'

'I am Regent while he is ill, he does not have to' she answered in Russian too, aware that this private conversation in front of *Prinz* Sebastian was incredibly rude. 'Forgive us' she said to him in French. 'Russia has devalued tin and has nearly starved my country into submission, and she has threatened us with invasion which will break the Treaty of Dalnerechensk she has with us. It is a deceit I will not easily forgive. So please Your Majesty, how do you suppose Kaiser Wilhelm the Second would appreciate the sale of our tin to Germany?'

'The Countess does not agree with your thoughts?' he asked, looking at Ekaterina.

'No Your Majesty' Ekaterina answered. 'Sale of the tin to Tsar Nicholas' cousin will deeply offend him, especially after the losses she has experienced. It would be a dangerous gamble.'

'They are not fond of each other now' said *Prinz* Sebastian. 'Russia has signed the Triple Entente agreement with France and England, and Kaiser Wilhelm finds himself encircled by powers that are isolating him in Europe. As for the sale of tin, it will benefit his country enormously and promises to draw him even closer into hostilities with Russia. It would suit his militaristic megalomania very well.'

Laura said nothing, sipping her brandy again. Fredrik, Karl and Axel had explained the attitudes of the Bayern led south to Kaiser Wilhelm as they had walked in beautiful City Centre Park together. Bayern had been ruled by a Prince Regent, Prince Luitpold, for nineteen years, since the death of the mad king Leopold, found floating in a lonely lake with his psychiatrist. Leopold's younger brother, Otto, was also clearly unfit for the throne, and neither had any children.

Prinz Sebastian was a relative of Luitpold and he shared the same attitudes as the Prince Regent. They both had disliked the anti-Catholic agenda of Bismarck's *Kulturkampf* and opposed Prussia's strategic dominance over the new German empire. They both had snubbed Kaiser Wilhelm, who was Prussian born, and Luitpold had even gone so far once as forbidding the flying of any other flag other than the blue and white Bavarian Flag on public buildings for the Emperor's birthday.

Laura was well aware of *Prinz* Sebastian's dislike for the Kaiser and how the von Schmidt family praised him. *Prinz* Sebastian would be very willing to point out Kaiser Wilhelm's faults to her. She would need to know what they were if what she was planning was going to work.

She finished the brandy and set the empty glass on the table, folding away the two newspapers carefully, vowing silently to take them with her to Dalnerechensk as proof.
'Forgive me for my behaviour' she said, lowering her eyes demurely.
'Of course' *Prinz* Sebastian said. Ekaterina still looked unhappy.
'Will you tell me about Kaiser Wilhelm, Your Majesty?' she asked, pouring him a cup of tea.
'He suffers from Erb's Palsy caused in a traumatic breach birth' *Prinz* Sebastian said. 'His left arm is withered and shorter than the right. He often carries gloves in his left hand to make his arm appear longer, though I am told despite being crippled he is tolerably attractive.'

Laura hid her smile at *Prinz* Sebastian's blunt description of his looks. *Prinz* Sebastian sipped his tea thoughtfully.
'He has been thoroughly indoctrinated in the hyper-militaristic society of the Prussian aristocracy. As such he is hardly ever seen out of uniform. He also adored his father and grandfather for their efforts in the Franco-Prussian War. So you see Your Highness, if you gave him the tin and caused tensions between Russia and Germany he would thank you most profusely for the excuse to go to war. He has already been accused of megalomania twice, and that was nearly fourteen years ago' he stopped and sipped at his tea again.

Laura shot Ekaterina a sly glance. The Countess had fallen into thought but her face was carefully blank of emotion as she listened to *Prinz* Sebastian's words.
'What is he like as a man?' Laura pressed.
'It is said he is highly educated, and possesses a quick intelligence. He is highly interested in science and technology; he has even begun building the large and powerful Dreadnaught Battleships to challenge the fleets of Russia and England. But, though he poses as a man of the world he remains convinced he belongs to a distinct order of mankind: Monarchy by the grace of God, and his vile temper overshadows his wit.

'He is presently meddling in Morocco, and has made a speech in his visit to Tangier which amounted to his favour of Moroccan independence. Needless to say this is causing friction with France who dislike Germany – especially Prussia – for their defeat in the Franco-Prussian War and the loss of the valuable region of Alsace-Loraine to the German Empire.

'These diplomatic blunderings will no doubt further isolate the nation of Germany in the eyes of Europe, and the conference they have called to take place at Algeciras cannot end favourably for Wilhelm. He insists on a foolish personal policy of dealing directly and intimately with kings and emperors and heads of state. If you are to offer him the tin expect him to visit Dalnerechensk personally.' He finished his tea and placed his cup back on the saucer.

'Your colour has improved Your Highness. We will have no more of this, the topic of conversation is distasteful. My valet will see to the costs; you are both to accompany me to the City Centre Park. It is too warm and pretty a day to be sitting inside discussing Prussian kings.'

He rose and Laura and Ekaterina rose too, following him out onto the street where he flagged down a carriage and helped the women inside, instructing the cab to their destination.

83

It was late when they returned to Varennikov Castle. *Prinz* Sebastian had escorted them all the way so Laura and Ekaterina had not a moment to talk to each other until they were alone in her rooms.

'Laura you cannot do this!' she burst out in frustration as soon as the door was closed. 'I know what you are planning. You are not the ruler of Dalnerechensk, Aleksei and the Council will not agree -'

'The Council will do as they are told' Laura interrupted coolly.

'It is madness!' Ekaterina cried. 'You cannot force Russia to pay more for the tin by threatening to sell it to Germany. It is too risky! She will invade!'

'We are desperate Ekaterina' Laura said, falling to her knees and taking her hands. 'We are *desperate*! If we do nothing Dalnerechensk will strike, revolt, I have heard what they say Ekaterina, I am terrified they will rise against Aleksei and me. They could kill us!'

'Laura' she moaned, falling to her knees too. 'You heard *Prinz* Sebastian. You are risking a war! Germany and Russia in *war* because of this! Do you think England and France will stand idly by while the third party of the Entente Cordiale is attacked? My God! Think of *that* war, because of us! Germany cannot win a war besieged by three nations, no matter what the von Schmidt family says. What will Russia do to us then?'

'*What else is there?*' Laura sobbed. '*What else can I do?*'

Ekaterina stayed silent, folding her arms around Laura, letting her sob quietly. *There was nothing they could do, and to do nothing would destroy the Principality.* She kissed Laura's head, stroking her hair gently.

Laura sighed and sat back, wiping her eyes.

'It is dangerous Ekaterina. I know that' she said tiredly. 'But Russia has starved us to the brink of revolution. I will not forgive that deception, and I mean to make her pay. If this goes wrong so be it. If the world descends into war so be it. If I lose my life -' she paused, fighting down the fear '- so be it. How my name will be written in history I can't guess. I can only hope they are kind, and realise I did what I did for the love of Dalnerechensk, and had little choice' she stopped talking, shutting her eyes tightly.

Ekaterina squeezed her hands tightly then stood, pulling Laura to her feet.

'Come Laura, let us pack, I am eager to be gone from here!' she cried passionately.

Laura felt the same way and agreed, catching sight of a letter propped up on the table. It was addressed to her and she lifted it, recognising the handwriting, detecting a scent of cologne on it. She paused, eyeing Ekaterina quietly.

'What is it?' Ekaterina asked.

'It is from Fredrik' she said, then gave it to her friend. 'You read it.'

Ekaterina eyed her then tore open the envelope, pulling out the sheets of paper. It was a long letter, and the silence dragged between them while Laura waited, studying Ekaterina's face as she read. Finally she folded the sheets and carefully placed it back inside the envelope. Without a word she dropped it all on the fire.

'It is better for you not to know' Ekaterina said, struggling with her emotions.

Laura said nothing, watching the paper curl and blacken in the hungry flames. She could guess what was written on those sheets of paper. Ekaterina came to her silently, linking her fingers through hers and resting her head on her shoulder.

'If the worst happens Laura, send word to Fredrik. He will help you' she said quietly.

Laura nodded, tears blurring the sight of the letter turning into ash. Ekaterina stayed with her quietly then finally tugged her to her room, helping her pack her clothes silently.

84

Laura woke early and slipped out of bed, dressing quickly and warmly. She padded down to the entrance hall of Varennikov Castle, determined in her course of action. The day was cool and faded in the early light and she accosted a servant, telling her 'carriage', the only thing she could say in her limited Hungarian.

The maid left, and she stepped outside, worried that her request would be ignored. After all, she was an unwanted guest here. Relief flooded through her a few minutes later when a carriage hitched to two horses trotted round the corner of Varennikov Castle and stopped at the foot of the stairs, though she hesitated when she saw the eerie groom sitting on the driver's seat. He leapt down and offered her his cold powdery hand.

She took it reluctantly, stepping up into the carriage. 'Post office' she said in French, not sure of the Hungarian word for it. The groom blinked, not understanding. 'Telegram' she tried.

He smiled then climbed up onto the carriage driver's seat, flicking the reins. She sat back nervously on the cushions, hoping he was taking her to the post office. She hoped it would be open, that there wasn't some public or bank holiday that would mean she couldn't send the telegrams she had lain awake in the night composing.

The carriage pulled to a stop outside the post office and Laura was relieved to see that it was open. The groom opened her door and she made a motion for him to wait by the carriage, hoping he wouldn't drive off while she was inside. He folded his long hands and stayed put. Laura smiled shortly, relieved, and slipped into the post office.

The man behind the counter looked up, surprised to see anyone inside at such an early hour. He greeted her warmly in Hungarian. Laura politely asked if he spoke Russian and was relieved when he said he did.

'I want to send two telegrams' she said. 'One is to be sent to His Royal and Imperial Majesty Tsar Nicholas the Second of Russia' she paused for the man to finish jotting down the quick notes, noticing he was writing in Hungarian. 'The telegram will read: The Regent of the Principality of Dalnerechensk invites His Royal and Imperial Majesty Tsar Nicholas the Second to attend discussions concerning the purchase of tin. Dalnerechensk will gladly receive His Royal and Imperial Majesty before the end of the month.

'The second telegram is to be addressed to His Royal and Imperial Majesty Kaiser Wilhelm the Second of Prussia. It will read exactly the same, except for the name.'

The man was quiet, quickly scratching down the message.

'Both those telegrams must be sent immediately' Laura said.

'Of course' he said, quickly adding up the cost of the telegrams.

Laura paid for them, her fingers brushing against the little melted lump of tin she kept in her purse as she fished out enough coins for the payment. She lay extra coins on the counter. 'Send them immediately' she begged, pushing all the money towards him.

He took the coins then turned, leaving the door open as he disappeared into a small room behind the counter so she could hear the beeps of Morse Code flooding down the telegraph wire. They paused once and then began again to send the second message. Laura thanked him quietly when he handed her the receipt for the payment and she turned, heading back to the coach, hoping she had done the right thing.

She hardly noticed the coldness of the groom's hand as she climbed back into the carriage, lost in her own thoughts. Whatever Aleksei and the Council would say it was done now. She shut her eyes, praying she would have the strength to withstand the Council's objections. She knew they would be horrified. *They didn't know what I know* she told herself quietly.

The carriage jerked to a stop, startling her out of her reverie. She was back at Varennikov Castle. She quickly composed herself and stepped down from the carriage, thanking the eerie groom absently. He had lost his frightening aura now she had met one of the Varennikov ghosts. He leapt back up onto the driver's seat and the carriage rolled away, leaving her alone before the doors of the castle.

She wondered if she should say goodbye to Fredrik, she and Ekaterina would be leaving soon. She wanted to ask him what was written on the letter but knew if she heard him confess what he felt for her she would ruin his good standing within his family and the eyes of society. He was lucky if his good name wasn't already smeared, he had been seen in the company of a married woman.

She sighed deeply, letting herself into Varennikov Castle. She would leave without a private audience with him. She stood in the entrance hall and looked up at the stairs, wondering if they would hang a wedding portrait of Marie and her ambitious husband in the castle like they had done for her and Aleksei. Her slander came back to her. *Had her husband bedded her last night? Did Marie feel like she had on her wedding night?* Laura shut her eyes, not wanting to think about that. It was a terrible thing to know your husband didn't love you.

Laura slipped upstairs, glancing out one of the windows as she did, catching her breath in her throat. Fredrik was striding across the lawn from the direction of the lake. He had his arms folded around his body and a dejected slump in his shoulders. He was still wearing the clothes he had worn for Marie's wedding. Laura wondered if he had been out all night. He certainly looked cold. *Did his letter ask me to meet him at the lake?*

She shut her eyes and continued up the stairs. Ekaterina was eating breakfast in the sitting room when she stepped in.

'Up so soon?' she asked, looking surprised and a flicker passed over her face.

So his letter did ask to meet me Laura thought and shut her eyes.

'I sent the telegrams to Tsar Nicholas and Kaiser Wilhelm' she said. 'God help us all.'

Ekaterina shut her eyes briefly. 'Come and eat Laura. What's done is done. We will leave in an hour.'

Laura did as she was told but could only manage a little to eat. Ekaterina noticed but said nothing, a painful and uneasy silence falling between them.

85

Laura sat quietly, watching out the window as the train hissed to a stop in Dalnerechensk's station. She had been listless for three days on the journey home, and as much as Ekaterina had tried to keep her mind off things she had slept and eaten less and less as they got closer to Liberty Valley. *They would have received the telegrams by now* Laura thought as the train puffed through Vsevolod's Gate. *No doubt all the Councilors are standing on the platform because they have received the answers.*

She could see several carriages and wondered if Olaf was on the platform, but couldn't see him because of the press of bodies. Her return to Dalnerechensk certainly had been different to the sad sending off. Before the train had even completely stopped Maksim and

Lev had pulled open the door, leaping aboard.

Laura sat waiting patiently. Grigory climbed on board too and took Ekaterina's hand, his eyes on the drama unfolding in front of him. Maksim held up a piece of paper with an angry flourish.

'I have a telegram, from Kaiser Wilhelm the Second which reads: Your gracious offer is gladly accepted. His Royal and Imperial Majesty will arrive in Dalnerechensk in seven days to discuss a treaty for the sale of tin. What have you done?!' Maksim cried, rounding on Laura.

'You have ruined centuries of diplomatic relations!' Lev added. 'You -'

'Do you want to be part of Russia or not?' she interrupted calmly.

The ministers blinked, caught off guard, then shot each other a veiled look.

'You are well aware that these matters are for private debate, not to be held in a riotous argument in the railway station. I assume you have already assembled to formulate plans to undo what damage you think I have done, and distressed my husband with this news' Laura went on calmly. 'I can assure you, gentlemen, the damage done was by Russia and not I. I will come directly to you in the Council Chambers as soon as we have arrived at the castle. Now if you will be so kind, I would like to get off the train.'

Maksim and Lev stepped back, dumbfounded with surprise. Grigory shot his wife a careful look, surprised at the air of strength and authority that had not been there before. There was a flood of thoughts competing on Ekaterina's face. Grigory squeezed her arm firmly, watching as Laura rose and strode determinedly past Lev and Maksim, smiling sweetly at Tsar Constantinovich as he reached out his hand to help her down from the train. 'Bring the parcel wrapped in brown paper with you when you come to the Council Chambers' Laura said over her shoulder to Maksim, knowing what kind of scowl that command would bring to his face.

She stepped down to the platform and Tsar Constantinovich drew her hand through his elbow, leading her to a waiting carriage.

'Hello Olaf' Laura smiled, seeing him standing beside the royal carriage, waiting patiently. 'It is nice to see a face without a scowl at my arrival. How are the kittens?'

'Inquisitive' he smiled. 'Anna is tearing her hair out.'

Laura's smile deepened and she took his hand, stepping up into the carriage. Tsar Constantinovich followed her, as did Ekaterina and Grigory. There was a strained politeness in their silence as they made their way up the hill to the castle, and Laura wondered just how hard Grigory was fighting the urge to pummel her and Ekaterina for information.

True to her word, when the carriage stopped she stepped out, thanking Olaf for his hand and went inside the castle, going straight to the Council Chambers, traveling cloak and all. Tsar Constantinovich followed her in, as did Grigory. The old Tsar sat in Aleksei's chair and Laura stood by it, waiting for the other ministers to join them.

Maksim dropped the brown package of newspapers on the table and sat, uncaring that the Princess was still standing. Other ministers eyed him, but none were quite so brave as to copy him. Ivan Gogol quickly retrieved several pieces of paper from a cabinet that stood in the room and opened a bottle of ink, ready to take the notes of this monumental confrontation. Laura noticed one or two sheets already had writing on them and she wondered what the ministers had decided in her absence.

She looked at Tsar Constantinovich.

'May I begin Your Majesty?' she asked quietly.

He nodded, and she eyed the ministers, masking her distaste at Maksim's behaviour carefully behind decorum then bade the remaining members of the council sit.

'My dear gentlemen, did none of you think to question the information Russia sends you?'

There was a stunned silence. Ministers looked at each other carefully. Laura went on regardless, unwrapping the newspapers and pushing copies at various ministers.

'Imagine my surprise then gentlemen, when I read several newspapers printed in French and Russian that confirms that what we know for fact, is a lie.'

'Ridiculous!' Maksim said, eyeing the Princess arrogantly. 'Russia has been our ally for hundreds of years! -'

'Russia has been bleeding us dry for hundreds of years!' she said, suddenly angry. 'She was never an ally, she sent a soldier to crush Vsevolod's town out of existence four hundred years ago! We are three valleys of irritation to Russia. She was forced to recognise us in Vsevolod's treaty but if Dalnerechensk collapses there will be nothing *to* recognise! She knows the tin is the only thing that keeps us alive! She has deliberately devalued it to starve us out, to beg for Russia to save us!'

'If you break the treaty Russia will invade!' Lev cried.

'And what is to stop Russia invading anyway? That was made plainly obvious when *Knjaz* Rurik was here. Russia is making her move to drive us out completely. But she is weak, she is plagued by internal strife -'

'We are surrounded by Russia!' Valentin Gogol cried. 'You cannot sell the tin to Germany! Russia will wipe us out before one scrap of metal leaves Dalnerechensk. You are risking a *war!*'

'Russia was defeated by Japan!' Laura said angrily. 'Great Mother Russia had her entire naval fleet destroyed by a land smaller than England! What little that is left has already mutinied. Germany is new and powerful. She is the height of industrialisation; they would be very grateful for our tin.'

'And how would you ensure our tin reached Germany across Western Russia?' Nicholas asked.

'It is not my intention to send it to Germany' she said bluntly, and explained what she planned to do. 'Trust me gentlemen' she said when she had finished. 'Dalnerechensk will not concede to Russia, I swear it.'

The arguments wandered back and forward for nearly an hour till the Councilors realised what she and Ekaterina already knew. To do nothing would damn the Principality. To begin this could end in a war encompassing the four greatest nations in Europe. But it could also save Dalnerechensk. There was no other course of action.

'These are high stakes indeed' Nicholas said quietly. 'And as you have said, Germany may be young and strong, but she is also isolated. Kaiser Wilhelm may simply refuse because he will realise it will put him in direct conflict with all of Europe. He may want a war, but will he want a war he cannot win?'

'I do not think she will remain isolated in Europe' Laura said. 'If I knew three great powers had united to surround me I would look for alliances too. Firstly, with my German-speaking neighbour, the Austro-Hungarian Empire. Then perhaps with Italy. She too is young and newly formed, Kaiser Wilhelm will find an understanding there I think.'

There was a silence. It was desperate. They all knew that. One detail still annoyed Grigory.

'Why so soon Your Highness? Aleksei is still not well, indeed he has almost relapsed with this latest information. The stress could inflame the ulcer. Would it not be better to wait until he is well?'

'I fear for Dalnerechensk if we do' she said quietly. 'We will tear ourselves apart with revolution if we do nothing. Nikita will return, with his army, to seize the mines whether we agree or not. He serves a mistress that has just been defeated and humiliated in war and paralysed with internal strife. She will desperately want to regain what she has lost, or if not, other territory to appease her. We cannot wait.'

'Who will argue the treaty?' Nicholas asked.

'I will' Laura answered quietly.

*

Ekaterina was pacing nervously in Laura's rooms, still wearing her travelling cloak. Laura pushed open her door, pulling off her grey cloak and dropping it on the couch.

'What did the Council say?' Ekaterina asked, coming to Laura and grabbing her hands nervously.

'They are not happy' Laura sighed. 'I think they will declare their feelings once it is done, but they know this is desperate.'

'Oh Laura,' Ekaterina breathed. 'Do you think it'll work?'

She shut her eyes, too frightened of the answer.

'Come, I will need your help' Laura said, changing the subject. 'I must have dresses in the colours of Russia and Germany. I will wear Romanov colours first, a yellow gown with black under skirts and white piping and trim, I will wear diamonds too, but I must look prettier in the Prussian colours, a white dress with black sashes and trim, and dark sapphires or black diamonds' Laura mused out loud, thinking furiously. 'And I must serve a national dish for each day, what do you recommend?'

'Frankfurters and vodka' Ekaterina grinned.

Laura laughed, smiling at her friend.

'Forgive me Laura, I'll bid you goodnight, I want to see my husband' Ekaterina said, squeezing her hand gently.

'Of course' she smiled, watching her slip quickly out the door, wistful they felt so strongly for each other.

She made up her mind and strode across the corridor to Aleksei's chambers. He was awake and dressed.

'Aleksei!' she gasped. 'You should not be up, go to bed.' she said firmly, coming forward to unbutton his shirt.

'I have a telegram' he said, halfheartedly deflecting her attentions.

'It is our last chance Aleksei, I am sure of it. Kaiser Wilhelm and -'

'It is from Marie Varennikova' he interrupted. 'It mentions an indiscretion with Baron Fredrik von Schmidt -' he stopped, pushing back his hurt.

'The woman you didn't marry, who is still in love with you, the woman as ugly as a horse sends you slander about me because she knows her husband does not love her, because she knows he only married her for her money' Laura said, pushing away his hands and continuing to unbutton his shirt. 'I'm surprised; we have so much in common…' she trailed off dryly.

'You are not a horse' Aleksei interrupted.

'Of course not, you ride your horses' she said, yanking open his shirt.

He gasped, shocked and amused at her words. He drew his breath in, noticing the pretty flush in her cheeks, roused by her boldness. Encouraged by that look Laura reached back and undid the back of her dress, pulling it off her.

'I desire you' she said.

She shut her eyes, stepping closer to him, resting her head on his shoulder, sighing as his arms came round her. Aleksei stroked her hair and her shoulders, shutting his eyes too.

'Marie told me about Alexander Andrei' she sighed, and felt him stiffen. 'She told me he was mad, she said you were mad, and that you would not bed me because our children would all be idiots' she sighed, tilting her face up to him, noticing the way his cheeks had darkened in rage. 'You are not your brother' she sighed softly. 'I do not think you are mad Aleksei. It is only the terrible, impossible situation you found yourself in.

'This gamble, the stakes are so high, it is desperate, desperate…' she trailed off, shutting her eyes tightly. 'But if it works…' she breathed, opening her eyes. 'If it works, if Tsar Nicholas realises he can no longer starve us out, if he realises that others are willing to fight for us…' she sighed. 'Dalnerechensk will prosper again, her citizens will be happy and well fed, and they will praise you for their deliverance.

'You will grow well as this terrible stress falls away, no more juggling money, robbing it from one need to pay another, and we will spend the time we need to together. In the winters we will hitch the sleigh and ride laughing through the fields, and in the summers you will take our sons to the little stone bridge and teach them to fish, and I will sit on the banks and teach our daughters to embroider, and then you and I will ride to the glen by the waterfall where on the warm grass I will make you forget all about your stables…' she trailed off, smiling as she felt him stir.

She pushed his shirt off his shoulders, reaching behind her to help him undo the laces for her corset.

'I want to bear you' she said, kissing his neck. 'I want to bear your sons.'

'How many will I have?' he asked quietly, stripping away the corset, throwing it onto the floor.

'Hundreds!' she promised, feeling his lips close on hers hungrily. 'All healthy and grand -' she stopped, unable to talk for the press of his mouth.

Aleksei lifted her then stopped, grunting in pain, letting her go quickly, pressing his hand to his stomach. Quickly Laura ran to his bedside table and measured a dose of laudanum for him, bringing it back. He tried to wave it away but she insisted, pushing it into his hand. He sighed bitterly and swallowed it, shutting his eyes.

Laura helped him to his bed, pulling off his boots when he lay back then joined him as he groaned, the drug's effects washing over him. She lay quietly beside him, resting her head on his chest, feeling his arms slide round her. Aleksei kissed the top of her head, lingering.

'I love you' he whispered quietly.

'We will survive this Aleksei' she said gently. 'Don't take a mistress, my heart cannot break any more times.'

He was silent. Laura planted a kiss on his chest and shut her eyes, letting sleep claim her.

86

Laura entered the Council Chambers early, noticing most of the advisors had already arrived. Tsar Constantinovich was absent, and Laura was slightly disappointed, she would have liked his quiet support here faced by a contingent of scared and angry old men.

Valentin Gogol held up another telegram.

'Tsar Nicholas and Kaiser Wilhelm will be arriving on the same day' he said, disapprovingly. 'Do you want them on the same train together realising that they are being manipulated? Perhaps giving them time to come to their own agreement?'

'Would you like them to discover it together when they walk into the Council Chambers and take their anger out on us?' Laura said sitting in Aleksei's chair, motioning for the ministers to sit. '*Prinz* Sebastian of Bayern assures me Kaiser Wilhelm has a cantankerous temper and I have no desire to be yelled at anymore' she shot her ministers a look. 'Tell me of Tsar Nicholas the Second.'

There was a sullen silence from some of the members. Ivan cleared his throat.

'I have heard he has had an excellent education' he said. 'He has excelled in History and speaks French, German and English. They say his English is so good he can fool an Oxford professor into mistaking him for an Englishman.'

'His memory is unusually keen' Nicholas said.

'He is terribly indecisive' Lev said. 'He is influenced by his wife.'

There were chuckles and a few derisive comments from the chauvinist elite in Dalnerechensk.

'He is a playboy' Maksim said dismissively. 'Too busy watching the clock in the meetings of the Imperial Council to be bothered to learn the art of politics.'

'He is well travelled and one of the richest men in the world' Nicholas continued. 'In fact he got his dislike of Japan on a visit there, long before his empire clashed with theirs.'

'He still has the scar on his forehead from the assassination attempt' Lev said. 'Attacked by a sword-wielding man because he had visited a temple no unbeliever had visited before. Were it not for his cousin, Prince George of Greece and Denmark he would not be alive.'

'What a shame' Maksim said dryly.

'It is said he rides well, and dances quite gracefully' Ivan said.

'What good does this all do?' Maksim blurted out, frustrated. 'You should send Kaiser Wilhelm a telegram saying there has been an embarrassing mistake -'

'Your opposition is duly noted Maksim' she said coolly. 'But I assure you it is necessary. I cannot undo what I have done now. To do so will destroy Dalnerechensk. So perhaps we should be focusing on what we can do to make it work. If I know their likes, their temperaments, their dislikes; it will help me. It is our only chance to make it work.'

They were quiet then reluctantly began to reveal more details of Tsar Nicholas' personality. Laura listened quietly, asking questions when she needed information clarified.

'Your Highness,' Ivan suddenly said quietly, interrupting them. 'What are we going to tell the people? If there is unrest or a miner strike or a rebellion while they are here it will not be to our advantage.'

Laura was quiet for a minute. 'We must make it absolutely clear that there are to be no demonstrations whatsoever when the Emperors are here' she said. 'We will need to tell the people that the Emperors are coming.'

'We cannot tell them their visit concerns the sale of the mines, or anything of the kind' Grigory said. 'That will start a mad panic, it would cause what we want to avoid.'

'True' she said. 'But we must tell them something. Perhaps a state visit, something festive' she mused out loud.

'That will be a weak excuse' Maksim said. 'The people will not be fooled.'

'Very well, Maksim you will be in charge of a suitable excuse that will be acceptable to the people' Laura said sweetly. 'The streets must be flooded with news of their arrival, and what behaviour is not acceptable while the Emperors are in Dalnerechensk. If there is any civil disobedience it will not be tolerated.'

'And what punishment will there be for those that do not obey?' Lev challenged.

Laura was quiet. It was a part of ruling that she didn't like. She knew the punishment had to be severe enough to deter them but not so severe that they would rise up in revolt against the monarchy.

'What do you suggest gentlemen?'

'Confiscate their property' Lev said.

'Too severe!' Laura warned. 'They have little left and will not take kindly to that being taken away from them as well.'

'Imprisonment' suggested Ivan.

'Too lenient' she sighed.

'A fine' Maksim said. 'They can little afford it. Thirty rubles.'

'That is too high' Ivan said. 'A week's wage? It is even more if you are a miner!'

'It is right' Laura said quietly. 'I would grumble unhappily about a weeks' worth of lost wage, but I would not risk it. If it were less I would risk it, if it were more, I would revolt, and that is what we want to avoid.'

The ministers sat back and argued, the morning dragging on as they made preparations for the arrival of the two most important men in Europe. Laura's temper frayed as the bickering continued but she did her best to hold on to her composure, delegating the overseeing of menial jobs to the ministers that annoyed her the most.

Finally she called an end to the meeting. Some issues were not resolved and some had not been raised but she was tired of them all, and knew they could always argue about it tomorrow. The ministers stood and bowed, looking unhappy. Laura didn't care and slipped out of the room, heading up to her chambers.

Anna greeted her warmly, happy to have her back from the Austro-Hungarian Empire, teasing a piece of string across the carpet where the four kittens pounced and jumped around, their tails puffed up in delighted fun. Laura returned the greeting, her tongue wanting to blurt out everything but knew she couldn't, as much as she was fond of Anna she couldn't risk the possibility that she might gossip.

Instead she dressed in her riding habit and slipped back downstairs, finding her stallion already saddled in his stall, waiting for her.

'Ah Olaf, I see you desire to escape from your duties as much as I do' she smiled.

He said nothing but boosted her up onto her mount, swinging himself up onto the saddled mare. Laura led them down Castle Street, noticing how few people looked at her anymore, and while they dipped curtseys and bows there was no respect in the movement, only hollow compliance. She had to force herself to resist the urge to gallop away into the Hunting Forest.

Olaf rode beside her, eyeing her surreptitiously as they left the wide cart track, heading into the quiet of the trees. *She's thinner, her jaw is sharper* he thought as they rode.

'Olaf, swear you'll defend me, no matter what happens' she suddenly said, reaching across to grab his hand.

The mare snorted as her grip pulled up on the reins. Olaf opened his mouth to swear and was cut off as she poured out her fears, the hand on his trembling. She told him everything, Russia's deception, what she had learned in the newspapers, her desperate gamble, the preparations they were making, the intent to inform the people and the punishment for lawlessness while the Emperors were in Dalnerechensk.

'Olaf!' she stopped, shutting her eyes. 'Can I do it Olaf? Can I bend two men to my will, can I save Dalnerechensk?'

He unfolded his hand from the rein and took her hand gently, feeling how small and delicate her fingers were in his large paw.

'You will charm them' he said quietly. 'You charmed Aleksei into damning Dalnerechensk for you. And I will defend you, no matter what happens.'

She looked away, shutting her eyes.

'Thank you Olaf' she said softly. 'You can't know what that means to me.'

She squeezed his hand then withdrew, sighing gently.

87

Ivan touched her arm lightly, startling her out of her reverie. She blushed prettily and quickly scanned her slate, wondering where they were up to in the lesson.

'Your Highness' he said gently. 'You have not spoken for ten minutes, and you are pale, are you ill?'

Cold fear slid over her and she glanced at the door to her sitting room, wondering if anyone had heard it. *If they believed both of us were ill…* she trailed off, not wanting to think about that. There would be nothing to stop the revolution. She shut her eyes tightly.

'Am I doing the right thing?' she asked, terrified.

'You are doing the only thing' he answered, folding his hand over hers. 'Your Highness, the Councilors support you in this. It is only that they are frightened of the outcome, of how much is at stake if something goes wrong. They do admire you and the efforts you have made in the Chambers; despite what they say sometimes' he managed a small smile.

She smiled faintly too.

'Your Highness, you are so pale…' he trailed off.

'I am worrying myself ill with this' she confessed. 'I cannot eat, I cannot sleep -'

'Your Highness, you should let your husband negotiate this -'

'No Ivan' she said quietly, firmly. 'I mean to insult Tsar Nicholas, to smile and call him a coward, to flatter his German cousin until he is angry enough to make a decision about the tin. It will only work because an insult is forgivable if it comes from a pretty smile' she dropped her eyes. 'I fear Aleksei is not reckless enough, and he worries Ivan, it drives him -' she stopped, avoiding the word. 'I don't want to make him ill anymore' she finished.

Ivan was silent, thinking.

'Then you must make every effort to stay alluring' he said. 'You are attractive, Your Highness,' he said, blushing, 'but you are growing thin. Even if you cannot taste your food for fear you must eat. It will keep your strength up and your body healthy. I would also suggest you see Doctor Pushkin for a tonic for your nerves.'

'I cannot' she said quietly. 'The Principality has not seen Aleksei for weeks, and when they hear that his poor American wife is quaffing tonics for nerves there will be no end of unrest and rumour. It would bring in to question the succession to the throne and a whole myriad of other grievances. Even enough to risk a thirty ruble fine. I cannot ask him for that.'

Ivan was silent, knowing she was right. Then he said:

'My mother has an old recipe for a calming tea, Trauma Tea she called it. A very soothing blend of mildly anaesthetising plants. It will make you somewhat drowsy, but will soothe the anxiety. Would you like me to bring you the recipe?'

'That is most kind of you Ivan' she smiled.

'I would also suggest you spend some afternoons with Countess Ivanova, teasing each other until you laugh and sparkle as you did when your Polish nieces and nephew were here' he went on. 'There is an alluring charm about a woman amused.'

The blush deepened in his cheeks. She laughed then, unable to help but feel amused at his words.

'Excellent' he said. 'Now, we were discussing the declensions Your Highness.'

Laura groaned but forced herself to concentrate on her lesson.

88

Laura stripped off her dress, pulling the strings of her corset tighter, wondering where Anna was. She had been gone all day, and part of Laura was jealous, remembering the dreamy smile on Anna's face, thinking she had spent the day with her lover instead of with her. She could have done with Anna's gossip today.

She was listless, so listless Aleksei had sent her from him when she had read to him, unable to sit still and pacing around his room. She had returned to her room and paced some more, picking up some embroidery to occupy her and then tossed it away again, unable to concentrate. *I hope Ivan remembers to bring the recipe tomorrow* she thought, tying her strings firmly then pushed up the shapely mounds of her breasts.

A quiet cough behind her interrupted her thoughts.

'How kind of you to look in on me now you have finished with your paramour!' Laura teased, turning to eye her maid.

It was Olaf, his face turned away from her. She gasped, aware she was standing in her corset and petticoats, and clamped her hands over her breasts in shame.

'What are you doing here?' she asked, fright making her shrill.

'I have been at the pub' he answered, deeply embarrassed. 'There was no answer – I let myself in -' he stopped.

'Wait out there' Laura snapped, scared and angry, gesturing to her sitting room.

Olaf did, closing the door behind him. Laura put her face in her hands and took a shaky breath then pulled on her day dress again, yanking open her door.

'What is so urgent it could not wait?' she snapped.

Olaf's anger rose.

'Would you like me to stand outside your door and knock while everyone can see the stable groom by the *Velikaja Knjaginja*'s rooms? You don't need any more rumours.'

Her cheeks paled and darkened with rage at the same time. Olaf had never seen anything like it before.

'What did they say at the pub?' she asked faintly, her voice barely slipping past the restraint she had on herself.

'Aleksei hides himself in his castle because he is afraid of being assassinated. His wife goes riding every afternoon when he comes out of Council Chambers to avoid him. They say there will be no heir. -'

'What do they say about the Emperors?' she broke in.

'Plenty' he answered. 'Half say the Treaty of Dalnerechensk is being renegotiated. Some want to believe Aleksei is trying to help them. Half say the mines are being sold to Russia, or to Germany, or being sold to Russia and then to Germany. Some say that Russia is absorbing Dalnerechensk into her territories again, but no one is really sure why Germany is here. They are suspicious about the fine for disruption. It makes the absorption into Russia theory more plausible.'

'Will they revolt?' she asked, clenching her fists tight.

'I don't know' he answered truthfully.

Laura shut her eyes tighter, clenching her fists till her knuckles were white, shuddering with the tension. Olaf suddenly took her by the arms and pushed her to sit on the chaise lounge.

'You are going to shake yourself apart' he said quietly.

'What am I going to do?' she moaned.

'Act like you've already done it' he answered, pouring her a small sherry from the decanter that stood on the small table near the fireplace.

He gave the sherry to her, watching her swallow it all then unconsciously lick her lips at the burn of it. The firelight glistened in the moisture her lick had left behind. He shut his eyes quickly.

'*Tsesarevna*, if you are confident that you will not possibly fail, then how can you?' he said gently. 'Do not focus on the *what ifs*. Focus on the *it wills*, and make it happen.'

She shut her eyes tightly then sighed, letting go of all her fear.

'They will not revolt' she said softly. 'They will wait' she looked at Olaf. 'Wait to see what the Kaiser is here for.'

She stood and crossed to the fire, carefully putting delicate glass back on the silver tray that sat on the small table.

'Thank you Olaf' she said softly.

The groom took his leave of her. Laura slipped into her room and shut the door behind her before stripping again, pulling out the beautiful white silk that had made Fredrik fall hopelessly in love with her. She fixed her hair and dabbed on perfume, aware she was just going through the motions, she had no desire to sit with the court, no desire to eat.

She pulled Aleksei's emeralds out of the jewelry box that sat in her dressing room, fastening it around her neck. She had hardly worn the pretty gems, ever since she had realised it was the only thing of worth in Dalnerechensk. She looked at herself carefully in the mirror, stroking the way the emeralds dripped down her throat. *You are of worth in Dalnerechensk* she told herself. *You will do this and Aleksei will chide you for wearing such poor jewels, and you will answer.* But my love, they are good for rough play with our children.

She managed a smile at that silliness and patted her coifed hair carefully before slipping out of her room. There was a gasp when she stepped into the dining hall and she made her way to her seat beside Aleksei's empty chair, greeting the few that sat at the table.

Ivan sat opposite her, talking to her politely, a slight pink in his cheeks. She smiled, aware of how attractive she was in the silk, and did her best to make her way steadfastly through a meal she couldn't taste. *It was all very well to know she was pretty; it would not give her the confidence she would need. Not with Ivan holding himself with perfect decorum* she thought.

Nikita would have flirted part of her said. *He would have looked at you through his lashes with that raw desire, his breath hard in his chest, pushing you up against the door –* she stopped herself. *What of Aleksei?* she wondered. If he saw her in this dress – *it was all he could do to keep from having her right there!* Ekaterina laughed in her ear again.

If he saw her he just might… She smiled then. *Sex was power and power was politics* Ekaterina had told her. *I will show Aleksei this dress and after a night of sex I will take that power and play politics!*

'Music!' she called, hiding her laugh, wondering if the musicians had always been there, sitting silently.

When was the last time I heard music? When was the last time it had played here? She didn't remember. Ivan stood and bowed to her, then walked around the table to take her hand. *How silly it seemed* she thought dreamily as she danced, noticing the way Tatiana and Natasha eyed her unhappily.

Ivan held her as they danced, and she could hear his breathing quicken as the dance stole their energy. The sound made her think of Aleksei's breathless lovemaking and she stopped suddenly, pulling away from Ivan.

'Court is dismissed' she said, then turned and ran up to the second floor, pushing open Aleksei's door.

He was asleep, snoring gently. She called his name quietly but there was no response. Cheated and angry Laura let herself out, shutting the door hard behind her.

89

The butterflies were panicking in her stomach when she woke, making her feel sick with dread and worry. She sat up, folding her arms across her middle, knowing that today of all days she could not be at the mercy of these feelings. She took a deep breath, expanding her lungs till they pressed down on her stomach and forced the butterflies to stop.

They rose again when she let her breath out so she stood, finding things to keep her occupied. The sun was coming up and she would need to be at the station soon as the train was due to arrive shortly. She paced, running through the list of things to do today, the phrases and topics of conversation that she would raise with the Emperors, her thoughts interrupted with Anna's soft tap on her sitting room door.

She let herself in, smiling shyly at the Princess. Laura greeted her absently, crossing into her dressing room, combing her hair with her fingers.

'Oh Anna,' she moaned when the girl followed her in. 'I don't think I can eat; I am so full of nerves I don't believe it will stay down!'

'I will run you an extra hot bath this morning, and fix the Gogol's tea to settle your stomach

Your Highness' she said, quickly filling up kettles of water to heat over the fire then went down to the kitchen for the teapot.

Laura checked her face carefully in the mirror for imperfections. She was pleased to see there was not a blemish and no telltale marks under her eyes to attest to the amount of sleep she had lost lately. She stroked the skin on her cheek and noted with satisfaction it felt as smooth as it looked, turning her head this way and that to see her skin catch the glow of the morning sun.

She was attractive and had practiced behaving confidently, knowing it was a strange aphrodisiac that men found absolutely irresistible. She had carefully watched the way Ekaterina turned men around her finger with the right look and the right smile. It looked easy, but Laura wondered if it would be enough to turn the two most powerful men in Europe. *They are still just men* she told herself, but it wouldn't stop the horrible butterfly feeling.

Anna returned with a pot of tea balanced on a silver tray. She set it on the table beside the chaise lounge, pouring Laura a cup. She took it from her and sipped the slightly bitter brew as she watched Anna disappear into the dressing room to run some cold water into the bath. Laura drained the cup, fanning her mouth as the hot liquid burnt it, then poured herself another, drinking that as well.

Anna checked the boiling water on the fire then used her skirt to protect her hand as she lifted the hot kettles, pouring the water into the bath. Laura followed her into the dressing room and stripped off her nightdress.
'Anna I must look heartbreaking today' she said, sitting in the tub and pulling her knees up. 'Whatever tricks you know of to make someone beautiful use all of them. Twice' she added.

Anna giggled then poured a little of Laura's perfume into the water. The room quickly filled with the steamy aroma and Laura breathed deeply, pleased. Anna washed her hair, rubbing in oils to clean it and bring it to a high glossy colour, massaging her shoulders and back to ease the tension she felt there. Laura moaned at the exquisite sensations and began to feel drowsy, letting herself relax.
'I wish my skin was as good as yours, Your Highness' Anna said wistfully, knowing nothing bolstered a woman's confidence more than knowing others envied her. 'Everyone is livid with envy that your hair is so glossy.'

Laura smiled, standing up in the tub. Anna folded a towel around her and Laura stepped out, seating herself at the dressing table. Anna combed out her hair, drying it with a towel and pinning it up in a simple, pretty coif. Laura shut her eyes as Anna combed her hair, liking the sensations on her scalp and shoulders. She sighed softly when Anna was done and dried herself carefully, pulling on her soft chemise. The tea was working wonderfully, and Laura had to caution herself not to become so lethargic she fell asleep.

Anna laced her into a corset tightly and helped her to pull on a beautiful emerald dress, smoothing the bodice down against her.
'You look beautiful' she sighed enviously.
'Thank you Anna. Take the teapot down to the kitchen, I must see to some last minute preparations' she said.

Anna dipped a curtsey then left. Laura slipped down the stairs and crossed the courtyard

318

to the stables, looking around for the carriage and the plumes for the bridles, hoping they were all clean and gleaming.

Olaf was not in the stables. She spied a flight of stairs at the far end of the room and climbed them into the loft, eyeing her surroundings. The stairs reached a small square landing on which sat a plain chair. Olaf's livery jacket hung over the back and a pair of polished boots stood on the seat. From the landing she turned and stepped up into the loft itself.

It was large and warm; heated by a crackling fireplace glowing in the warm light slanting through the windows. Over the fire a black pot bubbled sloppily and the smell of oats filled the room. A bed was pushed against the wall and a narrow wardrobe stood beside it. A small table stood between the bed and the fire, two small stools pushed under it and a wooden bowl sat on the rough top, a bent metal spoon beside it.

At the opposite end of the loft stood Olaf, stripped to his waist, standing in front of a small wash stand and peering into a small mirror, shaking his cut-throat razor in the bowl of cold water. Flecks of shaving foam stuck to his cheeks and he turned his face this way and that, catching sight of Laura's reflection.

'*Tsesarevna*?' he asked, surprised. 'You should not be up here.' He picked up a rough towel and patted his face clean of shaving foam.

'Perhaps I wanted to catch my groom in his underwear' she answered dryly. 'As such, I have decided I shall do exactly what I please today.' She lifted the livery jacket from the chair and crossed the loft. 'Put on your uniform, Tsar Nicholas the Second and Kaiser Wilhelm the Second are arriving today. As it looks to be a nice day we will need the open carriage and -'

'*Tsesarevna*' he interrupted with a small smile, tugging on his white shirt. 'Anna will make you the tea to calm your nerves; you do not need to be here.'

'I have already had a whole pot' she sighed. 'I'm afraid if I drink anymore I'll fall asleep standing up!'

Olaf laughed and left the towel bunched on the wash stand, crossing to the fire, swiping the wooden bowl from the table as he did so, spooning in a helping of oats from the thickly bubbling pot, dropping the ladle back in the oats.

'Have you eaten *Tsesarevna*? Those butterflies will drive you mad. Sit and eat, I have plenty.'

'No one has plenty' she said absently, folding the jacket and putting it on his bed, pulling out one of the stools and sitting at his table.

Olaf put the warm bowl of oats in front of her and quickly fetched another from a small cupboard under his wash stand. Laura dipped her spoon into the oats, tasting the simple meal. She breathed deeply, smiling, her eyes wandering around the room, reminded of her own simple living in the canvas tents of Texas.

Life was so much simpler then she thought, licking her lip, distracted. They had had very little, but Luke had always made sure they had food on their table, and no one had gone without. *No one had been reduced to stealing or risking a flogging.* She stopped, dropping her spoon back in her bowl, folding her hands tightly in her lap. Across the table from her Olaf eyed her carefully, his spoon poised halfway between the bowl and his mouth.

'Olaf,' she started then stopped, her cheeks draining of colour. He set his spoon down in the bowl and sat watching her. 'Do you know about the hog?' she whispered, chewing her lip.

'Did – did Fedor obey Aleksei? Did – did he -'

'*Nyet*' he soothed. 'He didn't harm a single one of them.'

Laura put her face in her hands, weeping with relief and guilt.

'It was my fault' she sobbed. 'Only I know how poor everyone is, she gave me that tin statue, it couldn't go unrewarded. It was all I could think of -'

'No one is blaming you' he said quietly, fishing out a handkerchief for her.

She took it, thanking him sheepishly, dabbing the folded fine material to her eyes.

'This is all going to make me go mad, never mind the butterflies' she said, wiping away more tears. 'I don't envy Aleksei or -' she stopped. 'Olaf? How long have you worked here? Have you ever heard the name Alexander Andrei?'

He paused. 'Everyone knows the name Alexander Andrei' he said quietly.

'He was Aleksei's brother wasn't he. The real *Tsesarevich* of Dalnerechensk. That's what Tsar Constantinovich meant when he said Aleksei was never meant to rule this. -'

'*Tsesarevna*' Olaf broke in gently, stilling her.

'Is he dead?' she blurted out.

'Maybe' he said. 'There was no funeral for him, only one for the Tsaritsa. Unless they buried them together, they always said he was very fond of his mother. There are rumours he lives in Siberia like a monk in the wilderness, but others say the Vakhtangovs are so embarrassed that they have locked him in a secret room in the castle because he now is no better than a child, only pushing his food or a new toy through the door before shutting it again, terrified someone will see him.'

Laura unfolded the handkerchief to dab her eyes and a pressed flower that had been hidden in the folds fell onto the table. It was one of the national flowers of Dalnerechensk, and Laura remembered Aleksei had plucked one of the flowers from her hair and given it to Olaf on her wedding day. She eyed him, aware of the way his cheeks had darkened.

She reached out and touched the flower, stroking a dry petal gently. She was surprised Olaf had kept this memento. *He could barely look at me* she reminded herself. *He thinks I am attractive.* She smiled softly and folded the flower back into the handkerchief and smoothed the initials embroidered onto the material before handing it back to the groom.

He said nothing, his cheeks still dark, and tucked the handkerchief back inside his shirt.

'Thank you for breakfast Olaf' she said quietly. 'Hitch the open carriage and put on your livery jacket, the Emperors will be here soon.'

She stood, pushed the stool back under the table carefully, stopping when she reached the head of the stairs.

'You must bow for them today, and every day they are here' she said, turning to look at him. 'I came to beseech you Olaf, as much as I enjoy your charming ways they cannot take offense at any slight. You must bow' she sighed then turned and slipped back down into the stables below.

90

Laura resisted the urge to smooth down her dress, to pat her hair quickly as the train rumbled to a stop, hissing as the engineer eased the pressure in the boilers. She stood on the station feeling terribly alone and paraded, aware of all the eyes on her. The station was momentarily engulfed in a clammy, hot cloud that hid the crowds of people, the open carriage and the shining guards of Dalnerechensk, mounted on elegant horses, their helms glowing in the warm midday sun.

The crowd of Dalnerechenskers behind their protective line was relatively quiet and well behaved. *They are probably more curious than anything else* Laura thought. She forced her fingers to stop from straying to pluck nervously at the blue sash she wore, the sash she had sewn for Aleksei's wedding regalia, and resisted the urge to play with the demure emerald necklace she wore at her throat.

The steam evaporated from the station and she smiled radiantly at the waiting train. Peter Kaminin stepped forward, resplendent in his uniform, and opened the door to the royal carriage, offering his hand to those inside. There was a hesitation then Tsar Nicholas stepped onto the platform, followed by Kaiser Wilhelm. They looked a little sour, and Laura wondered if they had fought on the train ride into the city. Neither wore faintly amused smiles that meant they had conspired together to make Dalnerechensk pay for her trickery.

Laura stepped forward and curtseyed deeply before then, knowing both pairs of eyes followed the descent of her curved breasts, taking a deep breath for her introductions.
'His Royal and Imperial Majesty Tsar Nicholas the Second, Emperor and Autocrat of All the Russias; Tsar of Moscow, Kiev, Vladimir, Novgorod, Kazan, Astrakhan, Poland, Siberia, the Tauric Chersonese and Georgia; Lord of Pskov; Grand Prince of Smolensk, Lithuania, Volhynia, Podolia, and Finland; Prince of Estonia, Livonia, Courland and Semigalia, Samogatia, Belostok, Karelia, Tver, Yugria, Perm, Viatka, Bulgaria and other lands; Lord and Grand Prince of Nizhnyi Novgorod and Chernigov; Ruler of Riazan, Polotsk, Rostov, Yaroslavl', Belo-Ozero, Udoria, Obdoria, Kondia, Vitebsk, Mstislavl, and all the Northern Lands; Lord and Sovereign of the Ivorian, Kartalinian and Karbadinian lands and of the Armenian Provinces; Hereditary Lord and Suzerain of the Circassian Princes and Highland Princes and others; Lord of Turkestan; Heir to the throne of Norway; Duke of Schleswig-Holstein, Stormarn, the Dithmarschen and Oldenburg!' she announced to the crowds. 'And His Royal and Imperial Majesty Wilhelm the Second, German Emperor and King of Prussia, Margrave of Brandenburg, Burgrave of Nuremberg, Count of Hohenzollern, Duke of Silesia and of the County of Glatz, Grand Duke of the Lower Rhine and of Posen, Duke in Saxony, of Angria, of Westphalia, of Pomerania and of Lunenburg, Duke of Schleswig, of Holstein and of Crossen, Duke of Magdeburg, of Bremen, of Guilderland and of Jülich, Cleves and Berg, Duke of the Wends and the Kashubians, of Lauenburg and of Mecklenburg, Landgrave of Hesse and in Thuringia, Margrave of Upper and Lower Lusatia, Prince of Orange, of Rugen, of East Friesland, of Paderborn and of Pyrmont, Prince of Halberstadt, of Münster, of Minden, of Osnabrück, of Hildesheim, of Verden, of Kammin, of Fulda, of Nassau and of Moers, Princely Count of Henneberg, Count of the Mark, of Ravensberg, of

Hohenstein, of Tecklenburg and of Lingen, Count of Mansfeld, of Sigmaringen and of Veringen, Lord of Frankfurt!'

She straightened, a small smile playing on her lips, pleased she had made it through their impressive lists of titles flawlessly.

'Welcome to Dalnerechensk!' she said then switched to French as it was the only language she knew as well as English as she came forward, clasping each of their hands and dipping another curtsey in front of each man, welcoming them again.

Both of them had enormous moustaches that ticked the back of her hand as they kissed her, thanking her for inviting them to Dalnerechensk. Kaiser Wilhelm grasped her hand with his right, holding a pair of elegant gloves in his left hand, hiding his disfigurement.

'Please follow me' she said with a smile, and led the men to the open carriage. Olaf stood beside the carriage and for a second Laura wondered if he was going to ignore her instructions. He looked uncomfortable in his uniform, but he bowed low then opened the door, holding out his hand for her.

Laura stepped in lightly, perching on the seat where a large basket of fresh oranges sat, opposite the two Emperors that climbed in behind her. She smiled sweetly, starting a charming discussion of the attractions in Dalnerechensk, diplomatically avoiding any mention of Vsevolod. The men began to relax and smile, pleased with her charming company, and began to exclaim politely at her words, and ask questions about the city.

Olaf climbed onto the driver's seat of the open carriage and Peter Kaminin remounted his horse at the head of the guard of honour. The ranks of mounted guard took up positions around the carriage, and Laura was glad to see that although the crowd blossomed after them, filling the platform of the station, there was not the desperate need to see the Emperors as there had been the need to see her when she arrived in Dalnerechensk.

The procession moved slowly off from the station, winding its way through all the streets in Dalnerechensk. Laura smiled prettily, calling hello to the people who stood on the street. Some called back, some threw flowers into the carriage, most waved, but a few did nothing, watching as the royals rode past.

'I must offer my personal congratulations on the birth of your son last year, Your Imperial Majesty' Laura suddenly said, smiling at Tsar Nicholas. 'We are most grieved to hear he is ill, and pray daily that he grows healthy and strong.'

'Thank you, your thoughts and prayers are most kind Your Highness' he answered.

'I must also congratulate you, Your Imperial Majesty, on Crown Prince William's upcoming marriage to Duchess Cecilie of Mecklenburg-Schwerin' Laura said, smiling at the Kaiser. 'You must be very proud!'

He chuckled and said he was, and the banter between them all bolstered Laura's confidence. They had warmed to her, listening pleasantly as she talked, asking questions and jesting diplomatically. They smiled at her as if she was a charming child, and it was clear that neither thought she was the one who had sent them the telegrams. She hoped they did think she was an innocent child because the next part was going to insult the Tsar greatly.

The mounted guard and carriage pulled to a stop and Laura could see that they had reached the hospital. Olaf leapt down from the seat and opened the carriage door, bowing deeply but awkwardly, then held out his hand for Laura. She passed him the large basket of oranges which he quickly switched into his other hand then stepped down from the carriage, balancing delicately on his arm.

Kaiser Wilhelm and Tsar Nicholas stepped down from the coach, eyeing their surroundings.

'I simply must show you the hospital we have here' Laura smiled. 'We are very proud of the highly specialised skills of our physicians and their innovative technological advancements. Will you accompany me?'

Her charming smile hid her thoughts. *They were specialised because they were adept at treating injuries that occurred in the mines and innovative because they had to save lives with the little resources they had.* The men decided not to let down their pretty host and Laura smiled gratefully, taking the heavy basket from Olaf.

'Allow me' Kaiser Wilhelm said, taking it from her, smiling.

She thanked him and led the men up the short pair of steps to the door of the hospital. Not to be outdone Tsar Nicholas opened the door for her and she flashed him a brilliant smile, greeting the hospital staff that stood in the wide reception room. Doctor Pushkin and Mother Matron swept low bows and curtsies to the newly arrived Royals.

Doctor Pushkin offered Laura his elbow and began a tour of the hospital in French, hesitant in his explanations as he was unfamiliar with the language he had not used since his school-boy days. The Emperors listened politely and Laura was pleased to see Doctor Pushkin was leading them through the warren of rooms and corridors to the children.

The excited chatter behind the door stopped as Doctor Pushkin opened the door. Voices called out and those that could walk rushed towards them happily. Some quickly remembered themselves and bowed deeply then rushed forward again, throwing their arms around Laura.

She hugged and kissed as many as she could, her royal guests momentarily forgotten, and Kaiser Wilhelm found himself set upon by children wanting oranges. They thanked him, dipping bows, and rushed back to beds to eat. In the silence that followed as they ate Laura explained quietly to the Emperors that they were the lucky survivors of a great tragedy.

The two men were quite moved by her dedication and her love for her subjects. She smiled sadly, turning away from the room, letting Doctor Pushkin lead them out.

'Will you read us a story Your Highness?' asked a voice beside them. They looked down to see a plucky boy in a wheelchair.

'Not today my dear boy' she smiled. 'But I will come back and read you a story soon, would you like that?'

Kaiser Wilhelm looked perplexed at the conversation and Tsar Nicholas graciously provided a translation.

'I wish I was leaving' the boy said suddenly. 'Mama cries all the time and I want the doctors to allow me to walk. I have to go back to the mines to help mama.'

The Tsar faulted in his translation, eyeing Laura. She ignored him for now, her attention on the boy.

'You're a good child, your mother will always be proud of you' she said quietly, ruffling his hair and kissing his head. 'Take the rest of the oranges to the others.' She took the basket from Wilhelm and gave it to him.

The boy placed it on his lap and wheeled away. Laura straightened up and turned to the two Emperors.

'What great tragedy did they survive?' Tsar Nicholas asked, suspicious.

'These children are survivors of a cave-in at the mines' She explained in French. 'Boris had his back broken in the accident, and no one has had the heart to tell him he will never walk again. He so wants to help his struggling family...' she trailed off, tears welling up in her eyes.

Tsar Nicholas looked embarrassed and Kaiser Wilhelm looked taken aback. *Tears were a treacherous manipulation, but I am pretty, and men fall over themselves to comfort a damsel in distress* Laura thought, and knew her carefully orchestrated insult had worked. She had shown Tsar Nicholas how much her people were suffering because of his deliberate devaluation of the tin and Kaiser Wilhelm a glimpse of being thought a savior, rescuing them from this dire situation. She pulled out a pretty lace handkerchief and dabbed her eyes surreptitiously, but obviously enough so that the men knew what she was doing.

She smiled sweetly again, apologising for her tears. Pushkin led them out of the hospital, bidding them a goodbye at the entrance. The mounted guard was still waiting, perfectly poised in the street despite the warmth of the day and the curious crowd that had gathered outside the hospital. Olaf bowed deeply again, opening the carriage door and offering his hand to Laura.

She climbed up and sat again, waiting for the Emperors to join her. She looked around for a topic of conversation and settled on the church she could see nearby, telling them about its design and architecture, and the Emperors were glad of the distraction. Laura let herself smile, enjoying their company, glad that the ride to the castle was almost over.

As her back was to the direction of the way they travelled Laura didn't notice Aleksei standing dressed on the steps of the castle, surrounded by ministers of the court, until the carriage and guard of honour stopped at the foot of the stairs. She hid her surprise carefully, smiling sweetly at him. He looked strained, and she wondered if his laudanum had worn off, leaving him at the mercy of his pain.

Olaf leapt down from the carriage and opened the door for them. Aleksei came down the stairs and offered his own hand to Laura and the two Emperors, welcoming them to his home. They called thanks and Laura slipped her arm through Aleksei's elbow, noticing how stiff he felt.

He led the way into the castle, taking over the duty as host from her, outlining the festivities that would take place that afternoon for the Emperors. Laura could do nothing but smile sweetly and behave as dutifully as she could, seething inside.

So he does think I have cuckolded him she thought angrily. *He is just as awkward as Tsar Nicholas; he is not reckless enough to risk everything; he must risk everything! If he does not ask for the highest price, all of this will be for nothing, and Dalnerechensk will still suffer!* She shut her eyes briefly, trying to get control.

Aleksei led them to the dining room and guided Laura to the chair beside his, bidding the two Tsars to sit on either side of them, in places of honour. Laura looked around, wondering where Tsar Constantinovich was, wondering how he would feel that the Tsar of Russia was sitting in his chair. Laura said nothing, keeping a pleasant conversation going, glad when she saw Ekaterina join them.

She introduced her friend to the two Emperors, watching the way she charmed the both of them delightedly, turning her face into Aleksei's neck.

'The laudanum has worn off, hasn't it' she whispered.

He didn't answer, but she saw the pinched look in his face. Laura called Anna over then sent to her to find Mikhail, to retrieve the laudanum from his room and administer a small dose in his drink. Anna scurried off and Mikhail soon returned, splashing a little of the drug in Aleksei's wine. He swallowed some of the diluted drug then pulled a face, refusing to drink any more. Laura didn't press him, mindful that they needed to keep the Emperors relaxed and entertained, and seeing a fight would not do that.

Aleksei ate with relish, and Laura realised it was the first meal that hadn't been especially prepared for him in weeks. She hoped the food would not upset his ulcer, and hoped his apparent gluttony would not be detrimental to the talks with the Emperors. *If they think we are greedy, they will not give us the price we want* she thought despairingly. She said nothing, smiling and laughing with the Emperors, hoping above hope that this desperate gamble would work.

91

Laura sat on the rug before the fire in her rooms, glad she was alone. She groaned softly, massaging her sore feet. She had treated the Emperors to a spectacular evening of dinner and dancing, several performers entertaining them as they ate, and a quartet of musicians started a lively dance when the dishes had been cleared away.

'Are you not going to ask a pretty girl to dance?' she had asked the Tsar, and smiled when he offered his elbow to her, leading her to the floor.

She had been careful to share her time equally with both, no matter how much she liked one's company or the other she could not forget Dalnerechensk's future rested with one of them taking offence. It was better to keep them rivals but devoted, and Laura hadn't realised how hard it had been to deliberately lead on two men and hold them off diplomatically at the same time.

Aleksei's pain had become unbearable as the evening wore on and he finally took his leave of the Emperors, unable to keep the pain from his voice as he insisted they stay at the party but forgive his absence. Laura had wanted to rush out after him, to hold him in her arms, frightened that he was still so ill but knew she could not. Instead she had stayed at the party, telling witty jokes and dancing prettily.

They had laughed and enjoyed themselves, Ekaterina helping to carry the fun of the dance, whispering suggestions in Laura's ear on how to hold a man's attention, on topics of conversation, of how to hold her neck just so, how to bite her lip gently when mulling over their words.

Laura sighed heavily, massaging her calves. She was aching from the dancing, from the flirting, from the witty banter. She wondered if she could do this for two more days. Russian and German Emperors were a lot more sophisticated than the Dalnerechensk court. Laura began to wonder if she was out of her depth.

I am not yet seventeen! she moaned inwardly. *The man on the bar top was right. What do I know of politics and evil Russian devils?* She shut her eyes. Tsar Nicholas was not evil. He was kind and charming, but hopelessly indecisive, and while he doddered his people grew restless and angry, and Dalnerechensk grew restless and angry. She would force him into a decision. And in two days. Her plan would work.

The fire had burned low in her room, casting dim shadows in the darkness. Laura wished Aleksei would tap on the door and let himself in, frightened of being caught entering an unmarried woman's chamber, and sit talking to her while he massaged her sore feet. She knew he wouldn't. He would be asleep, blissfully out of pain with a large dose of laudanum.

She sighed, wishing she too could drift off, unburdened by this stress. She had argued with the ministers in the days before the Emperors had arrived. At nine thirty tomorrow morning she, Grigory, Ivan, Nicholas Riminov and Vasilievich Chekhov would be the only ones to enter into the Council Chambers with the Emperors. That had been the bitterest argument of all, and Maksim had dared to intrude in Aleksei's bed chamber, resentful at being left out.

Laura had been surprised when Aleksei had muttered *Do what she asks* and dismissed him, rolling over away from the two of them. Perhaps he had known what she did; they could not argue in front of the Emperors, Maksim could not challenge the Princess tomorrow. The fewer ministers in chambers the better.

Nine thirty. She was both impatient and dreading the hour, doubting herself. *What if everything all fell to pieces?* She shut her eyes, pushing the thought from her head. She was too tired to worry, and too worried to sleep. She thanked God she was still too young to look as haggard and ill as Aleksei did.

She crawled to her bed and peeled back the covers, climbing in then pulled the warm material up to her nose. Anna had heated the sheets with several hot water bottles, and left two at the foot of her bed to warm her feet on. Laura smiled gently, blessing her friend absently. She was very fond of her servant. The warm, thick sheets were a blessing, a feathery cocoon of bliss that sapped the hurt out of her limbs and soothed her head, sending her instantly into sleep. She nuzzled deeper into the comfort, sighing contentedly, and dreamed of the scent of hay.

92

Laura woke before dawn and pushed back the covers, padding across into Aleksei's room. He was asleep but woke when she climbed onto his bed, folding his hand over his stomach. Laura's face fell.

'You're still not well' she said unhappily.

'I will still come' he said, sitting up then groaned, lying back down.

'You cannot' she begged, resting her head on his chest, folding her arms around him. 'How will I ever cope if this kills you?'

'You are young, and only a woman!' he groaned, agonised. 'What do you know of politics!'

'I know nothing' she said softly. 'But I know how Russia has cheated and deceived us, I will not forgive that. I know that your ulcer eats at you and the stress of the negotiations will inflame it and cause you great pain. I cannot bear thinking of you in pain!' she shut her eyes tightly.

'I should be there' he moaned.

'I can do this Aleksei' she said softly. 'I will come and tell you everything, I swear I will.'

Aleksei was silent then sighed, long and deeply, a man knowing there was no other choice.

'Do not push them too far in your desire for revenge' he said hollowly. 'Keep me fully informed of their moods and the progress. If you feel at all as if this is going wrong call a halt to the negotiations and I will take over, regardless of my pain' he said. 'It will not hurt for you to flatter the opening discussions. It may even do some good.'

Laura bit down the bitterness at Aleksei's lack of faith in her and kissed his shoulder gently then sat up to measure a dose of laudanum for him. He drank, but instead of giving the glass back to her he sat up, grimacing, and put it on the bedside table then reached for a small velvet box that sat near it. He opened it, looking at the contents in the box before holding out the necklace of black diamonds for her to see.

'They belonged to my mother' he said quietly, reaching over to fasten them round her throat. 'My uncle gave them to her after the birth of my brother' he shut his eyes momentarily, stroking the gems where they lay against her skin. 'She called them her lucky diamonds. You should wear them today.'

Laura stroked the gems, her fingers coming into contact with his. She took his hand but he pulled away.

'Go and dress' he said quietly, lying back on his pillows.

She leaned down and kissed his forehead then slipped out of his room.

Anna was in the corridor. She looked surprised to see her coming out of Aleksei's room and then she grinned. Laura hadn't the heart to counter what she was thinking. *Some good rumours floating round the castle about me will be a nice change* she thought. She opened her doors and stepped in; crossing into the dressing room where Anna poured cold water into a basin and Laura washed her face, knowing the cold water would bring up a rosy blush in her cheeks.

Anna combed her hair and twisted it back in a simple bun. Laura watched her work then stood and stripped, letting Anna lace her tightly into a corset. Laura tied on her petticoats while Anna retrieved the dress she was to wear today. Laura eyed it approvingly. They did not have enough yellow silk in Dalnerechensk to make a dress at such short notice so Ekaterina had graciously allowed the tailors to cut up one of her own gowns.

Laura had protested, but Ekaterina would have none of it, and had made the first cut herself. Laura had then hugged her friend and spent an hour standing on a stool in her corset and petticoats while the tailor had cut an elegant, shapely gown. The yellow bodice was decorated with white trim and the edges of her sleeves and hem were edged with white piping. The yellow skirts were cut to reveal the rich black underskirt and Laura sighed gently, letting Anna pull it over her head.

Laura stood for a long time, eyeing herself in the mirror; pushing up the bodice, turning around to eye the curve of her back and shoulders, turning back to stare intently at her face. She wondered briefly if she should wear the blue sash with the Dalnerechensk coat of arms on it then dismissed the idea. *It will clash with the colours* she thought. *Besides, the Romanov colours covered with the Dalnerechensk seal?* She didn't want to think of how that could be interpreted symbolically.

At last she blew her cheeks out, shutting her eyes tightly. She had not eaten but dared not in case her fear and anxiety made her vomit. The mad butterflies were creating tornadoes in her stomach but she dared not drink the Gogol's tea either.

'Pray for me Anna' she said as she turned from her reflection. 'Pray with all your might!'

Anna dutifully dropped to her knees and clasped her hands together in front of her, beginning fervent prayers and Laura smiled softly, closing the door gently behind her. She ignored the urge to run into Aleksei's chamber and slipped down the stairs to the first floor, pushing open the doors to the Advisory Council.

Ivan, Grigory, Nicholas Riminov and Vasilievich turned when she entered and eyed how regal she looked dressed in Russia's royal colours. They bowed deeply to her and waited till she had sat in Aleksei's chair at the head of the table before sitting themselves. They sat at the other end of the table, away from the chair where the discussion would take place, as instructed to do so.

A quiet, strained silence filled the room, the held-breath feeling of expectancy washing over them all. Laura had left the door to the Council Chambers open and they heard the footsteps of the two Emperors approaching. She rose from her chair and the council members rose too. Tsar Nicholas stepped into the chamber, smiling in delight when he saw her dressed in the colours of his household. Kaiser Wilhelm followed the Tsar into the chambers and smiled too.

Laura smiled at them beautifully, calling a good morning to them both. She introduced her ministers to the two Emperors and they each bowed low as their name was mentioned. Laura then called for the door to be closed and Ivan shut it carefully.

'Please forgive me, Your Imperial Majesties, my husband is very ill and cannot be with us today. He has given me his blessing to negotiate with you in his steed. I trust you will not find this change inconvenient?'

'Not at all' Tsar Nicholas said after the cousins had taken a careful look at each other.

'Please be seated my sires, and we will begin' she smiled, gesturing to the seats closest to her, sitting in Aleksei's chair.

Tsar Nicholas came to her right hand side and sat, Kaiser Wilhelm sat opposite him on her left, his withered hand hidden discreetly in his lap. Ivan came forward and poured each of them a glass of water from a crystal decanter. Laura thanked him absently and took a sip of the cold liquid, wishing it was something stronger to calm her nerves.

She waited till Ivan had sat again and opened an ink bottle before beginning.
'Your Imperial Majesty,' she started quietly, looking at Tsar Nicholas. 'Dalnerechensk's economy relies on the income generated from the sale of tin from her mines. To sell the mines outright will ruin the economy and the Principality will be plunged into suffering and misery' she dropped her eyes and outlined that the price Russia was paying for a ton of tin had already caused unrest. Kaiser Wilhelm looked shocked at the amount. Tsar Nicholas looked embarrassed. 'There are children in the mines of Dalnerechensk working long hours because if they don't their parents can't afford to feed them and they will starve' Laura went on. 'I must think of Dalnerechensk's wellbeing. It is therefore, with regret, that I cannot accept your generous offer of ten thousand rubles for the purchase of the mines.

'But perhaps between the three of us we may reach another agreement. Both your great nations have an interest in the tin we mine. We humbly ask for an increase in the price of tin.' She dropped her eyes again. 'I am at your mercy' she finished.
'I will offer you double the price for a ton' Kaiser Wilhelm said immediately.
'That is most appreciated Your Majesty' she said gently.

Not to be outdone by a powerful nation with a new navy, and pained from the losses he had recently suffered, Tsar Nicholas offered a few hundred more.

And so the debate began, Laura gently playing them against the other with innocent words and smiles at each new offer. She was firm and yet coquettish too, spending almost as much time talking about the Emperor's interests and countries as she did on driving a bargain between the three of them. When the price per ton had nearly tripled and Kaiser Wilhelm held the leading bid Laura called a break for the midday meal.

She rose from her seat before they could protest, causing all those in the room to rise as well. She curtsied sweetly, laughing that they would grow delirious if they did not eat soon, then led the Emperors down to the dining room where a lavish luncheon had been set out for them. The four Dalnerechensker ministers bowed deeply as the royals passed by them, amazed at what had happened in the room, slipping into procession behind them as they descended to the dining room.

Laura was surprised to see the dining room was full of the court and other notable persons in Dalnerechensk. She wondered how many were here to see the Emperors, and how many were here for the lavish celebrations. She knew they rivaled those of her own wedding feasts. *It does not matter* she told herself bluntly. *If this works, every day will rival your wedding feast.*

Ekaterina and other wives and daughters of the ministers joined them for lunch; the banter light and the mood a charming one. Laura let herself relax slightly, knowing the pressure was off her to carry the conversation single-handedly. Tsar Constantinovich sat beside her, sitting in Aleksei's chair so there would not be an empty space between Kaiser Wilhelm and himself. The ripples of rumour had fluttered up and down the tables when he had done so, and Laura noticed the looks they were shooting her too.

She sighed inwardly, knowing that rumours in the castle would be rife right now. Aleksei was missing while two important dignitaries ate at the table with the Princess and the old Tsar, who sat in his son's empty throne at the head of the table. But no one dared comment, not even Tatiana.

They were entertained as they ate by a jester who made bawdy jokes and pranced about like a strange pony, getting roars of laughter from the two Emperors. Tsar Constantinovich smiled at the mood in the dining hall, knowing how delicate the situation was that Laura was handling. No doubt when the younger members of the court went riding this afternoon Nicholas Riminov would whisper in his ear how well she was doing.

Laura excused herself from the Emperors' company briefly to slip into her rooms and change for their afternoon of hunting. Anna was still on her knees, her hands clasped before her. Laura was surprised then threw her hands round her friend.

'He was listening to you' she smiled, kissing her cheek. 'Come Anna, help me dress for the hunt, and then take the afternoon off, you have served me well.'

Anna smiled then got stiffly to her feet, following Laura to her dressing room. Laura dabbed on perfume then slipped a pretty, sapphire blue dress over her head, shrugging into a green jacket. Anna fastened her riding hat, making sure her hair was neat and tidy under it then Laura grabbed her gloves and went down to the stables.

A large contingent of palace guards was standing in a row by one of the castle walls, the bridles of their horses in their hands, waiting for the royals. As Laura stepped out of the castle they all bowed, the movement pulling the heads of the horses down too, and Laura smiled to think that the horses had bowed to her as well.

Livery boys had come to help Olaf in the stables and horses were brought to various ministers and boosted up. Several more livery men carried guns for their masters and two sat on the board of a wagon in which they would bring back any trophies they shot today.

The soldiers and horses bowed again as the two Emperors joined them and Laura turned, dipping a low curtsey to them. Out of the corner of her eye she saw Olaf bow as if someone had hit him in the stomach then straighten up and go back to what he was doing. Laura fought the urge to giggle, promising him silently that there would only be one more day of this.

'You cut a dashing figure on a horse, Your Majesty' Laura smiled, looking up at Tsar Nicholas as he mounted. 'I have heard you ride very well.'

'He does' his cousin said, mounting too. 'Now what say you *Princessin*, what figure do I cut on a horse?'

'Commanding' she answered, knowing the word would appeal to his militaristic vanity.

He laughed and Olaf boosted her up onto her stallion, handing her the reins. The court and the guard mounted too, Peter and another taking up the head of the hunting party's column then lead them out of the castle grounds, the wagon bringing up the rear.

The company laughed and joked as they rode into the forest, flirting and boasting of their prowess on horseback. Ivan told the Emperors how Laura had beaten the Polish officers in a race though he did not mention Nikita's name. Tsar Nicholas had laughed and asked how she rode against Emperors and a race was quickly organised.

Laura had been very tempted to push her luck, she had a magnificent stallion and knew that Franz and his friends had been accomplished riders. They had thundered through the pass neck in neck, but Laura had diplomatically allowed the Tsar to pull away from her, conceding the race, laughing at how she couldn't best an Emperor. Tsar Nicholas praised her as a horsewoman and they rode back to the hunting party.

'You ride magnificently' Peter said to Laura, the admiration clear on his face. 'Watching that race was quite inspiring!'

'You are an extraordinary woman, *Velikaja Knjaginja*' Tsar Nicholas said thoughtfully.

She laughed, blushing at their praise, and the party turned into the Hunting Forest, looking for a prize buck worthy of Emperors.

93

It was late when she pushed open Aleksei's door. She had worn the white silk that had made her look heartbreaking and had danced and flirted winningly with both Emperors, slightly more with Tsar Nicholas. She was now at the crucial part of the negotiations. She had almost tripled the price of tin, but it was still under what the tin was really worth. She had purposely called the negotiations off while Germany was in the lead to make Tsar Nicholas think of his country without Dalnerechensk's tin. She had talked incessantly with Kaiser Wilhelm about his industrialisation, about his booming economy, ensuring that he too knew that the tin would be valuable.

She sighed, climbing onto Aleksei's bed, shoes and all, and lay against him, resting her head on his chest.

'You're trembling' he said quietly.

'Oh Aleksei, I'm so scared' she moaned quietly, tucking herself tighter to him. 'So much is at stake! I just want to do what's right for Dalnerechensk, and I think it's working, but I'm so alone' she stopped, shutting her eyes tightly for a moment then outlined the discussions that had happened in chambers, the new price they had already achieved. 'Now it is the crucial point' she sighed. 'Russia must pay what the tin is worth, and she must pay more than Germany. I don't know how much Germany will pay for the tin. I can only pray it is not more than Russia can.'

'I should be there' he said, starting to sit up.

'No Aleksei' she said, pushing him gently back onto his pillows. 'You must get well. You must give your people the better life they deserve, to lead them into prosperity. I can't do that. I want you well again my love, I have missed you.'

'This is too much pressure to put on one no more than a girl.'

'Yes, I am a silly girl' she said, keeping all reproach out of her voice. 'But I am also a wife, and a princess, and many things are expected of me. I promised you I would serve you and Dalnerechensk to the best of my ability, only, I didn't expect to be tried so by fire.'

She shut her eyes and stroked his rough cheek with the backs of her fingers.

Aleksei stayed silent, torn by conflicting emotions. He too had his spy in the Council Chamber, a little bird that had whispered how Laura was charming them, how she had flattered and heckled, firm and flirty, and raised the price of tin to three hundred percent, fifty percent more than what he himself had dared to ask in the redrawn Treaty of Dalnerechensk.

That figure alone would ensure stability of the economy. If they called an end to the discussions right now he would be able to lift the heavy taxes off the crops and food, would be able to raise the wages of the miners three fold; would be able to raise everyone's annual income by three percent. Dalnerechensk would have money to spend on repairing public buildings and a sewer system to deal more effectively with waste; he would even be able to afford to put running water in the castle.

He was torn between admiration for her achievements and a bitter resentment. It should be him in Dalnerechensk's hour of glory, not his wife. She had questioned the Russians while he had been terrified of their military might, surrounded by Russia and cut off from any allies; she had discovered Russia's deceit and taken action to get revenge and reparation, and had come up with a solution that may just save Dalnerechensk, something he had worked himself sick over for eight years and had found nothing. *She had shown him how truly ignorant he had been.*

Her delicate hand brushed against his chest then, and she nuzzled closer to him, pressing kisses against his chest, pulling open his nightshirt.

'Go to your rooms, I'll not have you tonight' he snapped shortly, pulling the shirt closed again.

Laura stopped, surprised and hurt, then lowered her eyes.

'But of course, what is another month?' she said softly. 'We must put aside our own desires for your speedy recovery.' She stood and brushed at her clothing, smoothing back her hair.

Aleksei said nothing and she left him, shutting his door quietly, slipping across the corridor to her rooms. She closed her doors and leant against them, trying to control her tears.

So his bitterness has finally stopped him loving me she thought sadly. *I will save Dalnerechensk, and it will cost me the love of my husband.* She shut her eyes tightly, folding her hands on her stomach. *He will be kind if I become pregnant* she thought miserably. *Our marriage can still be comfortable and fond, even if there is no love anymore. He may even grow to love me if I am pregnant.* She stopped, shutting her eyes tightly. *The Revolution would go easy on me if they knew I was pregnant.*

She opened her doors and slipped through the silent castle, heading across to the stables. 'Olaf' she called, low and soft.

He was sitting at the far end of the stables on the stump he used to chop firewood, his back to her, polishing his boots. He hadn't heard her, so she crossed over to him, touching his shoulder as she whispered his name again. He jumped, whirling around, then his mouth dropped open.

'You have been at the bar' she said, smelling the mix of tobacco smoke and cheap alcohol on him. 'Tell me what was said.'

He shut his eyes. Laura dropped to her knees, grabbing his hands.

'How bad is it Olaf? Please! I beseech you -!'

'Don't beseech me on your knees *Velikaja Knjaginja*' he said, standing, dragging her up then turned away.

'Olaf you're frightening me!' she whispered, clasping her hands tightly and shutting her eyes.

He sighed gently, pained, trying to forget the sight of her in the white silk dress.

'They know that Tsar Constantinovich is sitting in his seat for meals, and that Aleksei is not eating with the Emperors' he said dully. 'They think he is ill or he is mad' he stopped.

'What will they do?' she whispered.

'They are maddened that they don't know what is going on -'

'What will they do!' she cried, grabbing his arm and forcing him to turn back to her.

He refused to look at her.

'They think Tsar Constantinovich has taken back the responsibility from his son. They think he is renegotiating the Treaty of Dalnerechensk. They still wait, but it is growing dangerous. I do not know what they will do if they think Aleksei is ill. If they believe he is mad -' he stopped.

'Tell me Olaf!' she demanded, shaking him a little.

'They love you, *Tsesarevna*' he sighed. 'If he is declared mad they will petition the Tsar or you to reverse the Law of Propriety.'

'What will that mean?' she asked, not understanding.

Olaf shut his eyes tighter. 'It means that while you are fertile you can take lovers. That you can have the marriage annulled if need be. That an illegitimate son may come to the throne.'

'That Tatiana's son can claim the throne' she said bitterly. 'What will happen if I am already pregnant when they petition me?'

He stopped, then dared to look at her quickly. 'Are you pregnant?'

'No' she sighed, shutting her eyes miserably.

He looked away again.

'If he is declared mad and you are pregnant, pray it is a girl' he said bluntly.

Laura shut her eyes tiredly.

'You are certain they will not revolt in the next few days?'

'No' he said truthfully. 'I can't be certain. But their complaints are against Aleksei, not the Tsar or you.'

'So they will wait' she sighed softly, letting go of his arm. 'Thank you Olaf' she smoothed down his hair absently, aware how untidy he looked sometimes, how much he reminded her of a child.

She sighed and slipped back into the castle, wondering if Anna had left hot water bottles in her bed again.

The second day of negotiations began at nine thirty and Laura sparkled in a white dress with black underskirts, the Tsaritsa's lucky black diamonds completing the Prussian King's colours, much to the delight of Kaiser Wilhelm. Again Laura sat at the head of the table with the Tsar on her right and the Kaiser on her left, the four Dalnerechensk ministers seated quietly at the far end of the table.

Tsar Nicholas opened the negotiations by offering one hundred more than Germany's closing bid yesterday, as she had bargained he would. Laura gave him a dazzling smile and charmed him with a witty comment that pleased him immensely.

But the negotiations bogged down soon afterwards, climbing by only a few rubles with each counter bid and Laura had to use all her powers of charm and persuasion to raise it any higher. The price finally reached the amount that had been printed in the Hungarian paper, and when Kaiser Wilhelm offered a bid just under the quadrupled former price Russia had paid for tin the Tsar conceded.

'That is a high price for tin' he said regretfully.

Laura blushed like a school girl, catching up Kaiser Wilhelm's good hand which she kissed, exclaiming:

'*Danke viel mal Ihr Majestät!*'

Kaiser Wilhelm laughed, pleased, and watched her pretty cheeks deepen in colour.

'Baron Fredrik von Schmidt told me the tin is a most excellent material for preventing steel corrosion' she said, girlishly excited, innocently playing another card she held. 'It must stop all those fantastic Dreadnaught battleships from corroding and sinking themselves!'

She saw the Tsar's face change out of the corner of her eye, and Wilhelm found her so charming he hadn't the heart to tell her most ships were made of iron. Laura was growing hotter, knowing she was at the most terrible moment of her plan. She took a deep breath and turned her attention back to the Tsar; playing the trump card she had in her deck, praying it would be enough.

'Now we come to negotiate the logistics of the arrangement with Germany' she said. 'Dalnerechensk realises that her borders are within those of Imperial Russia. It is Russia's benevolent blessing that allows us to use the railway to connect to Chelyabinsk and the lines Southwest to Constantinople. We understand that to uphold our agreement with Germany large quantities of tin will move along the rail lines and prove cumbersome to Imperial Russia. We also understand that should Germany station troops in Dalnerechensk to protect her interests it would prove uncomfortable for Russia to have the German army trooping over her soil to reach the Principality.'

'What do you propose?' Tsar Nicholas said quietly.

'Simply a strip of land from Dalnerechensk to Prussia to come under Dalnerechensk control, just wide enough for a rail and a road, a corridor that Dalnerechensk will maintain to free the Russian Rail lines so Germany may receive the tin and come to Dalnerechensk without causing concern to Russia.'

The Tsar's face tightened. Laura kept her face pleasant, wondering if she was holding her breath or had stopped breathing altogether. She dared not flick her eyes around the table to see the reactions of the four ministers. *She is hurting from the loss of Port Arthur, her entire fleet and her evacuation from Manchuria* Laura told herself. *She is in no mood to lose any more territory, not even a railway width, especially not if it means young and war-like Germany can penetrate into her unhindered as far as the Urals.*

There were a few tense seconds then Tsar Nicholas offered an amount that was four times what he had originally been paying. Laura's card had paid off.

This time Kaiser Wilhelm conceded. 'My last amount was generous' he said. 'I will not pay more for it.'

Laura smiled at him, feigning disappointment and thanked Tsar Nicholas for his generosity.

'As I am not needed to discuss land for a railway I will take my leave' Kaiser Wilhelm said, excusing himself from the discussions.

Laura stood, curtseying to him deeply, and the four Dalnerechensk ministers bowed low as he left the chambers, retiring to his rooms. Laura sat again, and Ivan began to write up the new treaty. Tsar Nicholas looked uncomfortable. Laura thought he was on the verge of reneging on his decision so she smiled at him.

'The terms of the Liberty Treaty are very simple Your Imperial Majesty. Russia will uphold the Treaty of Dalnerechensk, recognising the Principality of Dalnerechensk. She will agree to pay the amount negotiated for tin and will renegotiate the terms of Liberty Treaty every two years to ensure fair and current prices for tin.'

Grigory stood and came to them, handing over the treaty. Tsar Nicholas read it through carefully while Ivan brought over the inkwell and a pen. Tsar Nicholas took the offered pen and paused for a moment, reading the Treaty again. Laura had begun to think his indecisive nature had taken over again then he pressed the pen to the parchment and signed.

Those in the room let out a collective, relieved sigh, eyeing their Princess with awe. Like an impetuous girl she caught up the Tsar's hands and kissed them firmly, making him smile.

'Kind, generous man!' she whispered. 'How you will be praised, you have saved Dalnerechensk!'

'Your Highness?' Grigory urged, handing her another pen.

She took it and signed, writing the title: *Acting Regent of Dalnerechensk* after her name. Grigory took the pen and signed as a witness, as did the others of the court. It would still need Aleksei's signature to be recognised as law but the treaty was solid and binding as it stood. Laura felt dizzy with accomplishment.

95

Somehow Laura had made it through the rest of the afternoon's festivities, laughing and witty, though feeling as if she was floating. It was whispered from ear to ear as they danced, Ivan and Grigory unable to contain themselves, and there was great feasting that night. Both Emperors were smiling and enjoying themselves, laughing as Laura whirled them through energetic dances until they begged to be relieved, unable to keep up with the youth of the day.

Tsar Constantinovich glowed with pride for his daughter-in-law and the court turned to watch her as Ivan waltzed her past, beginning to see her with a newfound admiration and respect. Ekaterina had rushed over and kissed her warmly on the cheeks when Grigory had told her what had happened, and praised her so much Laura had begged her to stop.

Laura had wanted to hug herself, to go riding in the forest and scream with joy, to spend the afternoon with Aleksei making love, crying, both! She had rushed in with the treaty and pressed hard, excited kisses against his mouth, apologising that she couldn't stay, rushing out to keep the Emperors entertained.

She had allowed herself this shining moment of achievement.

But there was still one more card to play. *Tsar Nicholas was unhappy with the price of tin; he was unhappy with the Liberty Treaty.* Russia could still invade and forcibly absorb Dalnerechensk. International outrage meant nothing when it was only for small bits of land. The outcry at the annexation of Alsace-Loraine had been only that. No one had tried to make Germany give it back to France. *No one would care if Russia forcibly annexed Dalnerechensk.*

Laura had quickly dragged Ivan aside.

'Write me a new treaty' she said quietly. 'Have it ready in one hour and leave it in my rooms. All the ministers who signed the Liberty Treaty must sign it.' Then she outlined what was to be written in it.

Ivan looked surprised, but went to do as she bid. When the gloriously drunk court had been dismissed for the evening Laura went to her rooms and read the treaty carefully, approving of the word choices Ivan had made.

Instead of dressing for bed Laura sent Anna secretly scurrying down the corridor with a message to deliver then reclined back on the chaise lounge and waited. She was nervous, but tried to hide it, lowering her eyes in a way that always made Ekaterina appear so exotic. There was a quiet tap on her door and Anna returned, ushering in a surprised Kaiser Wilhelm.

He was half undressed, his splendid uniform jacket gone and his shoes taken off. He eyed the pretty Princess on the lounge as she dismissed her servant girl and invited the Kaiser to sit with her on the seat. He bowed and obliged, wondering if the secret looks she had sent him this evening would amount to a union, diplomatic or otherwise.

'I have asked you here this evening because I believe there is one other arrangement we could come to' she said, with a small smile that could have been quite seductive.

'You have me all intrigued Your Highness, do tell' he smiled, enjoying the flirt.

'Baron Fredrik von Schmidt had praised Germany so much I have quite fallen in love with her' Laura smiled. 'She has grown powerful and industrial, it is said that your navy rivals England's.' Her smile faded and she dropped her eyes. 'Dalnerechensk has no navy to speak of, not even an army, only a handful of palace guards. We cannot fend off Russia if she decides to break the Liberty Treaty rather than pay what was agreed. She has suffered devastating losses, and I fear she will look elsewhere for territory to appease her esteem.

'I propose another treaty with you Your Imperial Majesty, one of aid should Dalnerechensk be threatened. Would you consider such a cordial agreement?' She looked at him, knowing that the French translation of "cordial agreement" was the title of the treaty that had isolated Germany in Europe.

'Ah so it is business and not for pleasure that you have invited me' he teased.

Laura feigned innocent surprise.

'This alliance of ours would please me very much, my Sire' she said quietly, flirting with the deliberate pun on his informal title. 'The terms are simple: You would agree to protect Dalnerechensk and recognise her sovereignty. If the Liberty Treaty is broken you will provide military aide to uphold it. It will not be our concern what you do with the Russian territory you capture. If you claimed all of Western Russia up to the Urals we would not care' she flashed him a quick look to see the effect of her tempt of more land and power. Kaiser Wilhelm looked as if he were considering the terms seriously. She took a deep breath and played her last card.

'In return for providing this aid Germany will receive no less than fifty percent of the tin mined in Dalnerechensk, and there will be provision for a permanent garrison of German soldiers in the village of Tcherepnin, provided they are paid by Germany. All we ask is that Germany does not breach Dalnerechensk.'

She flashed him a look at her sexual pun. The Kaiser laughed and agreed to sign the treaty. She smiled, dropping her eyes and turning her neck elegantly as she pulled the piece of parchment that lay on her small table beside the couch closer to her. She dipped her pen nib in the bottle of ink and signed it, then passed the pen to Kaiser Wilhelm, knowing he had to lean across her to add his signature to the document. He smiled as he did so, and leaned a little too close, lingered a little too long.

'I trust Your Imperial Majesty will keep this matter discreet?' she whispered suddenly, a conspirator in a plot.

'There are many things one could promise to keep discreet in a lady's chamber' he teased quietly.

He leaned back to look at the girl on the edge of womanhood; at her firm beautiful body, her sweet innocent face. For just a moment he thought of his children, of his only daughter, twelve-year-old *Princessin* Victoria Louise, named after her English Great Grandmother, and his desire went.

He took her hand and kissed it gently.

'*Sehr gut* Your Highness, you have played a good hand this round. Your quick mind and youthful beauty have made fools of two old men' he smiled. 'I will look forward to meeting you again, *Princessin* Laura Vakhtangova, but I hope it will not be to honour this secret treaty' he stood and bowed to her. 'With your permission I will leave and retire for the night, I have indulged in excesses that will haunt me tomorrow.'

'Of course Sire' she smiled. 'Good night.'

He kissed the back of her hand then turned and slipped out of her room.

Laura hugged herself tightly to repress her emotions then lifted the new treaty, blowing on the ink carefully, waving it gently dry in the warm air of her chamber. She read it then read it again and fingered the dry signature of Kaiser Wilhelm, drunk with delirium and wine. Unable to contain herself anymore she pushed open her doors and fled across to Aleksei's chamber, bursting in.

He was sitting on the edge of his bed, dressed in black trousers and a loose white shirt, the Liberty Treaty in his hands. The look on his face instantly drowned Laura's elation. Mikhail was standing near the door to Aleksei's dressing room and she eyed him for any hint of reason for Aleksei's anger.

'What is the matter Aleksei?' she asked, worried at the look in his eye.

'You have asked too high a price. Russia will not pay, and she will invade' he snapped, throwing the parchment onto the floor in disgust.

'Russia agreed to the price' Laura said. 'But in any case, she will not dare, I have come with more news for you.' She handed over the Secret Treaty.

Aleksei read it in stunned silence then his face darkened with rage. His fists tightened, crumpling the paper in his grip. He threw it in the direction of the fire but it floated harmlessly off course.

'Pray tell me Laura, did you secure that one on your back?'

'What?' she gasped, shocked, her eyes flicking to Mikhail.

'Did you moan for him Laura? Tell him just how you like it?'

'You dare to call me a whore?' she cried, outraged. 'Why do you suspect me so?'

'My entire court is talking as though you were a whore!' he exploded furiously. 'They shuddered to think of you as a Russian whore and now you are a German one!'

'Perhaps they will not blame me for seeking solace when their mad king refuses to sire me anymore!' she cried, her temper snapping.

Aleksei flew off the bed and struck her hard, making her nose bleed. He grabbed her arms tightly.

'You will not rape me in front of your servant!' she said, wrenching one arm free.

Aleksei let her go with a shove, eyeing Mikhail quietly. He raised his hand once to strike her again, but lowered it, seething.

'You have disgraced me!' he hissed. 'This is the last time you will embarrass me. You have tainted the reputation of the monarchy and fueled the fire of rebellion in this country. You will be deeply sorry for this.'

'I have loved you and done my duty as any wife should' she said, wiping away the blood from her nose, smearing it across her cheek. 'But even now, violently abused by you, I will submit to your will Aleksei. When will you reverse the Law of Propriety and divorce me? I will need to send word to my father -'

'I didn't mean that' he interrupted, angry.

Laura dropped her eyes, fighting the tears.

'You had better tell Dalnerechensk from the walls tomorrow what you have done.'

'What *I* have done?' he cried, rounding on her.

'Of course' she said, wiping more blood away. 'You will claim what I did as your own work to save your people thinking their new wealth and protection was gained by a whore.' She turned on her heel and slammed the door behind her.

Something smashed against the door, making her jump, but she was not surprised. She tried to hold back the bitter tears but failed, sobbing as she stumbled out of the castle and across to the stables, flinging herself down in an empty stall, crying hard.

She had worked hard to woo and sign Russia, she had tossed and turned sleeplessly for two nights, she had worried and fretted and doubted herself, and although she hadn't given herself an ulcer, this was her victory and hour of triumph. She had worked hard to become accepted by the people and had grown to love them painfully, her thoughts turned constantly on how to please them, to fight for the best for them.

Olaf had told her the people loved her more than their own bloodline, and she had heard it for herself in the bar, how they had fought to uphold her good name at a slight. She knew the Council would talk to the other members, to their wives, who would gossip to others, until all of Dalnerechensk knew it was her that had negotiated the treaty. How would they react to Aleksei then when he stood up on the walls and claimed the glory for himself?

A small part of Laura suspected he no longer cared what his people thought about him. She shivered, frightened that Aleksei truly had lost his mind, and she would live the rest of her days in fear of his fists or his body, or the day when his rage consumed him so completely that he killed her.

The thought made her go cold and still in fear, then shake violently, pushing her face harder into the hay she lay on. She took several deep breaths to contain her fear that was threatening to make her scream out loud in terror, the soothing scent of hay filling her.

She desperately wished she was in that barn all those years ago again, with her father's arms around her, her mother sane and singing happily, combing her wet hair. Laura sobbed bitterly. Emily's bursts of hysteria had strained the relationship with her daughter, and had turned her into a stranger that frightened her, though Laura would never admit it. *I don't want to live frightened of my husband!* she wept.

She buffed her tears and hurt her assaulted nose, wincing and cursing quietly.

A hand grasped her shoulder and she whipped around, scrabbling away. Olaf visibly relaxed and lowered the shovel he was holding to strike her.

'Tsesarevna' he said, relieved, then his face changed. 'My God!'

He dropped the shovel and knelt beside her, reaching to pull her into his arms. She moved away, shutting her eyes, shaking to control her tears.

Olaf's hand tightened into a fist and he punched it through the stable wall, startling her and the mare in the next stall, who snorted in fright, stamping her hooves. Olaf bent his head, shutting his eyes tightly.

'He did it again didn't he' he whispered, shaking in anger, and Laura realised it was not the punch in the nose he was talking about.

Her cheeks went hot and her body went cold at the same time and she burned, too ashamed to even look at Olaf. She shut her eyes tightly, her tears flooding down her cheeks. She knew she was scrutinised at every moment, and every single action was talked about behind fans and over teacups; she had no idea that every action in her marriage bed was talked about as well.

'Oh Laura...' he whispered, all his anger and hate summed up in that quiet groan.

Olaf has feelings for me she realised, surprised. *He hides them well behind his gruffness* she smiled, a tear running down her cheek.

'Did he break my nose?' she whispered.

Olaf looked at her carefully, rising to his haunches. He reached out and gently inspected her nose, apologising when she winced at his touch. He told her it wasn't broken and pulled out his handkerchief, giving it to her, watching her wipe away her tears and the tacky blood from her cheek.

'How long have you known him?' she asked. 'How long have you served him? Why did he ask you to spy for him? Has he gone mad?'

'*Tsesarevna*,' he whispered softly, stilling her.

She sniffed loudly, wiping at her tears. 'Tell me about Alexander Andrei.'

Olaf was quiet then sighed softly. 'He was the oldest son. They said he was very handsome, full of life. Reckless too, like *Knjaz* Rurik perhaps. He sparkled; kept the whole court on its toes.'

'What happened to him?' she asked, wiping away more tears.

'The rumours say after the death of the Tsaritsa he lost all his sparkle, he just – lost all his vitality. He loved his mother and her death nearly killed him.'

'Is he still alive?'

'I don't know. They did not bury him, or if they did it was done in secret. He was loved in Dalnerechensk, moreso than his awkward brother. I do not think they could bear to think of him mad or dead. He simply disappeared. Some say he is still in the castle because the old Tsar cannot bear to send him away.'

'That's ridiculous, I have been through the castle, and there was not -' she stopped, the horror flooding through her as the memory of the distraught head of staff swam back into focus. 'Oh God, it's all true' she whispered. 'Alexander and Aleksei are both mad.'

'I am sorry *Tsesarevna*' he said gently. 'The complications of the Principality were not meant for a child -'

'Don't patronise me Olaf, I am the one who had Russia and Germany eating out of my hand despite what Aleksei will say on the wall tomorrow' she said angrily, then dropped her eyes and sighed tiredly. 'I have fought hard for this and lost' she sighed. 'I have humiliated him, though it was never my intention to do so. I love Dalnerechensk, but I cannot live here a spurned princess. I cannot live here in fear of my life.'

She shut her eyes then stood, leaving Olaf alone in the stables and made her way back to the castle, closing the kitchen door against the cold.

96

Laura woke, rubbing the sleep tiredly out of her eyes. It was still dark, and Anna slept on beside her, snoring gently. She smiled softly at her servant. She had been terrified when she returned to her rooms that Aleksei would come, inflamed with rage and lust, and she had begged Anna to stay with her, to help her if Aleksei came.

Anna had agreed, crying at the blood that was still on Laura's cheeks and washed her face clean, then helped her dress for bed. Laura had given her servant one of her own night dresses to wear, and Anna had giggled, stroking her hands on the sleeves of the dress, unused to feeling such luxurious material against her skin.

Laura slipped out of bed and washed quietly in her dressing room, then pulled on her corset and a pretty blue dress.

'Your Highness?' Anna suddenly cried out in fear.

'I'm here' she answered quietly, and Anna padded to the dressing room, relieved to see she was unhurt.

'What do we do now Your Highness?' Anna asked uncertainly.

'You will go and dress, and then you can take the day off' Laura smiled. 'I am going to have breakfast with the court and farewell Tsar Nicholas and Kaiser Wilhelm.' She turned and took Anna's hands. 'Thank you for staying with me last night' she added.

Anna squeezed her hands gently then stripped off the borrowed night gown, pulling on her own uniform again. Laura left her to dress and swept down the stairs to the dining hall.

The court and the two Emperors looked worse for wear after the excesses last night. As Laura stepped into the room the court rose to its feet and bowed deeply to her. She was surprised, then a small smile twitched at her lips. *They know what I have done* she thought. She smiled radiantly despite her third night of little sleep and took her place beside Tsar Constantinovich, who still sat in Aleksei's chair.

The conversation turned to the interests of the Emperors and the atmosphere was polite and one of mutual respect. Laura watched them all carefully as she ate, and Natasha smiled at her. Laura was surprised, Natasha had never shown her any warmth before, and all her smiles had been twisted with malice or mean humor at Tatiana's spite. She smiled tentatively back. Tatiana saw the exchange and she elbowed Natasha discreetly, who dropped her eyes and her smile.

When the meal was finished Laura rose and led the two men out to the waiting carriage, watching the livery boys load the Emperors' trunks onto two other waiting carriages. Olaf bowed jerkily then offered his hand to help the Princess up into the open carriage, uncomfortable in his dress uniform. Laura avoided looking at him and sat, waiting for the Emperors to climb up into the carriage with her.

The mounted guard arranged themselves around the open carriage, escorting their royal guests down to the train station. Laura noticed there were more people on the streets waving and calling out to the carriage. She didn't know if that was because the gossip had already reached them, or because they were glad to see the last of the Emperors.

The carriage stopped at the station, the mounted guards quickly forming a line to stop the people of Dalnerechensk flooding onto the platform. Olaf leapt down from the driver's seat and opened the carriage door, forgetting to bow. Laura smiled absently and took his hand, stepping down from the carriage.

The Royal train stood before them on the tracks, gleaming in the morning sun. Laura knew it would only go as far as Chelyabinsk, Russia was still paralysed with her railway strike. She guessed the two Emperors would travel on from there by private coach, or the new horseless carriages. The steam engine hissed, and Laura saw that a good number of the court had followed them to the station, all calling their goodbyes to the Emperors.

Laura took Kaiser Wilhelm's hand, kissing his cheek.

'God bless you, Your Royal and Imperial Majesty' she said. 'May your return journey be safe and your son's wedding be fruitful and happy.'

He thanked her, kissing her cheek as well. She let him go and turned to Tsar Nicholas, clasping his hand and kissing his cheek.

'God bless you, Your Royal and Imperial Majesty' she said. 'Travel safely, and may your son grow well and strong.'

He too thanked her, and kissed her cheek, then climbed on board the train. Kaiser Wilhelm was already on the train and opened a window, leaning out to wave goodbye with a fine white handkerchief. Tsar Nicholas joined him at the window, waving too.

With a blast of the whistle the train hissed then began to move, gliding slowly along the track. Laura waved, blowing girlish kisses after them that made the Emperors smile, calling her blessings after them.

The train slid through Vsevolod's Gate and disappeared. Laura dropped her arm, fighting the urge to hug herself in public. There was a strange sound behind her and she turned back to the assembled guards and ministers to find them all down on one knee, their heads bowed deeply with respect for her. Even Olaf was on his bended knee, who Laura thought had never knelt to anyone before.

Her surprise gave way to pleasure and she smiled softly, placing a hand on Grigory's head and then the other on the Captain of the Guard's helm, stroking the soft blue and green plume surreptitiously with a finger.

'Rise Grigory,' she said softly. 'Rise Peter, and lift your men up too.'

'You have saved Dalnerechensk' Grigory said softly.

'Rise Grigory' she said, pulling him up. 'You will not think so highly of me when it is whispered what it cost me.'

'I would not care' he swore, looking at her levelly. 'It has cost all of us.'

She squeezed his hand tightly then bid the court to rise again. Olaf offered her his hand and she stepped up into the waiting carriage. Peter and his guards remounted and saluted Laura, taking up positions around the carriage and riding back to the castle. In the courtyard Laura stepped down from the carriage, watching the mounted guard close rank and salute again as they left the castle grounds, heading back down to Tcherepnin.

Laura eyed the castle then turned to Olaf.

'Saddle my stallion and your mare. I have no desire to be indoors today' she said.

The court came forward, kissing her cheek and pressing her hand, swearing their love for her, promising to dutifully serve her, even Maksim. Laura thanked them all graciously, waiting while Olaf unhitched the carriage and dragged it to the shed at the back of the stables where they were kept then returned to saddle her stallion.

She swung herself up on her horse and Olaf mounted too, following her at a respectful distance as they wound their way into the hills of Liberty Valley.

'Come Olaf, do not hang back there' she called as they disappeared into the trees.

'What have you done?' he asked.

She turned to eye him, surprised.

'Why did you kneel to me if you did not know?' she asked.

'Because if Maksim Yegorov had knelt you must have done something awe inspiring.'

'I have written two treaties, though Aleksei will tell everyone from the walls today that it was his doing' she said, dropping her eyes. 'The price of tin has been quadrupled and Russia has sworn to uphold the sovereignty of the Principality in accordance with the Treaty of Dalnerechensk. So she will not break her word I have signed a treaty with Germany who promises us military aide in return for fifty percent of our tin if the outcome is successful.'

Olaf's mouth fell open then he laughed.

'You have done it!' he laughed, amazed.

'Yes, I have' she answered, dropping her eyes. 'It has only cost me my reputation and the love of my husband' she looked away. 'Come, a race to the Northern Border!' she cried, wheeling her mount and spurring it forward.

She felt the wind blow against her and catch in the folds of her dress like a sail. Olaf quickly overtook her, galloping past and calling back that she would have to do better than be a pretty figurehead for a ship if she hoped to win. She laughed and tucked the folds between her legs and the horse, spurring it on faster.

They raced up to the ramshackle Northern Wall in the Hunting Forest, Laura twenty paces behind and declaring herself the winner because she could do what she wanted, making Olaf laugh, wheeling the mare back to her.

'Go and buy some bread and cheese and bring it to the waterfall' she said suddenly, smoothing down her hair.

'It is not a fitting lunch for a princess' Olaf laughed.

'Oh let's not stand for this now!' she said irritably. 'There is no princess and stable groom here, only two friends riding in the wonder of Dalnerechensk.'

'Very well, I shall find the bread and cheese that suits us' he grinned, and spurred his horse towards the hamlet of Kalach.

Laura walked her stallion to the waterfall, sighing as she rounded the bend into the secret glen. The sun was shining on the water and the green trees made a pretty, dappled curtain to block out the rest of the world. She dismounted and let the stallion roam freely, avoiding the grassy spot where she and Aleksei had made love and sat down, sighing gently at the tranquil scene before her.

Olaf returned, riding into the glen with some food wrapped in packages. He too dismounted and let the mare wander, dropping the parcels of food beside her.

'Since you are not the *Tsesarevna* anymore I won't wait on you hand and foot' he teased, then kicked off his boots and stripped off his shirt, running down to the lake where he dove into the clear waters.

Laura laughed, amused then unwrapped one of the packages of cheese, lying back against the grassy bank to watched Olaf swim back and forward, occasionally climbing out of the water onto the rocks to dive in again. *He is a strong swimmer* she noticed, watching the way his shoulders moved through the strokes of his swim. She wondered if he swam a lot as a child, it was clear he didn't get much time to do anything these days.

Olaf surfaced, breaking the calm appearance of the pool and shook the water from his head left and right, then turned his face up to the bright sunlight, his smile clear even from this distance. He wiped his face, pushing back his hair. Laura envied him, wanting to strip off her dress and petticoats and corset and join him in the water to feel the coolness wash over her in soothing waves. She knew she could not. Her undergarments were see-through when they were wet, and Lady Ramkinson had discouraged swimming. Laura wasn't very good at it.

Olaf strode out of the water and flopped himself down on the grassy bank beside her, stretching out to dry in the hot sun, folding one hand behind his head. He grabbed a hunk of bread, lying back to eat contentedly. Laura tried not to stare at him and quickly looked away, a pretty blush coming up in her cheeks.

It was peaceful here, she sighed quietly, breathing in deep the smell of the wet, lush glade. They ate their fill of bread and cheese then lay quietly, enjoying their own thoughts and each other's company. Laura shut her eyes, resting her head on one arm, turning her cheek to rest on her elbow, shutting her eyes dreamily in the warm sun. She heard Olaf roll over once and imagined him stretching out to dry the back of his trousers.

Laura dozed contentedly, too lethargic to care if the sounds she heard from Olaf were him eating or snoring gently. It was nearly half an hour later when she realised that the noises had stopped and she could feel the weight of his grey eyes on her. She opened her eyes carefully, watching him through the veil of her lashes. He was looking at her unabashedly, a slow and careful, deliberate observation of her.

'Did no one ever tell you it was rude to stare at your betters?' she teased without moving.

'Breeding does not make you better' he said bluntly.

'Ah Olaf!' she laughed. 'You still forget I still have the dirt of my childhood on me' she sighed.

He paused then said quietly: 'Even diamonds and vibrant treasures spend their time in the dirt.'

She looked at him sharply. He looked away. She sat up, her mouth dropping open. *You possess a rare and vibrant treasure...* They had been the words Aleksei had used to describe her in the letter to her father Nikolai Ryzhkov had given them all those months ago. Laura knew both letters off by heart.

'You told Aleksei what to say in those letters' she said, astounded.

'*Da*' he admitted.

Laura turned away, her thoughts whirling in her. 'All this time Olaf I have been looking for the man that wrote those words in him. But they weren't his.'

'*Da Tsesarevna*' he said. 'Just the ones he couldn't find.' He dropped his eyes. 'We all have ways to help others. There is no man better than another.'

'Ah! So you are a socialist at heart' she smiled, turning back to him. 'All men are equal! And

344

why not? Dalnerechensk may as well be ruled by a stable groom, her mad royals are no good!'

'Don't tease me' he interrupted quietly.

'No need to swear your life to serve another's -' she went on.

'You are worth my life, I have sworn it to you!' he suddenly cried, grabbing her arms to still her.

She gasped, there was a high colour in his cheeks, and his grey eyes were burning intensely. She had never seen him so moved with passion before. He suddenly let her go, turning away from her.

'Forgive me' he said awkwardly. 'I would never hurt you Laura.'

'I know Olaf' she said softly. 'You are a good servant to me. But you forget yourself.'

'You asked me to' he answered huskily, swallowing down his emotion.

'I did, didn't I' she said sadly, then sighed and stood, dusting off her dress. 'Come Olaf, catch my horse for me, I need to return to the castle.'

'As you command' he said quietly.

He pulled on his boots and his shirt then went to call the horses to him.

97

Laura stared at her embroidery without seeing it. She and Olaf had not spoken as they rode back to the castle and she had left him in the stables to see to the horses. Grigory had been pacing nervously in the entrance hall of the castle. He stopped when he saw her, rushing over to her.

'He has locked himself in his rooms' he had said. 'He has not even signed the treaties.'

'Where are they?' she had asked, feeling cold.

'With him' he answered, surprised.

'Will he burn them?' she asked, eyeing Grigory carefully.

They had looked at each other then raced up to the second floor together. Laura had been even more surprised to find two guards armed with pikes stationed outside Aleksei's chamber.

She stepped towards them but they crossed their pikes before the door.

'His Royal Highness says no one is permitted to disturb him' one said, looking uncomfortable.

'Stand aside!' Laura snapped.

'We cannot, we have been ordered here, on penalty of death' the other said, just as uncomfortable.

'On whose authority?' she demanded.

'His Royal Highness *Velikij Knjaz* Aleksei Stephanovich Vakhtangov's' they both answered.

'I am his wife, stand aside!' she said, losing all patience.

There was a laugh from inside, a low, sultry woman's laugh.

Laura shut her eyes tightly, the sound ripping her heart apart in her chest. Behind her Grigory swore under his breath. Both the guards looked sickly, but they stayed where they were, their pikes crossed and barring the Princess from the room.

'What are your names?' she asked softly.

'Basil Barad' said one.

'Roman Prokofiev' said the other.

'Well, Basil Barad and Roman Prokofiev, I shall recommend the both of you to Peter Kaminin, for carrying out your duties under difficult circumstances' she said, turning away to open her door.

'Your Highness -' Grigory had started.

'Thank you Grigory, that will be all' she had said dully, then closed her door against them all in the corridor.

She had paced to keep the tears at bay, had picked up a book she tried to read without seeing it, had picked apart an embroidery project until she had quite ruined it with her fingers; and now sat, staring at it sightlessly, wondering if she had any more tears to cry.

The knock on the door interrupted her. She wiped her dry eyes quickly, looking around for Anna, surprised to see her gone again. She called out and Maksim pushed open her doors, a rolled up piece of parchment in his grip.

'Good evening Your Highness' he said pleasantly, closing the door behind him.

'To what do I owe this pleasure?' she asked dully.

She knew Maksim had not come to simply congratulate her, or to apologise for his treatment of her in the past few days. Lev was usually with the minister when he came to postulate or yell at her, and she wondered what new insult he had for her.

'I have a petition, Your Highness' he said, brandishing the roll of parchment. He presented it to her and bowed deeply.

Laura took it and unrolled it.

'It asks that you and Tsar Constantinovich invoke and reverse the Law of Propriety' he said.

Laura froze, feeling the white hot anger rise up and push away all her tears. She carefully stood and moved closer to her fire, reading the words slowly. Maksim waited. She turned to him, rolling the paper back up and thrusting it into the flames. Maksim gasped and she held it out to him, warding him off with the burning end.

'You dare to come to me to sanctify your plots to overthrow my husband?' she asked quietly.

Maksim blanched, horrified that she was mad, but he saw that she was neither hysterical nor emotional. In fact she was calm and deliberate. She dropped the burning petition on the fire.

'It is no secret that your daughter is my husband's mistress. Any child she has will not be fit to rule for some time yet, and who would that leave for the throne, Lord Protector?' she arched her eyebrow at him. 'It is a dangerous game you are playing Maksim. Why has your daughter not beseeched Aleksei to reverse the Law of Propriety?' There was a flicker in his eyes. 'Ah! So she *has* beseeched him!' she guessed. 'And I can only assume that the answer was no, and that is why you are here in my chambers pressing this suit on me' she turned away, eyeing the charring remains of the petition. 'Leave me now' she commanded.

'It will not be the last petition' Maksim promised, opening the door.

'It will be the last that ever bears your signature Maksim, or I will take it to Aleksei as proof of your desire to have his throne for yourself. I wonder how long you will remain in Dalnerechensk with all your favour, estates and titles intact if you are guilty of that? You know that is a treasonable offence.'

Maksim's face hardened and he turned, stamping away from her room. Laura eyed her door, knowing Basil and Roman had heard the last part of their argument. She sighed quietly, wondering if Aleksei had heard; if Tatiana had heard. She wondered if she was still in Aleksei's room, if he was whispering the things that he had whispered to her in the Ivanov garden. She shut her eyes tightly and looked away, closing the door.

98

Laura sat silently at dinner, ignoring the looks and the fluttering fans. Tsar Constantinovich was no longer sitting in Aleksei's seat, but it remained empty and whispers shot up and down the table. Everyone knew that Aleksei had stationed soldiers outside his door. Tsar Constantinovich eyed Laura worriedly and tried to prompt her into conversation once or twice but she did not respond, and he too fell silent. Laura pushed at the food on her plate, and reached too many times for her glass of wine.

She eyed Tatiana from where she sat, scrutinising the shape of her stomach in her dress. *Was she pregnant?* she wondered. It was too soon to tell if she was. *Is Aleksei the father or was it too soon to tell that too?* she thought meanly. She dropped her eyes then stood, forgetting to tell the court they were dismissed and slipped upstairs to her room.

Basil and Roman had been replaced by two new guards but Laura ignored them, slipping into her room, shutting the door harder than she needed to behind her. She leant against it, wanting to feel Nikita's breath on her throat, to feel his hands on her, to be looking everywhere but in his intense hazel eyes – she stopped. *Nikita had brown eyes. Olaf's were hazel.*

She flushed deeply at that, then tried to force back the memories of the sight of his body drying in the sun, still lean and hard from the physical work he did. Desire rose up in her. Giddy with her drink and lack of food she pulled open her door again and slipped down to the stables.

He was not in the stalls so she climbed the stairs at the far end of the stables. Strong arms grabbed her and yanked her off her feet into the loft, wrestling her bodily to the ground. She grunted in pain.

'*Tsesarevna!*' Olaf gasped, letting her go. 'What the hell are you doing up here?'

347

'I don't know' she hiccupped, sitting up.

Olaf realised she was drunk and pulled her to her feet, helping her over to his table where he sat her on a stool.

'Tatiana is pregnant' she said miserably. 'Her father came to me with a petition to reverse the Law of Propriety. Tell me Olaf' she said, grabbing his hand. 'Should I reverse it? What will the people do?'

'If you do that, it will tell them there is something wrong with you' he said quietly. 'There are already -' he stopped.

'Already what?' she pressed.

He shut his eyes, ashamed. 'There are already rumours that you are – disfigured' he said, and didn't tell her about the hermaphrodite slanders. 'Your better hope lies in declaring Aleksei mad and transferring power to you' he went on hurriedly.

'He is not mad' she said softly.

'Why are their soldiers barring everyone from going in his room?'

'Everyone except Tatiana' she corrected.

'Why has no announcement been made?'

'I don't know!' she yelled. 'He won't even see me!'

She stood, stamping drunkenly around his room.

'Wasn't I a good wife? Wasn't I so understanding of him spending all that time away from me? Wasn't I so understanding that I was just his property? Of him sending me to whore myself with Nikita for the good of Dalnerechensk? Of his need to fuck his mistress?' she tripped over her feet and sat down heavily, dissolving into pitiful tears.

Olaf crossed to her and took her in his arms. She fought him then gave up, resting her head on his shoulder and sobbing into his neck. He let her cry, rocking her gently, stroking her hair as he soothed her.

'You should not be up here *Tsesarevna*' he said gently. 'I will not be the man that brings shame to you.' He pushed her back to look at her, stroking away her tears with his thumb.

'You love me don't you?' she said, wiping away more tears. 'Someone must still love me in this Principality.'

'Yes' he sighed quietly. 'I swore to love the monarchy. Now go back inside *Tsesarevna*.'

Laura stood and unsteadily made her way down the stairs.

99

Laura rubbed her temples disgruntledly, shutting her eyes tightly against the glare of the sun reflecting off Vsevolod's table. The council members sat with her, fussing over her, pouring water, shutting the drapes to block out the sun, lighting all the candles so they could see the treaties and papers laid out on the table before them.

Laura only had herself to blame for her poor state but she glared at the ministers around her, wishing they would leave her alone. They kept asking her opinion on where the money should be spent, on what public works, on what would be reasonable wages for the miners. Laura reached over and fingered the water glass beside her, pushing it irritably back and forward on the table. *Can't these men make any decisions without me anymore?* she whined to herself. *Surely they are capable of deciding what colour paint for a building without asking me?*

'What is the good of all this gentlemen?' she snapped, breaking angrily into their argument. 'These plans are useless until he signs the treaties.'

There was a quiet, careful pause. Laura stopped playing with her water glass and looked at each of the men suspiciously. They dropped their eyes then Ivan pulled out a sheet of parchment paper. Laura stood sharply, making the ministers rise too. She backed away from the paper, as if trying to run away what she knew was coming.

'I won't hear it!' she cried.

'Your Highness, please,' Ivan begged. 'It's a petition -'

'Don't!' she said, pushing her hands to her temples, stopping the pain her own yell had caused. 'It is treason! I won't hear it; I won't reverse the Law of Propriety!'

'It is not for that Your Highness' Ivan said, trying to soothe her.

She paused and took her hands carefully away from her temples.

'Then what is it for?' she asked quietly.

They looked at each other carefully.

'Your Highness,' Nicholas Riminov started, coming to her and taking her hands. 'It has been two days -'

She pulled her hands away but Nicholas went on determinedly.

'There could be no reason for him to delay announcing this to Dalnerechensk' he said. 'There is no rational explanation. -'

'He is not mad' she said quietly, shutting her eyes. 'He is struggling with his pride and anger and illness -'

'Your Highness this is the only thing that will save Dalnerechensk!' Lev cried. 'You must sign this and absolve him of his power -'

'I will not declare him mad!' she cried, pressing her hands back to her temples. 'Leave me! All of you!'

They hesitated, eyeing each other carefully, then bowed and began to file out of the door. Ivan looked around him helplessly then put the petition on the table.

'I am sorry, Your Highness' he said quietly, then closed the door behind him with a careful click.

Laura shut her eyes, trying to push away the terrible pain in her head, the misery in her stomach. She tried to avoid looking at the petition then picked it up, reading the signatures at the bottom. *All of them have signed* she thought miserably. *Only she and Tsar Constantinovich had not.*

She suddenly pulled open the door and ran up to the second floor, taking the petition with her. Basil and Roman stood guard at Aleksei's door again. She knocked on the door, aware they had looked at each other uncomfortably. There was no answer from inside.

'Aleksei' she begged quietly, taking a step towards the door.

Roman's arm shot out, brushing against her stomach, then retreated a little, aware of the punishment for laying a hand on the monarchy. But still he held it between her and the door, ready to push her away if he had to.

'Aleksei, please…' her voice faded away.

The door remained stoically shut. She dropped her eyes then pushed the piece of paper under the door.

'Take this and burn it' she said, turning to go.

The three in the corridor looked down in surprise as the corner of the parchment disappeared under the door with a whisper against the silk rug. *So he was directly on the other side* she realised. She stepped closer, aware Roman's arm was pushed between her and the door.

'Aleksei' she whispered. 'They want me to declare you insane -'

Something slammed against the door. Laura took a frightened step back, wondering what had struck it, his fist or something else. She shut her eyes then took a deep breath and stepped forward again.

'You must sign them Aleksei' she whispered. 'You *must* make that announcement! It is done, but they need to know. Please, my love, *please…*'

There was a soft sigh on the other side of the door, a whisper of a word. It had sounded like a promise, but she wasn't really sure. She raised her hand to knock again, to beg to be let in, but didn't know what his reaction would be.

A floor board creaked in his room, and Laura knew he had moved away from the door. She dropped her eyes and stepped away from his room, releasing Roman from his awkward position of laying his hand on the monarchy though unable to remove it without being derelict in his duty. She cast one last sad look at the door then padded dejectedly down to the stables.

'Ah, and how fares you head today *Tsesarevna*?' Olaf laughed when he saw her.

'My head is a thousand splinters of pain' she moaned.

'Come, fresh air will do you good' he said, opening the stall door and led out her stallion, saddled and ready to ride.

'I must apologise for my unseemly conduct' she said, trying to be diplomatic and flushing horribly. 'I let the drink get the better of me.'

Olaf chuckled quietly and boosted her up onto her horse. She waited till he mounted then spurred her horse out of the courtyard, heading for the Hunting Forest. Olaf rode quietly behind her until they turned off the wide cart rack.

'Have you been back to the pub?' she asked, turning to meet him, unaware that he was riding up beside her.

His thigh grazed hers firmly and she flushed, looking away, turning her stallion back, and didn't miss the way he smiled at her embarrassment.

'I will go again tonight' he said.

'They asked me to declare him mad today' she sighed softly.

'Did you?' he asked bluntly.

'No' she sighed. 'I could not. I am not in the best frame of mind for making decisions' she dropped her eyes, sad. 'What will happen to him if he is declared mad?' she sighed, pained. 'Will he disappear like his brother? Will he be found floating in a lake like poor King Ludwig Wittelsbach?' she stopped, closing her eyes tightly. 'Will he live in the castle where his spite and anger will – will -' she stopped again.

Olaf looked away.

'If you declare him insane, you must send him away' he said.

'I don't know if he is insane' she sighed sadly. 'Come, to the waterfall, and no more of this sad talk. Pleasant places and pleasant company is what I need.'

A small smile twitched at his lips and he followed her silently to the pretty glen. Laura dismounted and let the stallion wander, sitting down on the lush grass. Olaf dismounted at a run, kicking off his boots and stripping off his shirt, diving headlong into the cool waters. Laura laughed at his eagerness, watching him swim back and forward.

She sighed, wondering if she should send him for bread and cheese again, knowing he would probably need to wait till he dried off. *Should I go myself?* she wondered, then pushed that thought from her mind. She dared not go out unescorted anymore. She desperately wanted Olaf to take her to the bar, to hear for herself what was being said, but knew she could not ask him. He would refuse anyway, but now she was too scared of what they would say, of what they would do if they saw her.

She sighed then pulled off her cloth shoes, pushing her hand up under her skirts and the elastic of her bloomers to unclip her silk stockings, stripping them off as well. She then stretched out her toes, wiggling them in the grass, unable to remember the last time she had walked outside barefoot. Certainly it had been before she went to Lady Ramkinson's school. And before her family had moved to Texas.

She smiled to herself, thinking she should walk barefoot in the grass more often and stood, padding back and forward as she picked wild flowers, making a floral crown for her hair. Olaf floated on his back and watched her as she lifted her hems a little, dipping her feet into the cool waters of the lake.

'Did you swim as a child Olaf?' she asked, watching him.

'*Da*' he said, lazily flapping his arms under the water, drifting towards the waterfall. 'Did you?'

'Once or twice in the water troughs' she grinned. 'Lady Ramkinson detested swimming. I'm not very good at it.'

'Then I will teach you' he said bluntly.

'Right now?' she looked flustered.

'If you choose' he shrugged. 'But you cannot swim in all those layers, you will sink like a stone.'

Laura blushed at the thought of taking her clothes off. Olaf laughed, splashing at her playfully. She kicked water at him but slipped, sitting down in the water at the lake's edge.

Olaf laughed harder.

'Well! Now you are all wet *Tsesarevna*, perhaps you would like to join me in the water?'

'I cannot' she said, getting to her feet again and retreating with as much dignity as she could muster.

All her skirts were soaked and she stretched out in the sun, shutting her eyes to protect her head from the glare of the hot afternoon, wringing out her dress. Olaf came out of the water and flopped down next to her, folding his hands behind his head and sighing quietly as he eyed her. She shivered at the uncomfortable weight and coldness of her skirts, shifting irritably.

'Come *Tsesarevna*, take off your petticoats, they will dry faster hung over branches in the sun, and do not flush so, I have seen you in your underwear and in men's trousers' he laughed at her embarrassment.

She stood and stepped away a few paces, one hand snaking under her dress where she found and pulled the ties for her petticoats, feeling them fall off with sodden squelches. She draped them over several tree branches then lay back, spreading her damp skirts widely and lay back against the grassy bank, throwing an arm across her eyes to protect her head.

Olaf chuckled again and Laura tried to make the heat in her cheeks go away.

100

Laura woke when he nudged her. The light had faded and the glen was gloomy. She sat up, surprised with how late it was. Her skirt was dry, but slightly damp where she had lain on it and she stood, quickly pulling down her petticoats that hung like dull ghosts on the trees. Hurriedly she pulled them on; glad the dusk afforded her some discretion and then sat to pull on her stockings and shoes.

Embarrassed to be struggling to find her suspender clips to put her stockings back on she gave up, tucking her loose stockings inside the leg of her bloomers where she would not lose them and pulled on her cloth shoes.

Olaf had caught the two horses and stood waiting patiently to boost her up on the stallion. She blushed again and swung up onto the horse's back, taking the reins from him quietly. He mounted the mare and they slowly made their way out of the glen, letting the horses pick their way carefully over the dark ground.

Night had fallen when they trotted out of Hunter's Pass. Laura reached over and grabbed Olaf's arm in warning, stopping her horse. The Tcherepnin Beacon had been lit in the tower.

Olaf peered carefully through the silent darkness. They could hear no shouting, no rumble of mob or war, the town and village of Dalnerechensk and Tcherepnin looked peaceful and undisturbed except for the strong light in the tower. He reached over and pulled Laura bodily onto the mare, turning the stallion loose.

'Olaf -'

'It will find its own way back' he said. 'No arguments *Velikaja Knjaginja*.'

He used her title Laura thought. Now she was really scared.

Olaf quietly nudged the horse forward, watching carefully as they approached King's Gate. The portcullis was still up and there was no sign of disturbance around the gate, no tell-tale marks of a breach assault on the city walls.

The town was humming. Doors and windows were shut tight, no lights shone out of houses into the streets. Dalnerechensk suddenly seemed malevolent and menacing, pulsing with a strange mixture of fear and excitement. Castle Street was littered with debris, boxes over-turned and not righted; here and there were loose items that seemed out of place on the street; even flower pots looked riffled and harassed.

Laura felt Olaf's grip tighten on her as they made their way through the city. Fear slithered over her icily. *Something's wrong, something happened on this street. Has the Revolution begun?* she wondered. But the streets were too quiet for that. *Surely it could not be over already!*

There was a shock waiting for them when they rounded the s-bend of Castle Street before the gates to the courtyard. The thick fire-hardened gates had been shut against the street. Laura guessed behind them the portcullis was lowered too. *Never, even in the recent days of unrest, had the gates to the castle been shut.* The men on the walls were in a state of nervous alert; Laura could see it in their bright faces, shining in the torches they had lit along the walls.

'Who goes there?' called a soldier, hearing the approaching hooves on the cobbles.

'It is only the stable groom' Olaf answered.

Above them on the wall came the grinding clanks as the chains for the portcullis were wound around the windlass, raising the iron blockade. Olaf and Laura then heard the scraping of wood against wood as the thick bar was lifted off the gates. One was pulled open and Olaf spurred his now nervous mare through the breach. Behind him the gate was shut and barred again, and the portcullis lowered back into place.

Several soldiers stood in the courtyard. Peter Kaminin was among them. He spotted Laura on Olaf's horse and rushed to help her down.

'What has happened?' she asked, frightened and searching his face in the torch-lit courtyard.

'There was a riot' he said uncomfortably. 'At the commons where they were handing out the deer meat. The soldiers were attacked and the alarm was raised. The deer were dragged away, but the unrest was put down.'

Laura didn't ask what he meant by that. Behind her Olaf swung down off the mare.

'Was anyone hurt? Was anyone killed?' she asked.

'No one was killed' Peter said. 'There were injuries.'

'Did this happen before or after Aleksei made his announcement?' she asked.

'What announcement?' Peter asked, confused.

Laura turned to Olaf.

'Go to the pub. Report to me afterwards' she said under her breath then turned and stamped into the castle.

Basil and Roman stood uneasily in the corridor on the second floor. At first Laura thought they were nervous about the unrest outside until she realised they weren't guarding Aleksei's door anymore, but straying between his rooms and – *he's in my rooms* she thought. The thought was confirmed by the way their eyes flickered to her door then each other and back to her again.

Laura slammed open her door, glad the two soldiers had not been given instructions to bar her from her own rooms. Aleksei was dressed, sitting on her chaise lounge beside the small table. The pretty knick-knacks she had arranged charmingly on it had been dashed to the floor and now only her little melted tin keepsake sitting on two sheets of parchment graced the table top.

Laura slammed the door against Roman and Basil, seething that he had invaded and upset her sanctuary.

'You arrogant bastard!' she yelled. 'You would throw away your entire Principality to punish me? Sign the treaties!'

'Did you see them out there?' he asked calmly. 'You see my people? Taking up arms against *me*?!' his words ended in a shout and he leapt to his feet. '*My* people! *My* entire Principality!' he mocked her words.

'They are frightened Aleksei! Frightened and tired and worried and angry…' she trailed off, stopping. 'They have not seen their Prince for weeks and two foreign Emperors traipsing over their soil. They are listening to vile rumours because no one has told them what has happened; why they were here. Aleksei please, you must sign them! You have worked too hard for this country; don't punish them to spite me. Don't punish -'

'You!' he yelled, interrupting her. 'What good is standing up there and telling my people what their Princess did on her back for them?'

Laura struck him.

'Don't you ever call me a whore again' she hissed.

Aleksei was surprised by the slap but his eyes narrowed, too angry to care.

'Then what are you?' he asked bitterly. 'A good wife supports her husband; she does not undermine his authority.'

'Everything I have ever done was to support you!' she cried, frustrated. 'I have done nothing -'

'*You wrote that treaty*!' he screamed, rounding on her. Laura leaned back from his anger, but did not back away. '*You* saved Dalnerechensk! I worked myself *sick* for *eight years* looking for an answer and *you* just – just – *it should have been me*!' he cried, waving his arms, helplessly jealous and bitter.

Laura shut her eyes and the silence folded thickly around them.

'It was you' she said softly. 'By law I am yours; my body, thoughts and deeds all belong to you. I asked myself: *What would you do, if you knew what I knew? What would you do for a better life for your flesh and blood out there?* And I knew then it *was* you, because you would do whatever it took for them. It was you Aleksei, just the words you couldn't find' she stopped, aware of his eyes on her.

'Please,' she said, her voice strained. 'I have not slept for three days. I have worried and panicked and felt ill for two weeks; I understand what you have gone through. I can only imagine how terrible eight years must have been. I do not want to take this from you.

354

'This is my gift Aleksei,' she said softly. 'The wedding dowry I cheated you out of. I surrender it and me all to you. *You* will be the one to give it to your people; you are their blood, their hero, their Prince and savior. I am only your vassal.'

He turned slowly away when she finished speaking, reaching out to touch the little lump of melted tin that sat on the table.

'You kept this?' he asked.

'Yes.'

'Why?' he turned to her, unable to bring himself to look at her completely, holding himself carefully in check.

'Because I remember what it once was' she said. 'It was a cherished thing of beauty, grace and pleasure; and I loved it' she shut her eyes. 'I can still see it when I look at it. I still love it.'

Aleksei's knees went weak and he sat down stunned, his hand pressing against his mouth, his eyes wide with realisation.

'My God,' he said, moved. 'You must hate me…'

'Nikita begged me to be his mistress' she said. '*Begged me.* And I refused him, because I loved you and had promised myself only to you, because that is the duty of a wife -'

'Spare me duty!' Aleksei interrupted then stopped, dropping his eyes and whispering: 'Do you love me?'

'Yes.'

He was quiet, the silence stretching between them. Then he sighed, softly agonised; running his hands through his hair, suddenly seeming older than she had ever seen him look before. Gently he moved aside the little lump of tin and turned the two sheets of parchment over. Laura saw they were the Liberty Treaty and her Secret Treaty.

'Bring me a pen and ink' he said quietly, and Laura did as she was told, watching him sign his Cyrillic script across the bottom of the papers, writing *Regent of Dalnerechensk* after his name.

He dropped the pen and slid his hands through his hair again. Laura crossed behind the chaise lounge and lay a timid hand on his shoulder, feeling the way the tension evaporated as he slumped in his seat.

'You must tell them tomorrow Aleksei' she whispered. 'There will be no more starving children in the mines. Even those who have cursed you will praise you once again' she whispered. 'Tomorrow Aleksei, promise me.'

'I promise' he sighed, deep and empty.

He took her hand from his shoulder and kissed her palm, folding his fingers round hers firmly. She stayed still, resisting the urge to pull her hand away. *Had he kissed Tatiana's hand like this?* Aleksei stopped, aware of her stillness.

'Come sit beside me, wife' he said quietly.

Laura did as she was told, folding her hands in her lap and dropping her eyes. Aleksei reached out to smooth the backs of his fingers against her cheek but stopped when she flinched. He dropped his arm again, knowing that she was frightened of his touches, hating that cold and distant way she held herself from him.

'You once sparkled so much!' he said quietly.

'As did you' she replied, smiling sadly.

'You are frightened of me.'

'No' she said quickly.

'And you are lying to me' he said quietly, shutting his eyes in resentment.

'Aleksei -'

He stood and left her. Laura heard him dismiss Roman and Basil in the corridor then the quiet click as his door shut behind him. She sighed softly, shutting her eyes tightly, then turned to look at the two signed treaties, stroking his name silently.

There was a soft tap at her door. She stood and opened it quickly, but it was Grigory, not Olaf.

'Your Highness, we were worried when we could not find you' he said, eyeing her as he stepped in, closing the door behind him.

'I was in safe hands' she answered. 'He has signed the treaties, and will announce them from the walls tomorrow' she sighed, gathering the precious papers from her table and handing them to him. 'If he does not go to the wall tomorrow I will.' She stopped, shutting her eyes. 'I will say he's relapsed in his illness after negotiating brilliantly for the treaty.'

'You would give him that?' Grigory said, surprised.

'Eight years has brought him nothing but pain and suffering' she said. 'It has humiliated and shamed him. It is his honour to accept.'

'You are a good woman Your Highness' he said quietly.

Anna's knock on the door interrupted them. Grigory bowed and left her, closing the door with a quiet click. Anna hugged her mistress, thanking God she was alright, then bustled about heating hot water bottles on the fire and spreading out her nightgown to warm before it.

Laura eyed the nightdress tiredly, knowing she could not let Anna help her undress. Her pair of stockings were still tucked into her bloomers, and as innocent as her explanation would be as to why they had been removed everyone had known she had gone riding with Olaf that afternoon, and not returned till after dark.

Instead she sent Anna down to the kitchen to bring her something to eat, quickly righting her clothing again and stood by the fire to chase out the lingering damp from the folds of her skirts. Anna returned with a serving tray laden with hot morsels and placed it on the little table. Laura sat and ate with relish while Anna bent and picked up the little knick-knacks that had been dashed to the floor, arranging them on the table top again.

When she was finished Anna took the tray back to the kitchens then returned to the rooms. Laura was surprised, she had seen little of her servant in the past few days, but was pleased for the company. Anna pushed several of the heated ceramic hot water bottles between the sheets of her bed to warm them up, putting many at the foot of the bed.

As the minutes passed Laura grew increasingly restless. She paced her sitting room for two hours, sitting down intermittently to try to write a speech to give on the walls at sundown should Aleksei fail to climb them during the day. Her mind wandered, looking for words, snatching at some then letting them slip away again, drifting back to her words to Grigory.

I will say he had relapsed in his illness. Which illness? She asked herself. Half of Dalnerechensk believed he was mad. All of his ministers believed it too. Tsar

Constantinovich had not signed the petition, and she wondered if he even knew of it. *What would it do to him knowing both of his sons went insane?* Laura hated to think.

The candles began to burn low in her rooms. Olaf had still not returned from the city and Laura worried something had happened to him. She sighed anxiously, catching Anna yawning.

'Oh Anna, go to bed, I shall see you in the morning' she smiled apologetically.

Anna curtseyed and thanked her, closing the door on her way out. Laura sighed and tried to concentrate on her words, irritably scratching out sentences and words that conveyed different meanings or were ambiguous. She suddenly paused, a bead of ink swelling from the poised pen, splattering down onto the paper. *Will she have to declare him insane if he does not go on the walls?*

She stood, unwilling to answer that, unable to continue writing unless she had. She paced her room again then finally decided to strip for bed, hoping Olaf would not return to find her naked. She folded a shawl round her shoulders and sat up in bed, forcing herself to read until the candles began to gutter in spent pools of wax. Sleep tugged at her from the warm sheets but she couldn't lie down, too anxious to know what was going on.

She shut her eyes, listening for the sound of footsteps outside her room. She wondered if having the citizens of Dalnerechensk at peace with their rulers would put Aleksei at ease again, wondered if the ulcer would heal and the stress melt away. *Would the madness leave too? Would he become that boyish man she fell in love with again?*

She sighed. They were not getting any younger. Each day that past made them more set in their ways, more infirm, more – *old*. Would she become frustrated with his emotional awkwardness? Would she resent a man who could not find the words, who would not tell her how wonderful she was, how much she meant to him except in the strange moments of post coital intimacy? *Intimacy that was now lost* she told herself quietly.

Their last act had been heated and angry. *Had she truly known the man she had married then? Had she just been seduced by his titles and the vain pleasure that she had bested the spiteful cows in Lady Ramkinson's school?*

She shut her eyes; the warmth of the bed was sapping her will to stay awake. *Had he always had a cruel streak?* she wondered. *What kind of a man would have grown up in the shadow of Alexander Andrei?* She opened her eyes again, suddenly cold. *What did it do to anyone when they realised their sibling bested them in every way, when they realised the sibling mattered, and not them?*

So he had been cruel then, she thought, trembling. Would she now live in fear of that cruel streak turning to her? Would she fall victim to violent outbursts of pent-up emotion?

Was he mad?

She decided to find out once and for all. She had to see Alexander Andrei.

She pushed back the covers and picked up her guttering candle, hunting for another. But it was the only one and she sighed, hoping it wouldn't go out. She opened her door carefully then tip-toed along the silent corridor, stopping before the room that she had been forbidden to enter.

She looked round the silent corridor carefully then placed her hand on the doorknob, hoping it wouldn't creak or make any other noise. To her surprise she found the handle turned easily and practically sprung open as the bolt slid out of the frame. There was no squeak as she pushed the door further into the room beyond, pushing her gloomy candle into the darkness before her. Inside the room beyond she could make out a wide and comfortable couch, covered in a dust cloth. Shadows cloaked most of the room but it didn't look very large, about the size of her sitting room.

She hoped it was empty; checking once behind her before stepping in, closing the door and shutting her almost in darkness. She raised the candle above her head to see the room better but the gloom was too deep. She took a steadying breath, listening carefully, her eyes adjusting to the darkness.

There were a few pieces of furniture all covered in dust cloths. She could make out the shapes of them, the white material looking like hunched ghosts in the gloom. It appeared to be come kind of greeting chamber, long disused. *Was this the parlour for Alexander?* The flame guttered even lower, but she could make out the outline of a door hidden amongst the shadows in the wall across the room.

She took a step towards it, accidentally sloshing the hot wax of the candle, a long drip landing on her finger. She winced, juggling the candle to pop the hurt finger in her mouth then stopped in shock.

She strained her ears in the silence, hear heart clogging her mouth. She heard it again, a small sound, like a gasp or somebody moving, changing position on a couch or a bed. She looked around her carefully, trying to see if the person was in the room with her, but could see nothing recognisable as a body. Laura swallowed, her heart loud in her ears, trying to listen past it to hear where the noise was coming from, wondering if she had heard a noise at all.

She crossed to the door steeped in shadows, imagining she heard noises at every step, and caught her breath when her flights of fancy were a little too loud to be imagined. She reached out, delicately dropping her fingers onto the cold door knob, wondering if Alexander Andrei was behind the door, wondering if she was ready for the things she might see. She turned the knob, expecting to feel it stop, the room beyond locked from her timid pry.

But it was not. The candle was no more than a tiny lick of blue, clinging desperately to the wick and useless for illuminating anything, but still Laura did not blow it out, holding it redundantly out in front of her as she pushed open the door. She could see a child's rocking horse near the door, regal and proud, a wooden horse fit for a prince. Soft shapes sat scattered over the floor, huddling on a dust cloth covered chaise lounge. They seemed to make the darkness friendlier, little soft lumps of comfort. *They're toys* she realised.

They have locked him in a secret room in the castle because he now is no better than a child, only pushing his food or a new toy through the door before shutting it again Olaf whispered to her again. So she had found him then. The secret mad Prince of Dalnerechensk.

There was another soft sound, and Laura took a deep breath, steeling herself, wondering what his reaction would be.

'Alexander?' she called softly.

A woman suddenly appeared before her and they both screamed with the shock of seeing the other. Laura had jumped, sloshing the candle wax over her fingers, dropping the candle and holder. She turned, flying out of the room but tripped on the scatterings of toys and furniture, landing heavily, grunting with pain and becoming disorientated in the dark.

There were footsteps behind her, a high keening wail that terrified her. In her panic she couldn't tell how many people were chasing her. She found the door and scrabbled at the handle, yanking it open, looking over her shoulder as she raced out, crashing into Aleksei's arms.

'Oh thank God!' she gasped, relieved, clinging to him.

'*What were you doing in the nursery?*' he thundered.

'Nursery? I – Alexander -' she stopped, confused and frightened by the look on his face.

He seized her arm and dragged her after him, ignoring her frightened words. He threw open the front doors of the castle, startling the guards on the wall. Laura did her best to cover herself, humiliated that she was outside in her night dress with all the servants looking at her, horrified that the windlass on the wall was grinding and the portcullis was up.

'I tried to be lenient with you Laura, I really did,' he was yelling, towing her mercilessly after him, her bare feet cutting and bruising on the gravel as he dragged her over to the stables.

'Aleksei stop! Please -'

'Don't beg, it's so unbecoming of a princess' he sneered, seizing a rope that was hanging on the wall of the stables.

It was fastened around her wrists before she knew what was happening, her head whirling with fear and confusion. He looped the rope over a hook that hung from the eves of the stables, jerking it taut. The ropes bit into her wrists, yanking her arms savagely above her head and wrenching her shoulders as she was almost pulled off her feet. Her hands tingled ticklishly, her big toes brushing at the gravel and Aleksei ripped open the back of her night shirt.

She cried out, begging, seeing him reach for a length of raw hide out of the corner of her eye then screamed as a red tongue of fire licked across her back. The whip slashed again, frenzied, and she screamed louder, begging for help.

'What is it?' Tsar Constantinovich cried, bursting out of the castle, followed closely by Fedor and Mikhail.

They were rooted to the spot in horror at the scene before them and the whip ripped open another line on her back.

'*Stop it! Stop this madness!*' Tsar Constantinovich cried, hurrying down the stairs, suddenly crying out and pressing a hand to his chest.

He clutched at his heart, groaning as he sank to his knees, his face turning ashen. Aleksei looked up, dropping the whip and was tackled by Fedor and Mikhail who wrestled him to the ground and held him there. Castle guards arrived from where they had raced down the single staircase from the walls, two helping to restrain the struggling Prince, more running to help the stricken Tsar. Laura whimpered quietly, suddenly released from the strain of the rope. She slumped forward, finding herself in a strong pair of arms. She screamed as his rough hand pressed against her cuts and he pulled away, staring at her blood on his fingers.

'Laura! My God…' Olaf gasped, his face streaked with horror and fear.

She was dimly aware of the rattle of the portcullis as it descended again, the shouts, the noise of the courtyard, a growing rumble in the air, or perhaps it was in her head. Olaf unbound her hands and threw the rope away, disgusted with it, keeping her pressed tightly to him.

'Tsar!' she blurted out, half coherent when she saw his pale face. 'Don't die!'

'We must get to the hospital!' Fedor cried, shouldering the Tsar and lifting him to his feet, worried by his colour and his fluttery movements.

'No!' Olaf shouted. They looked at him, dumbfounded. 'It's the people, the Revolution has begun!' He explained desperately. 'If they find us tonight they will kill us!'

Laura moaned, twitching.

'Where are they Olaf?' she asked, struggling to stand up on her own.

'Close' he answered, unwilling to tell her it was already too late.

'Castle Dalnerechensk!' she suddenly called out loudly. 'Go to your homes, to your loved ones and your family. Be with them now. I cannot ask you to kill your brothers.'

'But it is our duty to defend the castle' Roman said, standing near the group that was holding Aleksei down, unwilling to put his hands on his sovereign, watching him warily.

'Roman you serve the city; your duty is to protect her from outside attack, not from her own citizens. And you will still serve her, no matter how she is ruled. Do not take arms up against your own brothers. There must be no bloodshed. It is only stone; the heart of what Dalnerechensk means lives in each of you. Go now, all of you, to your families before it's too late.'

There was silence then someone called:

'God bless the Tsesarevna and keep her safe.'

There were the sounds of destruction outside the castle walls, a rumble that was approaching from her utility street, and a roar from Vsevolod's Way. The portcullis was once again cranked up and the gates pulled open. Those in the courtyard began to move, slipping away into the shadows. Olaf swept Laura up in his arms and carried her inside, racing up the stairs to her room.

Anna was inside, terrified and in tears, torn between staying to help her wounded mistress or fleeing to safety herself. Olaf pushed his way into her dressing room, sitting her at her small mirrored table and grabbed a pair of shoes, pushing them onto her bare feet, accidentally hurting her in his haste.

'Take Anna and save yourselves' Laura said, stroking down his unkempt hair.

'Never' he swore.

'You must leave me!' she said, starting to cry, the roar of the mob audible in her rooms.

Olaf ignored her, folding a shawl around her shoulders. She winced at the touch on her back and he pulled her to her feet, sliding his arm round her hips to help her walk. Anna followed them out, her face white, clutching her hands to her chest as if they could protect her from the horrors of what was happening.

Laura's knees felt wobbly and she clung hard to Olaf, convinced at any moment she was going to tumble down the stairs. He tightened his grip on her hip, knowing it was awkward but couldn't slip his arm around her waist as he would hurt her back.

She suddenly stopped as they reached the first floor, glancing along the corridor towards the offices and store rooms of the castle. Olaf tried to tug her along but she resisted.

'Where is Grigory?' she asked.

'Ladozhskoye' he answered, trying again to pull her along.

'The treaties' she said, twisting out of his grip and trotting unsteadily along the corridor.

Olaf followed, aware of the shouts and slamming doors down in the entrance hall, knowing they were running out of time. Anna waited in the corridor near the stairs torn between leaving and helping, calling down stairs for Mikhail.

The two treaties were sitting on Grigory's desk. Laura grabbed them, grateful they would not have to spend precious minutes hunting for them or breaking open Grigory's drawers. She folded them carefully then slipped them inside her nightdress, securing them against her stomach with the elastic of her bloomers, wincing as her skin pulled uncomfortably and her back chafed against the torn ends of her nightdress and her shawl. She did not know if she would ever return, but if she did, or they were captured, the treaties would be her best bargaining tool.

Olaf slid his arm round her again, helping her out of the room. There were more shouts from downstairs, and banging at the castle doors. Peter Kaminin spotted them from where he was standing in the entrance hall, one supportive arm around the grey-faced elderly Tsar. Mikhail and Fedor stood nearby; Aleksei sat on the floor a few paces away, his hands clasped behind his back. Peter waved wildly at them.

'Quickly! Follow me Your Highness, they are here!'

'Are we trapped?' Laura asked, hardly daring to breathe.

'No, there is another way out of here.'

Olaf, Anna and Laura quickly descended the stairs, and Laura could see Aleksei's hands were tied behind his back and his nose was bloody. She wondered which one of them had dared to strike him. She wondered what Olaf would have done to him if he had not had his arms around her. His body had gone stiff with anger though there was a gentleness and a tenderness in his movements. She wondered if his body was having trouble co-ordinating his limbs. Fedor and Peter half walked, half carried the Tsar; Mikhail, Anna, Olaf and Laura falling into step behind them. Laura looked back over her shoulder.

'Aleksei' she reminded them.

There was a pause.

'We can't leave him to be murdered by the mob!' she cried.

The sound of something slamming into the doors startled them and a long splinter of wood from the inside of the door clattered to the ground. Mikhail seized Aleksei and they raced after Peter as he dragged the Tsar towards the kitchen. It was empty, the fires banked down, every pot and pan in its place, all ready for the day workers to come in the next morning and prepare their breakfast. That innocent expectancy of it all caused the tears to well up in Laura's eyes as they rushed past, heading down the stairs to the cellar.

She slipped on the steep stairs and Olaf's grip tightened, steadying her against him. Her back ached but they rushed on, past the racks of wine. Laura was glad the snowy grit that had covered the floor last the time she had been down here was gone, there was nothing for their footprints to leave tell-tale tracks in. In the far recesses of the cellar Peter threw aside two large barrels of wine, revealing a grate in the floor.

Laura was surprised, the grate led to the underground river that flowed from the spring in Tcherepnin. She had thought that the tunnel had been blocked off and forgotten about over the years of peace with Russia. *Perhaps it was opened again after the recent unrest* she thought to herself. *Perhaps it was opened when they discovered Nikita's army camped on their borders.*

Peter tore open the grate and pushed Aleksei bodily through. Laura heard the splash and the grunt as he landed, his voice loud and hollow with the echoes of the tunnel. Fedor dropped through next and reached up for Tsar Constantinovich, Mikhail and Peter maneuvering the old man gently into the tunnel from above. He was mumbling, and semiconscious, but still alive.

Olaf took her arms and passed her down the grate to Fedor who caught her carefully round her waist. He and Peter then jumped down, closing the grate behind them. Laura wondered how they were going to disguise their escape route but then realised it didn't matter. By the time they discovered it they would be long gone.

The tunnel was dank, the walls were covered with a slimy moss, and it was difficult to see in the darkness. Laura hoped she wouldn't slip and fall face first in the ankle-deep water. Wet, illegible treaties would serve no one. Olaf's arms found her in the dark again and slipped round her, pulling her close. She was glad for his presence here, in the most terrifying situation she had ever found herself in.

Together the little company moved off into the night. Their footsteps echoed loudly, bouncing off the walls and echoing back until it sounded like there were footsteps behind them, chasing them. Their wide eyes searched the darkness around them but saw nothing.

Olaf kept his arm around Laura, feeling her trembling in pain and shock. He had been surprised with how many more had crowded into the bar; surprised how bitter, angry and hardened they had been, frightened by Aleksei's disappearance and the Emperors on their soil, and the ghastly silence from the castle that had followed their departure.

The socialist on the bar top had whipped them up into a frenzy of rebellion, but he had underestimated the mood in the bar, they weren't willing to be pacified by his crafty arguments anymore; and several parties had slipped out the door. Olaf had despaired, not knowing which group to follow, and had sloped through all the streets to find trouble. The hour was late when he heard it at last, breaking glass and the rumbling discontent of the mob. He had turned and run then, they were reckless, murderous; he had sprinted all the way back to the castle to warn them.

He shuddered in fury, remembering the sight that had greeted him when he had slipped through the portcullis and gates of the castle. *What the hell did the poor girl do to provoke that?* he wondered, his hands tightening in anger. She gasped beside him and he relented, whispering an apology. She turned her face into his neck to whisper back to him, aware how loud their voices were, her breath misting on his throat.

'Olaf, help Tsar Constantinovich, he needs you more than I do' she whispered. 'I will be alright.'

He paused, reluctant to let her go, but then noticed how stiffly she was holding herself. *I'm hurting her or embarrassing her* he thought then released her, slipping back to Fedor and Mikhail who were struggling with the enfeebled Tsar, sliding his arm around him and shouldering his weight.

They struggled on in the endless night, one hand on the wall of the tunnel so as not to lose their way and get turned around; one hand in front of them so as not to walk into anything. Laura was thankful Olaf had thought to put shoes on her feet but wished he had thought of some socks. They were water logged and stung with every step. She knew she would soon be sporting bloodied blisters as well as the cuts and bruises from the gravel. The only thing that kept her going was knowing somewhere behind her in the dark was Aleksei.

She shut her eyes and tried her best not to sob. *He had been shocked at my scars* she thought miserably. *I saw him hold back tears when I told him about them, and now he has inflicted even more pain…* she stopped, trying to force those thoughts away. *It wouldn't matter if Aleksei had whipped her if the Revolutionaries killed her* she told herself, and forced herself to concentrate on putting one foot in front of the other, ignoring the pain.

But she couldn't stop her mind wandering. She knew Dalnerechensk monarchs were allowed to punish their civilians and property with archaic and barbaric methods. She knew she had been foolish looking for Alexander Andrei. For all she knew he could be dead. *Why had he been so angry that she had been in the nursery? Did this mean Tatiana was indeed pregnant? That the Law of Propriety would be reversed? That her husband's mistress would raise her son to become a prince?*

She shut her eyes. *Not anymore* she told herself. *There were no more princes or monarchy…* She wondered if there would even be a Principality when the Revolution was over.

Her thoughts turned to Ekaterina and Grigory, wondering where they were, and what had become of them. She prayed that they had escaped unharmed, prayed that they would make it back to Varennikov Castle where they would be protected by her father, or even to Constantinople. She begged God silently that they had been spared from murderous intention.

The attack had been so quick on the castle she thought. *But they would see the mob coming for them from their home, please God don't let them be sleeping, oblivious to this.* She didn't want to think of her friends dead, butchered in angry revolution. She wondered if people were dying, if the castle guards were fighting back as the Revolutionaries stormed into the castle. *Will I die?* she wondered.

She was bitterly disappointed and angry. *If Aleksei had climbed the wall like he was supposed to none of this would have happened. They couldn't wait just* one *more day —*

Her hand hit something in the darkness, jarring her thoughts to a stop. It was crumbling metal, and felt like the bars of another grate. Peter, who had been walking beside her, quickly ran his hands over the metal, finding the catches, the hinges and the weaknesses in the grate. Laura realised the water in the tunnel was flowing over a lowered sluice gate from the room beyond the metal bars. Peter set his shoulders then grunted and pulled. The bars ground out of the way, rumbling and whining.

Quickly he stepped over the low sluice gate and reached back to take Laura's hand, helping her over. The room beyond felt cavernous and was filled with water. Laura guessed they were in Tcherepnin's water reservoir and the natural spring waters that flowed up into the fountain in the centre of Tcherepnin's market could be directed underground here, where it would flow through the sluice gates into the underground river to Dalnerechensk's reservoir, protected from poisoning attempts by besieging enemies.

Vsevolod had thought of everything when he designed the valley strong hold, Laura realised. *Except internal revolt* she added dryly, then wondered what he would have thought seeing what his people had become. She sighed softly, pushing the thoughts from her head. They had escaped the castle, but were by no means safe yet.

The water in the reservoir was knee deep, and Laura could hear the sound of water splashing down into the basin. It didn't sound like a large volume of water was pouring in, and she guessed only some of the spring had been diverted, most was still flowing through the fountain above them in the market. *If the water had suddenly stopped flowing it would create a panic* she realised. It also meant they were not in danger of the water level rising alarmingly fast to soak the treaties, or worse, drown them here below the city.

Peter led the way across the reservoir, feeling ahead of him carefully in the darkness for the bottom step he knew was there. He found it and guided them up carefully; aware the roughhewn marble was slippery from years of water polishing it smooth. The hem of Laura's nightgown tangled around her legs, uncomfortably clingy. At the top of the stairs was a door and Peter hesitated, pressing his ear against the cold steel to listen to the street outside.

He pulled open the door and ushered them quickly out into the unassuming service alley between two office buildings. The night outside seemed bright in comparison to the dark of the tunnels below the cities. The village was in confusion, they could see people in the streets at the end of the alley in their night clothes, all gazing up towards Dalnerechensk and asking each other worried and confused questions.

'This is as far I as I can go with you' Peter said. 'I can't leave the army ungoverned.'

'Thank you,' Laura said, pressing his hands tightly. 'Thank you for all you have done for us, I will not forget it. Do not let them kill each other, if you win they will hate you, if you lose, they will hang you. God bless and be with you.'

Peter kissed her cheek and her hands then bowed and turned, pushing the door to the reservoir shut behind him. Laura eyed the door sadly, there was only a lock on this side, she could not open the door and follow him to safety again.

Olaf looked out into the street and beckoned the small fugitive party forward. They stepped out into the market square of Tcherepnin. No one paid any attention to the small group that crawled out of the reservoir, their eyes locked on the horror of the orange flames that were licking from windows in the castle, the blaze dancing like gleeful devils against the old stone, lighting the walls and watchtowers.

Laura moaned quietly at the sight and hoped no one was hurt, looking around at her companions carefully. She and Tsar Constantinovich were still in their nightclothes though the others were dressed and she thought they would pass for other bewildered citizens of Tcherepnin, as no one seemed to be paying attention to their surroundings.

Alarms were ringing, people were riveted to the spot in awe and fear or running back and forward, trying to organise volunteers still willing to risk their lives to rescue the monarchy. Olaf bore the old Tsar as discreetly as possible through the throngs, the rest of the party following him. The guards at Tcherepnin's Forest Gate were too busy watching the flames to notice the party slipping down the road to the trees of the Hunting Forest.

Once inside they began to breathe again, the fear and tension abating somewhat. Olaf carried the Tsar for an hour inside the trees before he finally stopped, setting the old man gently down on a moss covered rock. The exhausted party sat too, finding stones or tree logs or just making do with the ground, catching their breaths and shivering slightly in their damp clothes.

Olaf pulled open the Tsar's nightshirt and pressed his ear to his chest, listening. Laura sat on her knees before the Tsar, taking his hand while Olaf knelt beside her, listening, his face unreadable.

'His heart is weak' he said finally. 'That nearly killed him.'

Laura shut her eyes against her tears then stroked back his grey locks, looking at him carefully. The forest was dark but even then she could see how frail and tired he looked.

'Laura my dear, I'm so sorry' he whispered, squeezing her hand.

'Shh' she soothed. 'Rest Your Majesty, you have had a bad turn.'

The Tsar sighed and shut his eyes. Laura stroked his hair again, eyeing Olaf who stayed with his head pressed against the old man's chest, his arms round him tenderly. *Olaf loved him* she realised. *Loved him fiercely.* Tsar Constantinovich stroked his messy blonde hair, shutting his eyes.

'I'm sorry' Olaf said quietly.

'You are a good boy my son' Tsar Constantinovich answered quietly then added something that Laura didn't quite catch. Olaf shut his eyes against his tears.

She bit her lip, moved by his emotion and turned away, looking at the others in their company.

'You should leave us' she suddenly said quietly. They looked up at her in surprise. 'Our fate is not yours.'

'We are not leaving you' Olaf said and Mikhail, Anna and Fedor swore to follow until death parted them.

Laura smiled, shutting her eyes against the tears, pleased that she would not be alone with Aleksei on the run from revolution.

They sat quietly, recovering from their exhausting flight, and the company could not stop their eyes from drifting between Laura and Aleksei. They had seen what he had done, or heard her screams of pain. *What were they going to do now?* they asked themselves. *How dangerous was he now? Was he insane? Could they abandon their sovereign leader to his fate alone here in the forests of Dalnerechensk?* They burned with a torment, torn between hatred for him and their duty to serve him. Aleksei glared back at them, proud and unrepentant.

'You know what the punishment is for embarrassing the Monarchy' he snapped at them. 'Get up, we have rested long enough.'

'He will not make it' Olaf said quietly.

'Leave me here' the Tsar said and was hushed by Laura.

'Olaf, find some branches we can make a stretcher from, we will carry him' she said. 'We cannot stay here; we are still too close. They will look for us.'

Olaf kissed the Tsar's cheek, leaving him to quickly hunt for some suitable branches. They had nothing to cut suitable lengths and so had to make do with what they found. Laura took off her shawl and gave it to Olaf who used the material to create a make-shift hammock sling. She flushed, bowing her head, sitting in the Hunting Forest of Dalnerechensk in a ripped nightdress, the material sliding off her shoulders. Anna slipped behind her, tying it closed as best as she could to give her some dignity, gasping when she saw the damage to her back.

Laura stood, thanking Anna quietly and helped the ashen-faced Tsar to ease onto the ground. Olaf and Mikhail came forward, helping her, arranging the Tsar carefully on the stretcher sling. Olaf, Fedor and Mikhail took up a position around him, ready to lift the poles then stopped, turning to look at the only man left. Aleksei's mouth twisted down.

'I am not a common labourer' he sneered.

'For Christ's sake he is your father!' Laura cried. Aleksei was unmoved. 'Anna help me' she said, moving into the last place at the foot of the stretcher.

Anna stood inside the sling hammock, taking hold of the pole Laura grabbed. They counted to three then lifted the Tsar, praying that the poles were strong enough, the shawl was strong enough. It held and they began to shuffle along, heading deeper into the Hunting Forest.

Aleksei sloped after them, eyeing the party distrustfully. *That artful witch had turned my whole Principality against me, had defied me and made herself a whore and a laughing stock but still they flocked to her like moths to a flame. I should never have married her. At least the Hungarian horse would have been obedient.*

Laura stumbled over the uneven ground, her shoes torturing her with every step, the weight of the pole dragging at her sore shoulders, rubbing her hands raw. They were winding their way through the dark forest, running parallel to the Tcherepnin road to Kalach. She understood why they were not walking on the road itself but as the shoes twisted and rubbed her feet to ribbons she couldn't help but wish they were.

They stopped to rest once more and Laura clutched her hands to her décolletage, trying to shield them from the pain of the stretcher sling. Fedor sat beside her, blowing on his raw hands, trying to ease the pain as well. Olaf took her hands and she winced as he brushed them roughly, accidentally, as he inspected them. He apologised then tore off the sleeves of his shirt, ripping them up to use as bindings for their hands.

They thanked him quietly then stood, taking her place by the stretcher, knowing they had to move on. Fatigue was making the Tsar feel twice as heavy but Laura said nothing, trudging wearily on, pushing the pain she felt into a corner of her mind, locking it away so she could still function. At least her hands didn't hurt as much, and wished he would wrap bindings around her feet, wondering if he had enough shirt for that.

The trees of the Hunting Forest fell away, leaving them exposed on the flank of Eastern Valley. Before them was a stretch of open ground and the single farm house and mill that was the hamlet of Kalach.

'Quickly now' Olaf said, and they glanced nervously at the empty road that wound down the flank of Eastern Valley to the house.

They reached the silent house without seeing a soul on the road and Olaf pounded on the door with his fist. There was movement inside, a light was lit and the frightened farmer peeked out, asking who it was. He was greatly surprised to see the Royal family and four servants on his door step. Laura saw he was the farmer who had hurt his arm all those months ago in the market, when her father had stopped his barreling milk cart and saved Natasha Riminova's life.

'Help us' she begged quietly.

He quickly looked up the empty road to the trees then opened the door, ushering them in. Laura thanked him, stumbling with exhaustion and felt the warmth of his house fold round her comfortingly.

'You saved my life once, I'll save yours now' he answered.

A woman's frightened voice called down from the loft. The company looked up to see his wife on the stairs, a shawl thrown over her nightdress. The farmer explained why the Royal Household was standing in their living room and she quickly came down the stairs, giving the servants orders to bring in wood, stoke the fire, prepare food and drink for them all.

The farmer and Olaf gently lay the ill Tsar on a wooden cot near the fire and covered him with blankets. The farmer's wife checked the temperature of his forehead and cheeks with the backs of her fingers, shooting a worried look at her husband.

Laura sank down wearily on a hard wooden chaise lounge, glad to be off her feet. She was dimly aware of the throb in her back and feet and hands, dimly aware that Anna and the farmer's wife were preparing food for all of them, knowing the meal would leave the family poor and strained for a week. She was dimly aware that Mikhail and Fedor were carting in firewood and stoking the fire. She didn't know where Aleksei was. Perhaps he had gone up to the loft to sleep.

Olaf sat beside her with a bowl of water and some clean soft linen rags. He shifted; putting the bowl of water beside him on the seat, turning her so her back was towards him, whispering that it would hurt while he cleaned the wounds. She felt him stroke her hair out of the road, felt him tug out the hastily tied knots in her ruined nightdress. She flinched once when he pressed the warm wet cloth against her, balling her hands in her nightdress.

Olaf worked gently, patting away the blood, squeezing the water into the bowl, marveling at the way she did not cry out as he worked. He gently pulled out another knot, opening her gown further, moving aside the material to wash another wound, catching sight of a white scar. Unable to stop himself he pulled her dress open wider, staring at the mess of scars that criss-crossed her lower back, gasping in horror.

She half turned, the dress slipping off her creamy shoulder and she pressed her hands to her chest to stop it falling off her. Olaf shut his eyes.

'It was not the first time' he said huskily.

'I had just arrived at Lady Ramkinson's School of Decorum, sent away from Texas where my father had struck oil. I had had no schooling prior to that, my father was drilling holes in the dirt and my mother was going insane. I was left to fend for myself a lot of the time' she smiled sadly then it faded away.

'Lady Ramkinson always carried a riding crop, but never went riding. She beat me for climbing one of the trees in her garden. It was the first lesson I learned at the school: *to fear the riding crop*. I was nine years old.'

She dropped her eyes and turned away, biting her lip at the look on his face. There was silence and she wondered if he was struggling with his emotions like Fredrik had, fighting with what he knew he couldn't say. She heard him swallow thickly behind her then the splashing as he dipped the cloth back into the water. She winced again and Olaf apologised, carefully pressing a freshly made poultice to her wounds to help them heal, retying her night dress when he was finished.

'My feet' she whispered.

Olaf slid off the couch and knelt on the floor, pulling off her shoes, his mouth dropping open.

'*Tsesarevna*, I'm so sorry' he said, gently beginning to wash away the blood, apologising each time she flinched.

They don't seem so fine and dainty now she thought when he was finished, leaving her shoes off, laying her hand on his head in thanks. She bid him good night absently then sat on the floor by Tsar Constantinovich's bed, resting her head on the mattress. His face was pinched with pain and she shut her eyes, trying not to think of what Aleksei had done to them. She ached all over but was too frightened to sleep and hoped her tears would not disturb the Tsar.

101

Tsar Constantinovich's fluttering hand on her hair brought her out of her doze. She had only slept for a moment and felt the agony of her wounds all the more sharply for having sat still so long. She took his hand, aware of his eyes on her.

'Go and eat *Tsarevna*' he said, pain slicing the roundness and richness off the vowels.

Laura got painfully to her feet, her back hurting too much to stretch out her cramped muscles. The farmer's wife came to her, curtseying as she handed over a plain dress and some socks.

'It is not much Your Highness, but it was our daughter's before she wed' she said.

'It's beautiful' Laura answered and took the dress, slipping away from the company to strip off her nightdress awkwardly, whimpering with the pain the movement caused then pulled on the course blue dress. She could not reach behind her to struggle with the buttons so she left the dress undone and pulled on the socks and shoes then went back to the company, patting her stomach carefully to check the treaties were snugly in place.

The table had been set for two people, and the servants and the farmers stood back, waiting for her and Aleksei to eat first. Aleksei was sitting at the head of the table already eating.

'Come! None of this now' Laura said. 'Sit, all of you and eat with us, we owe each of you our lives, some more than others' she said, her eyes straying to Aleksei.

They shot a quick look at the Prince, noticed it irritated him and sat happily, setting their places with wooden bowls and tin spoons, blessing their Princess. Olaf watched how little she ate, giving what she didn't eat with those who were still hungry. Her dull eyes would tighten when she moved and he guessed her clothing was hurting her.

'What will you do now?' the farmer asked, setting down his spoon in his empty bowl.

'We must leave Dalnerechensk' Laura answered.

'We will hide you here till dark, you can cross the wall then' the farmer said.

'We must go immediately' Olaf answered. 'They will send people to the four corners of Dalnerechensk, telling everyone that there is a new government. They will have discovered us gone by now. No one in Dalnerechensk should be found harbouring us.'

'What about the Tsar?' the farmer's wife broke in. 'He is too ill.'

'I will go' he answered. There was to be no argument from the tone of his voice.

Laura dropped her eyes, shutting them. She knew his chances of survival were slim.

'Then we give you our milk cart, you cannot carry him all day' the farmer said matter-of-factly. 'I will go and get it ready.'

He stood and bowed to the table then hurried outside.

The others set about quickly readying the company to leave, washing dishes, sweeping the floor. Anna quickly buttoned Laura's dress for her and although she was pleased to have some form of modesty again she winced at the feel of the cloth against her cuts. They looked around them carefully, wondering if there was any trace of them that would implicate the farmers in their escape.

The farmer's wife pressed a satchel of food into Olaf's hands. Laura gasped, exclaiming the gift was too generous.

'We are farmers; we are better off than those in the mines. You must take it, you have nothing' the wife said, waving off her protests.

Laura cried at their generosity, blessed them and promised not to forget them.

Olaf and Fedor carefully helped the Tsar to his feet, shouldering his weight between them as they carried him out of the house. The cart had been brought to the front door and Laura saw that it had an oilskin covering a metal frame that rose above the bed. The oilskin would protect him from the sun and the rain, and the sides had been rolled up to let the fresh air in. The bed of the cart had been filled with soft hay and Olaf and Fedor gently lifted the old Tsar inside, lying him out carefully.

'Are you comfortable Your Majesty?' Laura asked, folding her shawl over him to keep him warm.

'Da' he answered, smiling weakly. 'You're a good daughter Laura.'

She smiled and kissed his forehead. Anna placed the satchel of food and some bottles of milk and water into the cart with him. They said their goodbyes to the kind farmers hurriedly and began to walk, heading for the border wall. Laura couldn't help but remember how quickly it seemed the wall had approached while she had been neck and neck with Filip in a race that seemed so long ago now. *How quickly and how drastically the world could change in one little moment!*

The low stone wall grew larger and more distinct as they drew closer and they held their breaths, their eyes darting around nervously, expecting any minute to hear a shout of alarm as someone recognised them and shot them on the spot. But they reached the stone wall unhindered and carefully lifted and maneuvered the milk cart over it, not wanting to break an axle or jolt the ill Tsar too much.

On Russian soil they increased the pace nervously, frightened of being caught so close to the border. Laura was glad of the thick socks she was wearing; her shoes did not rub anymore and padded her feet somewhat from the uneven ground. They slipped into a valley pass of the Eastern Urals, Dalnerechensk disappearing behind them. Laura wondered if she would ever see it again then didn't want to think about that.

It was well into the afternoon before they dared to stop for a brief lunch. Laura climbed into the cart and gently lifted the old Tsar's head, spooning cold broth into his mouth and wiping his old whiskers. He rumbled in his chest then coughed, spluttering the broth into his beard. Laura soothed him and wiped the mess away quickly, smiling at him tenderly. He stroked her messy hair and smiled, the pain he was in evident in his eyes.

'Laura, dearest in Dalnerechensk' he said softly, coughing again.

'Shh, you must rest Your Majesty' she said, placing a gentle kiss on his forehead then slipped out of the cart.

Olaf gave her a bowl of cold broth and she sat quietly, eating a little, then gave the rest of her broth to Anna. Olaf felt her forehead and cheeks with the back of his fingers, wondering if she was beginning a fever, then gently turned her around, opening her dress. He poured a little water into a clean bowl then bathed her back gently, reapplying the soothing poultice on the wounds before fastening her dress again. She thanked him quietly, shutting her eyes tightly when she saw the strange look of anger and pain on Aleksei's face.

'Why did you go into the Nursery?' he asked finally, his voice hollow and agonised.

There was a gasp and Anna, Mikhail and Fedor crossed themselves. Laura was surprised by their reactions and felt fear crawl across her skin. *What was so wrong with the nursery?*

'I was looking for Alexander Andrei' she said, shutting her eyes. 'I had been told he was locked somewhere in the castle and no one could see him. I thought because I was stopped from going in –'

'You stupid wench,' Aleksei laughed, but there was no malice in his voice, only the tired pain of giving up. 'It was because of the curse you weren't to go in there.'

'What curse?' she whispered.

'Natasha's curse, my lady' Fedor said quietly. 'She was Vsevolod's wife. She oversaw the building of the nursery; the colours, the material, the fabric for the upholstery. She poured her life into that room, and it all came to nothing. She was barren Your Highness. She died miserably of an illness, cursing barrenness on the wombs of all wives of Tsars who entered thereafter. For four hundred years since then no Tsaritsa has ever set foot inside the nursery before the heir was born. Some refused to *ever* set foot in there. All descendants of Vsevolod come from his second wife Agnessa'

'We will never have children now' Aleksei sighed.

Laura dropped her eyes, fuming at the stupid superstition, feeling a bawdy comment about having to try harder wiggling on the tip of her tongue, and an even deeper ache in her, one that said: *If I remain childless it will have nothing to do with a stupid curse.* She turned away and shut her eyes tiredly.

'Your Highness?' Mikhail suddenly asked. 'Where are we to go?'

They looked at him then their eyes flicked between Aleksei, Laura and the milk cart where Tsar Constantinovich lay, wondering who was really in charge now.

'We will go to Prussia' Aleksei said. 'We have a treaty with them and they recognise us. When we are safe we will figure out what to do.'

There was a brief silence. The advice was what they had expected of a leader, and Aleksei looked calm and in control again. Laura realised that they had no doses of laudanum with them and wondered if he was in any pain at all. He didn't look it.

'They will have expected us to go to Europe, but by the quickest route west, through Davostok' he went on. 'We will continue East till clear of the Urals, then cross back through and head towards Prussia.'

'That will take us close to Moscow' Fedor pointed out.

'What else do you suggest? Walk across Siberia?' Aleksei asked. 'Prussia is our only option.'

The company fell silent again then stood and wiped their bowls clean, putting the food into the cart before trudging on through the forests of the Russian Urals.

102

That night in Russia was thick with rain, a torrent of misery that thundered down onto them, drenching them through to the bone. They had trudged on wearily from their short lunch break, the sky darkening over them until the afternoon had swirled into night. The only sound they could hear was the chaotic plinking of the droplets crashing into the oilskin and the wood-sodden rumble of the wheels as they bumped over the uneven ground in the forest. No one spoke.

The ground turned to mud under them. Rivers ran between the tree roots, carrying away leaves and the forest debris. It rolled pebbles under their feet or clung suddenly at their boots, making their legs ache with every step. Olaf, Mikhail and Fedor sweated and strained to move the cart a few feet at a time.

Laura finally stopped, exhausted and numb with pain, unsure what the time was or even how far they had walked.

'I cannot' she moaned. 'We must stop, we must rest.'

Her words were lost in the drumming of the rain on the muddy ground. Slowly she sank down, sitting on a wet boulder and smoothed her hair off her cheek, sopping and miserable, her back aching and chafing inside her wet tightened dress. Olaf, Mikhail and Fedor sat down with a squelch where they stood, panting and exhausted.

'We can't make a fire here' Aleksei said, sitting on a stone under the wagon, pulling his legs up and getting as far away from the rain as he could.

'We must stop, I can't keep walking' Laura said quietly, too exhausted to move now.

Anna crawled under the cart, sitting at a diplomatic distance from Aleksei, mopping her sopping face. After a pause the three men crawled under as well, huddling with each other for warmth, trying to ignore the wet ground beneath them, their boots poking out into the rain. The wagon creaked as Tsar Constantinovich coughed and shifted on his bed of hay.

With some effort Laura crawled over and pulled herself into the cart, sitting beside the Tsar and taking his fluttery, gnarled hand in her own, brushing his hair tenderly with the backs of her fingers. His skin was the colour of sallow ash, his cheeks purple hollows under his eyes. His breathing had become ragged during the damp day and the pain in his eyes made her wince.

He managed a gentle smile for her.

'My beloved daughter' he said softly.

Tears welled up in Laura's eyes and she kissed the back of his hand, smoothing his hair again.

'I am sorry, my dear -' he started.

'My lord, you have nothing to be sorry about' she said, kissing his hand again.

She reached for a bottle of milk and unstoppered it, holding his head up and pouring carefully to help him drink. She then opened the food satchel and pulled out the last loaf of bread, tearing off a hunk she sat on the hay beside her, putting the rest back in the satchel. She poured a bowl of cold soup from a wine skin, maneuvering the Tsar till he was propped up against her, protected from the wetness of her dress by the hay she raked up between them.

'I'm sorry Your Majesty, this must taste terrible' she said quietly, soaking bits of bread in the soup and gently dropping them into his mouth, wiping his whiskers as he ate.

Olaf lifted the oilskin and reached into the cart, pulling out the satchel for the others, his face lined with concern when he saw the Tsar's state. Laura tried to ignore the pain in his eyes because it would set her crying, and she wiped the Tsar's whiskers again. She could hear the company beneath her talking quietly, hear the sounds of them pouring cold soup and drinking from wooden bowls.

'Tell me of Alexander the Great' Tsar Constantinovich said, breaking into her thoughts. 'Tell me of Gaugamela.'

Laura sniffed, lying the Tsar back down, tucking her shawl around him warmly.

'His most famous of the three battles against the Persian king Darius the Third' she said, knowing he knew all this already. 'Alexander faced a vastly superior force on a battlefield that had been especially cleared for the scythed chariots. During the battle he used an unusual and risky strategy to draw much of Darius' cavalry to the flanks so he could strike a decisive blow at Darius' centre. The weakened Persian centre broke under Alexander's wedge assault and Darius was forced to turn and flee for the third time' she stopped, understanding why he had asked her to tell him of the battle.

It was Darius' third and final defeat by Alexander, he never got to pit his fourth army in battle against the Macedonian king as he was wounded mortally and left to die in the road by an usurper.

He knew he was dying.

Laura put her face in her hands to hold back the tears then tucked more hay around him, pulling it over him then lay against his chest, trying to keep him warm.

'Darius was an opponent worthy of Alexander the Great' she said. 'Defeated three times and yet still he fought; still he came to keep his home safe from an usurper. *We will not leave you to die in the road*' she promised, shutting her eyes against the tears.

She lay beside him, the cold folds of her dress clinging to her, and the night air slithering along her back, warmed only by the livid red and raw kisses of the whip. She began to shake, whimpering, listening to the rain attack the oilskin and the Tsar struggle for life. Despite her exhaustion sleep refused to come and her hand drifted to her midsection where the treaties had been carefully wrapped inside a section of the waterproof canvas she had cut when it had begun to rain.

She had no idea how long she had lain there with her face in the hay, had no idea how long they had walked into the night. Time had seemed to stand still, stretching away into long hours of saturation and cold. But the darkness was now lightening and she sat up, eyeing the fluttery, twitchy body of the Tsar.

His colour was worse in the morning light, the sickly grey of those at death's door. He groaned softly under his breath and his eyelids fluttered unceasingly. Laura stroked his hair and tried to rouse him but he didn't respond, murmuring restlessly.

Anna knocked quietly on the cart side and opened the oilskin flap looking wet and uncomfortable. It had not stopped raining. Laura managed to slip to the ground with Anna's help and turned to eye the men sitting miserably under the cart. She shut her eyes and gathered every inch of will power she had left.

'Tsar Constantinovich is dying' she said, clenching her fists as she tried desperately not to sob. 'He -' she stopped, deciding against saying anymore, turning away from them.

The men scrambled out from under the cart. Fedor lifted the flap of the oilskin, his eyes drifting into the darkness in the cart, the men behind him looking in too. For a long while Fedor stood there quietly, rigid with emotion until he finally lowered the flap, dropping his head and swallowing with difficulty.

'He is -' he started thickly then couldn't go on.

Anna gave up a high keening wail, throwing herself onto the forest floor where she was as nearly drowned with the rivers of mud as she was with her tears. Laura put her face in her hands, her body wracked with her sorrow, an aching hollow feeling starting deep inside her chest. The men dropped their heads, even Aleksei, who had seemed to have recovered his dignity while the rain had washed away that of the rest of the company.

We won't be able to give him a proper funeral Laura suddenly thought. *He's lying in state in a milk cart.* The thought made her cry even more. The old Tsar had ruled a nation that no one in Europe cared about, and had a pain in his lower back which made women take him by the arm and lead him around like an infirm child. *The only practical thing to do now would be to bury him* she told herself, *and he will lie in an unmarked grave in Russia.* There was nothing more degrading for a Tsar of Dalnerechensk.

'Olaf, Fedor, Mikhail,' she said thickly, screwing her eyes tightly shut to control herself. 'Over there by the mossy stump. That's a fitting place to bury a Tsar.'

It *was* a fitting place, the green stump twisted and twirled like a new vine pirouetting towards the sky. It sat on a raised mound of earth that had once overlooked the bend of an ancient riverbed, a watercourse that was now turning into a river again with the rain pouring out of the hills. On either side of the elegant stump was a flanking curtain of young saplings which drew the eye up towards the centre. The whole setting looked majestic and tranquil.

'To bury him in Russian soil is an insult' Aleksei said.

'We cannot carry him back or they will bury us beside him' Laura said quietly. 'He will lie in the forests he loved so much.'

Aleksei was silent, shutting his eyes, knowing she was right. He turned away from them, retreating into the wagon to sit privately with his father, pulling down the oilskin. Laura sat down in the mud, sobbing quietly, reaching out to take hold of Anna's hand tightly. She would have liked to have sat with Tsar Constantinovich, to have held his hand one last time, but did not want to be with Aleksei, and knew he had to make his peace with his father.

Olaf, Mikhail and Fedor looked at each other quietly then climbed the low embankment. The only digging equipment they had with them were the spoons, they would have to dig Tsar Constantinovich's grave with their bare hands. It was not a prospect any of them relished.

While they cleared the forest floor of debris and began to scoop out the soft black mud Laura and Anna continued to cry, watching the men work. Once they had climbed the embankment to help dig but the men had turned them away. Unwilling to do nothing Laura tore branches off the saplings and retreated to the milk cart where she sat out of the rain weaving wreaths from the branches. Anna too tore branches from the trees and sat with Laura, working silently.

They decorated the wreaths with wood roses and leaves, listening to the sounds above them from the cart, masked and distorted though they were by the rain on the oilskin. It took the men the better part of the morning, but at last they had dug the soft earth deep enough so wild animals would not disturb the grave. Olaf and Mikhail sat by the grave, panting from their efforts, the rain pouring through their hair and down their faces.

Fedor came down the embankment, reaching down to help Laura and Anna to their feet. Laura winced at the pull in her back and shifted her shoulders uncomfortably inside her dress. She was dreading this moment. She knocked quietly on the wooden side of the cart, not willing to push open the oilskin, not wanting to see what was inside.
'Tsar Stephanovich' she said, pushing away her tears, calling Aleksei by his new official title: The son of Stephan. 'It is time to bury your father.'

There was a hesitation then the cart creaked as Aleksei shifted, sighing quietly. He pushed aside the oilskin and swung himself out. Fedor flipped the oilskin back, reaching in carefully. Aleksei, having once refused to bear the stretcher, now carefully lifted out the dead son of Constantine by his shoulders, carrying him with Fedor's help to the grave.

Anna and Laura followed them, trying not to look at that damp black hole in the ground. It took a few moments of negotiation as they tried to give his body as much dignity as possible before they had the old man laid out in the muddy ground. He was still in his nightshirt and Laura's shawl, though it managed to look like a robe and mantle through the blur of Laura's tears. She and Anna lay the wreaths on his chest and feet, folding his cold hands on his stomach. *We don't even have a sword of state for him* Laura thought miserably.

Olaf suddenly darted away down to the milk cart, slamming his fists into it, smashing the wooden sides and mutilating them. Laura shut her eyes, letting him express his grief in his own gruff and blunt way, saying nothing as she heard the low metallic groan of bending metal.

To her surprise he came back to the grave, a metal bracket he had wrenched from the cart in his grip. He leaned down and placed the top of the bracket in the Tsar's hands, arranging the long part of the copper support to lie against his body, pointing at his feet. It looked like the dull blade of a bronze sword in his hands and Laura managed a tiny, brief smile at his thoughtfulness.

'Forgive us for burying you without a priest' she whispered to the Tsar as she knelt down and kissed his forehead gently. 'I pray your soul finds its freedom and paradise.'

Aleksei sighed gently, standing at the head of the grave in a posture of misery. He began to talk, a long, awkward eulogy that lurched between the pomp of state ceremony and the heartbreaking intimacy of a son who loved his father and felt responsible for his death. Laura felt sorry for him, aware of the agonies and intricacies of public grief. He finally stopped, sighing something softly under his breath then lifted a clod of soggy earth and crumbled it over the old man's body. He then turned and walked away from them all, sitting by himself in the cart, pulling the oilskins down again.

As Aleksei had talked Laura had watched the rain splash down onto the Tsar, gathering in pools and rivers that settled in the hollows of his eyes and between the press of his lips, waiting for him to stir and push the water away. Now she shut her eyes and lifted a wet handful of earth, sprinkling it over his legs, unwilling to do so but knowing she had to participate in saying goodbye.

One by one each of the servants said their goodbyes and their apologies, sprinkling his body with wet dirt. There was a long pause as they all tried to avoid the inevitable then Olaf sighed, beginning to carefully place the sod back into the hole. Mikhail helped him but they were unwilling to dirty the loved man's face. So they covered his body like children burying their father in the sand at the beach. Once, when the mud had accidentally splashed onto the Tsar's cheek, Olaf absently wiped it off with a gentle caress for the man who had shown him such affection.

When all but his face had been covered Mikhail and Olaf looked at each other, pausing briefly. Olaf shut his eyes and cried *God help me*, turning away and weeping as he pushed the earth to cover the Tsar's face. They finished quickly after that, filling the hole by pushing the dirt in haphazardly, not wanting to think who was buried under the mud. They then collected stones from the ancient riverbed and piled them high atop the grave, stacking them into a loose pyramid. Laura eyed the finished grave, thinking how beautiful it was, and how awful at the same time.

Olaf threw himself onto the muddy ground and sobbed for the man who had loved him like a son, whispering his grief to the ground that held him. Laura tried not to listen, but couldn't help overhearing a few words. They had a strange inflection, an unusual pronunciation. Laura thought it was his grief slurring his speech until she began to suspect the words were in another language.

That surprised her; she had thought Olaf a man of no education, and certainly no schooling in other languages. She wondered if he was a foreigner, and wondered how he had come to Dalnerechensk. No one came to the Principality unless it was to work the mines or to – *or to marry*. She wondered if Olaf was married, and then couldn't explain the sense of hurt she had at that thought. She shut her eyes, pushing away the pain, wishing it would all just leave her alone.

'*Tsesarevna*?' Olaf prompted softly.

She looked up. He was standing before her, streaked and patched with mud, his face lined with pain and sorrow, holding out a wiped clean hand to help her up. She accepted his hand and stood, wincing at the chafe of the dress on her back, looking down on the grave one last time. She saw someone had carved an epitaph into the mossy stump, the brown of the tree bark making the Cyrillic letters stand out against the green moss.

'Time to leave *Tsesarevna*' Olaf said quietly. 'We are still in danger.'

She sniffed, wiping a muddy hand across her face as she buffed at the tears, then turned and walked away.

103

Olaf opened his eyes and sat up, peering into the night and wondering what had woken him. The rain had finally stopped after three days and the night was still and quiet, a few pale stars shining in the clearing night sky. He glanced up at the oilskin they were lying under as a large droplet splattered down from the trees above them, landing with a hollow *plunk*. It had not been what had woken him; they had grown used to the deafening roar of torrential wetness on the oilskin.

Although they were pleased they had taken the oilskin, leaving the cart behind was another sad reminder that Tsar Constantinovich was dead. They had trudged on for three days, soaking wet, only stopping to eat a meager ration or to catch a few hours of uncomfortable sleep, wading along paths that were more mud and river than trails.

There was another scuffing noise and he looked over the sleeping party carefully, realising the Princess was missing. He crawled out from under their shelter, stretching and looking carefully around.

'*Tsesarevna*?' he called softly.

She was sitting upright on a rock a few paces away, her body swaying with exhaustion, her eyelids fluttering against sleep. She tried to rouse herself but couldn't, shutting her eyes and saying faintly:

'I'll be alright Olaf, go back to sleep.'

'*Tsesarevna*, you must sleep' he said, taking her arms and pulling her to her feet gently. 'You don't eat or sleep anymore. I've watched you, you eat less and less each day -'

'There's not enough' she said quietly. 'We barely have enough for one person's breakfast tomorrow -'

'I will hunt' he smiled. 'We will not starve, I swear. Come, -'

'I cannot' she said faintly, interrupting him. 'I cannot bear to lie on my back, and I cannot sleep with my face in the mud...' she trailed off, miserable and too tired to cry.

'I won't let you drown in the mud' he said quietly, folding his arm around her hips.

She hesitated, but Olaf pulled her gently back to the small shelter, sitting on the bed of small branches they had laid down in an attempt to sleep out of the mud. He pulled her down beside him with a gentle tug, noticing how shy she was suddenly. *You would think I was bedding a young virgin* Olaf grinned to himself and pulled her closer, feeling how she resisted as he lay her against his side. He slipped his arm around her shoulder and she gasped, arching hard into him to relieve the pain on her back. He apologised and folded his arm low across her hips, making her flush and hide her face in his chest. Olaf shifted, getting comfortable, stroking back her hair. She trembled then was instantly asleep, exhausted and spent.

She had gone when he woke in the weak morning. He stretched, shrugging his shoulders inside his damp shirt then sat up, looking around their makeshift campsite. Laura was already awake, collecting dry wood for a fire. After the non-stop rain there was precious little of it, but she had managed to find an armful of twigs and slim branches that would start the fire for their breakfast. He eyed her carefully, noticing the way she refused to look at him, her cheeks darkening.

Olaf allowed himself a smile at her discomfort and crawled out from under the oilskin, dusting off his muddy knees and thighs, wiping his hands clean on his lower back. Laura was doing her best to ignore him, moving off deeper into the trees. His smile grew and he pulled the knife out of the food satchel, cutting another thin strip from the oilskin, fashioning a crude sling from it. He selected a small stone from the ground and tested the sling, sending the pebble flying at a tree, meeting its mark with a satisfactory crack.

He collected several stones from the ground set off into the trees, swinging the sling absently. The sun rose, warming the air, and the forest smelled fresh and clean around him. It did not take him long to spot a rabbit and he sent a stone flying at it, missing by inches. The rabbit darted off, its cotton-tail bobbing frantically, but Olaf knew there would be more and was not concerned by the loss of the stone.

It took him the better part of an hour, but when he returned to the camp he had four rabbits and two large birds tied to his belt. The party greeted him warmly, astounded that he had found such rich supply of food and Laura smiled, bringing him the bowl of soup they had saved for him.

He thanked her, drinking it quickly, eyeing the blush in her cheeks. The soup was weak; they had used up the last of their water to make more of it to go around. He wiped the bowl on the cuff of his shirt then put it into the food satchel, noticing there was nothing in it but the bowls and empty wineskins and a few glass bottles. He unhooked the birds and rabbits from his belt and dumped them in too, while Mikhail and Fedor folded up the oilskin.

They set off again, following the new Tsar as he strode through the trees, Mikhail carrying the food satchel, Fedor with the oilskin rolled up under his arm. By mid-morning the hot summer sun was glaring over them, the green earth steaming as the mud evaporated. Their dried clothes became stiff with caked mud, and wet again where their sweat soaked the material. It made their steep climb round one of the hills uncomfortable and Laura pulled open the back of her dress to stop it chafing against the new scabs.

They reached a lush plateau above a rushing waterfall in the late afternoon and stopped to rest. Laura guessed that the waterfall would usually be sleepy, but rain was still pouring out of the hills into the watercourses, and it would be a few more days before they returned to their natural levels. She brushed off a boulder and sat, eyeing the pretty forest.

Anna and Mikhail went to explore the cave in a rocky wall and discovered a large supply of tinder dry wood. The company quickly decided to stay here for a day or two, enabling them to wash and dry their clothes and sleep in a dry place. Mikhail dragged the wood to the mouth of the cave to start a fire while Anna sat down to clean and pluck the two birds and Olaf and Fedor skinned the rabbits.

Laura slid off the rock and folded her arms on top of it, resting her head against her forearms, allowing her mind to wander for the first time in days. *What had happened to Ekaterina and Grigory?* Ekaterina may have been loved by the people, but Grigory was the Treasurer of Dalnerechensk, responsible for the budget and Aleksei's closest friend. There was no doubt in Laura's mind that some of the blame for Dalnerechensk's strife would be laid squarely at their feet. *They had burned the castle, the national symbol of what it meant to be a Dalnerechensker. What would they have done to the beautiful home above Ladozhskoye?*

She shut her eyes against the tears, hoping that her friends were alive and well. *Were they political prisoners in Dalnerechensk? Or were they on the run too? Where would they go? To Varennikov Castle? Will they ever return once the unrest had settled down, or had they left forever? Were they heading to America?*

The tears started at the thought of America. Her father would not know about the Revolution, or if he did, would not know where she was or even if she was still alive. She no longer wished to be a princess, to be accepted in high society. She was caught in the middle of a dangerous adventure and decided it sounded much better in print than the reality of sleepless nights and starvation. It was so much less painful to read about the death of loved ones then to count the handfuls of earth you cleared away for their grave.

I want to go home she thought miserably. *I will buy a place in Montana or Utah, farming the land for a living and fall asleep in the barn breathing in the soft scent of summer hay.*

She stopped then, steeling herself against reality. She was still married, was still the property of Aleksei. She could not buy her own land. If she left her husband she would have to return to her father, and he didn't have the money to support her, it had been swallowed up by Dalnerechensk. And her freedom rested on Aleksei's whim. He could still refuse to divorce her.

She opened her eyes and looked over at the new Tsar, watching him through her lashes. He had not spoken since his father had died, and she heard him weeping in the night once, when he thought the others were all asleep. They had not spoken alone and had avoided each other as he had not apologised for whipping her. Laura wondered if she could ever forgive him that.

If he were mad, if he was not in control of his thoughts perhaps she could she thought, eyeing him carefully. But she didn't think he was mad. *Sick with stress and jealousy and broken pride, but not mad.* He had whipped her to punish her for cuckolding him.

She shut her eyes, turning her face away.

'Your Highness?' Anna asked, stepping up to her. Laura opened her eyes to look at her. 'I can wash your clothes while the sun is warm enough to dry them.'

Laura stood, pushing herself up from the rock.

'I'll come with you Anna, I would like to bathe' she answered, and followed her upstream where the river curved out of sight.

Anna found a calm eddy in the water and hitched up her skirts, dropping the bundle of men's clothing she had with her, grabbing one item at a time and washing the mud and sweat stains out of them. Laura helped her, but as her dress kept falling into the river and chafed at her as she moved she finally stood, told her servant to watch out for the men and stripped off her dress and her bloomers, tossing the oilskin wrapped treaties onto the bank, continuing to wash the clothes naked.

Anna giggled then stripped off everything too, sitting down in the cool water. It felt divine on their skin and Laura sighed, draping the clean clothes over tree branches to dry, returning to sit in the water and scrub her skin and hair clean. Anna helped her when her skin pulled painfully, telling her that the cuts appeared to be healing nicely.

When they were thoroughly clean they sat on the bank and pulled her knees up to their chins, feeling the grass tickle their bare skin and the warm sun bask on their faces. Laura turned her face up to the sky, beginning to feel the stress and exhaustion of the past week melt away from her, draining from every limb.

She sighed then, detecting the acrid smell of the smoke from the fire.

The comfortable silence dragged out between them, each lost in their own thoughts. When the clothes had dried and the smell of roasting meat could be detected on the smoke Laura stood and dressed again, liking the feel of clean linen against her skin. Anna dressed and gathered the clothes, carrying them back to the men. They were all sitting around the fire, somewhat embarrassed at their half-naked attire. At once they jumped up and grabbed their clothes, heading down to the river to splash about in the cold water, washing their bodies and hair.

Laura and Anna sat quietly by the fire and tended to the bubbling pot of rabbit stew and roasting birds.

'My lady?' Anna suddenly started, flushing a little. 'Please don't think me too bold, but I want to ask your blessing. For Mikhail and I to marry' she flushed, dropping her eyes.

Laura looked at her surprised. *So that was her paramour* she thought, a small smile touching her lips. *That had been why she had called his name when the revolutionaries were at the castle doors.* Laura couldn't but help feel a little ironic that while Aleksei's and her love had waned, the love between their servants had grown. Anna was watching her, her face strained with hope. Laura grinned. 'You have my blessing. May he make you a good husband and an even better lover.'

Anna laughed, flushing to the roots of her hair, her eyes turning dreamy and pleased. Laura looked away and tried not to feel jealous.

The men returned, scrubbed pink and dressed again, and they ate a hearty meal that night, talking quietly around the golden ring of the fire. Laura shut her eyes contentedly; warm, dry and feeling safe for the first time in days. She knew they had already turned north and were following the mountains towards Moscow. She wondered when Aleksei would turn them west, when they would leave the mountains behind completely as they made their way to Prussia.

She shut her eyes. *What would they do once they got there?* Would they go immediately to the Emperor's residence and throw themselves on his mercy? Perhaps he might be inclined to be charitable, but the Secret Treaty had no grounds to be invoked. *Besides, we cannot ask him to give us soldiers to take back Dalnerechensk from rebels. Russia will take it as an invasion and start a war*

Europe could ill afford.

Could she send word to Fredrik? She paused, deliberating. Ekaterina had said to send word to him, that he would help her. In what way she didn't know. *Would he agree to help her husband?* She knew the answer to that was yes. His impeccable manners would let him do nothing less, even if it killed him to do so.

That wouldn't be very fair.

'What are we to do once inside Prussia's borders?' she asked Aleksei, opening her eyes to look at him.

'It will depend on the charity of Kaiser Wilhelm will it not?' he answered. 'Your treaty is to protect Dalnerechensk from Russian invasion, not from her own people revolting against her. Perhaps you could let the Kaiser press his suit with another little union' he sneered. There was a shocked gasp from those around the fire. Aleksei went on regardless. 'We will go to America, raise an army and return to crush the rebellion.'

'*What??*' Laura gasped, sitting upright, staring at him. *Are you insane?!* wormed at her tongue but she didn't let it out. 'You cannot be serious!'

'You are American are you not? You can commandeer troops for -'

'I cannot do that!' she gasped. 'I have no standing to do that! -'

'You are a princess!' he snapped.

'A Dalnerechensk Princess, I am an American nobody!' she cried, angry now. 'America does not wish to get involved in European affairs! The only army you could raise would be mercenaries and criminals! We could not pay them unless we were successful and if we are not they will kill us. And even if we do succeed in re-establishing the Monarchy they are not the sort of men you would want in Dalnerechensk. The people rebelled because they were suffering and if you punish them with those kinds of men they *will* rise up against you again. And they will not let us escape again. This is madness Aleksei!'

'And what do you propose?' he snapped, his tone implying that whatever she suggested would be worse.

Laura shut her eyes, thinking. Olaf added another log to the fire, and the eyes of the servants darted between her and Aleksei, waiting for her to say something.

'You are right, the treaty with Germany is only for help against Russian invasion. Therefore, it is useless to travel that far. We should go to St Petersburg.'

'What for?' Aleksei asked, annoyed but strangely interested.

'We need safe passage back to Dalnerechensk' she said. 'I will drop the price per ton of tin by ten percent, which ensures that Dalnerechensk is still getting a fair market price for it. In exchange we would ask for a small personal guard to escort us to the borders of Dalnerechensk. We will meet with the leaders of the Rebellion. We have the treaty, they do not. They will quickly realise that there is nothing they can do to alleviate Dalnerechensk without it. I do not think this man is a thug. He will listen to reason. Perhaps we may reach an understanding.'

'But you have brought Russia to their doorstep, they will hate you. What will you do then Laura? Use the Imperial Army to subdue your people?'

Laura laughed suddenly. 'Russia is always at our doorstep, our back door, our windows, our hearth! She is in our mouths and on the tongue we speak; she is even in our thoughts!

Dalnerechensk still has distant family in Russia' she stopped, eyeing them all. 'Russia is already in Dalnerechensk. But she will not rule her. Ever. The people will forgive me that at least.'

Aleksei was quiet for a while, shocked at her words. Then he stood and left the circle of light, bedding down away from the flames in the dark of the cave, his back turned towards them.

104

Olaf stood and stretched, eyeing the sweetly erotic image of Anna and Laura sleeping in each other's arms. The sun had not yet come up, but the sky was tinted salmon pink and all the birds had begun the dawn chorus. He slipped out of the cave with his oilskin sling and went down to the river, collecting a few pebbles he rolled dry on his thigh before dropping them into his pocket.

He knew the birds were bountiful just before dawn. It was the third morning he had gone hunting from the cave. He knew Aleksei was reluctant to move on; Laura's plan had been the more logical, the more reasonable of the two. The Tsar didn't like being proved wrong by his wife. He had hardly spoken at all to the company in the days since then.

Olaf sighed, knowing they could not stay in the cave forever. He fitted a stone into the sling absently, whistling a bird call. A bird answered to his left and he sent the stone flying accurately at its head, picking up the stone and the body, tying it to his belt. He was glad to know the Princess was eating again, and that the colour had come back to her cheeks, her jaw losing some of the angular sharpness it had recently acquired. He smiled to think of the blush that had warmed her cheeks whenever she had looked at him.

He heard a twig snap delicately behind him. He smiled to himself, knowing it was the Princess.

'Morning *Tsesarevna*' he said quietly.

'You have a fantastic aim' she said, joining him with a small smile. 'I do not know what we would do without you here to hunt for us.'

'Did you come all this way out here to tell me that?' he teased quietly. His smile deepened as her cheeks darkened.

'I came to ask if you were married' she said, flushing hotly.

Olaf looked surprised. 'Why would you think that?'

'Forgive me; I heard your words at the Tsar's grave. They are not Russian, perhaps Hungarian -'

'Polish' he said quietly.

'- and no one comes to Dalnerechensk except to work in the mines or marry' she stopped, biting her lip. 'Did you come here to marry?'

'No. My mother did. It is her tongue' he smiled.

'Why did you speak it to the Tsar?' she asked, confused.

'I loved him. It seemed right' he shrugged, looking away. Then his mood changed back to a mischievous one. 'Come *Tsesarevna*, why chase me into the woods to find out if I had a wife?' he teased.

'I wanted to spare your feelings from the others if she had died' she said, starting to feel hot.

'You are too kind' he teased with a sly smile.

Laura burned and turned her face away from his amused gaze. Olaf took her arm, apologising.

'It is only your good name I am thinking of' he said. 'Even here there are looks and whispers.'

'I have endured worse slanders, and worse hurts' she said quietly, dropping her eyes then shook herself. 'Come, teach me how to use the sling.'

He grinned and turned her around, showing her how to hold the sling, which way to swing it, when to release the stone. Laura tried several times, trying to get the trajectory right. 'It is much harder than it looks!' she cried in frustration. Olaf laughed at her. 'They will be hungry now' she sighed. 'We'll take your skillfully caught breakfast back to them.'

Olaf snickered quietly and offered his arm to her. She accepted, smiling and walked back through the forest with him, chatting pleasantly. When they reached the cave Mikhail, Anna and Fedor were sitting rigid at a smoldering fire, strange looks on their faces. Instantly Laura and Olaf were alarmed; she felt him stiffen beside her. Her eyes darted round, falling on the soldier beside Aleksei.

She was grabbed roughly and yanked away from Olaf. He swung out at the soldiers and was roughly clobbered with rifle butts, pushed to the ground. Laura gasped, crying out for them to stop. She was yanked around from his beating, finding herself thrust forward at a handsome, familiar face.

'I knew you would come after me' Nikita smiled, his eyes dropping to her breasts then he leaned close to her white throat. 'You smell of filth' he said distastefully, and his soldiers laughed.

He took hold of her jaw forcefully, leaning down to kiss her.

She turned her head violently away. 'I thought only pigs wallowed in filth Nikita' she said.

There was a horrible, stunned silence from the company then Nikita turned away, laughing off her insult. His company laughed nervously; politely. Nikita was not a man to suffer insults lightly, and Laura knew this. He turned back to strike her but she was quick, raising a knee hard into his crotch, smiling with cruel satisfaction. He struck her cheek hard, then limped off a few paces, one hand cupping his injured crotch.

'That was not very lady-like' he hissed.

'At least I won't be subjected to your lust' she said.

'You fool!' he laughed. 'I have the command of a company, and they will not find you unappealing.'

'But *you* will not have me' she said, eyeing him triumphantly.

Nikita struck her again then turned and seized Aleksei, dragging him over to the Princess, forcing him to kneel on the ground again. He pulled his sword out of his sheath and shoved back Aleksei's head with the tip at his throat, hard enough that a trickle of blood ran into his collar.

'You panted after me you whore, so do not stand there with such sickening false modesty. I shall make this very easy for you Your Highness. Give yourself to me and I'll spare his life.'

'No' she answered.

Nikita thrust Aleksei's head back with the sword point. Aleksei made a pained, choked sound.

'Laura!' he grimaced through clenched teeth. 'Do it!'

'I *will* kill him' Nikita warned, twisting the point of the sword in the skin on his neck. 'I could kill him right now.'

'And you think that if you killed him, I would be somehow grateful to you?' she asked. 'You think that you would ever find solace in courts again if you are guilty of regicide? If you had raped his wife or ordered your soldiers to?' she asked levelly. 'You won't ever have me Nikita, not even under this impossible choice.'

Nikita swore and yanked the sword away, thumping the hilt into Aleksei's head, knocking him unconscious. He shoved his sword back into its sheath, wiped his mouth then rubbed his sore crotch, eyeing her distastefully.

'Tie her' he snapped. 'And the others. Bring them with us.'

Laura's wrists were seized roughly and her hands were tied behind her back, as were the rest of the company's. Aleksei was thrown unceremoniously onto a cart of chattels and soldiers roughly manhandled the small party to their feet. The birds Olaf had caught were stripped from him and put in a bag for Nikita's own table and the slighted Prince returned to Laura with a length of rope in his hands. Olaf struggled when Nikita slipped it round her throat, pulling the noose firmly against her skin, and several of the soldiers dealt another blow or two to him.

'Come, my obedient little bitch' he said laughingly, tugging her after him back to his horse, walking with a slight limp that made her feel nastily satisfied, despite her humiliation. Nikita tied her to his saddle then swung up onto his horse's back, leading the company of soldiers southward through the Urals.

We're heading towards Dalnerechensk she thought as they walked, and wondered if he had been ordered to take the Principality, wondered if he had ever reached Vladivostok. She stumbled and the rope pulled tight against her throat. She forced herself to concentrate, she didn't want to trip and accidentally strangle herself.

The soldiers marched until late afternoon when they reached a glen and Nikita called a halt for the day. The soldiers set down their packs and set up a camp hurriedly while Nikita sat on horseback surveying the progress and giving orders. Laura stood behind the horse, breathing hard, her shoes and hem covered in excrement, watching the soldiers hewing down thick logs for fires, carrying several large poles inside a small tent that had already been erected.

A quick look around told her that the rest of the Dalnerechenskers were safe, if not tired, and were watching with as much amazement as she was as the canvas city sprang up in the clearing. Smoke began wafting from the large fire before the mess tent and they could hear the clangs of cooking equipment as the camp began to settle in for the evening.

Nikita dismounted from the horse and dragged Laura over to the tent she had seen the poles disappear into. At Nikita's order the rest of the Dalnerechenskers were dragged in too. The poles had been driven into the ground and each of the captives was forced to sit with their backs against them, their hands tied behind the pole, forcing them to sit uncomfortably upright. They were then left alone and armed guards stood outside the tent.

'Are you hurt Your Highness?' Olaf asked.

'No' she answered quietly, twisting her hands to see if she could pull undone the knots.

The twilight faded into darkness while they shifted uncomfortably, trying to ease the tiredness and pain in their limbs and bodies. The fires outside cast the shadows of the guards on the walls of the tent and Laura's belly was rumbling painfully, she had not eaten all day and had been weakened and exhausted by the march. She could hear the sounds of soldiers in the mess tent, could smell their food on the night air. She winced and struggled harder against her bonds.

A soldier pushed open the tent flap door and strode in, seizing Laura's arm and untying her from the pole. She twisted violently to get away but he was ready for it and dragged her out after him, ignoring her protests and the curses of the Dalnerechenskers. She was taken to a richly brocaded tent and pushed past two armed guards at the entrance flaps.

The soldier did not come in with her and she eyed her luxurious surroundings. There were tables and chairs, a large bed, a wooden bath; even a chaise lounge of sorts. Nikita lay sprawled back on the lounge, his shirt open at the neck and watching her. She composed herself carefully; aware she looked a frightful mess and stank of horse shit.

'Tell me Laura, my little bird, where were you flitting to in Russia's forests?' he asked coyly.

'Just flitting' she answered. 'Tell me Nikita, were you marching your company back to seize the mines of Dalnerechensk?'

Nikita's eyes narrowed and he sat up.

'You were fleeing from a little trouble Laura? A little rebellion perhaps?' He smiled at her surprise. 'Oh yes, word travels fast even in a forest. Were your people rising up against you?'

'Were you the man who murdered Gapon's followers or did you arrive in Vladivostok just in time to see the Japanese destroy Mother Russia's battleships?'

Nikita jumped to his feet in anger.

'Enough of this!' he snapped, seizing her arm and dragging her over to the table. He pushed her into a seat and called for food.

Two corporals entered, pouring fresh water into finger bowls and wine into goblets, setting out dishes of cooked meat before disappearing again. Nikita sat, wiggling his fingers in the cold water, patting them dry on a napkin.

'Hungry, Your Highness?' he asked, pushing a plate laden with tasty morsels towards her.

She turned her face away, feeling her stomach knot painfully and hoped it wouldn't growl loud enough for him to hear. Nikita laughed at her stubbornness and began to eat noisily, sucking his fingers clean with loud smacks, moaning with culinary pleasure.

'*This* is the only way to travel in this country!' he laughed, pushing back Laura's hair. She moved her head testily away from him. 'Come now passion flower, am I not being a gracious host?'

'I am not your only guest *Knjaz* Rurik' she said, shooting him an angry look.

He fell silent. 'Very well' he said after a pause and called for a guard. Another corporal stepped into the tent and bowed, waiting for orders. 'Take our Royal guests an evening meal fit for a king' Nikita said magnificently. 'There Laura, will that not make you happy with me?' He cocked his eyebrow as the corporal left.

'Of course not' she said. 'Perhaps you could loosen the ropes?' she twisted her hands again.

Nikita laughed mockingly. 'I fear not Laura, you are stubborn and wily, I'm sure you would try to stab me with a bread knife.'

I'm wilier than that she thought, surreptitiously eyeing the fork. Nikita drained his wine glass, picking up his fork again.

'But tell me, where were you headed?'

'Just flitting' she answered.

Nikita threw down his fork.

'Guard!' he snapped. Another soldier burst in, bowing to Nikita. 'Take her back to the others' he said, then rounded on her. 'I have tired of your games Laura. I will ask you again tomorrow night. See that you give me a better answer.'

The corporal dragged her out of the seat and pushed her ahead of him, taking hold of her arm to pull her back to the captive's tent. Inside, the plates of food Nikita had ordered had been put down in front of each captive, just out of reach. Laura was dragged back to a pole and tied again.

'Are you hurt? Did he touch you?' Olaf asked, the others echoing him.

'I am alright' she soothed, shutting her eyes and trying to get comfortable. 'He's taking us to Dalnerechensk, isn't he.'

'*Da*' Olaf answered quietly.

Laura sighed, pulling her feet up and felt the oilskin against her stomach, pleased that the treaties had not been discovered. Olaf was still watching her, concerned, and she eyed him quietly.

'He was never your lover' he said. 'I am sorry, Your Highness.'

He shut his eyes, his breath ragged in his chest. *He had told Aleksei we were lovers* she realised. *That information and Nikita's behaviour with her in the days following had led directly to her rape. And he knew it.*

'I forgive you' she said softly and shut her eyes, trying to ignore the rumble in her belly.

105

The captive company was woken at daybreak, stiff and hungry. They were untied from the poles and their hands were retied in front of them, allowing them to eat the stale bread they were given. They were hauled to their feet and dragged out of the tent, watching as the camp was taken down and packed into wagons and rucksacks the soldiers carried.

Aleksei had slept all of the long march yesterday but was now awake, eyeing his surroundings but saying nothing. Laura too looked round her carefully, noticing some wagons were covered with oilskins and others were not. One of the oilskins was flipped back and she saw wooden crates stacked in the cart, and large quantities of grapeshot packed beside the long muzzle of a cannon. The oilskin was righted and fastened, and she eyed the shape of the cannon carefully, then the other wagons, trying to guess what else was hidden.

She guessed from the similar shapes there were five cannon, and an untold amount of guns and ammunition. Nikita's army was marching towards Dalnerechensk with enough heavy artillery to reduce the Principality to rubble. There was no doubt in her mind now. They were going to be invaded.

Her mind turned to ways of escape. Olaf might be able to get away, he was strong and would be able to reach Dalnerechensk, to warn them, to help Peter organise the army to resist. She cursed herself quietly. Nikita knew all of Dalnerechensk's defenses, she had told him herself on her official tour of the Principality, pathetically eager to please the handsome man at Aleksei's insistence and her own desire.

How he must be laughing at her, how much fun he had twisting her round his fingers and watching her — pant after him. She stopped. She couldn't deny it. She shut her eyes when she saw him striding towards her, the rope in his hands. Aleksei gasped when he saw him drop it round her neck, pulling it firmly in place.

'Let her go!' he snapped, pushing away a guard that came too close.

'Oh I don't think so Your Highness' he said, grabbing Laura's hands and tying them behind her again so she couldn't take the noose off and escape.

Again she was hitched behind his horse and forced to walk as the camp moved off. Despite her hunger that the stale bread had done nothing to abate she looked around her, taking careful note of how many soldiers there were, of how far they could march in a day with all their equipment, of how many wagons were for food, for ammunitions, for furniture.

She knew the numbers would be helpful if one of them managed to get away. She caught Olaf looking around carefully too, and when they stopped for a quick break around midday he managed to catch a quick minute with her.

'How many men, cannons, days of supply do you count?' she asked softly.

'Five hundred men, five cannons, I think, and plenty of supply, enough for a siege if it came to that.'

'Try and get free' she said as the rope at her neck was pulled tightly.

'Heel!' Nikita laughed, dragging her away.

Laura suddenly stopped, causing Nikita to jerk to a halt, looking at her.

'You sure know how to treat a girl to a good time *Knjaz* Rurik, and goes nowhere towards endearing me enough to throw myself in your bed.'

He eyed her then suddenly took the rope from her neck, rubbing gently at the marks it had left on her throat. He retied her hands in front of her and attached the rope to her wrists, then remounted his horse and led the column of soldiers onwards.

With her neck free she was able to look round her more carefully. She was pleased to see that the other Dalnerechenskers were unharmed and walking in single file, several soldiers walking guard around them but not harassing them as they had yesterday. They trudged on through the afternoon till Nikita called a halt and the canvas city sprang up in the trees. Once again they were roped to poles in a small tent and watched over by an armed guard.

'How far have we marched?' she asked Olaf quietly.

'About fifteen miles' he said.

A soldier stepped into the tent and told them to stop talking, then unlooped Laura from the pole again, taking her back to the brocaded tent in the middle of the camp.

Nikita was sitting on the chaise lounge, his boots propped up on a chest that had not been in his tent last night. He ordered the corporal to untie her and Laura stood, rubbing her wrists while the soldier left. Nikita eyed her, the seconds dragging out between them. Laura brushed down her hair, aware of how dirty and smelly she was.

Someone cleared their throat and the flap was pushed open, several soldiers stepping inside with large pots of hot water they tipped into Nikita's wooden bath. When they left Nikita took his boots off the chest and opened it, pulling out a bottle of perfume. He stood, pouring it into the bath. At once his tent was filled with the heady aroma of the perfume Hannah had given to Laura. Nikita emptied the entire bottle into the bath and Laura's sinful thought of buying enough to bathe in came back to her.

Nikita returned to the chest and pulled out a beautiful white gown, showing it to her.

'I was going to give you this when I arrived back in Dalnerechensk' he said, draping it on the chaise lounge. He pulled out a pair of satin slippers and sat them on the chaise too. 'Wash and dress in something befitting of a princess' he said, heading to the door. 'And don't think of using this opportunity to escape.'

He slipped outside. Laura waited five minutes then went to the wall opposite the door and tried to lift the wall to slip out under it. She was not able to and she sighed, relenting. She eyed the door carefully, wondering if Nikita would come striding in while she was washing, tired of waiting for her.

But the lure of the bath was too strong. She stripped, hiding the oilskin of treaties in the folds of her dress and sat in the water, massaging all the tension out of her body. She felt guilty for these pleasures, knowing how the others were still uncomfortably tied to poles in a small tent. That guilt drove her out of the hot water quicker than she would have liked and she dressed quickly, hiding the oilskin back against her stomach, toweling her hair dry and combing it with her fingers. She wanted a mirror to see how she looked but couldn't find one in his tent.

Nikita tapped on the canvas door and pushed it open, eyeing her.

'Truly beautiful' he said, smiling. 'Food' he called over his shoulder; and two soldiers brought in two plates of hot morsels, setting them down on the table.

Nikita led her to a chair and tucked her into her seat then sat opposite her. Laura picked up a fork and began to eat, too hungry to care. Nikita watched her, an amused smile playing on his lips. He poured her a glass of wine and watched her gulp it thirstily, amused. As she ate he stood and went to the chest, pulling out a velvet box. Laura ignored the jewels he dropped round her throat, pushing food into her mouth, unsure when she would eat next.

He stroked her arms and kissed her neck, his tongue licking along her throat, scooping the gems into his mouth and sucking them, letting them fall back wetly against her skin. Laura made a wild stab at him with her fork, making him jump back in surprise. She seized her chance and bolted for the door but crashed into the guards on duty. Nikita grabbed her, hauling her back into his tent.

'Now that ruined dinner' he said, pulling her with him to sit on the chaise lounge.

Laura tore the jewels off her and tossed them onto the ground, breaking the chain and scattering the gems. Nikita slapped her.

'You ungrateful slut' he hissed.

'I am tired of your boorish attempts to woo me' she said. 'If you are going to rape me do it. You will not hear me beg you.'

Nikita slapped her harder then shoved her away, calling for a guard.

'Take her back to the others' he said. 'You have till sundown tomorrow Laura' Nikita warned.

'For what?' she raised her eyebrow, unimpressed with his threats.

'For you to tell me what I want to hear, or Boris will loosen your tongue.'

He waved her away. The soldier marched her back to the tent.

'Who is Boris?' she asked him.

'A torturer' he leered, pushing her inside.

There was a quiet intake of breath when she appeared and she closed her eyes, not wanting to see the looks on their faces. The soldier tied her to a pole then kissed her hard, gripping her breast. Laura bit his lip, twisting away from him. He screamed in pain then drew back, slamming his fist into her cheek. Laura's head rocketed back, jarring against the pole. The soldier pushed her head up and held her throat against the post, laughing quietly.

'I just wanted the taste of you, before Boris got finished cutting every little bit off you' he said, kissed her again and left, his laughter floating back to them.

Laura slumped, exhausted and terrified. She could feel blood trickling down the back of her head.

'Olaf get free' she whispered as consciousness slipped away from her. 'Get free and warn them.'

106

Their third day of captivity dawned, the rays slanting across Laura's face and rousing her. Pain slated across her brain and she winced, turning her eyes out of the light. Agony roared up her neck and she cried out, jerking her head back to where it was, shutting her eyes tightly.

'Laura,' Olaf called quietly, cutting through her pain. 'Can you hear me?'

She groaned an answer, not sure what she had said, trying to open an eye without the sunlight sending glaring sharp stabs into her head. She groaned again and leaned forward, dry retching and trying to get comfortable. Her hands were untied from the pole and she moaned, crawling away from the light.

'Get her something, a doctor!' Olaf was saying.

'Leave me here' she moaned, pulling her knees up and folding into a ball.

Both of them were ignored, their hands tied in front of them and given stale bread to eat. Laura stayed curled up until she was dragged out of the tent they were dismantling around her. Olaf and Mikhail got her to her feet, Olaf doing his best to do a rudimentary exam with his hands tied, prising open her eyes and peering in them carefully, checking the blood that had stained her dress from where the back of her head had hit the pole.

'Are you seeing double?' he asked her and she shook her head, wincing as he pressed accidentally on her cheek. 'I'm sorry' he said.

'My head throbs' she moaned quietly.

The Dalnerechenskers were lined up single file, and Laura was glad she was not hitched to Nikita's horse today. *I have really fallen from grace* she thought. She lifted her bound hands and gently inspected the sore cheek. *His blow must have been glancing* she thought, as her cheek hadn't swollen like she thought it might have. *I wonder if it has bruised.*

Nikita's company headed off through the trees, pushing wagons of weapons and the single file of captives with them. Laura's head throbbed but gradually began to clear as they walked, giving her time to think. She knew she had to escape. She was terrified at the prospect of torture, of what could happen to her when the sun set. She worked at her ropes as they walked, trying to loosen the knots in it.

She hadn't realised how far they had gone on their escape from Dalnerechensk until they crested the rise of a hill and Nikita called for the midday rest. The Urals stretched out in front of them, unimpressive and wearied ancient mountains, lush and green with new summer growth. In the distance the horizon was a smudged mustard grey, and Laura knew it was the smoke from the burnt towers of Dalnerechensk.

Her heart ached to think of that beautiful city reduced to ash, and wondered if the crafted tin plates on the Gate at Vsevolod's Way had been smashed into the fragments of a breached door, or melted in the burning torches of the unrest. *What was left of the city?* she wondered. *Would Nikita smash the remains into rubble in spite? What would happen to her and Aleksei when Russia had subdued Dalnerechensk?*

She turned her face away from the smoke tinged horizon, eyeing the bound wrists of her citizens. Their only chance lay in escape, in slipping away and staying ahead of the soldiers. *We can walk faster than fifteen miles a day unburdened with wagons* she told herself. *We will only have to stay ahead of his scouts.*

It wasn't long before Nikita pushed them on again, eager now he could see his smoky destination. They trudged on, the path narrowing, following a thin ridge between a mountain side and a steep drop to a swollen river ten feet below them. She watched it as she walked, how angry it seemed, how it swirled around and over hidden things in the river bed.

Inattentive as she was she stumbled on a rock, throwing up her bound hands to steady herself.

'Watch where you walk' growled a guard near her.

Laura righted herself, took a careful look around her then ran and leapt, plummeting down into the torrent below them. She hit the bitterly cold water with enough force to stun her, slamming all her breath from her body. She struggled underwater, clawing as best a she could with bound hands and yards of skirts tangling her legs, realising it was more violent than she had first thought. She prayed to God she wouldn't strike a rock or debris hidden in the folds of the foam.

She broke above the water, gasping for air, dragging in lungfuls of cold mist. There were shouts from the bank above her, seemingly far away and faint, drowned by the roar of the monster she was riding. It dragged her along, thrusting waves into her face, pulling her under, crashing her body into stones, spinning her round and round until she was dizzy. Laura fought it, trying to swim, trying to keep her head above water, trying to avoid bruises by pushing herself away from the rocks and boulders in the river.

The cold water was frighteningly fast, and filled with unknown horrors from its quick descent from the hills of the Urals, terrors that brushed or clawed, snagging and pulling, bumping and slapping. A strong hand suddenly grabbed her, folding around her stomach. It was Olaf, his hands were free from their constraints. He had leapt in after her, swimming powerfully until he caught her.

Laura coughed, spitting out water that had flooded into her mouth, struggling fruitlessly. 'Don't let us hit those rocks!' Olaf shouted, trying to swim across the current away from some wicked looking boulders.

The rapids swept them down onto the jagged rocks. Laura put her hands out and pushed as they collided, managing to spin them away. As they twirled in the water she caught a glimpse behind them before they swept round a bend. Nikita's company were following on the river banks, falling behind and disappearing from view. Laura saw Aleksei was also in the river, seeing a flash of his face just before they were swept from sight.

Her dress snagged again in the water, pulling her under. Olaf tore it, releasing her and she spluttered to the surface.
'I've got you Laura' he said, trying to soothe her. 'Don't fight the water, let it carry you.'

She tried to do as she was told but her skirts were dragging her down, and her bound hands were almost useless. She did her best to help fend them from bumps and apologised each time they ricocheted uncontrolled into another hidden object. Olaf swore.
'Hold your breath!' he yelled.

The river tilted, dropping out beneath them. They plunged down the violent waterfall, the force of the river behind them pushing them under. Laura was torn from Olaf, feeling alone and frightened. Her lungs burned for air, and she could feel herself sinking deeper, pushed down by the weight of this restless monster. She struggled and kicked, fighting against the urge to take a breath.

But it was no good. When she began to slip away from consciousness her instincts took over, trying to find a way to release her from the agony of breathlessness. She inhaled, and her lungs filled with water, freezing her inside out. The shock of the cold inside her partly revived her and she struggled once more, feeling that swirling blackness threatening to overtake her.

And then Olaf's arms were round her, pulling her above the water. She coughed and drew in shaky, grateful breaths, feeling the blackness ebb away.

'Thank God' he said quietly, smoothing her hair away from her face.

She coughed some more then lifted her bound wrists over his head, clinging to him tightly, too tired to fight the current now. Olaf let her go and used both hands to fend them from the rocks and they received fewer knocks and bruises. The river was more placid here, the churning froth had lessened. *It's either very deep or there are no more rocks* he thought. *How far have we gone in this river? Are we safe enough away to get out yet?*

He glanced behind them, unable to see any soldiers, and hoped they had left them far behind, even Nikita on horseback. He began to paddle across the current, pulling them out of the middle of the river and towards the banks. Ahead of them he could see an old log of wood protruding into the water and he swam towards it, tired and sapped of energy, praying he didn't miss.

The water sped them past and Olaf hooked his arm round the log and hung on for grim life. The river pushed them round towards the bank and Olaf shifted his grip, pulling them out of the current. Laura sighed when her feet touched the bottom and she stood, keeping hold of Olaf, trembling with exhaustion. He slipped his arm around her hips to help hold her up, eyeing the bank where they stood.

It was not an ideal place to try and get out of the river. The water had hollowed out the soil beneath the bank and flaps of grass-woven topsoil sagged into the water. He gave one clump an experimental pull and felt it disintegrate. They would not be able to pull themselves up here. He could boost Laura up, but knew she didn't have the strength to pull him up. He lifted the sod and took a step towards the bank, peering under it to see if there were firmer hand-holds under it.

There was a shout from the riverbank close by and Olaf grabbed Laura, pulling her into the small hollow, letting the sod fall back into place.

'Did they see us?' he whispered.

Laura shook her head and they stared intently at the narrow patch of river they could see beyond their hiding place. Above them on the bank the shouting continued. Olaf guessed there were two scouts, most likely on horseback to have caught up with them this quickly. There was a moment of silence then one said:

'They have to be dead, that waterfall should have drowned them.'

'So where are the other bodies?' the second asked.

'Washing out to sea' said the first dismissively. 'And I won't be going after them there. *Knjaz* Rurik will be lucky if he is not court martialed for this.'

There were a few more seconds of silence. Through the small gap in the sod Laura and Olaf saw Aleksei float into view, face down in the water. Laura moaned hollowly and Olaf pressed his hand across her mouth, stilling her. She shivered as her husband disappeared, his hand caressing the water the last thing she saw of him, reminding her of the first time he had touched her cheek, and tears rolled down her face unmitigated.

'It's growing dark; we'll never find them' one soldier said finally. 'Let's go back.'

Olaf and Laura stayed under the bank, shivering as the light faded around them, their ears straining against the quiet of the night. Laura's arms were still around Olaf's neck, shaking with her tears and the cold, hardly able to stand up on her own anymore.

Olaf finally pushed up the sod and stepped out, towing the Princess after him. *Not Tsesarevna* he corrected himself. *Tsaritsa.* He boosted her up onto the bank, checking round them. She scrabbled up and lay quietly, listening to him struggle to pull himself out of the water. He managed to wiggle his torso up but kept slipping back into the water, grunting and cursing under his breath. She sat up, grabbing his arm when he wiggled up again, managing to pull him up beside her.

He lay, panting quietly for a moment or two, then sat up and sighed. He took her cold hands gently and found the knot, his rough fingers making quick work of the rope bonds. He threw them into the water and rubbed her wrists gently. He then stood and helped her to her feet, walking to keep them warm while their clothes dried in the balmy air.

107

Laura woke with a start, sitting upright and looking round her wildly.

'You're safe Tsaritsa' Olaf soothed, laying a calming hand on her arm.

Her eyes darted round her again, aware she was lying on a pile of grass he had quickly gathered to make a bed for her. She was dimly aware that they had walked a long time in the darkness, and when she had been too tired to he had slipped his arms round her and carried her. She had no idea when she had fallen asleep only it was now late morning and their clothes and hair was completely dry from their wild ride in the river.

'The treaties!' she said suddenly, sitting upright and clutching at her stomach.

'They're alright' Olaf said, holding up the oilskin. 'They stayed miraculously dry.'

Laura's cheeks flamed at the thought of him pulling the oilskin out from where it had been tucked into her bloomers in the front of her dress.

'You shouldn't have done that' she snapped, painfully embarrassed.

'I was checking you for injuries' he said.

'I am not one of your horses!' she snapped.

Of course not. You ride your horses.

Laura burned with embarrassment and cold misery at the same time. The tears swam up again.

'I'm sorry Tsaritsa' he said, dropping his eyes.

'Tsesarevna' she corrected absently then stopped. *She was not a princess anymore. She was the queen.*

She shut her eyes, not wanting to think about that. Aleksei was dead, but she had spent her tears for him. She was thankful her last memory of him was that he had jumped into the river to save her, and she felt herself forgive some of the pain and anguish he had caused her.

She sighed, pushing the memories away, eyeing Olaf thoughtfully. He had saved her life, and had aided her escape from torture at Nikita's hands. *There was a certain charm about him* she thought; something in the way he carried himself that Laura found fascinating. Although his blonde shaggy hair was going grey at the temples he still had a youthful strength in his face that she found comforting and almost familiar. He was watching her appraisal of him quietly, with no curiosity or disdain, simply letting her and watching what she found.

'You're all that I have left Olaf' she said softly, sighing and looking away.

So she was queen of a principality that didn't exist, wife of a dead king, lost daughter of America. She pushed all the thoughts away, screwing her eyes up tightly.

'Where are we Olaf?' she asked instead.

'Close to Dalnerechensk' he answered. 'The river carried us quite a distance.'

She wondered if the river flowed through Liberty Valley, wondered what the people would do when they saw Aleksei's body floating past the smoldering ruins of his city. She stopped again, shoving those thoughts away from her violently and caught Olaf yawning.

'How long have we been here?' she asked, wondering how long he had carried her for.

'Maybe two hours' he answered, rubbing his eyes tiredly.

'You should rest -'

'We should keep going' he answered, getting to his feet, handing over the treaties wordlessly.

She blushed again and turned from him, pushing the cold oilskin down her dress and shivering at the touch. Olaf started out through the trees and she trotted after him, neither of them saying a word. After a while Laura reached out and took his hand. He looked at her, surprised.

'You have saved my life more times than I can remember' she said softly. 'You have been my friend and confidante and protector...' she trailed off. 'I have never been in this much danger. I need you Olaf.'

'I know' he said softly.

They walked on in silence, holding hands.

108

Night had fallen when they reached the small tavern at the crossroads. Laura could hear laughter and music spilling out of the windows and she stepped closer to Olaf, thinking of the bar in Dalnerechensk with the rough, drunken crowd. This place sounded just as violent and rough, and to confirm her fears a bottle smashed and there were ugly voices raised in dispute.

The door flew open, light spilling out onto the roadway and an unconscious brawler was unceremoniously dumped on the ground, the door slamming shut again.

'Not in there' Laura said, resisting Olaf's gentle pull.

'Hot food, a warm bed' he tempted her. 'Trust me Tsaritsa, I will not let anything happen to you.'

She hesitated, but let Olaf pull her to the door. Quickly he bent down and checked the sleeping man, pulling out a small coin purse he quickly relieved of its contents. Laura was shocked but Olaf said nothing, sliding his arm around her and holding her gently as he pushed open the door and stepped up to the bar.

At once an interested silence fell around the new comers. Olaf glared at the man peering closely at him and he turned away, muttering into his beer. Laura could feel her breath struggling in and out of her as Olaf guided her over to the long wooden counter. The bar tender folded his arms, eyeing them.

'I don't want any trouble in my bar' he said.

Laura felt cold then, wondering if he had recognised her. Olaf smiled pleasantly.

'My wife and I have traveled far; we want a meal and a room for the night. We'll be gone in the morning.'

The lie had slid easily off his tongue and Laura found herself flushing at the thought of being Olaf's wife. The bar man was eyeing them both distrustfully. Olaf leaned forward and there was the clink of the brawler's coins on the counter.

'Her family did not approve' he grinned, giving the man a wink.

The barman laughed then, throwing back his head and guffawing loudly. He took the coins and led them to a door, opening it and ushering them through. The dim corridor beyond stank of vomit and urine and Laura tried to breathe through her mouth. Neither man seemed to notice the stench and the barman unlocked a door at the far end of the corridor.

'The Honeymoon Suite' he laughed, giving Olaf the key.

Olaf and Laura stepped in, eyeing the room. It was tiny; it had a small fireplace and a single, narrow bed. The barman shut the door with a promise of hot food soon and Laura flushed, remembering her own honeymoon night, realising why the bed was not wide enough to sleep two side-by-side. She dared not look at Olaf and forced herself not to think about him too.

'You're flushing like a schoolgirl' he suddenly teased.

Laura went hot to the roots of her hair. Olaf laughed, guessing the reason for her embarrassment.

'Come come! No Putting To Bed Ceremony for you tonight!' he laughed. 'No luxurious sheets and mountainous pillows for you!'

She put her face in her hands, hiding her blush.

'No maid to dress you in fine night robes!' he went on.

'I'll just have to learn to do it myself then won't I?' she said, eyeing him.

The smile faded from his face. They were interrupted by a knock and Olaf remembered himself, opening the door. They were given a large pitcher of water and two plates heaped with steaming morsels. Olaf thanked the barman, locking the door after him and set the pitcher on the hearth beside the fire to warm. There was no table so they sat on the edge of the bed and balanced the plates on their knees, listening to the springs squeak alarmingly loudly under them.

The awkward flirt momentarily forgotten they ate ravenously, even Laura, who would have shocked the girls in Lady Ramkinson's school if they could have seen her like this, shoveling food into her face. She grinned then licked the plate clean feeling devilish and carefree, ignoring Olaf's amused chuckle. He took her empty plate from her and stacked it by the door with his, dipping a rough cloth into the fire-warmed water and gave it to her to wash her hands and face.

She did so and handed it back, watching him wash his own face carefully. He dropped the cloth in the water and tested how secure the door was then added another log to the fire.

Laura yawned, pleased he had talked her into spending the night here and stretched gingerly, wincing. Olaf quickly joined her, sitting behind her and massaging her tense muscles gently. She moaned softly as he worked, noticing how careful he was being not to pull at her newly formed scars where the skin was still tender, liking the way his fingers stole up into her hair and gently pressed away the dull ache that had been in the back of her skull.

She let herself relax, shivering at touches so light they were almost a caress. She suddenly stilled him, folding her hands over his.

'You said once you loved me' she said. 'You meant it, didn't you.'

'Yes' he confessed.

She sighed quietly, gently, then pulled his arms round her body.

'I am too tired of imagining what this feels like' she said softly.

Olaf was quiet then he bent his head to nuzzle her hair, his lips opening against the nape of her neck. He shifted closer, the bed squeaking, and she could feel the heat of his body against her back. She gasped as one hand cupped a breast, the other slipping behind her to pull undone the small buttons at the back of her dress. She turned then, sighing as his lips found hers, stroking back his blonde hair.

Quickly he stripped off his shirt, turning her towards him more, the springs broadcasting their every movement. Her fingers knotted into his hair and he tugged down the front of her dress, his mouth bowing to her rosebud nipples, sucking them gently. She gasped loudly at the sensations, arching her back into the feel of his hot breath and lips on her skin.

Olaf had wanted this too long, to feel her young body responding to his, her fingers knotted in his hair, to hear her strange, accented tongue in his ear as she gasped and begged him not to stop. He took her hands and pushed them against his body, pulling her closer as his mouth opened, the springs squealing louder under him. He was not surprised at the need he felt in her, not knowing how to be a princess under a man, not knowing how to state her wants and have them met, and Olaf was not patient enough to teach her tonight.

He lifted her, stripping her dress from her, taking the treaties and dumping them on the floor, pulling her to feel the skin of her body against his. Her arms folded round his neck, holding him tightly as she gasped, her chest hitching against the languid licks he planted there. He took a hand and pushed it against his desire, sliding his own hand inside her bloomers.

She gasped then, thinking wildly: *So this is why they call him the stallion*; her grip tightening on him, his firm fingers seeking out a gentle passage to her, realising how much it made her tremble with desire, and how ripe she was for him. He tore her bloomers down, pushing her back on the bed as he climbed between her knees, freeing himself from his cloth constraints.

She winced, then again as his weight pressed on her, sitting up against him.

'My back,' she whimpered.

Olaf pulled her over him, rising to meet her, feeling her flesh part around him.

She gasped, going rigid. Olaf stopped, wondering if he had gone too far, aware she was watching him. She moaned then, a low moan of one who has suffered long and finally found their relief. He stroked her hair, kissing her as she moved experimentally, squirming a little, the springs screeching under them. Olaf thrust, glad to hear her pleased gasps, his hands brushing over the scars of the riding crop as he guided her into a rhythm on him.

'Loud, too loud' she said suddenly, stopping, ashamed of the noise they made.

Olaf slid off the bed, dragging the blankets with them, guiding her into a gentle rhythm. She gasped then, hungry for his kisses as he made love to her, his slow hands tracing the contours of her breasts, her cheek and neck, or brushing over the scars to guide her in a way that pleased her and made him gasp, till every movement on him was causing ripples of pleasure to fan through her body, tightening her aching nipples chafed by Olaf's chest until she wanted to scream out her enjoyment.

Olaf let her, not caring who heard them, vowing they would leave before daybreak, pleased just to hear her joy in their bodies, and felt himself flood into her in welcome release. She groaned again, and shuddered against him, spent in her pleasure, letting him stay comfortably buried in her, nuzzling her face into his neck. Olaf kissed her forehead, gently soothing her from their pulse-racing climax, whispering how much she had pleased him.

She stroked his cheek and moaned gently, letting him make love to her twice more, once again close and tender on his lap, and once on her knees before the fire, his arms sliding round her, his strong hands cupped on her breasts as he took her from behind; feeling his thighs slap against the backs of hers and his desire plunge deep into her sticky yearning with a quick rhythm, feeling his mouth at her shoulders and hearing him whisper how he loved her. One hand stole to feel himself disappearing into her, a movement that roused Laura so much she screamed again, stuffing a fist into her mouth to muffle her intense pleasure.

Olaf groaned and retreated, both of them collapsing onto the rug before the fire, exhausted and sleepy with contentment. He reached out and pulled her into his arms, sighing as she rested her head on his chest and kissed her hair, shutting his eyes. Laura sighed, her heart still thudding in her ears, knotting her fingers through his, liking the way he felt against her as she drifted off to sleep.

109

She woke when he stroked her hair, whispering to her to get up. She opened her eyes and sat up, aware that the fire had gone out and it was still dark.

'Get dressed my love' he whispered and she obeyed, pulling on cold clothes and running her fingers through her hair to tidy it.

Olaf tossed the blankets casually onto the bed, eyeing Laura as she tucked the treaties back inside her dress, not regretting one instant of last night. She managed a small smile and took his hand as he pulled open the door. There was a drunk snoring loudly in the hallway, sleeping where he had fallen down. They slipped past him and left the key to their room on the bar top, letting themselves out of the tavern, breathing in the fresh, cool morning air.

Laura glanced towards the dawn where the line of the hills was growing clearer, though the horizon was still tinged with smoke, and a small part of her died. *They were still burning Dalnerechensk* she thought, *even after all this time. Was there anything left of the Principality to burn? Or to invade?* Olaf sensed her mood and touched her arm gently, whispering they had to go.

'We're going the wrong way' she said softly.

'Nikita was looking for us, I had to keep you safe' he said, giving her hand another tug.

'I can't' she sighed. 'Nikita may be looking for us, but he is still marching towards Dalnerechensk to invade.' She shut her eyes tightly. 'They will die if he takes the mines from them!' she wailed. 'They will die, the treaty is the only thing that can save them!' she stopped again, sighing resignedly.

'But Russia signed a treaty with the Monarchy of Dalnerechensk. She will not recognise this new government, and the Liberty Treaty will be voided. Russia will invade. Don't you see Olaf?' she asked, taking both of his hands in hers. 'The monarchy has to go back. It is the only thing that will save Dalnerechensk. If we are too late and Nikita is already there he will have to leave or risk war with Germany. If he is still coming, he can be turned away.'

Olaf shut his eyes tightly.

'If you go back they might kill you' he said finally, his voice thick.

Laura was silent. It was the part that terrified her the most. She knew the rumours, the slanders that had kept the tongues of the Principality wagging for months. She knew the woman who had been in the nursery her last night in the castle would tell others the throne was doomed because of her cursed, barren womb. Dalnerechenskers were almost as superstitious as the Transylvanian peasants. She was well aware of how they revered children and stepping into the nursery would be as bad as committing infanticide itself.

It didn't matter now she told herself quietly. *There is no need for an heir to the throne.* It was a gamble, she knew that. But there was no other choice.

'Perhaps they will' she sighed softly. 'But they will still have the treaty.'

Olaf bowed his head, tears running down his face. She *was* a queen, regal and responsible, and he loved her even more. She turned and he followed, heading towards Dalnerechensk, following her because he had sworn last night that not even his own death would stop him from doing so.

She set a determined pace. The river had carried them close, but they had marched for hours in the opposite direction, and Nikita's army had gained a day on them. It was now a race against time. Laura knew how much it would take to move his army; she had taken careful note as they had been marched along. She and Olaf could cover the distance much more quickly unencumbered by the army's provisions, but they had no provisions at all, and she feared it would eventually work against them.

They marched until the sun disappeared on the Western horizon, stopping only for brief rests and a handful of berries for lunch. They made a quick camp and cooked the two birds Olaf had killed with a slingshot, plucking them and roasting the carcasses skewered on sharp sticks over the fire.

They said very little to each other but Laura didn't resist when he took her hand and pulled her into his arms, making love quickly before settling back to sleep, cradled against his body. They woke after dawn the next day and stood, shaking out their stiff muscles, glancing eastward to the mustard grey smoke drifting lazily up from behind a hill, dissipating into the pale blue of the sky.

'Are they still burning Dalnerechensk?' she asked, turning to look at Olaf.

'It is the smelting works in Macherna' he explained. 'The mines are still operating.'

'Oh' Laura said, feeling cold.

There were only two things that could mean: That the new rulers of Dalnerechensk had established control and life was beginning to return to its familiar patterns, or that Nikita and company had reached Dalnerechensk, invaded and annexed the mines for Mother Russia. Neither Olaf nor Laura knew which one it was and she bowed her head, shutting her eyes.

They took each other's hand and walked on silently, picking berries absently as they walked, spotting a wide, disused road in the distance, knowing it was the one that lead to the borders of Dalnerechensk and the tiny village of Davostok. In unspoken agreement they avoided it, keeping north of it, reaching Dalnerechensk's low stone wall at midday.

Olaf hesitated but Laura swung over the wall determinedly, knowing that if she paused she would never climb over it. There was no shout, no alarm, not even anyone around to see them and they walked on, making no effort to hide themselves, climbing up the flanks of Western Valley to reach the pretty settlement of Macherna.

They had crested the rise and just about reached the village when Laura heard the shout they had expected to hear since crossing into Dalnerechensk. She stopped, waiting calmly for the pair of soldiers in strange green uniforms to rush over, carefully concealing her fear from them. *They are not the navy and gold uniform of the Imperial Army* she told herself. *Nikita is not here yet.*

The soldiers looked shocked when they saw who it was, unsure whether to bow low or remain upright against a ruler they no longer recognised. In the end they compromised with a curt nod of the head Laura remembered seeing so many times from Olaf and fought the urge to grab his hand for comfort.

'The Republic of Dalnerechensk no longer recognises her autocratic family' one said, who Laura recognised as the father of the boy Ari who had died in her arms. He dropped his eyes and shuffled his feet then, almost apologetic. 'By Order of the Government' he said by way of explanation.

'Why have you come back? They will try you for crimes against the Republic and hang you!'

the other cried.

The Republic didn't exist when I committed my "crimes" she thought, shutting her eyes to compose herself.

'I belong here' she said quietly. 'I will accept the wishes of Dalnerechensk, whatever she chooses.'

The men looked shocked, then they withdrew, holding a quick conversation and shooting Laura worried looks. Ari's father left and the other waited nervously, switching his gun from hand to hand and wishing desperately he had been in the privy when the Princess had arrived.

Laura stood on the road in the hot summer sun and waited, noticing how quiet Macherna seemed now. There were no children swinging in the tall trees calling down to the guards in Davostok and Dalnerechensk, no wives or daughters walking along the forested path to the mines carrying baskets of food for the workers, no one hanging washing or tending to small vegetable patches in the neat rows of houses. The only person she saw was the father returning reluctantly.

He had something in his grip she couldn't quite make out this far away, but realised a minute later he was carrying a rope. She carefully steeled herself for the worst, keeping her face carefully blank. He looked disturbed, and two soldiers driving a black carriage were following him along the road to where they stood.

'By order of the Republic of Dalnerechensk you are to be taken into custody and taken to the Head of State' he said when he arrived.

Laura thanked God silently he hadn't been ordered to hang her right here, but now feared she would be bound and marched through the streets, a mocking, sneering crowd lining the road throwing insults and rotten fruit where they had once thrown flowers and blessings.

She held out her arms and his eyes widened when he saw she had already been brutalised with rope bindings. He swallowed hard then slipped the rope round her hands so loosely she almost laughed. *I can shake my hands free!* she thought.

But they were not so kind to Olaf. They eyed him distrustfully, and bound his hands tightly. Instead of being ordered to march through the streets as Laura had feared they were pushed into the black carriage and the curtains were pulled. Ari's father and one of the soldiers who had driven the carriage climbed in too, sitting in silence. The other soldier stayed in the driver's seat, flicking the reins when the carriage had been firmly locked. The soldier who had warned Laura of her fate patted the door of the carriage and it jerked, starting down the hill to Ladozhskoye.

Laura begged for the curtain to be open a chink to let in the fresh air. The soldiers looked uncomfortable, but let a small sliver of daylight into the carriage. Through the gap Laura could see the empty streets of Ladozhskoye, and the remains of the Ivanov home smoking on the hillside. She shut her eyes tightly, knowing this was not the time to grieve for her friends.

Instead she turned her mind to the man waiting for her in Dalnerechensk's fortified city. She guessed he would be the man who had spoken so craftily in the pub all those nights, that man who had sparked the Revolution. With some horror she realised she didn't even know his name.

'Who is the Head of State?' she asked.

'Ilich Rukavishnikov' all three men said together.

110

Laura paced back and forward in her cell, her quick mind working. As the carriage had rolled through Dalnerechensk people had hissed at them, their hard faces frightening Laura, but she had quickly realised no one on the streets had known who was inside, and were probably hissing at the soldier they could see on the driver's seat. *We were driven secretly and quickly* she told herself. *Dalnerechensk is not happy with her new ruler.*

The thought had given her some hope and she had sat quietly, beginning to formulate plans. The carriage had jerked to a stop and Laura had heard the familiar crunching of the castle courtyard gravel under soldier's feet. The carriage door had been unlocked and pulled open. Laura had blinked, blinded by the light, and had been pulled out by Ari's father.

Roman had stood before her dressed in the green uniform of a Republican Soldier. His mouth had fallen open when he saw her then he had dropped his head, deeply embarrassed. 'Take them to cells in the tower' Ari's father had said, climbing up onto the driver's seat as the carriage rolled out of the castle grounds again.

Laura had looked up at the ancient stone walls of the castle, still as solid as ever, and thanked God silently that Dalnerechensk would never become like Varennikov Castle. It hadn't escaped completely she noticed, there were black sooty streaks against the light stone, and some windows had been broken. The rooms inside had been gutted by the flames. *They burned the throne room* she had thought.

Roman had avoided looking at her, taking her arm and leading her across the courtyard to the tower. Olaf had been pushed along behind her by another soldier as they walked up the spiral staircase, passing intermittent doors. When they had reached the top Roman pushed open a door and led them into a short corridor. One thick iron door had been unlocked and Olaf was untied and pushed in.

Roman had opened another cell and untied her, still unable to look at her.

'I'm sorry' he had said finally.

'Come Roman, I do not begrudge you earning a living' she had said, rubbing her wrists. 'Men still have to eat; life still has to go on.'

Roman had bowed his head and closed the iron door, locking it behind her.

'Please give the Head of State a message that I would like to see him' she had called after him.

'Yes Your Highness' Roman had said dutifully.

Laura had heard their footfalls crossing the stone and spiraling down the staircase. She had sighed then, looking around the small cell. There were still rusting manacles attached to the walls but a layer of fresh hay had been strewn over the stone floor. She could see the windows of her apartments from the small arrow-slit window of the tower and thought her rooms looked undisturbed, though she couldn't really tell.

So she had paced as she waited, crushing the fresh hay underfoot as she walked, breathing in deep the soothing smell, thinking and plotting. The more she thought and paced the more the smell soothed her until she finally stopped, sitting down calmly on the hard bed to wait. *He's not going to come today* she thought. *He's going to make me wait at least one night to prove he is the ruler of Dalnerechensk, and not I.*

She heard the sounds of footsteps approaching up the spiral staircase and the door to the corridor opened. Two soldiers came in, carrying plates of food for them. Roman politely knocked on her iron door then unlocked it.

'Something to eat, Your Highness' he said.

'You're not supposed to call her that' growled the other, locking Olaf's cell again.

Laura thanked Roman quietly when he gave it to her.

'Is there anything else I can get you Your- *Tsarevna*?' he said. 'A doctor maybe?'

She shut her eyes, remembering he had been in the courtyard when Aleksei had whipped her. It all seemed so strangely far away now.

'Was anyone hurt Roman?' she asked. 'Was anyone killed?'

The second guard joined them, hovering at the door, eyeing the returned Princess. Roman's eyes flicked to him then he began to talk earnestly.

'It was bloodless, despite all the fires and confusion. Commander Kaminin forbade anyone from taking up arms against them, and forbade anyone from joining in under pain of court martial and dishonourable discharge – at the very least, he said. So we just – watched' he shrugged helplessly. 'Watched them burn the castle and smash the windows, stealing all the things -' he stopped, swallowing his anger. 'They were really angry that you were gone' he went on. 'We thought you hadn't, thought they had killed you. I guess if they had found you they would have' he stopped again.

'How has it been since then?' Laura wanted to know. 'Are they still giving out the meat rations?'

'Well, they declared the forests were no longer private property of the monarchy' Roman said. 'As soon as they said that everyone flooded down to the forests, you should have seen it!' he grinned, but it faded again when he remembered who he was talking to. 'They culled all the deer' he went on. 'Wagons and wagons of them came out of the forest, all shapes and sizes; does, bucks, pigs, even fawns and birds! I don't think there are any animals left in the forest.'

Laura was quiet. She would miss the sounds of the forest when she went riding, but didn't know if that would ever happen again.

'He raised everyone's wages' Roman went on. 'The army's and the miners'; lots were employed to make the new uniforms -' he stopped, suddenly looking down, shamefaced that he was wearing it.

'No one's been paid yet' the guard at the door broke in, speaking for the first time.

Laura detected a note of bitterness in his voice. *Ah...* she thought. *So they had all been seduced by the promises that things would all be different, and yet, it was still the same...*

'The miners are on strike' Roman said.

Laura's mouth fell open in surprise.

'But the smelting works is still going' she blurted out.

'That's because he bribed them'

The guard at the door took Roman's arm, realising he had said too much and pulled him out of the room.

'My lords?' Laura asked, making them both stop, surprised by the title she had used. 'I would like some water, and if possible, a clean dress. I would like to be presentable when I go before the Head of State to answer the charges of Crimes Against the Republic.'

They looked at each other silently then nodded and left, locking the door behind them. Laura sat quietly, pushing around the cooling stew with her spoon, digesting this new bit of information.

The guards did not return and Ilich did not send for her, and now it was dark. Laura put aside the plate of uneaten stew, knowing there was nothing to do now but wait and sleep and plot.

111

Early the next morning Roman arrived with a bowl of warm water and a dress for her. She thanked him quietly and washed her face free of grime, smoothing it over her hair to tame the wisps and get rid of as much dirt as possible. She dressed quickly, and would have liked to have had clean bloomers but in all fairness she had only asked for a dress.

Roman tapped on the door quietly.

'Ilich Rukavishnikov requires your presence in Parliament Chambers' he said.

Laura held her hands out to be tied again and Roman eyed her raw wrists.

'That won't be necessary' he said quietly.

Laura was secretly glad, and followed Roman down the spiral staircase to the courtyard. She couldn't stop her eyes straying to the stables looking for Olaf. It seemed strange to be back here with everything so different. She wished he had not been separated from her; wished he could have kissed her, or squeezed her hand to reassure her as she left to face her fate.

Roman led her inside the castle. Laura paused, eyeing the entrance hall, noticing how little had changed, except that her marriage portrait was missing. Roman gently motioned her along, leading her up to the first floor to the Council Chambers, now renamed Parliament Chambers. He knocked and opened the door, ushering Laura in before shutting the door behind her. There was a soft sound and Laura knew he had leaned his weight against the door, either pressing his back to stand guard or his ear to listen in.

She was relieved to see only one man sitting in the large room, sitting in the Tsar's seat, the seat she had occupied for two days, negotiating the Liberty Treaty. Now she was the one who found themself in the position of not knowing how to behave, and nodded curtly at him before her eyes drifted around the room.

The Royal standard of Dalnerechensk had been torn down from the wall. Instead a new flag hung in its place and Laura studied it carefully. It was white with green trim, and still bore the black silhouette of the crossed pickaxe and shovel, under the three watch towers of Dalnerechensk. Laura guessed Ilich was wise enough not to break completely with tradition.

Her eyes were drawn back to the man at the head of the table, watching him flick through piles of documents. Ilich Rukavishnikov did not look like the young and passionate man she had seen on the bar top. In fact he looked haggard and worn, and prematurely old. Laura almost smiled, remembering how many times she had seen Aleksei with the same wearied look on his face, but stopped herself just in time.

She waited for him to speak, wondering why he had brought her here, why his new Advisory Council or Parliament or whatever he called them were not here accusing her of adultery, improvidence; crimes against the Republic. Her eyes narrowed slightly, tiring of his theatrics. She knew now what real fear was.

'I see you have built up a large standing army Ilich, what did you offer to pay them?' she suddenly asked.

His eyes flicked to hers and they were hard with distaste, but they looked away again, dropping to the parchment he was holding. *He had promised high wages* Laura realised, *probably with some brilliant story of resurrecting the glory of Vsevolod's army, and had realised now that Dalnerechensk was too poor to even afford her castle guards.* That one look had told her how naïve and foolish they had all been; her with her dreams of wealth and love, Aleksei in his awkward and gullible reliance on Russia's deceitful information, Ilich with his prejudice and dreams of glory reborn.

He's a man realising just how desperate this all was she thought. *He had promised wages he couldn't pay, ordered work and contracts he couldn't honour; his grandiose dreams of being the man to lead Dalnerechensk to glory and prosperity had crashed down around him when he realised that his party was in danger of having the same disgruntled followers rise against* him *in bloody, murderous revolution.*

Ilich sighed, dropping the parchment on the table, eyeing her. He rubbed his forehead tiredly, his eyes drawn back to the piles of paper. *He's wondering what he missed* Laura realised, and watched him stop himself from reaching for another sheet. He eyed her again.

'There was nothing anyone could have done' he said finally.

'There was something I did' she said, reaching into the front of her dress.

Ilich's eyes flicked to the door, then back to her, slightly embarrassed.

'It is not a knife, nor am I going to undress for you' she snapped as she approached him, pulling out the oilskin.

She reached him and tossed it onto the table before him. He eyed her then picked it up, unwrapping the two treaties. They were creased and crumpled and slightly dirty, but the ink was dry and legible and he began to read, his mouth dropping open in shock. He looked incredulously at her then read on in detail, a shadow of doubt crossing his face. It was erased when he read the second treaty. He was so shocked both pieces of parchment slipped from his shaking hands to the tabletop where they stared blankly up at him.

Laura was pleased to see he was not a man who spluttered with half started questions because she was about to shock him even more. She slapped him hard and he cried *Oh!* in surprise. The door burst open and Roman and another guard raced in, not too sure who had slapped who, but knowing their ruler had cried out.

'Both those treaties are dated three days before your little rebellion!' she said pointing to the table, her voice hissing in anger. 'Russia and Germany signed them with the autocratic Rulers of Dalnerechensk, from one Monarch to another! They will not recognise this ramshackle, ill-prepared parliament of disgruntled socialists! You have damned my people! Aleksei was ill, he was going to take to the wall the next morning to tell you all Dalnerechensk was saved but you couldn't wait!'

'It was supposed to wait!' Ilich cried suddenly, frustrated. 'It was not planned for another month!'

Laura laughed suddenly, astounded at this man's naïvety.

'Did you not think what effect your words had?!' she cried. 'Those men were poor disgruntled drunks that you whipped into a frenzy of hate and you just expected them to sit back and wait for you to tell them when to revolt?!' she slapped him again.

The two guards grabbed her arms, confused as to what was going on but trying to do their part. Ilich's face hardened.

'I know about your spy *Tsarevna* and he will be dealt with as a traitor. Take her back to her cell while I decide what to do with her' he snapped at the guards.

Laura stiffened, not letting her face show the horror and grief she felt.

'Take me to the cell under the kitchen, I don't want to be in the tower when Russia arrives with her cannons' she said to Roman.

Both guards stopped, looking at her in horror.

'What?' Ilich croaked, then cleared his throat, embarrassed, wanting to keep his resolve but unused to manipulation with this high level of bluff.

'I said you had damned my people' she said coldly. 'Rebellion is juicy news Ilich. *Knjaz* Nikita Rurik is en route with his company to crush Dalnerechensk and seize the mines. Will your unpaid soldiers fight for you when faced with five hundred professional Russian soldiers and five cannon?'

'Will they fight for you?' he snapped.

'Perhaps' she shrugged. 'They will fight for Vsevolod and Dalnerechensk. But if you want to avoid war those treaties are our only hope.'

The soldiers looked at each other and then at Ilich, wavering.

'What's done is done!' he finally cried. 'We cannot use them now! It would throw away everything I worked for!'

'You don't have anything you worked for and if you are going to be as pig-headed and stubborn as Aleksei this government will never exist either, and Dalnerechensk will be another Russian territory' she snapped.

'I cannot reverse the rebellion *Tsarevna*, they will not suffer Aleksei's madness on their throne anymore.'

Laura shut her eyes against the tears then said quietly:

'Tsaritsa.'

'Pardon?' Ilich said, confused.

'Tsar Constantinovich died from a shock-weakened heart on the run from the rebellion. He lies in his nightclothes in a grave in Russian soil.' She let a tear slide down her cheek. There was a moment of discomfort; the old Tsar had been respected in Dalnerechensk. 'Tsar Stephanovich is also dead, he drowned a few days ago, and his body is washing out to sea. I am Tsaritsa Stephanovna Vakhtangova.'

The two soldiers looked at each other then let her go. She was no longer just an imprisoned princess; they could see what was happening in the room, and they still had a deep respect for four hundred years of autocratic rule. The punishment for laying a hand on monarchy was a death they were not willing to risk.

'What are we going to do?' Roman finally asked, looking at both rulers, not too sure who was going to answer.

Ilich looked at Laura surreptitiously. He had been over confident and ill prepared for the takeover of power; and had definitely underestimated the Princess. *So the rumours were true then, it* had *been her in the Advisory Council negotiating a treaty with Russia* he thought. *And* what *a treaty it was too. He had thought rather maliciously at the time that the talks had come to nothing because no announcement had been made. He had ranted about it in the bar that night,* raved *even. And all the while this* was waiting for them…

'Are green and white the Republic's colours?' she asked suddenly, breaking into his thoughts.

'Yes' Ilich said, confused. 'What does that have to do with -'

'Find me a white dress and you a blue jacket' she instructed. 'Not navy blue, Dalnerechensk Royal Blue. I don't care if you need to destroy a dress to make one. We need a green sash and then you are going to take me up on the wall.'

'What?' he blinked, caught off-guard and trying not to feel like the Republic was slipping out of his fingers.

Laura ignored him, turning to the two soldiers, gathering up the treaties and rolling them together, folding the oilskin over them.

'Swear to me you love this country and will do everything you can to protect her, not because I am Tsaritsa, or even because they loved me once, but because I have the blood of Vsevolod in my veins too' she said. It was a technicality, but both men dropped to their knees, swearing their loyalty. She gave them the treaties. 'Take this to the printers. He has no other work but this' she swore. 'Do not leave these with him but keep them safe and bring them back to Ilich. Shower the streets with paper. They must know what was won for them. They must know that there is hope.'

The soldiers bowed and disappeared. Laura turned back to Ilich, whose jaw was jerking, aware that he was no longer in control in these rooms.

'Do you have a Council?' she demanded, not in the mood for nursing egos.

'Parliament' he corrected absently. 'Yes.'

'Do you have a military commander or any strategist?'

He shifted uncomfortably, not liking where this was going. 'Not as such' he answered.

'Then perhaps you should find a man familiar with the city's defenses, such as Peter Kaminin, and take me up on the walls in two hours, that should give the rumours enough time to reach Ladozhskoye and Macherna.'

And before Ilich could stop her she left the newly christened Parliament Chambers and went up the stairs to the Tsaritsa's Apartments.

Now they truly are mine she thought as she stepped inside, casting her eye around the room. She was pleased that they had not burnt her chambers though they had been ransacked. All her dresses and jewelry were gone, including the Tsaritsa's lucky black diamonds. Even some of the furniture had been taken from her room and a few of the nick-knacks were broken, scattered on the floor.

Laura spotted the small melted lump of tin and picked it up, holding it tightly in her fist and trotted into her bedroom, aware Ilich had followed her, not quite sure if he should return her to the cells or leave her alone. Laura crawled onto her bed and lay face down, the first proper bed she had slept in since their panicked flight from Dalnerechensk.

She sighed softly, shutting her eyes, and was instantly asleep. Ilich closed the door and left her chambers, stationing a guard outside her doors with strict orders that she was not to leave; then went to do as she had instructed.

112

Laura eyed her reflection in the parts of her mirror that had not been smashed. The white dress they had found was not one of hers, but it was made of fine silk, even if it was rather plain. *It would not do to appear on the walls draped in luxuries* she told herself. *They must fight for an ideal, not a rich and pampered Monarchy that made them so miserable.* She smoothed down her loose hair and checked the graze on her cheek from the punch Nikita's soldier had given her. It had not bruised, but it was obvious she had been attacked.

There was a knock on the door and it was pushed open. Ilich looked uncomfortable, holding the two treaties and a sash, and wearing a blue silk ceremonial jacket. It had been Aleksei's and was too large for him. Laura couldn't help but think it was a fitting metaphor for the disgruntled peasant in her husband's job. He swallowed when she turned and she knew with her hair down and her plain white dress she looked exquisite and virginal.

She took the green sash he was carrying off him and pulled one of his arms out in front of him, placing hers over the top and bound them together, looping the sash all the way up to their elbows.

'A *wedding*?!' Ilich gasped. 'I *am* married! My wife will kill me!'

'A political wedding' Laura corrected. 'I have no intention of bedding you.'

He flushed at that. Laura paid it no head, taking one of the treaties off him.

'Has the printer run out of paper yet?' she asked as she led him down the stairs of the castle.

Ilich didn't answer.

The entrance hall was full of soldiers in green uniforms and men wearing white sashes across their chests. Laura realised they were the new ministers of his parliament, and not one of them was a grey-headed old man. She wondered what had happened to the members of the Advisory Council, wondered if any of them had left Dalnerechensk, if any had been arrested. She wondered if Ilich would be foolish enough to put all his faith in young, inexperienced advisors, as Aleksei had put all his in doddering, conservative old men.

There were more soldiers and ministers in the courtyard. Laura could hear the noise of the crowds gathered on the commons already. *One rebellion could not single-handedly overturn four hundred years of tradition* she thought wryly, and hitched her skirts carefully to make her way up the stairs to the wall.

It was crowded with ministers and soldiers and at first their presence on the wall went unnoticed by the people who had flocked to the commons below the fortifications of Dalnerechensk Castle. The townsfolk were buzzing with rife rumour and one paperboy was rapidly disappearing under a swarm of curious people who were shouting and grabbing at the papers, reading them out loud to each other.

But the eyes of all those on the wall were fixed at the Northern Border of Dalnerechensk, where a dark smear on the horizon was slowly spreading like a plague towards their golden city, lit with the burning rays of the setting sun. The new parliament fidgeted nervously, and Peter Kaminin, re-employed and renamed Chief Strategist by Ilich's hastily addressed caucus, could not take his eyes off the growing horror. Nikita's army had arrived.

Laura looked round her testily. Ilich had let her sleep too long while he had gathered his caucus of ministers and had explained what was going on, and the hour was getting late.
'For heaven's sake, there are too many here!' Laura snapped. 'Get them off the walls or none of them will notice us!'

He eyed her but did as he was told. The ministers began to leave reluctantly, all eager to be part of this moment. The crowds below them were too busy fighting and squabbling over bits of paper, reading out the conditions of the treaties, arguing that they couldn't hear, jeering loudly that it was all a joke. The paperboy was knocked to the ground, his fliers grabbed from his hands and tossed through the crowds.

The people looked up to follow the arc of the paper and saw their beloved Princess on the walls. Their unvoiced cheers died in their throat; she was dressed in the colour of the rebels and she was with Ilich Rukavishnikov, who was dressed in royal colours, their hands tied with the green sash that was common in both flags. Unrest swirled through the crowds then they fell silent, expectant; more people flooding into the already packed commons.

Laura looked pointedly at Ilich, and he nodded to let her speak. She took a deep breath and shut her eyes, knowing this was the most important moment of her life. Then she began. 'I am sorry' she said, her voice pushing out from the deepest parts of her. There was not a single person in the commons who did not hear her. 'I am sorry Dalnerechensk; my people, my love; my blood. I promised you when I stood here all those days ago, that I would serve you as best as I could; but I promised to submit to the rule of my husband too. I am sorry that we did not listen when we should have; we did not speak when we needed to.

'Our Prince was ill and you were not told. And foreign kings came to your soil, and you were not told why. It is time you were told. There is a new treaty with Russia, a new price for tin, and you will not suffer anymore. There is also a new treaty with Germany, for protection if Russia ever decides to break our agreement. It is time you were told of such things.

'I fought for you, Dalnerechensk, in the chambers every day while my husband was ill. It's time you were told that. I forced Russia to cease in cheating you out of wealth that was rightfully yours. It cost me my reputation and the love of my husband. But I gave that honour to him, gave it to him to tell you from the walls because I wanted you to love him as I did.

'But he was too ill, and you were too angry...' she trailed off.

'It's time you were told Tsar -' she stuttered over the name as the tears came close. 'Tsar Constantinovich and Tsar Stephanovich both died in Russia a few days ago' she paused to let the shock of that sink in. 'We have lost men that we once admired; once loved. I stand here, today, as your Tsaritsa. I came here because I loved a prince; I came back because I loved a Principality.

'I have loved you; laughed with you, cried with you, prayed with you; buried the children with you. I have been there with you in our darkest hours, but a new darkness is drawing closer' There was a murmur in the crowd as they looked at each other, uneasy.

'Russia had decided to take action, to take advantage of the recent confusion. She signed the treaty with the Monarchy, not the Republic. She does not recognise their authority' There was another murmur, louder and discontented. 'But I *am* the Monarchy' she went on, louder to be heard above the crowd. 'I have returned to you. Even if you choose not to acknowledge me the Tsar of Russia *must*, and he cannot set one foot inside Dalnerechensk without risking war with Germany.

'Now an army approaches our gates' she said, and shouts of fear sounded in the crowd. 'Russia is here at our gates and means to have what is ours. Germany is too far away! It is us! It is the children of Vsevolod! We will repel this Russian Rebel again!' she cried and a cheer rang out through those gathered below. Laura let silence fall before continuing, her voice softer yet no less audible.

'I do not ask you to fight for a government, to fight for a Princess, a President, a Head of State. I ask you to fight for Dalnerechensk, for Vsevolod's city, for your brothers and sons and neighbours and friends! For the very blood in the veins that runs through each and every one of us, the blood of heroes and saints and saviors! I ask you to fight for your freedom, your existence and your pride! I ask you, – *I beg you*, – not to turn against yourselves, but to reach out and help each other in our hour of need. We need the sons and daughters of Vsevolod on the walls again, to save what we dearly love!'

They cheered again, folding their hands over their hearts and singing the national anthem. Ilich was watching Laura with something close to awe, wondering at the strength and artfulness in one so young. The anthem finished and another cheer went up from the gathered crowd.

Laura turned her face northwards to where the dark smear of advancing troops had stopped. She could make out the white speck that was Nikita's tent in the middle of the uneasy mess. She waved her hands for silence, waving Ilich's hand too and waited till the crowd obeyed.

'Arm yourselves and do not fear the Russians' she said. 'We have beaten odds before; we will do so again. Russia will never again dare to step foot on Dalnerechensk soil. Offer your help in any way that you can' she pleaded, letting the arm bound to Ilich's fall back between them. 'God save the Tsaritsa!' someone cried, and the blessing was taken up by others.

She touched her fingers to her lips and blessed them all then bowed low and stepped back, leading Ilich down the steps.

'Now what do we do?' Ilich asked in the courtyard, turning to a woman he was coming to deeply respect.

'You must take me to Nikita's army' she answered. 'They must see us united and supported by the other.'

He looked surprised then smiled. He was suddenly quite transformed and Laura smiled too, letting him lead her to the stables. Eagerly she looked for Olaf, wanting to share with him her feeling of triumph but was disappointed when a boy she had never seen before appeared, leading horses to a carriage and hitching them together. She turned to Ilich, carefully composing herself.

'What will become of Olaf?' she asked quietly.

'By Dalnerechensk law, the penalty for treason is hanging until the bones fall from the noose.'

Laura shut her eyes tightly. 'He saved my life; he is just a simple man… Please don't do anything yet.'

Ilich said nothing and helped her into the carriage. Laura did not say any more, knowing that she could lose the upper hand if they knew he was her lover. The carriage jerked and started down Castle Street, picking up speed once it passed under the King's Gate and headed towards the low stone wall marking the northern boundary of Dalnerechensk.

Beyond the wall they could see flickering torches along the border, illuminating the line of perambulation. Behind it was a strip of darkness where sentries and patrolling soldiers walked, out of the light to avoid being shot at by Dalnerechensk snipers and being counted by Dalnerechensk scouts. Beyond the darkness the canvas tents rose like chalky hillocks in the valley, lit here and there by torches or camp fires the soldiers had built to warm themselves, to see to gamble by.

Quickly Ilich climbed out of the coach and helped Laura down, moving awkwardly with their arms still tied. They mounted the wall and unfurled a white flag made hastily from a large handkerchief tied to a stick. It wasn't long before a sentry scout appeared; his rifle ready but not pointed at them.

'What business do you have with Russia?' he asked rudely.

'Boy, don't trifle these international relations and cause a war when you are still too young to shave!' Ilich snapped. 'Send for *Knjaz* Rurik before your blundering embarrasses Russia!'

He shot them a filthy look but went to rouse Nikita from his dinner.

The Prince's face turned ugly when he saw her atop the wall with a man he guessed was Ilich Rukavishnikov.

'*Velikaja Knjaginja*!' he called with mock delight and barely concealed disdain. 'I am pleased to see you arrived safely.'

'Thank you *Knjaz* Rurik, sadly it was not under your protection' she said sweetly.

'Dalnerechensk thanks you for the dedicated protection you have shown her citizens on your soil *Knjaz* Rurik' Ilich said. 'You can be sure Tsar Nicholas will receive excellent commendations about you.'

Nikita smiled like a snake, and Laura realised even if it wasn't too late to send word to Germany it was now impossible, the Russians had severed the telegraph wire. Dalnerechensk was cut off, and no one would know what Nikita had done until it was too late. Perhaps he would be reprimanded for his actions, but it would not be harshly. Russia needed the tin from the mines.

'Thank you, that is most kind' Nikita said, and there were fangs in his voice. 'I demand an explanation for Dalnerechensk spies on Russian soil.'

'Spies?' Ilich asked, surprised. 'You had the Royal Household of Dalnerechensk and their servants.'

'Do not insult me' Nikita snapped. 'The Royal couple does not travel like common peasants.'

'Of course we did *Knjaz* Rurik' Laura said. 'The parliament was set up to rule in our absence, but I fear we left too quickly, there were a few incidents' she said. 'We want the return of our servants.'

Nikita looked like he was carved in ice.

'It was revolution' he said softly, dangerously.

'An ambiguous choice of words,' Ilich said, shrugging. 'A very quick change of style, much like your new Duma. Perhaps you have been misled.'

'Perhaps' forced its way out of Nikita's lips.

He turned and barked several instructions at soldiers that were standing behind him. One or two detached themselves and disappeared into the village of tents. Anna, Mikhail and Fedor suddenly appeared and were waved over the wall, the Russians watching them disappear with distaste.

'We thank you for the safe return of our citizens' Ilich said. 'May God save and protect you.'

Nikita turned on his heel and disappeared into the darkness of his camp. One by one his soldiers disappeared into the night, though Laura knew they were watching them from just outside the reach of the light. *It's such a lonely spot standing here so exposed* she thought. She and Ilich carefully maneuvered down from the wall, awkward with the sash tying them together and got back in the carriage, sitting opposite the three servants, noticing how Mikhail's arms were round Anna.

'What will happen now?' Ilich asked, watching her unwind the green sash from their arms.

'We wait for them to attack' she said simply.

He blanched, his mouth dropping open, shocked.

'Nikita is rash and impudent' she said, eyeing him. 'He will not think of the consequences until it is too late. He will attack, we have till dawn to get ready, but he is lazy, so I wouldn't expect five hundred soldiers knocking on our gates till midday.'

She freed her arm and slid away from him on the seat. Anna threw her arms around Laura, sobbing and uttering unintelligible things in her relief and grief.

'They said you were all dead' Fedor said, his characteristically blank face furrowed in the dark carriage.

'Aleksei is dead' she said quietly.

There were gasps, but not the outpouring of sorrow that should have been expected. Laura knew they had probably grieved for them already, and were torn between their loyalty and their hate for him. She looked away, out the carriage window, the silence falling around them. Dalnerechensk was eerily quiet. Hardly any lights shone from buildings and the air was thick with fear and tension; a besieged city humming with barely controlled panic.

'Who are you?' Fedor asked, eyeing Ilich.

'Ilich Rukavishnikov' he answered. 'Head of State of the Republic of Dalnerechensk.'

Their eyes flicked from him to Laura and back again.

'What does that mean?' Mikhail asked. 'Are we under arrest? Do we go back to the castle? Where are we to live?'

The carriage pulled to a halt in the courtyard. The eyes flicked between Ilich and Laura again.

'You are free to go' Ilich said.

There was a pause.

'Go home to your family in the town' Laura said quietly. 'I am glad that you are safe and thankful for your service to the Royal Family. Go home to your families.'

There was silence then Anna threw her arms round her, holding her tight. Laura stroked her hair then gently pushed her away. She leaned over and kissed Mikhail's cheek.

'Keep her safe. May you live long and happily' she said, then kissed Fedor's cheek. 'Thank you, my friends.'

The door was pulled open by Basil and they slipped to the ground. Laura slipped out too and Basil took her arm, waiting till Ilich gave him an order.

'What is to be done with Olaf and me?' Laura asked.

'He was a spy, and I don't know what to do with you' Ilich answered, stepping down to the ground.

He took off the jacket as if it detested him, tossing it into the carriage and closing the door. Laura was quiet for a minute then asked:

'Tell me Ilich, do you know how many oppose you? Who they are? What they would be prepared to do?' Ilich looked uncomfortable. 'That's dangerous information to be without' she continued.

'According to your little speech Dalnerechensk is united to fight against the Russians' he snapped.

'So there are no spies, only – liaisons' she finished.

'Tell me *Tsarevna*, how did *Knjaz* Rurik know about the Revolution?' he asked, rounding on her.

Laura blinked. 'You think Olaf was spying on you and telling *Russia*?!' she asked, astounded.

Ilich said nothing, beckoning Basil to bring her with him into the castle, leading them up to Parliament Chambers. Peter Kaminin had brought maps from the military archives in the Tcherepnin Barracks and had spread them out on the long flat table. The room was crowded with men wearing white sashes all huddled around the table, eyeing the set of defenses around Dalnerechensk.

Ivan Gogol stood near them, wearing a white sash, too embarrassed to raise his eyes from the note pad he was jotting on to look at Laura. Basil let Laura go and closed the door behind her. She eyed Ilich then stepped closer to the table to see what was going on.

'What is this circular defense?' someone asked, pointing out a clearly marked line that ran from the river in the north around Dalnerechensk and rejoining the river south of the city.

'An old moat, it has been filled in' Peter said.

A messenger burst in, bringing a note from Tcherepnin Barracks. Peter Kaminin took it and read it quickly, dropping it on the floor. Laura saw the carpet was littered with such scraps of crumpled paper.

'We don't have enough ammunition to hold off a sustained attack, let alone a siege' he said, bending over his maps. 'They will surround the city, stretching our defenses thin. The little we have will be of minimum effect and quickly used up. We will either be pounded into submission or starved out in a siege. We need to let them breach.'

There were shocked and outraged gasps of horror from the men gathered. They erupted in noise, shouting down the suggestion, small arguments breaking out between them. *The more things change…* Laura thought wryly. Peter bellowed for silence, his voice lifting easily over the rabble in the room. Laura found herself wanting to snap to attention, and hid her grin when two of the men did. They looked sheepish and cleared their throats, shuffling closer to the table and out of their two-man line.

'We cannot sustain a circumferential attack. Our hope of success lies with a focused attack. Their initial assault will come from the north' he indicated on the maps before them, 'and then fan out around the walls. If they breach they will pour their men into it, drawing away from round the walls to the open gate. This will contain them -'

'Inside our city!' someone interrupted. He was silenced with a look from Peter.

'If they think they have won they will stop trying to gain entry via the other gates. -'

'Permit me to interrupt Peter Kaminin, but I think I could safely attest that *Knjaz* Rurik doesn't not simply mean to cease when the gates are breached' Laura said. 'He would think it such a shame to have brought so much ammunition to take home again.'

'We will take measures to deal with the guns' Peter said.

'If they breach King's Gate then the containment will mean vicious fighting from street to street' another minister said. 'A lot of property will be damaged.'

'King's Gate will not be breached' he said then tapped the map. 'Vsevolod's Gate will.'

The ministers eyed the map then eyed Peter.

'There is a chance that they might try to reposition the guns when the gate is breached, which will buy us some precious respite -'

'They would have to be mad to position themselves there, between the walls of Dalnerechensk and Tcherepnin; it would be slaughter' Ilich said. '*Knjaz* Rurik may be arrogant, but he would not -'

'Is he arrogant enough to think we're stupid enough to leave a gate undefended?' Peter asked.

'What do you propose?' Ilich asked suspiciously.

'He believes that Dalnerechensk is backwards and stupid, but he will have spies here, assessing our preparations. We will march the entire Tcherepnin garrison into Dalnerechensk in broad daylight, and stockpile our grapeshot only on the Northern Wall of the city. We will let him see only what we want him to see. We will fool him into thinking that he is right.

'Prepare barricades along Vsevolod's Way - board up the houses and shops. We have approximately three hundred and fifty able bodied men that have sworn up since - this afternoon' he said, his gaze resting on Laura briefly. 'They have been divided into seven units of fifty men: A, B, C, D, E, F and G. All Units except E and the Palace Guard will be stationed on the North Wall at the beginning of the attack. Unit E will line the barricades in Vsevolod's Way and direct the defense with all the citizens. The Palace Guard will hold a line hidden within the forests that line the slopes of West Valley -'

'What?' several people asked.

'You mean that the Palace Guard, the *only* men who have had any kind of training, will be *outside* the fortifications *hiding* in the *forest?*' Ilich demanded.

'*Yes*' Peter said forcefully. 'Our trained men, our *only* trained men, will be outside the fortifications hiding in the forest because they will hold the line. They will stand and watch the attack, they will listen to the sounds of war and the cries of the Principality's Patriots, wounded and dying, and *they will hold the line*. This will only work if men are there, holding the line until the signal is given. If they break, if they rush down before everyone is ready, this will fail, and Dalnerechensk will be lost.' He glared at all of them in the room, taking another message from a soldier from Tcherepnin and reading it quickly.

'We must make all effort to disable the cannon while all the units are on the North Wall' he continued on a quieter note, tapping the map to the north of the filled-in moat. 'When the breach begins all Units except A will retreat to the castle. Unit B will reinforce E along the barricades and C will hold the line at the castle. Units D, F and G will take the underground tunnel to Tcherepnin's water reservoir. Once they reach Tcherepnin F Unit will make their way to Dalnerechensk Gate' he tapped the gate in Tcherepnin's wall, closest to the city. 'Units D and G will leave Tcherepnin via Forest Gate and head into the Hunting Forest, moving into position here' he tapped the slopes of East Valley between the Dalnerechensk and Tcherepnin, opposite the line of the Palace Guard. 'When they are in position I will give the signal.

'*Knjaz* Rurik will have had to pour his men into the breach so as not to lose the advantage he once had, to force back the resistance. When I give the signal C Unit will begin a push down from the Castle, reinforcing Units E and B, who will attempt to block or at least choke Vsevolod's Gate. Units D and G and the Palace Guard will attack from the sides while Unit F will attack from the walls.'

'Box them in' Ilich said, impressed with his strategy.

Another messenger blew in with another strip of paper. Peter read it then dropped it to the floor, beginning to set his plans into action.

Men were sent to Vsevolod's Way to empty houses of furniture to build the barricades and others were sent to ensure the cannons were working perfectly. More were sent to load carts with hay and buckets of pitch, positioning them inside Vsevolod's Gate to be set alight and pushed into place. More still were sent to the underground river, muffling the echoes with any cloth they could find, praying the noise would be lost in that of the battle above them.

It was late when the war room was shut. The new ministers left for an uneasy few hours of rest and a grim Dalnerechensk moved into position to wait for the first light of dawn.

Laura was put under room arrest; instead of being sent back to the tower she was taken to the Tsaritsa's apartments. Roman bid her a quiet good night, filled with a nervous energy, torn between babysitting a queen in relative safety or standing with the nerve-wrecking fear beside soldiers and civilians alike, staring out into the dark and wondering which bullet had his name on it.

She thanked him, infinitely weary, but still had one request to make.

'Roman, Olaf is still in the tower cells. Please don't leave him up there to die in Russian cannon fire.'

Roman looked uneasy.

'I will not run away Roman. He saved my life and he is going to be executed for being a Russian spy. I shall like to see him again before then. Please Roman, just one more time. Give me that before they kill me too.'

He hesitated then gently shut the door and locked it. Laura shut her eyes and sagged, feeling the weight of events pulling her down. *Had it only been two days ago that he had held her on his lap, buried deep in her beside a small fire they had cooked the birds he had killed with a slingshot?* She pressed her hands to her neck, pushing away the thoughts of him.

She sighed, her eyes straying to her uncovered window. She could see the dark outline of the tower that had been her bedroom last night, and beyond it; the twinkling glow of firelight in Nikita's camp. Peter's plan was ambitious and glorious, but the defenders of Dalnerechensk were untrained farmers and parade soldiers, and they were pitted against a professional army. Laura wiped her eyes quickly.

The door behind her opened then shut again, and at once she knew Olaf was with her. She turned as he strode across her sitting room to her, taking her in his arms, kissing her feverishly.

'I heard you on the walls' he whispered between his kisses. 'Oh Laura, you will save Dalnerechensk.'

He lifted her up and she felt him hungry for her, pushing her against the thick castle walls, urgent and passionate, tearing the drapes from the window as he struggled to please her. She cried out and shuddered, feeling his pleasure respond to hers. Olaf stopped, breathing hard, groaning as he set her down again, pulling away from her and turning to look out the window.

Laura swallowed, her breath still hitching hard in her chest, wondering why he seemed so strange and distant. She slid her hand along his back, planting a kiss on his arm.

'What is it?' she whispered.

He turned to her, his face etched with deep pain and anguish.

'Olaf?' she whispered, frightened.

'I love you Laura' he said fiercely. 'I love you and will always, no matter what. But I can't protect you anymore. I swore I would die for you. And I will' he said, looking away, back out the window. 'They will execute me.'

'They cannot -'

'Laura' he interrupted softly, his voice full of pain. 'There are secrets in this castle, in the

Tsar's locked vault. They will find it eventually, if they have not already, and then not even your clever words can save me.'

'Olaf' she started and was interrupted with a soft, pained sigh, a whisper of something familiar.

She stopped, feeling slivers of fear creep over her. Olaf shut his eyes, slumping.

'I am Alexander Andrei' he said, turning to look back at her.

Laura gawped at him, too flabbergasted to respond. 'Don't be preposterous!' she finally snapped.

Stunning her, Olaf switched to English and cried: 'You asked me why I spoke Polish, the Countess was my mother, the Tsar was my father. You asked me if Alexander Andrei was mad, and I muck out the castle's stables instead of riding the horses to hunt, they will kill me because I am the first mad prince!' he stopped, his eyes flicking to the door, swallowing down his passion. 'I love you like I have loved no other Laura, but you cannot save me from my birthright.'

He put his face in his hands and sobbed. Laura stared at him, a whirl of maddening emotions and thoughts swirling through her. *He spoke English, what would a Dalnerechensk peasant need to know English for?* she asked herself. *If his words were true they would kill him for sure.*

'I led you back here' she said, incredulous and pained.

'No, Laura, don't blame yourself' he said, seizing her tightly and pulling her into his arms. 'I swore to follow you.'

She felt his lips in her hair, soothing her, hungry for her and surrendered, undoing the buttons of her dress. Olaf helped her, stripping it from her then carried her into the bedroom, setting her gently down on her bed. She lay back and guided him above her, asking him to take her like a Tsar in her bed. He obeyed, stroking her hair gently, covering her mouth with kisses, feeling her arch and squirm under him. She groaned at the sensations as he made love to her again, tender and gentle, finally sleeping exhausted in each other's arms, his tears drying on her cheeks.

113

It was the explosion that woke her at dawn. It was followed quickly by two others and she pushed back the covers of her bed, rushing to the window. Nikita's troops were on the move. They had blasted away three sections of the border wall before their camp and men and five cannon were pouring through, dragging the guns closer to the castle. She had known the attack was coming but hadn't realised it would be so soon. *The cannon would make it difficult to keep the Tin Gate and King's Gate firmly locked against the Russians* she thought. *I hope this plan works.*

She turned back to call to Olaf – Alexander – but her bed was empty. A note and a key sat on her pillow. She looked wildly round the room then rushed out into her sitting room. He was gone. She turned slowly and went back to her bed, picking up the short note, knowing they were his last words to her.

The script had bold, confident lines and swirls, but was wobbly, as if the person writing it was drunk, or shaking with emotion. It was written in French. Laura shut her eyes against the tears, picking up the key to the safe and clutching it tightly, pressing the paper against her breast as if she could somehow embrace Olaf through it.

There was a shout from the walls of Dalnerechensk and Laura saw soldiers uniformed in green and black race along the parapets, carrying guns and bows and quivers, one or two with leather strips she guessed were slingshots. She quickly dressed again, having nothing else to wear but the white dress she had worn yesterday, and pinned her hair up simply with a few clips she found scattered on the floor of her dressing room. *None of the clips with seed pearls are here* she thought ruefully.

She slipped across the sitting room, ignoring the torn puddle of drapes by the window and opened the door. No one stood outside to prevent her from leaving. The castle was eerily quiet, no ministers, no soldiers, not even any servants were around. She headed determinedly along the corridor to the library. She was going to find the proof in the Tsar's vault and take it, to keep Olaf safe. *They would not kill him if there was no proof.*

The room had been ransacked in the rebellion and a sizeable pile of books had been thrown together and set alight. Several of the books were charred but the fire had stopped, leaving a large number of books untouched. She wondered if someone had put the fire out and thanked God it hadn't spread.

The book she was last reading to Tsar Constantinovich was still sitting on her chair and she avoided looking at it, crossing to the portrait of the beautiful Polish Tsaritsa, stopping briefly to eye her features. She was blonde like Olaf but that was where the resemblance ended. Olaf didn't resemble the Tsar or the Tsaritsa and a flash of doubt washed over her. *Why would Olaf lie to her?* He was her friend and lover; she didn't care that he was a stable groom.

She reached up and took hold of the heavy, ornate frame the picture stood in, lifting it aside and carefully setting it on the ground, leaning it against the wall. Out the window she could see the approaching army, the five murderous cannons pushed before them, fanning out to take positions along the northern walls. Laura quickly pushed the key into the locked vault and twisted it open, hearing the clicks of the tumblers above the noise of the approaching army.

Inside were several sheets of thick parchment paper. She lifted them out carefully and flicked through them. They were bonds, dated three hundred years ago and totaling a million pounds. Laura looked at them all carefully, knowing they were her inheritance, stacking them carefully and setting them aside, reaching to pull out more papers.

She found three wills for Tsar Stephan Constantinovich Vakhtangov and pulled them out, reading them all quickly. The first was dated from the beginning of his reign, naming his younger brother *Velikij Knjaz* Radomyr Constantinovich Vakhtangov as heir to the throne and the wealth of the Principality. The next will was dated a few years later, naming his new born son, Alexander Andrei Stephanovich as heir, naming his brother Lord Protector of the Principality until Alexander was eighteen.

The third will was dated ten years ago. In it the Principality had been left to both Alexander and Aleksei, but Aleksei was to manage Alexander's half until he was either fit to rule in his own right, or married and produced a male heir. *If Alexander had had a child, regardless of whether Aleksei and she had had children, his son would have come to the throne and not hers* she thought.

There was a shout on the walls and she realised she was running out of time. She reached into the vault again, her fingers brushing against stiff, glossy cardboard. She pulled it out, her breath catching, her eyes filling with tears. It was a photograph, old and creased, but the young, carefree and stunningly handsome man in the picture was Olaf. He was dressed in fine clothes and casually scratching the neck of a magnificent stallion, smiling through his boyish blonde hair at her. There was a slight circle of discolouration and she turned the photograph over to discover a short testimonial marked with the Tsar's personal wax seal.

It stated that it was the wish of Alexander Andrei Stephanovich Vakhtangov to abdicate responsibility to his younger brother, and would disappear from public view. It was signed by Tsar Constantinovich, Aleksei, Nicholas Riminov, *Velikij Knjaz* Radomyr and Alexander Andrei himself, his signature shaky and uncontrolled, like that of a child still learning to write.

It was the same script written on Olaf's short note to her. He was Alexander Andrei.

Her vision blurred and she wiped at her tears, turning the photograph over to look at the handsome, young face. *What had caused him to abdicate the throne?* she wondered. There were more shouts from the walls and she put down the photograph, rummaging in the vault for anything else of importance.

She found Alexander's birth certificate and her marriage certificate, and the death certificates for the Tsaritsa and *Velikij Knjaz* Radomyr. Laura checked the date then grabbed the photograph again, checking the date of Alexander's abdication. *Velikij Knjaz* Radomyr's death certificate was signed three days after the abdication. His cause of death had been 'self-administered poison'.

How much more did this family need to suffer? she asked herself piteously. How terrible it must have been for Tsar Constantinovich, to lose his wife, his brother and his heir so close together. She took the photograph with the signed abdication, Alexander's birth certificate, her marriage certificate and all the bonds, pushing them down her dress, wondering if Ilich could be bribed to save his life, or other guards.

The bonds were his birthright she told herself. *And I'll be damned if I'm going to leave them here for the Revolution to discover and steal. I have given them what they needed anyway.*

She closed the vault and locked it, lifting the heavy portrait and placing it back on the wall, turning to the windows when she heard the agonising crunching sound followed by a muddy, watery splash.

There were cheers from the men on the walls and Laura saw that a large, slightly semi-circular trench had opened up in the ground. *Vsevolod's defenses had thought of heavy, modern artillery after all* she thought. The heavy guns had broken through the boards and earth that had covered the old defensive moat. It hadn't been filled in after all, only covered and forgotten about. Three of the Russian cannons plunged in, dragging their screaming operators with them, who were crushed and killed or pinned and drowned under the heavy equipment.

As she watched the two remaining cannons were pulled to the edge of the moat and loaded. *It is different to a medieval castle moat* she thought. *There is a good distance between the moat and the city walls. Vsevolod was a true military genius.* There was a puff of smoke from one cannon and she watched the metal ball sail towards her. The sound of the cannon reached her, making her jump and the ball smashed into the stone of the eastern tower. A puff of dust and grit exploded outwards, and large lumps of mortar and stone fell into the courtyard.

She heard the second cannon roar and looked up to see the metal ball heading straight for the library. She spun away from the window, throwing her arms over her head. The cannon ball smashed through the window and plowed through the pile of charred books, smashing into the shelves of books, overturning the Tsar's chair, which crashed into the fireplace, destroying one side of the marble.

The wind rushed in, snatching up pages and dust, tearing at the drapes and fluttering them all around Laura, dragging the smell of gunpowder and fear into the room, swirling the shouts and cries even louder in her ears. Dalnerechensk's cannons roared, deafening her and she turned to watch them fly towards Nikita's army.

Soundlessly the dirt fountained up around a group of men, and Laura gaped in horror as their bodies tore apart. Then the noise hit her, the dull, wet thump of impact and then the terrible cries of those wounded; choking and drowning in their own blood, screaming out for their limbs, calling piteously for their mothers and God. A dull red misty dirt rained back down onto them.

Laura turned her head from the sight, throwing up on the carpet. She heard the Russian cannons roar again and quickly rushed from the room, running down the stairs. The castle was deserted and no one stopped her as she raced out into the courtyard, eyeing the walls, trying to find Peter and Ilich. A cannon ball sailed overhead and smashed into the wall of the castle, raining down stone and mortar. Laura jumped aside and felt something *zing* past her ear. *A bullet!* she thought wildly. *And I nearly jumped right into it!*

She saw Roman and screamed out his name, rushing over and grabbing his arm. 'Where is Peter and Ilich?!' she cried. 'Is it working? Why isn't it working?'

A bullet ripped through Roman's shirt sleeve, grazing his arm. He yelled, clamping his hand over the hurt.

'Go inside and stay there!' he snapped. 'This is no place for hysterics now.' He shook her off and headed to the wall where several ladders had been placed against the ramparts, helping move troops around the defenses quickly. Another bullet pinged off the ground near her and she ran back into the castle, banging her fists in frustration on the doors.

Above her in the castle another cannon ball ripped into a room, smashing furniture and fixtures. *Downstairs was safest* she thought, and headed into the left wing of the castle, eyeing her surroundings. The ballroom was empty and the centre of the floor was gouged and marked where the chandelier had fallen to the floor. Not one trace of the expensive crystal was left; even the candles had been taken by the ransacking mob.

She could see soldiers running back and forward through the large windows and decided not to stay here, moving on to the torched throne room. The acrid smell of smoke and fire still clung to the room and it was black with soot. She wondered how long it would take for the room to become musty like the wing in Varennikov Castle, and wished she would hear Fredrik call out to her now, to pull her hand through his elbow and walk through this haunted place.

She turned away from the lump of charcoal that was the remains of the throne and headed into the east wing. The dining room was not touched by the riots save that the canopy had been torn down. They had not burnt or damaged the chair Aleksei sat in for meals. *It was once Vsevolod's throne* she reminded herself. *He still commands too much respect in the Principality, even if he was a king.*

She sat tiredly in the throne, alone in the dining room, thinking it was fitting for a queen who was not recognised by her people. Another cannonball smashed upstairs and Laura was surprised to hear gasps and small screams floating up from the kitchen. She stood and crossed to the doorway, seeing the kitchen was filled with all the members of the staff who had not run away or been fired after the Revolution.

They stood and curtsied or bowed when she arrived. Several of them were in tears, holding handkerchiefs they had balled in their fists or relentlessly torn as their hard fingers worried at the material. She was disappointed to see that Anna, Mikhail and Fedor were not here, and wondered briefly where they had gone. She stood for a few seconds, appraising them all, noticing how scared some of them looked.

'We have our men out there fighting a war for us' she said, beginning to roll up her sleeves. 'I'm sure many of them will be very hungry by the time it is over. Let's not stand here crying, they will need a meal fit for heroes tonight.'

She grabbed a rolling pin, brandishing it like a sabre as she headed to the bench, pulling tubs of flour and sugar towards her. The head cook curtsied and began barking orders at the girls. Some of their fear abated as they gained a purpose, making tray after tray of bread and pot after pot of stew. Laura was set to work rolling pastry for pies and deserts and she worked determinedly, pushing away her fear with each roll of the pin.

There was a shout and servants quickly scurried out of the way as soldiers and peasants poured through the kitchen, heading down the stairs to the cellar. Some were wearing green uniforms, others wore black, some were bloodied and wounded, most were not. They carried guns and swords, bows and quivers, pitchforks, knives and pikes. One was even carrying a quarterstaff.

The surprised kitchen watched them pour past, calling out questions in fear, wondering where they were going. Laura heard the grate in the cellar crash aside and men splash down into the river beneath them. She saw Roman and Basil rush past and fought the urge to call out to them too, to ask if the plan was working. She dared not ask how many had died already. *So the breach has begun* she thought, bowing her head over the pastry. *God help us all.*

114

The kitchen was stiflingly hot and Laura's dress clung uncomfortably to her. She put another tray in the oven and stood, placing her hands in the small of her back, arching to ease the dull ache in her spine. A loud roar startled her, making her glance upwards nervously. The noise bounced over the walls, soaring above the ramparts, penetrating deep into the ruined soil and the solid stone of the castle till everything thrummed and echoed with the sound. She recognised what it was though she had never heard it before. It was the sound of hundreds cheering in victory.

She quickly took off the apron she was wearing and rubbed her face, cleaning it of flour and sweat. She smoothed back her hair and carefully composed herself.

'Stay here' she told the nervous staff. 'If it is us, bring out the wine; if it is not, eat everything, we did not do this for the Russians.'

She slipped out of the kitchen and trotted through the dining room, her stomach knotted tightly. Just as she reached the wide entrance foyer the front doors of the castle swung open and Nikita strode in. Laura froze in horror, she had not prepared for the fall of Dalnerechensk. Nikita eyed her attire distastefully, then was roughly prodded from behind.

He cursed and stepped forward, and Dalnerechensk guards followed him in, singing the anthem, prodding Nikita with rifle butts. She sagged with relief, taking hold of the door frame but sat down on the stone floor, feeling weak with liberation and exhaustion. Peter and Ilich swept into the castle like grand masters, their faces shining with accomplishment. Dalnerechensk was safe.

Laura put her face in her hands and began to sob; relieved, fatigued, pained for those that were lost or had been left behind. She didn't see where they took Nikita but assumed he would be put under house arrest in one of the rooms in the castle that was undamaged by his cannon fire. Peter took her arm gently, pulling her into his embrace and kissing the top of her head, mindful of how young she still was.

She sobbed and he let her, knowing she needed the release, stroking her sweat dampened hair to soothe her. With a supreme effort Laura got herself under control, sniffing and wiping away her tears.

'What is to be done now?' she asked.

'Now? We celebrate' he said simply. 'And we mourn. We will leave everything else for tomorrow.'

She nodded, straightening herself.

'We prepared food for the soldiers' she said. 'I think we made enough to feed everyone. Bring them all to the castle, to the dining room. Every man that saved Dalnerechensk will be thanked.'

'As you wish, Your Highness' he said gently, smiling.

She turned and went back into the dining room, calling to the servants who stood crowded in the kitchen doorway to bring out the food, setting it out on the table. At once they beamed and clasped each other tightly, laughing in relief, scurrying into the kitchen to do as she commanded.

Soldiers, ministers and peasants alike all poured into the castle and fell ravenous on the table laden with food. Peter had stationed soldiers on the stairs, preventing anyone from going up to the chambers where Nikita was being kept. More still had been stationed with the remains of Nikita's surrendered army. Others were ferrying wounded and dead to the hospital; both Dalnerechenskers and Russians.

Laura thanked each of the men in the dining room personally, her tongue growing sore with the repetition of thanks, her lips detesting the taste of blood and dirt and sweat as she kissed each of their cheeks. Hundreds of grizzled old men and youths barely in their teens had fought for Dalnerechensk, and she made sure each and every one of them knew their efforts had been appreciated.

They had spoken to her, telling her of the defense; tales of fear and agony and courage that made her cry to hear them. When she could take no more she excused herself, blessing them all, and slipped past the soldiers on the stairs, heading to her rooms.

They had been damaged by cannon balls; glass littered the floor and wind swirled around her room. She glanced round it all, picking up the little lump of melted tin, sighing tiredly. She turned and headed to an empty bedroom on the third floor, slipping inside and falling down on the unmade bed, tucking her limbs up and wondering where Olaf was as she cried herself to sleep.

115

Laura rode on horseback beside Peter, listening absently as he pointed out the work that was taking place. At first light that morning the army had been organised into work details and sent out into Dalnerechensk. Broken stone rubble from the towers and castle was being lowered from the rooms in buckets on a system of pulleys and loaded into carts that took them to stone masons working in a small camp near the old moat. It had been decided to return Dalnerechensk to the original state of fortifications and soldiers were breaking in the boards of the moat, the masons were using the castle rubble to build pretty stone bridges to keep the city connected to the rest of Liberty Valley.

One group of soldiers was clearing the rubble from the destroyed sections of the Northern Border. Two masons had already completed an archway over one of the small breaches and were quickly completing the second arch. The large, central gap of the three breaches was to be left open, and a new road was to stretch there, branching away from King's Gate.

Work had already begun on the new road, two companies of soldiers were paring back the grass and digging a shallow trench that would be filled with scoria and pebbles to keep the road well drained before the hot asphalt was laid down. The wagons of Russian dead had to swing wide of the work, bumping over the uneven grass to the Russian side of the border wall.

Prisoners of War were digging graves for their fallen comrades along the wall, their commanding officer identifying each body, whole or dismembered, as they were placed in a deep hole. Their name and rank was scratched quickly onto a grave marker and placed at the head of the hole. A stone mason took each grave marker and chiseled the name carefully into the stone while the Russians silently shoveled the dirt back over the bodies, moving on to dig yet more graves.

Dalnerechensk's new road was to be called The Avenue of Heroes she thought absently, her eyes drifting over it again. She and Ilich had named it at dawn in his Parliament Rooms, sitting in chairs they had found amongst the rubble of Vsevolod's shattered dining room table. *At least it hadn't been his throne* she had thought, eyeing the destruction of the room. *That would have been a blow Dalnerechensk could not have taken.* The graves of the fallen Dalnerechensk were being dug alongside this new road, dug by soldiers and civilians alike, and Laura wondered if they were counting the shovels, if they felt every inch as she was sure Olaf had, digging the grave for his father with his bare hands.

She shut her eyes, turning her attention to the moat where it was being dredged. Ten men tossed a grappling hook into the waters for the three cannons, dragging them up onto the banks. They then used the hooks to retrieve the ten bodies that had disappeared into the moat with the cannons, stacking the bodies beside the dripping, waterlogged guns.

Misery, it was misery everywhere she thought, shutting her eyes again. She turned her horse sharply away and headed into the forest. Surprised, Peter followed her, keeping a respectful distance behind her. People waved to Laura, walking along Hunter's Pass, and she waved back with a smile that never reached her eyes, thanking them for their blessings. She rode to the glen, disappointed to find a family swimming in the lake beneath the waterfall and quickly turned her horse away again, feeling aimless and hollow.

Peter gently rode up beside her and took her reins, looking at her carefully.
'We should go back Your Highness, you should eat and rest, you have seen enough for today.'

She was quiet then nodded, letting her horse trot dutifully back to Dalnerechensk stables. As they emerged from the forest Laura saw the dark smeared earth before the moat had been set alight. The coppery smell of boiling blood was mingling with the stench of burning flesh and she shut her eyes tightly, forcing her breath in and out of her mouth so she didn't gag.

Peter said nothing, watching her carefully as they made their way back to the castle. Laura kept her eyes shut, not wanting to see the misery on the faces of the Dalnerechenskers who had lost ones they loved, not wanting to see damaged buildings and rubble, not wanting to see the boy in the castle stables instead of Olaf.

Ilich was waiting for her on the castle steps when she dismounted.
'Good news' he said. 'The engineers found the break in the telegraph wire and have repaired it. I have already sent a telegram to Tsar Nicholas the Second informing him of *Knjaz* Rurik's arrest, the charges and a demand to know why the Liberty Treaty was violated.'
'Very good' Laura said hollowly.

Ilich looked at her sharply then at Peter.

'Come inside my dear, I will send for Doctor Pushkin to take a look at you' he said, taking her hand.

Laura let herself be led inside, too miserable to care anymore.

'Did they find Alexander Andrei?' she asked suddenly.

Ilich stopped, surprised. 'He has been dead for ten years' he said, eyeing her.

Laura turned away, lifting the hem of her dress to step up the stairs.

'What is to be done with Olaf?' she asked.

'It is done' Ilich answered.

She gasped, eyeing him, then pulled away and ran up the stairs, shutting the door of the room on the third floor behind her. She sank down onto her side, sobbing with grief, biting her knuckles to try to muffle the noise.

116

Two days after the Defense of Dalnerechensk the new road and cemetreies were completed. Russian soldiers were buried in neat rows in Russian soil, each in an individual plot with accurate information on the grave marker. The rubble archways housed the two Russian cannons that had not fallen in the moat, concrete poured into their barrels to make them quite useless. The Avenue of Heroes stretched from the Russian cemetrey like a black ribbon, joining Castle Street. The Dalnerechensk graves lined it, a solemn tombstone at each head, a torch at each foot, and the topsoil that had been taken from the road had been packed down over the black scarred ground where the fire had burnt away any remains that could not be interred.

Laura and Ilich had stood atop the walls of the castle where work on the repairs had ceased for the ceremony, and Dalnerechensk was clothed in black, standing pressed together on the commons below the walls. Laura had spoken quietly from the walls, and those who had gathered here ten years ago to listen to the Tsar's speech at the death of the Tsaritsa remarked to each other how similar the two had been, how hollow and small and lost the young queen looked now.

Ilich had spoken too, and when he was finished the bells of Dalnerechensk's cathedral tolled out the number of the dead. Laura had then taken the torch and walked down Castle Street, followed by Ilich, Peter and a new *Episcop*, as *Episcop* Vasily had fled from Dalnerechensk when the Revolution began. Laura had lit all the torches herself and the *Episcop* had blessed the ground in which they lay. Ilich had promised to let the torches burn for seven days and then led the Tsaritsa back to Dalnerechensk, concerned at the dreamlike way she moved.

The ceremony had been her first appearance in two days; she had shut herself in the unmade rooms seeing no one, eating nothing. There was a gauntness to her now, a sharpness in her jaw, a dullness in her eyes. Ilich had given priority to the rebuilding of her rooms and some effort had been made to retrieve the furniture taken in the riots. Laura was touched by the thoughtfulness but still could not bring herself to care.

'A telegram came for you today, from Countess Ivanova' he said as they sat privately in the Parliament Chambers that evening.

Her eyes flicked to his.

'She and Grigory have reached Varennikov Castle. I have sent a telegram back to say that you are well.'

Laura closed her eyes, pleased that her friends were safe, but did not say anything. Ilich wiped his mouth, eyeing her.

'The Russian Ambassador arrives tomorrow for the official apology and hand over of our prisoners of war' he went on. 'Tsar Nicholas the Second has also offered to pay for the repairs needed.'

Still Laura said nothing, her eyes drifting from the Republic Flag out the window to the new cemetreies and the vanished tent city of Nikita's army.

Dalnerechensk is changed she thought sadly. *How had Vsevolod felt sitting in his castle, listening to his people cry for their dead, knowing he could never go back to Russia? Leadership was lonely...*

Her eyes drifted back to the Republic's flag. The Royal colours had been stripped from everything; the seals had been prised off and melted down. All the brilliant tapestries were gone, even the three silk ones of Vsevolod that had hung in the entrance hall. They had all been destroyed in the fire, or in the river between the city and Tcherepnin, torn to bits under the boots of soldiers.

Now the castle was brocaded in green and white, filled with statesmen sporting white sashes and not a grey hair between them. Not one of the old Advisory Council save for Ivan Gogol had set foot in the castle. They were not even consultants for the younger and inexperienced politicians. *I am the last Royal, the last of the old ways* she thought, closing her eyes.

She could not bring herself to leave the castle, indeed, could not bring herself to leave the rooms she had taken over. The stables called to her but she could not bear the sight of the boy there, couldn't bear the thought of Olaf's body swaying from a tree branch somewhere in the forests. The library called to her too, with books to tempt her away from her misery, but she couldn't bear to see the two chairs and know Tsar Constantinovich would never again sit opposite her and lean back rumbling contentedly, quietly correcting her pronunciation.

'I have something that might interest you' he said, pulling a sheet of parchment out of his jacket pocket.

He held it out to her. After a pause she reached over and took it, opening the letter. It was a signed confession, from Tatiana and Maksim Yegorov. *They had both sworn Tatiana was not pregnant.* She dropped the letter on the table, her hands resting lifelessly on the top.

'Laura –' Ilich started, folding his hand over hers.

She pulled away. 'Good night Ilich' she said hollowly, standing and leaving him.

117

Laura folded her hands gently on her stomach, quietly walking the Avenue of Heroes. The torches that had burned for seven days and nights had been removed and grass was beginning to push blades of green above the humps of brown earth before each headstone. She often walked here now, thinking as she did, shadowed by Fedor. Ilich had rehired him as her own personal attaché, and Anna as her own maid in an attempt to break her depression.

She liked to be walking the Avenue of Heroes, it gave her some of the solitude she had enjoyed in the Hunting Forests with Olaf. It was better than sitting uselessly in the Parliament Chambers.

For all their inexperience the Parliament was enthusiastic and hardy and the room echoed with laughter every now and then. A new system of government had been negotiated while Dalnerechensk mourned. It was still to be called a Principality presided over by the Monarchy, but power of legislation lay with the parliament, headed by a Head of State. Laura's first Royal Act as Tsaritsa of Dalnerechensk had been to sign over sovereignty to the new parliament. She was no more than a token queen confined to rooms in a country that held too many ghosts.

She sighed, turning at the border wall and making her way slowly back to Dalnerechensk. The Ambassador had gone, taking with him the disgraced Nikita Rurik, stripped of his titles and position of command, and the remaining three hundred and twenty-two Imperial soldiers in his company. Russian money was now pouring into Dalnerechensk; money to pay for the damage caused by Nikita's invasion, and money for the first few shipments of tin at the renegotiated price.

Ilich had paid his army and honoured his contracts then tripled the wages of all the workers in Dalnerechensk. The newspaper had reported the next day that every single tavern in the Principality had been drunk dry of alcohol. Laura had not been surprised, and she had sat in Parliament, listening as the Council voted on new building projects, on improving the school and the hospital, on the creation of a jail to deal with public drunkenness and other crimes that were committed in the Principality.

Laura's footsteps had taken her back up the hill to the castle where soldiers in smart green uniforms standing guard at the gate snapped respectful salutes for their poor queen. Laura thanked them absently, crossing the gravel courtyard and heading for the Parliament Chambers.

They looked surprised to see her and rose, shooting each other looks. She was quiet for a minute, looking at all the strange new faces in the room.
'Tsaritsa?' Ilich prompted quietly; surprised. 'We did not expect to see you this morning.'

She closed the door to the chambers. It was a new door, the old one had been smashed by a cannon ball. It was a shame, it had been original, and she would have liked to have run her fingers over the gouges Aleksei had made by throwing the tray of food after Nikita. *How the past all felt so distant and removed.*

'Tsar Constantinovich once said that a man with no heart is not the man to be in charge of a Principality' she started quietly, turning to face them. 'It is no secret in these walls that I have no heart for this. I have seen Russian money flood into the country and Parliament deal with incidents that arose in a fair and just manner. We understand that while I retain the title of Tsaritsa of Dalnerechensk I have no illusion of power.

'I am but a ghost here now, and I am haunted by those I loved who are no longer with us' she stopped.

Ilich and Ivan came to her, aware how fragile she looked.

'I will be seventeen in a month' she said, looking at Ilich. 'I have seen too many lifetimes in my days here. I am widowed, without friends, and I am not needed here. I want to -' *leave.* She couldn't bring herself to say the word. As haunted as she was in this place she loved it, and had nowhere else to call home. 'I want to travel to Varennikov Castle to see the Ivanovs' she finished.

She dropped her eyes, waiting for Ilich's answer. He smiled sadly, coming around the new table to take her hand and kiss it gently, studying her face carefully.

'We understand how difficult these days have been for you, Your Highness' he said quietly. 'I am so very sorry it has come to this. We will honour your wishes' he said.

She nodded then, and turned slowly, sweeping gracefully out of the room she no longer recognised.

118

Laura sat back in the plush seat, sighing as she watched the world slip by the train window. She rubbed at the small lump of disfigured tin with her thumb absently, the fingers of her other hand resting on a large, leather book balanced on her knees. It had been tied shut with string to keep the secret bonds hidden safely between the pages.

The train whistled, and Laura thought of the handsome carriages of the Royal Train that had taken her to the Russian Railway in Chelyabinsk. It was to be the last run for the train; Ilich had already painted out the coat of arms on the side of the engine and had given her the papers to present to a Sultan who was now the proud owner of the luxurious carriages. Laura had been polite and pleasant, watching as the solitary engine steamed back to Dalnerechensk, but it had left a bitter taste in her mouth.

Laura shut her eyes, pushing away the hurts. The echoes of the whistle died away and she thought about the railing of the *Queen of the Atlantic* where she had stood, just sixteen with her tutor and friend, waving goodbye to Boston for an unknown life with an unknown love. She thought about the adventure Ekaterina had promised her, thought about the love she had wanted to find, and decided she had found both in Dalnerechensk, though love had scarred her and broken her heart, and adventure was not as wonderful as it had seemed.

Part of her had been left in Dalnerechensk; part of her had died in a small Russian grave, her childhood had died in Aleksei's marriage bed. *She would not forget them* she vowed. She couldn't forget the tragedies that had shaped the lives of the Vakhtangovs, their poor mad heir and his jealous, awkward brother.

She sighed deeply, feeling another wave of the frightful nausea wash over her. She had not left her berth in the first class carriage for the entire trip; miserable and sick, and the journey had seemed restlessly endless. She had wished more than once that Ekaterina had been with her, had been some comfort to her in her time of need.

She was glad she had left Dalnerechensk for this brief respite. Although Ilich had promised to pay her a comfortable salary he had refused to return her dowry, and refused to surrender the contents of Aleksei's will, arguing that he might not be dead at all, as his body had not been found even though the river and estuary had been scouted. *I will have to wait seven years before I know if I am free of him or not* she thought unhappily. She thought again of the letter she wanted to send Fredrik, not knowing how it would be received, wondering if he would drop it unread onto the fire as she had done to his.

Another whistle interrupted her and she looked up. There were people standing at the windows now; she could see the houses of Debrecen. She slipped the little lump of tin into her drawstring purse and stood, clutching the leather book to her tightly. She joined the people at the windows, wondering if the train was visible yet, if Grigory and Ekaterina could see her from the platform. She knew they would be there.

She sighed, stroking the little lump of tin through the velvet of her purse. *And so I have changed too, little tin princess* she told herself quietly. She had been melted and broken down, but now she could start anew. *I still am queen, even if I have no country* she thought, gazing down absently at the purse for a long time, remembering what it once was, knowing it could be beautiful and desirable again. *I will make you sparkle again* she promised herself.

The platform was closer, and teemed with people who stood and gazed at the approaching train. Laura wondered if she could pick their faces, if she could somehow see Ekaterina. The Hungarian Countess shone like the sun in Dalnerechensk, but Laura could not for the life of her find her in the sea of bright faces.

There was suddenly a shout of joy and Laura shut her eyes tightly. The world melted away then, and she raised her hand to wave.

~~******~~

ABOUT THE AUTHOR

Rächal Monigatti was born in New Zealand and studied History, Literature and Linguistics at Waikato University. She has been writing as a hobby for twenty-two years but *The Tin Tsaritsa* is her first published novel. Rächal is currently completing the sequel to *The Tin Tsaritsa* and teaches English at a high school in Auckland, New Zealand.

www.ingramcontent.com/pod-product-compliance
Lightning Source LLC
Chambersburg PA
CBHW080817020726
47501CB00009B/2325